A BOOK OF
death
AND
FISH

Ian Stephen

Saraband

Published by Saraband
Suite 202, 98 Woodlands Road
Glasgow, G3 6HB, Scotland
www.saraband.net

ISBN: 9781908643971
ebook: 9781908643674

Printed in the UK by CPI on paper from sustainably managed sources.

Publication of this book has been supported by Creative Scotland.

ALBA | CHRUTHACHAIL

*Editor's note on spellings and punctuation: In keeping with its subject
and principal characters, this book is written in a blend of Scots and
English with some words and phrases of Gaelic – and occasionally
other languages and/or dialects occur. For the purposes of clarity for the
widest audience, words and phrases in Gaelic are italicised. This is to
avoid any confusion for readers unfamiliar with the language by what
might appear to be the indefinite article (in English) in common Gaelic
phrases such as* a ghràidh. *Readers should not infer any other motives
for the author's or editor's decisions on this subject.*

1 3 5 7 9 10 8 6 4 2

THIS BOOK IS DEDICATED TO TORMAD CALUM DOMHNALLAC
(NORMAN MALCOLM MACDONALD) OF TONG, LEWIS,
A PLAYWRIGHT, NOVELIST AND POET; AND TO
MAIRI NIC DHOMHNAILL (MAIRI MACDONALD)
OF GRIMSAY, NORTH UIST,
A TEACHER, POET AND PHOTOGRAPHER

Always you stare at the purple water, looking for the smoking signs of the herring. It's good when the water's dark for then you can imagine it swimming with fish.

When the day's clear you're sailing over safe sandy bottom, nothing to be seen but the smooth green ground. A crab slides along sideways. A speckled plaice stirs up the sand like a puff of smoke, gone at once like blood in the water. Yes we like the deep indigo sea. Even though the colour also hides the rocks, it hides the fish from us, we say, planting the nets.

We say to each other, "They're down there in shoals, millions. Soon they'll be in our net, a year's money in one night."

After the psalm and the supper and the waiting, the hauling of the nets, the capstan turning, we shake out the gasping fish, the hold fills, the boy coils, coils in his wet cubbyhole, in his weaving world of black wet rope.

We turn for home. Portrona beckons in the pearl and gold dawn. The wind with us, she takes it, hear her hiss through the water. The Zulu boat heeling, straining boards and sheets and canvas.

Hear her chuckle past Tiumpan, Bayble Island, The Chicken. She heels so far, at The Beasts, herring slips from her decks back into the sea.

Arnish, Goat Island, Number One. Portrona Quay before us. We're not the first but we're not the last either.

from Portrona – *a novel by Norman Malcolm MacDonald*
(Birlinn, Edinburgh, 2000)

CONTENTS

BOOK ONE: **Migrations**

Book Two: **Turbulence**

BOOK ONE

Migrations

Attic

Seamus was renovating a place just up from Bayhead. Not a bad little town-house with a nice bay window. Enough space in the attic to make another small room. He needed a fit young cove like myself to swing a sledgehammer. He could shovel the debris out, bit by bit, in his own time, once I'd brought it down.

Seamus ran a Coastguard watch and took part in training the coast-rescue team. We got on. I did a couple of shifts with him, as an auxiliary, once I got my radio ticket. First day I learned to skin a rabbit. Learned a couple of other things from him as well. It was the done thing then, favour for favour between coastguards.

He issued me with the heavy sledge. He took up a dainty five-pound club for the tidying up. We were in our Coastguard boiler-suits. Seamus pointed to the partitions which had to come down. Some of them were plasterboard but some were the older type of construction: plaster on a strapping of lath.

We got on with it. We had teacloths over our mouths and noses. Health and safety, late-Seventies style. Earlier in the decade you'd have had nothing at all.

We became possessed as we swung. The walls fell and the dust rose. I opened the skylight, which was about to be replaced by a larger Velux, and both of us gulped in air. It was all suddenly very quiet.

Some good wood here. Might be pitch-pine. You could smell the resin in the splintered bits. But we were horrified at how little time the demolition had taken.

'Aye, it doesn't take long to pull things down,' Seamus said.

I thought of The Who and 'Talkin bout my generation'. I also thought of Pete Townsend smashing up a beautifully built guitar, for dramatic effect. I was acting under instructions but I felt implicated.

I didn't voice any of this. Instead I asked why the low attic was divided further, into stalls. I was thinking of the Arnol black-house. It wasn't that different from other European peasant houses. The accommodation for animals was in touching and smelling distance. But this was an attic. It couldn't have been for beasts.

He could see it all. The whole plan would have been simple. Tiers of bunks at both ends with a cubby-hole in the middle.

'Look, that's where the chimney's bricked up. They'd have worked shifts, just like ourselves. That's where they'd have done their cooking. One shift shoving some hot foot down, quick as they could so as not to lose their sleeping time. The kettle back on for the next folk. One lot would be out into the cold of the morning, the next fall into their warmed bunks. All the women packed tight in here, like herrings in a barrel.'

Seamus could decipher the system at a glance. But what would have happened from midnight Saturday to midnight Sunday? They wouldn't have worked then.

'I suppose half of the girls would walk out to their homes out of town. They didn't think much of ten or fifteen miles back then. If the other half were from away, they'd have the bunks to themselves. Go together, arm in arm, to the kirk round the corner.'

He asked me to stay for a dram. But I wasn't drinking then. And I wanted to get the dust out of my hair. Up the road, the olaid had a big fire on for the hot water. The new council houses still had an open fire but now you got the radiators off it.

I told her about the room with the bunks, over our fried chops. She came alive when I told her what Seamus said about the herring girls. This was where East and West Coast folk had come together. It all got joined up in the towns of Stornoway or Wick or up at at Baltasound, in Unst. The Baltic trade. That never really recovered from the First World War. She'd never seen the big days of it but she could say she'd caught the tail end.

She was on form.

My Broch grannie, her own mother, had been to Stornoway long before that Lewisman danced herself off her feet. 'D'ye mind thon row o ornaments i the pre-fab i The Broch. Peterheid tae Yarmooth. Takin trains tae follow the fishin. Trying to save a few pound to send hame.'

Then it was saving up to get married. 'Your grannie aye said she'd hid nae a baud life.' Hard work but always amongst friends. She definitely mentioned Stornoway. It was a long time ago. Bayhead, Keith Street, Kenneth Street, Scotland Street – they were all full of attics like that. In between the barrel stores. Keith Street rang a bell. Now she thought of it, my grannie always said there was a lot of banter about being billeted so close to Al Crae, the undertakers.

My bit was done but Seamus asked me back. He'd finished the big sweep-up. The wallpapers were stripped, layers and layers of them. He pointed to the beams. The slants of light from the skylights were making them shine. There were waves and waves of lightly chalked names. *Dolly MacDonald, Garyvard. Ishbel Mary MacLeod, 12 Habost. Milly Strachan, Inverallochy. Henrietta Stephen, Brightsea, Fraserburgh.* And more and more.

I went home for a shot of my mother's camera. A wee Olympus Trip. Easy to use. Some of the snaps were a bit blurred with the slow explosure. The olaid went through them all, a few days later. We never sighted the name she was looking for. Her eyes misted over just the same – a thing you didn't see very often.

Providence

I was born one street back from the hoil. My arrival gave the olman and the olaid the points they needed to get their first council house. They already had a healthy daughter but one child was not enough to get up the list. They had to escape the brush. The cove in the flat down below would bang the end of a wooden handle on his ceiling, their floor, whenever the baby cried or there was any other sign of his tenants surviving. My father had survived a war. He wasn't scared of what lurked under the stairs. He just didn't want to lose the rag. Shoving that brush-handle up or down an orifice belonging to the landlord. I never saw or heard this, because I was only the baby who brought the points for the council house. But he talked about it himself, later on.

My mother's health wasn't that great then, he said. It wasn't an easy time for them. A weaver was self-employed. If you didn't get the hours in, you didn't finish your tweeds. No tweeds, no money. And you were down the list, for the next delivery of warps.

I don't remember the flat we escaped. But Westview Terrace is loud and clear. This was and is a pebble-dashed house, part of a row, wearing a blaeberry roof of best Penryn slate. The individual houses have faces and I've seen similar groupings of similar shapes in towns on the mainland and on other islands. Kirkcaldy and The Broch. Kirkwall and Lerwick. But the harling or the slate can vary. I don't suppose anyone was making concessions to local architectural styles because there wasn't a lot of any style, in towns that had grown big on the backs of squashed herring or on long rolls of linoleum.

We couldn't look out to sea but it was never very far away. Stornoway was still a herring port. I would be sent to the corner shop to buy a score. A different fish from the ones you saw swinging over, in dripping baskets. But the same species. They came from a firkin. That sounded like one of the measures laid out, black on pale blue, on the back cover of our school jotters. You had to know how many chains were to the furlong. Down the hoil, some cove off a boat would let me gather one for every digit I could hold out. I think I said that, instead of finger, because it's like a cubit, which maybe wasn't on the jotters, but it was in the Bible. The fry was taken from spillage from the crans, swung ashore in creels filled from the hold. We'd go back to the Terraces with handfuls, held out ahead. We'd leave behind, drying on the concrete, the cuddies we'd caught. These were small fry of lythe, saithe, cod and whiting.

Later I learned that the cuddy was strictly only the young of the saithe or coalfish. In other parts of Scotland the word means horse. Coves from away are welcome to use the word any way they want but we know what it really means. These fish had gone for a sliver of bait, torn from the bone with your hand. That was offered on a halfpenny hook to brown cotton line. When you had a bite, you pulled so the fish made an arc through the salt air to finish against the weeded concrete. I don't know why we had to kill them.

One of our neighbours worked on a boat, not a drifter. She was stacked high with pots. It was lobsters then. Prawns were trawled up, amongst the fish. These days, an occasional fish appears like a miracle among the prawns. We'd get a bucket of tails now and again from a Broch boat with a Strachan or a Tait *fa kent Sandy Sim's quine*. That was my olaid.

She'd do them there and then. The sister, Kirsty, and me would get to wait up. You'd to let the pale pink prawns cool that bit so you could give them one squeeze inwards, one out. The white meat would then come out clean and whole, from the shell. You couldn't stop till they were all gone.

Then we'd sleep. We didn't know then that the lobster and langoustine, the high-status shellfish which boil red, are the scavengers of the sea-floor. They tear and eat dead things.

Westview

When you interrupt yourself in a story, for any reason, you go back. Not always the full way but you backtrack before you gain forward momentum. It can be long enough before you overtake your original point. This is good. The first telling has raised ghosts but their friends have had time to wake up by the time you're on the second.

I can't go back further than Westview. This is no dead end. All the houses are double-skinned with cavities left between the walls, linked only with galvanised fixings, spaced for additional strength. I've seen enough being built to know the construction. We were already in ours when the streets around it were still to be completed. Finished in that pukey pebble-dash.

Round the backs, space was left for the peat-stacks and tattie patches. Most tenants had only just moved in from the rural parts of the Island. They brought their ways of life with them, in the removal vehicle. Usually it was a works' lorry, out of hours, driven by a mate, on a dry evening. My uncle said we had enough ground at the back to keep a cow. We did too, but he was only joking. That's what folk were leaving.

The front was for show, with annuals and roses and cured paths. People who cared for their gardens got upset when the football went over the privet. The hedges were slow to get going. In a few years, they'd be dense and cropped or high and wild.

Westview turns on to Jamieson Drive, which turns on to KT. Kennedy Terrace. I don't know who Kennedy was. Jamieson must have been from Shetland but we said it as Jimson. Cul-de-sacs, mapped into the overall design, made a turning place for these peat lorries, rubbish collections, mobile shops. It was also a self-contained stadium with a lamp post for a floodlight. At first, no-one had cars so there was nothing to interfere with the games. It was mostly football by day. At night, those who had been to Cubs or Brownies taught their own versions of British Bulldog. Whatever the chants or questions in these games, you always had to run for some base. Get home to an established point. Kick the can. Start again from that.

There were groupings of names in the guessing games – Gold Flake, Woodbine, Bogey Roll. Our Kirsty was great at them all. There would always be a sprinkling of older kids with the main gang, all about the same age. She would organise us, a bit.

My mother sent me for ten Embassy tipped and a packet of Ryvita. The word Embassy wasn't in our game yet. These fags only arrived after the tape was cut on MacLennan's Corner Shop. I had money for a thru'penny toffee. I didn't have to run to Johnny Og's on Bayhead for the plain loaf. A baker's batch or two now came up the road in the van for eight o' clock. You could ask for your rolls soft or crisp. The loaf was always crisp, the top was near-black, over the pure high sides.

Going into it from the top was dangerous. By the time you got what was left home, the thing would fall apart. You could usually get away with tackling it from the side. First, the flakes which naturally came off in your hand. Then you found yourself pulling a bit, like with a scab. Instead of blood, steam would spill out. You could remove and swallow some of the doughy bits, as long as you concentrated. If you didn't, you could easily arrive at the back door with a good crust and a hollow loaf. You weren't too popular.

You'd to watch for the herring coming in. Maybe a notice would be up in the shop saying that salt-herring were in at two and six the score. They wouldn't have been long in the small barrel of bleached wood beside the ha'penny tray of spongy goodies. That was just the word we used. It sounded childish when a visitor said sweetie.

In *Commando* books or *The Victor*, you were either a Kraut or a Tommy. Some editions had Nips as well. An older guy might call you 'my china' or just 'mate'. You wouldn't find these words in the lists on our jotters but you'd find how many drams were to something else. And a gill wasn't a part of a fish. It sounded like a girl's name and it was another measure. But you'd soon get to know that a gill was also a quarter-bottle, the way a firkin was a quarter-barrel. It was a full, whole container and then again, it wasn't.

The gang would get out to the castle grounds. They were given to the people of Lewis by Lord Leverhulme. He realised at last he could only do things for this Island if there were no strings attached, so my olman said. You could imagine him addressing a gathering of peasants and soldiers and sailors and curers and labourers, with a sprinkling of the more educated. 'Here's all this bloody ground, bought courtesy of Sunlight Soap. Now do with it what you will.'

But we didn't set out to destroy the bushes we dived through, launched from rocks. Maybe it was seeing Elvis doing a dive from Acapulco. In the ninepenny seats, you were that close to these big stars that you were blinking for half the movie. There was always a chance of a runner to the back-rows when the torch was on someone else. They were mostly empty, on a Saturday afternoon, the snogging seats.

Sir James Matheson Bart commissioned these forests, mostly broadleaves and conifers, native to the United Kingdom but interspersed with Tibetan rhododendrons, South American monkey-puzzles and North American sequoias. There was yew and there was cypress. This cove, the great benefactor, was only modestly represented under a life-sized marble statue of his noble lady. She lost her stone hand, like the statue of Venus in the Arthur Mee books. Sir James's head and shoulders just came out a few inches from the marble block that supported his wife. This was better than the trees for scratching your initials. The script doesn't hold back on praise, for himself. I wonder who wrote it.

All these grounds, for the marble lady to stroll through, sprouted from opium. That explained the bulging poppy heads, frozen in marble, repeated as a decoration all around the canopy above the pale dame's gentle head. None of us noticed them, back then. They were a lot higher up at that time.

The other place was the pier. In the evening we'd go down to observe the *Loch Seaforth* berthing. We'd bide the time by leaping on bales of wool. I always thought these were related to the fanks my uncle brought me out to. The olman didn't want too much to do with the family croft. People were giving up on the single cow and going more for sheep. You got wool from sheep. So I thought this was used by the weavers in a park of sheds, round the corner from the auction mart.

I was beginning to notice that common sense didn't always work. We went down the road, in a gang, to the Nicolson Institute buildings. We started off in the clock-school and moved across to Matheson Road. These were the original sandstone buildings. The pink-school was bigger and newer. I think it was yellow, by the time we got in there. We still called it the pink-school. Still do.

We learned that Manscheefend was to glorify God and enjoy Him forever. It took longer to find that the first word was three words. And some day we were told that our Island's wool normally went for carpets. So the bales on the quay were Cheviot wool, from the Borders, imported to make our tweed softer. As sure as linoleum was made in Kirkcaldy. Jute and marmalade were both Dundee.

Our Island had fishing and tweed. Kenny F lived across the road from me, in the house with the garden full of lobster pots. We'd both have to stand, in turn, and say what our fathers did. You usually got offered an extra bottle if you performed like this. One third of a pint. Another full container that wasn't. In the clock-school, your bottle of milk would be heated by the coal fire, if you wanted. I didn't like the taste or feel of it warm. The crate would be divided into milk for sheep and milk for goats. So my own bottle was left out in the cold, by request.

Kenny F took his milk cold, as well, but he had treacle on his porridge in the morning. Tate and Lyle. The tin had the lion from the bible story. Out of the strong came forth sweetness. In black and red. Golden Syrup tins were green and gold. If I called for him on a Saturday or a holiday, I'd get that porridge with the black swirls, as a second breakfast. I took it, joining in the grace before it. These patterns are connected with their religion, in my mind.

Free Presbyterians. The olaid said that fishermen were mostly very religious. She loved to see the kirk full, if there was a big gale and the East Coasters couldn't get home. Sometimes we'd have a visitor, in his best gansey, a Brocher fa kent her people.

Kenny F's olman never seemed to be around. He was always out in the boat, along with Kenny's big brother, except on Sunday. The only time you'd see him was when he was mending creels, stacked in their front garden. They didn't have any flower beds. The two of them worked away with what they called needles. The tools were called that but they looked more like the shuttle my olman sent skelping through the warp. These guys didn't talk to you much.

Not that my olman, the weaver, talked much more, when he was setting up a tweed, in the shed. But Kenny F and me would earn extra money by filling his bobbins, on the machine by the door. Maybe six feet from the loom. That was a fathom. I can't remember how much of a chain or furlong. The oil from the wool would smell, along with the oil from the Hattersley, but the door would always be wedged open. On a windy day, it would be held by two hooks and eyes. The shed could be shaking. The olman never shut the door completely.

Mostly it was grey herringbones. I remember once there was a glut, with American markets saturated. The word made me think of guts and more fish landed than could be sold. That happened sometimes too. My olman carried on weaving. He'd to keep the loom and himself in condition, he said. And he couldn't go laying off his squad whenever things went quiet. So Kenny F and me still got to fill bobbins.

In these quiet times, the colours were different. He would be trying this, trying that. He talked to us more, not having to go all-out to finish three tweeds for the week. And how was the fishing?

He said this, only to hear Kenny F say, '*Mì-chàilear.*' It wasn't just the word but the tone and the shake of the head with it. The other stock answer was 'I suppose we'll just about cover the diesel'. I think that meant a good week.

'You fishermen are as bad as farmers,' the olman would say. The

Inland Revenue chasing them and them writing off everything from their underpants to their pork chops, against the tax. The weaver got his standard self-employed allowance and that was that. No negotiation. But you couldn't grudge the fisherman what he got when you saw some of the weather he was out in.

Funny thing was, he said, they always say the weather's *Mì-chàilear*. If it's any better you don't want to risk breaking it by saying so and if it's worse, that's a thing you don't spell out.

What sort of night is it? This time *Mì-chàilear* meant something damn near a hurricane. Same word, different tone of voice.

I knew the word but didn't know it was real Gaelic. Thought it was maybe like a stroll down the hoil for a fry of mogs and skeds. Our own words, found nowhere else, except for a pocket or two in Drumchapel or Christchurch, New Zealand. This means going down by the harbour to scrounge mackerel and herring.

Gellie is another of our words. This one sounded Gaelic to me. It could be any fire, like your own living-room one, when the shovel of coal was flashed up by a good draught. Or at Kenny F's when a bucket of *caorain* was thrown on. We'd all gathered these up. Most people in and around Westview still cut peats and everyone helped to bring them home. Us kids gathered up the broken and small bits and got goodies while the grown-ups were at their feast, the work done.

My olman said he hadn't moved in town to import big chunks of the moor in with him. He wondered who the hell ever discovered that the brown soggy mass was combustible.

Stella

Kenny F's olman went fishing in the *Stella*. I thought it was called after his big sister. She was a nurse, away on the mainland now. But my olman told me it was a name for a star before it was a name for a woman.

The *Loch Seaforth* took passengers and sheep. Now and again you'd see a car slung in a net. The *Loch Dunvegan* took cargo. You got boats and you got smallboats. The *Stella* was a smaller boat than most of the smooth black hulls. But, she did have a yellow-gold line, finished near the bow in an arrow shape, just like the big boats. My olman would look and comment now and again, on all the piles of creels. Old ones, taken home for repair or new ones, rigged in fleets. That sounded like something to do with the Navy. If you had all that gear shot and there was a big blow coming, you were forced to sneak out, trying not to look at the sky, just to haul and haul, recovering what you had. If you managed in time, you had all this gear piled up high on your decks, round your wheelhouse, cluttering everything while you ran for home.

The olman knew a lot about fishing though he had no time for it.

Here's how it happened, on the day of the gellie. Apart from being a big fire, any big fire, it was also our Guy Fawkes fire. Two cul-de-sacs and a long run of street, two Drives and Terraces pulling weight together for a month. We'd be wheeling lorry tyres, bigger than ourselves, up from the tip between the pink-school and the shore.

A green van had come to our site, with a full load of cardboard and wooden boxes. Someone in the next street had a relation who worked for Liptons. Amongst the boxes were white shop-coats, clean but frayed. We wore them as a uniform, trailing to our ankles but tied at the waist with twine which we also found amongst this load. There was a freshening wind all day, but it stayed dry and we had all of the lighter rubbish weighed down with broken timber and tyres. We marked every single tyre with a number and our code, in chalk. A protection against raids. Three months of gathering.

Keeping them moving was the thing. Kind of tricky, crossing roads if anything came along. They didn't come with brakes. Even now, just before the gellie was to be lit, you could expect the Goathill boys, or a squad from Manor, to come and snatch stuff for their own pile.

So you could see the white coats milling about. Smaller guys like Kenny F and me nearly tripping up. It was always the coves who collected the tyres. We were the warrior gang. But a few of the blones helped gather and pile the other stuff. Kirsty was allowed into our gang then. Some big coves thought she was too bossy. But the big sister and her pal got the wee fellows running about for them. Kenny and me were now in the middle.

We were soon gazing up to recognise the big vinyl armchair or the dark, heavy-looking cupboard that hadn't been any bother at all to tumble up there. Matchwood all right. A sprinkle from a bottle. Plenty of Esso Blue about. The match going to the thing and getting a hold so it didn't matter when the cold rain started to come. We never realised there was so much wind. It blew right into the crevices of the pile. Soon our white coats had to go over our heads as shields from that heat. But it wasn't long before everyone started to look away, ready for the fireworks. We were the builders so we remained, loyal to our gellie, even after it had started to die down. Kenny F and me staying close to the fire, after the others were drifting to where the boxes were being opened by someone's Da. Of course Kenny's olman and the oldest brother, the crew, weren't home yet.

Then his mother appearing, nearly running, gathering her young son in to her, then hunting amongst all these white coats for his middle brother. Everyone starting to shush amongst the talk and roar of the gellie. The rockets were going up in Goathill. Then still more powerful booms from round the corner, at Leverhulme Drive. The Coastguard depot. You'd think you'd never know the sound of these maroons from all the other sounds that night. A bad time to get in trouble at sea.

But people had started to run. That's for us. It was the signal for both the Lifeboat and the LSA – boat and shore rescue parties. No-one in our scheme had phones at home then, so they depended on the maroons. The fire station, round one more corner, had a siren fixed to the roof. That went off most Guy Fawkes' nights, but not, so far, this one.

There was nothing anyone could do about the fire, short of calling the brigade. It was in a clear space and could be left to burn out. Flat, bright boxes were getting closed again. They had pictures that might have been from the *Dan Dare*. Rockets were taken back out of bottles. I was crying. Kirsty grabbed my hand and hauled me off. My crying was nothing to do with realising why Kenny F had been dragged off home. I thought that was just his mother, laying down the law on heathen bonfires.

The olaid quietened us, dishing out pancakes by the fire, after our baths. The radio purring away with a serial we liked. She only said it was the weather, a big storm coming. I got going with divers from the cornflakes packet. You used baking soda in a bottle with a screwtop. They were grey and ascended and descended slow and calm. Some of my mates had sea-monkeys. You could create life from dry seed in a packet. A bit of salt water, you could do anything. Walking on water was tricky but the word was, it had been done. We'd all had a good go at it but nobody had lasted more than a second. Better not try it down the hoil. Big bastard conger eels down there.

I did hear the gale, through my sleep. Slates rattling. But I was exhausted and got back down under.

In the morning, the curtains were still drawn in Kenny's windows, across the road. Before I went to school I saw people going in, wearing their church clothes. My olman didn't leave at the usual time, to go to the shed. Instead, he also had his good clothes on, dressed as if he was going to church though he never did. He went across the road for a few minutes. The olaid went over when he came back. She took some packets of tea and some sandwiches she'd made up.

My olman said he'd get me up and down the road today. Kenny F wouldn't be going to school. He met me at the gate. On the way home, we had to pass the Coastguard store at the bottom of Leverhulme Drive. There was a stack of creels and buoys. Some of them were crushed, the bamboo hoops all splintered. They're like chimney-rods, bent to take the netting over them. Everyone was whispering things.

About two weeks later, Kenny F was called away from school again. A teacher's car took him home. When I came in for my cup of tea and a roll, to keep me going, my mother told me, in a low voice, that Kenny F's father and brother had been found. No, no, they weren't alive, poor souls, there had been no hope of that but it still meant a lot to the family to get them back. Now there would be a funeral. Kenny would be off school for a few more days. I'd to promise not to ask him anything.

So I was left wondering about the return of the bodies. I imagined them in clothes like all the neighbours wore now, going to visit. They weren't in their bobbin-wool genseys and overalls. There weren't any haloes or anything. Just the father and brother in dark suits, the older one in wider trousers, big lapels and a wide tie. The younger with the thin tie over the white shirt and tighter suit. Probably I had seen them dressed like this on Sundays. But I heard it from someone at school that they'd been found in a fisherman's net.

I could see pure bodies, from the Bible, returned from the nets as a present. Dressed in these suits. The nets were not the usual black stuff but made of something silvery. Those cast on the starboard side of a vessel afloat on the Sea of Galilee.

I asked the olman about it. He said it didn't matter how the bodies came back, my mother was right, it made a big difference to the family. It was the same in her town – The Broch. They'd lost two lifeboat crews there, at different times. Both within sight of the harbour, everyone watching as the boat went to help someone who'd been caught out.

It was so many years later, more like twenty, that the olaid told me how my father had gone across the road, when everything was quietening down. He went to sort out arrangements that nobody else could cope with. Everything from legal statements to insurances. The way he put it, there was plenty of people to see to the spiritual side. Since he wasn't so tied up with prayer meetings, he could do his own bit. The olaid told me the tweeds had picked up, about then. The markets he thought he'd escaped from, had recovered. He was one of the few with a stockpile because he'd kept on going to the shed, not really because he saw it as an investment but because he wanted to make cloth. There also seemed to be a demand for these unusual designs.

That's when they spoke to him about coming into the Mill, setting up patterns. But anyway he was doing all right just about then.

So he'd gone to gather together the gear collected by the Team and still stacked at their store, down the road. Uninsured loss, it was called. The creels, ropes and buoys, what was left of them. Seems the way he put it to Kenny F's mother was there was plenty at the lobsters down in Lochs, now, crying out for gear. He'd get her a fair price for it.

He got hold of a van. I was in tears, not allowed to come with him. This was one time I couldn't come. Me grabbing at his arm and crying louder but still not allowed to come.

When he came back, his boiler-suit didn't smell of my grannie's shed the way it should have done. There was something I'd only smelled before each year on the night of the gellie. The paraffin hints around the burning wood. Then he went across the road to give the widow her money.

Strandings

The blue of these doors was deep. It was a dark, navy shade, no green in it. Stornoway harbour was pea soup and the beaches you reached out to, on Sunday school picnics, were as much green as blue. A colour I'd seen called 'mallard' in the plates of the Arthur Mee encyclopaedias. A locomotive was called that and coloured it too.

Three words, 'Life Saving Apparatus', were painted across the double doors, in white and you couldn't see any drips from the letters. When you passed by here, it was always worth a look to see if anyone was inside. Same thing, passing the fire station. Just round the corner. Doors open. Abandoned bicycles. A car or van left with its wheels on the pavement, parked in a hurry.

Sometimes I'd walk down for the paper, with the olman, him stretching his legs after pedalling at the loom all day. This was before we had the car and before he moved to that other office, up the far end of town, near The Battery. It was while he still got the *Express*. We'd to remember the *Woman's Weekly*, if it was the right day for it. Then he'd wind me up. '*Harold Hare* for you, isn't it?' But he knew fine I got *The Eagle* now. A *Bunty* for Kirsty. I'd learned it was no good asking for a *Beano* or a *Topper*. He'd always get our *Eagle* and *Bunty*, our choices, and a *Look And Learn* to share.

Back up the road, this day. The small door, set into the big double LSA doors, was open. It was there so you didn't have to go undoing all the bolts to get in. You only opened the big doors if you needed to get all the gear out. Some of our neighbours were in the team. We might see Uisdean, a neighbour, sorting out stuff.

Then one of the big doors opened. A man appeared. He had a white shirt and a white-topped cap. I wondered how he'd managed to bend through that small door, to open the big doors from the inside. Like in *Alice In Wonderland*, I thought, though I'm sure I didn't say that.

'What do you have in the Aladdin's cave, these days?' the olman asked and the tall Coastguard said, as it happened, he was just going to do his inspection so we'd get a look.

The second, wide door opened to brass lamps, wooden crates painted the same blue shade, wooden pulleys, shining with oil, neat coils of rope. Faint creosote. Dusty hemp. My father lifted one of the pulleys and said there was quite a trick to it.

This was the snatch block for the hawser. The breeches buoy would run on that, pulled out on an endless whip of lighter rope. I liked the words but couldn't see how that gear could rescue anyone, till the Coastguard started chalking a picture on a blackboard for me. Now I could see it, how people were brought ashore from wrecks. First the big rocket took out a light line. Then the crew had to pull out the thick rope – the hawser – so it all went from the shore to get tied round the mast of the wreck. That big rope was pulled tight and then it was like a runway for a cable car. The whip was the lighter rope that pulled the thing like a lifering back and fore, running along the thick hawser.

Survivors had to climb into the buoy. It had thick canvas leggings roped to it. Just in case you didn't get the idea, there was dark lettering which said, 'Sit In Breeches'. You were pulled ashore by the endless rope as your breeches ran along the thick hawser line. The empty buoy was then pulled back out again, for the next survivor in line.

The olman had gone very quiet. I thought this was just his usual trick of stepping back to let me figure things out. Then his voice came but it was very low.

'So why couldn't they use all this stuff at the *Iolaire*?'

'Feel the bloody weight of it. Even if you rounded up ten hardy crofters and a horse and cart, in time, it would be a struggle. When it gets wet, it's heavier still. No Land Rovers then. The access at

Holm wasn't great either. And it was New Year's night – the first one after the War. It would take time to round up your squad.'

At school, we were always told the story of the *Iolaire*. It wasn't a proper warship. Just a big motor yacht trying to carry the survivors of the First World War home for the New Year. Most were lost, about a mile out from Stornoway. The Beasts of Holm were really close to the shore. My olman took me out a walk to the memorial a few times. Most of the lost men were naval reserve. Most could have piloted the ship into harbour.

My father and the Coastguard were talking about it. One lad swam ashore with a rope. A few got off. What's the tide doing then? Falling. That's it, then. She'll be over. A watch was recovered, stopped at the time water entered it.

'And the *Stella*?' It was my father's voice again. Kenny F's olman's boat.

More recent history. They were all running for home but she was behind the rest of the fleet. He'd been on watch, at Holm. She was still showing her fishing lights, as well as her steaming lights. Red over white, up top, for fishing other than trawling. Most of the boats never bothered to put out the fishing lights, when they were steaming home, and most of them showed green over white – the trawlers.

'You know what I'm talking about, don't you?' the Coastguard said.

I saw him get a nod from my olman. Something passed between these two then, I wasn't sure what.

Knowing she'd be stacked up with gear, he'd watched her go under the blind spot at Holm. Off the Beasts. You could start counting then till you saw the lights re-appear. A slow count to fifteen or so, usually. But she never came back into sight. He called out the lifeboat and LSA then.

'Aye,' the olman said, 'the word is she just lost steerage, surfing in there and couldn't turn in time. Could have been the same with the *Iolaire*. Or maybe just underestimating what speed she was making in that following sea.'

'So you're a seaman, right enough?' the Coastguard said.

'Not now and you still don't know me, do you?'

Then my father did something I've only seen him do in our own house. Took his beret off. You didn't even notice it was on, after a while. Outside the house, it was always there. But that wasn't too unusual, round the town. We even have a word for it – your caydie, not just any hat. Like your trademark.

When I say he was bald, I don't mean just in the centre. He didn't have any hair on his head. You didn't even notice this after a while, even when he had the caydie off, in our house. And I suppose our neighbours were used to it, too.

But as soon as he took the beret off, the other man knew him. He couldn't say a word.

'I'm not a ghost yet. Remember, you got me out alive,' the olman said. 'There was nothing wrong with our own steering that night. Just the guy on the bridge.'

The Coastguard was recovering. Leaning against that rescue equipment. Remembering. Then he could speak.

North African coast. Ben Line. I was bosun. You were shaping up that way yourself. We hadn't been that route before. We thought Casablanca was only in the movies. This was a wind-up. We couldn't be heading there for real. Hogmanay and we were off watch. We'd taken our skinful early and were sleeping it off so we'd be ready for the next shift. Pity everyone hadn't done it that way.

The apprentice was left on the bridge on his own. Poor wee cadet steering when the mate went off to try to quieten down all the whoopee getting made down below. 'Just be a minute,' he said.

The baby sailor had the course to steer, safely round the top but he got into a daze. Instead of putting the helm over to keep her off the land, fighting the drift, he just calmly went with it. The compass started swinging.

What a crunch when we hit. Then the bloody klaxons went off. Everybody was going for a door. Drunk or sober. In their clothes or not. Bloody shambles.

Four to a cabin, those days, in steel bunks. Hellish steep companionways. The captain was shouting for the bosun to get a count going. None of these boats is getting lowered until every man's accounted for.

'Where's MacAulay?' he asks. Bloody hell. I had to get back down below with another guy to look for you. There was bit of a list on the ship already. She was settling. Not falling any further.

We found your cabin door and the bunk was collapsed in there. The steel beam of the top one was lying across your bunk below. You saw the torch and started shouting out in Gaelic. But you weren't in pain. Nothing lying on top of your body. Just the way these steel beams fell. They'd caged you in. We shifted one and you were free. Unhurt. We all got up on deck together.

But you were still shouting. All in Gaelic. The captain said, 'MacAulay is panicking the others, what's he saying?' I told him you were back in the war. Something about a tank. You were trapped inside.

We got told to shut you up. Someone found a bottle and we got a fair bit of rum down you. Then we got on with the counting and checking lifejackets. The boats were all ready to leave. But the ship didn't list any further.

In the morning we could all look at these bloody great lumps of rock. Shit, we were lucky. We could just sit tight for now. The weather was good. She was wedged solid. Then a squad of harbour launches was arranged to get us in to port. Nothing to write home about. We didn't get to Casablanca. We were in hotels for a couple of days before they decided to write off the ship. In that time, something was happening to your hair. First, it turned white. By the time we got home, it was gone. All of it. Your own mother was going to have trouble recognising you.

And you never did go back to sea, did you? Well, you didn't miss much. The Last Days of the British Merchant Fleet. We saw them. On the decline from then on. They were giving the Japanese builders guided tours of the Clyde, don't ask me why. Missionary work to show our way was better than the Communists, I suppose. Who was doing the kamikaze now?

Hell, this must be hard work for the boy. Must be some emergency rations here somewhere. Yes, here's an issue of chocolate bars. What about putting your name down for the LSA? Could do with a few guys who knew the arse end of a block from the other. No?

Well, I can understand that. Hell of a night on the way to Casablanca. Could have been worse. That was close enough. We got away with it.

'Most of the boys on the *Iolaire* didn't get away with it,' my father said.

'He was some lad, the man who got the rope ashore. The boat builder at Ness. The Royal Humane Society gave him a medal but they say he never talked about it.'

'No, I don't think he did.'

I heard the olman say that, even though I was getting stuck into the chocolate ration. That's all he said.

Yarns

My grannie with the Spangles was always telling stories. So was my uncle Ruaraidh. He'd get his mother started and then something she said would get him going. My aunty Sheena said they were like collie dogs chasing each other out on the hill.

Usually my uncle took me out in the green Austin van. I liked its badge. It matched the chrome of the stick-out indicators which showed other drivers where you were going. Better than sticking your arm out the window in the rain. Ruaraidh showed me how to save petrol. He'd turn the key as we took the left fork, off the Ranais road, down the hill. We'd see if we could coast all the way to my grannie's door.

It wasn't like our house. You could see the stones it was made from. Some of them were huge. It was easy to see how the lower ones would get moved but how could they get the big ones up when the walls were already high? There were never any cranes out here. I never got a proper answer to my question.

The mantelpiece was wood, not tiles. It had china dogs, big as real ones, not collies but terrier-sized. It was usually just myself, the uncle took along. The sister would be helping the olaid, baking and things. There wasn't an open fire like our house but a creamy Rayburn. If it was cold weather, my grannie opened the bottom oven door and told you to stick your feet in for a while. We'd have a cup of tea to start with. Then Ruaraidh would say, 'This won't pay the rent, *a bhalaich*. Nor put bread in the mouths of the bairns.'

Fanks were best. Other people would come and then there would be two or three dogs and a smell like Dettol. I liked that smell. So did most of the people. One man put his dog in to the bath when the sheep were finished. Another said, well if he hadn't gone bald he'd give his own hair a wash now. But when he took off his caydie his head was nearly as shiny as my olman's. I wondered what had happened to him.

At first, my grannie came out to help a bit. She got carried away when she was shooing the sheep. She always said, 'Kirie, Kirie, Kirie.' Maybe the sheep know that means to go on ahead, the same way the dog knows to crouch down or to start chasing, from a word or a whistle. Then my grannie stopped coming out but she still made scones, stacks of them. They came off a thing like a heavy frying pan. They didn't come out of the oven. She always timed it so there was a pile, still warm, when we came in. 'Help yourselves now, you'll get no waitress service here.'

People always started off with the weather then the news.

A coorse, coorse winter this, worst one for snow I can remember and I wasn't born yesterday. That Eichmann was found guilty on all counts. The world's getting smaller. You can't run away forever. That was a terrible plane-crash in Rhodesia. The Secretary General on his way to talks on the Congo. Was it an accident? A man swam the Channel both ways, an Argentinean. Must be all that corned beef. Get some of that down the wee fellow. Even if he is a Catholic that President Kennedy is a lovely man. Aye, some would say the first lady is a fine specimen too. It would take more than pretty speeches to stop them building that wall in Berlin. Will Real Madrid take it again this year? Big challenges. At least we can't do much worse than last year. We'll need to watch that Charlton fellow. And Greaves is deadly.

I didn't always know what they were talking about. But I got pictures in my mind, like listening to the radio. The Secretary on the Congo – you could see people typing letters, really fast while they were sitting on cushions floating on a wide river with jungle on each bank.

Then they'd get laughing, jumping back and fore between Gaelic and English. 'I'll tell you after,' Ruaraidh would say but I'd tug at my grannie's sleeve while she was laughing away. '*A ghràidh*, it's not the same in English. Here, do you like Spangles?' Each one was wrapped separately in the packet. Sometimes it was fruit ones and sometimes it was sharper ones.

You only got the other kind of stories if it was getting dark early. My grannie would sometimes ask Ruaraidh to tell me one of his yarns, so I wasn't left out, with all the political talk and the Gaelic. A story. For himself – that was me. Ruaraidh or someone else would say, 'Listen to herself trying to stir it up. What about one of your own Mac an t-Sronaich stories?'

'I don't want to frighten the townie,' she'd say. 'They only go to the pictures to get scared. They don't hear the real stories any more in Stornoway.'

So of course I'd to push out my chest. Proud because I'd done my share at the fank. Even got blood on my hand when the ram pulled me against the fence and they all said I'd seen too many Westerns at the Playhouse.

My grannie with the Spangles would top up everyone's tea then Ruaraidh might start.

'Did you hear now, the Ranais seaman's story about the coffin?' So of course everyone laughs and asks which of the thousand and one stories about a coffin this is. 'The true one,' he said and they all laughed again, but once my uncle was in full flight they'd all be leaning over to catch every word.

Someone said these yarns were better when the Tilley lamp was whirring away. But my grannie said we were supposed to be moving forward, not going backward. 'It wasn't that long ago electricity and running water came to this house. Maybe you'd rather just go out the back to the old chemical toilet but you can all use my WC if you ask nicely.'

My grannie admitted, though, that she kept the Tilley handy for power-cuts. 'What about Mac an t-Sronaich now before the boy had to be getting home?' someone said. Why did he have to get home tonight at all? There was a spare bed made up. His father could surely pick him up tomorrow.

'What about me though?' Ruaraidh said. 'I'll be scared stiff driving across the moor on my own after one of my mother's stories.'

But my grannie got me to phone home and it was decided.

'Have you seen Mac an t-Sronaich's cave, out the castle grounds at the mouth of the Creed?'

'Course I have.'

That big smooth slab, out there, where he cut up any animal he could steal. And the chimney in the rock where he roasted them. Now when the Creed river is low it's an easy crossing, maybe at the island and you're well out the Arnish moor. Then you wouldn't have to go near the lighthouse, not even the farm. You could dodge round the back at Prince Charlie's loch and get across the burn that goes into the Tob. Sometimes it's slow going in the heather and bogs. But it's not a long walk for a fit man. And they said Mac an t-Sronaich was fit all right, wiry as they come.

See when you come out at Griomsiadair, if you come over the shore way, you stumble on the last croft, a bit apart from the rest. You'll still see them, the lazy-beds, for oats and potatoes, enough for half the village. They're mostly out that way. So he wouldn't risk coming out there, in case there was a squad from the village working late. But see if you follow the lochs, you come to the end of our own croft and the houses were further apart then. Now you've got to think back a few years. They didn't even have the chemical toilet. No corrugated iron even. Just a blackhouse. Just a thatch and a rough door and the fire in the middle of the floor. A lean-to barn so you got the heat of the animals as well.

Mostly it was big families then but this poor wee boy's mother had died, having him. So the boy and his father just looked after each other and the boy helped with everything. Now they only had the one cow and they were very attached to her. She was Anabladh — a proper Highland cow, hardy as anything. Every evening she would come in from the grazings on her own when it was milking time. Without fail. And she had a fine calf, a red one so that was Anabladh Ruadh. She'd be worth a bit, end of the season.

So this night when the cow and calf didn't appear, they were worried. It crossed his father's mind that there were stories Mac an t-Sronaich was on the prowl again but he didn't want to frighten the boy. So he just said, 'Look now, you stay here and don't open the door to anyone till I get back. I'm just off to the end of the croft for the cow. I'll not be long.'

It was just on dark, the dips as they say, and the boy pulled the wooden bar over on the door. It was just against drafts really because nobody locked doors then.

His father was out near the moor and there was still no sign of the cow. He went further, careful with his footing in the dark and he was calling, 'Anabladh. Anabladh Ruadh.'

Then he was hearing the cow but she was distressed, you know, bothered about something. He found her then but there was no sign of the calf.

So the poor man started calling out again, 'Anabladh Ruadh.'

Next thing, this gruff voice came back and he couldn't tell where it was coming from. 'Half your Anabladh Ruadh is in the pot now and the other half will do for my breakfast.'

The father was really mad now and he would have had a go at Mac an t-Sronaich with his bare hands. He stumbled out further and heard the voice again. 'Half your Anabladh Ruadh is in my stomach now and the other half is roasting for my breakfast.'

He couldn't guess where the voice was coming from till he realised he was now a long way out from the village. It could be coming from the other direction, back where he'd come from, nearer the house. They say Mac an t-Sronaich could be very cunning. Maybe he was just being lured further out so that thief could circle back towards the house. They say he'd just take what he wanted, steal your food and he'd be away back over the moor with it. They say he could jump over the moor like a goat. They say he wouldn't let anybody stand in the way.

So that father started running for home but he twisted his ankle in the bog and it slowed him down. He could only hobble back towards the house. And a big squall of wind and sleet got up so no-one was going to hear him trying to shout. All the pain in his ankle was nothing to what was going on in his mind. He wasn't worrying about his fine calf any more.

Now back at the house, this very spot. Probably some of the same stones are in the walls of this house we're in right now. The boy heard a tapping at the door above the wind and hail. He ignored it and the door started rattling and shaking. Then there was a tapping at the one window. He could just make out a thin figure, bent over. 'Will you not give a minute's shelter to an old man on a night like this?'

But the boy just said they've been told not to open the door to anyone. 'Your father would want you to help a poor stranger.'

And the hail is rattling till the boy is thinking he has to take pity on the old fellow. 'You'll be alone in there now?'

He's saying nothing but he's thinking maybe Mac an t-Sronaich's been spying on the house, looking for his chance. And just then the figure outside starts hurling his frame at the door. There's real force there and something's got to go. The boy is looking at the wooden pin. A short piece of wood is a very strong thing but it's a matter of time before the door gives way. The rattling and thumps and the creaking wood – noises that go right through you.

Till the boy shouts back, louder than the hail and the rattling door. 'I'll need to get my brothers and sisters, through the house,' he said. 'We'll see what they have to say. Mairi. Calum. Torcuil. Ishbel. Sheena. Coinneach. Tormod...' *The boy was shouting out the names that came into his head. But he soon heard the scurry outside as Mac an t-Sronaich ran for it, fleeing back out the moor.*

His father was so happy his son was unharmed and so impressed with his quick thinking that the loss of the calf was no worry. As long as they had each other they could build everything up again. And Mac an t-Sronaich never bothered the village of Griomsiadair again. So that boy got the better of him.

Migrations

Like a lot of folk on this planet I owe my existence to herring. That and the Ross and Cromarty Council points system for allocating new council houses. The market for abundant herring brought the trade which created rafts of black small ships across bays and harbours, following the routes of the migrating fish. Stornoway was a main port. You could smell the scales along with the cotton nets and the burning coal. Diesel was in the air too but all the boats, with their slanting or rounding sterns, had chimneys. They all had black ranges then, though the Calor Gas shop was open on the pier. There was usually a smell of chops and bacon, from the boats.

When we visited The Broch, I knew that smell. But there was a different one, too. Some days there would be a tearing, sour stink behind the general mix. If the wind was blowing in from the outskirts, out Rosehearty way, you'd get a whiff of the gut factory. We used the same name in SY. Ours was out Seaforth Road. It wasn't just guts went there. Scad and mackerel, caught amongst the herring – there was no market for them. And if the herring catch missed its own market, sometimes you'd see the baskets getting tipped into lorries.

When you see fish in that amount you don't really notice the details of the species. The Arthur Mee books also had colour plates with different fish and the herring looked like a tropical species. All sorts of colours. I don't know why, but I got interested in fish. All these single herring swam in shoals which could keep the boats chasing them for days on end.

I think the gut factory smell was stronger in The Broch than it was at home.

But in SY or The Broch they had curing and kippering and commerce. So a Broch quine could typewrite her way into the iron-clad hexagon that was Stornoway fishmart. She could chaave awa wi the merchants o th borough. She might hear a hame voice on the quay. 'Na ye're nivver Sandy Sim's quine, Andra's sister?'

Maybe her own pedigree would show in a foxtrot. And her sure sense of rhythm would find the equally certain timing of the Lewis weaver. The relationships of the day were built on dancing as much as conversation.

Once I heard my mother, back in the voice of her hometown, I realised how her language was never really flowing, when she was on the Island. The Morris Traveller got us to The Broch more than once. That's where I heard the olaid clacking away, steady as the olman's Hattersley loom. It all happened in the pre-cast walls of the pre-fab house. The buildings that were only going to have to stand for ten years, as an answer to the post-war housing shortage. When she got home to SY, I think she might have typed out her story, right away, before going back to work. This is it.

I'd ging aff tae a dance wi ten Woodbine in a Players packet. Aa the quines did. The few men still hingin aroon likely didna hae tae bather. A lot o them didna bather muckle aboot learning tae dance aither. Ane o the qiunes quid get the works truck, nae the bus like. Jist the richt size to tak the sax or seevin o's, fae The Broch tae Peterheid. Aa aboot the toon. Ane o oor crood fae Inverallochy, anither fae Cairnbulg, ane fae Rosehearty if I mind richt. Syne ane awa oot in New Aberdour.

The time we spent gettin deen up for the Peterheid dance. You'd tae get the big reid lips richt and syne the thin black line doon the back o yer legs tae mak it look like proper stockins. Heels an aa. They aye had a real swing band in the blue toon - trombones, the lot.

Ae wye it was the loons in uniform you went for. Anither wye ye kent they were aa gettin ready tae ging awa, an there was a fair chance they widna be comin back. Us quines wid

agree tae shy clear o the navy types if ye quid. The odds
werena jist that great for thon puir loons. An the Merchant
Navy loons might get a hard time o it ashore, in their civies
but we kent they'd likely nivver be comin hame. The convoys
wid sail gey close in, past us.

Fair gettin the sangs goin on the drive there. Best time
I ivver hid, in a wye, if that disna soun terrible. Working
aa thae oors at the Toolies, gettin a wage and kine o pleasin
yersel.

But the claik atween us wis the thing. We fixed the van
oorselves ae nicht. That quine that drove kent fit she wis
aboot, so fan the thing dees on us, the lichts gingin doon,
she kens it's the fan-belt. An she heard someplace or ither
a stockin's the thing for a temporary repair. Only thing is
naebody's wintin tae admit they've a real pair o stockings
on because they ken they'll lose them. So we're aa grabbin at
each ither's legs, sayin tae come clean - and sure enough ane
o the crood has the real MacCoy. So we gie her a good slug
fae the half-bottle o gin as compensation, like. That driver
o oors ties a gweed ticht knot and we're aff again. Took us
there, got us hame again.

The crack wisna quite the same though efter that puir
loon in Orkney wis kilt. D'ye ken aboot that? Think he's
in the history books as the first civilian casualty. Plinty
eftir him. The Broch got hit mair than aince. Some fowk said
it wis the defences they were aifter, ithers the fishing
industry, feeding the country. Ithers again said na, na,
they werena targeting The Broch, like, we shouldna flatter
wirsells. They were jist dumpin their boombs if they hidna
seen a Convoy i the North Sea. Bofors guns were getting made
i the toon but we were makin Merlin engines for Rolls Royce.
We coulna admit til wersels that we were the targets. There
wis ane or twa terrible nichts. The fifth o November, 1940,
that wis ane.

Souns bloody terrible to say it, like, but it wis gweed
times for us workin quines. Tell ye a funny thing, though.

Some nichts, dance or no, we'd tak that van, us aa packed in, jist for a spin, like. Richt there on the back road, oot the wye o the lichthoose, Kinnaird Heid, there. It's my shotty up front, ridin shotgun and I think I'm seeing this aafa dim licht up aheid.

There's a lot o gigglin gaun on as per usual, but I'm telling aabody tae shoosh, as if that's goin tae mak me see better. Slow it richt doon, noo, slow. It wis a tail licht on a bicycle run affy a dynamo. So of coorse it's helluva dim there, wi the slope gaun uphill. We damn near ran that puir lassie doon.

She wis on her last legs. I said tae her, jokin like, it looked like she'd come aa the wye fae Aiberdeen. Fae Surrey, mair like. She wis a Land-Girl. Cyclin, and gittin lifts fae lorries part the wye. Kippin doon far she could, an that lichthoose was the eyn o her road. That's far she'd been makkin for the hale time.

It's a strange kinda story this. A lang time ago. We kent we quid bend a bike into that van, for we'd deen it afore. So we did, and first we're just gaun to help her alang tae the Lichthoose. Then, ye're thinkin, like it's such a queer story, is this gaun tae be aa richt? Nane o' us kent the keepers oot there, or their faimlies. So we didna funcy jist drappin her aff again.

Naitral like, we aa end up back for a filie at ane o the quines wi a bit mair space in the hoose. So she's tae bide there for the nicht. But of coorse we've aa got the late nicht hunger noo. There's nae breid; nithin. She's still in thae khaki breeches, gey strange things, blouse and gansey.

She's nae lookin sae roch for somebody that's been sleepin oot or takin a chance on a bed here an there. We aa tak til her. Nae a Scot, but nae a strang English twang aither. And some o the pack are gabbin tae her fan I'm awa oot the back wi a graip and liftin new tatties. Some ither biddie's heating up the fat and seen we're aa sitting tae egg an chips at that time o nicht - an us aa due tae ging tae work the next day.

You quid aye get eggs that bit oot o toon.

Then we're aa cravin for somethin for a sweet tooth an it's back oot tae the van for a wee stashie o tins. Emergency rations. Condensed milk to bile up wi a handfu o puddin rice an a puckle raisins. Talk aboot ambrosia! The land-girl quinie jist laps it up. Energy gaun back intil her.

Suppose that wis aa there wis til't, like. Missed some o her yarn fan I wis oot the back and scraping tatties. Then she was awa on her bike again, afore we were feenished.

Canna mind hoo she kent aboot Kinnaird Heid. Wis it her faither or her man that was stationed there? Bit we nivver saw her again. We aa meant tae drive oot tae speir if things had worked oot and she was aaricht, but we quidna get hud o the van for a while. Talked aboot her though. Maybe she'd just faan heid ower heels for a loon that had been stationed doon her wye - bit I dinna think so. Somethin aboot her. As if she was migratin. Like geese or that, nae choice. She might hae been the dochter o a lichtkeeper raised in the loom o that licht and needin tae get back til't, jist tae cope wi somethin. Or else she was gaun tae hae a bairn by a loon that wis noo tendin that licht on Kinnaird. It's nae jist ma memory. Nane o wis quid get that muckle sense oot o her that nicht. But I'll nivver forget her gettin stuck into that rice puddin we'd biled up. Lickin the spoon she wis, an us aa grinnin like mither hens, lookin aifter her.

Telt you it was a strange kind o a story. Dinna ken noo fit pynt I saw in it fan I started oot. That mony bits missin.

First free nicht efter that we got hud o the truck again, and of course heided straight aff tae the Peterheid dance. That was our ain wee migration. Desperate tae get there. She just went oot o mind efir that.

I'm seeing her again. Richt noo. First that dim, dim reid. And her nae lookin much at the road in front o her. Jist following the big wide sweep o Kinnaird. She'd taen a sense o that licht a the wye fae Surrey.

But I didn't think the Land Girl was like a stray goose, out of the formation. I was thinking of her first in her uniform, in a line of others in a field. Working in that moving line, a shoal of girls in brown breeches and greenish jerseys. That one breaking away, one night. Finding a way north, up the east coast of Britain. Getting lifts on lorries. Taking short cuts she found out all by herself.

So she became more like one single herring in a colour plate in Arthur Mee. A brown and green herring swimming along B roads. I was thinking that when I heard my mother tell it on her home turf. Then I smelled what was cooking. Sandy's quinie, my olaid, was helping in the kitchen. She was showing my sister how to edge the backbone out with your thumb – you didn't need the knife for that. Then they were dipped into the oatmeal and then put in the pan.

The coating turned more yellow than brown and got crispy. First the bones tickled you a bit then you stopped bothering and ate the whole thing. Then I forgot about herring being single things with eyes that could catch the glint of plankton, mouths that sucked in food from the sea.

The Move

It was the job that brought her to the Island in the first place. Good money for a woman. Not so much typing skills as a certain kind of toughness. She'd need it all in the fishmart offices. Up over everything, the weathercock was a salmon.

The olaid handled the wholesale side of the coal-merchant's trade, maritime insurance matters and an agency for the sale of charts. Whenever The Broch, Buckie, Banff or Peterhead boats were in, she'd be busy. I'd need to go in next-door, after school. I'd still get my roll and salt butter with my cup of sweet tea, to keep me going but it wasn't the same.

She'd really been employed as an interpreter, my olman said. She'd need to get across the gist of what some irate East Coaster had to say about arrangements made on his behalf. He'd not be best pleased if his vessel had to be slipped at Goat Island for some inspection, when the herring were running.

She'd bought a new three-piece suite, to replace the brown vinyl one that had ended up on our gellie. Before that, it had been used, in our big back yard, for committee meetings, discussing raids to increase our stock of code-marked tyres.

She bought fish knives. They came from the catalogue, in lined boxes and were shown to people who came in. The olman didn't argue with any of this as long as we could still eat herring and kippers with our fingers, as usual. These knives and the matching forks were laid out anyway. She reminded Kirsty to put them out with the usual ones. I think we used them once, when we had boiled ling in a white sauce.

I noticed that the olaid wasn't using the fish knives either, next time we had fish. For some weeks they were still laid beside soup and pudding spoons. Then they just stayed in their special box with the brass clamps, in a drawer of the sideboard.

Now we had one of these electric fires with artificial coal. It had wood surrounds to match the radiogram. I found that the flickering effect came from a small propellor which was turned by the heat of a red bulb. I could switch one bar on for myself if I was home before she was back and next-door was out. At the weekends, the electric fire was put out to the hall and we had a real one again.

The way she put it to us was, how would we feel about moving to the mainland? Our father had been offered a very good job. It was down near Stirling, the castle and the Forth. They taught nursing at the infirmary in Stirling. That's what Kirsty wanted to do.

I thought of the battle of Stirling Bridge. But the mainland was the absence of Griomsiadair. No more going out, first in the uncle's van then the olman's Traveller. Best with the uncle – getting your hands full of red sheep paint. That was called keel, like the bottom of a boat.

But the mainland was also brown paper blinds, so you could watch *The Fugitive* without the flickering light interfering. You got Grampian reception in The Broch. We could only get one channel on the Island, picked up on a hill outside town and plumbed in to most of the houses.

And on the mainland, ice-cream vans with oysters and sliders, stopped at the door. There were fish and chip teas with as many scones and pancakes as you could eat, in dining rooms, up over bakeries.

They must have been trying to tell us for a long time because it all happened very soon after that. Just when the new term was starting. The olman went first, to find a house and then we were staying on the *Loch Seaforth* instead of getting off at Kyle. After breakfast she put in to Mallaig and we caught the train. We saw deer, running from the tracks. We got in to Glasgow, Queen Street. The olman had been staying in a B&B from hell. He was talking more than usual. And much faster. The Morris had a new engine and was running sweet, on the long straight road from Glasgow to Stirling. We'd been over the Forth Road Bridge, last trip to the mainland. The olman said it had cost six lives. A lot less than the railway bridge. Now the one over the Tay was open. I don't know how many lives that one cost.

We'd have to go a wee trip. Clock that one as well. And the house? There were some beauties on the scheme but all out of our reach. This was a neat small one but the attic had been lined and there was space for another room.

Then I was being led into a class in a sandstone school and introduced as the new boy. Was I another Wee Willie? What? Football?

But I couldn't conceal the fact that I wasn't great at football.

When they asked me what Stornoway was like, thinking that was the Island, not the town and the whole place was up near Iceland anyhow, I talked too much about the great fishing and the woods and the pier. But they had plenty of woods, a pier at Gartmorn Dam and as much fishing as you wanted. What about the sea? Aye, if that's what yer wantin there's flounders in the Forth. Doon at the docks.

That was the year when I escaped the 11-plus, the big exam at the end of Primary, the one that decided your future. They'd already done away with it, down south in the Central Belt. That was also the year when the Island was in the news. When the Caledonian Hotel burned down. We'd had a high tea there, maybe the last Saturday night before the olman left to start his new job. A lassie was trapped in the building.

Then the murder took place, the first on the Island since the days of Mac an t-Sronaich. Maybe even longer – some people said that there was no evidence our Island fugitive ever killed anyone. There was no doubt that a person was killed, this time. She was Mary Mackenzie, aged eighty years. She lived on her own and had a small amount of money. A young neighbour, a weaver, would visit her. He was aged twenty-one years at the time. Some say his visits happened when he was short of cash.

In the village they say, she would sub him, from time to time, glad of the company. In the court, the defending QC introduced a story about a stranger seen that night at a petrol station. I remembered the episodes of *The Fugitive*, seen in The Broch, but I don't think there was a suggestion that this stranger only had one arm.

In the papers and in court, there was no disputing the evidence that Mrs Mackenzie's death was not an accident. She was beaten to death. It might have been an axe. It was certainly not a fall.

In the court, the police claimed that the evidence linked that twenty-one-year-old neighbour to the murdered woman. The defending QC said there was no disputing the fact that this young man visited his elderly neighbour from time to time but that the police evidence had failed to show the proof required to link him to her killing.

In the village, some say, a family closed ranks, helped by the failure of the local police. Some said they hadn't made a proper job of screening off the area before the experts arrived from the mainland.

Let's go back to Brue. This is a couple of lines of croft-houses, following the road that leads down close to the shore. We're just a bit south of Barvas. That's the beach we were always told was dangerous. We were never allowed to swim there. You reached Brue, visiting the Westside cousins, by taking the bus till the end of the main road, then walking towards the sound of the surf. You went a mile down the single-track, over the cattle grid. Even with everyone selling their cows then, they were still not called sheep-grids.

That history has another echo, for me, now. I recognised the story when I read a similar one about ten years later. It's a different setting, more urban than rural and it's fiction. There's an elderly woman who has certainly more money than she can use for her needs, that stage of her life. A young man, a student with strong powers of reasoning, has more need of it than her. He will make better use of it. A police Inspector has his suspicions. He uses reason and pressure and the murderer confesses and is punished. It's fiction but there's a lot of history in it.

No-one confessed to the Lewis murder. The young man from the village appeared in Inverness court, in his best suit, with a look of bewilderment caught by the flash-guns which popped as he arrived and left. Some questions were never answered.

It was plastered all over the national headlines for weeks. If I claimed that the opening headline when the story appeared in the *Stornoway Gazette* was 'Incident At Brue', would you think I was winding you up? There were two key issues. A sum of money was missing from Mrs Mackenzie's house. And there was much discussion of a pile of bloodstained clothing. The forensic evidence was confused.

The verdict was unanimous and it did not take much more than an hour for the jury to report. There were cheers of celebration from the accused's family in the public galleries, quelled by the judge. The charge against the weaver from the same village as the murdered woman was found 'Not Proven'.

The photographs were also on the front page of the nationals. Pints of beer being raised by the twenty-one-year-old and his family, to celebrate. He was a young man, they said. He would have plenty of time to rebuild his own life. He's also dead now.

A good day for the lawyers – that's what the olman said.

That verdict was the same finding as in the Madeleine Smith trial. She claimed to have bought arsenic for her own cosmetic treatment. There was no disputing the cause of death being arsenic poisoning or that Miss Smith had a clear motive. But there was still a need to prove that the arsenic bought by Miss Smith was administered. There was no evidence that the deceased and the accused had met in the period immediately before his death. A witness came forward but the trial had already started so this possible evidence was not admitted.

But what kind of a place was that Island? They kept asking that, in class, in Sauchie. It sounded worse than Glasgow, my classmates said.

Even the weather. I think it was that same year, hurricanes in the Approaches were in the news. The concrete beacon, set at the limits of the Arnish Reef, was toppled. You can see the surf break on it or just swell up on it close to High Water. The remains are in two parts now and the ruin is still listed in records of archaeological sites. Thomas Stevenson, the engineer, described the challenge and the technology which provided a successful solution. A small lighthouse was built on the Lewis mainland, west side of the bay and that small beacon, on the rock, reflected its light.

But the *Iolaire* grounded at Holm on the eastern side of the Approaches. And so did the fishing vessel, *Stella*.

I was beginning to spend a lot of time at library bookshelves. More than once, our teacher would ask if I didn't want to take the book back to my seat. But I'd have read most of it already or found what I wanted. Then I started knowing that I was different. That's because I talked different and some people thought I was English, some Welsh. Maybe that was why I began to hear my own voice, shouting above the rest, when the Catholic bus passed our school going to another. We went to the railings, swung and chanted. Our opposite numbers piled over to the windows on the kerb side of the upper deck. The Catholics cast out their reply in a net of sound, up louder than revving BMC diesels, up over our own wall.

Ghillie

The olman went alone to the funeral of his mother. She was my grannie with the Spangles. The one who knew all about fishing and dipping as well as scones. He wanted me to come with him, on the train, bus and ferry. The car was in the garage again.

The olaid said we could just get the plane, Glasgow to Stornoway, and worry about it at the end of the month but the olman said he couldn't do it. It wasn't the money. It was when they shut that tin door and you were up there. At least on the ferry you could get out on deck. You could open the window of the train – it was all diesel or electric now, on the passenger lines. But a very few shunts of sooty smoke still went up behind our house as the coal-train went out along the valley of the Devon river. Further upstream, they called it Glendevon, but not down here.

The olaid tried to persuade me. My heels, in their new brogues, were digging at the vinyl-covered floor. They weren't the leather-soled ones that were back in fashion again, expensive ones worn under expensive blue jeans. But the uppers were leather, over cheaper moulded soles. And we couldn't afford to carpet our semi so my shoes made a noise on the new vinyl, as they kicked out resistance to all this duty of death.

The olman let me off the hook. The olaid had already come back from the Co-op with the decent clothes I needed, bought on tick. That was a thing she was never going to do. The dark cord trousers had decent pockets, she said. Her own father always said, if times were tight you couldn't afford not to buy trousers with decent pockets. If they bothered about the pockets, all the rest of the breeks would last longer.

But she didn't take the clothes back when my father said he'd go alone. Maybe the wee man had a point, he said. It would be fine at the bread-van and the fish-van, the right things would be said. But at the wake, in the house, all the borrowed seats filled with people in dark clothes, and in the church, no-one would be saying anything good about a woman that never harmed anyone. There was no mention of maybe my sister going up. She was in the middle of exams and it was a long way to go to make the tea and the soup. That's what women did at Lewis funerals after the short service which never mentioned the person you were going to bury.

I was hearing them talking, late on. Kirsty's voice was there, too. The olman was saying his mother managed without a husband most of her life and she kept you laughing with it. Didn't spend on herself but saved from what she had. A woman who could produce what was needed from behind the wally-dugs on the mantel-shelf, at the exact moment. She'd lost her own man when the First War was over for the rest of Great Britain. And she'd given a son to the convoys that kept the supply lines going and the alliance together.

Hell, he knew the world was falling to bits and we were all sinners without having to be told it again. And all the nods in his direction as one who had left the fold and needed this lesson of the transient nature of our lives.

Maybe there might even be a mention of this Gomorrah in the Central Belt. It was Alloa's turn to be in the news. An interpretation of the law in Scotland allowed local councils the yea or nea on censorship, when it came to cinema. So cars were coming from other regions where other councils had taken a moral standpoint on *Ulysses*, the film. They came from far and wide, maybe to see what was behind the two-page inserts in the papers or maybe to express solidarity with Clackmannan, who refused the power of censorship. You couldn't guess at the motives of the occupants of all these Anglias, all these Cambridges, Cortinas, Beetles. Triumphs.

We tried to get a look at the boards, walking through the park to the town, to catch a later bus home. But the usual gallery of stills had been replaced with a discreet rough board, giving the times of the showings.

The olman was subdued, on his return from Lewis. It could have been the travel or it could just have been sheer guilt from us not having returned to visit, as a family, since the removal van. But I heard them talking late. You could hear a lot from up the sliding ladder into the converted loft. Shares of the croft. Long before leaving the Island, he had forfeited all right to anything in Griomsiadair. He couldn't argue with that. But something would have been handy enough to keep the Building Society at bay.

Then my mother's voice came stronger. That bloody car would have to come off the road. We could hardly afford to put petrol in it anyway. We wouldn't get anything for it but at least we wouldn't have to go taxing and insuring it. And the no-claims was gone since that knock on the way home from that damned football match.

So we were green before our time, courtesy of the Abbey National. The Morris went into the garage and stayed. He had to catch the workers' bus at the corner and she would just walk up and down Hungry Hill. I lost the contact with my father that came from him driving me out to Crook of Devon or Rumbling Bridge and collecting me at the end of the day. He'd make a token moan about it but once or twice he'd even shown some interest in this angling after small trout, under hazels, over brambles.

He'd knock them on the head for me. Gut them with the small sharp smooth-handled knife that every crofter's son carried in a pocket. He quite liked being my ghillie. At least it was out in the open. Nothing would get him into a small boat of any sort again. He could just about cope with the *Loch Seaforth* as long as he could get out on deck.

But my corduroy trousers and pink nylon shirt and mock brogue shoes got put to use. The olaid got the word from The Broch. Grampa was failing fast – his lungs of course and Granma was jist broken-hertit. We ended up staying on after one funeral for the next. They were no more than three weeks apart, all in the summer holidays so I didn't have to get time off school.

People were quite cheery but I was sad about the pre-fab and the garden. There were still jars and jars of greenish onions in the cupboard and enough Tunnocks biscuits to stick to the teeth of half the population of Scotland. My granma could never believe there would ever be enough to feed the whole family. There were tins of ham and a fridge full of bacon. She was a hefty lady and maybe that had something to do with the massive strokes, one after the other. But everyone was saying it was a mercy really, she couldn't have gone on long without Sandy.

There was a brass band in full uniform at her funeral and the minister said what a good woman she was. They only carried the coffin the very last bit, here, just family. So a lot of men didn't get a shot of carrying it on the black frame.

The olman was not very long back from going to the Lewis funeral. Now he hired a car to drive up the east coast to join the family for The Broch ones. We all went back down together. It was a Fiat 500. We all fitted in and we came across the Tay Bridge.

Pike

Gartmorn Dam was sided by pines. They'd probably been planted in a post-war panic, anticipating the future demand for pit props and wood pulp. They kept most winds off the water.

The pier had standing room for three anglers. It led out away from sloping walls to the flooded area. A rusty steel cylinder was linked to the concrete bank by an iron walkway. The whole construction must have been there to monitor the supply, or pump it, when the water, captured here, had served the area. You reached onto the pier by stepping round a locked gate and going out onto the lattice of metal.

From there, you could catch the reflection of a real island, forested and about half a mile out. The picture in the water was something worth looking at, in the algae soup of insects, collected here. That's probably why the shoals of small perch also gathered around the pier. The smaller fish would chase the sticklebacks and perch fry that chased the insects. In turn, bigger solo perch and long pike would come up from deep water to take their fill of the intermediate-sized fish.

It was like looking into the diesel film in Stornoway harbour. You could catch the first dimples of disturbance. Could be just a breeze escaping through branches – until you saw fry break the surface. Maybe you'd catch the chrome glint of an accelerating fish below. I leaned over to watch all this and could have been looking at mackerel chasing sandeels.

I took my first pike long before I took a salmon. I was well prepared. A big reader then. Everything from *The Old Man and*

The Sea (because of the leaping fish on the cover) to all the comics. I had a paper-round – newspapers in the morning and magazines after school. I read all the comics before I delivered them. Some customers complained they were getting their papers late. I'd read anything but I liked fishing books best. Manuals and stories. Salmon weighed sixty-four pounds and were taken on long poles of greenheart by a Miss Ballantyne, in tweed, wielding gear over swollen water. Monks bore witness to pike, snapping at water-fowl.

I would sit in the Public Library, between buses back from school, turning the pages of *The Manchester Guardian* till I came to the hot bits. The angling column was by Anthony somebody. He could be casting for sea bass, from storm beaches in Atlantic Ireland. That was another fish with a spiny dorsal like a perch but a silver bar, foreign to me and so pure and strange.

The paper-round money would get spent, between the blue-painted Sports Shop and the Co-op fish shop across the road. Wire traces with treble hooks didn't come cheap, even if the white-haired lady knocked a penny or two off because of your ginger hair and soft voice. Herring fillets made bait that shone and sent a message of oil into the non-tidal water. That catch must have come from the Clyde or Canada. The boned bodies were so clean that they didn't smell of fish. They might have been netted from the chlorine waters, inside the sandstone Public Baths, the other side of the junction.

It must have been New Year's Day because I had no papers to deliver. It could easily have been the first day of the Seventies. I was stocked up with gear, between Christmas and Hogmanay tips. These came from the first few parts of my territory, up from Main Street, before the railway line. These were all council houses.

Further up the hill, there were too many people like us. Refugees from council schemes in other parts of Scotland and now saddled with mortgages they couldn't afford, for a bungalow with at least one dormer window or porch to make it different from next door. Further up the hill again, was the real money. Some of them got *The Times*. There was a lot of *Scotsman*s for every *Record*.

You didn't expect anything, that far up, except for a polite directive to stop using the short cut between gardens and start going the long way round. Please. That was when there were semi's which didn't really want to be connected. My part of Hungry Hill was the place where people went into the Spar grocers for two ounces of cheese. Up the hill, they had the money because they hung on to it.

I was beginning to realise that I now lived in a reservoir. Maybe we were all near enough the same species but there was a pattern of territories. If you walked all the way around the silver birch to find a quiet clearing, at The Dam, you could ledger a worm all day and hope that a survivor of the stock of brown trout would take it. These had been bred to be angled for with Greenwells' Glories and Bloody Butchers. The survivors were forgotten about when the pike and perch took a hold. Rowing boats were removed.

Attempts to control the angling were abandoned. It became free to all. These trout could be bottom feeders or they could snap at smaller fish of several species. The perch territories encouraged float-fishers. But all these areas intersected around that old pier. All substantial fish gravitated towards the small fry.

So when I could, I would catch baitfish like cuddies in a harbour, on the smallest hook you could find, tied on a handline. The trouble was you got too occupied in this and forgot you were collecting them for bigger things. And I learned not to call them cuddies. I didn't like being laughed at. People kept asking me to say salmon and worm. Hebridean indicators in the voice. Like the way we say 'soup'. I was ready to give way to a new accent the way all these Poles who'd settled here after the war, had dropped a syllable or two out of their names. A concession.

I cast the herring fillet from the narrow walkway and paid out line, going round the spikes to take me back to the concrete. Big guys arrived on bikes with drop-handlebars. They normally went after salmon but even on the Tay there was a couple of months closed. They had Barbour jackets and gaffs. They had reels with numbered grades of tension, worked from the back. They told me to wait for a run. Don't hit him till he's turned.

'Like conger?' I asked. 'Like conger,' they agreed.

One of these guys hit a fish. There wasn't much bend in his rod because all his line was running out as he fiddled with the drag. I watched my own nylon go out the three feet they said it would. I waited then hit it and it worked. At first it was a weight then it came in with me. I wound fast and it slashed at the surface. I remembered to give line like the books said, then, next time it surfaced, I just held on. The tension in the rod was pulling it by its wide-open mouth, a treble hook visible in a jaw. The teeth were prominent, like those of a ling, but the marblings, the camouflage, were shades of reed and waterlily. It came to the net in a strange tangle of light, bright enough to be shocking, from that thick water. It was three and a quarter pounds on their spring-balance. 'Do you want to put it back?' I shook my head.

Well, some of these Polish guys will take one from you. A lot of them had been airmen who got stranded here at the end of the war. Or met local women. There was a back-street shop in Alloa where you could buy salami and stuff.

But I brought it home. The olaid made an effort. She didn't know why the book said it was an ugly fish. Mrs Beeton claimed that they were good eating but inclined to be dry and so required plenty of basting. We forked at the baked fish but no-one really liked it.

Most days I caught none but once I caught four, all of them smaller than the first one. When my mother said I shouldn't have taken them home and my sister said it was cruel to kill fish, I said I knew someone who would take them. One of the names on the morning newspapers was foreign enough to be someone who would eat pike.

Instead, I buried them to make maggots. I'd read about this in one of the angling books, from the main library. When I dug up the rottened and softened flesh, some weeks later, it had worked. The skulls and teeth and shrunken eyes were recognisable. That resilient skin still showed a smudged print of the pattern. The maggots in between everything were smaller than the ones you bought, for trout or perch, in the tackle shop. I couldn't get the smell from my hands.

One Sunday we went through to Glasgow. The olman had found

the money to get the car tested and taxed. That bloodymortgage was now another single word in our house. He waxed the Morris so it shone like the other cars in the street. Then we were away. I remember his points like a route to fishing-grounds: Dobbie's Loan; Great Western Road; Kersland Street. This was an aunt-by-marriage on my father's side. She'd lost her husband in the war. He was on the convoys.

Folk she knew, back on the Island, said, by way of condolence, 'So you're still in Glasgow?' But she said she loved it, here. We'd all to come with her now, on the Underground. It didn't go anywhere you needed to go but she brought all her visitors this way. There was talk of doing away with it so you had to grab these chances.

She bought our tickets and we sat on leather benches, holding chrome rails. The smell of the seats made me think of old books. The chrome was the pipework of our Stornoway neighbour's BSA. The glimmer of brass was my first pike from Gartmorn Dam.

We got out at Kelvinbridge. This is near the Botanics. My mother and father were ready to get back to the flat to catch up on the news and have some tea. Kirsty wanted to walk by a few shop windows. Didn't matter that they were shut. Better that way. Yes I could go to the Botanics on my own. I was sure I knew how to get back to the flat. My aunty said she'd write the address and phone number down on a card, just in case. My landmark was a snooker-room. Smoke spilled out of the windows. A blackboard at the door said, 'Private Club.' The flat was round the next corner.

I was hit by the sweaty smell of the Camellia rooms. I took in all the names, going down a gear into sleepiness. Sunday afternoons were still like that, trapped near a bar of the electric fire. The olaid never bothered with the coal fire now. The olman wouldn't let me go fishing on a Sunday but I don't think it was religion. Just trying to get me to think of something different to do.

Still in the Botanics, I found carp. You couldn't say they were merely goldfish. These fish were bred to bring out decorative features. One had a stark colour scheme of red and white. Another had a dorsal fin like a sail. Pectoral fins would move like orange seaweed. They were big and lazy and mouthed at any items that fell into their oxygenated pools.

'Bet you wouldn't mind dropping a line to one o them.' I started because of the accuracy. It was spoken in a soft tone, a Glasgow voice but slow in pace and without the hard edges of the mining towns of the Central Belt.

'Hold on and I'll see if they'll go for a Mint Imperial,' he said. 'Aboot your age, we used to figure oot ways to catch wan. No tae kill it or eat it or anything, jist tae get a right look at it.'

He'd have been about forty to fifty. Dressed like anybody else, in a jacket and good trousers. A cap but I think it was an open-necked shirt. Could have been a polo-neck. I don't remember a tie.

I found I was talking. Telling him I fished for trout and pike where I lived now. Where did I used to live, then, with that accent? No, he liked it, a change. The Hebrides. Aye, he'd guessed aboot there.

'So you're a pike-fisher, then. Quite far up the piscatorial pecking order an that?'

I liked the way he talked like the angling books. We were out of the hothouses now. I was talking again and we were gravitating towards the Kelvin. 'Any fish there?' I asked. I wasn't too keen on the laugh that was his answer.

'Is it too dirty, then?' I thought of the maroon colour that came on the Devon before it met the Forth. Someone else had laughed when I'd asked if it was peat, washed into the water after a spate. It was from Tillicoultry paper-mill, whatever shade was being done that day.

'Aye, it's dirty,' he said, 'but they've made a start on it. They're trying to clean up the Clyde an all. Talk of the first salmon for God knows how many years. Now, if you wouldn't mind being lookout, I've had one lunchtime pint too many the day.'

'Are even the pubs open here on a Sunday?' I asked. 'I kent ye were a real teuchter,' he said. 'Well, the hotel bars anyway. Here's the ideal place, if you would jist keep a wee eye peeled for any old dears coming along.'

It was a sort of tunnel, with the grass turfs growing over it and the path passing all the way through. It had turned dull and not many people were about. I said the coast was clear.

He carried on speaking as he was pissing, looking over his shoulder towards me. I lost the thread of what he was saying. Just hearing the tone of his voice. Then he turned, shaking the drops off and said, 'No a bad size o cock, eh, would you no like to have one like that, yersel, eh?'

My own fins were bristling then, ready to drive me out of the confined area, back to the light. But I didn't try to run or anything. I would have had about two yards start, more really because he wouldn't have been able to start running until he'd got his zip up.

I just stayed still. He said, in much the same tone, maybe a wee edge of something that wasn't there before, 'I suppose you're too shy now, to show me yours.'

I still didn't get into gear. Just backed off.

Now I can see it, instinct serving you, just keeping it slow, getting you away from the hazard. Hearing my own voice saying yes I was too shy and then getting towards the surface, out of that tunnel. Some fifty yards later, not running but walking fast, looking over the shoulder.

He made no effort to come after me.

Back at the flat, over pancakes, back in the car, back in the bungalow on Hungry Hill, I never said anything. It wasn't exactly a big debate going on in my mind but I remember considering whether to say something. Maybe he'd be bothering someone else. Maybe it was more than bother.

It takes a while to get a focus. Now I can observe the tone, the skill in letting me do the talking, homing into my subject. It seems to me now a real tint of danger. I never did say anything though.

That afternoon went right out of my mind, till one time I was back in the West End, maybe twenty years later. Round at Bank Street, remembering the way to the Botanics. Within a mile or so of that tunnel, I saw it all again. Felt my muscles quiver like fins. Looked for the open space, people swimming by.

Torcuil's Olman

If I was in the back garden when the first rumble of a train began, I'd go down to find some empty cans. They'd usually be Ind Coope or Skol. They were from Alloa breweries. Old ale was out. Even the girls on the Tennents cans were perfect. No signs of wear on their skins, hair or costumes. And the colours were pure, no fuzziness from area to area. I'd lay the beer can on the rail, bashing it down a bit so it would hold in place. Then I'd retreat into the whins. The locomotives were all diesel now. When the train had passed, I'd go to inspect the compressed steel. These clear pictures went psychedelic when the metal was pressed to follow the profile of the rails.

You could follow the line out away from the housing. That's how I got fishing. That's how I met Torcuil. I thought Torcuil was from Dollar Academy when I first met him by the Devon river. The railway line formed the boundary between public and private houses. The garden of our own house ended right where the embankment started to slide. So we were at the edge. The rails went to Dollar Mine. That sounded like the goldrush but it was on its last few seams. One or two people from higher up our hill went to school in Dollar. Tall and hairy guys walked around in flannel shorts. Their knees and their ears must have got hardened to it all. Sure he was disguised in jeans for the Saturday but I thought he'd just escaped from the Academy boundaries, to throw a line out. Maybe he wasn't much older than me but he looked it, the fair hair already well over the ears. Once I took that in, I knew he couldn't be at Dollar.

It turned out he lived just up the road from me, the next village out towards the hills. He showed me a trick. The track passed over a high steel bridge, down from Tillicoultry. We'd find a boulder that took the two of us to roll it. Then we'd lift it by getting our weight under it and lever it over the edge. Like a depth-charge.

The splash would come all the way back to us. It would cross all that height very fast. The power of it came close to scaring you. Maybe one day we'd see a huge salmon there, stunned by us after straying up the Devon, from the Forth.

Torcuil's father was a Merchant Navy skipper. He didn't really like us following the railway line out, even if the trains were slow and scarce. But that's all navigation was, these days, he said, following rhum lines.

When you left port you followed electronic railway tracks on the water. Only thing was, you had to keep an eye out for some bastard coming the other way along the same line. These would take you out a few hundred miles. Then you steered along your course-line. That's when the sextant and the chronometer came in. You took a sun sight or a star sight to determine where exactly you were in relation to that theoretical line. Within a certain margin, of course.

I'd been nudged away from Torcuil's collection of LZ and Jethro Tull. His olman was from Dundonnell way and still spoke like it. He was pretty shocked to find I didn't have Gaelic. Torcuil had been on the move quite a bit, only going back to the northwest for holidays. He had an excuse. But someone growing up in Stornoway? That was demoralising. But did I ever go sea fishing? Aye and what gear did we use?

'Only the *dorgh*.'

That wasn't bad for someone who didn't have Gaelic. And what was our *dorgh* like?

So I described the paternoster of bent galvanised wire. A lead weight cast in the middle, swivel above it. You'd feel the bottom and pull up half a fathom so your baits would be out of reach of the crab. Somehow the bite was transmitted, amplified by this gear so you'd feel the nudge at the line on your finger. Even at twenty fathoms.

'Like sonar,' he said. 'And where did you fish?'

'The Dubh Sgeir.'

His eyebrows were a bit scary. It's amazing how many men in authority have eyebrows like that. Deputy headmasters. Just greying. Under them, everything would be neat. Torcuil's father had a white, open-necked shirt. The V-neck looked new. I saw the Pringle label and knew that my own father might have checked it. It was mostly women seated along the line. He was the supervisor. He didn't bother with the beret any more. People called him Yul Bryner, of course.

Torcuil's olman reached for a book. *Indicus Nauticus*. It didn't go out of date like charts and almanacs. He showed me the page with about fifty rocks of the same name. Some variations in the spelling, he said. I wouldn't know the Lat and Long, but did the southern approaches to Loch Erisort sound about right?

It did.

And on the soft ground, between the hard patches, it would be mussel bait for adagan. And lugworm for leopag. I nodded. And what did we consider leopag on Lewis?

That was any flatfish, I said, the way my mother said dabs for all small flatties. My father said leopag to mean flounder, plaice, lemons or dabs.

Next he tested me on peat. I found I could go through this grammar for him, not realising where the knowledge had come from. Our own cul-de-sac in Stornoway or the sorties to Griomsiadair. The fad was just under the cep. You cut the outer one thick because it was fibrous. They did not dry so completely but were good for finishing off the cruach. Regular, even peats from the top row went to build the shell. Then creelfuls of darker peat, broken smaller, were just piled inside. Some places they did them herringbone style like tweed because they said it kept the water out better. The *caoran* was the bottom peat, cut last so it wouldn't go to smoor, which was peat–dross. These were the ones your grannie wanted to start the fire and to get heat up in the Rayburn for baking. The dampened smoor kept the fire smouldering overnight.

Torcuil's mother, coming in with cups of tea, said it was easier to be interested in peats when you were sitting in your armchair in the south of the country, well clear of them. There was a lot of heat in peats when you were cutting them. Plenty heat when you were lifting and turning and gathering them. Only time there was no heat in peat was when you put them on the fire and tried to burn them.

But Torcuil's father was back in the *Indicus Nauticus*. Gob Rubha Usinis, not too far south from the Dubh Sgeir. A lot of people confused it with Usinish light in Uist. There, at the Sound of Shiants. Did I know that place?

I told him I knew a spot just north of there. You kept a house in Calbost open on a point. We put on bigger hooks if we had a drift off there. One day there was a thumping on the line like I'd never felt before. A big green head came to the surface and a long white full belly under it. I saw the hook, not looking so big any more, just in the skin of the mouth, above the barbel. Someone tried to get a hand in the gills but the fish rolled over and flicked a huge tail and was gone. It didn't sink. It swam. It was alive.

Aye, he said, it's the ones that got away you remember best. He had a story about that. It had happened not that far out from Calbost, out on the Shiant Banks. But when it happened he didn't know anything about it.

I could see that Torcuil and his olaid had heard this one before more than once but I was hooked.

I was second mate on the Loch Ness *during the war. We were always chock a block, taking fellows only a few years older than yourselves, on the first leg to join their ships or regiments. There was a scare or two but we never saw much trouble.*

A couple of years ago, I met this fellow at a conference. He was very well turned out. We all were but he was noticeably smart. I thought he might be Danish. He wasn't giving away much. The smoked salmon and tab-nabs were getting passed around. He asked me if I'd served in the Merchant or Royal Navy during the war. So I told him I was in the Merch but on the ferries for most of it.

He asked me which ferries and he seemed to know the area. He said it must be rough for a surface ship in that place when the north wind blew.

The hairs were standing on the back of my neck then. I had a feeling.

Sure enough he described the Loch Ness *pretty well. Told me we were making good about fourteen knots.*

'We had you in our sights,' he said.

The thing was, their main mission was to gather information on the places where Atlantic convoys mustered. They had judged it was not good to give their whereabouts away. They would find other prey out to sea after they had passed their information.

I wasn't going to thank him for my life. I didn't get through the war without seeing the destruction that follows a torpedo-hit. The smell of burning oil is something you remember.

So, in this case, we were the one that got away. That's why he remembered our ship so clearly. The way you remember that big ling, off Calbost.

Andra

The summer after the one when all the grandparents disappeared, the olman had to work on, get some overtime. This was a new word in our house. There was no more talk of having to earn your crust in a decent number of hours. And it wasn't only pattern-making. The olaid said he was just a foreman really, overseeing all these rows of knitting machines. They were getting all the rest, out of him, free, gratis and for nothing.

So I'd need to go with my mother to The Broch. I couldn't be left alone all these days and my sister had her own summer job.

They were worried about my fluctuating moods. One day I'd be hitting the glottal stop with the rest of them, the next pissing them off by saying that Stornoway ruled OK. Even if the Aths or the Rovers weren't even in the Highland League. At least Alloa was in the second division. But I only boasted out loud to those my size or smaller.

Maybe it was just the time of life. Hair was starting to appear all over the place. At last you felt you could hold up your arms when you were diving, at the baths. But you were worried that the almost constant erection would come out over the top of the swimming trunks. So you didn't focus too long on these older girls, swimming slowly by with the upper parts of their costumes pretty full.

That was about the time that sex started to rot my teeth. Or maybe it was the lack of sex. This science teacher had bobbed black hair. I'd study the bare part of her neck while she wrote on the board. Even now, there's a faint hint of the erotic when you click to light the gas – the smell of a Bunsen burner. Normally distant and aloof, she hated anybody chewing in class. So you got attention. OK, you got belted as well but that was attention too.

That item of Lochgelly craftsmanship would go back over her shoulder and then she'd catch your eye before she swung it. She put plenty into the swing but it wasn't like when a male teacher belted you. If you got even one or two on a cold morning, from a man, that was something you wouldn't want to go through again, in a hurry.

The ritual was also a kind of status. Sometimes a female teacher would send you to be belted by a male. But the science teacher was maybe too proud for that. We kept a score. I ate a lot of toffee. I was in the lead.

Maybe I was just seasick. Defined as a growing awareness of the lack of the stuff around you. Not only sea for the purposes of floating vessels or for providing a home for mackerel whose dorsals made a zig-zag of vees in calm harbours, broken by the leaping cloud of small fry.

Your line going first one way then another in a pattern you couldn't predict. The sheen and phosphor hints of the belly. The back turning against the source of light to show something of a crazy pattern of greens and blues and blacks.

But the sea as something on the move. Just there. So a day trip to the gritty and probably contaminated Burntisland shore beat the Trossachs. We weren't too fussed about the Aberfeldy-Auchtermuchty Scotland where you could find the Broon's But and Ben round the next bend in the road. Too much scenery. Bonny enough. Damp enough. Not salty enough.

So I did grieve for the loss of the harbour, the inner loch at Griomsiadair, maybe even for my grannie with the Spangles and the stories and the bloody great forearms that would wrap you all up in a wrestle just when your temper was at its fiercest. You couldn't win that kind of struggle with your grannie. Even if she wasn't related to Grannie Broon.

Then there were the plots across from the Toolies at The Broch. The hard wee onions that came from them and came to you from out of wide jars. The wind blowing sand between the barriers at the beach. Ice-creams from Jimmie Sinclair's van, eaten amongst the dunes. Out along the rocks to Rosehearty and the cold blue pool, the tiles concreted in to a smoothed-out hollow, near the black breakwater.

Andra would pick us up from Aberdeen Station. Dr Beeching had got to Fraserburgh station first. I used to mix up his name with the Dr on the powders for colds and flu. The adverts were still new to us and we concentrated on them, still.

Andra was the oldest. Maist o his loonies and quinies were gang aboot the planet. Satellites jist. Comin back to base jist when they were wintin fuel.

Maggie let him talk most of the time, just throwing out a line when she felt he was totally off the beam. Andra loved Scotland. Loved his family, loved life. Fairly keen on the fitba as weil. Mebbe he'd jist manage to git doon the roadie tae us, next time Aiberdeen hid an Old Firm game.

Family suppers, aabody jist caain in by West Road fanivver they took a notion for't. A ham or a tongue in the centre wi pickles aa roon aboot it. Jist lke the aul man's.

Maybe it was these suppers gave Andra his stature. He was keeping the big family going. I thought he was a big man. So he was but eventually I noticed he didn't have a head over me. Just big arms, big shoulders, big chest and belly. Big legs. Flicking big heart.

My Aunty Maggie wasn't the thin woman you'd expect as the other side of the act, from all these cartoons in *The Sunday Post* and *The Weekly News*. Everything about her struck you as normal. Just as well.

It was strange staying in the Swedish house even if there was a bit more space than the pre-fab down West Road. Somebody else was in there now. I had to take a walk down, the first day. So I saw the overgrown roses. I never stepped across the low wall but was right back into that garden and through the door, smelling my Broch granma's shreddy beef casserole and the mealy puddins.

The strawberries and sweet peas faded from the orange-red and grass-green after a few days. They just became normal. The colours stayed strong in the crates of skoosh. Back in SY this was all called lade. You got limeade and raspberryade and plain lade and any colour so long as it was bright. Round about Sauchie and Alloa, it was all called ginger. But my Broch granma called it skoosh and she was always digging out crates from cupboards that smelled of old people's clothes. Once or twice, a gill of rum would appear from a cranny and the grampa would kind of look the other way. Evenings were best. The TV was always on but nobody ever paid much attention except when there was sport on.

The Fugitive was still tracking the one-armed man. Bitter veterans of the Korean War. Andra learned to appear when my cousin and me were deep into *Top Of The Pops*. Grampa Sandy would always join forces with the loons, in defence, whether he liked the records or not. Andra would throw out his lines. 'Fit the hell d'you see in yon galshick? Gie me Bothy Nichts ony day o the week. Is that a loon or a quine, that ane?'

'Leave the loons in peace tae enjoy their music.'

My granma was keen on music with a bit of get up and go. And she didn't mind dressing up. The olaid told me how she and my grampa had been local champions at roller-skating, dancing on wheels, when it was a big thing. She was a fully dressed member of the Sally Ally and went to the kirk with the bright sound of brass ringing over grey stone. Old Sandy always wheezed a bit – he'd had a whiff of gas in the trenches but was always tense with energy. He'd never sit for long. A glass of rum helped. He'd argue with Andra just to keep things lively. But usually you saw the old man on his bike. Pedalling away on the single gear, between the plot and the harbour. Always a string of veg or a string of fish dangling from the handlebars.

My cousin Willum (Sandy's Andra's loon) was collecting LPs to play on the Dansette. I'd seen the same player in my mother's catalogue but knew not to ask right then. I'd to keep the paper-round going, when I got back, that was for sure. Willum was going to be doing Navigation at the College but my cousin had his own sideline, for the summer.

He'd point the head of that old yole in towards the boulders strewn between Fraserburgh and Rosehearty, as long as the wind was taking us offshore. I'd haul up the few old pots he'd patched up, with him bumping the clutch of the big *Seagull*. A few kicks of that crazy big prop were enough to put her nose back in. I'd be dangling half over the side, looking for the first sight of a dark blue shape. Seen as a break in the block colour of the netting – a dark patch within International Orange. Willum showed me the net knot, come from his yellow plastic needle and I thought of my own olman, missing something about him for the first time, that holiday. He'd put his own flash of colour into the shuttle. It might look weird to anybody else till they saw the effect of it, against some other background shade.

So the pots would tumble back aboard, one by one. There was a transformation of that dark blue into sunburn red, shouting from a blue-patterned plate. This would be the centrepiece of the supper table, that night, at West Road. Willum had a wee contract with our grampa. A lobster in exchange for two-stroke mix, for the outboard.

I asked if it was a marrow, that strange torpedo-shaped vege-table, laid out as a centrepiece.

Even when others were laughing, our grampa was defending me. A homegrown cucumber wasn't all neat and regular like a shop-bought one.

'As close a relative tae a marra as you're a cousin o Willum though ye widna ken that fae the colour o your skins.'

I was as red as that lobster and Willum had gone black-brown. Granma or Grampa or both of them had matched the money that lobster would have fetched so it could sit here and get scoffed by folk that had as much right tae it as the toffs. Aabody kent boats hid expenses.

And now the old couple just weren't here. Their pre-fab was that few hundred yards down the same road but it wasn't their's now. A mercy they'd gone, so close together, people would say.

When the olaid had to go back south to work, there was no objection to the idea of me shuffling into the back room made up there wi naebody bidin in it. Willum didn't mind having somebody to do the hauling for the rest of the holiday. Looks like he'd be waiting forever for the hydraulic capstan that Andra was working on. Aye he kent ye couldna hurry an inventor. 'Watt an Simpson and Curie an aa yon crood widna hae produced the goods if somebody'd been hoverin ower their shouder half a the time.'

First day with them, Andra took me to his work. He hid a big share o the responsibility o keepin The Broch alive. While Maggie was pumpin they wee bitties o history and geography an readin an rithmetic intil aa the loonies an quinies, he wis seein til his section o production at the Toolies. Hydraulics maistly.

He'd learned his engineering in the Army. The units were being finished in paint as bright as skoosh. Queueing up for export.

'Hydraulics are simple, ken. Naethin bit oil in a tube. Jist the pressure. Bit aa your fittins, your crimps, hiv tae be up tae the job. That's fit it's aboot, lookin for a weak spot. Sortin it. Still I willna hae to rush that hauler for young Willum noo. He still his the teuchter cousin tae pull up his bitties o string.

'I wis at the big Macfisheries afore this. Nivver mind the bloody Common Market. We hiv to keep oor ain fish. They Icelanders hiv the richt idea. Writin on the waa. That's fit wye I took the job when it was offert. We're exportin aa over the world jist. Be supplying a station on the moon next. Bit the stock tae keep the processin and smokin on the go is gettin gey tricky tae find. I've seen us buyin in herrin fae Canada tae mak Broch kippers. Maybe caught by Brochers or Lewis fowk wint oot across the Atlantic fan there was nithin left tae eat here. I've a sister oot across the pond yet. Yer ain auntie. And yer Grampa workin at the coal, barrowing it on tae the drifters and trawlers, we were nivver short o fish. Best o stuff and we'd aa be saying, nae fish again. My ain faither, he'd said it often enough like. *There'll come a day. Ye'll be mindin back tae aa this fish, an ae day – nae aa that far awa – it'll be rich man's food.*'

Young Willum gave me the justification to go daily to the pier for podlies. Just big enough to be bait in his pots. The prickies were our cuddies, the same species but smaller. What they called harvesters in Kirkcaldy. I'd taken one or two there when our car was on the road. My father just smelling the sea while my mother and sister were at the shops. I watched the coming and going of the bigger boats through the gap in Kirkcaldy breakwater. They had white painted whalebacks at the bow and rows and rows of marker buoys. The last of the great-line boats.

Here in The Broch, the flags were still flying over the beach. Red for danger. The breeze was too strong today. But the miniature railway was pelting its way among the dunes.

Everywhere, I saw colour. Even the telly was colour now, as opposed to black and white, which was the only possible thing, back on the Island. The technology was no problem in the Central Belt but colour cost more ready money than we had now.

In Fraserburgh, the podlies would show an orange hint through the dense green of their backs, until the moisture burned off their skins and dark spread over the whole fish. Just the white of the lateral line, loud and prominent.

The Toolies, on the Aberdeen road, was a neutral sort of concrete colour. But, all outside the building, you'd see rows and rows of orange and green compressors, all checked by my uncle. They sat, waiting, on their new tyres. And, just across the old railway, were the boatyards. All the brushes were cleaned on the wall outside. Remnants, weakened with spirit, were brushed off against the rough-cast.

'You tak a piece o that waa back wi ye like, loon,' Andra said. 'Bloody Picasso, man – naethin on The Broch, ken.'

Six of the seven weeks of the summer holidays had gone by. Just gone.

I phoned and got the extension for the last week. I'd need to get the train from Aberdeen to Stirling, on the Friday. Change at Perth. My auntie Maggie would be back at work, The Broch schools going back earlier, this year. Willum said I could tak the boat oot fan he was at the College, startin Monday.

But I wasn't confident enough, on my own.

I got stuck into the books. There wasn't that many in the house – no book club editions but there was a whole library of paperbacks. Twelve volumes. They had black and red covers with Churchill's name at the top. His *History of The Second World War*. Once I started

reading I was stuck in it. Things must have looked bad that first
two years. Andra would come back from work to find me turning
the pages.

'You and your sister still hae the Churchill croons your auntie
sent doon?'

He told me my grampa had been against the idea of getting
one for all the cousins. The aul man remembered Gallipoli. 'That
wis a disaster, sending these great ships intil a tight corner to git
hammered. And leaving all these good men, the Kiwis an Aussies,
all jist stranded. Churchill gave these orders. Maybe so but it was
the same chiel's speeches held it aa together afore the tide turned,
next war on. Peace and love is all very fine, trying to stop that
nonsense in Vietnam but it widna hae stoppit an invasion nine-
teenbloodyforty. We cam close enough. And it widna hae stoppit
Rommels Panzers in North Africa neither.'

I could make the quote now and I think my uncle might have
joined in it then. 'Now this is not the end. It is not even the beginning of the end. But it is, perhaps, the end of the beginning.'

That was 1942. A lot of deaths to come but the myth of the
invincible enemy was shattered. A poor start to the war at sea, that
same year. The code machine used by the Germans was adapted so
there were four rotors instead of three. I might not have been great
at maths but I could guess that was a hell of a lot more combinations. Our codebreakers had been ahead of the game. They'd been
given a helping hand by Polish intelligence, just before the 1939
invasion. This change was a huge setback. It was going to take a
long time to crack the combinations delivered by the new model of
machine. So we lost the power to intercept key messages and more
and more ships went to the bottom.

But in the autumn of that same year a U-boat forced to the
surface of the Mediterranean was going to cough up a codebook.
These clues would be fed into our own tonnage of machinery,
manufactured by an American cash-register company. The results
would prove decisive in the Atlantic.

I learned that the battle against the Nazis was gaining hope,
by the end of 1942, in the desert, the sea and the huge snowfields

surrounding Stalingrad. Churchill's rhetoric probably helped. So did his ability to hug uncle Joe.

Andra let me show off my new knowledge but then he pulled another book off the shelves. Another volume by Sir Winston, *The World Crisis.*

'Aye, the same chiel had the giftie o the gab richt enough but ye ken he blew his ain trumpet that much in this book, it's what led to the German code machines in the first place.'

And sure enough, my uncle read me the passage where the cocky author is boasting about the British ability to anticipate every move of the German High Seas fleet. Even then, I could see the writing was over the top. Stuff about the Russians picking up the body of a German sailor from the *Magdeburg*, clutching the cipher book to his breast. A bit unwise for an ambitious author to go revealing privileged information in 1923 when an enemy laid low by the Treaty of Versailles was wanting for an advantage.

History really shouldn't be written by the people making it. It's either unreliable or dangerous. Or both.

Never mind 1942, there was a fair bit going on in 1967. By the end of the year there were 500,000 American troops in Vietnam. In one demonstration, that same year, marching in Central Park, New York (neighbouring city to Stornoway, looking west) near enough the same number was claimed, by the protesters. And it was all coming in, sometimes live, to the TV in West Road, Fraserburgh, a few miles along from the United States listening installation on Mormond Hill.

Next day when I switched on the news, Andra was not yet back from the town, on his day-off and Maggie was not yet back from the first half-day of term.

All these rows of rifles. This time it was Washington D.C. Last time I'd seen all these tanks on the telly, in black and white, I was in Stornoway and it was Poland and the Russians were taking over. Now it was the National Guard, in colour. Strange thing was, all these people in uniform were frozen in black and white. The colours all belonged to the people in long hair and long clothes.

Another image. So common now you can't honestly remember

when or where you saw it first. But it's definitely monochrome. You know the picture. A person drops a flower down the barrel of a rifle held by a tense guardsman.

Auntie Maggie saw it repeated on the one o' clock news. Andra had so far failed to appear. She went at a run when the doorbell went. Caught him as the taxi-driver dropped him. 'Give me a hand, then,' she said but she didn't really need it, getting herself under one shoulder and levering all that weight around. He made a fair attempt to get into the sitting room. He was maybe aiming for the self-assembly rocking chair he kept having to glue up. But my auntie wasn't having it. 'Come on then, gie us a hand till we get him in the door.'

I did and he went through easily, offering no real resistance when he saw he was going to his bed. He was asleep as soon as she had his shoes off.

'Does your ain faither git himself intae states like this?'

She asked but she didn't want a reply. She had to say something. She said quite a lot. It was time to make myself scarce. I went to the shed for the bike and the fishing gear. But the window went up and Andra's feet appeared. I wondered how he'd managed to get his shoes back on. He hauled a shoulder out next. When his arm got itself liberated, Andra held a finger up to his lips. I could hear his phrases, as he was climbing.

'No names. No pack-drill. We're maybe no Top o the Pops. But we did oor bit.'

He was away down town again.

I didn't tell Maggie and got sheer hell from her, the first time in all these weeks. 'Why did ye nae tell me? Him gaun back doon t' that Legion t' mak a feel o himsel. Fit why did ye nae tell me? That's aa you'd t' dee.'

'I thought he'd sobered up.' I said it and it sounded as lame it sounds now.

'Sobered up. Sobered up, fan he's climbing through his ain bedroom windae. That man's jist a bairn fan it comes t' drink.'

The Swimmers

It was June. A settled Scandinavian high was bringing great weather to the Island. It was all timed for our family's return. The sister was starting her nursing studies down in Stirling. And we were staying with Ruaraidh. One night, I got to go out late, with the net. We'd struck lucky and I posted my share of the salmon money to my sister along with detailed instructions. Kirsty scored me Levi's with an orange tag and a slight flare. And the big prize, a Levi's jacket. Every radio, every jukebox, was belting out Mungo Jerry's *In the Summertime* and *Badge* or *White Room* or *Born to Be Wild* could easily sound out between the wall-to-wall Motown. Even my mother was glad to be back, free of money worries. The Mill was renovating an old house for us. Tweed was in demand again and so was my olman's skill. We'd be down Inaclete Road, by welders and builders' yards but who the hell cared.

On Friday afternoons, after one double period of schoolwork, you strolled out to your Activity. I thought the guys were winding me up, the first week. Last two periods, Friday, you could choose anything from ping-pong to sea angling. Of course you chose partly for the thing itself and partly for who else was doing it. My first choice was badminton because there was a girl I liked. She was the first dame to play snooker at the YMCA. All that stretching and sweating was kind of engaging.

I think swimming was my second choice. I wasn't ready to give up on the badminton blone, yet. At that time the Swimming Pool was only a plan. The proposal was for the site of the original Primary, but leaving the clock-tower, jutting up, sandstone over concrete. That's how it happened. The clock-tower is still standing but it's stranded now. The first indoor pool was demolished and the new one is in the Sports Centre, along the road.

Back to the day before the Mark 1 pool was built, somehow two seasons had slipped by, back on the Island. Mungo Jerry were about extinct. Cream had split. Hendrix was dead and it was January.

Even when the guy taking the Activity gave us one big shit of a lecture to state that swimming meant swimming, in the sea at the end of the road at Melbost, I wasn't sure he was serious. This man was a music teacher. He had given up on teaching us notation, even songs. One day you would bring in your LPs of Leonard Cohen or Deep Purple and he would play them first and comment afterwards. Another day you would listen to Shostakovich. Fair trade but we didn't find his week-two sessions all that cheery.

True, others in the Activity nudged you and said no he really wasn't kidding and it wasn't as bad as you thought. But that was like a good con, rehearsed with collaborators. Of course it would be classroom instruction. Techniques, maybe a film. Wasn't there a wee covered training pool, somewhere on the island? And I did seriously want to swim better. Get a bit of muscle on my slight frame. I'd grown too high, too fast. Now I needed to fill out the shoulders of my jacket.

Most of us, the new additions to this Activity group, had been together years back, making our first attempts to swim. In May, with sun catching dust, we'd raced when the bell went. Got our gear and gone down the lane to the saltings at the Cocklebb. The tidal pools were warm and shallow. We floundered and practiced what we'd seen others do, on the flickering black and white set.

There was a sewer outlet half a mile away but the tide came in over the bar and everything was flushed out twice a day. We watched that tide once, nearly caught by its speed. No waves, just advancing movement, right up to the tussocks and muddy pools where we caught sticklebacks. Once we'd seen it, we remembered the warnings. Primary School stories of the tide in the Solway Firth, flooding faster than a man on a horse. It was only ten years since the last local drowning. We were just far enough away from that time to be able to persuade parents against their better judgments.

We never went alone.

My father couldn't swim at all, my mother only slightly. A lot of seamen and fishermen didn't believe in learning. It would only prolong the agony if you went over the wall. But herself wanted us to be able to swim properly. She believed in it, for companionship as well as for safety. She bought us lessons, at the Bon Accord pool in Aberdeen, when we were on holiday. Ian Black swam there. These people trained every day. My mother pointed him out, quietly, the Aberdeen celebrity who'd won the medal. The one the whole street had watched one Saturday afternoon, on Kenny F's telly, the first set to be connected, on Westview Terrace.

After one lesson, I was able to put together the movements we'd taught ourselves at the Cocklebb. I could get from one side of the wide pool to the other. It was nearer breaststroke than anything else.

But you got to Melbost by following the tidal flats, watching for soft mud, then down along the Airport beach and round the rocky headland. A shifting shore, mainly shingle but with moving sandbars. Sometimes deposits build up, after big North-Easters.

That's why I was interested in the Activity. I think the wind was from the northeast that first day, but not a storm. Only fresh. It was a tough initiation. We all changed at the back of the bus. The small but hardened squad, from the last season, didn't hesitate. That group filed out after our leader and waded into the surf. He was out in front, furthest from the beach. His hair was cropped, as close as the crew-cuts which had been in fashion when we'd paddled at the Cocklebb. I hadn't realised he was such a wee guy.

An onshore wind is probably best for swimming from a beach, depending on tide, but Melbost is the other side of that sandbar so there's not a big tidal flow. We were right at the head of Broad Bay. It was about three in the afternoon, perhaps the best part of the day. Our new group watched at the back of the bus. We made jokes between ourselves. We'd shout down the aisle to form an alliance with a driver who thought we were all crazy but it kept him in a job. All us new boys put our clothes back on. A collective decision made.

None of the swimmers followed the length of the beach. They would make a few strokes along the line of an incoming wave. Then, when they reached the shallows, they would jump a bit before wading back out to immerse themselves again. The grouping of figures, perhaps five, was an arrangement. They were white to begin with and then began to shade lobster-red, livid against the pebbles, as they ran back for the blue bus.

Our leader was shaking with rage as much as from cold. He had even less meat on his body than me. As he rubbed the towel hard, to generate warmth, he spoke from between clenched teeth. If we didn't get into the water next week he'd see to it that we got the Activity we wanted least.

Kenny F said that was fair enough by him. Swimming ability wasn't going to help you stay alive for long anyway if you went over the side. Our music teacher controlled himself. He didn't respond.

Instead, he concentrated on furthering the comradely spirit of the real swimmers. I could see he did have leadership qualities. If you were in the team. He knew it wasn't worth trying a 'Come on in, the water's lovely,' with us.

The next week, with the exception of Kenny, who was here for the crack on the bus but just wasn't going for this winter swimming shit, we swam. Not for long. But long enough to find that the initial shock does dim. I believe now it's dangerous when that lull comes over you. Maybe that was partly why the swimmers went, what they were looking for. A strange tranquillity in the searing wind on the shore. Cheaper than LSD at thirty bob the tab. Bloody one-pound-fifty, new money, the price of an average six-pound fish, to a guesthouse with a back door.

The breaking surf inviting you to enter it, under the wind. More difficult to imagine any sexual undertone. Everyone became equal. You'd need tweezers to find your knob, if you'd needed to, when you came out of that water.

Maybe dope would help. A wee blast before you went in. Trouble was, it hadn't done much for me. You'd to take a legit roll-up now and again to keep in training so you could hold the smoke down long enough. My head swam just as much with the Old Holborn. Maybe more. The hash was probably that old and dried up by the time it got across the Minch.

Kenny transferred to the Castle school. He was only interested in preparing for the fishing industry. His mother kept trying to bribe him to study something else. I never heard her say anything upfront. 'I lost your father and your brother to the sea. Isn't that enough?' Nothing like that. Instead it was the new shoes and the jacket she could run to if he decided to stick in at school. Something that would lead to a clean, safe job.

The Swimming Activity became like Shostakovich – we entered the water every second week. One of the hardcore – the few guys who went in every week – he shone when he stayed to do Sixth Year History. The run-up to the Second World War. He was an expert. He had subscribed to all these magazines that build up week-by-week or month-by-month and are bound in embossed folders. He kept me right. I thought things only got really dirty towards the end of the war. No, he said, the murders and mass killings happened as soon as the German armies were blasting through Poland.

I met him at the class reunion, the year most of us turned forty. He was there, only I didn't know him at first. Now he was near bald, with the little hair left at the sides and back of his head cropped almost to the skin. Lean and looking well on it.

I mentioned the swimming group when we got into a huddle over the fourth or fifth pint of the night. He was away. Every New Year, he said, when his olaid was still around, he'd be back. Of course he'd to be home for the bells.

Early on Hogmanay evening, he'd take a drive out, whatever the weather. He'd park at Melbost and put the headlights on the surf. He might have the wetsuit in the back and the board on the roof but that's not what he'd come for. He'd study the water for some minutes, then strip off. Not much chance of anyone else being there. He'd enter it. Going back somewhere or carrying an experience forward, he didn't know which. Didn't really want to know. Just went for that feeling, when you got over the shock and your every muscle was tuned. Your senses picking up everything for a range of miles but not overwhelmed. You were coping with it, calm. Of course he knew there was a risk. And he hadn't forgotten about the boy who never reached our own age, the one who didn't walk back from the shore at the other side of the tidal bar.

Maybe it was that first ingestion of choking seawater that took you down. If you couldn't clear your lungs, you'd be bound to take in some of the airborne spray. But he had to keep coming back to that shingle between the conglomerate down from the Airport and the conglomerate below the old Ui churchyard.

I thought back to the leader of the Activity. He never tried to hide his addiction to cigarettes. He told us how you got in the thrall of a thing you didn't enjoy any longer. He put that very well. But maybe there was other stuff he couldn't talk out to any of us. Not even the swimmers.

He would find plenty to discuss though, in the intervals between playing his records and ours. Which was, that term, in the intervals between weekly excursions to the turning-place. To swim or not to swim.

Talking of choices. The music teacher waited till there wasn't an audience. There was maybe an option, he told me. He said he knew I wasn't getting on so well with most of the staff. But he'd seen me find the will to join in a few times, the winter swimming. But that's not what he wanted to say. That drumming of fingers on the desk. It was distracting for the others, but it happened to be in time.

He meant it. I had a sense of rhythm. It was flawless. Like a machine. He could arrange access to a drum kit. I could just go to a music room, in spare periods and at lunchtimes. Get it out of my system. Learn it by doing it. I wouldn't need any tutors. And the school band might be looking for a percussionist.

He did me a real favour, there. Stuck his neck out. The drums were good for a term or two. It took me a while before I realised I didn't need to make the beat, just identify it. It was machines I liked. The pulse of a motor.

And what happened to our music teacher? A lonely life, with not much more than us and all these difficult LPs. I think he still stayed in the teachers' houses. They still called them that after dear Mrs Thatcher got her way and they got sold off. Along with the police houses, the coastguard ones and the health board ones.

I think he still stayed in the teachers' houses. They still called them that after dear Mrs Thatcher got her way and they got sold off. Along with the police houses, the coastguard ones and the health board ones.

You never saw him out and about. All round the town there were plenty of curtains that would part when the taxi drove up. The basic provisions and something that would chink in the carrier bags. I don't know if the swimmer was one of that number.

I never thought of calling by. Could have said that Uni was working out okay and history was making me tick. You don't really do that. You just keep a weather eye on the notices in the windows, the paper-shop and the butcher's. If you're home at the time, you need to take a lift at the funerals of your teachers.

Back to the reunion. The historian got me thinking. I might have turned a corner, that night. Looking back to try to analyse what was really going on.

A long blue bus at the end of the black road, at the start of the cropped green turf. That first time you plunged into cold surf. When your heart kicked fast to get the blood where it thought you needed it. The sheer, bloody beauty of the water in winter light. And it wasn't pain any more. Maybe I'd been in the wrong number. We shouldn't have disrupted the cohesion and the intimacy of that small band. Brave guys who let themselves go for these short moments into cold water. But the swimming pool was to open only a few years later. So the Activity could not have survived, in any case.

East

My journey to the east started on the wall outside the Renden. OK, why did the meeting not happen in the Rendezvous Café? Because I was banned from there at the time. And we couldn't go to the Lido because there was no way Kenny F was going to get in. He got very protective if people had a go at us for our hair or anything. Like in *Easy Rider*. He wasn't really aggressive, just looked a bit threatening when he stuck out his big fisherman's chest. Then it could all escalate.

So this guy comes up when we've got our arses parked on the wall and says, 'What is there to do in this lousy town of yours?'

I liked him already.

'You're seeing it, cove. What brings you here?'

He was a member of the Bahá'í Faith. Couldn't place his voice, his looks, short, tight curly hair. Egyptian, he says, but he was living in Reading now.

He was surprised I knew the name of an English town. Alcocks of Reading, fishing tackle manufacturer, of course. Later to become Norris-Shakespeare, with a noticeable drop in average quality.

He nodded. I was sure of a lot of things then. I was wrong about Reading, though. Alcocks manufactured in Redditch. A different town.

'So what do you guys believe in then, apart from fishing?' We told him that one day, on this island, there'd be a group of crofts and at the middle there'd be a big barn and every waif and stray and passer-by could just crash there and that would become a known thing.

The dudes doing the talking are of course the same dudes whose Da's couldn't get them to dig the garden. We did go fishing though. So we'd do just enough digging to get a tobacco tin full of worms.

We'd talk about anything. Sitting on the wall. All weathers. Religion was worth half an hour.

He told us his beliefs. The essential one-ness of all the major world religions. It's just the hair-splitting and dogmas that create confusion.

Sounds appealing doesn't it, put like that.

So our gang ended up going to what they called 'Firesides', next door to the new auction mart. The word might sound a bit weird but it's just imported American-speak for ceilidh. A wee gathering. The mart used to be on Westview Terrace. I could talk as fast as the auctioneer and swear with full grammar before I went to school. Life-skills. The sheep-pens still smelled much the same but the slaughterhouse was a bit of distance from most of the houses, now.

You'd know he was Egyptian when he got a shot of a car. With an SY influence – something in the way you take both hands off the wheel, hit the horn and flash the lights when you clock a mate. His sidekick was doing a PhD on the sugar flow of plants, concentrating on hogweed. You found specimens in abandoned yards in cities. Another guy with hair like ours was from Glasgow. He built chopper motorbikes.

'Aye, sure, man, like in *Easy Rider*. Aye the Faith got me aff the drugs an tha.' We were in the house of an NZ/Iranian couple. And the Iranian cove's mother lived with them. She couldn't speak English but one night her son said his mother would like to cook for us.

We were trying to cool it on the drink and one by one we would repeat the mantra, no chemicals man. So we just drifted by there, most nights. We were all about seventeen years of age.

So how did these religions fit together then? They seemed pretty different.

That was because prophets or Manifestations of God brought the same message, renewed from age to age but adapted to the needs of the time. So the law of Moses was a harsh one for a desert tribe. Jesus spoke to the individual and Muhammad built nation-hood. Laws for society. The message of Bahá'u'lláh was for a new world order.

The new message was that science and religion should go hand in hand. Other principles were the equality of men and women and co-operation of all nations in a world commonwealth.

Sounded like pretty radical guys for nineteenth-century Iran.

I couldn't see it then but it's pretty clear now, it's all about stories. I'd been fed stories with my milk and then with tea and three sugars. The river of Jordan had flowed into Westview Terrace and the waters of the Red Sea parted when you got clear of the lighthouse at Arnish. Catechism wasn't so good. Remember, it was a big surprise to find that Manscheefend was three different words. Some of the phrases stuck with you, just the same.

There were a couple of nutcase teachers who had you learning chunks and chunks of psalms. This was mid-primary – before the shift to the Central Belt. You just couldn't keep them all the lines in your head so you had to work out which verse you were going to get, plus one or two either side in case someone mucked it up and she'd stomp on to the next seat. An insurance policy really but it was good practice for arithmetic.

And it was worth the time to learn these few verses. Otherwise you'd probably get belted. Of course the idea of a scented woman in crisp clothes swinging a slim, split thong of top grade saddlery from over her shoulder – that does things to the Scottish male psyche. Did I mention this before? Don't get carried away. I can tell you, ladies and gentlemen, there was nothing erotic about getting the strap in P5. Very specialised stuff.

Bri-Nylon outfits and hairs on her chin. A straggly moustache and slavers running from her mouth when she got worked up about something. A roar in the back of the throat which changed to a smiling softer tone when the headmaster took a look in to make sure there were no serious casualties. She had this habit of throwing the wooden-backed duster. So you had to get good at putting the lid of your desk up in time, as a shield. There was a cloud of chalk in the air. Then it was more psalms. It was good for developing your reflexes. Mine are still pretty good. So it was all education of a kind.

They couldn't get rid of her so they made sure you got a good teacher before and after. The good ones – and I think all the others were good ones – they told stories half the time. New and Old Testament and Pinocchio on a Friday afa. Do you say that in other places? Our word for post-noon.

Staffs pointed at rocks, causing them to open and release sweet running water. Bushes burned but never fell to ashes. Loaves and fishes were shared between thousands. Two fishes to be precise. Now speaking as a guy who wasn't that keen on the salt herring, I could still appreciate the fact that they did look like they'd come from the Bible. They lay in their brine by a new batch of crusted loaves (more than five) at the cornershop. And I'd long borne witness to the debates as to whether my father or the sister should get the last one after half a dozen each had been scoffed. I was well placed to understand that satisfying a multitude with a couple of them was pretty good going.

The new stories, down by the new auction mart, took us into Iran. Only it was called Persia then. It was near the middle of the nineteenth century. A change was coming. There was a figure, a bit like John the Baptist, who paved the way. He was called the Báb, which meant that he was the gateway to the new religion. But the Bábí Faith was seen as a breakaway from Islam rather than a new religion. So the Mullahs went all out to stamp it out. Devotees were publicly tortured before execution. Reports of European observers include descriptions of people shod like horses and driven through the streets. The leader, a merchant from Tabriz, was shot in a barrack-square. He was suspended from a fastening to a wall, along with a disciple. When the dust cleared he was not to be seen. He was found in a nearby room, continuing the dictation of a last letter. He then said something like, 'This task is completed, you can do your business now.'

So the story goes.

I was ready to give up on drink and drugs. I wanted to believe. I read the main account, *Nabíl's Narrative*, in a fine edition, bound in dark green, embossed in gold leaf. Edited by the Guardian of the

Faith who honed his grasp of rhetorical English at Balliol College, Oxford.

I'm not seventeen now. I've been back to that book. The translator and editor's main stylistic influence, he said, was Gibbon's *Decline and Fall*. There could be a whiff of Sir Winston in there too. The editor's notes and footnotes add observations of Western commentators in English and in French but, with the exception of an account by the doctor who examined the leader, after he was beaten with the bastinado, these are not first-hand accounts.

Nabíl's own account was gathered, many years after the events, while sharing the exile of one Mírzá Husayn-'Alí, who claimed to be that next Prophet or Manifestation of God. In that respect, his narrative is similar to the way that the events surrounding a carpenter's son, from Nazareth, became fixed texts. Nabíl is a very fine storyteller. Author and editor list their sources. The genealogy of stories.

No disrespect to *Nabíl's Narrative* but the best stories came from our mentor's mother. She cooked us chicken, marinated in crushed walnuts and pomegranate puree. This is a day's work, in preparations. I ate slowly to taste every mouthful. By this time I wasn't smoking or drinking alcohol. Yes, I quit on the drink when I was seventeen. Food was always important but it became like a religious observance.

I don't think it was just that chicken dish. It was the drama of the stories and there were a few warning signs in our own latter days. Waking up covered in puke again. The deaths of Brian Jones, Janis Joplin, Jim Morrison.

One of our number had already met his death, like the Stones guitarist, in an outdoor pool, at a party, far from home. Some mates were becoming Jesus-freaks and others were talking about Guru Maharaji. Some of us were just inquisitive but the real devotees were the storytellers. Or maybe their conviction is what gave them the power to yarn for Scotland. Our local radical Christians didn't have long hair. Well, maybe the women did but you couldn't see that. It would usually be tied up in a bun or in a hat. (There will now follow a short digression on the subject of hat shops. Omit the next paragraph if you cannot see the relevance of this indicator.)

If you wish to appreciate the cultural forces at work in the Long Island it is important to observe and appreciate the central role of hat shops. In a fragile economy, then based mainly on the world fashion industry's taste for Harris Tweed and the international restaurant trade's appetite for prawns, SY could boast not one but two specialist retailers of hats. If it were not for this data, an observer would be tempted to conclude that hats worn by the religious community would all be in the style of sober head coverings, essential for modesty. More systematic sampling, without prejudice, will produce the following results:

Wide brims and narrow;
Red as well as blue or black;
Yellow, less common but noticeably present in the congregations and not only at Easter – not a major Festival, anyway, in Long Island religious observation.

Then there are the additions:
Lace trim – completely acceptable;
Feathers – mandatory.

And that's only the menswear.

But whether we were still religious believers or no, we were also doing the 'Stop The War' chant with Country Joe. I would sign up for any band called 'The Fish' anyway. It just couldn't go on, this missile against missile balance of international power, not for much longer. Took a lot of arguing that one, with people who remembered being caught out, ill-prepared for the blitzkrieg of '39. My olman for one. In an alliance with his brother-in-law fae The Broch.

It already seemed like another mythology, talking about my generation. I was born in 1955. Ten Years After – the name of a rock and roll band with a very fast guitarist by the name of Alvin Lee. Ten years after VE day, prisoners were still awaiting repatriation. Or exhumation.

I read the Qu'ran in translation. I couldn't tie in all the loose ends. We'd sit up talking till after closing time. Keeping us out of temptation.

'What about the Hindu religion?'

'Well, that was so far back in history and there was so little written material that traditions developed. That's why it's now impossible to reconcile all the details.'

'The Buddhists – these guys don't really have a god, never mind heaven and hell?'

'Cultural layers are so dense that it's impossible to know what the original message was. But you can still see the influence of the Buddha's positive energy. That's why there's a need for a new Manifestation of God from age to age.'

'So another guy could appear tomorrow?'

'In theory yes, just that Bahá'u'lláh specifically wrote that his message would be valid for a full thousand years.'

Now I can see how that's a time period with a ring to it. We should do a study of architecture designed to last for a full thousand years. Albert Speer would be to the fore and maybe Nicolae Ceausescu's favoured few would sneak in to be in that number. What's with all the columns and domes?

I thought there would be a bit of resistance to this mystical period, from the olman and the olaid. Not so. They'd observed everything I was doing, the drugs and all and just held back. My olman could sense a tide turning and this was it. The direction was right, even if he couldn't get his head round the details. As long as we were talking shit we weren't smoking too much of it.

My olaid was almost envious when I said there was a new wind blowing, enough to stop the war in Vietnam. 'Do you not have doubts?' she asked.

'No,' I said, 'I know we're all part of something though we can't agree on the details.'

'I envy you,' she said.

I was amazed to hear that my Brocher olaid had underlying doubts. She'd been brought up to full churches of fishermen in genseys, while hail blasted outside. There were even trumpets and other brass.

I got doubts later but I suppressed them. The food helped. Let me run by a few highlights. The food, not the doubts.

A Basque dish where the singed and peeled red peppers are marinated in walnut oil and cayenne. That was when my SYtalian mate brought me along to the wee Roman Catholic Church. We were invited across for tapas after the Mass which was a wee bit ornate for my taste. See, the Presbyterian vibe stays ringing in your ears, after all.

Basmati rice, cooked till al dente then placed on a covering of thinly sliced potatoes in oil. The pan is then placed on top of three crushed cans so the heat at the lowest setting steams gently through, so it all comes out from the pan with the cloth under the lid. Like a pudding with the potato crust gone brown around the white grains. Yes, you've guessed, that was the Egyptian Bahá'í.

A thick mutton curry where leaves are added towards the end of cooking time and you don't have to do like the cook does and lift a green chilli and bite into it absentmindedly, as you're finishing the dish. And by the way you shouldn't do as I did and gorge yourself on the rice with the subtle spices, not realising it's just a starter before the high pile of thick chapattis arrives with said steaming bowls of meat. That was my taste of the Punjab on Newton Street, before a discussion on Islam in the modern world.

The gammon, marinated in molasses and rum and studded with cloves before boiling and baking by the not-so-young rebel from the Free Presbyterian church. This guy wasn't getting on very well with the new minister.

'I'm not expecting him to live in a stable but I don't see why he needs the church to build him a house that size.'

But that wasn't the main issue.

'I lent the man my wheelbarrow so he could get a start on the garden. Good to see him roll his sleeves up. But I'm having a hell of a job getting it back. And the question to ask is this. If you can't trust the man with your wheelbarrow, can you really trust him with your soul?'

My mother's liver and bacon casserole with tomato reduction in the gravy, waiting for me, just round the corner, after a New

Zealander's faithful copying of a dish of lamb in green herbs, taught her by her Iranian mother-in-law before she departed the Island to live in Holland. So I had two dinners in pretty quick succession. But by that time it was getting a bit late to get up the road for the first ever blood-donor session – because members of our gang had just come of age to donate and we were working on developing our individual social consciences to go with it.

So I legged it up the road, after the two quick dinners, made it just in time and did the business but the big hall started to go wooh wooh wooh like Hitchcock and I was on the deck. That wasn't the worst bit. The worst bit was that when I came to, they offered me brandy and I said, 'No, sorry mate, I don't drink now.' And I suppose that's when it was pretty public – hell, he's got a weird Oriental Religion. Pretty normal for a wild guy to get a dose of the *cùram* – hardcore born-again Christianity – or, to put it another way, fallen into the care of God. But this was different. As Kenny F said, 'What the hell breed of *cùram* are you suffering from?'

Soon there was thirty or forty of us, all 'into' different religious stuff and the tribe was seen as a threat. Which was great because we were the outsiders getting bombarded with letters to the *Gazette* from elders of the Last Bastion kirks. But we had some free-thinking champions who wrote punchier letters back than any of us could. This guy wrote, in answer to the issue of the possible threat posed to the youth of our island by Oriental Religions, 'Does the previous correspondent believe that Jesus Christ appeared in Kyle of Lochalsh?

Quo Vadis

I helped discharge the *Quo Vadis*. These were boom years. All the records were tumbling. There were different ways of doing things. Like in Athletics. Things had never been the same since Dick Fosbury made the straddle-jump seem just as outdated as the scissor-jump, when you saw people doing it, fast time, on old newsreels. You couldn't see how it could work, just coming in from another angle, turning and then he was over the bar backwards with his feet up in the heavens. Everything was changed. The heights went up and the times went down. Everything was moving faster.

The scale of *Quo Vadis* scared us all but we were in awe of her, the high red steel and the turning radars. The antennae that made you glance into the bridge – you could hardly call it a wheelhouse – with all the dials and screens. If anything, the talk had played it all down.

At least the herring wasn't going to fishmeal. All these Norwegians and Faroese tied up with their stock of whitewood barrels lashed on deck. They fixed a price with the skippers, then took on casual labour. That was us, Kenny F and me, in the line with the rest of them, queuing like the dockers in our history books.

I stuck close to Kenny and usually got picked. He was heftier than me and had the reputation of being a grafter. Flat rate, no overtime, no tea breaks. You worked right through till the load was done. And one woman of the few amongst us, spread a sweet, maroon salt on the fish as they wriggled up the conveyor. She was just old enough to remember this from before, with the belching steam-drifters. And the crack flying with the knives.

'But the hours, *a ghràidh*, the hours we worked.'

And we worked them again in the here and now. So the *Quo Vadis* could get out for another shottie. I took my turn, pressing the electronic counter, the Norskis' tally against the East Coasters'. Got distracted when my opposite number told me there was talk of a Daimler, for a bonus, company car like, if the accountant could swing it. No point givin it tae the bloody taxman, like.

The top fish they scooped for the sample looked much like the herring you'd cadged on a string from the *Daffodil*, the *Lily*, the *Ivy* – the Scalpay drifters. Deeper down in the hold, they became faded and soft. So the further into the shift you went, the more dull the fish became. There wasn't a lot of shine to them. No firmness left. That's it, you saw what was missing in the herring, not what was there. Except for the eyes. The bloodshot eyes of seven hangovers in a row. And hardness now in the sockets that contained them, the bony sunken mouth below it.

I met the *Quo Vadis* again a couple of years later. She was anchored to her quota, out in Loch Shell. She'd taken the lot on the first night of the season. Most of it had gone to the fishmeal factory. Markets weren't ready for them. They'd slapped the ban on fishing herring in the Minch. That included the Scalpay boats, and the last of the drift-netters amongst them – they were all tied up too. These boys were out of a job.

I had a summer job, up that loch. Up, over the burn, into fresh water. I'd to row anglers around and try to steer their casts towards the sea trout. It was as dry a summer as I can remember and the sky just got heavier.

Colin insisted on these patrols in the estate launch. We fired up a Merc inboard with a push-button start. A sweet piece of engineering in a planing hull. It was a novelty for me, being free of the laws of displacement for a while. It was supposed to be serious anti-poaching stuff but the real reason was just to get away from the Lodge for a while.

The paying guests were getting restless on a red diet of heather lamb and netted salmon steaks. There wasn't a fish could get up over the dry stones to be caught by these people.

Sometimes we'd take the old boat and leave it on a running mooring, the other side of the loch. We'd get up the hill so Colin could get the telescope out. Once, he took me over the hill, right to the wreck of a World War Two bomber. Forget the type but it wasn't a Lancaster, Wellington or anything I'd seen in Airfix models. Maybe an Anson. It was impossible to get near by sea or road so it had just been left where it fell, once any bodies or survivors had been removed.

Belts and belts of ammo. Even the machine guns in the remains of turrets. Whitened needles, gone like bone that would never shift again, round black dials. Good bloody job the Orinsay boys hadn't taken the arsenal back across the loch yet. One of these ex-Merch engineers with a lathe in his lean-to would probably get these guns going. Then woe betide any gamie and ghillie trying to flex muscle in the environs of Loch Shell.

That one didn't win a smile from big Colin. Now at the end of the ridge, looking seaward, he'd get muttering when he caught the glint of monofilament as someone was cleaning their net. Maybe, in turn, the Lemrewayites were glancing across and seeing the flash from that glass – we were the Hun in the sun.

Colin knew better than to ask the ghillies to go with him to pick up any of these nets. I didn't mind angling all day, weeding radishes and rowing out to a few pots in the bay. Non-combatant role only.

But on our way back from the outpost, he had me pull quietly upwind to the *Quo Vadis*. She was in good holding ground, good shelter and no tide to speak of, this far up the loch. If this ban continued, they'd have to steam for Cornwall, for the mackerel. Say what you like about Colin, he knew the tricks. Right enough, the grey floats, not that easy to see from any distance, were out astern and he pointed at once to the few that were down. He took one drowned fish out of it and laid it on the bottom boards while I kept to the oars.

'A good nine-pounder,' he said. 'That one was meant for the fly.'

There wasn't another so he had me glide up alongside but most of the lads were on deck. Colin started off very politely.

'Aye, boys, plenty herring around but you can't land them. Just biding your time, aye. Well, that's very decent, yes, a few won't go amiss.'

And a boxful, creamed from the very top, still decent fish, was passed to us. A few chafed scales but these were all right, though they'd come from a net that could trap everyone in Hampden Park, spectators, players and all. I could already smell these, frying in their own oil, the oatmeal coating getting toasted.

'Aye, now but there's another matter, boys. That drift-net astern. Sure, sure it's just for the mackerel, yes, bloody big mackerel this aye.'

And he got me to hold it up by the tail.

Card-play. I wouldn't fancy a game of poker with Colin. They just quietly said, 'Aye a richt, nae fit we wis efter like but it'll dae jist the same. Ane for the frying pan. It's no exactly on a commercial basis. Jist whilin awa a bittie time.'

Maybe not very commercial, Colin said, but it was illegal. As long as the net came in he wouldn't take it any further.

'Aye, but the cook has his plans for a bit change in the diet.'

I was amazed when he held firm. Didn't say another word. Just sat impassive at the stern and motioned me to pull away. Their fish was on our bottom boards.

I felt the eyes burning into the back of my head. The daggers between my shoulder blades.

'Come on, Colin. Hell, you've got to give them that one. We're going to be heroes when we come back with the herring. Fair trade.'

But he pulled the outboard cord instead. I couldn't look up to the high decks any more. It wasn't that one of the guys might recognise me from when we were discharging her at Stornoway, or that one of them might be related to me. Just sheer embarrassment.

We never said another word, the way back into the loch. I was now looking up to the high ground. For the first time I was seeing how history worked. You leave traces as jets leave vapour. Propellers leave a paraffin whiff in the air, a less viscous slick in the water. The picture won't last long, bust up by chop or the gradients of isobars as air masses move with pressure. When that movement shifts to work against wind-driven water, the waves stand up. They become dangerous.

Our craft can now venture into water and into air. The breath of airmen was frosted on canopies but their craft still moved over the high ground. Some got caught in low cloud, the crews trying to decipher instruments that were slow to respond to changes. A failure to climb quite high enough. A hand on a stick.

Far below it, an eye on a periscope, a hand still as it could ever be, over a firing-pin. Another individual adjusting a heading but hearing a voice naming reefs. Particular hazards, named over time, said by one voice but moving on from what was said before. A long way over land and water, terrain burned-out even before new machines strafed it. Named people were left there too. Men trying to breathe, in a loud, hot tank when the lid clanged shut.

Not only humans. The known routes of flocks from cool to warm or back again. The grazing herds, sniffing water. The lithe eels from the Sargasso or bars of muscle, following krill in the North Sea, northern part. Maybe strangest of all, the herring. Even these masses were now proven to be finite. All these swimmers gone before, in the wake of plankton. All these trails of all these hunters in all these craft following herring. And the breathing women, gutters and packers fae The Broch tae Yarmouth, following the followers.

Colin just said, when he'd shut off the fuel and we were gliding to the buoy, 'You'd have given them that fish?'

'Sure I would. These herring are priceless. And we've a glut of salmon.'

'Aye and you're half East Coaster, with it. Blood's coming out.'

The cook didn't thank him for the *bradan*.

'You can stuff that if you like and stick it in a glass case or anywhere else it might fit. Give me the *sgadan*.'

And her fingers were pulling at the backbones, to open them out, ready for the oatmeal.

The Dry Summer

That was the dry summer. Shoals of salmon and sea trout arrived to cruise by the mouths of the burns. Fish jumped often, trying to shake off the sea-lice. These would fall off, soon after the migratory fish entered the fresh water systems. But the fish couldn't run the burns because there was hardly any water.

We rowed guests across the bay and they cast teams of gaudy flies. The sea trout fins would follow the lures but the fish wouldn't take. The visitors, English, French, German and Austrian groups, were paying plenty for wild fishing. Soon it would be the stalking season and still the fish hadn't been able to run. The seals were cruising across Loch Shell, taking their pick.

I found out that I could use my fly rod like coarse-fishing tackle. I could put a small float and a hook with a worm on and let it go from the burn into the sea. There would still be traces of the fresh water, enticing the fish in. The float would dive and I'd hit a fish of two to three pounds. It would jump and I'd take a long time to get it ashore. There were rocks with bladderwrack and kelp at the edge and the mouths of the fish were very soft. I lost a few and landed a few. You had to be careful, hitting the thick head on a rock because they were so lively. The speckles and spots continue deeper into the flank than those on a salmon. And you don't feel the bone in the tail the same way, so they're difficult to keep a hold of.

They took them from me for the kitchen. They'd go in the freeze for the next guests. We had the salmon we'd netted, for this week. Then they saw my tackle at the end of my rod. I didn't try to hide it. They never spoke to me directly. That's not how things were done.

They got Colin to tell me, the owner was not too happy with the fishing method so it was back to fly-only from now on. The guests would get angry. Or jealous.

So at the end of the week I asked for my sea trout to take in town. One for the folks and one to bring round to my uncle's. Sheena wasn't keeping that well. The owner wasn't used to you talking to him direct. He didn't put up much resistance.

He shot a seal from an upstairs bedroom. Colin said he was very proud of the shot. Bad news. The owner had noticed me swimming the other night. When I'd stayed underwater quite a long time, looking for scallops till I got the shivers.

The three of us went out in the estate launch. I thought it was a poaching patrol and I'd need to stay away from the Island for a while when the word got out. But no, the cove himself had another idea. He handed me a rope. He'd taken a bearing of where that seal was hit. He was sure he'd got it and it sank. It wasn't deep and it was about Low Water, now. If I got a line to it, that would feed all the dogs for weeks.

But Colin tipped me a nod which said, don't you bloody dare find it. The stink of boiling up that thing would choke us all. A very eloquent nod. The carcass was deeper than I thought and I got scared in the kelp anyway. That could have influenced the decision to run with Colin's wishes and not those of the boss.

And then it was the stalking. I thought I'd be rowing fishermen around all summer and into September. But then a new lot of guests were being taken down to the bay. There was a rusting steel shape, cut to the rough shape of a deer, a good distance off. Target practice. The guests thought they were checking the sights of their guns. Colin was checking how close he'd have to take them, so they wouldn't just wound a beast. I didn't know I'd be expected to lead a pony into the slopes around Ben Mor and hold it till a stag, still warm, was strapped on its back.

The old Eriskay pony was fine. She was used to it. Colin warned me that the young Highland – a heavier animal, might panic when he smelled the blood. I'd to take the pony close when I heard the shot or saw smoke from a small heather fire.

I'd been present when a wedder was killed in the byre, the week before and I'd seen the innards of sheep and cattle often enough in the slaughterhouse at Westview.

This time, after the shot, Colin rubbed his hand across my face – I took a step back and then realised he'd smeared the blood of the deer on me. Like my uncle did once with the thick slop of the peat-bank when we were bantering, near the end of the day.

Archie did rear up, when the carcass was put on his back. I'd been warned to dig my heels in and let him turn the circle. Talk quietly to him. I did that and it worked. He carried the stag after that.

It was all sweat and smell and warm close weather. I hadn't even brought a thick gensey. Next thing, it all just went black and this cloud dumped its hard hail on us. We couldn't believe it, kicking it on the ground to check. Then my teeth were chattering. I was hugging myself and beating my elbows trying to get some heat. Then, before we were back at the Lodge, the air was warm again.

I was looking forward to the venison, a change from lamb and salmon, but Colin told me these people hang it for quite a long time. But we'd get a fry-up of the liver for our breakfast tomorrow.

At the end of the day I found my new boots weren't quite broken in. I got a plaster for the blister but Colin said he'd find me another job – he needed me fit for later in the week – they'd be working the high ground.

I wasn't too bothered because I liked weeding and grass cutting, inside the walled garden. No-one bothered you. But the owner showed me the boilers inside the dog pens, where they used to cook up offal and seal meat. He was carrying the head of the stag we'd killed. It wasn't much of a head but the guest wanted a trophy – the skull with the horns. So all traces of the meat and hair would have to be scoured.

I don't mind the smell of game cooking. But that wasn't much of a job. I'd to keep going back to it, topping up the fire from waste and rotten timber. The eyes were a good indicator. When they'd fallen out.

Sometimes we'd row a bit then start the outboard in a dinghy and get some mackerel or lythe. They're common fish but they're still fine to look at. The zig-zag pattern on the back of the mackerel can shift from deep green to indigo to black. There's a lot of colour on the flanks below that when they're fresh. The lythe has a bronze sheen and the lateral line takes a dip. It's broken, like the trace of an old track on the moor. The sea-fish were a change of diet. We hit big shoals one night. I was for stopping when the blood and beat of the tails was up over our boots but Colin said no. Fill a few boxes and we'll salt them for pot-bait.

They just went in whole into plastic tubs with plenty rough salt. I found an old wooden firkin and put it aside. My own share of the catch. I was up till the early hours. I'd seen village guys do this, when I was out at Holm Point with Kenny. One guy on the long bamboo pole. The other splitting and gutting the fish as they came in and packing them in layers of salt. There and then. Going home with the firkin full of salt fish. They'd a way of carrying it too. Efficient.

It was just about September and still warm and dry. But it was almost true dark again. I scrubbed at the smell for a while, in the shower and then slept sound.

I'd to come back to the Lodge to collect my gear. It was a break from all the rounds of people coming to the house to offer sympathy. There wasn't really anything to be said but there's a way of doing things. My mother told me to try to make a day of it. Get out a walk or cast a line before I took my stuff back. It would do me good to get out and she was going for a hurl with my sister. Kirsty was able to stay at home for another few days.

I ate lunch in the kitchen of the Lodge. My radishes and cos lettuce were doing well. The fish had run at last. Now they were catching sea trout where the burn came from the loch. Yes, on the fly, one after another.

Down at the pier, I went to roll my firkin out to the road where the van could pick it up. I was going to be the hero of the out-of-town brigade of relations. I heard it before I saw it. Hatching bluebottles. The maggots were bright and fast, all through the backs of the split mackerel. I'd seen this before, but that was a plan to create bait for trout. And I'd seen it once when I was very young. I hadn't followed the *Blue Peter* instructions for hibernation. I'd neglected the large tortoise. I remember crying and my sister thinking I was making a big fuss.

When Colin arrived he said, never mind, my work wouldn't go to waste, they were needing more pot-bait.

They paid me till the end of the broken week. Insisted I take some brown crab, yes from our own pots. The lobsters were moving in now. Colder at last. I didn't fancy digging out Mrs Beeton again to look up *Crabs, how to dress them*. You can just see one in a tuxedo, can't you? But you couldn't say no. I never got a lobster, though. Dead and red, or alive and blue.

I don't like putting crabs into boiling water. You've to jam the lid down for a minute or so after when you do it that way. Mrs Beeton says you can kill them instantly if you pierce a metal skewer through each eye, diagonally, once in each direction. That does seem to be faster. That night the olaid led the way, picking out the meat from the shells. The sister, herself, myself, two hammers and a pair of pliers. The sister was saying how the olman had to dig out the tools to make the tea on a Sunday – opening a tin of sardines.

The three of us were learning how to make a smile again. We were filling two bowls of sweet flesh, the brown meat and the white.

The News

The olman could never do much damage to anyone because he always had his doubts. I think he cherished them, really, as proof he was still human after a certain six years. So it couldn't really have all been Yorkshire puddings baking over petrol fires, his personal history of World War Two. He was a restless body, for as long as I can remember. You might expect that of a man who was trapped in a confined space, not once but twice in his lifetime.

One day, in my room in the SY flat owned by the Mill, all the revolutionaries were doing sweet FA as usual. This was us settling back in the hometown after us all getting disorientated in the Central Belt. Kenny F, me and the boys did nothing much except learn to smoke and wear out vinyl discs, in a dark room, shutting the curtains on the decent weather outside. The cove himself came in to us with a tray of coffee. He was more or less his own boss since we moved back to the Island. He was under contract to design for new markets but trusted to do it his way, like Frank Sinatra. In fact he was quite bloody capable of bursting into that song just to embarrass me in front of the mates. This time he dropped a line in our direction.

'Surprised to see any of yous in here when there's big money to be made down the hoil.'

The Klondykers. We hadn't heard the Norskis were back? Pound an hour, here we come. That was two full-price LPs for the dawn till dusk shift.

'No, better than that. Two-fifty, or maybe it was up to three quid now. But nobody could stand more than a couple of hours of that.

No, not the herring. A Geest boat. Banana-carrier. The refrigeration's gone bust and the hold's stinking. It's got to get cleared. They're issuing masks and everything.'

We were off. Searched both Number One and Number Two piers. Nothing to see. The coal boat was in, that was about the lot. We took another looksee before we could admit to ourselves he'd hooked us. A bloody banana boat, how the hell had we bought that dummy? The gang came back, livid, to find him trying to continue being deadpan. Giving it up and just falling apart. But he'd a hell of a laugh when he got going. Big laugh for a slightly built guy. A tall man but still, nothing much of him.

Back further than that. Fast rewind. Before we left the Island in the first place. We played war most of the time, back in the cul-de-sac. Think we were playing it when I fell from the rafters at the second storey of brick houses, going up fast in the field behind us. OK, there was blood then and it could have been bad. Must have looked bad. Someone saw me and screamed. No, don't start, I wasn't that bad looking a kid. Kirsty was standing out with the older coves in the street. She led me by the hand to our own house. Just needed a clean up. Herself and the olaid just gently wiped the blood away. Nothing needed stitching. Just as well, I was thinking of the sewing machine when they said that. It looked like a normal one but they'd got an electric motor fixed to it now.

Could have been it, I suppose, if I'd made the wrong landing. But most of the time you never came close to the thing. Death, I mean.

War games got exciting again when the Bay of Pigs was on. The themes changed from Second to Third World War. But Sputniks made stronger pictures than missiles. You couldn't get them yet in Airfix kits, but the American lot, Revell, they had missile models. Andra had given me a set, one holiday. Jeeps and U.S. personnel guarding a missile installation.

About that time I used to go to the slaughterhouse, round the corner, to get the innards of a sheep so my grannie could make *marag* – black and white puddings. These streets still had village ways then. My mother – she was in hospital. The Broch stomach had bothered her for years and she was having a big chunk of it removed. She was home in a week or two, taking it easy for a short time. The operation seemed to work.

We had plenty of visitors. Never heard so many war stories from the olman and my uncle Andra, who'd got a flight over. They hit it off. Yarns.

There were stolen geese and a scrawny turkey that needed fattening. A sack of almonds that was worth a fortune if they could find a buyer. Petrol traded for anything. Plenty of petrol. Trouble was, the British Army used more petrol when it was static. The brass were getting suspicious.

What the hell do I know? It was all *Commando* comics to me. I was born ten years to the day after that rat took to his bunker. That's an insult to rats and I retract it. The great orator gone shabby.

That wasn't the end of it. Not by a long way. A lot of people got killed after that. What about Japan? And Andra had a brother killed when his Jeep fell off a bridge when the whole show was over.

One day, my Lewis uncle, Ruaraidh, called by with a dram in him and the yarns with his brother really did get going. But they stopped, mid-flight. The olman asked why they had to keep doing this, just telling the funny stories. Nothing about the rest of it. Shivering under trucks. The sound of shells, falling close.

Now fast-back to later summer holidays, 1968. When the olman was putting in every hour of the day to keep us in a bungalow on a hungry hill in the Central Belt. And my mother was working and worrying about money. They were only too happy when I wanted to be packed back to the Island for the whole of the holidays.

So I was billeted with Ruaraidh and Sheena. Getting spoiled rotten. They didn't have a family of their own. I'd come back early from Goat Island because I'd caught a sea trout instead of a mackerel. I didn't want that sea silver to get cracked and dry.

He was day-off, down town. She was working in the morning, a history teacher at the Nic, because school was to start for the kids in a couple of days. She came home to make a late lunch. She didn't believe me when I told her about all the tanks on the news. Rolling, one after another. The downfall of Dubček. A young guy setting himself on fire. With petrol.

Ruaraidh came back from the garage, scrubbed down and sat, dazed, in the armchair, still in his overalls. This was the man who told me stories with shadows and big laughs and the big laughs always won, in the end.

Jan Palach died a public death. A martyr who knows he's going to heaven, that could have a shade of self-interest, he said. But Jan's act was the ultimate thing one young guy could do against all that armour. The message went out, with some time-delays, out over continental Europe. Out across the North Sea.

Over Aberdeen and West Road in The Broch and across the Grampians and bouncing across the Minch. It got picked up at the remote aerials up from the new landfill site that was still called the òtrach. Only for us, grown in the town, it was now the okeroch. Part of our English. Then these signals were routed by cables. Into houses all over town.

God, I loved Ruaraidh and Sheena. But I never told them or showed them. Like the famous Lewisman who loved his wife so much that he very nearly told her. Can't make amends for that to either of them now, anymore than I can ask my olman more about who he was. Or about when he was trapped in that tank. How it felt when he saw sky over him again.

Fast forward now. We're all back on the Island. It was Ruaraidh who told me my father was gone. He didn't tell me exactly. Just shook my hand, clasped me really and said what could he say?

Colin had waved us ashore. We'd been out at the pots. Bantering about sharing out the sheep and goats, one for our lobster curry in the bothy, one for the Lodge. The days were getting shorter and the water was getting cooler. But big Colin was just standing there and looking grim. I was thinking, shit I must have left the gate open when I fed the ponies in the morning.

Then, Colin said something like, 'There's some not very good news for you. Your father's not well. The car's ready. I'll drive you in.'

Ruaraidh coming to meet me, once we arrived in town. That embrace was waiting to happen. Should have happened when we'd cut peats or dipped sheep or succeeded in something or other. Then me saying, I'll be OK, just got to get some air. Him not wanting to let me and then realising I had to get out the back garden for a minute.

Talk about clarity. Everything embossing, printing. Every stalk of grass stood out on its own.

My sister coming home. Some comfort for our mother. The olaid just looked stunned. She couldn't believe it yet.

We all went through a year at that heightened pitch. Stories came fast and furious. I got the feeling that maybe so many of them were like Ruaraidh's own stories. And most of the olman's. So many of them skirting around their real subject, maybe because they had to. Maybe their very purpose was to help cope with what had come to your senses, unasked for.

After so many stories you can come one day to the body you never saw because it had all been so sudden. The undertaker, I mean the father of the present one, taking care of everything, all in safe hands. There had to be a P.M. So the lid was put on the box, after the body was released. The only thing to see was a brass plate with his name and age.

And the job which now looks like therapy but was pure chance. Me taking the year out from Uni. It was Kenny's uncle Angus who steered me to it. Ruaraidh was trying to get us in touch, see if they could get the two nephews to piss off to sea now and again. Get me out of the books and the hushed houses.

Angus had seen the card in the window. There on the board of the Buroo, was the hospital porter's job. Shift work. So I got to meet the folk who dealt with local life and death. I got involved. Got my hands dirty, as they say.

One day, I took a look-in to see one of the guys, in the beds I kept having to move. This was one of the ambulance drivers. We'd give them a hand with the trolley, in the doors. You got to know each other over a cup of tea, after the patient was delivered. He'd had a wee stroke. Taken a turn, as they say. The job didn't give you immunity. I went in for a yarn and he told me then, he was the one. My olman, he meant. He was first on scene. They were just too late. Cardiac arrest is like that.

We shook hands. He made a good recovery. Every time I saw him in the street there was something there between us and it wasn't a bad thing.

Then there was the mortuary and I never thought much of it at first. Fact of life, as they say. One of the additional duties, you had to do, along with the medical staff. Then this night, this male nurse started clowning around a bit, not out of hand. Just his way of showing a trainee nurse something she'd need to get used to. He was only bantering, to make things easier. Part of hospital life.

But then he says to her, putting on an eerie sort of voice, 'And this is where they do post-mortems.'

And I realised I was about to strangle the bastard and I knew I had to get outside before I laid hands on him. The night was very clear.

Bhalaich Ghriomsiadair

There wasn't a lot to sort out. He'd kept the shed going. It wasn't the same one he was in, before we left the Island. It might have been a second cousin of it, as the saying goes. Second generation corrugated iron which of course is zinc-coated mild steel and likely to rust faster than the old bit you're improving by laying the new sheet on top of it. So the main result of the repairs is art. Oxygen reacts with exposed metal but fails to eat into areas which still cling to their coating. I was looking at random etching. Varied resistance to weather. Colour and texture altering within each individual shed. When you stepped back to try to take in the whole park of sheds, with a few contrasting timber ones, islands in the waves of metal, you were swimming in lush imagery, SY style. Greening bitumen. Burnt-orange oxide. A bakers' dozen shades of chocolate.

The number eleven was stencilled on a door which might have been Lifeboat blue, one time. I now know the cause of the heightened vision, heightened everything. Eat your hearts out, users of mescaline and pimpled mushrooms, the proximity of death is the thing that really alters perception.

The olman had jumped at the first chance to buy one of these sheds though we no longer lived round the corner. Hattersley looms were easier to find and cheaper to buy. A slump in the tweeds was looking permanent and looms weren't far off ten a penny. I don't know if he'd become more reclusive or if it was just that I was away at Uni for a good chunk of the year so I didn't see it happen. It looked like he'd been hankering back to a community of sheds. This one had been thrown up by rows of houses. It wasn't far from the site of the old one where me and Kenny F used to fill the bobbins.

The tiny key turned easily in the greased padlock. I'd kind of hoped it would jam and break and I could make a decent excuse to my mother. But I was in. OK, there were cobwebs but the light was now bursting through the small panes onto the loom. His tweed was a beauty. This one looked quiet and fine enough till you came nearer. The harmonic threads had some startling colours amongst them. I'd need some help to get the olman's last cloth off his loom intact. Couldn't trust myself to that.

My eye went to a curved wooden tray on a deal table. I know it's called a *scumaig* but I don't know an English word for it. There was a coil of cotton line resting in it. The hooks had gone brittle. Snoods were strange stuff, maybe horsehair. There was a round tobacco tin on the scrubbed wood top. You had to use a coin to lever it open. A military badge on a pad of soft cloth. A strong red on black. I knew it was a tank regiment.

I was sure I could smell the gravy. His stories always came after Sunday dinner. He'd made the big mistake of volunteering. In his own house. His best efforts at making Yorkshire pudding collapsed before the olaid's hardest glance. He'd made it worse by saying he was a bit lost with the electric oven, really needed a petrol fire. 'Weel you can light one oot the back next week,' she'd said.

The ledger in the drawer didn't have many figures in it. It was careful but brief. And then there were grids and letters, like a code. I was back in Enidbloodyblytonland, as he called it, till I realised it was his pattern book. All these single letters would amount to cloth. And now I noticed a few patches, samples, tacked to a board.

I turned over a few pages of the tall, lined book. Plain, black, board covers, without any tables of weights and measures. This was something different. Letters joined to others, arranged to make a complete design. I recognised the rhythms and listened to his voice. It came from a sloping handwriting that you somehow knew.

The Parker 61 was there too, in its box. The box of navy Quink. I remember the olaid showing me what she'd got him for Christmas. She knew it was the right thing.

This was my father's testament. I read it first, standing up. I've typed it out for you.

PATTERN BOOK

I grew up by Loch Griomsiadair. It's better in Gaelic because the English says Grimshader and for me it was never a grim place. It is the first sea-loch as you proceed south from Stornoway, on the east side of Lewis. There is excellent shelter to be had, up through the narrows into Loch Beag, a sheltered Tob. But first you have to be sure and leave Sgeir Linish, on the north side of the mouth, to starboard and watch for Sgeir a Chaolais. That is a reef which covers at about three-quarters flood tide but there is navigable water, to be found, on either side.

This is the approach from seaward, of course. You will probably be driving, over the cattle grid, up the other side of the hill. From there, the village looks across to Ranais. You must turn the corner before you can look out to the open Minch at the road end.

We were never far from boats. We were brought out and the marks were pointed out to us and named, from the beginning. After a few trips they were with you forever. On that northern side, between the two dangers I mentioned earlier, there is a conspicuous rock. It is known as The Sail and that is exactly what it looks like, even from a distance out, in good visibility. It is not like the tan sail of a working boat but a new sail as delivered before treatment, or one for a yacht: white with a hint of yellow and green in it. Perhaps the colour is derived from the lichens growing on it but when you sight that rock from the sea, there appears to be a tint in the white.

If you hold that mark open on Gob A Chuilg, the headland on the south side of the mouth of Loch Griomsiadair, you have a back bearing, also known as a stern transit. This will take you out as far as The Carranoch – a pinnacle where the fish take shelter. When I was a boy we never had to come further than the mouth of the loch to catch all the haddock, whiting, codling and gurnard, the whole village could eat. Going to The Carranoch was more of an adventure, seeking larger fish and other species. Cod, ling, large mature coalfish and, if you anchored, conger eels.

It was a matter of honour to know which was a haddock and which a whiting before they surfaced. The haddock thumped at the mussel and thumped again on the line and if you had two, one on each hook at each end of the wire *dorgh*, you had quite a pull. The whiting mouthed at the bait and you sometimes thought you'd lost it. Then you'd feel the weight of it again and it would come swirling up.

The men went out late for herring but I was too young to be considered for that – they were not back till the early morning. One night, though, I joined the old boys.

All the able-bodied men, my father amongst them, were away fighting a war we now know had little to do with them or us: 'The Imperialists' War' or 'The Industrialists' War'. My own father, like so many from our Island, had been in the Naval Reserve – that was money coming into the house after all, so he'd been called up right away. I can only remember a fearsome moustache, the smell of pipe tobacco and a laugh that had the momentum of a following sea. He was always making jokes. He was probably making jokes aboard whichever warship or auxiliary he was serving on. But the herring did not know that he was away, along with most of the able men. The word was that the shoals were coming in from the Minch, to the entrance of our sea-loch, the same as usual, late summer.

You could tell something was brewing from the amount of smoke going up into the air, down at the narrows. The village boat was being tarred but I heard my mother say there was as much smoke coming from the bogey-roll as the tar barrel. The older men had got together over the boat and I don't think there was one of them under sixty years of age, though I've heard some say that none were under seventy: the boat of the old men. To me, then, anyone over fifteen years of age was old.

My mother could be quite a hard woman at times but a delegation came up to seek official permission.

The spokesman took a step forward.

'We are a man short for the boat,' he said. 'Your boy is strong for his age. He has a keen eye on him. We will look after him well but it might be a late night. We could do with him, on the tiller.'

'And what are you going to take the herring with?' my mother asked.

'Well, the boy said his father's nets were...'

'Yes, I'm sure he did. But have you had a look at them yet?'

So they filed out after my mother to the barn. The nets had been put away properly but unless they are treated with preservative, they fall rotten. When you treated the nets, you treated the sail and cordage.

'Well, I cannot see how you think you will keep a herring in those.' Her scrubbed hand went through the black cotton.

The *bodaich Ghriomsiadair* were crestfallen but she took pity on them. My mother led them back through the house. She reached behind the wally dugs on the mantel shelf. (Some peddlar must have made his fortune because there is a pair like that in every other house in the island.) She brought a couple of small packets out. The old boys were looking at each other. They did not know what to make of this.

My mother took out some very small new hooks, ones with a glint to them.

'In the Shetlands,' she said, 'they take herring on these. At Baltasound, at the gutting and packing, I saw them rig lines like that. A dandy, they called it. My husband was going to try them.'

Then my mother sent me for a *dorgh* – that is a bent wire a bit like a coat hanger with lead fixed at the centre. It keeps the two hooks separate so they cannot get into a fankle. She fixed these fine hooks to light gut, more like stuff you would use for trout, making a rig with three of them suspended on each side.

'Yes, we saw them going out in these narrow boats, with tackle like that,' she told the old men. 'If you all make up a line like this one, you might take herring if there are herring to be caught. You need not bother starting in full light and you can stop right away when it falls dark.'

Well, to be told how to fish by a woman was something but

a woman from another village instructing them in a technique from another group of Islands – that was something else, again. And when that other village was on the West side (my mother was a *Siarach*) and that other group of islands was Shetland – the home of pagan Vikings – that was pretty close to the limit. I was desperate in case the whole expedition was cancelled there and then but our village needed that fishing.

So we set out. The boat was sound enough and she took in very little water. She had been hauled up and tied down where the spring tides could reach her and keep her timbers from drying out too much. The first thing was to clear the narrows, going out into the calm loch under the sweeps. I had to take a wee go at the pipe. I cannot say I enjoyed it much. Then I got my lesson.

That was my place, at the tiller but I had to look to catch the eye of one man – I suppose you could say he was the skipper though we never called him that.

This was my lesson. First, if I was worried about anything I just had to catch his eye and he would keep me right.

'Aye.'

'Second, this is the starboard side. That is the port. You will need to give her starboard helm to go port, port helm for starboard. Do you have that?'

'I do.'

They tested me when we were still under oars. I had the hang of it.

Did I know Sgeir a Chaolais? I nodded. Sgeir Linish? I nodded again. Well, when we were under sail we had to give these an even wider berth, in case our way through the water was not as direct as we thought it was. But there was a good keel under this boat. I would learn to trust it. Did I know the transit on The Sail?

'The what?'

'How to line up the marks.'

'The Sail on the point.'

'Well, that should do you for now.'

Then I got the nod to put her nose into the wind. Where was it coming from? 'Southerly.'

'Aye, now just you hold her there,' I was told, 'and the boys will soon have the lugsail up.'

They had done that before, I could see. It was still pretty smooth. I was so involved in watching how one was fastening something while another was hauling, that I lost the eye of the man guiding me and was slow to take her off the wind. But we found momentum again all right and I got a look, as much as to say they wouldn't hold that one against me.

The old boat really got going then. I was amazed at the way we made under sail. I was to take her as close to the wind as I could without losing power. I was guided into steering her upwind till there was a small shake at the front edge of the sail. Then the skipper on the sheet took in the slack and when I eased her off the wind we heeled a bit. The breeze was on our starboard side, so the sail was out the other way. Nobody said anything but these boys were easing their weight on to the windward gunnel as neat as dancers.

The sheet was never tied. If that was released, the strain would come off. And the halyard too, the rope that held the sail high on its bending spar, just a few turns. No knots, so it could be let go in a hurry. The friction would be sufficient to hold it.

We were now further out to sea than I had ever been before. Someone asked, were we making for Sutherland, but one old fellow knew exactly where we were going. To the herring. He talked me through tacking the boat. I had just to take her all the way through the wind, quite smart but nothing sudden. The sail would be dipped round to the other side of the mast and the sheet shifted from one hole in the top plank, across to its opposite number.

I could tell they were happy with the manoeuvre, pleased with themselves for not losing their touch. The whole boat was smiling. And we were fair shifting, beating into it, with the wind on our port side, now. The sea hadn't built up yet. Our course was taking us closer to the land again but further down the east coast of Lewis.

How that man knew they were under our keel, I could not even guess. It might have been his sense of smell, sight, taste or sound – or all of them. Perhaps he just knew where they usually shoaled at that time of year. I had seen the porpoises in the loch but these were dolphins around us, leaping like salmon. Maybe it was their excitement that provided the sign.

These old boys and myself, we all sent the *dorgh* over, I could not say with how much faith. The light was just starting to fade. It was a strange feeling. You know when you take a mackerel, the line goes everywhere. A spray comes off the line. Well the herring are not at all like that. They rise to feed on the plankton and must go for the glint on these bare hooks, mouthing softer than whiting. You feel only a shimmer.

The old boys were wondering if there was fish there or not. They were hauling at speed and shaking them off. It was maybe just my curiosity at work but I was pulling very gently, hand over hand and there they were: five herring for six hooks. Then everyone was into them.

You think you have already seen a herring. If that fish has come from a trawl, you have not really seen a herring yet. If you have seen one that fell from a drift-net, you have come close to what I witnessed that night. You might think they are silver but that night I could see purple, brown, grey and other colours on the broad scales of the *sgadan* as they fell into our black boat. I do not know names for these colours, in Gaelic or English.

One thing was sure, the Minch was thick with fish. We had to ditch some of our ballast of round boulders, over the side. We cast out more, as the weight of fish amassed. We only knew the light had gone when the fish stopped taking.

There was more than the whole village could eat. It was later in the year you wanted them for salting. The old boys knew there would be a hell of a price in Stornoway, with the wartime shortage. What about the boy? Someone said what they were all thinking. But I said I'd be fine. It was a fair night.

We were drunk with it, including myself, left on the tiller as *Bhalaich Ghriomsiadair* set course for harbour. The Stornoway fleet were a long way off. The word was, they were working out off The Butt, these nights. We would be the first to land.

I was told that you did not run with the wind up your backside. You kept it on your quarter so the sail could not back. Even so, the boys put one reef in the sail, showing me the seaman's way with the slipknot. So nothing would jam. Where is she coming from now? And I could tell the wind had backed a touch to the east. Not good for fishing but we had all the catch we could carry and a fair breeze to take us to the Market.

We were creaming in, on the surf out from the beacon off Arnish light. I could feel real weight in the tiller now and I had to lean against it to keep her steady. I can still hear the voice of the man who was directing us.

'Here is a trick for you. Harden her up a bit as you hear one coming. That's it. Now relax your grip completely when the wave has a hold of us and we will just ride with it. Tighten up again, ready for the next one.'

He had a wee word for us all before we took her in, alongside. There would be none of this dropping the sail and dragging her in on the sweeps. The village boys would take her in under sail.

I only had to keep watching for that eye and we would be fine. So she turned into the wind for the few souls on the pier to see us arrive, first at the market, our larch kissing the greenheart. The iron traveller slid down the mast. It was gliding on the linseed oil we'd been rubbing in, only a day before.

We landed these fish and they sold themselves. There was blood in their gills and pearls in their scales. Wads of money started appearing. The share-out would come later. We had to take a dram, only the one, from a clay piggy that was not supposed to be for sale. The boy, that was me, could take a sip. 'Hold it down now,' they said. 'Don't you go looking green about your own gills.'

Now the way they said it, afterwards, was this: you learn a

thing and you think that is that. But it is not. You think you know a thing but you have to find it out again. Then when you grow old, surely you have made all your mistakes and that is finally that.

But all these men were boys like me. The signs were there for anyone to see. The sixty and seventy-foot Zulus and Fifies were coming in when we were going out. The big fishing ships were well reefed-down and that is a sight you did not see often, when they were racing to land their catch. A big tide was still ebbing so you got a confused sea, just off the beacon.

'The ebb is good for us,' they said. 'The wind is well in the east now so we will have no need to beat against it so hard on the way home. It will not take us long. We will grab the chance before she veers back to the south.'

We were still making good way with two reefs in but the motion was not good, banging right on our beam. Then I could sense another shift but she wasn't veering, she was backing further. Even a bit of north in her.

It was then our skipper put his hand over my own. He nodded back towards Holm Point and I could see dark low clouds. We all knew there would be a blast in these but we were not going to try to fight it. It was too late to turn back to harbour. We were well out the door now. I was to hold my course and they would drop the sail altogether.

Nothing was being rushed but the whole rig came down as gently as before. A blast of hail hit us with the wind: the edge of the front. You will often get that with the anvil clouds.

'There will be more to come, *a bhalaich*,' said himself. 'But we can take it, with your help. We are in a real seaboat here. This is what they use in the Pentland Firth and they have worse conditions there than anything we might meet tonight.'

Even so, the smallest scrap of cloth we could show was too much for what was happening on the Minch. So we had just to run, on the bare pole, as they said: steering as before. There was still no hope of coming through the wind to fight back to Stornoway. They left me on the tiller.

I do not know if it was because my muscles were young and they needed me there or if they were keeping me occupied so I would not be too scared. If these old boys were scared, they did not show it. There was a lot less spoken but it was still all calm in the boat itself. And I still had to catch the eye of himself, with the rest of them slumped all around the boat, snatching some rest.

My arms were heavy but you found a way of wrapping yourself around the tiller so you were a part of it. The veins were up in my own arm, like the grain of the wood. The cold was something that bit at you. Hail is more fierce in the late summer because you are not prepared for it. The spray that just comes over the tops of the waves is very nearly a pure white. The old boys warned me not to bother looking back. There was no use in seeing these big green ones coming from a distance. I would hear and feel them soon enough. I knew what to do now.

We were surfing on but that old stick of a mast was our sail.

'We've nothing to worry about,' the old boys said. 'We have the whole Minch to play with.'

So we were just responding with the tiller while we still had way, when you felt the surge. He said I was doing just fine.

You have to be slower or faster than the wave to keep steerage. If the speeds are equal you have no power in the helm. It was that night I learned that the same transit that takes you out away from home, will take you back in again, if you can find it.

When the squalls were down a bit, I got the message to scan that skyline, coming towards us, up out of the dark.

'Can I borrow your eyes, now?' himself asked. We had run past our entrance. They reckoned we were well out abeam Loch Erisort. Better that way, further off the land. But I had it, The Sail and then the Gob. None of them could make out the marks but they trusted my younger eyes and sent the smallest, reefed-down sail up the traveller.

That took us in. There is a huge relief in recognising what you already know: a course well clear of the reefs, nothing fancy, and we were at the narrows. *Bhalaich Ghriomsiadair* had been sighted. Some figures were running along the skyline. Then, with the old boys awake and drawing on their last reserve, we rowed to the muddy shingle. The whole village was out to meet us.

My own sense of relief was over when I saw my mother to the fore but a hand went on my shoulder. Now they had trusted me and it was my turn to trust them. This was something they could do for me.

The man whose eye had taken us through everything, waded ashore first. If he was exhausted, he did not show it. He went directly to my mother and had a quiet word. I could not tell you now what was said. When I came ashore I had first to do as the youngest aboard always did – turn his back as the fry of herring that had been held back from sale was shared into piles. There were five shares, to include the one for the boat. My job was to call out the names, while my back was turned.

'Who is having this one?'

'Murchadh.'

'This one?'

'Iain Mhor.'

'And this?'

'Aonghas Dubh.'

'And this one?'

'That must be my own, if I'm getting one.'

'Oh you're getting one all right,' Murchadh said.

'Well, the last one must be for the boat,' I said.

Then we did the same with the folding money. That was also counted into five equal shares.

Mine was a full share. But the fifth wasn't given to the owner of the boat. No-one could say who owned it anyway and the only expenses were a bucket of tar, some peats to melt that and a brush or two. No, but the fifth share was given in full to my mother: the herring-girl who had seen how it was done in the Shetlands. My own mother remembered it all, for the boat of the old men.

Ruaraidh

Angus, from South Lochs, and my uncle Ruaraidh were the best of mates. That's what they called each other – a mhate. The Gaelic version. I knew Angus first as my pal Kenny's uncle. He became our skipper but he never talked about being in the war, with my uncle Ruaraidh.

There were whispers of what they'd been through. Something in the war, for sure, but neither of them ever talked about it. I think I asked if they'd been in the air force or the navy or in tanks like my own olman but I think they just said they were foot soldiers. Common foot soldiers.

When they got going, one story sparked off the next. I couldn't say now which one of them told me this one. I heard it when I was a student, back home visiting. It was my first time out of town for long enough. Angus had his own stock on the croft at Griomsiadair now. Ruaraidh didn't have much stomach for it, these days. They were pleased to see I could still get my hands dirty even if I wasn't eating properly.

By God when you'd had nothing but one slice of bread with jam and the other with spam and you put the two bits together right away before the flies got to them and got it down you when you could, you wouldn't turn your nose up at food after that. But that's about the only detail you would get. Same with my father. It was as if the three of them had got together and made a pact. But their non-talking pact held up a lot longer than Adolf and Joe's non-aggression agreement. I can only remember a couple of hints that maybe Ruaraidh was almost ready to tell it as it was.

'A good job the Nazi-Soviet agreement fell apart. Do you think the Allies could have defeated the Nazis if Hitler hadn't taken on that mad assault into Russia? Aye and what if there had been no attack on Pearl Harbour? Would the Yanks have been in on it then?'

They'd talk out these issues all right but it was late on in their lives, when these men knew their number was coming up sooner rather than later. It was only then they'd drop their guard. You'd get a memory, from either of them, sharp and tight enough to steal the wind out of you.

Maybe some of the experience was in the choice of stories. There were funny ones all right but then you'd get something like the one I'm going to try to tell you. I couldn't say which one of them told me this. They were like twins when they got going.

So you walked over the moor today, Peter? You didn't take the short cut in by the loch? No? Aye, it was probably safer to hug the coast, in case the mist came down.

Well, you wouldn't be the first student to take that route to Lochs. There were two students, one time. And they were out gathering birds' eggs when they should have been studying. Out the Arnish moor, just the way you've come. One of them gets to an eyrie first and he's in luck, he takes the egg. The other is mad because he saw the nest first, and he thought they should share it, there were collectors would pay good money for that. So there was a quarrel. And the one that took the egg smashed it right against the forehead of the other. It didn't hurt him but he saw red and reached for a stone. His friend had turned round so he went at his head with the stone and that was that.

He got hold of what he could lay his hands on, some old bleached animal bones, lying there and used them to dig a crude, shallow grave.

No-one knew they'd gone out there together so the lad that did the deed, he made good his escape. He probably took a berth on a boat and one ship led to another and the years passed.

But after all that time he thought it was safe to return to Stornoway. Maybe he said they'd run away to sea together but then lost touch when they were put on different ships. Sure enough, everything was forgotten. Maybe they all thought the missing lad was making his fortune in the colonies. Or maybe he'd just turn up when his ship berthed in SY.

And the fellow who did that terrible deed, he was not long back, looking for work and visiting the relatives. Out here like yourself today, out from the town. Some things haven't changed. They'd make sure and serve up the best they had. And then they'd look to a story from the young man who'd run off to see a bit of the world. They'd want to hear about his travels.

Except that these people were as poor as you could get. You made use of what you could find. But there was usually fish anyway and maybe some meal. They'd have shown hospitality to their cousin some way. So the former student is sitting and eating and being back in the family. Usually you'd just eat with your fingers but they had a few simple spoons and knives made from staghorn and bone.

And this rough knife of bone slipped and made a small cut in the young man's thumb. It started to bleed and it just didn't stop. Now a rough blade can cut worse than a sharp one and that blood just kept on flowing. They wrapped it as best they could, in this and that, trying to stop it. But the blood came seeping through everything. That night, the cut became infected. By the morning, the hand was looking terrible.

They sent word and eventually the doctor rode out to them. But the infection had taken a hold. The doctor asked how it all happened. They told him about the bleeding. He asked to see the knife.

'Where did you find this?' the doctor asked.

They told the doctor they'd just come across a pile of old antlers and deer bones, when they were out at the sheep, out the Arnish moor. All just bleached clean. So one of the boys had just passed the time carving out the spoons and knives from what he found.

'Well,' said the doctor, 'I'll need to take these utensils back with me and any others you may have. We have to trace where an infection like that comes from.'

The returning traveller never recovered from that infection. When the results came back, the doctor came to see the family again. Most of the spoons and knives were made from the antlers and bones of a large red deer. But the knife that did the damage was whittled out of a human bone.

But if it was Angus who told that one, it was his sidekick who chipped in the next bit.

Remember I told you, you'd never stay a night out at Creag a' Bhodaich. Even if you got caught out in the mist. Most folk said they'd hear the voice of an old man with a story he had to tell to someone. Up until very recently there'd be sightings out that way, near where our road meets the main one. Other folk said it wasn't an old man at all. One fellow described a young man wearing something like a long woollen covering, not from our times.

Well, they found something when they were peat-cutting. They had to call in the museums people. They thought it was a preserved body from Neolithic times. But it wasn't that old. It was the remains of a lad in his mid-teens. His woven long socks and long plaid thing were pretty much intact. He'd been killed by a crushing blow to the back of the head.

See the appetite we've got for stories like that, on Lewis. We're insatiable. Once one cove or *cailleach* gets started, it prompts another and it could go on all night. Sometimes does. Same with songs. Only they're worse. We like them a few shades below the *mì-chàilear*, when it comes to grief. And people will be cheery as you like, in between the songs or yarns. Smiling away and teasing each other. The very dab, as we used to say. You don't hear that now and I've no idea where the phrase comes from. But you can bet someone will say, 'O shut up.' Which of course means, 'Please continue.'

Now, I ask you, do you find that one plausible? I wouldn't like to make a religion out of being sceptical – isn't that what that Krishnamurti guy did? But I'm not going to buy that yarn. Doesn't matter. You still want to hear them told.

The brass buttons on the dripping sailor's jacket. Only it turns out he was lost some weeks before he was sighted. He says something which helps to find his body on the sand. You'll meet him all the way from Sandwood Bay to the Ross of Mull. And there will be an Irish connection – either where his ship sank, or the origins of the mate who became the ghost.

Then there's the fine boots which you know will be stolen from the drowned seaman, whether you're in Uist or Shetland. You also know that they will be reclaimed by their dead owner.

The Carranoch

All these meetings. The memories among patent-mops, plastic folders. I met the skipper at the goodie counter. All roads meet here in December. If you don't see someone out at Marybank Garage, waiting for a tyre or exhaust, you'll see them in the Woolies. I was looking along the presentation boxes for Terry's Spartan. The olaid had never gone for soft-centres.

This was F W Woolworth, not long before the sign changed to Woolworth and the cheques had to be made out to Woolworth PLC. The skipper was Angus from Garyvard. Kenny's uncle. It might be enough to be all Jock Tamson's bairns in the rest of Scotland but in the Outer Hebrides, we need to know the details of the relationships.

The round face was even more round. A trace of white stubble coming through the red. The thick glasses. No Sellotape. The ones he had to hand on the boat were held together with the stuff. These must be his best wear. I'd first met this man, amongst others, in a fishing boat chartered for a sea angling competition. Then again when he bought my olman's Morris Traveller. He put the brush over it with Charlie Morrison's Paint – yacht enamel – wooden bits and all and it did him a couple of years. But that was as far as my track went. I didn't know he was Kenny F's uncle, till that first time out in the sea angling boat.

'Do you still go fishing?' It was his question, direct, no smalltalk.

It was like we were in the movies. Marbled vinyl of the floor going wavy. Here we go. We're away. A bit like LSD. But that's how it was. The shoppers passing us by like other vessels in transit. I was afloat.

Kenny F and me took turns being anchor-man and mate. A bristling rivalry between us. Usually, it was Kenny who was up the pecking order. He was ahead of me in seamanship. A guy who knew what he wanted to do. But we'd work as a team to start the Lister. One on the handle, the other ready to pull over the lever on the first cylinder when she was turning over fast enough. Then the second two got recompressed when she was chuntering. Since then, I've never fully trusted an electric start.

Kenny's uncle Angus gave us the marks once. Then he let us argue between ourselves until we remembered them and found anchorage uptide from the pinnacle. Quite a knack in judging the slack so you'd hold but not drift too far down. I learned not to coil that warp, on the way out, but to flake it, end for end, loose so it would run.

All around The Carranoch it's thirty fathoms and then it climbs. Twenty, then eighteen and you're right on it. Abeam the tits up on the hill over Loch Erisort, the mark open on the island – Tavay. We couldn't wait to get the lines down.

A real Christmas tree rig, Angus called Kenny's set of lures. I blame all these angling magazines.

But there was something to be said for hedging your bet between the bigger hook on the bottom and a smaller one on a snood. You might get something interesting half a fathom up. Maybe because the three of us fished a different set of terminal tackle, the box would fill with colours. Twelve species was nothing out of the ordinary and sometime we'd be struggling for names, between our town English and the skipper's Gaelic. Was a red bream the same as a Norwegian haddock? He would often start to sing but composing in English, for our benefit.

'If you catch a Balallan Wrasse,
You can stick it up your ass...'

Cuckoo wrasse had the tropical colours, ballan wrasse, often larger fish, had a soft shift of shading from kelp red to a green I haven't seen anywhere else. The ling coming up, mottled like pike but a valued fish in our parts. All sure signs you were over the hard ground. Every village in North Lochs would have its own set of marks for the reef.

Balallan was further up Loch Erisort, almost inland. Not taken too seriously by guys like our skipper from further down the loch.

All gasping colours, darkening on wrinkled skins as the day went on. The light always seeming to be refracted so it came from the clouds as rays from a protractor. Spreading to link us, over The Carranoch, spreading further west to Eilean Calum Chille – St Columba's Isle. If that Irishman visited half the islands that bear his name, he'd have got around as much as Bonny Prince Charlie. The Prince's cairn was another of our marks, muddy ground for thornback ray, in his case.

'Did you ever see such a fluke as –

A skate on a haddock hook?'

It was only a matter of time before Angus's big rod would go right on over, as far as the water and we'd think he had the bottom and was winding us up. But no, nine times out of ten, a grey slashing conger would come up on his single Scandinavian hook. Mustad. Best forged Swedish steel.

But it was one of Kenny's congers that nearly caused a mutiny.

'If that bloody thing is coming into this boat, I'm leaving it.' His uncle's judgement. And I played along. Kenny was getting worked up.

'Come on, I don't have a wire trace on. Just the thick mono. It's getting frayed. Don't piss about, gaff that eel before we lose it.'

I was guided by Angus. We lifted several of the bottom boards before taking up the gaff. Put them aside in order. As I swung the big black thing in, Angus took his knife to the thick nylon snood so the whole thing fell into the place prepared for it. He chucked the boards back and sat on them. There was a drumming. But you couldn't risk your fingers near that. He'd stun it, aiming at the spine near the vent, in a minute. That one would be in the salt by tonight. Feed half his own village unless we townies wanted it.

'No, you're welcome to it.' Kenny was recovering. 'You have to live at least three cattle grids out from town to eat salt eel.'

Even if none of it's said, sometimes you know the other guy is reliving it with you. Memories meeting. Passing vessels exchanging courtesies. Angus was still in the aisle of the shop. The voice that came through to me at last, said how was his nephew, Kenny, doing?

Hadn't he heard?

He wouldn't be blooming well asking me if he'd heard.

The skipper's language was more subdued these days. I'd heard he was on the tack. Religion usually went along with that. He looked well on it.

I told him Kenny F had blown it.

'Blown what?'

'Blown a good job at the Arnish yard.'

The yard out over the harbour Approaches, near the old quarantine buoy. I'd jotted the figures down for the surveyors who prepared the ground. That was one summer job. Next season I'd looked at the smoke from the town side, as they burned the farm cottage and bulldozed the hill behind it. Kept a lot of young guys at home. Brought a few travellers back. Jackets and collars in steel for North Sea platforms. Cash to be spent in the shops down town. Accommodation for welding inspectors.

To be weighed against the loss of the more adventurous townie's Sunday stroll. The pollution of one shore which was thick with horse-mussels. The clappy-doos you see at the Barras in Glasgow. Once, when it was blowing too much of a hooly even for us to go out past the light, the skipper had taken us into Glumaig Bay at Low Water to fill a fishbox with them. First you saw nothing. Then you became sensitive to the barnacled black stone that wasn't a stone. You needed a decent knife. Meaty shellfish, asking for a garlic sauce.

Angus told me my mate hadn't been out to Garyvard for a long time. I told him I hadn't seen him, myself. I'd been at Uni, back and fore. And on shiftwork, when I was working at home.

'Is he at the welding? He was at Nigg for a while.'

No, Kenny hadn't been a welder. A scaffolder and, the word was, a bloody good one. He had it all planned. A definite share, each week into the boat account. Sure as Pay As You Earn. He had the keel laid in a yard at Buckie. Small enough to work single-handed, if he had to, big enough to put out in a bit of sea.

'So what's gone wrong ?'

The twelve-hour shifts. You could see it coming. First it was only one on the way home, when you knocked off. There were a few places you could tap at the door, whatever the finishing time.

'Aye, I used to know a few of these knocks.'

Then it was after the night shifts, before you got to your bed. Only a matter of time before there was something in the back pocket or in the tea flask.

Angus only had to give the smallest nod. 'So it came to a head?

'In style. They thought he'd gone crazy one night. Nobody realised what he was up to, carrying all these poles outside the main shed. Then someone misses him for a tricky bit where they were welding. Goes out to find this amazing bit of scaffolding, pretty well the full height of the shed. And there's Kenny, swaying, with a big can of that indelible paint, making this huge mark.

'When you stood back, it was a big white cross. First they think it's a big Scottish nationalist sign and a lot of guys start cheering till it looks like a war's going to break out. Then somebody think's he's got religion in a big way. Could be that kind of cross.'

But the skipper knew what it was the way I'd known what Kenny was up to. Our northward mark for the Carranoch Reef was gone, since the old Coastguard aerial at Holm had been shifted. Then the Arnish sheds obscured another mark. So Kenny had painted a white cross you could see from five miles out at sea. Just what we needed to line up on the war memorial. Only of course some tidy so and so painted over it before we had a chance to test it out properly. And Kenny was down the road. I hadn't seen him for a while.

'He'll get his boat another way if he gets off the sauce,' Angus said.

And I could see now how the red in our skipper's face was somehow different, clearer, not broken by small veins. I remembered someone saying he was an Elder, these days. But he was saying something else. I hadn't answered his question, did I still go fishing?

No, not that way, not to sea, not for a while. But I went to fresh water. The longer the hike over the moor the better. Maybe that was like enjoying the clearing up more than the party. But I was a bit that way as well, believe it or not. And himself?

'Eels. No, not congers. Freshwater. Like reptiles.' He had a small business, laying traps and fyke-nets in the lochs near home. Then he had a stainless-steel smoker set-up. Got oak chips from the boatyard at Goat Island. They fetched a better price than smoked salmon, these days, with all that farmed stuff about.

He'd seen them often enough, Hamburg or Rotterdam, out on the stalls. About the only thing that stayed in his mind from the blur of all these shore visits. He'd never eat one himself.

'If you ever taste one,' he said, 'it might be one of mine. You'll need to report back to me, what they're like.'

The Trolley

I had rounds, like the consultant, but I delivered supplies to the different wards and I collected rubbish. There was an incinerator so you could get rid of a lot of waste on site. Other bags would be marked as sharps and you'd take special care to put these in their allotted place. Then there was the laundry collection and that was good for an extra cup of tea and a yarn.

A sample conversation: 'Maternity's busy.'

'Sure is.'

'You'd think that cold spell we had last March these men would be keeping it in their trousers.'

'So you'd think.

'But no, the zips must have been up and down like President Kennedy's.'

'Aye.'

One of the jobs you had to do was to help take a body out to the mortuary. You could go months without a death happening on your shift. When it did, you'd get a call from the ward. Then you'd go and fetch a different trolley. This one was long enough and it had a hinged metal lid so everything was discreet. If it was during the day porter's hours, you'd go and get him to help. If it was at night, the ward sister would lend you one of her nurses and see if she could get a male nurse from one of the men's wards.

The guys were good about swapping shifts but this day I was keen to get off an hour early to get to a meeting. I forget which brand of religion I was exploring at the time. Of course we were changing the world. History was on our side.

A new day porter had just got a start but he seemed OK for the crack. Glaswegian but he spoke slower than most so you could sometimes get at least two words in three.

So I asked him, any chance you could stay on an extra two hours and I'll be owing you? 'No bother,' he says, 'but just cover me for an hour. I'll get down the road. Get some dinner in me first.'

'Fine.'

But he's just out the door when the phone goes in the canteen – I've got the chairs up on the tables and the mop's out – but I get to it OK. 'There's been a death in female medical. You'll need to get the day porter. We'll have everything ready for you in about fifteen minutes.'

It needs two people to lift a body out of the trolley on to the slab.

Now I can't tell her I've just made a deal with said porter which means he's not where he should be right now. So I have to come up with a contingency plan. I happen to know that a guy who used to be a day porter is in the hospital pharmacy now. So I go and whisper a word in his shell-like and he says sorry, he'd like to help but the back's been a real bastard – that's why he got the move in the first place so he just can't risk it.

Plan B has to kick in. Accept the help of the nurse to get the trolley out to the mortuary and wait till the Glasgow cove gets back on scene. Then we can lift the body out together.

So it's a student nurse and she's not done this before. Everything is very discreet. The body is always sewn up in a crisp shroud so you don't see the features or anything. These nurses have the techniques for lifting, you wouldn't believe it. Slight wee things joining hands under a hefty patient and easing her where she needs to go. Impressive. So the ward sister, the student and me, got the body in the trolley with some dignity. I swung the lid over and we were on out way. When I say 'we', I mean the two of us, the nurse and me. Or the three of us if you count the deceased.

We've got to keep some flicking decorum. No fancy swerves at the corners.

The student was so relieved when I said, that was the job done for now. 'The other porter and me can see to the rest of it at the change-over.' So she doesn't ask any further and she's gone back out that door before you can say cheerio.

Fine, so far, except your man is a bit on the late side and I'm in that mind-set. We're talking religious investigation here – mission mode. And I'm that relieved at staying out of trouble so far. Trouble with a plan is once you've formulated it you think the thing is done already. So I just forget to say we've a wee job to do first. And of course when God's on your side too, it's possible to get a shade complacent.

I got to the meeting, more or less on time. I was oblivious to the fact that a law of the universe was kicking in. In the next hour, before the night porter came on shift, the new day porter took a phone call. Male medical ward. Another death. But no-one's done the full induction for the new man so he hasn't done a death before. So the sister – that red-haired, striking one – she talked him through it. Sure enough, the key worked. He was in the mortuary and the trolley was there.

But remember, he'd never pushed it before and the lid was down. So he was wheeling the body I'd not long moved out of the hospital back where it came from. With a bit of difficulty, he negotiated the bends. The sister and the nurse were holding the swing doors for him in the side ward.

Fine.

But when the nurse lifted the lid she jumped three feet into the air. As you know, but they didn't, that trolley was already occupied.

Like I said, they're all sewn up but when you're expecting an empty void in a covered trolley, the outline of a body in a shroud must be a bit shocking.

'Oh well, they'll be company for each other,' the day porter said. And of course, with a fair number of chess-moves, everything got sorted.

Meanwhile, our group was finished doing its bit to save the rest of the planet by prayer and were tackling the cakes and savouries.

The state of mild euphoria lasted till I came in to start my rounds next day. I got called to Female Medical.

'What were you thinking of?'

Some of the other sisters in that hospital would have gone straight to my boss. I might have been out the door and down the road that day. The red-haired one told me I'd nearly given her poor nurse her own heart attack but after that she had to say they'd all made a full recovery. Except for the two who were dead already.

The District

After a bit of a blow there's lobsters too dizzy to sell. Alive but crippled. Not a commercial proposition. Bootlace conger, rockling and wrasse – they're only a by-catch.

Put them all in the stock. The bony fish will hold together. Don't flood them with too much liquid of any kind. Let it be intense. Bay leaves, a big onion, sticks of celery.

Let the pan tick over long enough. Drain and salvage white meat from the debris. Save it to put it back in, right at the end.

If you've tomatoes gone soft or not quite ripened, chop them small. Shallots, garlic, leeks, chives – whatever's in season, sweat them gently in oil or butter. Pour in a half glass of fino. (A return trade for most of our shellfish.)

Add something fresh, maybe some well-scrubbed mussels. Adjust the seasoning but if you add any tomato puree, take it easy. You want it to taste of fish.

Some fine-chopped parsley can go in with the white shellfish meat.

Don't leave any of the soup or you might get bad weather tomorrow.

Kirsty was something else at the funeral. She really looked after the olaid. They used to chafe a lot. Fathers and daughters. Mothers and sons. I think the olaid was a bit jealous of the way they'd stand and gab. I remember he'd walk out to the back door with Kirsty when there was a very clear night. He'd point out the belt of Orion and his dog, Sirius, following behind. Then they'd turn to the handle of the pan that led you up to bright Polaris. I was eavesdropping. The names stayed with me though I didn't know what to look for.

All the arrangements were made for us. Ruaraidh was the go-between. Talking to the undertaker. We didn't care which coffin or if there were to be flowers or anything like that.

But I heard the voices raised in the kitchen. It was Kirsty's, quite strong, quite loud. Quite firm. Ruaraidh was talking about the done thing and offending people.

Kirsty said she wasn't going to go back home and stir the soup for the men and neither was her mother.

They might have been the first women who went to the graveside at a Lewis funeral. Maybe they didn't count because one was an East Coaster and the other half and half. But Ruaraidh's wife, Sheena – she went along with them. She was the bravest one of the three.

I was that proud of them. At the time I still had a faith of a kind but it was out of step with the majority verdict. I could say a short prayer but only to myself. It didn't help that much.

The service never said much about the olman. That was the usual then. I think they might have mentioned his name. They didn't always do that. 'We are here to bury our father and brother, husband, friend. This is the fate that awaits us all and none of us know the hour or the day.'

And that's about it but it takes a bit longer.

The undertaker and his helper take the coffin from the church to the bier. It's difficult, standing up in front, with the coffin. You get a cord to hold and later that's what you'll use to take your share of lowering it into the ground.

Ruaraidh and the rest of the male relations had the other cords. I nodded to the men I'd seen in their overalls at fanks. They all had black ties and white shirts so I had to look a few times to remember who was who.

The rest of the men lined up behind the bier which was chocked up ready, outside the church. Sometimes it's outside a house, but that's usually when the funeral is out of town.

So there were two lines forming, men who worked with the

olman in the Mill, more distant relations, folk who knew him in the town. Guys I was at school with, showing solidarity. I didn't catch Kenny F's eye any time. But he might have been there. You don't see the guys in the line when you're holding the cord. Except at the hearse. They don't come up to shake your hand then. That's at the graveside. They don't all come to the graveside. If they do, they share cars or take the bus that's always laid on.

Before all that, the weight has to be shared between the two lines. It's like two queues, walking slowly and slightly separate as the procession moves. When you come to the front, you nod to the guy you're taking over from. Then your right or left hand goes to the front handle. The other guy moves back to the middle handle. And so on. They try to park the hearse according to the length of the lines so everyone gets a share of carrying the coffin.

Most guys have done their bit then. A lot of the guys in the lines won't have gone to the service, in the house or at the church. They'll just have arrived outside, to take their share of 'the lift'. The undertaker says, 'We'll take a lift now, boys.'

At the cemetery, there's another lift to the graveside. And this time there were three women standing, waiting. The olaid flanked by Kirsty and Sheena. Since then it's been done quite a bit. It's not the usual thing now but it's done sometimes.

Kirsty had to go back to Canada to sort a few things out. I was holding the fort at home. No bother. In a couple of months she had things arranged – a temporary job on the District to come home to – a maternity-leave post. And she'd be staying with an old pal out of town. This was partly practical – a rural District. And partly because she knew it would be too much, the women nagging each other in the same house.

I wouldn't say we got close exactly but there was one evening, after the olaid went to bed. Kirsty would stay the night now and again. She told me a story. Something that happened on the District. Something like this.

I've always wanted to be on the District and that's what I'm doing. How many can say that? I've a neat red car, Essential Users

Allowance and I see a fair bit of life and death as well as drinking too many cups of tea. I'll probably go back at the end of the job, pick up my life in Canada. But this is fine for now.

So at home, I usually get my feet up by the box. But I always make sure and do a baking once a week. Sometimes I get a few visitors when they see my car outside. I was quite pleased at the company the first time Kenny F showed up on the doorstep.

I've seen your old mate a few times, lately. I know you're out of touch, with you going to meetings and not drinking. At first I thought he was a relation, on the olman's side of course. Then I remembered him from Westview.

His face is the sort that a photographer would find interesting. Quite a good-looking man in his way if you were looking for that. Weatherbeaten, I thought. Something quite kind in him. Just a year or two younger than myself. I remember us being only a year or two apart at school. I tried to make it clear I had no interest that way. My life was full but I was glad of the company. But Westview meant a lot to all of us.

I don't suppose I'd seen him for five years or more. He said it all in a breath that he'd had a bit of luck with his job on a boat and there was a bit of fish going spare. How was the brother doing? He was sorry about the olman.

Hadn't he heard, Peter was working in the hospital for a while. But on shiftwork. Out of step.

He said working on a boat was a bit like that too. But Peter would be going back to Uni. That was for sure.

Kenny wasn't going to come in but then he did. It was a job to get him to sit down. He was soon coming out with his yarn though and I felt his laugh was the sort you could trust. So I said he was to be sure and come back any time, fish or no fish. He left a good feeling behind him.

Well of course I went to see what was in the poly-bag then. It was one from the Mainland, Markies, I remember. The things you notice. How that was in circulation in the village.

It wasn't white fish he'd brought but prawns, the quality you usually only see in the big hotels. Not tailed but still whole. I know all this because I used to clear up the leavings of ones like that for a couple of years before I went nursing. But of course Kenny's offering would have meant the same supposing it was only a whiting or two.

It was more difficult with him next time. He sat for a while though he didn't say much and I don't believe we had a laugh once. That made me feel as if he was taking up more of the house. I didn't really mind for myself, only I was worried for his own sake. You notice more in the quiet.

He said thanks for the tea, though he didn't eat anything. The bag he left was cold. It was prawns again and as big as the last lot but they'd been in the freezer. Not that I minded, they taste the same and I could still take a few next door when they were thawed and boiled.

It was afterwards I heard he'd lost the job a week or two before that visit but he was keeping up appearances. I was annoyed he felt he had to put on an act where he was welcome anyway.

I asked him straight when he came again and he said yes, it was true, but he wasn't bothered. He was out on his own now and here was the catch in the bag. He didn't need any flashy boats bought with a big grant and a big loan hanging over them. He could fire up the old engine in the old boat and get out far enough to set a few creels.

So it was a lobster this time and still alive. That didn't shock me. I've handled them before, in big stainless-steel kitchens. But the black berries disturbed everything. That's what the lobster's eggs look like. The fishermen are supposed to return ones like that to the water but some of them scrape the stuff off the shell and sell the lobster as good. That's a waste of future stock. It would have been better that Kenny was honest at least and hadn't bothered to disguise things. But he hadn't even noticed the berries.

That seems strange, as if everything about him was numb. Of course it was obvious to me then and I wondered how someone in my job could have missed it for so long. You wouldn't believe how good some people are at disguising that problem. They often drink vodka rather than whisky so you don't notice it on the breath.

He wasn't excited or staggering or anything like that but I was left feeling sick when he went. The waste of the black spawn didn't help. I couldn't scrape the lobster or boil it. I hadn't even had a glass of wine so I ended up driving down to the jetty. The tide was out so I had to stagger over the rocks in the dark till I found the water. I don't know if the creature survived.

I found out afterwards that this was all on the day that Kenny went missing. In the village I heard the word 'disappeared' as if they were making a meal of it. Even next door they were talking about dragging the harbour, in these hushed tones as if drowning was a judgment from above. Inevitable for a big alky like that, always near water. He was crazy for the fishing. The lochs too. Freshwater. Pity he didn't drink more fresh water when he was alive, I heard someone say.

I lost patience at that and let go. I told them I'd seen a few recovered from the harbour when I was working in the Lewis hospital, before the midwifery. I'd to help wheel the breathing equipment and keep the manual cardiac massage going till they got all the electronic gear ready. Then I'd to keep the other fellow occupied, the one who'd dived in after his shipmate. You usually know if they've a chance of coming round. But sometimes you're wrong. This casualty had been down for a while. He was swollen and blue. He wasn't going to revive.

One night the consultant got called in to do the full resuscitation bit. Then had a cup of tea with me and told me, wherever else you die, stay clear of a hospital. Keep some dignity.

Anyway, it turned out that Kenny hadn't ended up in the harbour. He turned up at my doorstep a couple of weeks after. He'd been coming off the drink. Away on his own in a hut out on the moor. Not that I'm saying he's cured now. That's the wrong way of looking at that problem. But he'd have a better chance if people hadn't wanted to say so quickly that he must have fallen in the harbour.

Laws

Sexual repression gets that bit easier, with time, if the food is good and there's plenty of exercise. And there's a network – you're on a train and a family sitting opposite recognises that the fish-pendant is a symbol. It was a gift, made in stainless steel by a craftsman cousin who was glad to see you at the right end of Kenneth Street. I suppose I was going along more now for the stories and for the sense of being in a congregation when that huge groundswell lifted to follow the melody offered by the precentor. I usually went to the Gaelic services. I'd picked up a bit but not enough to follow the sermons. That was maybe just as well. The rhythms of the whole thing swept you along. And then there was the warmth in the handshakes, as you went outside. The anticipation of the Sunday dinner, roast meat and gravy, almost a smell in the air already, like smoke over the town.

The olaid went now and again to her own church up the road, the moderate Church of Scotland. There were two of these to pick from. I gave that a try but it was just like I remembered. The olaid reminded me I used to kick my feet that much they won a dispensation for me to take in the gory volumes on the Bruces and Stewarts, Wallace and Montrose. The olman would go along too, to keep the family together and because the olaid wouldn't trust him with the dinner and even himself didn't have the nerve to go to the loom shed on the Sabbath. He'd hand out the pan-drops before the sermon.

Now these you could understand and they usually seemed quite sensible but they didn't have the passion and the rhythms I was now experiencing in the Free Kirk Gaelic.

There were also letters to the *Gazette*, with names under them that you recognised. Sometimes an aspiring elder but nearly always from a male. Unless radical female evangelists from Lewis wrote under pen names, like George Eliot. The issues would alternate when the editor would come in to say that correspondence on the issue was closed for now. But they went in a cycle, with a few variations, as sure as a weaver's pattern. The tyranny of Rome. The need for vigilance in protecting our youth from the appetites induced by the unscrupulous makers of immoral films. The condoning of homosexuality by those in Parliament with a duty to legislate for the safety of all. The demon drink, of course.

The best one though was the guy who blamed the Roman Catholic Church for the Vietnam War. See, we're free-thinkers here. This guy was ahead of the game, dislodging the haloes from these Kennedys, of Irish background, lest we forget.

Once or twice another porter or a bored houseman doc, on the night shift, would ask me how I could go along to that church when these public statements were made. I'd just tell them I took the letters as entertainment, an extreme line to challenge and debate and most people on the pews would say the same.

There's something about hospitals. People would just ask you what you really thought, on a regular bloody basis. That didn't happen much at Uni. Take Transubstantiation.

I remember that one, watching the son of an ice-cream maker sip from the bottle of Bardolino along with the Spanish Basque priest, after I'd attended a Mass on the far, far end of Kenneth Street. I didn't dare risk it in case I'd get a real thirst and seize hold of said bottle. I was getting used to the non-taste of water.

This is the crunch. These guys have to say they really believe the other wine, sipped in church, becomes blood and not just any blood. The wafer, no kidding, becomes flesh and not human flesh. There's communion all right, even amongst the breakaways – the Free Presbyterians and now the breakaways from the breakaways – but none of these guys believe that the stuff has changed its physical character. Both wine and bread are symbols.

I could see that but I still couldn't bring myself to do the preparation for taking the step forward to take said bread and wine even on the understanding that you weren't expected to believe it had changed its physical nature.

Doubts are good shit sometimes. Believers can be dangerous. Political ones too. But what must it have been like for a guy who fought in the Spanish war, as a communist, and lived to see the tanks roll in to Prague and then see footage of poor Jan who set himself alight. At what point do you say, this is not what I signed up for?

I've got to tell you about a book. It's called the *Kitáb-i-Aqdas* which is Arabic for 'The Most Holy Book'. This is the Bahá'í book of laws for a new age. An early critic of the Faith translated it but that was from a hostile standpoint. I was at a seminar where a keen young devotee did some research by way of just asking an Arabic speaker, present in the room, to translate some passages. The legal code was pretty Islamic.

And sure enough, not long after, a Synopsis and Codification of the book of laws was published. But not a translation of the contents. Not yet the time, the introduction said. It did say that the penalties for certain crimes were listed. But it didn't say what these penalties were. Now one of the attractive things had been this phrase – 'Independent investigation of truth'. Maybe I'd failed to ask the right questions.

Someone else asked exactly what the penalties were.

They were meant for a future state of society, not applicable now.

But what were they? What about that slander about Bahá'ís believing in the death penalty? An eye for an eye. If a man should set fire to another he should be burned?

'Penalties are indeed listed but it is clear that these are not for society as we know it now and in any case there is the possibility of mitigating such penalties to imprisonment for life.'

I was struggling.

How could you not be struggling? Knowing that one prescribed penalty for an arsonist was to burn him or her. When the guy whose seed is in you escaped from a disabled tank in the battle of El Alamein. So that was one World Religion firmly in touch.

Or was it? Next week, *The Two Minute Silence* printed a single letter on a single topic, from a main man in our Last Bastion of the Faithful, the official Free Church of Scotland, accept no substitute. It was on 'The Majesty of Capital Punishment'. A later epistle under the same name likened predatory homosexuals to jackals. Appropriate biblical language, of course.

Which brings us to Palestine. Or rather the State of Israel which was then still occupying significant chunks of territories that their tanks had rolled through, during their own blitzkrieg in the Six-Day War. And perhaps it still is.

At the end of the year-out as a hospital porter I had plenty of dosh. I'd been depositing shift-disturbance allowance and I wasn't drinking or smoking. Not even tobacco. It was the olaid who said I should get myself travelling. Take another year out before I got back to the course. Maybe take my fishing rod along with me. I didn't take it on the first trip but it came along on the second.

Thomas

There's a couple of stories where some guy's in the cack, usually for carrying out his duty as a Hebridean citizen by carrying out the act of poaching. The laird, being a sporting gent, gives him a chance. There's three questions. They vary, story to story, island to island but one of them always is, 'What am I worth?'

You know the answer? It's 'Twenty-nine pieces of silver. Because our Lord was sold for thirty and you can't be worth more than that.'

I've heard that there's a sect which places Judas Iscariot pretty high up the pecking order of apostles. He was the instrument by which we all gained the possibility of redemption. I don't think he was the one Bob Marley was singing about, but.

I've a soft spot for Thomas. Remember he was the one who had to see the nail holes in the hand, to be convinced. Most guys in any of the churches I attended or in the mosque or shrine or maybe at the wailing wall, would say that it's better to have faith. If you really must, then you can go and weigh up the evidence. Maybe I became addicted to documentary evidence at a very early age. My olman might have had something to do with it.

There was a church group organising a trip to the Holy Land. It was tempting. Most of the arrangements would be made and the itinerary rang with the resonance of The River of Jordan and The Red Sea, The Sinai Desert. Jerusalem and Bethlehem. There wasn't a lot about the Gaza strip in The Brochure. I asked the olaid if she didn't fancy that one herself. I could help with the spondulicks.

'I dinna think so, son,' she says. 'Everybody on that bus'll be trying to be good as gold. It'll nae be a lot o fun.'

And Kirsty, back in Canada, was planning on a visit. What was winter to us was a mild break for her.

I signed up for a six-month spell as a volunteer on a kibbutz. It was not far from the seaport of Acre. I remembered the Bahá'í World Centre was close to there. There was a shrine in Haifa and a prison where the exiled leader had been held for many years.

And I didn't know much about Judaism.

I suppose there was still a bit of an idea of the kibbutz as utopian community crofting. Oranges instead of neeps. (By the way you should try roasting peeled swede with Middle East spices and a dribble of salt and honey.)

I didn't get much of a sense of oranges, far less milk and honey, when I got to the El Al office in London. These dames were scary. An up-against-the-wall search with what I assume, from my very limited experience of recent movies, was a sub-machine gun. I did not find it erotic, since you ask.

You might have heard that the flicks ceased to flicker in SY after they had the nerve to show *Jesus Christ Superstar*. The fact is that the joint was losing money. Bingo was out of the question and not even a succession of window cleaners' confessions nor Swedish soft porn fantasia could bring in enough to cover the overheads, behind the Art Deco frontage. Pity it was boarded up because the building matched the transit shed on Number One pier. As long as it stood. It's gone now because we've no shortage of period buildings worth listing, on the Island.

Still, I got the idea that the Israeli army was armed to the hilt and there was a ceasefire agreement that could make the Treaty of Versaille look like a model for a future Europe. Not much of a settlement. Sorry, bad choice of words there.

Which brings us to my jet-lagged arrival at a location which was a jolly minibus drive from the bus terminal at Haifa. I was not the only one on a quest for socialism in action. But I soon found there were other motives for signing up for a six a.m. start and porridge with warm black tea made from a stewed concentrate, served at eight.

There was a very good system to make sure that no-one was

isolated. Each new volunteer was assigned to one with a few months' experience and you both shared the same kibbutz parents. These were mentors.

First, I met Gabriele. I sensed right away I could do worse. She was pretty well my own height for a start, so it was a welcome change from stooping to get eye contact or to avoid intimidating some short guy. She was also wiry like myself but unbelievably fit. She'd go out running, in the cool of the evening, after a full day's work in the fields. She kept her dark brown hair cropped. This must have kept her cool but it also kept her streamlined. She had a sharp nose and that's where I got into trouble first. It was probably a mistake to say she reminded me of Concorde.

No amount of backtracking seemed to help. How it was a compliment – cordiality and co-operation and very elegant lines…I began to realise I was in the company of a very serious woman. I even learned to shut up for long enough for her to tell me why she was here. She was German. Her father was no Nazi – he had been a student of architecture, called up to take his share of sending high explosives, to destroy fine buildings and intimidate the Poles into a quick surrender. He had suffered, like the other survivors and that had not stopped when he reached Vienna, after deserting from the crumbling Eastern Front.

I saw how she sat at the feet of our kibbutz father. He was a very short man. I'd watched him lead work parties. I still couldn't figure out the physics of his strength and endurance. OK, he was low to the ground but that didn't explain the weight he could lift on his wiry frame. There was nothing to him but he was one intense wee bastard.

Gabriele asked him about his children. He lived with his wife in this tiny apartment. Their children would visit, like us, on different scheduled nights, to spend an evening.

'They are not our children,' he said. 'They are the children of the kibbutz.'

This time, I knew to bite the tongue. But I ask you to remember I'm from Lewis and at that time a fairly frequent attender of Free Church services. I should know a fanatic when I hear one.

But I think I fell for Gabriele when I heard her ask him about the people who had been on this land before.

'They made nothing of it. Look what we have done. One side of the fence is still desert.'

By their avocados ye shall know them. I thought it but I didn't say it. It wouldn't have helped.

Maybe he was the only one of his family who survived. Maybe the jewellery or savings, diminished by inflation, were just enough to send one child out, before that original blitzkrieg.

Who the hell am I to say that these guys can't see history repeating itself? As the high explosives make rubble out of concrete and bones in a place called Gaza. But you find yourself looking for a wee Palestinian boy with a sling and a sure eye. Only there ain't no evil giant to aim for. More conscripts, probably. Like the Yanks who did, or did not, return from Vietnam.

I did join the guilt-torn German volunteer on a few excursions, on our rare days off. We took a week, in the company of a few others, sharing fuel costs, to travel from hostel to hostel.

An Orthodox man took the time to explain the significance of one of the world's iconic Walls. He wasn't a guide and he wasn't trying to convert men. He was showing kindness to a visitor. Gabriele had touched the one in Berlin but women were not permitted past a fence erected here. The man with the ringlets then bought us steaming and fragrant falafel so he could continue his story.

An Arab shop-owner in Jerusalem old city made us tea and went out the back door to fetch mint, leaving his select items of Bedouin jewellery scattered about the table in front of us. I did think of getting an example for my new German friend but I bought one for my mother instead. We got talking. He just shrugged when we said we were kibbutz volunteers. Well, now we were travelling we would see what we saw and make up our own minds.

He met us in the street that evening and guided me to a café I could trust. He had a word with a man and fixed a price for our group. I was brought into the kitchen. We could have this or that. I pointed here and there and he brought out heaped plates for us all. We savoured the marinated aubergine, the roasted artichoke, wrapped in vine leaves. The saffron rice, the small pieces of grilled lamb on skewers, the round bread from the clay oven.

We happened to be at a hostel on another kibbutz by Ein Gedi on a feast night. They called it the Sabbath though it wasn't yet Sunday. There was chicken roasted with mild spices and there was white wine for those who wanted, produce of Israel.

Last day of freedom, I went with Gabriele to the memorial sites in the new Jerusalem which was not that shiny. We saw the stained glass windows, designed by Chagall. I was quite fit then but I was breathless. It was not enough to visit one place as a reminder. Even then I could tell there was something compulsive in the need to cross the threshold of every structure which linked to the Holocaust.

Peter

I heard this story through the olaid but indirectly. When I got back home, there was still six months to go before I rejoined the History Honours course at Aberdeen. It might have been panic, wondering if I could thread the shuttle again. Before long, I was surrounded with books and markers. The olaid could see there was something desperate there. She asked me more than once about who I'd met in Israel. There were a couple of Airmails from Germany. One from Finland.

There was still money in the bank and the grant came through OK. The olaid told me there was nothing she needed for the house but she'd been happy looking after the wee car for me. She took her old pal from Westview for a spin now and again. Folk didn't talk to each other the same, in the new houses.

She nagged me to get out of the history books and dig out my fishing tackle. She remembered I was always buried in angling books. Catalogues from Abu, Sweden. When I was young, I'd show her photos of astonishing and exotic pike and perch from Swedish and Finnish lakes. This fish pornography had taken over from Enid Blyton.

I remembered a standing invite, from two other volunteers. This was a couple, into boats and into catching their own supper. They lived on a small island in the Baltic. You took a ferry from Stockholm to Turku, then a bus which would drop you at a road-end. Half a mile walk to a regular ferry. They'd pick me up the other end. She had been born on the island. Her man was an American who had settled in Canada, after getting over the border to dodge the draft.

He still couldn't return to the USA. Everyone had good English.

They were still analysing their own experience in the land we called Israel. How the actual compared with what they'd imagined beforehand. What they now read about the settlers' determination to hold on to their hard-won gains.

Then there was the perch fishing. Saltwater perch grew to a very good size. You could cast a spinner from just outside the door. I took one that would do for a starter for us all. Two friends from another island were coming for a supper of elk.

That's how I heard this tale from a Polish artist on a Swedish-speaking Finnish island. (Did you get all that?)

'Please call me Andrew. I think you might have difficulty with the Polish version of my name.' Andrew had married a Finnish woman and taught at Turku and Helsinki universities, for years.

He picked happily at the white flakes still holding to the vertical-striped skin, baked in a crust of salt. 'Very Biblical,' he said.

He was retired now. He seemed amazed to find we were getting the banter going. 'Are you laughing to be polite?' he asked.

'No, I'm laughing because you're funny.'

'No-one in this country finds my stories funny.'

I thought at the time, this was strange. You would think Poland and Finland had strong similarities in their unfortunate histories. Both had been invaded and torn up between feuding empires. You would think there would be some common ground in the darkest breed of bitter irony. Maybe you needed to know the language to savour Finnish humour. But my new friend was completely fluent.

'All right,' he said, 'are you religious?'

'You know I am. Unless you've been asleep for the last hour. I went to the Holy Land to make comparisons. In my last week, there was one man who walked streets out of his way to make sure I found the way to the bus station, when I asked directions. It was like being in Glasgow. He was a Jordanian Christian.'

'Not a Samaritan?' the Canadian said.

Andrew continued. 'I mean religious with a capital R. Easily offended?'

'Try me.'

Good. The fish reminded me of something. It's after the resurrection. Jesus and Peter have got together again. The show is back on the road. But it's not as good as it was. I think it was Peter who said it first.

'Lord,' he said, 'forgive me for saying this but it's not as good as it was.'

Jesus said, 'Peter, you're an honest man. What can we do about it? Is there anything we can do? Support me.'

'Well,' said Peter, 'that walking on the water thing, that was good. That went down really well with the crowd. Could you do that again?'

But Jesus was nervous. He thought about it. Then he said, 'We could go out together to the Sea of Galilee when it's quiet. Have a trial run when there's no-one watching. Will you help me?'

'I'm there, Lord. I'm with you.'

So they did go forth together, united, and took possession of a suitable small craft. But Jesus was seriously nervous.

'Can you remember how we did this?' he asked.

'Yes,' Peter said, 'it was the starboard side.'

'Starboard, you're sure?'

'I am.'

'Are you ready now, are you looking after me?'

'I'm with you, Lord.'

So Jesus slowly eased himself over the side of the vessel and sank like a stone. Fortunately he still had all that hair so Peter was able to get a hold and pull him, gasping, back aboard.

When Jesus got his breath back he said, at last, 'That didn't go so well.'

'Have to say, Lord, it could have gone better. It must have been the port side.'

'Sure?'

'Of course I'm sure, it's the only one left.'

'Are you ready?'

'I'm ready.'

Jesus eased himself even more slowly over on the port side and sank down, just like before.

Peter got hold of his hair again and as he pulled him aboard said, 'Lord, Lord, I know what it is.'

'What is it?'

'Lord, You didn't have those holes in the feet the last time.'

I laughed. My new friend was surprised. He asked again if I was being polite. But if there was any ice intact on this mild June evening, on an island in the Baltic, circa 1978, it was melted now.

The geographies and the complex histories proved convenient for the invaders who came on the rampage, from either east or west. You just blame an atrocity on the other guy. Strange that both of them had a moustache.

It was a long time after the leader with the heavier and wider model shed the mortal, that there was any sign of the Russian state coming close to an admission of responsibility for approximately 20,000 counts of murder in the woods of Katyn.

You could thus argue that the Second World War began and ended in Polish territory. It was inevitable that the German-speaking areas of Czechoslovakia would be overrun by the Nazis. The borderline with Poland was the test of the standpoints and alliances. Polish authorities had no doubts about the invasion to come. That's why they handed over everything they'd discovered, towards the deciphering of messages encrypted by the German forces' Enigma machines. They gave their information to both Britain and France.

And sure enough an incident was staged to show an apparent infringement of the territory of the Third Reich. It was another couple of years before I'd see an example of how this was reported to the German public.

It was of course at another reunion of volunteer workers, wondering how the hell they had thought it a good idea to support the efforts of those who mainly denied any rights to the previous occupiers of the land they'd taken over. History implies the use of hindsight as a tool.

Gabriele Richter's mother was hospitable towards her daughter's friend. She must have been one of the few Germans who failed to destroy her cherished documentation of the myth of Adolf. Frau Richter's carefully bound copies of the collected, illustrated instalments of the life and actions of Adolf Hitler told me more than any analysis I've ever read. You know the word Führer might suggest a guide or teacher as well as a leader. There's a lot of children and dogs and smiling but on this occasion even the benevolent Führer has lost his patience with the threats from the Polish people. They were astray and in need of strong leadership. That's one way of presenting an invasion.

But since I really am preaching now, ladies and gentleman, I exhort you. Go thee now. Go and perform the latter-day action which is known unto the multitude as a google. Do a google on blitzkrieg. I did it to check the spelling.

The term is currently being applied to matters of commerce. That's worse than the guys in the temple.

'You have taken the house of my father and turned it into a den of thieves.'

You'll know me now – the use of language is sacred to me. I'm hearing the whine of these hellish Stukas. Using that fucking word, that fucking way, is criminal.

End of rant within rant. Back to my home island.

In the same way as the First World War did not end for the people of the Hebridean Long Island on the 11th of the 11th of the 11th, 1918, the Second could not end for the Polish people until a leader visited the site of the mass grave. In 1992 a step was made when the Russian administration released documents which proved that Stalin's Politburo had approved, on the 5th March 1940, the proposal to order the killings.

Vladimir V Putin did not apologise but he did say the following, as reported by the *New York Times* (Michael Schwirtz, April 7th 2010). The words within quotemarks are still qualified:

'In this ground lay Soviet citizens, burnt in the fire of the Stalinist repression of the 1930s; Polish officers, shot on secret orders; soldiers of the Red Army, executed by the Nazis.'

But a photograph does indeed show yet another powerful wee guy laying his wreath. I don't think the government of the United Kingdom has apologised yet for advertising the wreck of *Iolaire*, for sale to the highest bidder, before all the missing bodies had been recovered. There's probably a record on file somewhere but I can't tell you offhand how many pieces of silver they got, for all that bronze and teak.

Patterns

His mother and my father died within a year of each other. Robbie's loss came first. Our flat had become the Shetland family home while his mother was at Foresterhill Hospital. I made big pans of soup and we bought ham and things to go with it. His father seemed to be taking it not too bad, if you could judge that. It wasn't as if they weren't expecting it. Some weeks had gone by since she'd been taken down on the air ambulance. Still, it's hard when it comes.

Then came the complications of flying the coffin home. I don't know the details, only that Robbie and his uncle were trying this, trying that. Tension mounting. Then again, most of the family was in Aberdeen anyway. There were plenty of Shetlanders buried in that city and at least it was by the sea.

I bought and borrowed clothes that weren't jeans and genseys. Walked behind Robbie and his family and watched his mother's coffin lowered, under a skyline of steelwork, within reach of the floodlights of Pittodrie. Call it halfway between the estuaries of the Don and the Dee. You couldn't see them but I knew the stake nets were stretched out, between groynes, only over a wall or two. If an Islander had to be buried in a city, this would do.

Robbie's father gave me a pocketknife. It was slim with a very smooth wooden handle and a blade that took an edge. He made me give him a coin in return. So the friendship would never be cut. Did I know that one? He didn't say if each partner in the contract had to keep the knife or the coin, forever.

Then it was a blur of studies. I took to swimming, way back

in the wake of Robbie. But still using up all the useless physical energy that the anxiety in your body was providing. I suppose we were both fit as butchers' dogs then, so sitting on our arses in various libraries didn't come too naturally.

My year flowed into that summer job and the death of my own father, without any intimation. That was a word from all these church announcements – the following are the intimations.

The olman was already up, with the kettle on the go when I heard the alarm tell me it was half an hour till the mail van left. I was getting a lift out to the road-end. He'd been trying out a new pattern, laying colours together, trial and error, till they seemed somehow happy. He didn't do much weaving himself any more, just somehow got into this thing of designing patterns. In fact, pattern was the wrong word. He'd started off studying the market, coming up with the template for export goods. But the materials, texture as well as colour, were leading somewhere else.

In his hands they took on a life of their own.

He came out to the stairway, sniffing the morning. You could see a trace of mist in the gap between the buildings. The light was trying to break through. It would burn off in an hour or two. The flat still belonged to the Mill. Maybe the only one still active then, that part of town. Our very own wee industrial landscape. Power station and all. You got used to the timbre of the diesels, running on heavy oil.

In one way he liked a bit of bustle, getting breakfasts done, cups of tea for visitors. My olman was on his best form before most of the household was awake or after folk had gone to bed. If he'd outlived his wife, he'd have been a good hand at seeing to the visitors. As long as he had a window of the kitchen open. It wasn't a big room. The house had no outlook, except another roughcast wall but he needed to know there was an airflow.

I've told you how I heard the news. Out at the estate. My uncle and Colin, the gamekeeper, must have had a conspiracy going. Following the doctor's advice on how to break it. And they had some experience between them. They were both in the Legion. Give him time to prepare himself.

Tell him his father is not well and it looks serious. You don't tell anyone right away that a heart has stopped beating. A nose and a mouth are no longer registering the air, passing through a system.

I remember wondering if a body still shook and muscles moved with the nerves, after the blood stopped circulating. The oxygen missing. I'd seen plenty fish die. I hope to hell it was fast. The panic of being caught without the chance of air. Pure bloody merry hell for anyone. But what must that be like for a guy who already knew what it was like to be trapped in a tight space? Because his death was so sudden, a lot of people came up these cold concrete stairs to sit in the flat for a while. This was no bad thing because all the rounds of making tea, seeing to the fire and shaking hands – all that stuff gave us something to do. It was hardest on my mother who had just to sit. The sister came into her own, once she got over the travel. She was struggling all right but already she'd had a few years of attending people as they passed in and out of the world.

The olaid didn't want a real Island wake, for her Lewis husband. She got one all the same. Ruairidh took me aside. My olman always had his own way of doing things. But he wouldn't want to make a big fuss. The village people were here.

The olman wouldn't have wanted the sermon we got. But he'd have put up with it. So we did for him, as he would have wanted which was just the most normal way. It took my sister and the olaid to make a stand where it mattered. I'm not sure things were the same again, between us and our uncle.

It was easy to sort things out with the Uni, to arrange to take a year out. Everyone accepted the need. I phoned Robbie. Well, hell, he'd not long been there, himself. And he kent another Shetlander, on a one-year course, so he could take my room. We could all return to normal, after that.

I'd come to Aberdeen for a week, just to sort things out. I couldn't leave all that driftwood shelving, roped and balanced like a pilot-ladder. Some people liked to sit in a bit more comfort than a basket fender could provide. And it wasn't everyone who was willing to step over all the maritime debris before they could make a cup of tea.

Robbie met me off the train. The Shetlandic flatmate. We took as much as we dared back on the Number One bus to where we'd found it. The driver knew my ways. We got off at the Bridge of Don, on the north side where the beach carries on past the wreck of that trawler. All the way to Balmedie. We didn't go anything like as far as that. Only placed everything back above what seemed to us to be the High Water Springs mark. Our own ritual. It was easier than finding a skip with some space. Things you gather, things you dump. From the shore, back to the shore.

That year just went. But I got the details of the progress of the Russian Revolution and the events following the collapse of the Nazi-Soviet pact clear in my mind. I wasn't ready to go back to Uni. Then there was the kibbutz. That changed my life in a way I could never have imagined. Then there was the trip to Finland. Archipelagos and fish.

I also got to know my mother better. We'd sit a while in the kitchen having coffee after a meal. Mine black, hers made with milk. Maybe she needed a wee break from me. We got through the last few months OK. Maybe Gabriele's visit helped.

Then I'd to get the degree finished, in Aberdeen. Robbie's offer of a break in Shetland sounded good. Less of a jump from the quiet life at home back to the course and the city. A thing you had to do. Pick things up again. I still had a bit of money from the hospital job. Herself was cool as always. She just said, 'Aye, definitely. You should definitely dae that.'

Maybe she needed to pick her own things up. Her own way. Ready for it. Kirsty had a few more months on the Island. An overlap. She'd call by more often when I was away.

I had to go via Aberdeen anyway, to get the ferry to Shetland. I only stopped off long enough to dump my gear. The flat was sad. An orange carpet had been thrown down over the old Wilton in my room. It smelled of parties.

Maybe I had a lot of talking to catch up on because I got yarning to people, on the ferry. Drank a lot of stewed coffee and didn't manage to sleep much.

So this was Lerwick, the working harbour, with new buildings of sheet metal. Central streets more picturesque than Stornoway. The stone-built architecture had a bit more integrity. Less of the Sixties showing.

So here I was. 'Good to see you.'

Robbie's father had got painfully thin but of course I said, 'You're looking well.' I think I said too much. And it was daft to go raking about in the rucksack then and there. It was fine to take out the smoked salmon but I should have left the other brown paper parcel for the right moment.

I was thinking back to when I'd found it. Part of the clear-out. The design, in progress on my own father's frame. The one I found in the shed up from the town when the house quietened down at last. Wondering how to take it off without unravelling it.

Realising it was more or less complete. Two sections with a plain bit for a break in between. Of course it was all clear, a piece for the sister, piece for me. I don't think the olaid had ever been in the loom shed. That was a place her man went to, on his own, in the morning. Came back from it in the middle of the day. That used to be dinnertime and then it became lunchtime.

My sister was still white from the suddenness. She had never spent much time in the shed either. But I could see it meant a lot to her to see these signs of our father's creative work as well as his living. The only really personal signs of his life. It was difficult for her to book that flight back to her own life. She had some photographs and her share of that last cloth.

But there was another few small sections, already completed and stored, on the shelving, wrapped loosely in brown paper. Cloth my father probably had no idea of selling. My mother didn't show much emotion when I showed it to her. Didn't break down at the sight of it or anything. She unwrapped what was there. She took her keepsake, a throw to put over the settee that was now starting to show its own age. That's all she wanted. We were to share out the rest.

My sister chose another small piece. That was about all she could take on the plane. So I had one last section of the small amount of tweed that was made without an eye to any market. Here it was, in a new brown paper parcel, brought all these slow miles up the North Sea.

Imported to Shetland. For Robbie's olman. The guy who gave me a pocketknife after the funeral of his wife.

'I'm sorry,' he said, 'but I just can't take that. I've never been that good wi presents and that's a thing you should keep.'

Don't know how he just sensed that this was something that should have stayed on another Island.

Canny guys, Shetlanders.

Seagull

Robbie said he knew I was into diesel engines but I'd have to make do with a petrol two-stroke when I came to visit him. I said that a Seagull engine had plenty of character. At least it wasn't a Suzuki. Then I remembered his guitar was a Suzuki.

He lived pretty close to that guitar. You had to make an appointment to get into the toilet in the flat we shared. It was in a square box set right between his room and mine, neutral territory. The extractor fan used to make a big noise but hadn't worked for a while and the acoustics were good. He might have disconnected it.

When you did get to hear him play, it could be just about anything. Robbie alternated between chords to accompany the Shetland fiddle, contemporary jazz and a few acoustic versions of rock riffs. One of his heroes was Peerie Willie, the Shetlander who fingerpicked all that lot together, maybe with some bluegrass. And got away with it.

Robbie was also good enough to get away with it. But he could cope with a lot of things because he could adapt. Eat any food. Play Country and Western in some zinc shack he'd been driven to on a Friday. You had no choice when the motor stopped for you and someone who was needing a guitarist came knocking at the door.

My sleeping bag was stretched out somewhere in his Da's house. At the heart of a scheme in Lerwick which was the double of another one I knew well, on another island. In both towns, the council housing was back a good way from the harbour and up a slope. Maybe the site of the Lerwick one had been a cornfield too. Not that we're short of decent arable land in the outer Isles, you understand.

I wouldn't have minded being in the down cocoon, right then. His father had lodged a wee protest. You can't go hauling that boy out to sea now, after he's been on that P&O boat for fourteen hours. Robbie said he could, the forecast wasn't that great for the rest of the week so we'd have to grab our chance.

He knew I was keen to get out in a Shetland skiff. Shetland Model, they called them, here. Makes them sound like toys but they've a name as sea boats. More of a rowing boat you can sail, compared to the beamy, load-carrying boats of Orkney and Lewis.

The keel of the Shetland Model runs the full length of the hull, thus presenting sufficient area of timber against drift. That would be oak. Then there would be the lighter larch of the first broad plank. The Shetlanders would shift their weight to keep her well down in the water. They fair crowded on sail, to race them, so one man was there with a shovel, bailing all the time. The out and out racers would have some extra keel. That would help them keep a course close to the wind.

Robbie's father had never sailed this one. Even those who did sail might have a Seagull stashed away under an oilskin for when they just went fishing. I held the door of the shed open and Robbie carried the beast out. This one had a square cylinder and even had a clutch. It was a late-Sixties model. A good period. Think of Jimi Hendrix. As he said to me quietly, once, in that Aberdeen flat, you don't write off Hendrix's music just because the guy's dead. Where would that leave Samuel Taylor Coleridge? I couldn't argue with that.

He'd liked *The Ancient Mariner*, rediscovering the thing after it had been murdered at school, the Anderson High. It was the open-endedness that hit him, the way you couldn't fit it all into this moral framework it was pretending to illustrate. We traded studies in our better moments. I was doing a Literature module that year – reflections on the French Revolution and all that. Leading into a short course on the European historical novel.

Robbie swapped Basic Navigation for Literature. Not basic enough, sometimes. He had to get the star-sights in there. Capella and the like. Only high-sounding names to me. My olman would have hung on every word.

A bearing and a distance. A vector. A line carrying both magnitude and direction. I could get a grip of that. But there were a couple of wee complexities.

'Tell me more about Variation and Deviation.' They sounded quite sexy. You have to allow for the difference between True North and the way the compass points, varying slightly year by year. Then there's compensation for the vessel's own magnetic field, on a given bearing.

I'd seen his advert. Our flat was cheap but we had to pay the price. It wasn't that quiet. He'd grabbed the chance to rent it from another Shetlander, who'd got a job back home. It was just off Market Street. Walking distance from the Nautical College. Fish lorries passed under our window at any hour. We got the stale smoke from up the road, when the wind blew it down – the place with the sign we wanted to liberate and install in the flat.

REEKIE AND COLEMAN: Fish Curers

Robbie was soft-spoken, for a Viking. Younger than me but used to being attended to by stewards and so on. I taught him a few survival skills. There was the cheese sauce, roux method, livened up with some leek and Stilton. Your own curry paste, with natural yoghurt, lemon juice and coriander. A basic garam masala prepared in small quantities, for freshness. He was too easy to lead. I shouldn't have got away with it for so long.

The hint of his other side came when I saw him cruise up and down with the other half-dozen regulars of the early morning session at the Bon Accord Baths. His fair hair looked even thinner, plastered wet and still not much sign of a beard. But a bow wave coming off him as he swam miles, propelled by a steady breast-stroke. All these swimmers, navigating on lines of black tiles along the blue. They passed each other as courteously as ships following the secure rules of their roads.

He phoned me before I left from Lewis. Yes, the trip was still on. But there was something up. I'd get the story when I got there. Robbie wasn't a guy to give away much on the phone. I'd to bear with him but it was time I saw his home ground.

Robbie wouldn't let me carry the Seagull from the shed beside the running-mooring. That would have been the usual thing. One guy would pull in the boat and the other get the engine down.

'I know how to carry it,' I said. 'The gearbox end held below the level of the fuel tank.'

He let me take the oars and that was about it. Anchor, warp, spare fuel, spare plug and spanner. No lifejackets, no flares.

The sky didn't look too good to me. There was a couple of old guys yarning by the boats, leaning against the archetypal harbour rail.

'No yous are not going out today, boys, not far anyhow?'

Robbie told them he'd just get out to lift a few pots. He'd to recover them before the sea got up.

'Well if du lads are set on going, it'll have to be da sooth way.'

Robbie grinned. His look said, *Aye, northabout as planned.*

The trim of this boat was important. He sat me on the forward thwart then pulled her out clear of all the moorings. Then dropped oars and pumped fuel through the engine. It fired, second pull, on its bracket of bent galvanised bar. This was bolted to the stern post, where the rudder would have been hung.

I sat as directed. The Shetland Model seemed narrow, to the Lewis eye, and the seas were building up. It took them well, punching in.

'She's good in a following sea too,' Robbie shouted, over the motor. 'You won't ship a green one in this.'

That was about as much as we could say, over the engine. That type of unit vents directly to the grey air above the shifting water level. Water coolant gushed out in a healthy jet. The rich fuel mixture was smoking, even in this breeze.

He throttled back a bit and it was quieter or maybe I was just getting used to it. I asked if it was a ten-to-one mix.

Robbie nodded.

'You get a wee kit now,' I started, 'to convert the carb to take twenty-five-to-one.'

Shit, I couldn't keep my mouth shut.

'Ten-to-one sounds fine to me,' Robbie shouted above the exhaust. 'Keeps it smooth on short runs. Around the pots.'

I noted the direction of buoyage as we passed a cylindrical port-hand buoy. It was across from a yard. Just like the Arnish buoy at Approaches to Stornoway. The one that replaced the fallen beacon.

'Norscot,' Robbie said. A lot of guys who used to throw fishing gear out here were working in there, now. Lucky for him. Otherwise there would be no lobsters left for us. One for the fuel, one for the table.

'Da kens i Norscot recipe for kippers?'

On the night shift, you wrapped them in newspapers. Shoved them behind a radiator at the start of the shift. Dug them out at the meal break. That was it.

He throttled back up. I saw the seas were getting longer. Less breaking waves. Had to be deeper water.

He signalled me to move to the middle thwart. He was wanting to keep the prop down so it would bite more. I realised that I wasn't too happy. I'd been out in a lot worse seas but there was something about the situation. Not being in control.

Bare islands were close now. Could just as easily have been the entrance to Loch Erisort. Skuas dodged in the airways above our heaving boat.

'That rain'll keep the wind doon.'

But I came close to mutiny at the narrows. Robbie cut the engine.

'My gear is in the lee o that lot. It'll be no bother to haul. We can git through wi da tide like this but it's safer just to pull.'

Without thinking, I took up one of the narrow-bladed oars as he took the other. In the short swell, I missed one stroke.

'It's easier if there's only one guy pulling,' he said and took over my oar. I went forward to look for nasty stuff. It was worse when you had nothing to do with guiding the boat through. I swallowed words.

It was like a lagoon, through these narrows. He'd known it would be, of course, in this wind. I hauled the gear while Robbie handled the boat. That thrill of gambling with traps is the same everywhere.

A few crabs, just big enough to be worth boiling up. Two indigo snapping shapes, but just under the limit. And one decent lobster. I found the rubber bands in the fish box and doubled them round the claws then placed it in the other end of that box, with an old oilskin separating it from the crabs.

Robbie then motioned me to go forward while he stowed the six or so pots, with their ropes and buoys placed inside, to avoid tangles. When he was happy that the boat was back in trim, we were back on the go, him on the stern thwart. He told me then, he wasn't going back to Aberdeen.

He'd heard so many local versions of his own story, it was getting kind of difficult to explain the real one. He'd heard he'd failed his last ticket. He'd jumped ship in the Pacific, over a woman he was involved with. She was younger than him of course but he didn't know if she was Polynesian or not. Then there was the older woman theory, Unst, Walls or Yell versions. Met when he was playing music on one of those islands.

Let's just say the ticket he did have would do him for any North Sea job he wanted and he'd be back home for the two weeks off. He'd probably not get sponsored to carry on but so what? He wasn't so sure of the ring of Captain Sinclair anyway. Too many of them round here.

Sure enough, in front of our window in Aberdeen, the lines had been getting longer and thicker. Converted trawlers, built high to be reborn as supply ships. Painted in new liveries. Between that boom coming and the Lerwick connections, he'd be OK.

More important to him right now, to keep the music going, the two weeks at home. He was lucky. His father wasn't the sort to put pressure on him. He was glad of the company in the house.

He still didn't give me the tiller on the way back. I knew for sure then that I'd tried to steer him more than enough in the recent past. You think you know someone but maybe part of the person you think you're seeing is only your own impression.

Maybe it's difficult to really get to know anyone. For all the animated dialogue and shared meals. It takes more time maybe to be aware of what's particular.

Take a Shetland vessel, broad-planked for strength with light-ness but also for speed of build. Primarily a beach-launched boat, held by a bare minimum of sawn frames. Double ended and narrow in the beam. Light and strong. Like boats in Faroes and Fair Isle. But something unique. And this one that Robbie's father had once got built for him might have had more flare here or there, than specified. The cut of the larch. The way it grew. The way it bent.

Even if everything was scrupulously done to templates, it must have had additions or subtractions over the years. An eye bolt added or galvanised pins for the oars to replace worn iron ones. An anchor permanently aboard but carried in a slightly different position every trip.

All becoming factors of the vessel's own individual nature. Its own resultant deviation, valid for the time it has its effect. Causing a swing east or west of the magnetic bearing.

You couldn't put complete trust in any swinging needle. Any dial.

Sine

The room that's a haven for a while begins to constrain you. Your own legs start to hit against those of the table. You hear the door close behind you and you're on the stairs. Whatever the weather is doing, out there, it's welcome.

If there's a harbour near your room, that's perfect. There could be high jibs of cranes that run on tracks. There could be the spurts of unburned diesel as big Caterpillars start up in the early hours. There might be landscaped surfaces. Restored buildings. There could even be cobbles (surface of rounded stones) and cobles (flat-bottomed beach boats for salmon fishing) and rows of parlour-pots, stacked up for the photographs.

At Stonehaven you could round the shore towards Low Water and then see the smaller commercial boats discharging their codlings and fluke. The radars would still be spinning. All this in the foreground. A step or two back shorewards, you'd see the signs of leisure activities. Racks and racks of bright sea kayaks. And signs of dinghies, under canopies. A shelf of aluminium masts.

I slept in a garret right over the Bridge of Cowie. Might have been possible to catch a sea trout from the window. I was a bit preoccupied though. Trying to get right back into the studies. Final year. Comes to the stage you just want to get shot of them. Get back out into the world again.

Whatever the hell the real world is. Trouble is, the more you get into a subject, the harder it is to keep it tidy. What's the point of studying history if you're not making comparisons? To get steady good grades and deliver on time, you need to limit the fields. Or unlimited time.

I emerged, rubbing the eyes, to phone my mother. I was too late. Poor Sheena had gone down fast. A mercy, really. The funeral had been yesterday. I should phone Ruaraidh or send a card.

You know how it is. Memory sweeps by at a pace within the confines of a regulation King George the whatsit cast iron kiosk. Between the lines of a phone call to your mother, hours and weeks can flash back and fore in time.

Brave woman. I saw her with her hair gone, in the hospital. She was teasing me about the dungarees. Real Soviet-issue job. Very appropriate for the history student. I was thinking back to the summer holiday I'd spent with herself and Ruaraidh. She'd come back from work to find me and my uncle in the living room with the telly on. Newsflashes. I was not away on the bike, fishing. Unusual. She sat to join us, hardly believing the imagery of the tanks. She would call herself a Socialist. We were witnessing something different. That poor Jan Palach. Union of Soviet Socialist Republics. My arse.

I'd never heard her swear. Never heard any aunt swear. Not even one by marriage.

She was always witty and wry but she had nothing to say, that time. She never even went for the kettle, never put her shopping bag away. I was shocked when I saw some tears. She was tough and always won arguments.

Last time I saw her, she was home in bed. In remission. But there should have been a meal together. Ruaraidh was to pick me up after the early shift. A fank. Just like we used to. Business as usual. Back to the town homestead after. It would be *marag* and bacon and eggs though. Maybe get a bit of fried duff with it.

But we stayed over at Griomsiadair, at the next croft, for tea and sponge cake and stuff and this is the weird thing. My excuse was that the timing was getting tight for a meeting I needed to get to. But my stomach was in a knot all that year. I couldn't see me coping with a fry-up after a daft bit of light cake. As the saying goes, you're not cracking up if you know you're going crazy. But I didn't think I was going crazy.

In the phonebox on the Bridge of Cowie, about one year later, I knew it, all right. Fucking meeting. After the olman's funeral, there was only one meeting that mattered that year. That was eating with Ruaraidh and Sheena. And I'd ratted out of it. Aye, a brave dame all right. Probably the first local woman to a graveside on Lewis. Unless she was being carried. Brave cove, Ruaraidh. Maybe it was no bad thing he liked his dram.

When the olaid sent me the *Gazette* I saw the notice. That was the first time I realised that this woman who had fed me so often was called 'Sine'. I'd thought of it spelled the way it sounded – Sheena – not like the word from trigonometry. But of course it was a Gaelic name. Sometimes people called her husband, my uncle, Roddy. I knew his friend as Angus but he would be 'Aonghas', pronounced Innes, in the villages out of town. Many people on the island had to answer to two names.

Recovering to sound OK for the olaid. Mind, we're still in the phonebox. Bridge of Cowie.

No problem, no bother. Grades a wee bit down on before but the tutor said there was a good platform to work on. Sure, sure, I wouldn't leave it so long.

Fidelity

I couldn't go back up the stairs after that conversation in the phonebox. A good healthy whiff of exhaust down my lungs might help. I walked along the road first, not sure why. I'd got used to the traffic noise and lights. That was before the bypass. Sharp night.

The shadow of the swimming pool – it was closed in winter. Remember outdoor pools? Spaced along the east coast, Tarlair, Stonehaven, Arbroath, Eyemouth.

The olman had driven us from one to the other, one summer holiday, since we'd learned to swim.

And, of course, that night I took the path away from the bridge, the one that led round to the sea. Heard the sifting of pebbles down the shore. Heard a Gaelic song in my head. A tune I never knew I knew.

Coming by the breakwater. The smaller trawlers were landing. A few boats still worked longlines. Then there were smaller boats still, ones that could take the ground, as they say, fall over on one side when the tide dropped, keel in the mud.

Amongst them I saw the *Fidelity*. PD. Registered in Peterhead. But when you said the two letters it could be peedie, as in the Shetland way of saying wee.

She was half-decked, rigged with a bowsprit. The details, again. I was seeing with a close-up lens and the focus was sharp. When you're fucking hurt, guilty to the core, the perceptions burn bright.

A man in a fishing gansey and a Hamburg or Breton-type cap was checking her running mooring, taking up slack. There was a bit of a blow coming in.

When I admired the boat, he said I was from Lewis, had to be, from the voice.

'You're not, though. Northumberland? But how come you caught on to my accent so fast?'

Well, how had I caught on to his? Pretty fair stab, that.

'I went to hear some guys play tunes. Tapped along with them. The small-pipes player, he was Northumberland.'

'Aye, and so were his pipes. But I lived on Lewis enough years, to recognise a voice from SY. Well, I've started all over again here. New family. Come on up to the house.'

James led me, one street back from the harbour. Wilma was an artist; graphics, drawings, mainly. His boy played the piano. Electric one, though. They just called it playing keyboards, these days. Mostly jazz. One of his girls had made a career of music – clarinet. We could put a record on later. On the high-fidelity.

We talked about fishing boats.

The shape of the *Fidelity* was a forerunner of the decked drifters, great black smooth ships that carried a massive dipping lug forward and a standing lug aft, not much smaller. This was a little craft, maybe nineteen-foot six. The scaffies had often been built to thirty-foot or more. He didn't know of any of those which had survived. Being open to the skies, a lot of them were lost in famous storms. Government Inquiries recommended a move to decked boats.

There was a toddler and a baby. A large fish tank. Oriental rugs on the walls and on the floor. The hangings all had a twist to the warp or weft and the colourings were something.

The wee girl led me up the stairway to see the trains. We bypassed a blue painted spar with a white cotton sail bent on it. Aye, I've a very understanding wife.

'A wife as flipping crazy as himself, more like,' Wilma said.

The trains seemed huge to me. I forgot what gauge they were but many of the locomotives and trucks were handmade. Wilma came up and got it going and showed me photos she'd done where the speeding engines looked huge.

We usually spoke about boats. Now and again tunes were mentioned.

'Wait now, here's something you've got to hear. A new pibroch, off the radio. I been working on it all week.'

'Aye, tell me about it,' Wilma said.

But it was me glancing to the clock which said ten o clock. I thought he was going to produce a chanter or a set of Northumbrian pipes. But no, the big Highland pipes appeared from their box.

'That wee madam will be up another half-hour yet if I know her. She had a sleep in the afternoon and we've trained the wee guy to sleep through anything. And the natives are pretty friendly. They like the pipes here.'

'Just as well,' I said.

James played the pibroch, pacing slowly all the time. Their house was amongst others, a fine group of stone shapes but sandstone, not granite. The whole swaying big music with no-one banging on the wall to interrupt.

He took me for a dram, then. There was The Ship and The Marine. And I came close to breaking the tack. Taking a drink, I mean. It was a bit difficult when it came to the pub, here. Back home it was no bother. Folk just assumed you had the *cùram* or else you had a problem with the *deoch*. So it was an orange juice and another knot in the gut. And then back to my high room, able to work on for a bit, in isolation.

The Brails

The walk round the pier to their house became a feature of life in Stonehaven. Wilma tended to get the frying pan out as soon as look at me. Knowing that I couldn't fight against eating when she'd gone to the bother. Besides, my nose would be twitching, on its own. She'd dig out stuff like lambs' kidneys or a bit of frying liver. It was like being in *Ulysses*. I could still see that scene in the film with parts of a pig sizzling in the pan. I've never read the book but I read an extract somewhere and that was the bit.

Once, I stayed a day or two after the end of term, to get sailing. He'd recently installed a wee Ducati diesel. Very little vibration.

Wilma thought he'd sold out. They'd had some good cod last year. It was mostly long-lining, inshore here, which had saved the fishing. So far. I had my dinner with them and we waited for the wind to fall. Sides of cod from the freeze. Must have been a good-sized fish.

Did I like mine bare naked, like my women, or with a bit of sauce?

'A bit of HP,' I said.

'Oh well,' she said.

James and me walked as far as the seafront to check on the barograph, viewed through glass, at the corner. These were installed all round Scotland. Before outdoor swimming pools. After drownings.

It was steadier now, after a steep fall in pressure. We'd give it a go. Should moderate by evening.

'First, these are the brails. The light lines gather the canvas and pull it up tight. Faster than lowering the sail by the halyard, if we have to. We might need to. We should get the Ducati running and warmed up first. She'll probably fire, first go. The dynastart is pretty good.'

She did fire up, not too much smoke. James looked proud.

'We'll keep her running,' he said, 'till we clear the pier. A bit of tide off there. OK, I'll hold her nose in and you get that sail up but don't lose these brails whatever you do.'

So I hoisted, hand over hand. Then I made the halyard fast. I knew not to do any locking turns. You could feel the boat taking the wind already. I was sensing her lean right over. The adrenalin was kicking in. I was ready to shift my slight weight. Coiling the slack.

Not really seeing that the heel was now quite violent. Water shouldn't really be slopping in over an inboard engine. Even if it's under a painted plywood hatch. Not really seeing that the skipper wasn't looking that happy. Hearing it though, soon enough.

'Never mind the bloody slack. The brails.'

I yanked at them and the sail gathered together to spill wind. One gunnel dipped. James lunged forward and we got the yard down together.

'Hell's teeth.'

Too much wind. It hit you when you cleared the breakwater. He just turned her in a wide circle then took her through the gap so I could pick up the mooring buoy we'd thrown off, only fifteen or twenty minutes before. But this small circle had done something to us. I'd only had one minor role but had played it, on demand. Maybe James was keen on testing these brails, that engine. Now he knew. The new systems could get you out of trouble.

It was The Ship. I came close to it, not only getting one for him but one for me too. But James had already ordered his Glenmorangie, my orange juice.

He'd been in a seminary, training for the priesthood. Cycled bloody miles from there to a pub. But he was serious all the same. That's why he didn't laugh at people's beliefs. He'd been at the last hurdle. No, another story for another day. Enough drama for tonight, real life.

Two wives, five kids, maybe more to come, kids that was, probably not wives.

James never tried to steer me one way or the other. Get the degree, then decide. If you'd found a line you had to follow it. If anyone could make sense of the last century, they were on a worthwhile mission. But follow your own lines of enquiry, not the ones set by the other guys. You can surely jump through the hoops when it comes to the finals. Then get back to your real project. That's all he could say. He said he'd done too many daft things to be able to advise anyone. It had worked out for him now, though.

See pibroch, most folk thought it was improvised music. Like a series of cadenzas. It wasn't like that at all. There's a set series of variations but they've been composed by a piper who's gone before you. You don't have that much freedom to move within them, at all.

I was thinking that percussion isn't really that different. It's like the timing in an engine. If it's set right, you don't really notice it.

The reality of the situation. As it is. One orange juice, one malt. Like the modern inboard engine in the historic boat. Like the nylon covering over the shrouds to prevent the sail chafing. Like being late with the phone call, missing the funeral.

Then beginning to see more clearly, at last. Learning the pibroch. Falling into the rhythm. So there's a chance you can maybe keep momentum. Move on.

Mairi Bhan

This is a meeting that took place in Billy Forsyth's. That's a bakery but I went in there for mushrooms. Everything in Prestos or Safeways, or whatever the hell Liptons was called these days, was pre-packed in big quantities. The ones on the bottom would be liquid by the time you reached them. Running away through the drainage holes in the package. Forsyth's hasn't changed much. Don't go looking for that name on the sign, though. It never said that. It was always Hugh Matheson's. Same way Calum Sgianach's had a sign that said Malcolm MacLean's, but you probably knew that.

You know how it is, though. You always buy something else as well and they'd started to do rye bread. But I've got this vice. Maybe you share it, I don't know. Maybe these quirks you hide because you think you're the only one and it turns out every second cove is afflicted by the same thing. I can't avoid looking into other people's shopping baskets.

The queue is going down, getting nearer the till and your eyes are in there before you know it. This one had red and green peppers. I was looking for a jar of olives, thinking she was going to make pizza but there wasn't any and no aubergine, though they'd been on offer, at a price. So it didn't look like ratatouille, either. Maybe some colour for the winter salads. That tied in with all these mixer drinks, the ginger ale and tonic and other things you wouldn't want to drink on their own.

My eyes must have lifted for clues then because the beret caught me. Decent wool, but it was the angle. You can only call it panache. It had to be Mairi Bhan. She always had style. My mates couldn't see it. She was kind of petite but the wit was fast off the mark. Of course her hair was nearly black which was why she had the Gaelic nickname for 'fair'. Short and wavy. But of course she was a year or two down the school and that was called babysnatching.

I was right back there. Something in her touch at the back of your neck, under the revolving reflective ball, with *Whiter Shade Of Pale* still lingering. Getting off with her at the SY YMCA.

And Fleetwood Mac before the boy Green got fat. *Because I Need Your Love So Bad.* And the walk to the lane up by the hostel. Which could get crowded on disco nights. It wasn't a long walk but there was that one aberration of hers, the platform soled boots, which made it kind of slow. When she lost her own judgments to the pressures of marketing.

There was also a limit, though, in how fast I could walk, arm around Mairi, towards that lane. You might think twenty-six-inch flares, bought from an advert in *Sounds*, were enough for anybody. No but you could expand them by cutting the side gussets at the outside and sewing in an offcut of something else. A flash of colour to sweep and swirl from the black cotton. Flapping like hell on a course up Church Street.

There was a lot of sighing in the lane. It was a bit distracting hearing other people's noises and wondering how far they were going. But then her tongue would get past my teeth like it was shoving them out of the way, roots and all, and I'd hold her and hug her. I liked her. Her nose. Her earlobes out from her curly hair, not the fashion of the day.

'Garyvard. Hell, I could just about call in and see her by boat. Get hold of the Dangler's launch and get hold of a mate and that was us sorted.'

'Not quite m'atal. I'm going to be in Carloway for the holidays. Staying with my grannie. We take it turn about. My mother's a *Siarach*.'

So she was a *Siarach*-Lochie cross, just like my olman.

'Carloway. Loch Roag. Hell, that's round the top. The Butt of Lewis,' I said.

'Or through the Sound of Harris'.

'That's worse. The Board of Trade will never let us take the boat outside Lewis Territorial Waters.'

But I'd see her at the Carloway dance all right. End of term, everything seems possible. How the hell was I going to get from town out there? I knew a few guys who could get hold of a car. But none of them wanted to go west on a Saturday night. Buses didn't go that way after five p.m. and didn't come back till the Monday morning. A cab was possible. The poaching money would have stretched that far. Kenny F took a cab to Brenish, once. End of the road. Then the girl wouldn't see him. Or her father wouldn't let her see him.

But I'd spent my share of the salmon money on Levi's Originals. My olman thought I'd gone daft, sitting in the bath with them on. Shrink to fit. Took me two days to get the dye off the enamel. Then he'd caught me taking the scrubbing brush to them, against the roughcast. First time he'd seen me cleaning anything, he says. Maybe he shouldn't moan.

Should have been a perfect summer. But I was missing Mairi's peppery lips. I still had the taste of them. It was her voice as well. Not giggling. Bantering. There was a way to get out to her territory. We could take a borrowed tent with us, out of town. Kenny had himself together at the time. He'd take a creelman's holiday and go dangling.

We assembled the gear, together. The tent was light enough because there was no flysheet but the six-inch nails, as pegs, added up to a few pounds. The cooking stove wasn't so bad but the gas cylinder had to be carried on a stick between us.

Ruaraidh dropped us off, between Garynahine and Grimersta. We had the word on a couple of good trout lochs. It was too early and too dry for a chance of a salmon.

We got sunburnt so we punched each other when one rolled to brush against the other's tender form, in the short night. We caught trout in each of four lochs. Caught so many we had to start releasing them. We'd eaten trout and beans. Trout and stale white bread. Trout and black pudding looked better on the plate, the pink and the mottled brown-black.

But then my rod just stayed over when I hit a fish and it did the running. When she gasped ashore, at last, she was the biggest I'd caught, nudging the two pounds. I faffed about, unhooking her. A two-pound trout was something to boast about. Then I tried supporting her upright in the clear water till the oxygen could get through her gills. It was too late. We couldn't waste that fish but it was a struggle to eat the lot.

There were golden eagles circling the bays between the seacliffs. Wide wingtips breaking clear skies. It was Saturday and we rose early. We moved our base-camp to a spot near the crossroads. We'd get a few casts for sea trout in the seapool, near the road, before the toffs were at their breakfast. Kenny knew one of the watchers. We were fine till about nine.

We cast flies and watched the fins of a few bored fish follow them and flick a tail now and again. They weren't interested in taking. They had sex on their tiny brains and wanted water to get up that stream of fresh water. It was just as well, we were stuffed with trout and if we'd scored a fish it wouldn't be fresh by Monday, when we'd be back in the city. We could get a sleep and still have time to walk the whole way if we had to.

Karma was sound. Kudos could have been better, arriving courtesy of Massey-Ferguson. But we got there. Some of these village dances were two-bit jobs, with the accordionist propped against the back wall and fed occasionally from a half bottle. These guys had amplifiers – bass, lead with tremolo echo. I sighted Mairi Bhan's pal first. Made a small attempt to get Kenny dancing with her. Then I was in Mairi's smell and her wiry hair was over my burned face. Talk about 'Be gentle with me, my darling'.

But she was and she led me away from the band who were trying to tell me that my cheating heart would tell on me. Out the door and the weight of Rayburn fume came at us in the calm air. It made the swirling smoke in the concrete hall seem healthy. Always a few collie dogs slinking by.

We didn't go far. Down a croft, away from the road. Sad day we left it, the croft, not the road. We leaned back against the traditional backrest. A peatstack with a herringbone pattern. I could feel every hard bit of it, either side of my spine. My teeth didn't get in her way any more and she went easy on my sunburned neck. She said she'd make it cool. I don't know that she did but her tongue felt all right there, as well. Yes and there too. I stopped worrying about the peat-stack pattern getting embossed on my backside.

Maybe that's another wee fetish which possesses more than one Lewisman. We all think we're the only cove whose eyes roll at the thought of being gently guided backwards till your arse is hard up against a peat-stack.

Now, I'd know what to do, to play fair, to see her eyes smoke over. But the mind was racing with what you were supposed to do and supposed to be carrying and the only plastic or nylon in my pocket was a cast of fishing line.

If she was angry with me she didn't show it. She led me back to her sleeping house. Cut me a doorstep from that morning's loaf, the crust fired black. A slab of salty Anchor butter and another orange slab of Scottish Cheddar. More tea. And whispering talk and still more tea but on her lips this time, at the door. Not in a big hurry to leave.

Five minutes back to the hall and Kenny F was shaking his head. He'd had a lift arranged. No, not the Fergie. Some guys with a van were going to run us in, as far as Marybank. My mate had waited, not wanting to see me stranded and our lift was gone. There was one battered Cortina still there. How come they always had crumpled wings? Maybe these were the only ones allowed to be borrowed to get out to dances like this. Windows were pretty steamed up. That one wasn't going nowhere for a while. So we turned two sets of heels on the district of Loch Roag.

We came close to calling it a night when we stumbled on a digger left at some roadworks, with the sliding door unlocked. Gospel according to JCB. It would have done for one, not for two. It was a long time since we'd moved camp that morning and energy was failing. But one foot follows the other and we made progress until what might have been the last roadworthy Morris Minor on the Island stopped for us. He dropped us close to our tent. 'Help yourself to a fish from the boot.'

'No thanks, cove.'

We slept for most of Sunday but got back out the moor, out of sight in the evening. We picked up some more trout to take home for the relations. At nine sharp on Monday, we were out on the road waiting to get collected. Angus showed up. Ruaraidh was on shift doing his best to keep the GPO on the road. Another Morris. Would you believe it? This was my olman's Traveller, painted with the brush. My uncle had helped him with the brakes and put a new clutch in. The second engine ran like a sewing machine.

For the first time in my life, town felt strange. School went back. Word came from a go-between, older than me, that so and so, from the sixth year, was interested but only if I considered myself unattached. She had long blonde hair, blue eyes and she was my own height. Everyone thought she was something. There was kudos in being seen with an older girl and she'd probably know what to do.

I was still in the summer clothes of rebellion, with the peace-and-love patches now sewn on to my new jeans in a pattern you hoped looked random – I had to conform. So I lost Mairi. From some far but still wakeful corner of my daft eyes, I saw her run from the YM hall. I was shuffling around it with my arms full of fair hair. Status smelled good. Until I saw the girl I really liked and desired going for that door. I was seized in my tracks. She was gone.

Until I bantered with her again at the check-out in Billy Forsyth's. Of course, she recognised me. We're only talking ten years. I was still reeling, just catching her words. They always had an open house. The sisters were all up as well, for the New Year anyway. I should make it out to Lochs.

You say these things. Where was she working? Glasgow again. Training to be an archivist. Park Bar was the place. And me?

'Took some time out of Uni. Back there again but home to keep the olaid company for the holiday.'

'Time for a coffee, across the road?'

What a forgiving lady. But there was a car hooting outside, where it shouldn't be parked and she'd to gather up the bags and it was my turn to go through the check-out.

In another few weeks I'd be heading east. Far East this time – Aberdeen, in fact.

Peter's Fish

You slept for the best part of a day. Then you woke to inform me you were ready to do some walking. You realised then, it might sound pushy, put like that, in English. It's just that you'd been sitting on trains, aircraft, ferries. Now you were ready to get out into the open.

Only if that was all right with me.

I said it would be a bit better than all right and you smiled, a bit puzzled. You were tuning in to the local lingo.

As it happened, I was free till late in the afa. I was dishwashing later on.

You asked me if that's what I did for a living. Aye, I said, I was destined to be a porter of some kind. I used to work in the hospital. Now it was the kitchens. When I wasn't out with the boys, on the cliffs or breeches-buoy training. An auxiliary Coastguard. I hadn't got the grades so the PhD was out the window.

I told you how something happened during my finals. I was staring at the papers and they just didn't seem important. They said I could plead 'special circumstances'. The essays had been all right. They said bereavement was a strange thing. Often there was a delayed reaction.

Aye, but I'd had my therapeutic year-out and I'd even had a fishing holiday. I wasn't doing so bad.

Then you told me that's really why you were here. It was now a year since your father had been reported lost. As if it was during a war. You'd been trying to support your mother but now you needed to get away, to find time for yourself. You remembered how we could say what we liked, in our letters. We could talk.

So of course I said, no, we shouldn't talk, we should go fishing instead. That might have been the right response. We had a big event in our lives in common and that was that.

We didn't get fishing that day but we did get out for a walk.

I didn't start till late. No, your English wasn't so rusty. Better than my French and the German I didn't have.

I went across the road to the bakery for rolls and teabread. Girdle scones, fruit scones and pancakes, soft and pleasant after all the healthy real bread you were used to. We ate something and had mugs of tea.

We took the bus from round the corner – I'd checked the times. It ran past the airport, to Melbost. We'd have a couple of hours before the next one, back to town. We passed through a larch gate and we were on the marram grass under a yellow winter sky. It was August.

We passed someone with his dog. One of the regulars. They all had dogs. Working collies or the bigger breeds – the ones that needed to get out. This same man had stopped me once and told me that he remembered my uncle Ruaraidh running out here to swim, every day in the year. And he'd have the run back, ahead of him. A fit guy – he'd been big in cross-country running, in the army. Did they still have the croft? They were tough, out there, the Lochies.

'Lochie-*Siarach* cross,' I said, but no, the croft was let out now. Sheena was gone.

He said he was sorry to hear that. Then he admired your hat. Hand-dyed and spun. He seemed to recognise that. 'And your own father,' he said to me, 'wasn't he a weaver? Always his own man though, whatever he did.'

And he was gone again, bending into the breeze.

I could tell you how I'd come, one term, every Friday afternoon in a long blue bus. With other swimmers, people who had something to prove, in October or February.

It was the wind that got me, sapping will. Then and today. From the northeast, not so common a wind here but the one that funnels down Broad Bay. That area of blue not looking its normal benign self.

'You talk of a place like a person,' you said, and I said, 'Yes.' You were amazed at the scale of these sands, at low-water springs. They stretched from the outcrop at Melbost, broken only by the falling groynes and one more tidal island, to the more harsh rocks at Aignish. The MacLeod stones, in the old churchyard, were worth seeing. Heads of deer, hour-glasses. Skulls, of course, the markers of time. Strange weathering.

But while we were walking, you were asking, in that direct way of yours, what this bay meant to me. You sensed something. Something sad? A death of someone I knew?

No-one I knew had drowned here. Someone I used to go fishing with had lost a son. But I didn't remember it happening at the time. Not the way I remembered one of my class dying under the wheels of a milk-truck, a couple of miles up the road, the way we'd come. Closer to home. Anyway, that drowning had been further up, where the river went in, north of the town. What you might call an estuary, really. Broad Bay hadn't been too bad to me.

We looked out over the coiled patterns across the cold shallows. Lugworm casts in the muddier areas and bleached razor-shells in the cleaner ground. Rich feeding.

'The best haddock came from there,' I said. You asked why it was 'came' in the past tense and not 'come'.

'Bigger boats with bigger nets.' I said it all like that, unfairly. You were surprised at the emotion which you caught and I wasn't willing to expand.

We didn't hold hands. We were close, though, and left the MacLeod stones for another day. You pressed me for the story. I warned you it was easier to start me than stop me. I might not know German but I knew haddock were *schellfisch*. You recognised the word. You'd seen it on packets of frozen fish. You didn't have a picture of the fish to go with the word.

We looked again to Broad Bay. At a stretch, we could make out the tip of the Eye peninsula – Tiumpan Head. Shift your gaze from there and take a big sweep to the north. We'll start from that point, though we can't see it. We walked on and I gave you the commentary.

Running down from the Butt of Lewis, there's the harbour at Port of Ness. A class of boat called the *sgoth Niseach* worked from there but from other shores too. Steep swells rose just out of the tidal harbour and tidal eddies swept across it. The biggest vessels were over thirty feet long and worked up to forty miles offshore. Then there was Skigersta, with a slipway of stone, tricky in any swell. Going south from there, past the abandoned Baptist Chapel, we're abeam Cellar Head. Then there's a geo at Dibadail. A natural inlet in the rock. That was a fishing station, once. You can see the ruins of fishing-bothies built into the side of the hill.

Then we come to Tolsta village with a concrete breakwater. It's tidal and it seems dead, with useless, huge bollards now. They're rusty sculptures. It could never have been much good, close to Low Water but it must have been worth developing, in its day. A big fleet of *sgothan* worked from there. Let's make this clear. The fishing, out there, used to be good. Note the tense.

My description of the stranded pier made you think of the Aral Sea in the Soviet Union, when the water dropped back. The sources had been harnessed for irrigation schemes. Trawlers, or whatever they were, lay stranded and dying like beached whales.

But on Broad Bay, it had been line fishing. Commercial longline fishing from open boats to the north and smaller scale inshore fishing down near here. The villages of Coll, Back, Vatisker on one side and Portnaguran just up there. It was never great for shelter. You'd to haul a boat right up but the harvest had been worth the risk. Cod, plaice, dabs, whitings, yes, but the haddock was the fish.

'What does that fish look like?' you asked.

'Like St Peter's fish,' I said.

I was shown how to tell a haddock from a whiting by that dark thumb-mark. At the feeding of the multitude, when the catch was shared, the print was seared into the grey black flank of the haddock and it's there, yet. There was more than five thousand fed from Broad Bay.

I think I grew more self-conscious then, surprised at letting go to this emotion. But you were happy with me in this role. I wasn't giving you the standard tour. You wouldn't have been interested in that. So I was away. The boat was pushed out. Small lines had only about a hundred snoods – that was thinner, shorter pieces, spliced to the main line. Each had a small hook, baited with mussel or herring-strip and worked from a smaller vessel.

There was only one line-fishing boat left. She hadn't been broken at her keel or worn to death by being winched up that geo. Even stranger, she hadn't been burned or broken up when the fishing was done. She was moored in Stornoway Harbour, the *Peace and Plenty*. A Coll man had done all right on the fish and found the capital for a shop. Became a merchant. Some say he started voting Tory.

Others did the catching but he too must have had a memory because he wouldn't let that boat go. He had a Swedish engine put into her and placed her old mast up in a loft. And there she was, like a harbour launch, with teak seating. Some might say she'd gone up in the world, like the guy himself.

Others preferred her as she'd been. Lighter. Everyone you talked to in Coll seemed to have been on her at one time or another. She had a stern like that. I drew the curve with my hand and of course you laughed because I was so passionate about a shape in wood.

Aye, if you think we get excited about sheep, watch Lewismen's eyes when they're near boats. You laughed again. Then you looked surprised at yourself.

I told you how I'd done some research. Chasing for the history of the boat I'd fallen in love with. She'd been built on this Island, up at Port of Ness. I'd spoken to the Fishery Officer I knew, working in the office where all the old registrations were kept. No art in the asking. I said what came in to my head. 'Hey Joe, Where You Going...?'

Yes, he was still available for a gig. Didn't have to be Hendrix. Rock and roll was here to stay. What was I after?

He turned up the records of that boat. There she was, on a page of handwritten entries. She was built by the man who swam ashore with the rope from the *Iolaire*.

But you were cold. Even through the borrowed Harris wool gansey, worn over your own. Our first intimacy. And I was gabbing on.

There was some bite in that wind. You could almost believe sleet could fall. We were lucky to catch the long and nearly empty bus at the turning place. The driver was having a smoke.

You were caught by these fish. You asked to hear more, once we were warm. You were getting used to this way of taking tea, simmered a while on a ring of the cooker. I'd to get the uniform wooley pooley on now. Borrow the keys for the olaid's Mini. I'd the back-shift to do.

You were still up when I got home. Stretched in front of the coal fire. The olaid was in bed. You said she'd organised a big pan of prawns. You said the two of you had eaten a lot of them but we've left a few for you.

In our kitchen, you opened Davidson's *North Atlantic Seafood.*

'You know, some people are happy to read Raymond Chandler, on holiday,' I said.

You'd gone round the corner to find the bookshop I'd described. You'd asked Ian Beaver for a detailed work on sea fish and he'd reached for that one without even looking. I used to think he was called Beaver because he always tried to sell or give away books on North American Indians. But at school, a guy called MacIver became Beaver.

This was the one, he'd said. You told me that this Davidson man called these characteristic marks 'thumb-prints' as well. This is the quote:

In this the haddock resembles the John Dory and fishermen of Boulogne therefore call it 'Faux St Pierre'.

'Pity all these French coves have it the wrong way round,' I said. 'Haddock's the real one.'

You took my hook and quoted from the same work to say that John Dory was St Peter's fish to the Portuguese, Spanish, French, Swedish, Norwegians and Danish. It seemed to be Peter's fish in Gaelic too though in German it was the King of the Herring. And further, you said, wasn't the Sea of Galilee fresh water, like the Aral Sea, in Russia?

'Don't you go talking science to me, woman,' I said. Everyone I knew who'd given me instruction in fishing, they all said the same. That print on the haddock was burned into my own mind at an early age. Anyway, the story was only mentioned in three gospels. Matthew might have made it more clear, mentioned haddock by name, if he'd remembered.

We gave up on rhetoric then. I can't remember if our fingers touched by that open book. I knew I wanted them to. We were closest when our serious sides got a rest.

I slept late in the morning, tired from that last back-shift and preparing for the change to the killer first night-shift. You'd made a salad. I tried not to look wary as you blended mustard, cream and a touch of sugar with oil and vinegar.

You were impressed by my Webb's Curlies. They'd been grown inside a fish box. Converted into a cloche by nailing a half barrel lid at each end, to carry the curve of clear polythene. You have to defeat the wind, to grow anything here. Wait till you see my crop of courgettes. One sturdy plant to a box. Cousins of cucumbers. I'd had to tickle them with a feather, transferring the pollen. If my Broch Grampa had been alive, he'd have been proud of me.

Now, I could listen to you opening up, letting go. Not so many details in what you said. But the bits that mattered came out.

You're father had never been found but he was gone, for sure. Missing presumed lost. Just like in war – but that was too long a story for now. Your mother had her problems. It wouldn't get better in a hurry.

'And how about your studies? You had an idea for a post-grad, didn't you?'

'Language and literature, both. Now English literature. It was difficult, towards finals, when you knew everything depended on the grades.'

She'd needed to get away from the centre of Europe.

'But you are in the centre of Europe,' I said. 'If you tilt the map a bit and include the maritime territories and fishing rights. But let's not talk about them.'

I can't tell you now everything we talked about but fish came into the discussion again. Strange, that. You said you'd stopped by the Broad Bay fish shop. It had to be haddock in the window and you nearly went inside. But you were shy of cooking fish for me. I seemed to be an expert.

'Only obsessed. You should know not to get me started. You wouldn't let me shrug and play it all down. You really did want to know if I'd ever been a fisherman. So I could tell you that I'd never worked on a trawler but I had set lines once or twice.

'I could tell you about it. But not right now,' I said.

This really was history, even if it was personal. Maybe I could write something down and post it. Maybe you would write me back, keep us in touch, till we could meet again. That's as close as we got but it was past a point of no return. With the benefit of hindsight, maybe that's as close as we ever got. In the shadows of our lost fathers.

Broad Bay

I told you I'd write this down. I didn't know it would take so long. Well, the writing didn't take long but it took time to be able to say what's in it. I hope you're doing well, Gabriele. The teaching and your family and the cycling and everything else. Sorry, I can't write you a chatty letter right now. I need to stretch the legs. This is the story I promised you. I'll post it tomorrow.

Hope we meet up again, before too long, Peter

• • •

We went angling, with a fair amount of technology. We all read the catalogues. Bought the gear, when we could afford it. We even had a portable echo-sounder to detect a *bo* – that's an underwater reef which could foul a net and so couldn't be trawled over.

One time, years back, our plans to round Tiumpan Head into Broad Bay met with the right conditions. The twenty-five footer, *Heron*, cut glass most of the way. She was air-cooled and made a thump you could hear for miles. We'd have been excommunicated from the Sea Angling Club and banned from competition fishing for life if any committee members had been up that early to take a look. We had three longlines aboard, coiled in wicker baskets. Angus, the skipper, directed me in keeping the sequence as I baited each one. One loose flying hook would be enough to make a bundle of bastards. That's a technical term.

First, you threw out a float then paid out twenty-odd fathoms of cod-line to a weight. A fathom is a measure based on the widest span of the arms of a man of about your own height. Then the sequence of a hundred baited hooks, nice and steady, to another weight. After that went over, you paid out a further twenty fathoms to the second float. That way you had two chances of recovering the line.

Muirneag agus Tiumpean. The hill on the point. That was the mark if we'd been out the North Minch. But in here, we'd just watch for a patch of rough that the trawl couldn't bounce over. Judge it so our line would just lie on the edge of the soft ground. Too far away from the hard patch and the bottom would be trawled clean. Too near and we'd lose our gear on the rock.

The first line was heavy, rasping with dogfish that no-one wanted. My pal, Kenny F, and myself hauling. Our hands were rasped, tearing them off and throwing them back. Our second line had been on the nursery slopes, coming up with cleaned hooks and a few small fish, which we returned, save for a few reasonable whiting.

I won't forget our last line. That was another heavy one but not sluggish like dogfish. Your finger could sense the tugging haddock. Looking down, where it was going green, to see the string of washing going where all colour was lost. The bellies coming up white and grey. A few blank areas as if the wind had blown the clothes off the line. A few slimy snoods, bitten off by something strange. But groupings of decent fish, the ones we'd come for. They came up over our gunnel as our bow was held, just off the light breeze.

A scallop, St Jacques' fish, had been gripped on one hook. Angus took his knife to the shell and cut the gut off with one flick. Then he put the white muscle and the orange coral to his mouth. They eat oysters like that, he said. We shook our heads but both his crew had to try one when another pair came up. It wasn't so bad, salt, sweet and soft.

When we brought the boat back to the mooring and I'd

rowed us and the catch ashore, there was another ritual. Being the youngest, I had to turn my back and shout the names of the owners of the piles, as equal as they could be made. Your own. Kenny's. Mine. The boat's. The boat's share was divided between anyone who appeared at the pier, wanting a fry. Just given away. That's how it was done.

That's it, Gabriele, as true as I can make it. I remember us standing where the long bus turns, looking out towards Tiumpan. That's what I was remembering. I promised you I'd tell you.

'But surely there must be some of those fish left?' you said.

I said, 'Only the stragglers.'

It all seemed long gone. That's why you were surprised, a few days later, when I went down to help at the weigh-in. I was on the early shift so I couldn't have gone out with the club. I didn't do competitions any more, anyway. Neither did Kenny's uncle Angus. He'd gone off everything to do with clubs as well as competitions. He'd fallen out with the committee and wasn't too fussed because he'd lost his taste for weighing and photo-graphing big dead fish that didn't always get eaten. Kenny F was at another Klondyke at the time. Big money, making oil-rigs, at Nigg Bay. Gaining the skill that would get him back home when the Arnish yard started up, near the lighthouse. A mixed blessing.

When I went over to the west side of Number One pier, the boats, chartered for the day, were coming in. I had a full oilskin smock on, looking the part, as the rain came down thick. Not much wind behind it. I wore clogs, like the East Coast boys, working on the immense purse-seine nets, laid out on Number Two. Pelagic fishing. The last days of the herring industry when a couple of boats scooped up the whole quota.

I gripped the rope that someone threw and I supposed it looked all right. He thought I was ready. Made the nod. The man on deck below was not their skipper. That was maybe the thing. He should have shouted something up to me, from the boat to the pier, to keep me right.

I put weight on the rope but it was against the strain. Below me, hooks went into the cut-out handles of the bottom fish-box. There were three wooden boxes, all stacked together. This was one man's catch. He caught my eye. Big Iain.

They'd found a mark, the first for years. A murmur was going round the pierhead. I didn't have to ask where they'd come from. A last single fish was placed on the top box, the thumb-mark prominent. I was about to haul. Paused. Was about to say, wouldn't it be better to take them one at a time?

There was a lot of fish to move. I didn't say anything. I should have called to someone else, someone in the crowd forming at the point of Number One, trying to get a glimpse of the draft of haddock.

The boxes were coming up, bridled together and swaying. The block on the gantry was running fine so far. It was working after all. You could see at a glance that these fish had never been in a net. A haul from out the blue.

It was becoming jerky. I remember it was awkward suddenly, come through an arc so I was now pulling from the wrong angle. I wanted to shout again but nothing came out. The three boxes glanced against the concrete rim of the pier.

That guy on deck didn't even stir in his boots when the last of the Broad Bay shoals came tumbling on him from above. The boxes hit the gunnel just as the swell was taking the boat a yard or so out from the greenheart piles. The cluttered decks were strewn with grey haddock. But the matt black harbour water, between the smudged black gloss of the boat and the pier, now bulged with dead forms. These fish were dead before they fell. But I only saw them as dead now when they were floating, bellies up.

If I'd moved quickly, I could have recovered some of the catch. I just looked down. There had to be a gaff aboard. The booted figure kept his stance. He knew that there wasn't any gaff or long-handled net so there wasn't much point in rushing about. So he was calm. The few other people who saw what happened – they gasped. Big Iain's prize-winning catch. The fish would be wasted. The fat harbour seals would get them.

Maybe these watching people stopped me from trying something. Maybe it was just the thought of clambering down a weeded ladder, in clogs or bare feet, to try to recover the fish by hand. All this rational stuff comes only now, after it's all in the past.

We couldn't bring these fish back to the pier. So there was no point in stumbling around. That would have felt wrong, like the jerking tensions on the rope, working against the swing of the gantry. So I didn't make a big thing of saying sorry, looking down to the angler I knew.

Someone showed me then, to bring my end of the rope round to the other side of the post, so the angle was correct. Hooks went into handles again and this time boxes came up, smoothly enough, one by one. This time, hands were waiting, to take the handles in the boxes.

So, Gabriele, that's the full story of the 'Schellfisch'. I didn't tell it all, at the time. So you just saw it as a miracle, me arriving back at the house with a large Broad Bay haddie.

It was my mother's bridge night. We had the house to ourselves. I just pointed to the bundle of newspapers by the sink. We unwrapped them together and, even now it was faded, it was still a very fine, line-caught fish. It was you who said it then. This could be St Peter's fish.

All I said was yes, you'd been right, there was still some haddocks came in to that bay. Some people I knew had taken their share. No lies but not the whole story.

I took the knife to it and you shuddered. I left the head on and I took the white liver to mix with the oatmeal, seasoning and a touch of chopped onion. The stuffing went back through the mouth, down to the gills. You were horrified. But this was the most traditional Lewis dish. The whole thing poached in milk. Pale green rings of leeks. The milk thickened to a sauce. The stuffing eaten with the fish and our dry potatoes. I'd grown up on it.

After sharing all that, neither of us were bothering to move hands or feet out of the way. So we came close together over a gift of a dead fish. I could have told you a bit more of my own part in the waste of some of the catch. But that was too much. Maybe I was being kind, leaving the angst out of it.

That's what people do when they tell their stories. Leave bits out. It's all history once it's happened. The match is over and here are the selected highlights.

A Letter from Köln

I don't know why recycled paper always had to have squares. In a weak blue. The paper itself was the colour of the whites I tried to wash. So far, I hadn't managed to achieve the standards of either my mother or Kirsty.

Unbleached paper. Natural cotton. Gabriele's joke. There weren't that many so I can remember most of them. 'Why are the Greens having so many babies these days? Because hessian is better than plastic.'

Makes you shiver, doesn't it boys?

But it was Gabriele's letter all right. It was right there in one of the box files, the ones with three or four labels, with numbers or dates, marking a new attempt to organise the MacAulay archive.

The squares are a good grid for handwriting. The loops are never allowed to stray too far to impinge on too many graduations of the grid. I don't know why the pen was red – but it stood out from the grey and the pale scaffolding. Maybe there was a job lot of red ink for her fountain pen. Maybe it was a clue to a passionate side which had to surface somehow before being subdued again. I've typed it all in for you so it's with all this other stuff. It was a way of getting my head back there. I didn't really know what my heart was doing at the time and I probably still don't.

My dear Peter,

I hope you are well and in good spirits. Do you still cycle to work in winter? There were storms all over Europe. We had snowploughs but I think you had the strongest winds. I read that in the newspaper but I know you can't think in metres-per-second so I have not copied the recorded speeds for you. Perhaps my contact with British culture is now too strong (even if you are Scottish) because I now realise I have begun my letter with a discussion of the weather in Europe.

But I really wanted to tell you I've completely stopped smoking now. I know it was not fair on you, when you were trying so hard and I would arrive with my allowance of duty-free Shag. And all your friends saying of course, it was time for another shag and looking at me. British humour – it's really not improved since I was a student. Is it all still about farts and arses and suggestions about sex? We don't rate toilet humour so high in Germany.

You know what was difficult? I could remember my father – every time I smoked. That's something you do not want to lose. I think I know why. It was after sailing. I know you are more into engines but we share a love of wooden boats. My father had the boat built for him. I would visit the boatbuilder in the Netherlands with him and see how the shape grew on the frames. From some angles it looked quite fat, like a goose and from others it was streamlined. Also like a goose. We did the lacquer work ourselves. The wood is very light yellow, like a German woman's hair was supposed to be like. The timber grew a little darker after twelve coats of lacquer but it still shone.

My father would always hoist the sails. It was very funny, the day he realised I was now taller than him. He kept trying to reach a rope that was loose on the mast. The wind was blowing it away from him and he kept trying to reach it. I stretched out, by instinct, and he looked so surprised when I handed the end to him.

He looked even smaller because he was so thin. They say a lot of people who survived the war were small, thin types. They could stay alive on less food than people with bigger frames. You know I have inherited his build but perhaps not for very much longer. I thought it was propaganda from tobacco companies, the gain of weight when you stopped but it has started to happen. I remember you saying Lewis-men like their vessels a bit on the wide side. You might get tested, on that, next visit.

You said I was like Popeye with the round muscle popping up from a long bony arm. You might not win at an arm wrestle now, Mr Peter MacAulay, so you had better watch what you say in future.

And I must warn you I have let my hair grow a bit, just to my shoulder. It's cut straight there. It makes me feel good. I think you call it a bob. I know a shilling used to be a bob too. Five new pence, I remember.

Writing this, I am thinking back to being on the boat with my father. I became good on deck. There are two ropes to pull as the sail goes up. It's a lot of sailcloth for quite a slim boat. But when the mainsail is nearly up, you tie one rope and pull the other till the top of the sail – the gaff – stretches up higher. Here is a little drawing for you.

I learned to watch the sails and slacken this or tighten that to get the boat moving better. I read books and did training on a dinghy. I had to bully my father a bit to make him move his weight out to the side, or forward or back. When the boat is light, your weight makes a big difference.

Sometimes we argued. Some days he said he just wanted to get away from being the man in charge. Difficult phone calls with anxious clients. He didn't want to have to give his best performance on the water. But I did. I could not be happy if I saw a chance to make the boat go better. She would lean over a bit but there would be very little splashing. She could carry a lot of sail because she had a heavy, iron centreboard that dropped to make a keel.

The club became crowded. More pontoons were installed on the wide river. We could sail into a lake. It was a day-boat – no berths for sleeping but it was worth the long drive. Soon there were Saturday races. I persuaded him to enter. Our boat was new and still light. We would get her back on the trailer when were finished. I scrubbed and scrubbed till my father said I'd wear the wood away. A boat goes faster when it's smooth.

We were usually second or third. The day we won, the wind was behind us on the last section of the course. There was a big wave on the lake. I got the pole on the big foresail but I tied it to the shroud so I didn't have to hold it. Then I took my weight back, right beside my father and we crouched close so there was less of us to catch the wind. The boat made a hiss that told us we were fast. We were across the line first and all the boats were the same type. We hugged and then I said, 'God, I could do with a smoke now.'

My father looked a bit shocked because he had not guessed his little daughter (taller than him now) could possibly smoke. He just made a shrug and passed me his packet. Just this once. He had been trying to hide it too, to set an example. It was about the time people were starting to talk about lung cancer and warnings on packets.

Once or twice we had a smoke at the door of the house. It was not yet finished. You know about the shoes on the children of the cobbler? Well this was the architect's house. But my mother had her kitchen organised now. She was making *Sauerbraten* – like a marinated pot-roast, with vinegar. Mutti still believes in pot-roast. It keeps in the juices. It's her religion now. There was a lot of moving things from a bowl to a pan and Mutti got angry when I wasn't there to help.

'What are you two finding to talk about?' she asked. We were smoking at the door and talking about this and that. I knew she was apart – left out – but I just knew there would not be many conversations like this with my father. Before the weight came back on him.

Then my mother was banging pans and I had to go back in. He stayed out, looking at the unfinished walls, the piles of sand

and stones. It was his dream house and he looked lost.

He asked for my help later, with the cough mixture. I was to tell him if I found bottles in cupboards. Hidden away anywhere. I think I knew already my mother was always having flu and had sore heads and had to go to lie down. But it was after my father was reported missing that my brother and myself got Mutti to go for help. There were clinics. It was a common problem. People who could not cope with life, day after day, they would swallow spoons and spoons of this cough medicine.

Now, dear Peter, you know another family secret. I want you to know all about me. But I do not want to be always like a German full of angst, so now for happier matters.

Michel has a new camera. It is an SLR with three lenses. Our father's Leica rangefinder is old-fashioned now. I love it but I don't want to use it. Michel doesn't want it either because it is like something from a shrine. We still use his dark-room. The house was not completely finished until after he was gone.

Here are Michel's pictures. You can see the boat. You will get on well with my brother. He is mainly interested in engines. All kinds of engines, not sailing. That is why my father asked me to sail with him. Here is Michel's photo of the new me. Where's your Popeye now? I remember you saying how I was the nearest you'd come to having a boyfriend. You can see I don't have my hair cut short any more. You need to be thin for that. I hope you like my new look, all the same. I'm happy in my self.

Love, Gabriele

PS. Did you find out if we could take out the dinghy of your friends? I can teach you everything in two or three days. We could go to that island you talk about, the one with the stone arch. I will send my dates. Write back soon. Thank you for the sad story about the haddock. I think it was good for you to write your story. It was good for me to read it. It made me close to you again.

Another Letter

Another letter, fat in the envelope. Pale blue squares on flecked off-white with red ink, weak now. It's difficult not to change the phrasing, just reproduce the handwritten words, in type.

My dear Peter,

I've handed in my notice. Don't get anxious. It's nothing final. The city of Köln will give me a year's leave of absence. As a lecturer in literature I am a civil servant with terms of employment that includes the chance to take a sabbatical. It is also a time to think. I do not know if I really want to be a teacher, for life. I have the feeling that my own research in literature is not complete. To be specific, I feel that your Ms Austen has been accepted as a feminist icon without careful scrutiny of the work. Her status is secure in Germany as well as in Great Britain (I know not to say England) but I do not think enough attention has been paid to the study of how she achieves her results. I think she uses language the way a careful surgeon might use a scalpel. I must confess I have never witnessed an operation. I also think of my father working at a drawing board. There is a delicate balance, achieved by a system of suspended weights. There is a need for precision. I think also of my father's way of lifting his glasses and rubbing his eyebows.

Do you think that a careful author is a bit like an architect? She imagines buildings and gardens and draws them but the reader has her own pictures in her mind. Jane Austen draws and describes to provide a clear perception of the people who move in the buildings she has created – the structures she has imagined. But then there is something in her tone of voice. It is as if she can step aside and rub her glasses and let her characters say what they must say.

Your mother is very kind to invite me again but of course I worry about being a German person in Britain. It is not so many years and people still remember what it was like in the war. I think most families have lost someone.

I have enough savings to rent a room and this will also be good for my spoken English. But I do hope Peter that we will be able to spend time together. I hope we can spend long enough to know how our friendship might develop. What it is and what it might become.

Yes, history is certainly complex but our generation knows all too well there are some black and white issues. The generation of my mother and father kept their heads down and so the Nazis knew they would not be challenged.

I have to stop writing now. Please know I am thinking of you Peter. Please write and cheer me up,

Love, Gabriele

In Black and White

The olaid always says she wants it in black and white. That goes for an estimate from the plumber or a politician's promise. I got the chance she never had, nor her husband either. I went to the college of knowledge and found that truth seems to come between the lines of different accounts. Something in Gabriele's letter set me thinking. I always seem to be returning to the years when we settled back on the Island. That's when I really got into history, in reaction to a guy who said it was just another subject to tick off on the score sheet. Maybe that reaction was part of the cynical bastard's intention.

None of you have any interest in history. I know this. Please don't bother to argue. It's unlikely to be a problem. You are all here because you wish to pass Higher History at the best grade possible. Some of you will need the grade so you will be accepted for a university or college course. Your reasons for being in this class are not really my main concern. I can help you to achieve the passes you are capable of but only if we understand one another.

Some of you are diligent workers, some of you are lazy. You are all capable of achieving a good pass in Higher Grade History if you pay attention and are willing to put in a moderate amount of work into learning and arranging some information. I will be showing you some techniques for passing this exam. I will attempt to minimise the amount of time necessary to achieve a good result. With your agreement, ladies and gentlemen of the fifth year, we will start now.

When I write on the board, it will be necessary for you to take notes.

Let's take the example of the French Revolution.

Please copy this.

Standard Introduction Number One

• The Revolution which took place in France in 1789 had several underlying causes. A strong case can be made out for .... being the main cause.

(Select any one of the Causes and insert in the blank.)

Causes of the French Revolution – see handout A.

Change of Argument Number One

• However, many other causes also played a significant role. (List remaining causes from handout A. Take care not to repeat the one previously chosen as the main cause.)

Conclusion Number One

• In balance it would appear that .... was the fundamental cause.

(Choose one cause at your own discretion. If possible, give a sensible reason for your choice.)

The more intelligent of you here may be aware that it would be a little repetitive if the examiner had to read through twenty-eight identical answers. Therefore in the following weeks I will be providing you with Standard Introductions Two to Four; Changes of Argument Two to Four and a choice of four phrases to introduce your conclusion. We will then move on to apply the same approach to such questions as Constitutional Reform in Britain and the Causes of the First World War.

When we are approaching the Higher Prelims in January, I will be providing you with assessments of the probability of each particular topic occurring as a question, based on the frequency of its appearance in the past five years. We cannot of course be absolutely certain of all but a few questions appearing. Therefore I am sure you will agree it is prudent to cover a few eventualities.

Now, can I have four volunteers to distribute these handouts?

He was always dressed like a bank manager. Decent dark suit but not at all flashy. Shone shoes and slicked hair. That's back in fashion again (some histories do seem to go in cycles) but they call it gel now. He moved quietly about the room. Never seemed either slow or in a hurry. It was like the cove had Brylcreem under his shoes as well and he was gliding. I don't remember him losing the rag or shouting or anything. He'd have been good in wartime. Great organisational skills and he was an effective communicator.

In 1972 we wrote how the incident at Sarajevo was only the spark which caused the inevitable conflagration of the First World War. The war would probably have happened without it, unless you chose another cause to front the list, if you forgot that one, under pressure. So all these boys from Griomsiadair or Rügen would have gone away to war anyway. Archduke or not. Maybe.

The timing mattered a bit though. If the spark had come from the late race to carve up what was left of Africa, maybe the war would have started later. Finished later. So it might not have been in the early hours of the 1st of January 1919 when the Lewis boys were coming home. The Naval contingent channelled on to His Majesty's Yacht *Iolaire*. And it wouldn't have been the exact combination of contributory causes which had her strike the Beasts of Holm. And my grandfather wouldn't have been lost, a cable or two from the home island shore.

He wasn't the only one who could have taken the helm that night. Most of the uniformed passengers would have recognised the lee shore. And he wasn't the only one who failed to arrive for the big New Year homecoming. A change of clothes would have been waiting on a chair, in Griomsiadair or Garyvard, Aird Point, Aird Uig, Bays of Harris. Over two hundred changes of clothes put away again when the news came through. So even the next generation didn't speak of it.

Not for a long time. And my olman never did, not in detail, at least not to me. He wrote it down though. Can't say for sure when. Have a feeling it couldn't have been that long before he died. He was a good talker but he never wrote verse. Only that one poem titled *Iolaire*. It didn't rhyme but it had to be metrical. That degree of feeling needs a form.

So that's history. Causes of this, causes of that. People's pasts. Some memories you can substantiate, others you can't. The olman's stories. Andra's. Told often enough to become set pieces. Vernacular but formal. Convincing yourself the Second World War was all about what you managed to cook and eat in tricky circumstances. But if he'd been given a bit more time, my olman might have told us how he'd at last squared up to the death of his own father. He'd written it down for himself. Another brave one. This piece of writing was not in the drawer in the weaving shed. It was in Ruaraidh's house. I never thought the brothers had very much in common but maybe that was my olman trying to share something. Ruaraidh gave it back to me, when it looked like I might be settling into the Coastguard Service.

HM YACHT *IOLAIRE* **(formerly** *AMALTHEA***)**
Wrecked on The Beasts of Holm, Approaches to Stornoway,
1st January, 1919: 205 lives lost

'The tide now, rising or falling?'

'I think she's rising.'
'Aye, well, that's it then.'

Conglomerate backs
exposed then awash
with the pulse of each
individual surf.
The night of the killing wind.
Sure as shrapnel.

The grounded decking
now shedding
sailors like waters.
Numbered reservists;
Hands and ABs;
a Petty Officer;
Cooper 2nd Class;

Signalman; Gunner.
Slipping or jumping.

The shivering souls
are now the same rank.
Sometimes engaging
hard shoals.
Sometimes sliding
a way through
a choking gap
of troubled mudflats.

One man jumped
from the wreck to the surf,
towing a light line.
He was knocked back under
the pretty counter.
He'd have to find breath
and come in on a wave.

The few on the shore
dragged him and his rope,
hauled on a heavy one,
a thick hemp hawser,
ship to shore. But
'...all who tried did not manage to hold on.' [1]

The sodden lifeline
stretching out from
broached iron.
Bitter hands held
these three strands.

Late carts spilling
useless apparatus
on stony fields.

Three shapes hanging
on stretching tendons

to an arrow-shaft from
a broken-backed yacht
with the name of an eagle.
Two slipped to seas.
One held through dark
swept by spray and
the timed light
of irrelevant Arnish.

All the dials
around an island
seized at sunrise.
And soon the lot
was offered for sale:
pukka Burma teak;
Admiralty brass;
unrecovered sons.

[1] From a witness at the Court of Inquiry

We only went as far as the Causes of the First World War at Higher level. Causes of the Second World War – that was a sixth-year job. In our fifth year, when we were schooled in arranging causes of events, Kurt Waldheim replaced U Thant as Secretary-General of the UN. Which body of course has prevented all subsequent wars with a few minor exceptions, for example, Korea, Aden, Vietnam, Uganda and Ireland. (Random sample from a definitive list we never got, of wars since 1945, not run off from a master stencil to paper sweet with the smell of solvent, from a Gestetner machine.)

The Waldheim cove is another guy who had one hell of a yarn to tell. But he was never mentioned in our history class. He's another one who had to tell his own story so often it became quite tidy. Kurt had been a corporal in the Austrian army. Thus he was drafted by the Nazis. There were no choices. He'd become a lieutenant, wounded on the Eastern Front. So he was back home early, he said. Often. As long as he was Secretary-General of the United Nations, he could get away with that. But once he stood for power, at home, he was in trouble.

It so happened that some of the facts were trapped in written records by an obsessive Nazi bureaucracy. He said he was just another soldier following orders. He kept buoyant, afloat on his own story for long enough. But his time was coming. His signature was on too many orders, carrying out too many deportations, or worse.

Biology

One more of these letters – handwritten in that ink on that paper, but I've typed it up.

My very dear Peter,

Thank you for your last long letter. For me too, the visit was something big. Too short. Our relationship is something different now. Your typing is getting very good. Perhaps I can employ you to type my thesis. It is going to be a lot of work but it looks as if it may be accepted towards a Masters. They do not yet call a degree a Mistress of Literature (or Letters) even though my subject might well be a close look at the language used by 'The Mistress Of Irony'. So maybe you will be my sexy secretary and sit on my knee. My body is back to being bony again, so it might not be comfortable. No, I have not gone back to smoking. I have joined the rowing club. We meet every other day, after school. We are all quite serious. Perhaps that is what you would expect.

I like the way you describe your schooling. Your teachers. The history you were taught and the history you were not. I'm glad you didn't try to steal the Stone of Destiny back when you were twelve years old. We should make a film about it in the style of *Whisky Galore*.

You did make me laugh when you said how you found your strict lady schoolteachers sexy. Very, very British. I did not know the Scots were like that too – I thought only English public schoolboys. But I will make you a promise now, Peter MacAulay. You will never persuade me to dress up for you in any way. You must take me as I am or not at all. But so far I must say you do seem to be just a little excited by a bare naked woman. Even if she is not blonde and does not have big breasts like in the *Carry On* films. Do you think I could pass a test on British culture? Have you thought about corresponding with a French woman? I think they like dressing up a bit more.

But I hope you don't dare. Will you teach me to catch fish if I teach you to sail? Can we make a handshake on that. Very British again. See – I am learning.

To be more serious, your letter reminded me of a school-teacher, here in Germany. He is probably still alive. He might even still be teaching. I hope not. I cannot write like Ms Austen but I will try to describe him.

This man always wore a brown tracksuit. It had a metal zip and tight cuffs. It looked like wool or cotton, something like that, from an older time, not nylon. Already everyone was wearing modern materials, polyester and strong colours, blues or reds. This tracksuit reminded me of something I'd seen before, in films. You could not be certain of the time exactly. He wore it every season, every year. Perhaps he had many suits, all the same, like a uniform. All teachers were expected to help at Sports Day. When he stood beside the older pupils you realised how small he was. He seemed to be very fit for his age, with a build like my own. I'm not exactly fat now but you know I was very thin when I was younger. Then I grew up so fast and became tall and awkward. He had hair like a crew-cut in old American films.

He introduced himself as Maskulinski. The word for masculine is a bit different in German - *Maskulinum* - and you would say *männlich* for 'manly'. So it wasn't so obvious at first. But he told us, when we were doing Latin, we would realise what his name really meant.

The boys would get him talking about motorbikes. That was a guaranteed break from genes and chromosomes. A machine would last if it was well maintained. That meant you needed a system, a schedule with nothing left to chance. Lubrication was the most important element so metal would not wear against metal. He kept saying, *'Ich und meine Maschine.'* It was hard not to giggle. Even at our age, it was obvious. What do you say – a penis-extension? But he could not see that himself.

He said, if you could dismantle and reassemble a machine, it could be immortal. Some parts would wear out but you could seek replacements. If you could not find the parts but were strong in your resolve, you could make them. Usually you only needed access to a lathe.

Did we know that the speed of nearly 280 kilometres per hour, on a 500cc BMW in 1937, set a world record that stood for fourteen years? He was very proud of this as if he had built the bike or driven it himself. Did we know that the shaft-drive system was so successful in difficult conditions that these machines could continue operating in the desert. Even the harsh North African desert. These were great days for German industry.

He must have said that so often that the figures became ingrained, the way you might remember a telephone number. The way I've heard you quote the weight of a salmon caught by a lady on the River Tay. You could tell me her name and the river. Maybe even the date, as well as the pounds and ounces. We could see him out, a few kilometres ride from the town, if the weather was good. He would gather samples, plants and flowers. So we would watch him go past. We could see the shining chrome and black leather of the BMW. It was an old model, with polished badges. He wore high motorcycle boots but he carried a selection of flowers and grasses tied to the rack behind him.

He taught geography as well as biology. He would describe constellations and say they could be seen as bodies relating to each other. He'd pick someone with a brown jersey – the Earth. If you wore a red top you would have to represent the sun. Whoever was left, wearing a contrasting colour – they would be the moon of course. He'd have you out in front of the class and arrange you, pulling you about so your relative positions would relate to the seasons. He would be passionate, arranging and explaining. He would hold tight to your jersey.

When we did genetics, everything would happen between black, long-haired rabbits and white short-haired ones. So, with black people, negative attributes were dominant, he said. It was a long-term process but good white attributes would disappear. Think of all that tight curly hair, girls, he would say. And he would turn up his nose, make a bad face.

We would pretend to be confused and say how we could not see what was wrong with tight curly hair. Think of Art Garfunkel, we would say, quite cute sir, don't you think? And why exactly were black attributes negative? I do not quite understand, sir. Can you explain?

He would reply that we girls were to be careful. And it was not only black people. We were not to get involved with any Turkish men. Turks were only interested in one-night stands. It was not worth it. We would ruin our lives.

We asked him if he had been a soldier. Yes, he replied. But he would not give us any details. I think I heard him say once that it was the strong men in slight frames who survived.

When I think of him in the classroom I still shiver. And I can still see him now, on Sports Day, in that old brown tracksuit. But he was a different man when you saw him out on that beautiful bike, with its quiet and controlled roar. He would be riding like a king or queen, down the roads beside the farms with his floral arrangement, like a passenger, behind him.

Well, Peter, that was a surprise for me. All these words coming out. I hope I can still fit this letter in the envelope. It will have to go surface. But I am happy with our trade. Please write another of your strange letters. I like them.

Hugs and kisses, Gabriele

A Constitutional Question

The letters to and from the city of Cologne brought me right back to the subject of history, pre-Uni. While I was being navigated through the likely questions for my Highers, the British Army pushed for a result in a no-go part of Londonderry. The headlines on the banned civil rights march failed to prompt discussion in our class. Of course it wasn't history then. But it was, by the evening of the 30th January 1972. Or was it? Question: do you have to wait to the end of the day, the end of the month or the end of the year till events are indeed history? No, we never got asked that one either.

For the UK government this was a constitutional question, an internal matter. It could be a different story, abroad, if states wanted to break away or reunite. Also on 30th January 1972, Britain, Australia and New Zealand recognised Bangladesh. Pakistan then withdrew from the Great Commonwealth. For the new Secretary-General of the UN, the aforementioned former Nazi soldier, Northern Ireland was just another civil war. The United Kingdom was a bit curt (sorry) when the Austrian offered to act as a go-between.

So it was not even a thirty per cent possible question:

'Why were thirteen civilians left dead on the streets and many more wounded by British Army fire during a civil rights March in Londonderry on the 30th January 1972?' Let's attempt to apply my history teacher's methodology to the question that wasn't asked. I'm a bit rusty on how this is done. History was a bit of a different subject, at Uni. How far back can we go in the attempt to determine a cause for an effect?

The deaths and woundings which occurred in Derry on 30th January 1972 were the result of a complex combination of circumstances, which had developed over a period of centuries. William of Orange's victory at the Battle of the Boyne has remained a potent symbol, used by both sides. 'Remember 1690.' The vibrancy of the colour orange, as manifested on sashes worn on marches and mural paintings displayed on gables in Loyalist areas of Belfast and Londonderry, is set against the intensity of the colour green, which features prominently on murals in Republican areas.

Musical rhythms provide a further manifestation of two opposing cultures. The Lambeg drum has long been used by the Protestant side to project a steady, military and very loud beat, offset by high-pitched fifes. These expressions of the localised domination of one group over another are bound to lead to a series of reactions and counter-actions.

In contrast, Republican songs often work within a Celtic ballad tradition, where narrative and lyrical phrasing is to the fore. Often the lyrics are sentimental. There are many historical precedents for the use of an anthem by a group regarded as 'Rebel'. Despite the horrors of a more mechanised warfare, there are still romantic songs relating to the 'Rebel' forces in the American Civil War.

An additional tier has been brought into the tension by the military traditions associated with particular regiments, deployed with the aim of enforcing the UK government's policies in Northern Ireland. The distinctive maroon berets of 'the paras' or the green and black of Black Watch tartan bring their own associations into the complex mix.

The process of colonisation has left inevitable resentment. There are clear parallels between the encouragement of the Planters across the north of Ireland by King James I/VI and other historical situations.

Right, that's enough of that. I just don't get it that the Jewish settlers took over Palestinian farms and properties. Just like the Nazis gave confiscated lands to 'ethnic Germans' in Czechoslovakia after murdering or deporting the 'inferior' folk who were in them.

It was maybe inevitable that the Army would come to be seen

as a force of occupation. Violence escalated, in the form of killings and explosions. The degree of ruthlessness, in bombing 'campaigns' which were bound to lead to high numbers of civilian casualties, is World War Two again. The failure of successive UK governments to instigate enquiries into the conduct of their troops was another factor. On the thirtieth anniversary of 'Bloody Sunday' it's still not easy to decipher it all. Let's fucking try.

Civil rights, in matters of arrest and justice, had been withdrawn as a security measure. One side said that not enough terrorist convictions were being made under the normal judge and jury system, so suspension of these rights and adoption of 'internment', was a necessary measure. The policy of imprisonment without trial and its apparent application to one sector more than another, led to the decision to organise that civil rights march through Derry.

Now how the hell do we change tack on this argument? The slick teacher did indeed give us a choice of four phrases but I can't be arsed planting one in.

What about Heath's memories? It was the Wilson government which first ordered the troops across the North Channel. But Heath was at the helm when it became a war. Sorry. My chronology is arse about face. We're going backwards and forwards. But we're going to Derry now.

So, let's think of the paras in their signature maroon headgear, cooped up and hearing the usual rain of bricks. You're behind a hot metal wall, in a powered steel pram. You've been issued the rounds and told again. You are the agent of delivery. In your warpaint, psyched for the game, this is it. It's come from the highest authority that you 'scoop up the yobos'. Once you've got separation from the rest of the crowd, you go in. If you see anything, let this be clear, you shoot first.

The boys' bellbottom jeans are no longer flapping. The old guy who's gone to help the wounded chap on the ground is killed with him. The priest is waving the hankie that's more red than white. He's as near immortal as you can get. He's an image of the day. He stays at the age he was, on that day.

If the march hadn't been declared illegal; if the organisers had responded to the risk; if the Army had responded to the Constabulary; if the boys hadn't started throwing bricks; if the difference between the British Army's shots and the IRA's was clear; if the major had stood up to the brigadier; if the sergeant-major had more control; if the mother's sons under maroon berets hadn't been psyched up for a result.

The film-makers have taught me better than the historians. Two works appeared in close succession to mark the thirtieth anniversary. McGovern and Greengrass. They are both documentaries but events are dramatised. Is that fiction or non-fiction?

I don't know. There's a few things we can't know. What would have happened if...?

If the single inquiring judge hadn't been only one; if he hadn't been personally briefed by the Prime Minister; if the conclusion had not been composed before the evidence was heard... Maybe people in the streets might have thought they could still influence the course of history, without guns and bombs. Hell happened on the streets of more than one city and town and village and prison and home.

What about all the mother's sons dragged out from in front of the telly and shot on their own front doorstep by the guys who thought they were heroes? What about the bairns blown to bits? It wasn't till the 21st August 1976 that Betty Williams and Mairead Corrigan led the Northern Ireland Women's Peace Movement through the Belfast streets. It was out of desperation. The casualties that year reached the worst since 1972 with 175 killed and 1,470 injured. There's no statistics can get us into the minds of those who issued the orders. On best available information, at the time. That, of course, is information selected by higher authority.

The man at the helm, Edward Heath, must have had his own private hauntings in the years to follow. The latest version of the offshore yacht-racing gospel, according to Sparkmann and Stephens of New York, was commissioned by the then Prime Minister. *Morning Cloud II* went down, with loss of life, during a delivery trip in 1974. Crew had signed up for wages and no doubt for the kudos of sailing the PM's yacht. I can't even start to imagine how the 'highest authority' looked back on that decade. Remember that my own father was trapped in both a tank and a ship. I'm guessing that Heath was also troubled by the deeds of the paras but, politically, he could only pay his condolences to the crew he'd personally hired. There was no apology for Bloody Sunday, not in his lifetime.

At what point do you know that a plunging yacht is not going to recover? Maybe he could see the sheets being let go. Everything flying free but the sea still pouring into the cockpit and the heeling continuing to that point of no return. Or maybe the lads just heard a sudden bang. Then they were upside down with broken gear everywhere. Hissing electrics. The conscious ones braced, holding breath and waiting to see if she would come back up. Maybe she did but the mast was down, fractured, so the sharp bits were knocking holes in the hull. Where were the wire-cutters? But the noise factor would be knackering your normal ability to think it out. The skipper's voice would probably be calm. 'We'll deal with this.' But everyone would know that *Morning Cloud II* wasn't coming back from this one and some of the lads wouldn't get out.

No Foul Play was suspected. It was an accident, not an act of revenge. I don't believe it was a supernatural event, divinely inspired to remind the powerful that it is human beings who drive racing machines, and human beings who comprise a march.

And the conclusions? Not sure I believe in conclusions, now. Not sure I did when I was sitting Higher History. But trailing ends are slack bastard things that foul your prop. So let's look at a few strands again.

An obituary in the *New York Times* quotes the historian Robert Edwin Herzstein's conclusion on the war record of the former Secretary-General of the UN:

> *Waldheim was clearly not a psychopath like Dr Josef Mengele nor a hate-filled racist like Adolf Hitler. His very ordinariness, in fact, may be the most important thing about him.*

And let's look again at the careers of two teachers, one in the new (West) Germany and one who found his home on a Hebridean island. So what happened to the masculine man in the brown tracksuit? No-one complained, to Gabriele's knowledge. He continued to teach, as far as we know. And the man who taught us to arrange summaries of historical data in mechanical order? He got results, as assessed in exams. So if that is the aim of education, he was indeed successful. He was promoted to the highest level. He was promoted out of teaching. A strong case could be made out for that being a good thing.

A Local Issue

You'd been all through the Outer Hebrides, Butt to Barra, on a sit-up-and-beg roadster. Over the Clisham, with the German equivalent of three Sturmley-Archer hub gears. You might have been lean and streamlined before but you were the build of the average racing snake afterwards.

You ate at my mother's table and rolled out your sleeping bag in our living room. This was our normal way. Our house had a trickle of visitors, met on ferries, or friends of friends, who'd been given the address.

You were getting your kit together for the Keep Nato Out demo at the gates of Stornoway airport. You talked about getting ready for water cannons, in Germany. An anti-nuclear demonstration. My olaid was kind of impressed with your story of all these women borrowing oilskins. The guys making a token attempt at sewing up their own banners then making the tea while the women got practical and just took over. The first time we lay down together was like a real old bundling. It was a public place and we were pretty well insulated by layers of clothes. I had taken the Mark One oilskin coat, with rotting cotton lining, from a hook in the byre at Griomsiadair. Laid it on the mud, the town side of Branahuie. A standard Lewis Crofters galvanised gate to the park that was mapped out. Stage One of the 'Extension of Runway, Expansion Of Facilities' at Stornoway Airport. We were joined by a group of settlers from across the Minch.

Scoraig Peninsula, Little Loch Broom. Disparate souls, scratching out a crust from this and that enterprise, across the loch from Dundonnell. The very area my fishing mate Torcuil was from. My young mentor in fly fishing became a gaunt man with a problem. The musician's problem. His face came to me when the name of his father's homeland was spoken. Where was he now? Maybe he'd survive me. They say it's not the drug that kills but the associated lifestyle. Maybe mates I've lost touch with will show up at my own funeral.

These cool guys from Scoraig had long since swapped sandals for wellies. We were called Rent-a-mob by the contractor until he saw faces like mine. He had to stop to think then, tracing us to the housing Terraces of Stornoway, the suburbs of Sandwick, Peninsula of Bhaltos, Inlets of Lochs.

We were the latter-day locals, with all democratic processes duly done and won, the QC hired by our elected Council outdoing the QC paid by the MOD. Gladiators in suits had done the fighting on our behalf, mincing words. But the findings of the Public Inquiry, which, it seems, we needn't have had in the first place, were overturned by the Secretary Of State.

Our little local battle is a significant part of European history. The North Atlantic Gap made our Island's airport important. Excuse me if I go into some detail on our own strategies of defence?

Some were talking about night-visiting to put sugar in the petrol tanks. Others considered running a JCB through the whole thing. The trouble with Direct Action at an airport, with all these runways in civilian use, is that some daft cove would be bound to stumble around in the dark and damage something so some innocent somebody would get hurt the next day. I don't think the idea of yellow road paint on the runway would have done any harm though. What was the text, yes, NATO DEMONOCRACY. Not a bad scheme but we never did it.

Instead, we took part in one organised, symbolic day to say that we were taking action because the great democracies weren't behaving well, in our name. Hence the oilskin coats so we could lie down in front of the contractors' vans, when they arrived. We weren't expecting water cannons. We pitched my ex-hire Blacks of Greenock tent and spent much of the night talking to a strong old man from Maine, more about wooden boats than this heated-up cold war.

There are some strange heroes in the twentieth century and the one of this day was a visiting Chief Inspector of Police, imported from the Mainland for the big do. Along with video cameras and reporters from the Nationals. It seems there wasn't going to be a delivery of aggregate by the contractors that day. They shrewdly thought they'd just lose a few hours, rather than have all that hassle for a small result. Sensible, really. Things were still pretty small scale. The heaviest plant was coming in to the Island in dribs and drabs. These special flat landing-craft, hooting at the small boats, in no hurry to get out of their way, here in the Approaches to Stornoway.

The engineers didn't realise that the remnants of vast shoals of herring were still running, under their chartered vessels. So there was a flotilla of small craft, jigging lines of shimmering hooks in the dusk. The subsistence fishers were asserting their right to be on the water.

All the aggregate required for extending the runway was being removed from Carinish, the southwest of the Lewis mainland, then trucked through Glen Bhaltos and on to the outskirts of Stornoway. The local contractor had got done for running lorries without tail-lights.

That's why there wasn't a lot happening behind the gate, when morning light came to the flat sky. Even the single enemy vehicle, still operational, was trapped in rather than trapped out. The guys imported with it had read the signs and assumed there was no chance of overtime this first Saturday. So they'd all hit the spots the night before, while we were conserving energy.

But this blessed Inspector used all his contacts to get some action going. We hadn't thought to guard the side entrance and that one truck got out and filled up from the depot with its single load. Then it showed up at the main entrance we were blockading. To us, it looked as if this lonely wagon really had made the dawn journey from Carinish quarry.

The Inspector's motive was complex. The word is that he felt the police force in this whole area were a bit lacking in experience of crowd situations. None of them were veterans of Toxteth or Notting Hill, Wapping or the Murdoch Empire. Police, the country over, needed a bit of training. This was the local opportunity. A show-down with the miners was on the cards. And this was a mobile service.

It's possible that he was also being considerate to us, knowing that the Catch 22 at the tail-end of the Inquiry (verdict overturned in view of the National Interest) had detracted from the principal purpose of letting everybody let off steam. So he could allow folk to lie down in front of a lorry for a day and then they'd really feel they'd done all they could. As long as everybody behaved themselves.

As the actions of Messrs Bonaparte and Schicklgruber indicate, historical missions are beyond reason. The latter is Hitler to us. His olman changed his second name thirteen years before Adolf was born. That small action might have had a huge effect. Heil Schicklgruber just doesn't have the ring. Mind you, Comrade Stalin wasn't always called that either.

But Russia was the enemy now. That's why Stornoway could plug the Atlantic Gap for Nato.

Our own small historical event was a good day out. Lewis light finally broke on the zinc of that gate. The Inspector used his tannoy to voice the contemporary version of the riot act. We calmly followed, in the ritual, as arranged.

The old oily proved inadequate. I remember the initial cold, seeping through to the backside. Then I was past caring. A police-man's voice in my ear, still quite reasonable but a bit cheesed off. 'Don't you think you've made your point now? My back's not that great.'

'No, sorry, not really. We've got to follow this through. Careful with your back, though. Remember to keep it straight while you're dragging me.'

I remember the smell of the diesel and the sound of the engine but didn't see the wheels turning. Maybe the driver had been asked to rev the thing for a bit of realism. That cop really did me a favour. It was getting cold again from underneath. He'd hoped to avoid this – it wasn't just getting your hands dirty but everybody looking at you and cameras and things. Probably a crofter's son who'd been sickened of tattie-planting and peat lifting and gone for a clean job. So he manhandled me to the van, quite gently, really.

'Is your back still OK, mate?'

'Aye. We'll survive.'

I was in the first batch of the arrested – six or so of us in the Sherpa. I'd been separated from Gabriele. Our lot was driven towards the quay. 'How do you like driving the diesel, then?' somebody asked and the woman constable at the wheel said it was OK on a long trip, a bit heavy round town.

'And are we going on a long trip?'

'Only as far as Barlinnie,' she said.

We were driven to the quay.

'The ferry leaves in half an hour,' said the constable in the back. One of the arrested replied, 'Are you keen on Westerns, then?' And the woman constable turned to say, as it happened she loved them and did we know that John Wayne was from Ness. I did, the others didn't. Maybe that was a police trap for finding out if you were local.

So we were out in the sun at Number One pier, where the Queen had landed and a decorated lamp had been long since installed to mark the spot. There was no rule of the game to say you couldn't go back for another shot. This was like the cooling-off period in ice hockey. So we started to walk. We were recognised by a sympathiser driving a van and given a lift to do it all again.

That's why we missed the chocolate digestives which the second arrested party, including Gabriele, were treated to, at the station. She told me they were apologetic at Kenneth Street, not really prepared. So they handed round the cups of tea and the sergeant got the cleaner to run across the road to J and E's for the biscuits. A human touch, though we were all running through this exercise like hamsters.

No-one did anything sillier than getting their arse wet in public. More importantly, the course of the Inquiry slowed everything down long enough for further histories to play their part. The runway and the pier were completed and very welcome too, for civilian use. Installation of the hardened shelters is still somewhere on the books as a NATO project. Each year, the matter has been quietly shelved. But maybe we can risk saying that the idea of Stornoway as a key operational Nato airbase has died a death.

There was the Saddam factor, the Gadaffi, the proliferation idea but everyone except the UK government seemed to realise that the multi-warhead system developed against you-know-who wasn't quite the thing for other threats. The hard old reds might make a comeback on a tide of disillusion, the magic market being kind of a fickle business – but it's difficult to see how all these Tridents, aimed at all these cities, in all these new countries, could change things.

Those first stages, at the airport, gave us a new fishing mark. You could now line the grey and white shack, conspicuous at Branahuie with the third pillar of that amazing Nato pier. Then you kept Arnish lighthouse open on Holm to let you drift over a bank which can still yield a few small whitings. If the trawlers haven't been over them first.

Maybe by the time I shed the mortal, the trawling will be over. We'll be back to hooks and lines and small fish swimming free.

Who knows, maybe the Nato pier and pipeline is taking all the fuel for the Island, safely clear of the harbour terminal that's only a whispering distance from the town centre? There might be coin-slot telescopes organised by the Holm Community. German and Japanese and maybe Russian tourists could be scoffing their fill of mussels and scallops and razorfish, further down the pier.

You can just see all their heads turning to look seaward, out on a bearing to the Shiants. Catching a glimpse of a white-beaked or a white-sided dolphin. A pod of the heavy grey Risso's dolphin was resident, between Holm Point and Tiumpan Head. That was in the year we kept Nato out. But there have been few sightings since. We don't yet know all the factors which determine the migrations of these fellow mammals.

Emcee

I always got on OK with Emcee. Marek Cybulski, to give the cove his full name. He was in the class above us at school but he repeated French and History so I got a yarn with him, now and again. His olman was in the Air Force and met a blone from Lewis. His number was up.

When other guys were trying to lose their cherry and I was looking for a pattern to this world, Emcee took me down the bottom of Kenneth Street. I mean all the way down, just before it joins Scotland Street and slides its way downhill, to Bayhead. You passed the copshop, next door to the Lodge, on your right, and then went up a wee close behind the priest's house. There was a painted wooden building.

You won't see it now. It burned down – no foul play suspected – and they built a proper church, with laminated timber beams and all that. There's some interesting church architecture on Lewis but most of it's out of town. Like the place on the Peninsula. Amazing modernist building in the middle of peat banks and bungalows. They say one of the elders had a cousin in the States who was an architect and wanted to do something for the old community. The plans might have come buckshee but it put the breakaway group on the map, all right. All these splits in the church have been good for the Island building industry. Unless these guys are doing it buckshee, too. In return for a pass through the pearly gates. I don't think so.

The long, wooden hut, now replaced, was the official Catholic church. I'd been there once, with another mate, but that was just to a discussion evening. I went to a mass with Marek. It was a bit fancy for me but they were all friendly enough, after all the ritual. Can't be any more strange than what happens up the road. On the square. Honest, I've never been in any further than the bar. I only know what that guy Pierre told me, in *War and Peace*. I got asked along a couple of times, but that was much later, when I became a proper Coastguard. I don't think you qualified, being an auxiliary out on the cliffs or in the boat team.

The thing was, I got asked back home for scoff. It was amazing. Marek's olman was doing the cooking. That's a thing you never saw, on Lewis, unless you were on a fishing boat. I still remember the Sunday dinner. Wee bits of dark rye bread with dried salami, strings still attached. Then there was pork. The crackling was cracking and there was something sweet and something spicy there. There was cabbage, still crisp, with fennel seeds through it. Baked onions, stuffed with cloves.

I wanted to ask about wine becoming blood. I wanted to ask about the aircraft stationed on the Island during the war. But Marek's olman looked to his smiling wife and talked about the foxtrots they used to do, to the brass band.

A few years went by and I was on the bones of the bachoochie, not long out of Uni. I bumped into Emcee and he said, 'Hi Caulay, what's fresh?' He told me they could do with a KP in the Crown. I was up for it, as long as they'd let me off whenever there was a shout for the coast-rescue team. He was the main man on the pans and I was washing them. It's true what they say. He used every flicking one of them, every time, lunch or dinner.

I was in the Crown for about a year. All the seasons. Summer was shit, watching other guys chug by, out to the fishing. March was good, out of the wind that came from the Baltic. I felt good, putting your cold hands into water that was as hot as you could bear. Then there was the grub. Most of it was pretty plain stuff, roasts and stews and fries but Marek would do a special now and again. Word was getting around, it was the thing to go for, but if there was any of it left, that's what I always went for, when we took the staff lunch, job done.

This day, he put me on the spot. The sous-chef didn't turn up so I was giving a hand, stirring sauces and stuff. Then it came to our own grub and Marek says, 'Surprise me, Westview boy.' Flick's sakes, the same cove would be doing potato pancakes baked crisp with artichokes in a white sauce and all that.

'See what's left in the box,' he said. That was the mixed box of fish, sent over from the other end of the hoil. That time most of the hotels just bought boxes of frozen prawns and boxes of fillets, ready to deep-fry. Marek was up on the game. He was doing brill and megrim and serving up fish that looked like fish.

I was in luck. A few red gurnard pouted at me, spiny amongst the slimy stuff. The heads of monks, with their angling tackle and their wicked teeth. Marek would have kept them for the stock of his seafood soup. But he wasn't getting these guys intact.

'All right, you're on, but nothing fancy. Dangler's style.'

The new fibreglass sea angling club boat had a Calor Gas cooker with two burners and a grill for toast. Sometimes we knocked a mackerel or two on the head and threw them to the frying pan.

There was always a great wee knife handy. I put a new edge to it and attacked the heads. The cheeks take a bit of prodding out but soon I had enough. Gurnard are amazing looking things, armour plated, but I knew how to hold them so the spines in the back of the gills didn't catch you when you were watching for the ones on the dorsal. The blade found the backbones and followed them till it whistled out at the tails. 'Never mind that salad oil shit,' I heard myself saying. I just wanted light oil without any taste in itself. There was parsley, dill and chives, from Marek's window-boxes, out the back. I had these all finely chopped in the lemon butter.

You want to just sear the naked side then turn it to let the skin side fry itself till it's just about crisp but you can still see the red. Turn it to serve that way up. Meanwhile you've turned the monks' cheeks for a minute, in the oil. Let the herb butter trickle over them but aside from the red gurnard. That's the dish, simple as that. It got me the sous-chef job.

The pace was good when we got going and I learned a lot. Scariest day was when I made the borscht for our lunch. I'd made it when I was at Uni because it fed a few folk for a few bob and it looked good in the bowl. Marek tuned it up for me. You've to sauté the grated beetroot and waxy tatties long enough and slow enough. And like everything else, the stock's the secret. And that wee bit of lemon to cut the sweetness of the veg.

I went back with Marek a couple of times to catch his olman's yarn. The food was something else and once I did taste the borscht he'd been brought up on. That made me realise I was only half a cook and I'd never be able to put the hours in to get really good. See the intensity of that shade of broth and the surprise of its flavours on your tongue. But I never did ask the question I was thinking. I couldn't find the words to ask either Marek or the ex-airman if they really did believe that the wine became actual blood.

Peace and Plenty

Me and Gabriele never did consummate our union at sea but we came close. That blone didn't mind a fair bit of swell running. She was swaying slightly, to the motion. She'd let her hair grow but not by much. It was thick and brown and bobbed, plastered by rain on her light-coloured face. Then she'd come snuggling in closer.

Hang on, somebody's got to work the tiller.

The more variable the wave pattern the better, for her. Off the port-hand buoy at Arnish, at Low Water, with seas rolling in from the southeast. Out a bit from the fallen old concrete beacon at the limit of the reef. The shallowing always interrupts the wave length of the longer seas and shifts the shapes of the waters.

If we made it out past the Tob and the Bo to Loch Erisort we'd meet some even more confused seas off Stac Ranais, wind against tide. Maybe we'd decide to run into Loch Griomsiadair. I never needed much persuasion for that.

I think I caught Gabriele with an unused longline. I never thought she'd stay on this Island, once her official year-off was over. It's easy to be adventurous when you've a job to go back to.

But I told her how my olman's fishing gear was past it. I wouldn't have wanted to risk losing it anyway. But the scummaig, the wooden holder, was now filled by a replacement. Ruaraidh had a more recent one in his shed. When he'd had his retirement do, from the Poy-oy (General Post Office), one of his first moves was to go into the Lewis Crofters for a cotton small-line with ninety haddock hooks. But his mates in the Legion laughed at him. There was nothing to be caught on the East Side now. Join the club and go west like they did in the movies. The new line would have stayed hanging as a

symbol in his hallway. So he'd asked his nephew to throw it out and
see if the trawlers had left anything worth buttering the frying pan
about. Mind you, now he'd be claiming his share if we did.

That was a story you could be drawn into. Is that what it's about?
All our individual narratives frapping in the breezes, Baltic, North
Sea, Minch, Atlantic. Finding your place in another person's story.
So the eventual and necessary touch is only consolidating that.

I think I was for dropping that strange sail that came with the
boat. There were mounts for an inboard in the *Peace and Plenty* but
the old petrol engine had been fussy to run. It had been lifted out
by the previous owner. My hand kept going down to the space,
looking for a gear lever.

Gabriele stayed on the tiller, putting the helm down while I
backed the foresail against the main as instructed.

'This is not what the new woman means,' she said. 'Only gaining
respect by taking on the men at their own games.'

But she also said she liked this sort of thing. She'd learned it
young and it had stuck.

The terms for fish flew, then. I was trying to get a ling into words.
Bit like a sea-pike. '*Hecht*.'

'We'll have to catch one,' she said. 'A visual aid.'

This was a bo, a submerged reef that wouldn't dry in any combination of conditions and tidal sequence we could predict. Round the
corner, into the loch, there were reefs that dried and covered. These
are the ones you've got to watch. You can't take your eye off these
devious bastards. But we set our line while we were still over deeper
water. Gabriele wondered how I could tell, without an echo sounder.

The marks told us we were at the edge of that bo. We'd lose
hooks, for sure, but they were easily replaced. I'd rigged the line with
a buoy at both ends to give two chances of recovery, if it snagged.

That sequence went out miraculously, sweet as my memory of it.
Strips from the flank of a few expensive herring went down in an
orderly fashion to the stranger strata near the bottom. Now that's
real gambling, sacrificing the nourishment a herring provides for a
possible greater yield.

We'd to leave it an hour or so. So we did head into the loch. You had to recognise Sgeir Linish. See it now while the tip was dry. It would become harder to spot when the swell was breaking over it. We'd have to watch for it, both of us, when we came round, out the loch on the other tack. There wasn't a lot of sea room. Would that be a reach in and a reach out? I deferred on sailing matters to her much greater experience.

Had I done this with my own father?

'Only in his story,' I told her. Suffice to say he'd been keen on the sea but something had happened. A near disaster. Sometimes you had to skip a generation. It was all magnetism, attraction or repulsion.

Her own father could be a case-study on the rebuilding of Germany. Their own house was to prove a very sound investment – a good building of structural integrity at the edges of the fast-developing city of Bonn.

There were all these evenings at the drawing board, which took over the attic area of the house. The floored loft of a converted barn. Their mother never really liked it – the obligations of her husband's career were inescapable. Their own living space was too much part of his vision. His designs were original but not flashy. They usually had a good vernacular structure as a basis.

But when he sailed alone with his daughter, he told her of his dry baptism into navigation. It was by the pole star only but that was enough. Like thousands of the other survivors of the Wehrmacht, he was a shadow on the retreat from what is now part of Poland. It was all the Reich to them, then. Not for long. The Red Army was advancing fast. Desertion was almost certain death.

But he and his best friend whispered to each other. If they stayed, it was definite death. Just because you saw something coming didn't mean you could stop it happening. They delayed too long. The survivors of their unit were surrounded and exhausted and starving. They were rounded up and marched. They were being taken to a central camp. He'd heard the stories. They all said much the same. Once you were driven through a gate and kept behind wire, that was it. No-one would crawl out of that.

They'd all seen what had happened in Russia before the tide had turned. The situations he had not been able to photograph. The advancing Germans had starved their Russian prisoners. It was a very efficient and cost-effective method, perhaps learned from Comrade Stalin's own methods of dealing with the kulags who resisted handing everything over to the State. Or had they resisted handing over the food, because they were already starving?

So what could the German prisoners expect now that they were the ones behind the wire? It took a lot of organisation and resources to feed that amount of prisoners. Why should they keep Nazi murderers alive?

Burned fields didn't yield very much food. Once they went behind the barbed wire, into the collection area, that was it.

He might not have been able to do anything to break out of the script that was written for him if he had been alone. But his fellow student from the architecture class had also survived this far. They shook hands on it. They would crawl off into the woods together and take their chance.

So they waited till the vodka ration was issued to their guards, in the evening. That took effect quickly. They listened for the drunken singing then they crawled low to the icy ground and then kept on walking. They always walked at night. Mainly through woodlands, looking through the branches for navigational marks. Their route back, a bit south of west, was in relation to that one star. Follow the line of the handle up. Fix it from there. It worked. They came out in Innsbruck.

And the rest of the regiment? Their estimate had been right. Not one of the others found a way home.

He'd picked up the pieces and, like his old classmate, worked at repairs and rebuilding. The other survivor went on to specialise in public buildings. They met in the summers, on the Baltic coast. Family men, both of them.

Your telling of your father's story took us through the narrows into the inner loch. Now the outboard was behaving better, with its prop in the water most of the time. You could see the lines of disused lazy-beds, running down to the shore. All these ribs of ground, still showing green, as far as the rusty kelp. The boiler from a steam-drifter lay beside the rocks. The ground here hadn't been tilled for years. But there were a few cattle, beasts among the sheep. Maybe the village and a lot of others like it had never really recovered from the First War before the Second hit it further. How could they have known that the First had nothing to do with them? If they had stayed and others like them, East and West Coasts of Scotland, Lowlanders, Coldstreams, Welsh Guards and all – maybe there wouldn't have been that Second? Pointless to speculate, in the peace of this inlet, with our anchor holding us over deep mud.

When we headed out again, the wind that should have been at a right angle to the boat was right on our nose. It might not have shifted much. Even if I didn't know much about sailing, I knew it tends to funnel down sea-lochs. But I was running with Gabriele's story as much as with the wind. And in matters of sailing I was always to defer to her. The Lewis sailors of open boats must have possessed skills second to none. And their knacks and knowledge were all lost in one generation.

The course we could sail was too fine to clear the entrance with a safe margin. We'd to dip an oar more than once to tack clear. This was when we needed a bearing to clear the skerries. We had that. This is the situation where you want a decent inboard engine. We didn't have that and the outboard kept whining when the prop lifted right out of the water.

Wind and tide had both been on the move while we'd been tracing her olman's navigation from the Eastern Front to Innsbruck. Stories are dangerous. Now there were white horses all across the loch. So it was difficult to see which was the warning white, breaking directly around the covered reef. And which was innocent white.

I got the sail and spars down and lashed everything tight while Gabriele held her nose in to the weather with one oar out. Then I took the second oar and we made way. With the outboard helping from time to time. Long steady pulls were the answer. First we seemed to be just holding our own but then the skerry was astern and we had sea room for a fine reach, with a reef in the sail now.

Back on the tiller, she picked her moment to tell me I'd need to get a stronger outboard engine for next season. She said she shouldn't really be rowing for much longer now.

Glancing down at the belly of her oilies and gasping. Recovering. We could call that quits for me saying we might just as well get married, when the letter from the Home Office said that she should not have been claiming any benefits. Deportation was the next step.

We were both laughing. Maybe I'd already known, somehow. And to consolidate everything, there were three ling on my uncle's line, cast from my own olman's scummaig. Two haddock would have been truly biblical but these would do. Not a very economic return for the man, woman, boat and baby hours expended. But we hadn't used much in the way of fossil fuel. One for us, to share with my mother who had long since overcome the East Coast prejudice for cod. One for my uncle who gave us the line. One for a young guy we'd met on the Goat Island shore. He was doing up another clinker boat and given us some non-slip red for our tiny foredeck. It now looked sharp against the rest of the boat in navy grey.

That should have been it, a simple yarn, with a few droppers dangling off the main thread – a small-line of stories. But I showed you another ritual when we had the boat back on the mooring. This was normally done at the shore but as we were staying at the same address, it was easier to perform on the doorstep. I put down some newspapers from a pile of recent ones and separated the three ling. Laid them out on the printed sheets. You had to turn your back. Then you, as the youngest aboard, had to tell me one of the three names as I pointed to a fish you couldn't see. So it was as fair as it could be, who got what.

But Gabriele got sidetracked and missed her cue. She'd glanced at the papers she hadn't bothered with before. A front-page story in the *West Highland Free Press* caught her.

It was a protest from the Irish government. Yet another leak from Windscale, now Sellafield. Yes, I said, this is a British way of problem solving. You don't reassess things, which is far too messy a process, you just change the name.

Gabriele didn't smile because there was a map on the page with projected tidal currents setting northeast to meet with Cape Wrath and another story. This time the protest came from the Norwegian government, over the reprocessing plant at Dounreay.

'Yes, they haven't changed that name yet because they're looking for international business,' I said. 'But they've changed the name of the ship that carries its waste down the Minch. Everyone got to know the *Kingsnorth Fisher* so she was re-named *New Generation*. Never mind though, a decent radiation leak from the Other Side and we could blame the lot on that.'

Like the pollution in the Elbe. The powers in West Germany said it was all from the East.

Then there was one of those far-fetched chances that happens to be true. She was looking down on the paper I'd opened up, to wrap our own ling. Her hand went down to hold it open on a page. Neither of us had noticed it before. A proposed Superquarry bringing jobs to the Bays of Harris. To maximise the potential of the site, the resulting hole could be filled with harmless waste from Hamburg. As one bulk-carrier went seaward, taking high-grade anorthosite to the West German market, another would arrive to disperse low-grade industrial silt.

An efficient idea.

'The Elbe is one of the most contaminated waters in Europe,' she said. Protesters in Germany made an alliance from the Rhine to the Elbe. To show that their concern was not just the local issue.

So the industrial waste she had protested against might follow her around the fringes of the continent. All these traces of metals, the ones which induce cauliflower growths on eels. From the North Sea to the Little Minch.

Invasions usually cause some deaths. Organisms are attacked by aggressive others who have to establish themselves. Some people argue that beggars can't be choosers. The Harris Tweed industry was seriously frayed and the fishing industry was in a terminal crisis.

We couldn't live on fresh island air. But the plan to establish the largest quarry in Europe did not in fact go ahead. So there was no huge influx of either ballast water or landfill. And Gabriele went on to bring one additional new life to the Island.

Ordnance

I'd been accepted to train as a full-time Regular Coastguard Officer. We'd not long been offered the Coastguard house on Leverhulme Drive. We had a bairn on the way and I was earning a bit more than the Queen's shilling. It was walking distance from the olaid's new council house, where we'd shared the back room.

'It's no that your nae welcome but I dinna want to be on top o ye,' she said. 'And it could jist be that I've been used to hivin a wee bit space. I dinna mind yer Gabriele like.'

That's the East Coaster's way of showing love and affection.

I was working my way back into the town after the years of being back and fore. Wanting to be a part of its pulse.

'What's fresh?'

'You're seeing it. Yourself?'

We'd just met in town. The uncle took me for a dram in the Legion. He was grabbing his chance in case I went back to all that religious stuff. So it was a large Dewars and a half of Export. Each. That was his order. I had money in my pocket to ask for the same again.

I'd only recently re-started taking any alcohol. I knew I was out of practice but I remembered that there's that point of no return. Like in love and affection. And it sometimes comes across you a bit suddenly. Like in love and affection. So we went out for a stroll after he'd topped up the drams again and we'd sunk those.

If we were seriously interested in the historical aspects of the town, we should go and have a look at the Opera House, Ruaraidh said.

'The what?'

'The South Beach pissoire.' Maybe I was too young to have swilled hot whisky and cold beer, down the neck and then out against the wall. He'd spent a wee bit of his own life pissing against walls.

We walked to the end of the pedestrian precinct then risked a route across. Ignoring the indicators of fast Fords. Escorts now. They used to be Cortinas.

'Cairo is the only other town where they drive like this.'

'I've never been there,' I told Ruaraidh, 'but I've driven with someone who has.'

Then my uncle told me one more variation on the story of the guy who went to the gates of heaven.

This cove, a good Free Kirker all his life. He kicks it. He's up the road at the gates waiting for St Peter to finish a yarn with the guy in front. It's taking a hell of a time and the good man looks ahead and notices it's a brown-skinned gentleman and they're talking on and on, even though the cove's already through the gate. He's getting a bit impatient so he just says, 'Scuse me, Peter, my friend, sorry to interrupt but, there's just a wee formality here and then you can carry on with the old conversation.'

But Peter and the other guy are just blethering on so the Free Kirker says, 'Now excuse me gentlemen but, I've been a paid up member all my life and hardly missed a service and I've borne witness and —' 'No, you excuse, me,' says Peter. 'I have a conversation to complete with this good man, Abdul.'

'What's so special about Abdul,' the Free Kirker says, 'that you can wave him through and yarn away all day and keep me hanging on out here?'

'Since you ask,' says Peter, 'Abdul used to be a taxi driver in Cairo and he's put the fear of God into a lot more people than you have.'

And in Cuba they keep the wide and long Oldsmobiles and Chevrolets on the road because they have nothing to replace them with, their wings shiny as in the days when Kennedys were Knights.

'I watched a moon-landing in this town, no not a moon descending on the town. Hell, you know what I mean, Ruaraidh.

Squeezed it in between cycling back from Holm, me and Kenny, with tails of mackerel, haddock and flounder beating a song in our spokes. Staying with you guys for the summer. You let me watch BBC2. They got Pink Floyd to do space age music. We called it Underground. While we looked to the heavens. No wonder so many people's grannies still believed the whole thing was set up in a studio in London or Cape Kennedy.

'We were all talking about how crazy it was with Biafra going on and then we all shut up when the footage happened. Think of that still from Glen's Hasselblad.

'Then, just a few days after the moonwalk, splashdown. And that was the day Senator Edward walked, on this earth, away from a drowning car sinking into Chappaquiddick. Mary Jo sank with it. Put to the Democratic-ish test, he was re-affirmed as the candidate. He won and his majority was only slightly down on '64. The power of the Kennedy myth remained but the big dream of the dynasty was all over.'

'Hell of a story to tell me when we're trying to cross a road,' Ruaraidh said. 'Any road. But hell, this road?'

So the uncle and me were now two wanderers. OK, you're supposed to say so and so and I. It doesn't sound too good in the SY twang. All these years, all these teachers, good ones among them, and they never quite got me out of it.

One of the best of all was in the Clock School. We were a family in her classroom and you still nod to folk you recognise, in their greying hair. Frostiest time of the Cold War. Of course, we guys were still all Uri Gargarins. Did you know that our hero was 5ft 2ins tall, by the way?

The Opera House was still standing but only just, near Number Two Pier, across from the Weighbridge. A stink from the joined forces of whisky and ammonia still hung in the air around it. A stout wooden barrier bolted across the entrance. The Opera House WAS OUT OF ORDER.

'See that gate,' Ruaraidh said. 'It would keep a herd of bloody elephants at bay. But that's not enough. There has to be that sign as well. It says a lot, that additional KEEP OUT.'

We went to the café. Me and my mates all got banned from these in our day. They all changed their names as the next generation took over. Cabrelli's became The Town House, Scaramouchie's became The Coffee Pot.

The seat's got to be where you can look out, see who's going by, Ruaraidh reckoned. You flirt with muesli, revert to oatmeal porridge, not the flakes. But eggs are probably best. Two of them. Poached ones are all right but fried ones are better. He could remember when they were scarce.

'The telephone's a handy instrument, by the way,' he said. 'It's a long peatbank. That was a hint, young man.'

One to cut and one to throw. It was great, swinging them to fall with an inch between each one and delicate thuds sounding out to say they were mostly landing fine.

As for the cutting, I hadn't done too bad, once I started getting the iron closer in, flush to the wall of the bank. I must have had a good teacher. Or else it was genetic. No disrespect but you could always recognise an incomer's peatbank. Usually tried to re-invent the whole procedure. Unless they'd teamed up with the right squad. It could be funny until a sheep drowned in it. You're making a new edge, for next year, as you go along. And the village inspection committee would of course be studying what we'd done. So we shouldn't be too proud to adopt some kind of pride.

'Cutting peats is a piece of piss,' I said. 'It's holding your own in the philosophy, the religious, sexual and political discussions while driving a razor-sharp, long iron down to its hilt – that's what takes a bit of concentration.'

But we both had all five fingers and toes, port and starboard sides intact, with the job complete.

And then we strolled over to that loch, the deep one over the ridge. Ruaraidh said that stories came from it like vapours. Maybe the last water-horse was still down there.

In the village, the word was a Heinkel had gone over. Hadn't found a target out the Atlantic and had to drop its heavy load somewhere if it was going to get back. Someone heard the controlled thunder of engines, the loose whine of a falling weapon. But then a delay. Only the engines fading distant. No explosion. They'd gone out next day and hunted the moor. They'd want to find it sooner rather than later, not hit it with an iron, at the peats. Not a trace. No new mud. No visible holes in the wet coat of the Lewis moor.

But all eyes went to that deep loch. If there wasn't a sign of it anywhere else, it might be there still. That bomb might not be dead yet. Our lives could still be affected by the ordnance from a war that was growing distant.

The Gynaecologist

A pal of mine went for one of the ex-Health-Board houses. They were in a group, not so far from Westview Terrace. Nice part of town and in good reach of the Lewis Hospital. It was a good buy. There was a lot of timber under the roof. It was Welsh slate, outside that, and the construction was solid. Like the Coastguard houses. You felt bad at taking advantage of the offer at the time but whatever you said, the next guy was going to buy it. If by any chance he didn't, it would be sold on the open market.

These were the houses reserved for those with useful occupations. The teachers' houses on Ripley Place. The nurses' cottages on Westview. Police houses on Balmerino Drive.

But see, when it came to the plumbing in this house, he was expecting a nightmare of different layers of additions since the Sixties. But no, every pipe was labelled. Every tap, every twist and turn, joint and elbow. He said to me, 'I think this must have been the gynaecologist's house.'

I remember a gynaecologist from when I was a hospital porter for a year. He was very proud of his machines. He gave me dirty looks, for my cornering style. I remember this day, giving a young lad who was long-term sick, a spin round with me – a suggestion from one of the sisters. He was a born teacher, telling me the Gaelic for 'This way North' and 'That way South' and the lefts and rights. We didn't come that close really but parked up behind the machine outside Maternity. Too close for the gynaecologist. He had these classic authoritarian eyebrows and he told us exactly how much that machine had cost.

When it came to Gabriele's scans, it was probably the replacement model for that machine – so of course a lot more compact. That's the way machines go. I've a very early hand-held GPS and you couldn't fit it in a pocket. They cost a grand when they were new, about the mid-Nineties.

Anyway, when I was showing the new porter round, before going back to Uni, he thought the consultant was the day porter. That was the guy who was into sailing and vans and would stop for a cup of tea and a yarn with you. The gynaecologist was never so familiar. It's very educational, observing a hierarchy from the bottom.

Gabriele had an issue with his dates. This was a bit crucial for us because our son was due right in the middle of the Coastguard Training Course which we hoped would help feed him and educate him. We knew he was a son because the gynaecologist told us. But he didn't ask us if we wanted to know. I was a bit pissed off but Gabriele was livid. I had to press on her arm a bit to calm things down. Then she tackled him on the dates again. His answer is burned into my memory: 'I have never known this machine to be wrong.'

So we drove down to Bristol and swung on to Christchurch. We had found a cottage to rent, out of season but the occupants were caught up in a chain of buying and selling houses. Everyone was talking about buying and selling houses. The Coastguard houses on Leverhulme Drive were being modernised – double-glazing and central heating from piped gas – but we'd been promised one, soon after the end of the eight-week course. So we found an out-of-season holiday apartment for our nest. It was clean and fine and close to the river.

We'd drive to Boscombe hospital for checks and visits. But our son was not born there. Though Gabriele did give birth there. It was not an easy birth.

The labour took about twenty-four hours and all issues about natural childbirth and waterbaths so the new baby could swim soon after birth – these did not seem very important any longer. So when I went into uncontrollable laughter when our baby was born, the staff must have thought it was simply the relief after all that tension.

Our son was a healthy girl. One arrogant bastard and his machine had been proven wrong. He must have just taken a glance at the scan, peering under all that hair in his eyebrows.

So this is of course a memory of the beginning of a new life. Though a strong case could be argued for seeing the event as a death. Whether you want to or not, you have an idea in your mind, suggested by the abrupt words of someone in authority. So the idea of that son died when our Anna appeared. That stage of the game I don't think either of us could have cared what sex our baby turned out to be. Except that it was a very good result.

Gynaecologist nil. Anna one.

Flights

Razorfishing depends on the day and what's gone before it. An Atlantic depression will bump up the High Water, way above the predicted level. Wind-driven current, from a spell of strong southerlies, will hold back the tide, preventing the ebb from going as far back as it wants to. Tides are strange things. They can be predicted up to a point but events in distant geographies exert their influence.

You need a big, spring tide – one of only a handful in the year when the ebb goes far enough back – with calm, mild weather. No rain. You'll see the same faces at the shore. Everyone nods to a new arrival then returns to their own small area of patrol. It's a blood sport but the red you notice, leaking into the sand, is more likely to have come from the top of your own hand, when you've made an eager stab.

If you do get enough razorfish, you place them in a shallow container, maybe a lasagne dish. You pour the kettle, making sure they're all covered. They'll open. Meanwhile you've the cold tap running. You rinse them. This flushes the sand out and stops them from cooking further. If you leave them in the hot water too long they'll get tough. I've seen a TV chef, handsome chap, make an arse of it. Delicate things till you overdo them and then they're about the texture of a wellington boot.

There's a sandy gut to remove. You do this while the butter is melting in a skillet. Crushed garlic if you like it and a twist of black pepper. It's like making omelettes. Everyone's got to be ready to eat. You pat them dry and then just turn them in the seasoned butter. That's it.

I say all this just so you understand that we really wanted to leave the house and get to that shore, Gabriele as much as me. If you don't catch that hour, either side of the turn of the tide, you might as well not bother. I abandoned the dishes, unwashed in the sink, as Gabriele was hunting through the row of wellies for a pair which still fitted Anna.

The phone went. I was crashed from our kitchen into Glasgow, at the sound of my mate's voice. I was back in touch with Kenny F. He was living in a high-rise in Maryhill, very appropriate for a scaffolder. And staying sober, a good idea in that trade. I'd bumped into Angus, in town, and he'd given me the number. I hadn't given it long before asking the favour. Since he wasn't a kick in the arse from the city, could he take Anna's papers, photo and details direct to the Passport Office? The timing was tight. Delays were expected but if you got someone to go along in person…Kenny had indeed been along in person. That fucking office was Kafkaland. Something else. He'd already been an hour over his lunch break when he was given a card which said 'Turn No. 83'. He'd tried to explain that all the papers were ready with franked photographs but the woman was harassed and told him to wait his turn. He couldn't do it. He couldn't get off the site, long enough, during the day. It might not be the best job in the world but it was a job. Only thing he could think of now was to give a few quid to a mate who wasn't working, get him to queue.

'I took a look, of course,' Kenny said. 'The photos. The wife and the kid. Isn't your lady German? Quite tidy, by the way. I thought they were supposed to be organised, I mean with dates and stuff.'

'Exception that proves the rule?' I said it though I'd never understood that idea. 'Thanks anyway, man. Thanks for trying. Hold on. Gabriele's decision.'

She shook her head. So I asked Kenny if he could just post the whole lot to the Passport Office, registered. We'd take our chance.

What was I up to anyway, apart from international wheeling and dealing? 'Razorfishing.'

He wished I hadn't said that. Pity I couldn't send him some. Put some on the plane, maybe, like they do with lobsters. Remember the raw clams off the line on Broad Bay? But it would only take a delay of an hour or two and they'd be higher than we'd ever got.

He'd just need to come up and get some. They still printed the tides in the *Gazette* when they remembered.

'I'll see if I can swing it.'

Was he coming to visit, Gabriele asked, when I put the phone down and I said, no, only promising to. He could cope with it if he kept his distance. There was no work for him here and he went crazy with boredom after a while.

Gabriele said she'd need to cancel. There was no way she could organise a passport for Anna in time. There was an international panic going on.

Anna didn't like hanging about after we decided to get going somewhere. It took a while to get boots and hats and everything arranged but now she was kitted out and looking in despair at her mother dialling numbers. I lifted her, wellies and all, though there was a taboo on them in the living room. We went over to see what we could see, out the window. Bushes were only wavering. Nothing was bent over. Looking good, if we could get down there. Some brightness warming the equinoctial sky. It was ten minutes to Low Water but we'd have an hour the other side, if we got shifting.

Gabriele came off the phone. The girl who'd dealt with the booking was out to lunch. Someone else took a note. She didn't have the details. Best to call back later.

We drove to the shore at Holm. These excavations struck you again, even though you knew they were there. I said how the sight was not as hard to take as the first time we saw all the earth-moving equipment getting stuck into the quiet bay. Now there was some sign of the road being restored, with huge boulders being shoved to the sides to shore it up against tides that might advance further than they'd been known to come before.

I caught Gabriele looking again at the small house, last one before the water, down a croft. It was now renovated to make a holiday home. She said she'd risk it, a few metres increase from global warming, to have that outlook.

We turned our backs on the roadworks. We saw Holm as we'd

known it. From here, the airport, across Branahuie Bay, looked as sleepy as it used to. You didn't see the new constructions.

Slight and variable wind hadn't held the ebb back. A huge expanse of Branahuie was exposed. The piles of the fuel jetty now looked stronger than ever, driven in regularly, at set angles, out to the deeper water. A road of concrete went out on the structure to about halfway along. Soon it would carry the fuel lines.

Then Nato would at last have the ability to protect itself in the Atlantic Gap, from here to Iceland. Well, not quite. There was still the final phase, which was the most expensive. Installation of the missile stores and shelters. But for now, the runway extension was proving very useful for civilian flights. The construction of this fuel jetty was too far ahead to stop but could have its uses. The local word was that it would go right out to reach the mackerel in summer, codling in winter.

These Reds hadn't played by the rules at all. Move and counter-move have to be kind of predictable, fair's fair. You don't invest all these billions into an outreach of bloody, former herringville, SY, just for the planned enemy to fall apart at its own seams. The stitching holding the Soviet empire was failing – like the pale orange lines on my Levi's jacket.

So the Expansion of Runway, Extension of Facilities would benefit a few Bolshy Heb civilians and their visiting tourists. And the Nato fuel jetty would be about as useful as the World War Two Nissan huts, refusing to rust away. At least they'd had their day, sheltering the horseshide and fleece-clad flyers who'd ventured up in flying boats and seaplanes.

I felt a small weight hit my shoulder. Anna had gone off to sleep in the backpack. She'd be out for an hour now. She'd be safe enough in the child-seat in the car. We'd have it in sight, all the time.

A few figures were well spaced along the shallows. Some strolled gently, water to the ankles of their boots, plastic bags held behind their backs. Others trod backwards along the wet sand, looking for a spout raised by the pressure of their boots.

'Cartier-Bresson would have a lot of fun here,' Gabriele said. I'd seen some of the photos her father had taken. The ones she used to take, herself. I could also now see the photo that would not get taken.

The breeze was colder than it looked, from the car. We worked together and became involved. Gabriele did the backward bit. You forget how daft it is whenever there's a spout. Everybody around is quietly doing likewise. Our mood was recovering from the tension of the phone calls. I followed her and stooped fast when there was a show in the wet sand.

I'd glance my finger on a shell and be too slow. Then I'd feel one pulse, releasing the jet of water that would send it fast, deeper into the sand than you could follow. But my finger managing to nudge it against the side of its track. Gabriele would loosen the sand around it with the long trowel, until I had a safe grip. With patience, it was ours. Pull too fast and you left the meat in the sand.

Someone near me said they were deep today. I knew this cove. He had a small trawler and was having a day off. The prawns were there but the market was quiet. 'Not worth bothering, this week. Blame it on the Gulf.'

'Aye, it's some of that bloody plant up there we'd need to dig down to them, the day. JCB-assisted razorfishing.'

And the three of us glanced to the excavators, which had started again after the lunch break.

Gabriele and me looked to each other, both of us sensing the Caterpillar tracks too near our car. Digger shovels too high, up over it. We went, both of us, without saying anything. Anna was still dead to the world. But our peace of mind was gone.

I was left to the tide while Gabriele drove back with Anna. This business of the flights was worrying her anyway. She'd have to sort it out.

I knew something was up when she returned to collect me. Anna was bright again, so I sat in the back by her car seat.

'Get on OK, then?' I said to the front.

'Not really. There's a problem. No refunds. Mutti always pays for the flights but we can't ask her for that if I don't get to Germany. It's a lot of money.'

By this time I should have guessed that Gabriele was in her own dilemma. It was an increased state of alert. A car on the A9 this time of year was a more dangerous way to travel, even with a war on. Fear isn't all that rational, though – and we couldn't say it then – how it wouldn't have bothered us so much, somehow, if we were all going together, as a family, sharing our fate. But we'd used my leave. I had shifts to do and that was that.

It wasn't the best time to travel but she'd felt she had to do her best to get to Bonn this time in case it was the last time she'd see her mother. A big birthday. Michel had got in touch with the aunt and the cousins. But she'd left it too late to arrange to have Anna placed on her passport. The olaid would have helped me out but Gabriele was still breastfeeding. Not an option.

So I shifted into the driving seat when we got home, though Anna wasn't keen on letting me go away again. I left them and went down to the travel agents. These daft company clothes. I waited to speak to the right woman.

They had a special number for the Passport Office. There would be someone there, till about five. Not much time. Yes, they were through.

Not by post. A personal visit. Wait, what? Oh, that was unfortunate. Maybe the person who came had not made it clear the party was due to travel in two weeks. If someone else could come and quote this reference…

I said thanks but I'd need to make one more phone call. They nodded to the one on the desk. Kenny F was back in the flat. Early start, early finish. No overtime. Fixing some scran to make up for the missed lunch. OK, I felt guilty. Not guilty enough to stop me asking the question: had he posted the stuff?

'No.'

'That's the right answer, cove.'

My long-suffering comrade agreed as absolutely the final favour to go back to Kafkaland tomorrow lunchtime and quote this reference. It would work. And re lunches, what about a side of smoked wild fish, guaranteed illegal, posted, vacuum-sealed. Forget all that crap, chemical stuff at Glasgow Airport.

'Done.'

I felt proud. The great Lewisian network. They were shaking their heads at the travel agents' desk but not too bothered. The booking for Gabriele and Anna held. Mission accomplished. It was like going back to the elation of three-card-brag, played blind, with Kenny and me as a team on a Friday night. Go home early, skint, or get plastered. Nothing in between.

Gabriele didn't look so pleased with the news. I thought she was still doubting that this passport thing was going to happen in time. But it wasn't that. Mixed feelings about the visit. She didn't want to have to explain why she wasn't talking German to Anna. I refrained from saying how I still didn't understand that one myself.

A registered envelope arrived in the post, in time. So Gabriele had Anna's daft big passport, bound in black, to put beside her own more demure green one. I drove them to the airport, glancing across to Holm, on the way. The tides were not too huge now but still significant. It was Low Water and the ebb had left our own desert right out to the piles of the Nato pier.

I waited till the propellers were turning. Casablanca moment. Anna would be getting the royal treatment. Loving it. After all the arrangements, I was ready to get my head down.

Had a bit of a tidy up first. Breakfast dishes. Quick hoover. Things turn over when you're doing jobs like that. I thought of a prawn fisherman with his boat tied up all week, due to poor markets. The conversation. Blame it on the Gulf. No-one wanting to hang around restaurants in big hotels. There had been a scare. There was always a scare. If it wasn't Saddam, it was the other guys.

I found my oblivion. I didn't always manage a doss before the first night-shift but I was wrecked. At least there should be a break from teething now. For me, anyway. Not for Anna and Gabriele.

I woke up hot. I was seeing a shape cross a sky which was like sand. A desert landscape and the long razor-shell hurtling above it. Vapour trailing from an end but the detail of the shell amazingly clear. So clear that I could see the layers of growth, the swirls. As well as the rivets, holding the shell together. The rivets that were popping, the shell falling apart, quietly, as it continued at speed.

The Rescue of
the VAT Man

Don't trip over the VAT man. And there he was, full length on the lino, in his grey suit. A couple of bowls of crisps and stuff on the deck beside him. Of course someone had stuck a pay-slip in the saucer of nuts beside his head. Civil servants work for peanuts.

We were looking for space. The place was heaving. We were the contingency from Her Majesty's Coastguard. We arrived, the survivors of one office party, bearing gifts. A bottle of Trawler Rum and one of Grouse. Thus we could cater for most normal tastes. A space was being cleared on an office table. It was Mairi Bhan, shifting a case of McEwan's Export.

'Room for a discreet little arse here,' she said.

Then, 'Is that all you have? You're as bad as the Customs. I thought they would run to Cognac or Bison-grass, or something kind of special, half-inched from some poor bastard.'

'Fucks sake. When I was a lad there were only four drinks. Light, heavy, whisky and rum. And we managed to get pissed just the same.'

'Listen, Mr Her Majesty's flicking Coastguard in your pretty uniform, you've come a long way from Westview flicking terrace.'

She held out her glass and nodded to the rum. I said I didn't have any mixers, either. She said maybe Her Majesty's Customs could run to the Coke. But no, that team couldn't even run to Coca Cola. Good job she liked the black rum just as it came, if there was a tin of a beer to wash it down.

Mairi Bhan seemed to have forgiven me. Our first meeting

since Billy Forsyth's wasn't too hot. It was over a full pot of coffee in the galley shared by several departments. A liaison visit. We'd got talking. Was she a typist? No, she was a flicking Fisheries Officer as it happened and the Civil Service was an Equal Flicking Opportunities Employer, in case I hadn't got that yet. OK?

Things had improved over the coffee. Real McCoy. Remember Calum Sgianach's round the corner? They ground it there, the smell lingering over the worn maple counter. Her olman had developed a taste for the stuff, on his travels. A lot of folk still drank Camp then. Chicory and sugar included. It was a syrup in a bottle, like HP sauce. But there was a soldier in a kilt on the label. She'd liked going in town with himself. So now she insisted on decent coffee, any office she was working in.

The cove she was with had his head turned the other way. He was yarning with another Fisheries Officer, a guitar legend in the city of SY. I remembered his playing. Mairi's cove turned back to her, I couldn't believe it. Kenny F.

'Where the hell have you been hiding? I thought you were still in Glasgow.'

'I was but I got fed up of waiting for that side of wild fish you promised. You forgotten how to cast? That was a flicking year ago. Is the wife back in *Deutschland*?'

She was indeed. And I had knocked off the day shift with a sleeping day tomorrow before starting nights.

'I'd never have guessed you'd just come off shift. Nice braid, by the way. Must feel proud to be a servant of Her Majesty?'

I just nodded. My misspent youth was staring me in the face. He looked in pretty good shape. Considering.

'You guys have some catching up to do. Yeah, suppose you're both verging on the *bodach* stage.'

'Trainee *bodaich*. Lads really, I said. Sure I used to know Kenny F but hell, he wasn't on the orange juice in them thar days, Jim, lad. What have you done to the man?'

Kenny said he didn't mind being the driver if the crack was good.

'Thought we'd established there was none to be had? From Customs sources, anyway.'

'You can chalk that one up.'

She let that pass.

'Don't you worry about Kenny. I'll make it up to him when we get home,' she said and I got the feeling she wasn't going to be stopping to pour him a dram.

'Kenny, *a bhalaich*, let's make a deal. I won't go telling nobody bout the crazy things you done in the days of your youth if you don't tell nobody bout mine, man.'

There was a Gaelic proverb to that effect, he said, so he wouldn't go spilling the beans to Mairi Bhan about the day his so-called fucking mates left him for dead on the quay and pissed off fishing somewhere.

No and I definitely wouldn't tell nobody, man, bout the guy who went on a bender the one day in the year we'd got our flicking act together to get out to score some sea trout. But shit, I'd come in with someone, a New Arrival. I couldn't leave him swimming in this den.

I got my backside off the table and saw my colleague making conversation with another Fisheries Officer.

'This is...' I said but that's as far as I got.

'Never mind the fucking shop, do you still listen to Hendrix?'

'Strange thing is I dug out *Axis: Bold As Love* the other night and it didn't sound too bad. I can't listen to the Stones anymore. How can you take all this streetfighting talk from these bastards? Never mind my listening, do you still play the stuff?'

He nodded. 'Sure. Sometimes just for myself. Sometimes I get a shout. You still on the drums?'

I had to shake my head. Donnie, the Fisheries Officer, still had the Strat. The cove brought it out of the house when he got asked to jam but most of the time he just played for himself, the wee amp in his room.

'This guy was the best. Probably still is,' I said and my fellow Coastguard Officer politely said he'd missed out on Hendrix first time round but his kids were into it now so he was getting a taste. He wouldn't mind hearing more.

I topped their glasses and left them to it. Mairi held out hers for a rum. I kind of hesitantly offered Kenny again but you get the feeling some people know what they're saying.

'You have your dram,' he said, 'but some of us are better off without it.'

'Shit, the head's reeling,' I said. 'Not whisky, but memory. Stronger stuff, by far.'

'You got to move on. Someone, sometime did a song about that, too.'

I pushed it. Looking round, you could see that the whole room had broken up into a big number of small ceilidhs. Everyone was gabbing. Except for the VAT man. He was at rest.

'Times like this,' I said, 'people are supposed to remember what they were up to when President Kennedy got shot.'

'Go on,' Mairi Bhan said, 'take it away.'

'Yeah. I'd been at the Lifies – you know, junior Boys Brigade, uniforms and brass and string – just like the Coastguard, now. Thought I'd got away from that. Anyway, we went to Charlie's on the way home. That was Cher Ali. His son tried to get the Western Isles' first Indian Restaurant off the ground. Change from selling nylon drars and FLs but he was way too soon. We bought plates of chips there. I ate mine and went home and it was on the telly, but on the way, you could tell something was on. People talking in whispers, stopping each other in the street. Like, really mourning. Like it was somebody's brother, somebody you knew.'

Mairi poured me another Grouse, a rum for herself. Kenny got another orange juice. I caught her smile to him, looking like a promise.

She couldn't care less about John F flicking Kennedy. He had to get hold of a new bit of skirt every day. With the whole world ready to fall in about all our lugholes. It was the brother she felt for. That poor bastard was really trying to do something to stop the war and nail the Mafia. Must have been a hell of a shock for him to find that Daddie Jo had bought into the big firm and paid for elections with these same dollars. That wasn't Bobby's fault. And his death was even more weird.

Talking of death, I'd a rabbit called Floyd Patterson because they said he'd fought back and killed a cat that had a go at him when he was out of the hutch.

'What?' said Kenny, like the sober bastard he was. 'It's not everyone would see the connection. Pick a subject and we'll run with it.'

'Skip all this pseudo-historical smalltalk. What about the year of the herring ban?' Mairi Bhan said. Quite firm. Loud enough to break into the yarns going on a table away because Donnie's voice came over the top.

'No Fucking Shop.'

But he and the New Arrival were still gabbing away all right so we just carried on.

The Year of the Fathers

Kenny gave his nod to the choice of subject, like he was bidding for a box of fish at the mart. I don't think he'd heard this yarn of Mairi's either. Had the feeling they'd not been together that long so maybe they didn't spend so much time talking, yet.

She rolled herself a smoke and held the tin out. I shook my head and Kenny noticed. We'd both gone that way. She shrugged and took a big draw, to keep her going.

The year of the herring ban. First, everyone was talking about the big shots the *Quo Vadis* was bringing in. The records getting toppled. Then the Minch was closed. They'd even stopped the Scalpay drifters. What was the point of that, for all the herring they took? And the small ones swimming through. They could have chucked out the purse-seiners and left it at that. But you couldn't land a herring even if you'd caught one.

Now salmon that year – you couldn't give them away. It was a dry summer and they were going crazy at the mouths of all the rivers and burns. Everyone had their freezer full and there wasn't much point in going out for more. Mairi said:

This was the year after my father died. He wasn't that old, and it just wasn't expected. It happened in the winter so everything had already been put away. When I went into the byre, there it was, the drift net with the corks, a different mesh from the salmon net, stretched and dried. The Seagull engine, the big one with the brass tank, on its bronze bracket, all the old fuel drained. The plug loose in the cylinder. A new one in a box, ready.

So I put the boat back on the running mooring. My sisters — you know there wasn't a boy in our family — had taken her in, when we stopped setting the net in the bay. The estate had started lifting nets by then. Well, I'd never been out at night, of course, but I found myself following my nose. I'd his oiled gansey with the grey fleck in it, the Norwegian one that sheds the rain. I wasn't cold, wasn't scared and I knew where to go.

You know the east gap — out by Orinsay island? You can just about cut through the narrows to Loch Erisort in a dinghy on a big enough tide. And the south way takes you to a good fishing at Calbost. Or right clear down to the Shiants. There's a couple of rocks to watch out for, both routes.

Choke on. Fresh mixture. New plug. I primed it, pumping that nipple on the carburettor. There was a spark and clean fuel. It had to go first time. It did. I went out the south gap at half throttle. Once we were through, there was enough light to make out the marks. I opened her up then.

But don't ask me how I knew when it was time to stop. Just like himself reminding me to put the brass tap in to shut off the fuel. 'Enough vessels dropping their oil and muck in the Minch without us adding our tuppence-ha'penny worth.' It was his own voice, telling me.

I remembered something else he'd said. Something about a light that was very handy. No, not a lighthouse. One house up Calbost way. One old guy was always up half the night. He'd keep his light on. You could catch sight of that white light and hold it on the point.

I paid out the net then, just like going for salmon, only rigged to fish deeper and I held the rope. I wasn't sure where to tie it on but it was as if he was in the boat with me, pointing out the eye bolt at the bow. Round turn with two half hitches but I took the end back through the first hitch. Same as the anchor knot.

You know how you set the salmon net with a grapnel and hold off to watch it? I mean you know their runs, where they'll come close for a taste of fresh water. Well, I knew just to drift with this one and I wasn't cold. Wasn't lonely or scared. Don't ask me how I knew it was time to haul but I did. It was heavy to get in. I thought of these stories you hear of — a basking shark caught in it. But it was herring.

Again, it was as if he was in there with me, explaining how to shake them out in one part of the boat. Clear of the anchor and other gear. The light was coming back into the sky. The tide had gone and returned to about the same level so I'd have plenty of water, coming back in the loch.

I got the shovel from the byre and more boxes. Didn't fill them too full so I could drag them in under shelter. It was cold in there. Planks and a concrete block on top so the rats or mink or cats wouldn't get them. I'd phone around later in the morning for people to come and help themselves. But I put a decent fry in a bag in the fridge. That was going to be a special delivery, for the old guy who keeps his light on.

I pulled the ropes to put the boat back out on the running mooring. I could clean the scales off later. Found myself raking out the ashes in the Rayburn as he always did. A few bits of black caoran to get it warm for the breakfast and I went to my bed before my mother was up.

But it was all starting to move again, this room, at this time. Our personal ceilidhs were breaking up. People were saying they wouldn't leave it till next year. We'd keep it going, they said.

Kenny F said we wouldn't say anything. If we said something like that we'd think it was all sewn up. It would be in our minds as having happened already and we wouldn't do anything more about it. So we'd just shut the old gobs.

Mairi Bhan put down the roll-up that had gone out between her fingers and we made a move. People were putting the remnants into carrier bags and checking on taxis.

Kenny said the VAT man wasn't going to make it out under his own steam. We'd take a shoulder each. No bother.

'We'll get the blame for getting him like this. I've been there, man.'

'Me too and I'm fucking sober. Engage the anus in gear, now.'

The VAT man didn't weigh much. He didn't protest.

Then I was hearing another voice, sounding hell of a familiar somehow. It was saying that the floor of this room had started to ripple. Not that surprising really because the whole thing's built on reclaimed land and therefore still subject to the influence of tides.

But then another voice was sounding, even closer to my ear and it wasn't my own this time. Wasn't Mairi's or Kenny's. Wasn't Donnie the guitar man or my bewildered new colleague on his cultural immersion course.

'You are fucking rat-arsed, Mr Coastguard.'

It was the VAT man talking to me.

West Side Mayday

Once you'd jumped through the hoops and passed everything, you took charge of the watch when the senior man was on leave or sick. You usually worked with the same people and get to know them pretty well. When the watch was short, it could be filled on over-time. You'd find yourself working with guys you didn't really know.

This guy's just back from his training course. Pukka procedure. Time and a place for it, as they say. But he's been a Chief Petty Officer in the Navy. Mentioned in dispatches in the Falklands. So he's got kind of used to getting a bit of authority into his voice on the VHF.

We get this wee shout on channel sixteen. 'Hello Stornoway Coastguard, can you ring this number in Bernera? Can you do that for me? Over.'

I see his Adam's apple twitch under the microphone attached to the headset. So I catch his eye and stroll over before he gets his oar in. I know his script. Would have followed it myself, maybe at the trainee stage of the career. You come over as pompous because you don't know you're twitchy. Something like, 'That's Commercial Traffic. Call Hebrides Radio on channel two-six. Over.'

Instead I strolled over to the channel sixteen desk. 'Ask him what's up.'

'*Mallard*, this is Stornoway Coastguard. What's your situation? Over.'

'Yes, Coastguard, *Mallard* here. Thanks for coming back. Well, the gearbox is packed in and we might need a tow. Over.'

'Mallard, Stornoway Coastguard. What is your position? Over.'

They're talking now but I catch my Number One in the new gold braid and Persil Automatic shirt looking bloody amazed as I hit the Scramble button. Fair do's, he doesn't show it in the voice, just a wee bristle but when there's a wee break and he catches his breath he gives me a 'You're in charge but...'

I stop him short. 'We'll talk about it later.' And when there's a lull, I add, 'By the way, you've just heard the West Side Mayday.'

He's thinking of wind strength and direction, glancing at the whiteboards. If it's an offshore wind, that strength, what's the problem? The new boy's used to a few thousand gross registered tonnes under his arse. Hundreds of guys to run around the ship.

The West Side's different. The boys are throwing out creels there, as close to the reefs as they can get. Drying bastards, breaking bastards and every other kind of bit of brick. Doesn't have to be a lot of wind, in from Old Hill. There's something to collide with, any way you drift.

I ring the number in Bernera. A woman says she'll get a hold of her husband on channel eight. Should be all right.

The chopper's on scene in half an hour. 'Disregard the vessel's report of Force Four,' they say. 'A lot of white down there. Not very good conditions. Gusting over thirty knots. We'll stick around here till the tow's connected.'

It took about an hour before the 'return-to-base'. The boys got it sorted out between themselves, this time. No further assistance.

Couple of weeks later the *Mallard* breaks up. The guy's OK. He drifted onto one of the countless skerries in West Loch Roag. It all happened too fast to get on the radio. He got ashore on a reef that wasn't going to cover too soon. He was picked up from there.

Bits of blue-green fibreglass were getting swept up from Barvas to Cape Wrath. The gearbox again.

That Year Again

This was it, had to be. The croft was newly fenced and you could make out a pattern of plastic tubes, a strange faded pink, inside the wire. These were about four feet high and staked to protect trees at a vulnerable stage. There was shelter from the slopes on either side of the renovated house. As long as the drainage worked, the trees should grow, on this croft.

Kenny was turning a pepper mill over the soup when we came in. This was the New Lewisman before our very eyes, Gabriele said. Another voice said to come and we'd see the virtual Lewis. Through a sliding door, off the kitchen, in what must have been once called a scullery, Mairi Bhan was sitting in front of a colour screen.

'So you don't have Windows in South Lochs, yet, blone?'

'Flick's sake, a white c on a blue screen is all you need. You don't want all these icons jumping up to distract you, all over the place. You're looking at the appropriate amount of technology, SY cove.'

She had a coo at the sight of sleeping Anna. Kenny F was fair taken too. 'She's no bother,' I said. 'She always goes to sleep in the van. She'll be down for a couple of hours now.'

Mairi showed me where to put the carry-cot – a quiet, clean corner.

'A few jobs to do yet,' Kenny said.

'Tell me about it,' Gabriele said.

'Time was they asked you to take off your boots on a coorse day and warm your feet in the slow oven. Now they show you the pace of the modem.'

'You can still perform primitive rituals in this house. First thing I do when I get home in the winter. Cup of tea, feet in the stove.'

The heater in the van was on Kenny's list. A long way from the top. Another year and the South Lochs *Autobahn* would be ready. Good councillor, they had. European funds.

'Aye, it cost a lot of cod and hake and haddock, but.'

It was a 22-carat Lewis dinner – soup, lamb, rhubarb crumble. But the soup was a light fish broth with Erisort mussels and singed peppers. The gigot had been marinaded in olive oil, garlic and rosemary and the flesh was still pink near the bone. A dusting of nutmeg, freshly grated on the crumble with its toasted oatmeal topping. 'Hell, Kenny, that'll just about do,' I said.

Half the point of eating like that is the mood you're all in. The yarns get going when the scoff is done. The girls were on the CabSauv and the lads were on the water. We were also on the topic of uncles. A lasting friendship between North and South Lochs. There was hope for the world. I told him I still remembered a yarn with Angus in the Woolies a few years back. Was he still trapping eels? He'd been good to us when we were young. Hadn't seen him for a while.

So we got Kenny's story. I remembered he didn't get to tell his bit, at the office party. I'd been letting the hair down while there was still some left to do so. Now we were again back to the year of the herring ban. One mo time. Kenny said:

My uncle Angus seemed fit enough then, but he'd to watch the angina. We cracked about the heart condition. What else do you do? How many peats can you cut to one of them pills? If any bit of bare flesh appeared on the telly, we'd say, better get one of them down you, man, so you can cope with the shock. Then we'd be looking out for the first salmon of the year. When you saw a few corks go down, then heard the splash you'd say, pop a pill now, Angus.

Angus said he could handle all them things with only one pill but the first herring would be too much. He'd need half the bottle. Or a half-bottle. And that was definitely not a good idea. He painted the boat, though. Then put the antifouling on. We'd to pull it down to the running mooring he'd laid. He checked the endless rope for wear. He gave it the nod. Then it was time for his siesta.

You know him yourself. Glasses held together with sellotape. Not just the frames. One of the lenses, too. He keeps his good pair in the house, says he'd just leave them behind, when he got talking somewhere. But he never does. Leave them behind, I mean. He gets talking everywhere he goes.

You know what the weather was like that year. There was no fun in taking salmon any more. Fish were queueing from the Creed to Eishken to get up the burns but there was only a trickle.

We had all the troops from Glasgow home for the summer holiday. They weren't that impressed with the swimming pool and carnival and other town stuff. So there was this wee exodus to the uncle's, down Garyvard. Sure, sure, I know I never came clean about the Garyvard Connection — good name for a rock band. Think the olaid had the idea of getting me out of the Crit and the Star and back to the great outdoor life. The uncle's boat was the thing but I wasn't so sure about taking the whole gang out the loch. You know the tides sweep round the points. You're past the Kebock into the Sound of Shiants before you know it.

A good sea boat, though. On the heavy side but stable. Built by Matt Findlay, on Goat Island, for the seaweed cutting. We always had her painted plain grey. Think we got a job lot of it with the boat. Good colour if you don't want to be seen. Bad one if you're in the shit. Tidy transom stern and a decent inboard. The Norwegian one, a Sabb.

'The one with the big flywheel,' I said. 'Sabb with the double b, not to be confused with the Swedish car. Chemical cigarette for the cold start, in winter. Beautifully balanced. Not one of these bastards that shakes the ribs out of the boat.'

That's the one. Everybody's on holiday. Angus is off to his bed, next door after giving me a warning look. Kids are out of the game. The visitors are staying over. The bottle's getting passed about. Nobody's warned them their cousin Kenny's got to watch it. The word 'herring' was mentioned.

So the bottle was emptied and there might have been another and that went too so there was no chance of me getting a livener in the morning. A short night. Next day, the kids are jumping on top of you. Everyone was digging out herring nets, buoys. Making pieces, filling flasks, diluting orange squash, all that.

I'm not feeling that great. The weather's clear and I'm trying to backpeddle. I'm saying it's not going to get dark till late on. It's a bit dodgy with wee Murdo and Cathy. Angus is looking over the top of his glasses and telling me, I was out in the boat at night, at their age. It wasn't as if there was school tomorrow. And he's going over his marks and the tides. Telling me when we've got to start back, so we'll get the last of the flood come home on. There's a wee margin but we couldn't linger too long at the nets.

We had plenty of diesel, warm jerseys, the compass, all that. Angus checked it all over. No flies on him. He knew me as well as that boat. He knew I thought the world of these wee guys.

You stood up to steer that boat. One hand by the gear and the other by the throttle. Just like the old Heron. The tiller nudging against the leg of your jeans. The way a collie puts her snout against your knee. We were soon out the loch and no-one was trying to gab against the thump of the engine. The kids were right up for it.

So we sent a big pink puta over the wall and then the corks were going out. I got her going astern and it was all running sweet. We were getting the second net ready. The cousins were going for it.

When the last of the gear was out we'd just tie everything off. It would be a waiting game then. Time for a game of I Spy. That would be tricky. I was just giving her a few kicks astern now and then, to keep her moving away from the corks, leaving a line of them, well clear. And then one of the wee ones came running forward to tell me something and hit against the gear lever. So we shunted forward towards the net. I kicked the lever back but the screw was in it. Maybe my reflexes weren't as fast as they should have been.

I could have gone over the side with the knife to free the prop, but not in that tide. I didn't fancy trying anything heroic. We just cut it as close as we could so there wouldn't be much loose stuff trailing. I tied on our last buoy so we wouldn't lose the net. We dug out the big sweeps. There was no chance of turning the prop. Rowing practice, folks.

We wouldn't make the entrance in the time we had the tide with us. We had to get in close and get an anchor down. So I knew I'd got to involve the kids. They were right up for it.

I rowed till the blisters came up. When the tide turned, we threw the hook over. It held. Everyone was in a huddle, getting some rest. I rigged handlines for the kids and that kept them going. One of them got a big lythe and they thought it was all great. The kids got some more juice and another jersey on and there wasn't a moan.

Dolphins came close, the big ones, blowing, diving under our bow and that kept the kids sweet. Soon we had three heads settling, on the boards, beside their mother. It wasn't that bad a night.

Once we felt the change in the tide, we pulled up the anchor and made the most of it, with the oars. The tide did most of the work for us.

He was waiting for us, of course, old Angus. His shape, in the old funeral-coat, was pretty clear in the morning light. He helped the kids out and made sure their mother was fine. They'd had a grand time — it made their holiday.

Angus just slipped me the nod — I should get my head down for a few hours. He'd use the fall of the tide to get the prop cleared. Then we'd need to get back to our nets, when she floated again.

I knew he was coming this time and didn't try to argue. He had me take the helm, find my transit. I was cream-crackered. 'Where the hell were yous fishing last night, off Lochinver?' There was hardly a ripple and these big pink buoys should have been visible for half a mile. My eyes were on the skyline, trying to find the Last House, over Calbost way. That was trickier in daylight. I saw Angus make a reach down with the boathook, no hurry in the movement. Here was the blue warp.

I need to get myself glasses like these. Infra-red sellotape. He gave me the nod to start hauling. This net was full of herring. He pulled out one sample fish and grinned. Then he let me shake them out, maybe four full boxes. No, he didn't need to take a pill. The second net was heavy and sad. He thought it was maybe a basking shark but it was worse.

Long marblings, perfect black and white, in the leather. There were two types like this, he said. He leaned over. The white didn't continue above the mouth so it wasn't the more common, the white-beaked one. This was the more scarce one — the white-sided dolphin. Not so heavy in the body. Poor lass. Then he turns to me and he speaks, dead quiet. I can tell you every word he said to me.

'There's two things we can do,' he says. 'One is just to cut her free and let her sink.' A memory I could blame next time I took the top off a bottle

and threw it over my shoulder. Or I could help him take out the jaw. The
researchers wanted these, for positive identification.

   He handed me the knife and I got on with it. I did it. We let the rest
sink down to the crabs and the congers. That's what happens at sea.

   That was it, for me, I mean off the fucking sauce, and on the tack.

   We came home with the boxes of herring. The dolphin's jawbone, in
a bag. I'd to make a driftwood fire and boil it down on the shore. Hell
of a soup that would have been but it was better than posting the whole
job to the Natural History Museum in August. The dog days. It would
have been buzzing when it got there if I'd sent the whole thing. But I just
posted off the bone in a box.

   While I was dealing with that, Angus was driving all over Lochs,
dropping off herring and coming back with eggs and ducks and cabbages
and the rest of it.

Kenny was already up at the kettle as he finished his yarn. See a
Lewis cheerio, it's in stages. You do the first bit sitting down. Then
someone says how they've got to shoot the crow. There's always a
few more yarns when you're standing. At the door, you lean back
against the wall. That's how it's done.

   At the gate, he said we could bring a bottle over next time but
that would be some nice extra-virgin. Plenty of space in the VW
for that, next time we hit the continent.

   That could be arranged. But it might be a while before we were
in the olive latitudes again. You needed that much stuff, travelling
with the baby.

   'You're looking well on it,' Mairi Bhan said, to Gabriele.

   I'd never known Mairi so quiet so long. And she was looking at
her man like she'd just met him. It looked good.

   Just like Kenny F, I'd like to end the story there. It's a great knack,
that, knowing where to stop. Never cracked it, myself. People like
his uncle Angus, people like both my grannies – they had it. I can't
do it this time. There's more of this story to come. Not now though.
Maybe later.

   I think we got the van back down to Garyvard once. We remembered the oil but it came from the Co-op. First cold pressing for his

pizza dough that had to rise half a dozen times over. It would get beaten back and back and it would keep on getting up for more. Like Floyd Patterson. Until he met his Ingemar Johansson. Then he came back again and rose up again and again until he'd regained the title. But even Patterson would have to meet his Sonny Liston.

In the Crit

There's no point in telling you lies by omission. I bumped into Kenny F again, in the Crit, when it was still more of a fishermen's pub. Before all these Gaelic actors and journalists appeared. Nothing against them, it's just that it's a small pub. For a second I thought he'd be having a Virgin Mary, waiting for Mairi to finish work, round the corner.

No, he was looking like he looked ten years before. Eyes red, everything red, hair gone longer. Hair is back in fashion with Italian football stars but his was looking kind of forgotten. He held out his glass and I nodded to get another one put in it. Why not? If he was on it, he was on it. I asked for a pint of stout. We went over to a corner. There was going to be a story.

I was going to ask him to save it. If he was on the piss again, it wouldn't be a short one. He was straight into it. No introductions.

She must have been crazy to think she could hide it. OK, it was very early on but he was pretty sure of the signs. She was supposed to be going on another course. Pretty plausible, with all that new tech and her promotion board coming up. Adapting this database programme for the office needs. Fucking brownie points.

He'd a feeling though, even before someone from the office asked how Mairi was. Real concerned note.

Click.

To him, she was in East Kilbride, on a course. She'd even phoned him. Said it was going all right. To them, she was on the sick.

It was me who was slow, taking a sip of my stout. I thought we were talking about something on the side.

Kenny knew I hadn't got it.

I could have coped with her having a fling, he said. I couldn't have shared her but I'd have waited to get her back. Now he could have her back but he didn't want a blone who could do away with their baby. She hadn't even been going to tell him. Just wanted to get back to her fucking development programme. No choice, she said, since he wasn't working. Doing up the house. Debts building up. No choice. They'd have another chance later.

Not with me, you won't. That's what he'd said. He'd gone straight out the door. A woman's right to choose, he said. Well, a guy could choose, too.

He was choosing now. He'd found a place to crash in town, wherever there was a couch. All of us too fucking old for other people's floors. She could have the house and the croft and every other thing. It was her family croft, anyway. And she was earning the dosh. She could fucking pay someone to do the last of the finishing.

I was thinking of my own blur of shifts and snatched sleep. The things you're not proud of, the shouting and the huffs when the bairn's asleep.

But then there was the photo Gabriele took when I fell asleep but Anna was turning the pages for herself. She was just reading on before I even knew she could. When I was knackered from the shiftwork. And you knew then you could hold it together. Maybe not for keeps but maybe for long enough.

I turned back to the eyes of a guy I grew up with. The formative years. I couldn't ask him back to our house. Couldn't be that much of a bastard.

I put another dram in his glass and walked home.

Offal

We brought the olaid to Italy once. She always wanted to go there. The olman had been there in the war. There and North Africa. She wanted to go somewhere that had been a big part of his life. But she didn't want to go to the desert. We piled into the VW. She played with Anna in the back. Read stories out loud. Nothing was a problem.

Every night she'd eat spaghetti bolognese. 'Ah ken ah kin eat that. Ken fit it is.'

But when we were in Sienna, we found a trattoria with white painted roughcast on the inside. I asked what the local thing was and the guy said tripe. We ordered one portion of lamb's liver with sage and one tripe, to share. I asked the olaid if she wanted spagbol again. 'Did he say tripe?' she asked.

I said, 'Aye, but it won't be like you know it, with milk and onions.'

'Ah dinna care fits aboot it, if it's tripe ah can eat it,' she said.

She ordered another Tripe Sienna. It came in a tomato and herb sauce. She ate every bit and took her bread to the plate after.

The liver was seared outside. The sage was fresh, of course, and the flavour went right through the rare organ. It was the best I've tasted and I've tried to cook it like that ever since.

In the past few years I've thought back to that liver. Or rather to different dishes of liver and other sights of liver.

You know we eat fish livers, here on Lewis, but that's something different. I'm talking only about meat now.

There was the time I bought a wedder from one of my watch-mates. But the deal was you had to be there at the killing. It was all done on trestles. A fellow came round. He was the man. He did everyone's. You gave him some chops or another nice cut. I don't think it was illegal then.

My thinking was, this has got to be better than loading the animal into a trailer. Driving miles to town. Then it's waiting in a pen smelling what it's smelling and hearing what it's hearing.

Instead, you get the village expert round. I thought back to Angus, come across the loch by boat to preside over the deed in the shed at Griomsiadair. I'd thought of asking him along on the Italian job. Himself and Ruaraidh would have been company for herself. And entertainment for wee Anna. Then there would have been a vermouth or a last cup of tea, after the wee one had turned her last page of the day.

They would have memories. It might be time to talk about past events. But Ruaraidh wasn't keeping that great. We'd left it too late.

This time the man who was not Angus, but was like him in some ways, said, 'Well, you boys should know about knots.' That was a mistake. I think I went for a clove hitch with a locking turn. But see that moment when the animal struggles. The panic should only be for seconds. But that puts a jerking strain on a tie. Mine did not hold up to that test. He did the proper lashing himself then.

This time there was no mistake. There was just a tiny twist of a small sharp blade, a pocket knife really. Its eyes just glazed over and I remembered my job was to hold the basin close. Everything was clean with a trace of bleach. Someone else poured some salt in the basin and you had to keep stirring, all the time, as it filled. Otherwise the blood would congeal.

He showed us the bits we had to scrub to contain the *marag*. Black pudding. Then we left the carcass there to hang for a while and went home with the blood and offal.

Gabriele opened the Mrs Beeton edition, provided by my olaid, of course. I said, no, never, but sure enough, there was a recipe for haggis. So we made black puddings and we made our own haggis. I chopped the heart, kidneys and liver. There was a description of how to drain the fluid off the lungs so you could use them too but that sounded a bit much.

The hardest bit was scrubbing the doosh – the stomach that would contain the pudding. I remembered they used to take these to the shore and do them in the salt water. I remembered having to go to the slaughterhouse to get one for a relation so that proved you could do the job at home too, in Westview Terrace.

We did it and everything worked out.

I loved the olaid's own casserole but that was ox liver, cooked till tender. She hadn't been able to do much of her own cooking for a while, with the stroke. Her balance was not so good for standing at the kitchen.

Back in Sienna, there were three clean plates and the waiter was beaming. Four, really, because Anna was always a good eater too.

I remembered frying up thick slices of deer liver, out at the estate. That was a breakfast that kept you going. The smell was kind of pungent. The cook wasn't that happy but she had plenty to do so let us get on with our own breakfast on a corner of the Aga. You've to be really careful, selecting liver for eating. A lot of it is condemned. And wild deer get parasites.

After that, it was the hospital. The porter's job. Mostly, it was routine. Now and again something would come up. You'd to keep the incinerator going clean. Burn the cardboard and stuff, a bit at a time so it didn't get clogged up. One time a staff-nurse comes chasing out of Surgical. They were needing another oxygen bottle in a hurry. I looked to the store, and knew the trolley you used to wheel them in was at the other end of the round. 'Is it really urgent?' I asked. 'It is,' she said.

So I just let the cylinder fall onto my shoulder and ran with it, balanced there. She held the doors open for me. It wouldn't do to batter someone on the way. Save a life and take another. Net gain nil. But that all worked out fine. We saved some minutes.

But this time, there was no urgency. I was passing the lab. A woman in a white coat saw me and said they'd been meaning to phone round. Was the incinerator running? It was.

Well, there was some samples here. They'd had to keep them for a long time. Just in case. A legal thing. But they wouldn't be needed.

Could I dispose of them as soon as possible? They needed to clear the chilled storage.

There's this thing about authority. I was down the pecking order. She held out a small, thick, polythene bag. It was double sealed with a zip of some kind and labelled but it was still transparent. Something inside it looked like liver.

She saw my question.

A poor soul who shot himself.

There but for the grace of who or what. Maybe I'd been too eager to take my dose of the opiate of the masses but I might still be on a one-way nosedive if I'd not been given that support.

I was about to say, hold on, if it's been here for months, what's the hurry? I could go and get a box or another bag. But she was holding the top of the sample-bag out for me to take.

I took it.

I tried to walk as fast as I could, the most direct way to the shed where the incinerator was housed but one of the engineers saw me, holding it out a bit.

'That's a shit job you have there,' he said.

So I opened the door and closed it as fast as I could. That was it done. You couldn't hear or see anything now. I'll tell you this though. You could smell it. And it was just like meat cooking. I thought of eating a hare or a goose. Spitting out lead shot now and again. I thought of any stray shot melting instantly in there as the liver disappeared.

Will and Testament

Sand and gravel shift. Essential landmarks remain. Amendments, rather than corrections to your own chart, in your mind. Sounds like a thing you should be able to do. Say who you are. Say what you think. But now I don't think that's easy. All of us responding to moving conditions. Just a few things you can maybe be sure about.

The olaid dropped a not so subtle hint. 'A mannie wi responsibilities noo. A wife and dochter tae think aboot. If onything should, happen, God forbid.'

All right, here it is.

Everything's for you, Gabriele. I knew love before I met you but you taught me a different kind of love. I think we know each other's bodies quite well now. I have these strong impressions of the shapes your body makes, in different positions. If I'm away from home, more than a few days, these images stay with me.

I hope I learned to listen to you and your body. My mother once said you were made of galvanised wire and that was a compliment. No wonder you found you could live on Lewis. A place in a state of change, like all other places on our overstocked planet. But our Island home has become dependent on fencewire, as a means of holding everything together. These temporary repairs have a habit of proving more permanent than systems designed to last for at least a millennium.

You said, a long time ago, when it came to arrangements, you didn't want anything left to chance. You could cope with a lot in these strange islands as long as you got some bread that looked as if it might have come from a Bible story. You missed the stout, rye bread of home. That light loaf, with a scattering of grains in it – the one we used to get from Billy Forsyth's – it was called 'rye' but it just wouldn't do.

You didn't mind being imported, yourself, to improve the stock with a healthy bit of hybridisation. Looking at that fit daughter of ours, it seems to have worked. Suppose the question is, would it have worked the same if I'd gone to Cologne? Same genetics, another urban environment. The Rhine is wide. Barges ride down it with their loads, or slog up against the flow. They send their waves and wash to the built banks. But it's not the sea.

It's fitting, your mother living in prosperous Bonn – with your brother's support. But my own mother's offspring settled either side of the Atlantic. There's geography and there's language. Your immaculate English – well, it was better before you came to live here. We've roughened it up. But I didn't have a word of German. Then again, look at my sister, gone Canadian, fluent in French with a funny accent. So maybe language isn't the issue we think it is.

My job is about communication. That's the technical word we use, for an operator of the changing technology that sends wireless signals over water – a communicator. The idea of being out there, lost, out of reach of all signals, that's what really scares me. My mother keeps asking me if she's still making sense. Her speech is tricky but her mind is on the ball.

So I've already discussed a little deal with you, my own wife. If I go gaga, before departure, I'd be grateful if you could find a way of arranging something. And I'll try to do the same for you, if it should be the other way. Maybe all these intermittent shovels of aluminium sulphate to whiten the peaty water of the Island will have their effect. Or all these daft mercury fillings in my teeth. I got most of them the same year. You can do a lot of damage fast with McCowan's toffee bars on a daily basis.

That's a moral tale for you. But possibly also open to interpretation. Anyway, my point is, if I've lost the plot, I wouldn't want to linger on.

I know your own menu, for your send-off, even if you haven't written it down. Pretty sure, though, that you'll be burying me first, somehow, barring accidents. Statistics are on your side. But you stated your wishes, just in case. In this respect, they're dead right, all these guys in the hats who say you never know your hour.

A menu for a funeral. When you say menu now, it sounds like something that appears on the computer screen. Maybe restaurants will also be like that by the time you read this spiel.

You'll touch a discreet screen, built in to the end of the table. Maybe the font imitates fast handwriting. You'd say, that's typical of Westfalia, ox-tongue, served hot in its liquor. A bay leaf. An onion studded with cloves. And I'd go along with it as I told you about the tongue that my uncle Andra would still do, for the New Year, in The Broch. Maybe we'd walk into the house while it was cooling and get a slice, melting the butter on the white doorstep of loaf.

We both found shared ground, by the Rhine and by the Minch – and in more things than food. Where you draw the line is sin. Our daughter is full of mischief. She can be capable of hurting but also feeling sorry afterwards. Same as all of us – she just hasn't learned to conceal it yet. She's not evil, though, not unredeemed. So you won't have anyone go on about sin over your dead head. Instead, you'll have the Unst Bridal March. Keep cash in the kitty to pay the fiddler.

OK, it's a Shetland tune but let's face it, there's not much of an instrumental tradition on the Long Island. Big songs, though. One of them wouldn't do any harm. But your own only request is that one tune. There's an understanding that friends are asked to linger for a round-the-table dinner with the menu up to myself. Trouble is, if you don't specify things, things might get taken out of your hands when you're in a daze.

But I didn't set out to write your will. So here we go. Take two. Or it might be my third attempt to get practical. I'd no idea this floodgate was going to open. Where did all these words come from?

SPECIAL INSTRUCTIONS

BEING THE WISHES OF PETER MACAULAY,

COASTGUARD COTTAGE 1,

LEVERHULME DRIVE, STORNOWAY

No prayers, please. I don't mind flowers as long as they haven't been flown round the world to get here. But I want this to get read out, legal requirement or not. It's an audience, flick's sake. The epistle has spread off the red Post Office form it started on. It's taken on a life of its own.

I hope there are some good conversations going round our living room. None of these hushed tones. The traditional assortment of chairs pulled in from next-door or borrowed from the school down the road, if there's enough people to sit on them. If there's only a few, just get everyone seated round the kitchen table. Blast up the stove but don't dump me in it yet.

The registration plates will maybe have gone another cycle of letters. Maybe all cars will be made in Malaysia and Korea now, or in whatever powerhouse is being promoted. Or the Far East might have had its day and Romania or Bulgaria taken over any manufacturing that's still going on. An equation of low labour costs and a population desperate for economic advancement. Or maybe everything will be made in China. Military dictatorships are going out of fashion in a lot of places but they seem to be OK if the country is a trading partner. And we've got to sell our electronic weaponry to someone. That's about the only stuff we're making now, anyway.

Never mind the random shots, what about my own code of beliefs, now that I'm dead? Well, I'm not dead yet but I should be, when you're reading this. What were MacAulay's beliefs, exactly?

The act of writing this wee document started something going. I can't stop typing now. I can't say it in one word any more. Not Christian, Bahá'í or Buddhist or Marxist. I don't think I ever could. Just tried to do that, for a short while. My own story is tapping out into its own order now but these other complicated bits of history keep butting in. I'm nowhere near at peace with myself. I've missed too many chances to do something to help. Shit, sounds a bit like they're right about sin, after all.

Best get back to practical matters.

PRACTICAL MATTERS

I'm quite happy to leave the choice of music, at my funeral, to yourself, Gabriele, if you do indeed survive me. My critical faculties probably won't be at their best anyway.

If we both do peg out together though, and a third party is making the arrangements, what about laying on a bit of a show? We could have your Unst Bridal March with a PowerPoint slide of the late romanticism you're so keen on. Maybe we should have a couple of figures in misty mountains – Caspar David Friedrich woz ere. To keep it balanced, so to speak, we could have the Reverend Whatsisname skating, courtesy of Raeburn. Even if they do use that outline on the plastic carriers of Edinburgh Galleries. And they reckon it might have been some other cove that did the painting. Oh and the pond's not where the title says. Apart from that it's all pretty genuine.

What about if you're making arrangements for me? A good get-up-and-go South African-style funeral wouldn't be bad but it might take a bit of arranging on Lewis and I wouldn't want to give you the hassle. Who would have believed Mandela would get out alive and he'd somehow continue to inspire? I fancy one of these painted coffins but maybe there's a simpler idea. We'll come to that later. You might be mourning, for all I know. But if you fancy making a shindig of it, that's OK with me.

You'd go quite a distance for a good demonstration. Never mind all this asking if it does any good. The exercise of the democratic right to speak your mind. That's what brought us together. You were looking for a different father at that kibbutz. You weren't ready for a lover.

With all this said, Frau Richter, we come to the material arrangements and welcome back to any materialistic bastards who went to sleep during the above digressions.

MATERIAL ARRANGEMENTS

1. ALL MATERIAL ASSETS.

All yours. Then you can decide what's to happen to the stuff, when you've taken your own turn to pop the clogs. If you're not around by my demise, all goes to the offspring. The property is in joint names anyway so it's all yours, girls.

2. BURIAL ARRANGEMENTS.

Don't go planting me in the ground. But before I forget, let me state now – it's OK to use any bits, best Lewis tradition of spare parts, before you get rid of the rest. That's the only card I believe in carrying, these days. Let's be realistic. The only way to avoid being taken over by the aforementioned men in the hats is to do the business elsewhere. I'll be most surprised but willing to post-humously eat my words if there are women elders and ministers on this Island (Episcopalians excepted) by the time I vamoose.

Please ferry the bits to Inverness, to get burned. I would have no serious objections to a blazing gellie of driftwood but there's bound to be legal obstacles. I know that the vultures pick the bones in Tibet but don't feed me to the seagulls. The council wouldn't allow it anyway and they're fat enough on batter and chips. That's the seagulls, not the councillors.

Better to pay through the nose, I think, and get properly cremated. But you can tell young Al Crae not to go crazy with the varnish and brasswork. The box is going to be wrapped in a certain very distinctive bit of tweed. But do like they do at sea and keep the cloth for another day. A flag of the hill. Colours of a section of our moor, shifting from wet to dry in its own light. My own father's woven image of it, anyway. After this use, my own section of his last tweed goes to our daughter. This seems to have become unbusinesslike again. Back to the practicalities. I've no serious objections to a wee service at the house, with people reading what they feel might be appropriate, sacred or no.

Maybe while that's going on, it's a good time to get the Decca Navigator flashed up. No, I'm out of date again. That was looking good for a few more years but of course they flicked the switch on the UK's Decca chains on the 31st of March in 2001. The midnight hour. One hell of an April Fool's gag. I never thought they were serious. That's all history now and the three masts, standing up from the Ness Machair, were felled. All that rigging was scrapped and I hope some of it found its way into fences or hawsers. I still have one of the last Decca receivers somewhere in the garage. I was going to have it wired up so you could observe the historical moment when the data fell from the screen. But it all happened too suddenly. Maybe the Yanks' GPS is also as obsolete as their Loran C. They could throw the switch on that too. We're at their mercy, unless you've a paper chart, a compass and an eye for transits.

You've got to throw the ashes somewhere so we might as well go for the weather side of the Carranoch reef. Fine, I know I should stipulate that only visual landmarks are used but I'll be lucky enough to get thrown anywhere south of the back of Goat Island, by the old outfall pipe, without making things any more difficult.

Even if Kenny F is back on the tack (off the *deoch*) and got himself a small boat on the go, don't trust him with the job. Better not present them to my near-colleague Mairi Bhan either. People who are into the fishing are primitive hunters. I know about this and about the strategies they use to disguise it. Pleasure or commercial fishing, they'll only want to get the gear down as soon as they can. Mairi would forget about the ashes till she found them in the galley sink, months later, between casts with dried up mackerel skin and used teabags. Safest bet is the lifeboat cox. Calum's successor, Murtie, or the guy after him, if I last that long.

All these guys have a conscience, by definition. No use giving them a bottle of malt for their trouble because most of them won't even take a dram for fear of missing a shout. Another chance to get shaken about by turbo-diesels, get sick and thrown about. Great. Give a decent donation to the cause.

I don't suppose you can get wee self-propelled caskets, yet. One to drop a model anchor by remote control, when you're right over the mark. You can probably get one if you send to Florida. But don't bother. Just ask the Cox to chuck the burnt bones over, when he's updrift of the spot.

My various greys swamped by the deeper greys of the North Minch. That's not a bad picture to go out on.

But I hope I manage to do a bit more typing first. I got rhythm. Melody might have to take its place in the queue.

BOOK TWO

Turbulence

The Twist

For every story there's a lighter and a darker version. My uncle Andra, fae The Broch, talked about plucking the geese. They were in Italy in the war and the lads had done a deal. Jock Rose, the tinker, showed how it was done. He plunged the carcasses into near-boiling water and then the feathers just flew off. But first you had to kill your goose. They're big birds and none of the squaddies ever managed to do that twisting the neck thing. Except Jock.

So it was all done, in the right order, and they made a proper dinner. Invited their new friends and colleagues in the trade fuelled by British Army petrol to eat with them. The squaddies told their new mates to bring wives and daughters. The table was set. But Jock Rose arrived pissed. He'd got hold of a horse and cart and there were two hoors from the brothel, sitting one on either side of him. The guests evaporated. Some of them grabbed food, as they legged it out, stuffing it in the pockets of their good clothes. These were hungry times in the villages and the towns of Italy.

But Andra also told me about the dysentry. How no-one was reporting sick. If you did that, they wouldn't let you on the train. No-one wanted to stay on that continent any longer than he had to. You were so desperate to get home that you'd shit in overflowing buckets for three days and nights. That was the only hint that something had happened inside the minds of all these men in tin hats. Not just those with a story like my own father's – his escape from a tank. An armoured vehicle that had been mobile, just seconds before, became a steel coffin. A smouldering target. A hatch clanged shut for the last time and he was outside of it. By a whisker.

We kept hens for a while. Out the back. The daughter, Anna, and me had fun, building the housie with the nesting box on the side and the run out front. Long before that, I remembered my grannie just lifting a corner of the coop and grabbing a black one. She disappeared into the shed with it and we got it to take home in a bag. It might not be worth roasting but there would be good soup there.

I killed hens after making sure Anna really was somewhere out of the way. First I listened to advice then I did the twist thing just as I'd been told, so I thought. But you might as well have been doing the other kind of twist, chasing it round the garden when it came back to life. So I put an edge on the hatchet after that. They still quivered and moved more than you could think possible but you knew they were dead in most senses.

We kept two geese for a while. This was pushing it, even in a back garden stretching out for half an acre. The neighbours all had projects too. There was no hassle. We thought our geese would breed but one day we found two eggs. We phoned a man versed in these matters. When are you in town, next?

So my uncle's mate, Angus from Garyvard, officially sexed our stock and neither was a gander. But they were very protective about their fine eggs – it took a single one to make the richest omelette or scrambled egg you could want. I'm tasting them now, creamy without the addition of cream. I felt bad, keeping one goose off with a stick while I stole the egg they were jointly guarding. I knew I couldn't carry on doing this. So the deal was done – two live geese for two live lobsters. At least I knew how to do them, courtesy of Mrs Beeton. As per crab. That diagonal thing with the skewer through the eyes.

The latter days of the barter system in the Coastguard Service. I broke the news as gently as I could to Anna who liked to stroll down the urban allotment to throw grain in their direction. They were going to a good home.

'But I wanted to eat the gooses,' she said.

I don't think I could have swung the hatchet at one of those arching necks. And I didn't know any relative of any Jock Rose who would do that favour.

It was my Lewis uncle, Ruaraidh, arranged mattters, out on the croft. I must have been very young because they didn't want me in there at the time. I could catch some of my grannie's yarns for a change. It might even have been Angus, in there with him. In the villages there was usually an expert, in at the killing.

But I remember being proud when my uncle gave me my share to take back to town. 'You earned it,' he said, 'you've hardly missed a fank.' And the olaid was proud of me too, not just because there was a whole pile of chops and a gigot, shoulder and everything. Maybe my sister was scowling. It wasn't fair. I got to go driving about in the van and take part in all these things while she had to help my mother in the kitchen.

Ruaraidh was at the hospital when I saw him for the last time. I wasn't so good at reading the signs – he didn't give a lot away anyway, asking after everybody. He had cancer of the stomach. They say that's one of the most painful. But I was there in uniform, on the way home after the day-shift. Her Majesty's Coastguard, he said. That was maybe enough. He knew I was in a job that needed doing. That's all he would say about his own years in the war. Except for one new year's visit, a rare exchange with my olman.

'Aye, we were there when they were needing them. Not when they were feeding them.'

We came close to getting the real stories then. But they never came out that night. They never did, in my hearing.

It was a bit sudden when I said I'd better be heading now because Gabriele's brother, Michel, was over from Germany and they wouldn't eat till I got there. Something went, fast as a North Minch rainsquall, across his face. He knew that was it, even if I hadn't faced it yet. He did say something to me though. Very low-key.

'Don't wait till you're an old man,' he said. 'It might never happen. You tell your own stories when you need to.'

I never took the chance to tell him what it all meant to me, the runs out to fanks at Griomsiadair. An initiation into a world of blood, sweat and yarns.

Torcuil

Glasgow Airport doesn't run to recycled paper, yet. At least WH bloody Smith's doesn't. You couldn't fail to find the stuff in Germany. Either end of the process. Putting your shit down on paper or wiping it off you. Maybe it's all that guilt. Maybe now that there's signs of a lasting downturn in the industrial world over on the continent, things might change. Still plenty of new Mercs and BMs. It's getting difficult to find used cars because everyone sells them for silly money to the East. And they say there isn't a border any more.

There's an abundance of borders still to be clearly defined and agreed. Constitutional Questions.

The *Independent*, picked up from the vacant business class seats of this aircraft, quotes the revamped Cecil Parkinson, adding to his serious target, right from his conscience, going for three per cent less emissions from exhausts this very year. Cool. Until you find his footnote which says this means we can now increase production of cars by, wait for it, three per cent.

Public transport went up in price as The Wall came down. Even the bloody wall itself is now packaged in wee bits for sale. Of course that's only right. Since that system over the other side eventually corrupted itself to death, it naturally follows that the wonderful one, West of it, is necessarily correct in all its aspects. Course it does.

These wee bottles on the flight. Could they not just give you a slug from a litre into a glass? No, they've done the time and motion study. Modern Times in the air. The designer labels. I'm seated beside a young kid, going to Scotland, fed up with history. Fed up of all that money going to the East whether they work for it or not.

'We worked for it. They want it right away.'

'Hold on, you're still going to school, as the Yanks say. You're a college girl.'

'Well, my father worked for it,' she said.

Here's a seismic sensing opportunity. A sign of a backlash. Two generations on, a move to emerge from the guilty period. Mind you, let us remember this is a random sample of one kid on one plane.

Even with a couple of the complimentary (i.e. you've paid for as much as you can drink on your ticket already) wee bottles inside me, I can sense that my effort at finding common ground, a propos *The Tin Drum* isn't going to work. OK, there was the *Independent* but it seems to be all about food and where to eat it. I have another try at conversation, citing *Effie Brest* though I'm on the point of saying *Marie Braun*. The former is far enough back to be OK. She's had it up to here with National Guilt and asking whys. Or maybe I'm just forgetting I'm pretty well an old bastard myself and there's no reason this kid should respond to attempts at conversation just cause she's drawn the seat next to me.

I settle in the chair and think of Gabriele and Anna who have a couple more days in Bonn while I'm back at work. At least one Lewisman is flying Tornados in Germany. That's up the road a bit. Closer to Düsseldorf. The pilot cove was a bit vague about the location. Might soon get taken over by a budget airline anyway. It might be the Tornados which migrate norwest to plague us for a designated number of weeks in the year. That's OK really, to justify the forty million pounds sterling Nato spent on our airport. What's that in Deutschmarks? DMs rule these days and I don't mean Doc Marten boots though they're back in fashion again. That German lassie maybe has a pair though I can't see for all the folding tables and plastic cups and stuff.

In the olden days, I remember it was four to a pound. Mention Germany to old soldiers – ones who'd come through it – and they'd tell you anything and they meant anything – cost ten cigarettes in Germany. Amongst the rubble.

I'm off the plane and I'm realising that I'm not going to get home tonight. It's the old story of a slight delay and the Stornoway plane not waiting for two passengers. OK, I can understand that, what's the arrangement? So the car arrives to take me and one other guy from one other flight they didn't wait for.

I should phone back to Germany to catch Gabriele before she phones home and gets worried that I've not arrived. Which bloody way does this hour go? I always get it wrong.

First, the stairs. A better bet than lifts full of tired people, spilled from bus-tours. Forty-eight pounds a night to stay here, without breakfast, if you were paying for it. I remembered the asparagus, the pale shoots we bought direct from the farm, not the flashy green ones. There was no fridge in the room but I filled the sink with cold water. Eased them in there and hoped for the best.

Just looking out now and I'm glad of the height. Just as well I've been shuttled into this Stakis Glamourama. Looking out over the Renfrew boatyards. Pleasure yachts. Easier to come up the Clyde on a two-masted toothbrush than to have a ship built here now. Why exactly did we have to commit industrial suicide? Remind me.

Aye. The other guys were still massed the other side of the Steppes. Indo-China was getting weird. So it was better to build trade with our defeated enemies, Japan and Germany. And the fellows on the Clyde had created trouble before. These damned democratic socialists were all too close to the National sort of socialists. So Churchill said, in public, against advice. But he was only outvoted for a short time. He got back in office when times were hard.

Lest we forget, the technique was still worth trying again. After the Argentinians obliged with national distraction therapy, the focus shifted to the Yorkshire miners. There ain't no enemy like an enemy within. Ask Trotsky. Did you know that Arthur Ransome, foreign correspondent for *The Manchester Guardian*, married Trotsky's former secretary? Sailed her out of Russia in the *Racundra*, hastily launched in 1922.

Pity my old mate Kenny wasn't still in Glasgow. Just as well he was back home. It might be me leading him astray tonight. But the conscious part of my Civil Service mentality was still sober. I couldn't risk missing that flight, tomorrow. The whole reason I was travelling back without my family was to make that shift I couldn't swap. So I couldn't venture into Glasgow proper. I had to stay where I was put.

Here I was before the wide window of my room in the high-rise hotel. Observing the rise of the Ochils. The blip of Stirling Castle, the Wallace Monument. Startling visibility.

I could navigate to Coalsnaughton, Torcuil, if I had time and you can't navigate without that. Doesn't have to be a brass chronometer. A five-quid digital dial would do nicely, thanks. Mind that chapter in *Swallows and Amazons*, trying to get back in the dark. Trusting to counting. Dodgy. Without accurate assessment of how long you've been steering a given course, or a log to tell you that distance, you don't know where you are. Simple as that.

But Torcuil's mariner olman admitted to me once how he'd been caught out with a younger version of my pal aboard. Visibility was down so they couldn't find the entrance to Little Loch Broom. The pair, father and son, had been out of the loch, fishing to the north, towards Priest Island. The ship's master on leave naturally still had the compass bearing home, in his head, but you need to know how long you've travelled along it.

He told me they were caught north of Rubha na Cailleach, the wrong side of The Old Woman, you could say. Or was it a witch? No, that was Loch Maree. Witch's Point. There surely had to be a Dubh somewhere, for a proper witch. Or was that a nun? Maybe there wasn't much difference to a good Presbyterian.

That was the point in the story where Torcuil's olman admitted, from under these eyebrows, that he hadn't brought the watch. Something about being on holiday. But unforgivable for all that. A lesson he'd learned often enough not to have to learn it again.

They were well on course for the entrance. He didn't know how far he would have trusted his own judgment if he'd had no other option. Dense low cloud and pawing drizzle started to shift. A bit of a breeze but nothing silly. As the temperatures of air and sea became more equal, they could see again, as far as the cliffs and the Summer Isles. There was the brown cloth skin of the Priest. Priest Island, that is, now well astern. Just where it should be. They now knew for sure they had plenty sea-room if they needed it. Then the distant shape was showing its rocky sides, a touch of pink in the granite in late light, as religious as Iona. That monk of a rock held on the quarter, a back-bearing and the Old Woman stood up, too tired to hide from them any longer, fed up of the game and letting them come home into Little Loch Broom.

So that's another of your olman's stories, Torcuil. And I'm remembering it, marooned in the Stakis hotel, just along a line from the rise to the Ochil Hills. Even if I could find my way back to your folks' house in that street that isn't new any longer, I might not recognise the particular box. Your father had his stroke in the house he'd commissioned. First occupant and first to die in it. He did it all quite tidily, during his leave. I don't suppose there's a chance that you're in it now.

From this height in a high-rise, time is variable. Maybe it's the Saint Emillion, carried from the Carvery. Another glass. *Pourquoi pas?* I'm not going nowhere, tonight. Not in body. The mind is racing. Got to be backward. Only way to go. I'm going out of this window and along that motorway. The Stirling motorway was completed only the year before our small exodus from Lewis. My mother, the sister and myself were on the *Loch Seaforth*, calling at Kyle, breakfasting then disembarking at Mallaig. Our journey in hope to the Central Belt of Scotland. The scenic train run to Queen Street where the poor wee dog peed for half an hour solid. Half an hour liquid. Hell, you know what I mean.

My olman had a reconditioned motor fitted in the Morris Traveller and the new road was ready. The A series of Austin Morris engines went on with only minor modifications right up to the Metro. He was driving us to our own box. We were not the first owners but it was the first time they were paying a mortgage rather than rent. I can understand now, it was something for them to be proud of. It's shuffled right up front of the memory now, that card to the front of the file. 1967.

Does everybody's mind work this way or is this a leftover from that one damn microdot? The one that entered right into my own skull? All very virginal. Two cherries plucked in one week not so long after we'd moved back to the Island in 1970. My first fish, *Salmo salar*, spotted and snatched quietly, out on my own. Traded for the tab of acid. Full sex came a lot later.

I dropped the tab to the Yes album saying 'Yours Is No Disgrace, silly human race.' But all the daft stuff was everybody else. We really were the beautiful people. And at first all the scabby faces were the others. From Bayhead to Newton, the masks were melting. Then the buildings were shaking and the harl was peeling from the seaward walls. Bad trips only happened to other poor bastards. Couldn't be that. But some of these weird faces stayed with me for a long time to come.

I escaped the long trip, helped out by a couple of mates. Forget the fucking chemicals and get some of this down your neck. And they tilted the Lanliq. Most of it dribbled down to add a layer to the tie-dye vest but I swallowed enough to get plastered on top of the acid. Good move. Got home, stinking of the Republic of South Africa. Got hell. Got to bed. Next day was interesting.

Herself was damn sure I was going to school, whatever state my head was in.

'I dinna care fit you wear, loon,' she said. 'I'm jist past a that.' Three mugs of tea and I faced the bright. But the trip didn't stop. You'd get a bit of respite, think you were down and then the walls would move again. Fuck. Wasn't all bad now but you just wanted off the rollercoaster.

The flashbacks went on for a couple of years. My voice joined the gathering consensus that repeated, 'No chemicals, man.' But some of the rest of the gang carried on with the stuff from the Mill. We called it The Weavers Answer and we sniffed it from a hankie. Guys were going seriously bananas. Don't ask me how he found out but my olman was aware of what was going on. He just said to me, quietly, 'Look son, tell the boys, I used to work with that stuff. You're supposed to have a mask. A ventilated room. You're risking lung damage, the lot. You boys are taking serious fucking poison.'

I think it was the only time he swore when he was talking to me. OK, you can say, don't do it, to other guys. But that's like your music teacher saying, don't start smoking. They've already set the example. At least we stopped. It's about then I was getting quite good at smoking. Holding a blast down long enough to let the dope work. The tobacco didn't get me choking now. I was getting to like the mix of smells.

But I found that even the organic stuff was getting dodgy for me. Trouble was someone had got hold of some proper resin. Hell, this didn't only smell of something. Maybe it was just that we had a bit of money now from the poaching or the Klondyking. There's a lingering trace of alchemy in that trade. Minch herring sold to Faroese packers so providing us, the Hebridean labour force, with the ability to purchase some black Afghani.

We were blasting it from a hollowed out carrot but see some guys. Eating the fucking pipe. And then we reached a stage we hadn't been at before. No more daft laughing, everyone going quiet. But for me it was another acid flashback and I wanted out.

So that's a brief summary of the lowlights of what followed my Central Belt experience. My return to the gentle Isle of Lewis. Leaving Torcuil, my fellow teuchter, trapped down there, under the Ochils.

Let's come closer to now. Back one week only, from this day of the flight that departed without me, leaving me stranded in this three-star box. We left Anna with the Bonn grannie and took a great train ride to Essen. The main mission was to see a gallery. 'Never mind what's on the display panels,' she said. This building was designed by her father's best friend. They'd been students of architecture together and were drafted together and they deserted together. And survived the war.

'Is *he* still alive?' I asked.

'I think so,' she said.

I already knew Gabriele's father had gone missing in strange circumstances somewhere around Rügen Island, long after the war. But no-one in the family spoke about it much.

It seemed strange, not looking up his best friend. But of course that whole situation was so delicate. I didn't ask any further. But we did see the big Magnum Photographers show. See that photo – you've seen it printed all over the place. It's a billboard with the big Chevy or Buick or whatever it is, guzzling the gas with the happy white family that dreams are made of, driving into the sky, over the backs of the blacks looking at the poster from the street. We're on the move, it says.

And we fucking were, that day. I'm back again to our family move to the better life on the Mainland. This Bordeaux beats shit. It's transported me back to the new motorway. We're right under this window but back about one quarter of one century. Along that tarmac or maybe a layer of it that's now under a renewed surface. We were proceeding along the new road to the new life in the Central Belt. South to us. Maybe not a new Chevvy but a reconditioned 'A series', four-cylinder, 998cc design classic, under our green bonnet.

Torcuil, won't you join me in a glass of this fine red, courtesy of BA, which we don't own any more either. Wasn't there some dirty tricks there too, by some former Cabinet member? BA were still managing to squeeze out that upstart entrepreneur from certain routes. Just look at that beard, these clothes. He may be a credible example of Thatcherite values but he had to learn it was to everyone's advantage to operate on certain routes only. Lack of schooling, really. The things that shouldn't need to be said.

Torcuil, *a bhalaich*, we bought our LPs off that guy Virgin Branson for a while. Before he got airborne. This is pretty smooth stuff, but we can handle it. I should call up the other guy who got stranded. Didn't get a note of the number of the room he's in. Thought I might see him in the Carvery. There was an American lady, a lecturer in literature, judging from the conversation you couldn't help hearing, at the next table. She was talking to another lady. I was about to ask them if they wanted a glass and ask what she thought of this Bradley guy. Some writer, man.

I read his novel, on the holiday. Full of hot toddies and backwoods, trails and history – Civil War to Vietnam. Pointed out to me with missionary zeal by Mairi Bhan, my near-colleague in the

Fisheries Office. She even trusted me with her library ticket. The most personal history, that's what the novel's about. What you're carrying when you think you're naked.

But I didn't have the guts to move across and engage the professor in a literary discussion. I mean I don't even have the terminology. I only did a module.

Feel bad about that stranded guy, though, Torcuil. People placed in situations, even in Stakis joints, should stick together. We were the two teuchters, stranded in the Central Belt. And you taught me how to cast a fly. Could go down and find what room he's in but maybe he just wants to crash. Coming up from Sunderland. Tornabloodysunderland. Worse than the Clyde. It's all dead sheds down his way so he thought he'd just take up the offer and visit his Island relatives. He hasn't seen them since he was a kid.

And yourself? You don't have anyone left, by Loch Broom. Shit, anyone would think you can hear me just because I'm up here, a few metres of altitude. You might be in London. You might be under the ground.

This Sunderland guy said he just mentioned it on the phone as a possibility, the idea of visiting the relatives on Lewis. Next thing these tickets arrived in the post. 'They must be desperate to get their peats home,' I'd told him. 'Must be a bag-them-out job. Better than getting bogged down.'

I knew about that.

Here's the scenario. One tractor goes down to the axles with the last big load on it. You can't budge it even when you get the load off. You can't support the trailer to unhitch it. You have to send the young lads down the track for jacks and planks. These are brought to the scene of desolation by another tractor which gets bogged when it gets near. You risk a third, just skirting the danger area. That bit too close. Shit, another one down. Have you got the score so far? It's not looking great. There's one more neighbour and before you know where you are you've the Island record for the biggest number of tractors bogged down at the same time. Four down and resources are getting scarce. That was the last year we went over to Lochs to cut peats.

Gas central heating – the way of the town. Nearly as good as cooking on it, man.

Maybe all that kind of excitement has happened already and our Sunderland friend is on his way to help manhandle all these bags out of the wet area. After the monsoon. All these fertiliser bags. Now it's fish farm bags. Fish farms – looks like we've blown that one too. A sound idea rushed to viability. There's been a couple of scares with chemicals. So what do you do? Easy. Change the name of the chemical. Have you come across this way of dealing with a problem somewhere before? Windscale/Sellafield? Give it another year and there'll be another layer in the design of piles of bagged peat. All these graphics, logos, colours getting bleached under the attack of ultra-violet. Most people don't have a clue how strong the light can be, up our way, once it gets through the clouds. Rays of light, shooting like howitzers, over the Lewis moorland.

And you'd be amazed at all the houses getting built on the more stony areas. The ground might be hellish for any sort of production, barring sheep meat, but there was now one hell of a crop of houses on it. No bad thing, either.

Houses like the one your olman built, Torcuil. It'll be your mother's house now. It was out along the road, a bit nearer the Devon river, a bit more sheltered than most sites you'd get on Lewis or Dundonnell. Maybe your olman could have built his house up Loch Broom way if the ferry route hadn't shifted to Ullapool and the road link to Inverauchtin-shoochtin-glockamorra hadn't got so developed. Crofts became worth money. Buildings in need of total renovation sold at a wild price.

And the rest of the family wanted to sell when the price was so good. Easier to share cash than fall out over land. The share that got you the electric guitar and amp, when the windfall arrived. That got you into the band scene. That got you enough session work, to call yourself a musician. I listened to the tracks you specified and even I could hear you were better than most of the accredited guys. The way of the session musician. Studio to studio. I thought you were less screwed up too, until you found your way to Lewis.

Torcuil, the chronology's gone completely to Hell, again. It's just wine. I can't be properly pissed. I'm not going to try to retrace steps, sort anything out. Maybe I can say something if I just maintain the course and speed.

It's like we're looking out further, from this high room, altering our course and our sightline to the northwest, right over the submarine pens up the Holy Loch. The whole way north. Focusing on Scoraig peninsula for now, just in from the Cailleach. We're wondering where the hell everyone went to, hoping it wasn't to Tasmania or some such place to do unto others worse than had been done to them.

Some days at work, I get an insight into the colonialists' way of speaking to folk. Some guys go on about the Hebs – they seem to forget than I'm one of them – or a half-breed, anyway. Bit more complicated than that, of course. A fair bit of Norse bloodline in the east coast stock, too.

In Lewis and Dundonnell, Norse was filtered through Gaelic. Various systems of orthography until people like my old man gave up on the written form of his own first language as something only for those who'd been to Varsity. He accepted the majority verdict and clung only to the spoken word. He didn't speak to me or the sister in Gaelic, though.

We've a few bearings, still, Torcuil, if you're alive and awake. We're not going back, either of us, you to Dundonnell or me to Griomsiadair. But bearings, Torcuil. Hell's teeth, just having a few of the bastards to start with, that's something. Let's cross the Minch again, together, though you didn't get much joy out of me, last time.

Torcuil 2

Still here, mate. There's only a wee glass left but it's yours if you want to change your mind. I'm on the tea with the UHT milk now.

I'm working on the chronology again. Since I spoke to you last, I phoned back to Germany and everything's OK. They're not daft though, as a species, women I mean. They see it or hear it. My mother's the same. My Gabriele listened for one or two syllables before asking me if the wine was free.

We're close to something now, Torcuil, *a bhalaich*, pretty close. Things not said and maybe there was a reason why not.

Getting a good bearing on your family home now. We've left the motorway, staying clear of Tullibody. Who wouldn't, if they could? Some bloody kind people, mind you. More tolerant than they could have been. But we're not crossing the Devon to these houses up Hungry Hill, Sauchie, or going out your way, to Coalsnaughton. We're going down past Glenochil. It's in the news again. Some Young Offender putting an end to it behind the wire. Could have been us, *a bhalaich*. Pretty close. I was losing the plot down there till my olman knew we had to get back home. The olaid was resigned to it too – the mainland wasn't what she remembered.

We're going along Hillfoots now. Menstrie, Alva, Tillie, Dollar and all of them with burns running down from the hills above them. You showed the way. I wouldn't have got further than Gartmorn Dam and the Devon, where the railway crossed. You got me on to the right buses. We went up all these tracks and fished the hill burns for wild fish so you knew why they were called brown trout. Small fish with heads like bulls and only reticent hints of red you could hardly call spots. You got one once that must have got the size it did by eating every other trout in the pool. It was a struggle that might have come to life from one of the woodcuts in your olman's angling books. I helped pull your big fish from the gravel to the path. Rowans and resilient birch. That's where these colours came from. Refracted on to the skins of these thin trout.

Back to the bungalows and bookshelves again. How to cast? I'd got a cheap fly rod from the paper-round money and you were a few weeks ahead of me. You had it. Up, pause, cast. The pause was the most important bit and the trickiest. We were ready to fall out when you remembered you'd promised your mother you'd go on the bike for something at the Spar Grocers. You'd to go or you'd get shot. When you came back, I'd be casting. And I was. You probably just went round the corner and strummed the guitar, without the amp so I thought you were gone. Maybe you got the man-management technique from your olman but it worked. Get the hell out of it and leave the pupil to make his own mistakes. Gain the skill.

And what did I give you in return, Torcuil, when you made it to Lewis? One day's fishing and two bacon rolls, not much more.

The first phone call was the biggest shock. I was looking after a place and its pets, out of town. An old guy called Angus. A mate's uncle. An uncle's mate. He had to go to Glasgow. For some treatment. My girlfriend had just come across Europe to see how this Islander and this Island were, outside holiday times. Gabriele picked up the phone and said, 'It's Torcuil.'

I didn't get your face from the name or from the voice when I took the phone. Maybe all these years in London left their trace. If you'd said this is Torcuil who caught a one and a quarter pound trout, from the Tillicoultry burn, or, your mate who caught a twenty-two and a half pound pike from the Dam because he went round the back, near the Black Devon at Clackmannan, when everyone else fished from the Sauchie pier – well, I'd have got you right away.

You and your girlfriend and me and mine – we met in a rustified lounge in Stornoway. You know, chunks axed out of perfectly good 3 by 2s to suggest timber in a barn. I wondered if I should be drinking with you, trying to conceal the shock when I saw your hair long and lank as if trapped in time. Thin in a way common to rock guitarists of an earlier era. Not thin as in wiry as in the tough style of hill trout. More like the reared fish now in the cages of Loch Griomsiadair, the ones in pitted chrome, with torn fins.

We mentioned some fish, some family, some recent history. Planned a day out, on the top loch. I'd get a wee permit for us both. Changed days. The Trust had made the fishing affordable. They reckoned that would cut down the poaching. They were right. Yes, my boat was still in the water. But we had to get back out of town, tonight. We were looking after the ranch at Garyvard, for old Angus. Cats, dog and hens, anyway.

You never said it first time, Torcuil, but Gabriele caught on before I did. She said she'd seen plenty like you and your friend, in the city of Köln.

And me, Torcuil, I missed that scene. Thank the Lord. Even though I don't think I believe in him any more. As a generation, we imported plenty old shit and a tab or two of acid but, in my day there wasn't much talk of white powders. When there was no dope around we'd try this or that. There used to be a cough mixture which still contained opium. That worked. There were yellow pills called Nembies. Didn't do anything for me but two of my mates disappeared for two days, wandering under the rhododendrons in Matheson's forest. Would have been more appropriate, out there, if they'd been on Dr Collis Brown's mixture, since the Chinese opium trade paid for all the bloody plants and soil and bridges in the first place. That was still the active ingredient till someone asked why sales were going through the roof.

Then the Family song called *The Weaver's Answer*. Guys had already caught on to modelling glue. Shoe conditioner from Woolie's did the trick too. First there was a buzz in the ears and you thought that was it until the pulses got more rhythmical. Then you were away. You could top up the visions if you kept conscious but otherwise it was maybe five minutes oblivion on the concrete deck of a concrete hut.

That man Bosch, not the electrician, the painter. His spirit was alive and unwell and hanging out, in the old youth club, close to the Nicolson Institute. None of our lot died. The red eyes and streaming noses, going home dizzy, strange smells, found handker-chiefs. Enough clues for a small town. The school took the head-on approach, rooting out culprits, maybe the boss just not knowing that the thing itself wasn't illegal. He also couldn't cope with the idea that there were no ringleaders, pushers, only a collective madness. Whatever action was taken couldn't stop the younger guys taking over when our mania subsided. Simple exhaustion saved us.

But one of the next group died from inhaling fumes. In a confined space. An abandoned outbuilding funded by Sir James Matheson's unlimited wealth. The end result was the same but it seemed to us very different from the accidents that happened out in the open. A wee cove caught under wheels or trapped by tide.

Now, down this way, in the housing schemes of the Central Belt, in eyeshot of this block of windows, they say the kids are going straight to the powders. No preliminaries. They tell me the dope is back in fashion up the road and across the Minch but it doesn't stop at that. Where there's money, there's cocaine. I'm out of touch. Maybe I should make an effort to know, as a man with a daughter growing fast. But that's me, Torcuil. Let's get back to you, man. You were the session guitarist who needed to escape the scene.

We failed to phone you. Failed to ask you out to the croft we were looking after. There were trout in the lochs behind it and lythe in the sea in front of it. Gabriele said she could handle you, not your friend.

We met again in town and your friend did most of the talking. She'd been on the heroin for longer. For you, Torcuil, it was the music scene. You told us the way it happened. You weren't like the nerds who got hooked. You measured the buzz, took it when you had to get up there. Avoided it for weeks after. Then it was for days after. Then you just knew you couldn't play so well without it. Then it got expensive. So you had a hole in your back garden and buried the deal there. People came to your back door so you got watched.

You both knew it was closing in, a matter of time. You'd seen it happen to so many. Better to go through Cold Turkey in a place you planned to be. Better than a cell. You'd planned on escaping to France. A location passed by word of mouth. No scene there. Good weather. Good busking. Cheap living.

But the girlfriend's sister was a white-settler up here so it was a contact. She'd persuaded you, remembering that your dad was from somewhere up in the Highlands. She'd got you some gigs. There was the bar-lounge and the Indian restaurant. We went along. Nodded to the SY Pakistani proprietor. Great accent. We bought our meal. You two got yours on the house. There were no other customers that night but the word would get round. The guitar was good, really good. Singing needed work. She'd help you out with that.

She was a liability, you told me, that one time we went fishing. Casting for a late sea trout that failed to appear. You still had the knack, a far better rod arm than I'd ever have. Your line always landed lightly. Musician's touch? She was playing the manager, kind of aggressive, pissing everyone off. What could you do? She was on edge. She had all this stuff, fucking bottlefuls, for the withdrawals but she was still getting bad spasms. It had been a big chunk of her life.

I still remember your flycasting. Best pleasure to be had that day. The three movements. Up, pause then cast. The sea trout had long since run to this loch on a spate. They'd seen it all now, this late in the season. These fish wouldn't chase lures, wouldn't play with us.

My last pause was too long. Your phone call wasn't such a big surprise. Worst thing was, you were in the place at the time, sleeping next door. You'd had a few pints, just enough to get a sleep. She just went through the shaky door to the toilet. A holiday caravan. It was always shaking. You found her there, all the empty bottles around her. She hadn't taken any chances, just swallowed everything. You made the phone calls, ambulance, police, everyone. Couldn't go back there.

So I came in to my mother's house, back in the town. Down the road from the caravan you had to leave. It was the only time me and the olaid fell out in years. She said to me after you left, 'Fit kind o people are you mixin wi?'

She'd only slip back into Doric if she was really wound up. Me snapping back, out of sheer guilt because I knew I could have done more.

Torcuil, *a bhalaich*, you even gathered the mussels and moored them at Low Water, beside the boat so they'd be fresh. For bait. OK, I was on shiftwork. And coping with the pan-European relationship. Still and all, fuck's sake.

You waited a few tides, Torcuil, before I called you for that one day's fishing. I was caught up, reorganising my own life. Gabriele was trying to get her bearings. Cologne to Stornoway. Quite a shift.

The formalities over, there was no point in hanging about. If you returned to London, it was back to the scene. The only option was your own mother's for a spell. OK, she'd given up on you but she'd given up on you before and you'd always got a bed there. The numbers worked. You didn't have to say too much. Next ferry.

We didn't keep in touch like we said we would. I'm looking in your direction right now. Well, the direction of your mother's house, anyway. From this hotel height. I'd like to go back to you teaching me to cast with a fly rod, in your own back garden. My lungs and liver seem to have survived the dangers of adolescence in that period of history, in that place. But I've hurt some other people since then. It's not true what we used to chant at school – 'Sticks and stones will break my bones but names will never hurt me.'

The olman used to find it difficult, biting the tongue, when he had bosses hanging over him. 'Try counting to ten, son,' he said once. 'Just count to ten, nice and slow. Before you say a thing. That usually works for me.'

But usually, in my own case, it's been by neglect. You might be in the back-room now, that house in Coalsnaughton, with the amp switched on or off. You might have driven yourself up that hill path, to get back to a place where you hunted out a large trout. But I don't think so. A lot of people gravitate back to London, not wanting to go. I know some good musicians with good families, living down that way, don't get me wrong. But I'm seeing you now, navigating around your own veins. Losing tracks, losing way. Putting the needle bloody anywhere, to get a fix.

I've gone off this wine. Don't fancy that last glass. Changed days. Could have handled a dry white, scoffed the lot. This stuff is too red, too smooth.

Klondykers

'Not a McDonald's,' Anna said and I couldn't let it go. My daughter was growing up. Fast.

'Time was, we had to drive all around the outskirts of various blooming European cities just to find a Burger King,' I said. 'Now you're moaning because here it is, the big high yellow M, where you didn't expect to see it.'

We'd been well warned. The former East was changing fast. We drove by skips full of fine old windows with bronze furniture. It wasn't fair – these guys wanting neutral uPVC draftproof windows, just like their neighbours. They'd soon have to install vents, to provide an alternative airflow to that caused by expansion and contraction in natural materials, like the timber items they were throwing out.

How can anywhere be the former East?

The night-driving and the *Autobahn* gave way to A roads. The route took us across a long steel bridge.

We came upon a narrower road with high poplars swaying. We were still on that avenue and then another sign said 'Pitbus Circus'. We used to have to go and hunt the lions and tigers and efelants on loud posters. I remembered further back than that, when the Circus came to Stornoway. No big cats or bun-eating landwhales but I did remember the clown on stilts. Couldn't have been viable because they never came again. All these trucks, suspended in nets from the derrick of the *Loch Seaforth*. That was the best bit. When the show was all up in the air. Before the *Hebrides* worked the shorter Minch crossing, putting in to Tarbert, with its turntables and a lift to the car-deck.

I was curious to see what Baltic water looked like. I'd grown up with the Baltic shoeshop, where they had a foot gauge to get the right width of Clarks sandals. Now Birkenstock rules OK among the sensible casual brigade. If my uncle Ruaraidh bumped into me in the metropolis he'd steer me into the Baltic bookshop and if I was slow to choose between this and that, he'd take the both of them to the till. *Dinny Smith Comes Home* by Angus MacVicar and RM Ballantyne's *Among the Bushrangers*. I'd get all the Enid Blyton I could stuff down me, in the library, if I still wanted it.

What about herring? If there were still Baltic herring to be caught, how come all these Klondykers crossed the North Sea with their decks stacked with empty barrels, for the stated purpose of filling them up in SY? Gabriele said the Baltic fish were small, sweet and seasonal. It's a matter of quantity. I thought of the sister and my olman wrestling over the last salt herring from the score the olaid had boiled. She'd have to change the water at least once, sometimes twice. I wouldn't fancy eating a salt herring raw. I remembered the olman going to Henderson's on Bayhead for a bottle of wine to go with the New Year dinner. It was a once-a-year thing, then. I couldn't figure out why he was asking for salt herring in a shop that had nothing but bottles of drink. I found out much later it was Sauternes.

The grey empire, recently folded, couldn't have lived on pink salami alone. There were a lot of mouths to feed. Even though Adolf and Joe had managed to wipe out all these millions between them.

The herring shoals were now chased with electronic sensors on the purse-seine so the bag wasn't pulled tight till it was worth it. But then the markets might not be prepared for them, so the catch might get ground to meal.

And then you fed that to caged salmon or caged furry animals. We no longer had glossy minks in wire cages, back on Lewis. Only the escape artists whose teeth had coped with chicken wire, applying jittering leverage till the staples sprung. The escaped mink bred. They dined well, on hens, ducks, eels and salmon though they killed far more than they ate. Like people.

Frozen Minch and Westside herring, which had found no ready market, for human consumption, went to our neighbours who farmed both mink and salmon. And bizarre blocks of frozen sand eels. So our own puffins and sea trout had to cover more air and water to fill their bellies.

Klondykers had never paid the top price. But they bought in bulk. My own account of my first work, after school, is now definitely historical. Basket after basket would swing over the SY hoil. The Faroese would want them coated in sweet red pickle but the Baltic market wanted a dense packing in plain brine. I'd worked, topping up barrels, till a few midnights. And just maybe Gabriele had eaten some of the fish I'd packed. Matjes, taken soaked but raw, with boiled potatoes. Just possibly the produce of my home town.

Her and her father, the architect-sailor, eating as you only do when you've had the boat leaning and spray on your lips, and she's tied up secure, springs and stern lines, with a small amount of slack. The sweet Baltic herring might still swim but the shoals would be smaller and more scarce. Dense numbers ran for limited periods only. That's what we say. The herring or the mackerel or the salmon are running. Draw that picture.

Baltic herring were more suitable for frying whole. Minch herring had for centuries provided the full, pregnant matjes. There was a complete grammar of grades and stamps. Our words for different qualities of peat had nothing on it.

The talk of herring sustained us along the avenue and took us by a few missed turnings, a couple of backtracks. Gabriele was getting tired. Maybe this right side of the road was now an extra bit of concentration, after years on the left. We drove into the Pitbus Circus by sheer accident. There were no tigers, no clowns. It was a grass circle surrounded by a curve of buildings. Restrained neo-classicism. Robert Adams might have made a wee sortie over this way. If he'd been as far as Bath for a job, this was possible. More likely, the columns showed how the same movements in the arts went in waves across most of Europe.

These showcase buildings had been maintained. But driving

on towards Sassnitz, looking out for the turn to take us out the northern coast, the streetlights showed an island in transition.

Interior sides of gable walls are just like the inside covers of books, when the elevation is exposed, during demolition. Generations of wallpapers are caught in the glare. Abandoned picture frames tilt on their nails. The residue of soot and conversations hold to lime. A suspension.

Jibs of high counterbalanced cranes break the changing skyline. Fallen bricks remain in clumps and the new blocks are all in ordered groups, held by steel tapes.

We found the street with the right name. The family hotel was somewhere along this one. One or two hotels were newly completed but we found the older building. We could have been in Bournemouth. The long-established pine trees looked similar to those on the English Riviera.

Rügen needs the New Year business. This island did most of its trade, in much-needed foreign currency, till a couple of years ago. Now people from the inland cities of the former GDR drove here, for their holiday. The ones who were earning. There were no Trabants in this car park. People who had been on the waiting list for a decade now wanted to buy a big car from across the former border.

The pier was at the end of the street and we had to see it first. It was long and wide and lit up bright and there was a restaurant about a third of the way along. Even in all this artificial light, we could see that the shapes were right – an echo of the old form in sepia-tinted photographs. The postcards in a shoebox.

You hadn't expected a true restoration – weathered planks, numbered and returned but... it was all so shiny. The zinc on the galvanised rails was catching the lights of the restaurant and the waxing moon combined.

This was Gabriele's pilgrimage. She had not expected this scale of development, so soon. All those building sites. Anna was checking out her flapping jeans, making sure she didn't pick up dirt on the trailing hems. Looking forward to seeing the cousins again.

I'd already got good mileage out of the return of the bellbottoms as well as another coming of Jimi Hendrix. So I gave it a rest.

That look was already a common currency, both sides of the new Germany. The fashions in jeans went alongside the sports clothes that ruled over the new Europe. The logo is the indicator of the individual's income or debt.

Things had shifted fast. The cost of reconstruction. Not forgetting demolition.

Reunions

The reunion was painless. I was tense about the language. My German hadn't improved much and was slow enough to dull the conversation. People felt they had to stop and explain. Anna had chosen French at school and we hadn't pushed the issue. After a couple of Rostocker Pils, from the tap, things were getting easier, between the grown-ups.

Anna was next door. I was out of it as soon as my head hit the crisp pillow but I came to in an hour or so, knowing Gabriele was lying awake.

'Strange to be back?' I asked.

But Gabriele had never been to her father's birthplace before. She only knew the piers and the shores and the reed beds from the stories. Her father couldn't tell her what had changed and what had not.

So strange. This is where she should have come with him on boating holidays if it had all been possible, back then. The graves of the grandparents she'd never known were on this very island. The legacy of the district piermaster. Even in the 1930s, this had been the recreational pier, with pleasure boats and craft for hire. There were fishing villages with working jetties and her grandfather had looked after these too. We'd need to see them. Pity that, I said, so the Stornoway Coastguard would just have to go looking at boats and piers on his holidays. Well, couldn't be helped.

At last we slept. We made it to breakfast, just. We found the same selection of rye and white and birdseed rolls we'd get in Bonn or Cologne. Endless coffee and Anna just picking up where she'd left off, with the cousins. The older ones all wanted to practice their English. The younger ones wanted help with their new Lego kits. Nobody in the half-empty hotel seemed to worry about our noisy babble.

The forces would divide. Gabriele's man would of course want to see the harbours. Perhaps Gabriele would like to visit the cemetery and see the family graves. Then there was a very good swimming pool in the big hotel but the public could buy tickets for it. And of course there was the Rügen steam train.

We all wanted to do everything. There were enough days before the New Year to make this possible.

After the board games and card games were carefully packed away, Gabriele needed to talk before she could sleep. We'd share one last beer. This was a place she'd needed to see and we were just in time.

Next day, we saw a bit more of Rügen. For years the main roads had been developed as links with the high ferries to Bornholm and Trelleborg. Acres of tarmac parking were now in place. Containers. A bit like Felixstowe. But there were still unspoiled shores.

After a light snow flurry went through, the December brightness would intensify and pick out each individual bronze stem in the rushes. In the sway of a body of them, you could just make out a parting, like the habitual combed pattern of the head-hair of a man from some decades back. You'd decipher a channel and discover a black boat, lying snug, to its mooring.

The rushes would give way to shingle, shelving to make a landing place. The black boats would be turned keel up. Broad white calligraphy made from bold legal numbers in cracked gloss over matt bitumen. An arrangement of anchors lay beside the beached fleet. Flattened flukes were pitted where the oxide had failed to adhere.

The chemical film was smoky over most of the area of exposed metal. But clean steel showed where regular use had worn away all coatings. You could have spent a whole day arranging them and the sculpture of anchors wouldn't have been more startling. There were too many for securing the boats so they must have been for laying out fishing gear.

Gabriele told me more of the family history. How her aunt had walked across the railway bridge, fleeing Rügen at night, clutching her childrens' hands. Her own father had seen the writing on what was left of the walls. He'd remained in the West after finding his way back from the Eastern Front. He knew to stay well clear of anywhere the Red Army might have reached.

It took a while before the rebuild got going. When it did, he was in the right place with the right skills. He'd chosen well. In a few years, Bonn was booming and its neighbouring cities also prospered.

So Gabriele's aunt Erika had got out in the nick of time, before the watchtowers were spaced all along the shorelines. The good old democratic GDR was founded in 1949. Not so many years before Gabriele's birth in the emerging city of Bonn. Now, in 1999, the next generation of Gabriele's cousins had been given back the old family hotel on Rügen island. It sounds like a neat fifty-year cycle, put like that, but both ends were pretty messy.

We looked to the cliff line and from this angle the wooden towers were more obvious. At first I thought they were hunters' lookouts. Yes, they were, you said. But it wasn't tame pigs, bred to be hairy and gamey. Think about it. There was a lot of boats moored here and I'd said myself they looked like a seaworthy type. The islands of Denmark were just across there. Not that far to Kiel Fjord and Flensburg when you thought of it, in kilometres or nautical miles.

Swimmers had escaped. They'd stumbled ashore to start their new life with nothing but an out-of-date costume and a smear of pork fat. Usually, they were sighted and one walkie-talkie flickered to another. A launch, faster than the low-geared fishing boats, would be sent out to hunt with its searchlight. Often the swimmers left but just didn't arrive anywhere.

We looked closer at the clinker boats, larger craft than those we'd seen before. Twenty-footers, beamy but not too much draft so they could be hauled up the banks by large-geared winches. You saw the remains of winches like that in the geos of Lewis. But this too was small scale commercial fishing. While the colossal tonnage of the factory-ships had gone to the Atlantic to do their bit towards feeding the empire, these inshore craft set their long lines and fyke-nets. Red and black flags frayed on bamboo poles, projecting over the raised sheerline at their sterns. Big three-bladed props would be linked to hand-started diesels.

'So you wouldn't have needed a key?' you asked.

'No, the starting handles would stick out from timber hous-ings. Worn smooth where palms gripped them. You just flick the decompression lever over, get the heavy flywheel turning, then you flick the lever back.'

If the fuel was casting a fine spray at the injector you'd hear the universal language, the diesel creak. She'd have to go. There would be one puff of black smoke and then you'd put her in gear. You'd have to be sure the prop was clear of snags at the beach first. No rise and fall of tide here but a few shoves of the shoulder and you'd soon get her moving down the slope. Must be a few flounders or plaice left here to make it worthwhile.

I realised then you were telling me something more. This was how you imagined he'd done it.

You told me your father, the deserter and one of only two survi-vors from a regiment, had made another choice here, later in his life. He'd been invited to attend an architectural conference. The latter days of the Eastern Bloc. Even in these last years, he'd only have access to a few showcase buildings. The GDR still wanted to demonstrate a working system, to Western eyes.

But he'd given his guardians the slip and taken a boat. A Rügen boat with a shape which showed the same Norse ancestry as those of the Scottish islands.

He could have easily afforded to have a replica built. Had it shipped across. They'd gladly have taken the proper Deutschmarks. They built and exported Folkboats for currency, in the 1960s for God's sake. Or rather for the good of the state. And he had no need to escape anywhere. He'd done all that. He had freedom of movement. Up to a point and here was that point.

I'd never pushed Gabriele for the details about her father's death. I'd known they'd never been presented with a body to bury.

That it had happened over here, where her grandfather had been a piermaster. That was all she'd said.

The visiting architect had absconded from the conference. He may have taken out a boat. Details had grown no more clear, with the years. They'd had to make a thousand phone calls, write scores of letters, before getting the little information they'd ever received.

An uncle on her mother's side had come to represent the family. Her brother Michel had joined him. They might not have known which questions to ask. Michel had never had much interest in boats, only cars. The two men might have thought there was little point in asking any questions at that time.

Her father couldn't have launched one of the working boats on his own but he might have taken one that was moored afloat. Just waded out to it. But the diesel thump would have been a giveaway on a quiet night.

So a man was missing and a boat seemed to be missing. It was fair weather but once you were out, clear of the banks, you were an unlit boat, black in colour, crossing shipping lanes. Out there, the thumping of a big vessel's own seagoing cylinders would easily drown the noise of ten or twenty horsepower. If he'd just rowed out, the swish of oars wouldn't register on the decibel scale. If he'd seen danger coming and shouted out loud, he would not have been heard.

There had been no record of sightings, no shots, no news. There was a missing boat and there was some wreckage. But the number wasn't on any boat part washed up. So these splintered sections of bone-white pine, jutting from the black stain – they could have been from the normal annual wastage of Rügen boats. Ones broken from moorings or ones floundered at sea. Or tumbled down the beach in a February storm.

Had they considered their father might have survived, his stolen boat come ashore somewhere in Denmark? Some men wanted to start a new life. He wouldn't be the first. As to the matter of the boat, perhaps now was not the time, but there was a matter of compensation which would have to be faced. A comrade had lost the means of his productivity to the state.

Of course they'd circulated the story and the description to police in West Germany, Denmark, Sweden and Finland. Yes, Poland too. Was there a seed of doubt? Gabriele shook her head. Doubt as to the way he died, that was all. But it wasn't like in all these Cold War thrillers where there was a reason for everything. Why people had to disappear. When the plot was unravelled, the matter was satisfied. In her father's case, there was just no way of being sure of the ending.

It was hardest on their mother, the doubts. From the children's perspective, they'd just lost their father and had to mourn him without visiting the cemetery after church, before dinner on Sunday. At least there was a stone now, even if there was nothing under it. They had to wait for years before the loss was officially recognised. When that happened, it did make it easier for Mutti.

Some people got to see their body, dressed and looking its best. Other times there was a reason why the lid was screwed down. But now I knew there could also be a gravestone, with nothing under it.

The official at Bergen or Sassnitz or across the bridge wouldn't have known that this eminent architect from the other side, reported missing, used to row around these bays with his own father. A story unfolds. It doesn't fall into your lap, all sorted. You might miss the significant bits, or you might hoard and file details that just don't seem to matter.

Maybe now was the time Gabriele's family could talk about it again. Time I played some pool with the daughter and the cousins. They might let me play the *Best of Jimi Hendrix* double CD Anna had given me for Christmas. Just because she wanted to hear a bit of history herself.

Hearing it again, I thought Hendrix played the best version of the Dylan song. That opening – 'Must be some kind of way out of here'. This was the best or worst place to listen to it. The watch-towers remaining, though their ladders had been taken away. The spacing between each one maybe corresponded to what a watcher could scan, with the aid of 7 x 50 Zeiss binoculars, in average visibility. Or maybe they needed to flog these west for good currency and the guards just got Zenit ones.

Brickwork

Most historical events seem to me to be a fine balance of intention and cock-up. Here's one scenario, leaning towards the latter.

Her father needed to float that boat. He'd known his own father would really be in the boat with him, in spirit. All he had to do was to extend his evening stroll over a fence or two. Locate the vessel he'd sighted earlier and give it a shove out. But some twitchy guard saw him. This gangly, spotty, kid recited the rote-learned warning twice but the architect's mind was engaged in acts of memory.

The man who was able to reason out his run before the advancing Red Army – and survived – was vulnerable in his own home territory. When the authorities discovered the guy they'd shot had quite some standing, they got a shock. Things were supposed to be opening up. They couldn't tie it all up too neatly. So they followed the example of Mrs Thatcher's British Government Ministers, in courts of law, and were 'economical with the truth'.

Here's another version. Even a story that is fixed, secure in its train of narrative detail, is different every time it's told. And this one has very little fixed, except some background information which might be essential.

An eminent architect had been invited over to view certain designated sights. He knew he had to stick to the script. He couldn't stray. He was reported as having behaved impeccably up to that critical point. The delegation had been touring a fine piece of Baltic minimalism. Sympathetic designers from Finland had worked with the Party to produce the hotel. Rest and recuperation for those with onerous duties. The new hotel was set back a safe interval from the dunes. For more than one reason. Forecasts for erosion and encroachment suggested the need to allow a generous distance back from the water's edge, if you were to think of a projected lifespan of at least a hundred years. That would be enough because there are of course some unfortunate precedents in buildings planned to last out a full glorious millennium.

And then of course there were the shanty villages of caravans and bothies for normal workers, erected closer to the water. A sensitive degree of separation was clearly required. So the great and good would not be disturbed by inquisitive eyes, looking to the shine of the new modernism.

Now we could all buy a ticket to swim in the trapped rays of winter sun, but it would have been private functions only when your father made his officially sanctioned visit.

These wide, triple-glazed windows looked seaward but the angles had been cleverly thought out. You wouldn't see the line of watchtowers, close to the swaying tops of the pines.

Maybe the visitors really could believe that this was a sign of solid economic foundations. This was of course only the start of a building programme which would make that level of recreational and conference facility available to the many as well as to the few. Later.

At least one of these visitors from the West, however, had the mark of a survivor. As surely as if it had been inked under his living skin. Two youths from the architectural class of 1939 had been in it together. They had been transported across a continent, fought and then been rounded up together. This history had to be the key.

Gabriele's father and his friend had heard the stories. If you went behind that wire in that camp you would not come out again. The two men had lived through fire from both sides by lying low during the day and sighting the plough in the night sky. Their angle on the pole star had taken them all the way across the desolate kilometres. But one man's past life was still trapped here in Rügen.

I think he set a course, that dim night. He'd crossed more than one frontier by night, before. He'd emerged on the lucky side or at least the prosperous one. He hadn't even needed to walk across a long bridge. The survivor has to live with guilt.

But to put his Rügen past behind him, he'd have to sail from it, alone, on his own wits. A black boat in a dark sea, criss-crossed by the wakes of all these ferries and cargo ships.

I'll go for that story. It's like diving down the stairwell, in a solid apartment block in Turin, the very house where he was raised before the madness of fascism struck. That's what Primo Levi did. Or probably did. How can anyone know, for sure? Maybe he'd only kept everything together till he'd borne witness to all the things it was possible for a human being to tell.

It was me now, lying awake, trying not to move about. Gabriele had found the sleep she needed. It was worth two ferries and a long drive for that. *The Periodic Table*, in English, was lying unopened on the table, her side. She'd come late to bed after waiting up, drinking pear schnapps with her brother, when the rest of us had sloped off. Nothing was resolved but they had now held their wake.

We'd have one collective family walk on New Year's Day, out past the empty *Sekt* bottles and spent fireworks. Some said, this one, '98 to '99, was the real Millennium? And others said it was 2000–2001. Was that logic or maths? Where's the logic in the arbitrary marking of time, anyway? Hang on though, there's a bit of astronomy and natural physics involved. Difficult to argue with the sun and the moon. Shit, a party's a party.

The Caspar David Freidrich cliffs were reflecting the light, casting it back seaward. The flints in the shingle shimmered. The cousins were sifting for fossilised octopus. Sure enough, the brown tentacles were recognisable. You hoped for amber. It only took time for all these animal bodies to stop being so sinister. A bit unfair on left-handed folk, that continuing extension of meaning. Casting nasturtiums. But that's how language is.

We were stopped by the cops on our way home. A bored Sunday morning officer in Berwick-upon-Tweed when we drove in to hunt down bacon and eggs.

'This car's overloaded,' he said. ' What do you have in it?'

'Usual stuff,' I said.

'Open up the boot,' he said.

He just looked at me when he saw all these weathered bricks, the fruits of old Rügen, washed by the Baltic, sharp edges muted.

'Usual stuff for him,' Anna said. The two sage folks exchanged long-suffering looks and the cop just said to take it easy, up the road.

Back on the Island, we made a winter walk in similar bright conditions. We didn't go Griomsiadair way but out from Melbost, the beach behind the airport. It's still a civilian installation. We kept Nato out. Don't know exactly where these old bricks came from but there's plenty, washed by Broad Bay. Stamped 'Lewis Brick'.

Anna helped me with the mortar work. 'You're just doing this because you're too proud to play Lego any more,' she said. That was about right. The Morsø stove was imported to Lewis from the Danish Baltic islands. They sell hundreds a year, in SY. We were careful to alternate the Rügen and Lewis bricks in the surround. But, within that scheme, all these random variations in the tones looked fine.

Spare Parts

Charlie's wife was a very understanding woman but now that the four chimneys were only dimly remembered ghosts and the roof was fixed, would there be any chance at all of a clear up? There was the Audi and the one for bits. There was also the Lada. I remembered the conversations. Charlie's opposite number at the watch changeover winding him up, as you do, and Charlie coming back with the line, 'Aye, but I own my Lada. The bank owns your Ford.'

We'd done the concrete paths and the weathershield paint on Charlie's house. And my VW (Type 3) van had shining, resprayed flanks and was running sweetly. That was a lot of hours prep before the paint job. I was still owing him. So we had a boys' day out with Anna as an honorary member of the club and she said, years after, it was one of the best days she'd ever had, running dead cars to the dump, one after the other.

It started off with a boat-job since we had the big van on hire and the towbar had both types of fitting. So we took the dinghy, rebuilt in a colleague's garage, along Newton, the gang of three of us in the front. Charlie said, 'Oh look, some poor bastard's lost a wheel.' As we watched it rolling past us.

There was that second's delay before the crunching of the collapsed trailer sent sparks we couldn't see but could imagine all too well.

Our little breakdown was not a kick in the arse off a break in the sea-wall where the remains of a concrete slipway survive. There was a bit of collapsing here and there but it was no worse than the other slip at the far side of the harbour. We just hailed a passer-by.

The flashers went on and the dinghy came off the trailer and onto the slip to wait for the tide. Just as if we'd planned it.

'Now Anna, *a ghràidh*, you are at present accompanying no less than two coastguard officers on an off-watch mission. Both of us are completely capable of forgetting to come back to row that dinghy to the mooring at High Water so please dear, remind us gentlemen.'

She repeated 'gentlemen' with a question mark added. Then she nodded and the deal was done. The doctrine of shared responsibility. Good working practice.

So next it was the Lada. And we got a hold of trailer number two. This was a proper one for moving sick and dead vehicles. It's called an ambulance, in the trade. We agreed it was better to recover the boat trailer from the side of the road first. So we did that and the damage wasn't terminal by any means but a job for another day. We just left it in Charlie's back yard, though we were clearing up.

There's a lot of adrenalin in steering a Lada. That occurs when there isn't a seat and it's getting towed and you're steering. Then you realise the scraping is coming from the trailing driveshaft which is sending a regular hail of sparks for a wider arc than you would think possible. And you remember Charlie saying that the petrol tank isn't disconnected yet and, thank God, Anna's riding shotgun in the towing van but they must be bantering because they're slow to realise that their father and watchmate respectively is holding for his life with one arm and waving for his life with the other.

I don't think I've ever been so scared. But we all survived. The standard Lewisian repair of twists of galvanised fence-wire sufficed to tie up the shaft. The rain of sparks stopped and we reached the dump without incident. These were the former days. When the council boys were so grateful that you took in old vehicles, instead of abandoning them out peat roads, that they didn't make you complete multiple forms, drain off all liquids and oils and pay several fees.

So next was Audi number two and that was amazing because a guy just showed up. He'd been phoning for a while and he lived just out the peninsula. So Charlie said, 'We agreed fifty notes for the bits you wanted. Give us sixty now and we'll deliver the whole thing for you right to your door.' And that's what we did. But the day was getting on. Since Anna was along for the hurl, we couldn't just work on because we'd be sure to get reminded about lunch and stuff like that. And then there was the state of the tide to remember. You thought we were going to forget, didn't you? But we didn't and Anna rowed that boat to a running mooring for us and that was another tick.

So the light was just beginning to go when the final carcass of Audi number one was secure on the ambulance. If the last shall be first then this was the appropriate order of events. But it involved a fair amount of improvisation with several different jacks. And then we realised that even that lot wasn't going to solve our problem. So three sharp minds went to work. One of them had a good grasp of wheeled transport from the beginnings of a self-taught bilingual approach to life. Anna's early grammar was made up of composites of German and English so 'auto' was pretty much her first word.

Then I heard her say 'auto-shoes', which got me thinking till I saw her looking at roller skates. One day, from her car-seat, she said 'auto-see-saw'. I couldn't figure out that one, so I ended up doing a wee U-turn and looking back along the route. The Peel's crane was at work on a site by the road. Auto-see-saw.

And one of us had the advantage of a very good pass in O-grade Physics behind him. And Charlie was just bloody sharp, full stop. The logistics of vehicle removal were proving as much of a challenge as the dismantling of chimneys. See chimneys, when they're not on your own house, everyone is brave. Just put a rope on it and tow it with the tractor. It's got to come down. Aye, but it might not come down in bite-sized harmless portions. And the mass could fall the wrong way and gain velocity as it went. So we played Lego with scaffolding. I'm not sure our tower would have been approved by a missing old mate of mine who really was qualified in this subject. We took turns, nibbling into the tough, poured concrete, with a heavy Kango hammer. Good vibrations.

But the gang was getting tired, the day of the dead cars. The crack was still good but we'd all quietened down. We faced one more obstacle. The ambulance's turning circle was just that bit too wide for the turning place at the entrance to the dump. The gates of course were locked now. No-one likes a loose end after a good day's play.

Two young dudes drove up right then. They'd come by for a spruchle through the skip, outside the wire, to see if anything was worth salvaging. And their eyes lit up when they saw the Audi. Charlie is a good judge of human nature and said, 'A fiver and she's yours.'

Even Anna gave him a look. But these lads could look after themselves. 'Aye, but weren't you going to dump it?'

'I cannot tell a lie,' Charlie said, at the closed gates of said dump. And then they said, 'Tell you what, that's the ambulance from Lava's garage, isn't it? We've used it before. So what about we take this off your hands now? Get the trolley back to the cove in the morning and everything's cool.'

So that's what happened and it's very likely that the Audi made a mechanical version of the Lazarus trick. With some help from some talented skip-raiders.

But let us not forget that all our collective efforts could serve only to prolong the individual history of that Audi. Like the raising of Lazarus himself, only a postponement of the inevitable was possible. It wouldn't be immortal. I remember this point from the days when I was a believer.

And fair's fair, one of the guys who argued for looking at the real significance behind the miraculous was Abdu'l Bahá – son of the main prophet figure in the Bahá'í Faith. I don't know if I told you he gave public talks in Paris in 1912. On the sixth of January in 1913, he stayed in a fine family manse in Charlotte Square, Edinburgh, before delivering a similar talk. The rebirth of a man who was spiritually dead was more significant than the walk of a dead man. If I told you he was invited by the wife of a Free Church minister, you would probably think I was telling stories. So I am. But that's what the recorded information says.

So nearly six months after the Titanic dived down deep, bringing several millionaires and many of the poor of Ireland down with her, a prisoner freed by the Young Turks revolution gave public talks to argue for the establishment of a New World Order. And before July was over, the following year, the mechanised war would explode and take all these lads from all these villages and cities and crofts and fine houses. My grandfather would be one of those who failed to return from it. A dim figure from the village of Griomsiadair was only one of the many lost from the *Iolaire* (formerly *Amaltha*) on New Year's night, 1919.

And of course that chain of events which became the Great War would set in motion the punitive settlement and the circumstances which would let that bitter and believing, small dark man send out all that rhetoric. Members of the Bahá'í Faith did not suffer as badly as Jewish people, gypsies and homosexuals during the Nazi period though the faith was disbanded by an order signed by Himmler. No official meetings were held. The alternative was to sign up to a policy of expelling any members of the Faith from a Jewish background.

But in Iran the State is still involved in prosecutions of Bahá'ís, amongst others, for holding to the belief of a minority in that region. Images of the destruction of Bahá'í cemeteries evoke images of similar destruction of Jewish sites in Europe since the 9th of November, 1938. And of course we can't discuss the treatment of Buddhists in occupied Tibet because of our economic trading deals. Maybe they're also called 'treaties' now.

Back to resurrections. Audi, or Auto Union as it was then, already had the badge of four interlocked rings to symbolise merged companies. Of course their production lines were used for the war effort and of course they were bombed. The company was reincarnated in East Germany as a State enterprise. In West Germany, VW took over Audi in 1966.

Charlie told me that the DKW was a more popular car than the Beetle, just before the war. He told Anna where the name came from – *Dampf-Kraft-Wagen* – and asked her to guess why. She first guessed that this was a wagon, made in the damp. Then she asked if it needed damp to work.

'Think of power, think of pistons,' Charlie said.

'Steam?'

'Steam.'

Before they became the largest manufacturer of motorcycles in the world, DKW produced a light, steam-driven car. So the famous supercharged four-stroke in the Audi Quattro is only one in a continuing series of reincarnations. And there is still a dispensation for historic two-strokes to leave their blue-grey lines of vapour across a large part of Europe. A guy brought one, powering a Trabant, back to Lewis, about 1994. Thank the Lord, that one didn't end up in Charlie's drive.

Clinker

We can't evade the difficult subject of the deaths of boats. After these years in the Coastguard Service, of course I think of this boat and that boat. Ones we lost. But there were people aboard, too. I could intone the names of the vessels, over the years, like a prayer. But it wouldn't change a thing. Reports have been written and cases closed.

So I'm talking here about boats that were broken up. Incidents where there was no-one aboard. So it was more of a matter for insurers, if they were insured, rather than life-saving services.

They do say that if a vessel is seriously damaged, by accident or storm, then a total loss may be an easier situation than a partial one.

Even as the hospital porter, you could see that this could also apply to the human body. It might not have been a good thing if the owner of that liver I'd once burned, had somehow pulled through. The torture in the mind, which had led to the terrible bodily injury, would be prolonged. But I also know that you can write off a body too soon. I once met a cheery soul being discharged from the Lewis Hospital. His offspring told me that I'd met their father already. A month back, I'd wheeled him in for an emergency resuscitation, then made tea for his grown-up bairns.

The consultant had indeed got his heart beating and the air circulating. He advised that the old fellow was not likely to survive more than twenty-four hours. But that would be a mercy in itself because it would give their sister a chance to say goodbye. Four whole weeks later, here was that same old fellow telling me a parting tale, from the wheelchair. He told me about another man who came very close to stations with names in an unknown tongue.

'Did you hear about the Lewisman who got a job on the trains in Wales? He was to call out these long names of stations they stopped at. He couldn't manage that. So what he called out was this: If there's anybody here for there they'd better get out now cos this is it.'

There was light in this old cove's eyes all right as he delivered that one. His voice was strong enough. Good job no-one had written this man off. Similarly, I wouldn't want to be the one to make a final decision on whether to operate on a failing vessel or to put her out of her misery.

Remember the old *Peace and Plenty*. I was already patching the patches, when she was in my care, back when I first got together with Gabriele. In the following fast years of the new career, and the state of fatherhood and the building of extensions to a solid Coastguard house, her care was neglected.

In the case of a human being, it would be difficult to judge that one particular life was more worth more effort in its saving, than another. In the case of a historic vessel you could make a strong argument for putting your resources into the *Peace and Plenty*.

She had that full rounded stern. Just looking at her, you'd know she would rise to big water or jabble. Very beamy, not very deep in the water so she could be pulled up and down the shore. Something sharper towards the bow then fairing out and coming in, not too fast, to that ample backside.

The records showed that she was built by the man who swam ashore with the rope from the *Iolaire*. She was eighteen feet overall by seven-foot six in the beam. You could see the engine mounts and the cutlass bearing so she must have once had an inboard. Sure enough, there was the bronze seacock that would have allowed seawater to circulate and cool the head of the motor. Maybe a little petrol Stuart-Turner. Bonny, dinky thing. Designed and made by British craftsmen in durable materials to give you year after year of trouble. Or the Kelvin Poppett. Since petrol isn't nearly dangerous enough to carry on a boat, you have two tanks and a changeover. Two lots of fuel taps and two breeds of explosive vapour. You started her on petrol and switched to the cheaper paraffin when she was hot.

There was a rudder still fixed on rusting pins. She was painted up in white, greys and black. I'd just stand back to appreciate her from all angles. The fellow who sold her to me didn't really want to part with her. 'If you can save her, she's yours,' he said. That's love. Or maybe he just needed the cash to pour into the next vessel he was already in love with. It happens.

I looked closely but, by then, I'd given my pal Mairi a bit of help with a few repairs. Enough to guess it might be easier to build a new boat. 'What about the hysterical society?' I suggested. There were very few surviving examples of this type of craft because they were launched from hard shores and worked to death.

But plans for a maritime museum got a knockback. Eventually they would build flats instead, on the site by the harbour. You already know I took her on. My coastguard colleagues and my fishing mates gave me a hand. Their repairs kept her in use, which is the best way to preserve her. A dry wind will crack the shell of a wooden boat open in a day or two if she's left exposed, on land.

When it all became too much I knew enough to keep her under cover. When she was dry and the generations of paint burned off, it was clear that said paint had played a structural rather than decorative role, for quite some years. I thought there might be enough forensic evidence, to recreate her shape. The shape of a clinker boat is all made up of planks that were flat originally but cut in convex and concave curves. So there's not a single straight line amongst them.

A boatbuilder friend – a guy I got arrested with once, helping to Keep Nato Out – he gave me a hand. This cove ran a wind-powered workshop across the dark side of the Minch. I got him to take the shapes, transfer the lines of the planks. The original keel was still sound. The plank shapes were preserved. I suppose that's a bit like rich guys getting their bodies frozen. Who knows where the human spirit lives but the physical structure could be revived once medical science had advanced sufficiently to solve the problems of ageing and disease.

When you saw the whole set of curves for one side of the boat, these were enough to tell the full story. Everything was in the flat but all the information necessary to reproduce all three dimensions was in the cut of these planks. That's an engineer's approach to timber construction. It's a set of components which have to be joined together. The method of assembly should consider the possible need to dismantle some parts of the construction to repair or replace those parts most likely to wear out first. I don't know if human bodies are built like that.

I learned that clinker build beats carvel construction. The latter is when heavier planks are fixed flush on a pre-built skeleton of oak. The former Viking method has a better strength to weight ratio, up to a certain scale of vessel. In Norse-type boatbuilding, the norm in the Scottish islands, the cut of the overlapping planks produces the shape. Boats used to come across the North Sea, like flatpacks, generations before the Rana boat kits were brought in to the UK. Ikea before its time. I wanted to commission my mate to build another *Peace and Plenty*. Diesels were getting lighter. But I was outvoted. The democratic family unit. For about half the cost of building a small open wooden boat, we could buy a yacht big enough to go places and sleep aboard. Sounds convincing, put like that.

But when it came to getting a boat with a lid, I couldn't see beyond clinker construction. All through Scandinavia, they build simple yachts like that, the Nordic Folkboat. They were all to the same plan, for racing, but it all got going just before a series of events which put development of recreational sailing vessels on the shelf for a while.

The three main Folkboat countries suffered different fates during World War Two. Norway was invaded, Sweden was neutral. Denmark had a unique position, in being protected from British invasion but allowed to keep her own government. The independent administration allowed the Nazis to outlaw and subsequently deport members of the Communist Party (twenty-two deaths in a concentration camp) but refused to enact laws against the Jewish population. This legal step was of course the first move which would have inevitably led to deportation, by train to a camp at the edge of a town in what used to be Poland.

The sacrifice of these political opponents might have been on purely practical grounds. The administration had to give something to the occupying force. Like in yachts, where you have sacrificial anodes. You spend a little time and money installing zinc anodes in strategic places. So the corrosion will affect the weakest metal first. Steel will last longer before it's attacked. Bronze should look after itself anyway.

Post-war, the Folkboat class flourished. Of course Britain won a dispensation to build them with a significant difference to every-body else's. Smooth carvel hulls so you could sleep on them without such a loud rippling on the overlapping planks of the original clinker design. The addition of cabin tops, of various shapes and sizes, ruined the streamlined sweep of elegance but provided a little more space for cruising sailors. They were no longer Nordic Folkboats, in class, so their sail numbers have to say FB rather than F.

I looked at a good example of one authentic Nordic Folkboat. I brought along a friend, a little shorter than me. When he laid down on the third bunk it was clear that our fast-growing Anna wouldn't be able to stretch out to sleep on this boat, if she carried on sprouting. Gabriele was a bit wider than before but she hadn't gotten any shorter. So I searched and found a sturdy example of a British cruising Folkboat.

We were still looking at clinker construction, because overlapping, lighter planks are a very good thing in a 25ft sailing yacht. This cabin was kept low but was longer than in the original design, so you had three usable bunks and a simple interior.

Those of you with a sound grasp of physics or who have been listening instead of switching off when technical information enters a story – you will be aware that the speed of any displacement craft (i.e. one that floats in, rather than planes on top of, H_2O, salt or fresh) relates to its length. So if you have enough sail to get the boat leaning and the top is longer than the waterline, you can go faster.

Beyond a certain number of degrees, the turbulence will slow the boat and more than cancel out any advantage. But, up to that point, she'll like to lean. Of course you don't need to bother with all this if you just install a decent diesel with enough horsepower to drive her at a nice easy cruising speed. She'll not go quite as fast as these occasional little bursts in fair breeze but I'm willing to argue that the average speed, over a distance, will nearly always be better.

The British Folkboat, *Polaris*, was out on a mooring in Portree harbour. Her Yanmar looked like it hadn't done much running – a bad thing, I thought. Not much detail about that in the paperwork. Only miles of notes about bits of sailing gear and navigation aids which might have come from the original Ark if Captain Noah was into electronics. There was a recent Decca navigator which gave a display in lat and long so you didn't have to do a fiddly interpolation on a Decca chart.

I changed the filters while my boatbuilder mate dealt with wire and string. We bled her together and we were off. There wasn't a lot of wind. I nursed the Yanmar and we had a good push from the tide. We crossed the Minch, overnight, in good weather.

Next day, Gabriele and Anna came out for the gentle introduction. Conditions were squally. When she leaned over, we could stand up, vertical, in the cockpit.

'Is she supposed to do this?' Anna asked.

I said, 'Well, you flashed up that website, showing them racing.'

'Oh yes,' she said. 'That's alright then.'

And it was.

But just to make sure, I had the mast craned off and we replaced every bit of wire and searched for weak links and had bits welded and spent plenty of time and money. We bought a crisp new foresail and, come spring, Anna and her pal provided the child labour to scrape and paint till she shone. We'd have her in good nick ready for the season. Of course I had to get the Yanmar out. That took a bit of jiggery-pokery, with improvised derricks.

Anna must have sensed I was quite keen to get into the innards of the squat little Japanese unit. 'Will you be taking it to bed with you?' she asked.

I would not call any of the tasks we completed, to revive the Folkboat, major surgery. But maybe all our hearts are partly divided, if we are honest. I still thought of the keel and the plank-shapes of the *Peace and Plenty*, stored more in hope than expectation.

Tante Erika

It's about a voyage. Well, no, it isn't, it's about an arrival. It's about sailing up close to an island off an island, out from another island in the Uists. The Sound of Flodday. You know *Fraoch a Ronaigh*? An exile's song, remembering the place names, the features on the landscape of that group of islands. Mapping them by moving the melody from one place name to the other. This is one of several Gaelic songs used to strong effect in a film. No, I don't mean Talitha Mackenzie's voice in *Zena, The Warrior Princess*. I'm thinking about a low-budget and very strange Scottish film with gory bits but without much of the blockbuster effect. Some very good performances though and of course excellent scenery. But I can't remember the name of it, the director, or the names of the actors. That's why documentation is important. Memory is suspect.

Tante Erika was being navigated by Gabriele and me after dropping the offspring off in Lochmaddy. Anna had signed up for a week's drama workshop in the studio theatre in Benpeculiar. We sailed out of the loch in moderate to poor visibility and met dense fog. It clung to us so we sailed blind up to the entrance to the loch, referring to a hand-held GPS in the cockpit. I don't think I would have trusted Decca that far.

We said we'd only go in there if we had a hundred metres visibility. The Yanks could decide to go to war and flick the switch on all the satellites. Maybe fifty would do. Metres, not satellites. It's one of several anchorages known as Acarsaid Fhallaidh – a hidden place. There's a gap between rocks and you don't see it till you're up to it. The way you'd think to go – that's not navigable – rocks everywhere, just under the surface. But the narrow way has enough depth any state of tide and no obstructions. Like a parable.

The Uist boys had told me not to worry even if the pilot book is a bit guarded. You'll be fine. We were. We went in to find good holding in stiff mud. And then we looked around. The fog was moving. A tumbling burn appeared on the lit shoulder of a hill. And there he was.

Another of our icons. A proud and independent head. I couldn't count how many points. Just call it a fine tall head on a hefty stag.

I think I told you I had to boil a head like that once, though not as fine as the live one we were observing. I had to chop the wood from old furniture and decayed roofs of outhouses. Once you got it to the boil, it wasn't so bad to keep it going. I could get on with weeding the radishes and Webbs Curlies. But I'd to keep going back to keep the water boiling so the fur and meat fell off the skull. It wasn't that much of a rest for my foot. I'd have been as well on the hill.

The romanticism of the sight before us, made me think of Scott. I'd brought *Waverley* along on this trip. I wanted to decide for myself if the superstar author of the day had indeed taken a romantic line on the tragedy of the '45 rebellion.

You could argue he invented the historical novel. First, he composed long, rhythmic poems that sent hundreds of people, rich enough to travel, out from their drawing rooms to the Trossachs.

He was also the guy quoted by a landscape consultant, employed by one of the world's largest suppliers of aggregates, to prove that blasting away a whole small mountain on the east coast of Harris would be no great loss to the world. He maybe saw it on a poor day. Our mist is kind of wet when you're walking or sailing in it, rather than looking out from a castle window.

We had just navigated down the indented east coast of North Harris. That's Gabriele and me. Sir Walter wasn't really with us. We'd explored an inlet or two, tight channels between reefs, taking you into good pools under these grey hills. One navigator's log could say 'impressive' and another 'intimidating' when you were looking at the same geological faultline. A high fold, formed by extreme heat.

The same observations are open to conflicting interpretation. Take the Crusades. These reformed Viking raiders, settled in fertile Orkney. Some of them were converted and spent some of the great wealth they'd gained, from the taken lands, on expeditions to the Holy Land. So they saved their souls. Or they caused havoc on land as they had on sea. Depending on your standpoint.

I was getting the feeling that Scott was inevitably and profitably (in more ways than one) caught between the classical liking for order and an attraction to mountain chasms. There's quite a tendency for some of his characters to leap over them. The chasms, I mean, not the classical buildings. He was simply having a classical day when he witnessed the east side of Harris. Roineabhal was under dense cloud and all these complex shades of grey were lost on him. On that occasion. Next day it could have been different.

If we look to science we may learn that the suggestion of east Harris being reminiscent of a lunar landscape has a sure foundation. Although Lewisian gneiss prevails, Roineabhal itself is composed of anorthosite – hence the proposal to remove it and use it for making motorways. This is in fact a predominant rock in the samples gained from the Apollo expeditions. Trust me, I'm telling you a story.

To take it a bit further, let's look to the arts. Can I inform you, if you don't know already, that Stanley Kubrick composed his shots depicting the landscape of Jupiter, in *2001, A Space Odyssey*, from that of Harris?

A man made a fortune and made himself bankrupt in building his dream castle in stone. (But probably not anorthosite.) The same man produced dialogue which printed the voice of less privileged characters with respect and fidelity to their Scots voices. Not just for colour.

The easts and wests of islands. My olman had a foot in both camps. So he could see how all that luxuriance of machair and storm beaches on our wild west side needs the more plain heaps of lunar boulders that comprise the east side of Harris. The bursts of colour shining from that grey can be intense. Like the bright maroon garnets you'll sometimes find in the rocks. I was maybe beginning to understand a bit more of what the olman wove into that cloth, the stuff he made when the markets were fickle.

Let's not forget the west side's rugged shores are savage to a mariner's eye. Mangersta is brutal. And the Barvas navigators would only take the risk if there was documentary evidence that a fishing was to be had. Think of all these boulders strewn across the alkaline green strip back from the surf-line. The power that drove them there. And then there's Arnol, the murder-village. All these stones that were an asset if you were building dykes and blackhouses. But my olman would still tease our *Siarach* relations. Aye, he said, the good lord must have been cutting it fine on the Saturday night. The Sabbath was fast approaching so he gathered all the rubble left after making the world and dumped the lot at Arnol.

Strange how the bristling tension that seems to have become a background hum to your relationship, in place of passion, can ease without warning. The strain came off Gabriele aboard *Tante Erika*. Even after our daughter left the ship, we were easy together, most of that trip.

I was beginning to think I could get used to the way speed is bound to vary when you're indulging in this sailing carry-on. One or two days we even achieved a better average than the rebuilt Yanmar could give, without busting a gut and devouring diesel. I knew we could keep things secure for at least a bit longer. You just have to take it from one tide to another.

Loss

If I still believed in life continuing after death, I'd see Gabriele's aunt smiling down. The woman who'd walked across a long bridge to a chunk of Germany under a different political system – Erika. A share of her legacy let us buy our old Folkboat.

Even so, some people say it's tempting fate – changing the name of a boat. I'm not admitting to sharing the superstitious nature of fishermen but I looked up *Erika* after Gabriele had finished painting the name, by hand, on a teak plate to be fixed to her transom stern.

I didn't really mind dial-up internet. You had a bit of thinking time between the appearances of sections of data. Even if you've not had the great benefit of having studied Latin for one year, you might be a keen gardener. Maybe even a botanist. Then you'd certainly know we're talking about heather. The genre of girls' names linked to flowers. In turn, there's many a boat named after either the girl or the original flower. Look up the names of the herring fleet of Scalpay – the *Daffodil*, the *Lily*, the *Lilac*, for a start. And remember the White Heather Club – twirling dancers and the costumes and the sangs o hame. Well, we're surely nae the ainly anes, ken.

It could get worse. How's this for a set of lyrics?

On the Heath blooms a small flower
And she's called, Erika
Hot from a hundred thousand small bees
all swarming around Erika

then her heart is full of sweetness
Delicate smells stream from her flowery dress
And she's called, Erika

In the homeland their lives a small girl
and she's called, Erika
and that girl is my faithful little treasure
And my happiness, Erika
When the heath flower bloom's red & pink
I sing this song to greet her
On the heath blooms a small blossom
And she's called, Erika

There's quite a bit more but you've likely sensed the tone of it, now. If I was to make the claim that that lyric, set to an adaptation of a rousing German folk tune, was to become one of the main marching songs of the Wehrmacht, would you believe me? Granted, the words might not always be exactly as recorded in the versions made for the team working under Goebbel's direction.

And if I were to assert that the same song became particularly identified with the Waffen SS, would that be stretching your credibility further? Sweet heather and bare skulls. Not the skulls of stags.

What if I claimed that you can now obtain a recording of German soldiers singing this song in the form of a ring-tone for your mobile phone?

Operation Heather could well have been a commando-raid but it wasn't. Let's go back to 1942, for now. A big year. I wasn't even a twinkle and the guy who might have told us straight, is not to be found. Not even in his own empty grave.

But he was a 'pioneer'. A particular breed of private in the German army. Timber roads were laid across swamps. Good experience for students of architecture. The *Erika* corridor was a German advance which became a bit like netting thin spent fish in a trap. The Wehrmacht was able to cut off huge numbers of Soviet troops in the Volkhov 'pocket'. There are plenty of photographs. Mostly they show the more peaceful times for the German troops. A very few show the ceremonial funeral of fallen comrades about to be placed in their carefully prepared graves. A further few show the mass of captured arms and equipment, even the T-34 tanks which were acknowledged to be superior to the panzers, in that strange terrain. They had basic diesel engines, so there was less to go wrong and the fuel was less volatile. A good thing in a tank, I would have thought. And I know another guy who would agree with his son if we could hear him.

Variants of T-34s were still in service until 1996, a bit like British Seagull engines, built as disposable units for the Normandy landings but surviving till the present day. Panzer production was a bit inhibited by unsporting rivalry between manufacturers. This was perhaps a factor in the complexity of the petrol engines installed in their units. Not a good thing on the Eastern Front. Good job for us they didn't cope with cold the way the BMW motorbike propulsion seemed to function in extreme heat. According to certain sources, not guaranteed unbiased.

The trains didn't do that well, either. German-made locomotives froze and the army was unable to capture any of the inferior race's rolling stock, admittedly superior in that climate.

There are other photographs which passed the censor. Most of these were taken by enthusiastic amateurs who were soldiers of a Fatherland which had expanded with incredible speed. They hint at a huge number of Russian prisoners who seemed happy to be captured. Others revealed the photographers' interest in human faces and ingenious little bits of engineering. One or two such photographs did arrive at the home of the sweetheart of that one pioneer, Gabriele's olman. One of the few who found his way back. For a while.

But it was really a counter-attack, like the later last push at Arnhem against a later advancing front. Don't take my word for it. Go to the memoirs of Field Marshal Keitel. Written but unrevised in his last few weeks before his hanging at Nuremburg.

He saw the writing on the wall in 1941 even though the resolve of his noble but volatile leader (he admits) on at least one occasion, had delayed the echo of 1812 by carrying out such pincer movements as the one which occurred in the Erika Aisle.

No disrespect to brave aunt Erika, but I wish we hadn't changed the name of our yacht. In mitigation, do you really want to keep calling your modest Folkboat *Polaris* – the name it came with? A little bit sonorous on the VHF. And I think of that name as attached to a class of nuclear submarine and so associated with a vessel which spends too much of its time under the water, for my taste. But they do say that changing the name of a boat is inviting bad luck.

With a bit more research, it got worse. The World Wide Web provided details of another vessel going under the name of *Erika* – an example of a class of tanker (37,000 tonnes) built in Japan in 1975. There was some concern about the class's light build and their probable safe working life. However, she had passed an inspection by RINA – the Italian shipping classification society. And the rate of hire was comparatively cheap. So that was fine.

But *Erika* began listing, off the coast of Brittany, when carrying about 20,000 tonnes of heavy fuel oil. She broke up and sank in a storm. The data that will continue the story after that event of 1999, depends a little bit on your perspective. It was an environmental disaster, with all but about a third of her oil entering the sea, to cause havoc along a huge section of coast. Or it was a ground-breaking salvage operation with the remaining oil recovered from the broken ship – almost half of the original cargo, some accounts say.

As to our own *Tante Erika,* she was still afloat at the tail end of the year, with the varnish hardly dull on her proud new nameplate. Gabriele really got Anna and myself sailing together, after we'd picked her up at Lochmaddy, on the way home from our first wee cruise. But after that, she didn't come out with us very often. She just seemed to run out of steam, no matter how much sleep she got.

That autumn, the daughter and me sailed in sun and we sailed in snow squalls. Sometimes these things happened in the same day, the same hour. We learned that you could let the sheet go now and again to let some wind out of the sails. Or you could get everything really tight so you lost some of the curve in the cloth and reduce power that way. Anna's pal had done a fair bit of dinghy sailing and it showed. She was really teaching us. In turn, I enjoyed showing the girls the basics of driving under engine power. Testing them, so they could reel off the shapes and lights of Cardinal marks.

She was getting good use so we decided to keep her going through the winter. So I got another mate to dive on the mooring we'd borrowed and replace the rope and chain that joined the tackle on the bottom to the buoy at the top. The two sinkers were deep in shingle. We left them undisturbed.

Shipwrecks

I got the phone call at about six a.m. 'I don't want to be the one who tells you, but she's ashore.' It was a colleague speaking. One of the few new-generation coastguards who still looked out the window of the box.

I'd been awake listening to the wind for hours. I drove down. It was a white-out. The hardest edge of the front had gone through but there were still heavy squalls with the claps of thunder. The car rocked as I watched the lines come across the harbour from the northwest. The only exposed direction from our mooring. There was not enough distance for any build of sea. It was simply the extreme power from an electrical storm. Hail dented the roof and I feared for the windscreen. It was just past the top of the tide. We were on Springs but the low pressure had forced the water higher still.

There was nothing showing where the mooring had been. A white shape, still beautiful, was being lifted and pounded, pulsing on the shingle shore. At first she seemed to be intact but, as I watched, I saw small bits of painted wood, washing up here and there. You couldn't ask anyone to do anything in these conditions. I still had to watch.

It had gusted to 106mph that night at Stornoway airport. It was a clear day when the front went through. You could see that nothing had broken. Everything was dragged ashore. Heavy chain and two ground anchors. Not what I expected to see – I thought the mooring I'd borrowed was SY style. Two huge flat grids from the quarry. The diver had simply said everything was in good order. I had not asked the right questions.

When she was lifted by the crane, there was a gasp. One side was intact and then when she swung, there was a third of the boat missing, on the port side. I was thinking about not asking the right questions when the remaining two-thirds of the boat were swinging in the air. The phone calls you took when you were bleary-eyed. Could you have picked up on something between the obvious lines? Something that might have made a difference.

You could see her ribs and the trailing wires. It was indecent. I heard someone say I looked pretty cool. Would the insurance cover everything?

I'd wanted to get the electrics done, complete the job, before the survey. She was not insured but I can't say what difference that would have made to the way we felt. Anna was with me now. I knew it would be easier for her if she was involved in gathering the lifejackets, the sail-bags. Things we could save.

I just said I'd been a coastguard for a few years. The first question was, always, the number of people aboard. If there was no-one aboard, it was a sad loss but even a beautiful boat could be replaced.

People had gathered to help. Other boat owners, mostly. One was the former manager of an island estate, one where assaults and reprisals had taken place. He was therefore the enemy but he and his partner went to the last remaining Italian café and came back with coffees and bacon rolls for all. There was not much to do. At times like that you seek comfort in the words of those who have shared a similar experience.

I spoke to the GP and the poet in Kyle. Former custodians of the elegant *Isadora*. I'd got to know them when I installed their new engine. I was still trying to build up a trade, then, one that could get me free of the long nightshifts. Where did all these days go? They'd phoned to express sympathy. They'd seen the footage on the national news. 'New Year storms lash the Northwest.'

They weren't the only ones who phoned. Old Angus rang. He didn't remind me that *Erika* had been a material thing.

'I know what it's like when a boat is lost. Sorry for your trouble.'
Others came to drink tea and offer practical help.

Later, when I was able to listen to it, the GP (wife) and poet (husband) told me the full story of *Isadora*. She had huge long over-hangs, one of the metre-class, a racing boat, in her day. They only had an outboard motor clamped on. It worked sometimes. She was balanced and sailed herself. Spoiled you for sailing anything else. And you'd turn back from the dinghy just to look at her line. Of course she also leaned right over and people with modern boats thought you were sailing badly till you overtook them.

You had to watch not to underestimate her speed. She just glided along. One night they heard the sound of surf and rolling pebbles. They looked out in time to see breaking white surf and tacked fast. A bank of shingle they thought was not going to be an issue for some time to come.

It was after that they'd considered installing a modern inboard engine. They'd heard about me from the coastguard on Skye. I advised them I was not yet a recognised Beta agent but they didn't seem to mind. I took leave and lived in the grannie-flat attached to their house till the job was done. The grannie was no longer with us.

They grew anxious when they saw the two-cylinder unit was rated at 14bhp. I pointed out that the weight was considerably less than an older Volvo, Bukh or Sabb single cylinder, rated at eight or ten. Shortly after that, Beta marketed the same engine as an 11bhp. It was the same kit, just de-rated so people wouldn't think it was bigger or heavier than it was. The psychology of technical improve-ments which have happened too fast – manufacturers shouldn't scare people.

The job went very sweetly and the Kubota-based unit ran like the proverbial Singer even if it wasn't built by the Clyde. It gave them the confidence to use the boat more than they had. But it had no power to save *Isadora* on the fateful night.

She was on a swinging mooring, out from the harbour. Not far from the small naval base. Butec. It had been a busy time in their lives. The GP was over in Raigmore hospital for radiotherapy, following a mastectomy. The poet proved an excellent nurse. They were in the wrong place at the wrong time, for the wellbeing of the boat.

You get these localised squalls at Kyle. It funnels under the bridge and comes at you like a tornado. They had been getting a trolley welded up. The GP was welding, not the poet, so the job hadn't got completed, after her diagnosis. *Isadora* was due to come out for survey and winter storage ashore. The dates were set.

But they were in Inverness when the call came from the harbour-master. He'd spotted her dragging the mooring.

Detail is important. I've heard this story more than once. Each time, the detail is more clear. It hasn't altered. It's different when a survivor is talking. He might have to believe the others have a chance. We're talking about something much more analytical here. This is not an insurance report where the slant of the story could make a difference. This is more like a post-mortem.

But this is a P.M. without a body. More of a Fatal Accident inquiry really. I've been to one of them. Each minute has to be accounted for. The tone of each question. The answers you received and logged. The information you might have obtained if you'd asked the right question at the right time. The details are everything. Every receipt which indicates that welding was done. Anything which could indicate the addition or removal of weight from one part of the vessel to another. Any factor which could have an effect on overall stability and compromise the integrity of an approved design.

A detail like the strands of light line, called 'small stuff' in the trade. Found tied round the cuffs of oilskin-type protective clothing. You can see the turquoise and orange frayings on the blatant yellow. You can imagine the action of guys who know their boat's going to go over, caught, held by the creel-rope, in a swell she can't rise to. It might just have been possible to slow the seepage of water into the suit long enough to provide enough flotation to gain the shore. But it wasn't enough. Not for these boys, that night. The ones I'm thinking of now.

But no-one was aboard *Isadora*.

Conditions were too severe for any boat at the harbour. By good or ill fortune, a big naval auxiliary was running for home. The harbour-master asked for a favour. He'd managed to contact the poet by phone. He'd repeated the phrase, 'At my own risk.'

If she'd been a handier vessel they could have put a man aboard to turn the new key. *Isadora* would have been fine under her own power. But she was taken under tow. That's another equation entirely. How the bow will rise or dig in a chop, according to the angle of the pull. How the strains can be distributed so a hull that's not been designed to take such pressures can bear them.

If anything at all can be done after the bow section is pulled apart. If she dips she will take in water at this point. The flow of water at a high part of the vessel must then descend with increasing velocity to the lower area closer to the stern of the boat. So the stability is seriously compromised.

Then there is the issue of sideways rolling of a volume of water, which is nothing more or less than moving weight. A pendulum but one that will increase in momentum as the movement of water goes that bit further each time. As it has further to travel, the weight of that volume will be driven, side to side, at ever-increasing velocity. Until a point is reached.

It is certainly possible to calculate that point. But there's no need. In this case, the vessel was not manned or womanned. And once that point of stability has been passed, further changes to the outcome of the story are not possible.

I can remember that principle from O-Level Physics. So there might have been an element of learning, by accident, as I went jumping through the hoops to try to prove a different premise to the one being examined.

They lost *Isadora*. The tow had to be let go as the vessel dived down. There was a fierce combination of storm squall and tide rip. She was probably trundled along the bottom till her back broke. Then the tide would have scattered the sections in the deeper parts of the Inner Sound. Small sanctuaries for nehrops. Or maybe her sections might have been driven down the tidal sluice into Kylerea narrows. Wherever her remains lie now, she was buried at sea. They kept looking out for sections of wreckage but none appeared. The new Beta is down there with the rest. Tidy installation, if I may say so.

And we lost *Tante Erika*. Her own ruined body was recovered for a pointless examination. The conditions on the night were simply beyond what we'd been prepared to meet.

But the GP's course of treatment seems to have been completely successful. I cooked for herself and her man, not long ago as they visited Stornoway harbour in their fine cruising yacht. It was a type known as a Rival, manufactured in glass-reinforced-plastic.

Slate

The builder pulled a fast one on me with the slate. That's what made the roof a slow job. Guys were up there, rain or shine, day in, day out. Fragments spraying out in a sharp grey hail. He'd got hold of pallets of extra lightweight brittle shit instead of the heavy Spanish that replaces our own Ballachulish or Easdale. And my eye was off the ball. The saving must have cost him more in labour, with all the breakages.

One day it just had to get sorted. This time I got on the peat-driven telegraph system of local knowledge and located the right dude to sort out the other guy's mess. I was guided to a man who loved the material. He took apart all the detailing over the storm-windows and another whole section that had dozens of breakages. He suggested using reclaimed Ballachulish. That would outlast us all and it would be faster to strip a complete section than to patch up here and there.

If we did these whole sections, your eye would go to them. The good slater was on another job, stripping a roof. If I got up the scaffolding, on my days off the Coastguard watch, I could get hold of decent slate, in return for my own labour. So I unpeeled the roof skin for him and the olaid had enough in the kitty to buy a small number of selected Ballachulish longs. You could find any number of short slates to nail, up top, close to the ridge. Longs were getting scarce.

Scottish slate is graded by length as you go up. Welsh, and now Spanish, is graded by weight. The heavies are fixed down close to the gutters. My new mentor told me the Visitors' Centre, just completed near the old quarry, in Ballachulish, is roofed in Spanish slate.

The light was strong enough, the clouds were fast and it was a fine enough day between the bursts of hail. We often get that mild week or two in December but it wasn't happening yet. The oilies were the answer. They keep the wind out. You're sweating in them but you've got to keep the wind out.

The usual thing is to do a day for a day with a mate. But I knew there was no way Kenny F was ever going back to work on Mairi's house in Garyvard. Probably wouldn't get any other buiding project together, either. So I couldn't repay him. Some days too, I knew he'd be a liability on a roof. And paying that cove cash-in-hand wouldn't be doing him any favours. Physical labour beat arguing with the builder or fighting through the courts. We needed to get this house together for the olaid.

The roof was only one of the problems. The other issue was the chimney. The linings had been done. We had a neat multi-fuel stove with a dinky back boiler. One radiator ran off it and the hot water to the kitchen taps. She said she wouldn't move to any house without a real flame in it, disability-spec or no. But when we put a match to the new installation, the smoke came back where it came from.

'No, we tested it with smoke bombs,' the builder said. 'Some chimneys are like that. Must be the wind. Maybe it never worked.'

So I got it all set up outside. A pile of concrete blocks, and shingle by a small stack of ceramic liners. The dark art of chimneys. When I studied this gable, there was no way I wanted to break into it, to hunt the blockage. So I got the good slater, also a roughcaster, up to see it. He shook his head.

'You can't do that without a serious bit of scaffolding. Anyway, you don't want a crack on the outside. Why the hell don't you tackle it from inside? Where do you think the problem is?'

So this cove took the boots off in the kitchen and said hi to the olaid on the way through. She was in the high-backed chair now, telly blasting away. She was in her scarf and thick genseys. The room was like a sauna – the storage heaters were all blasted up but she didn't feel warm since she couldn't see a fire. I knew she'd manoeuvre her way over to the Dimplex control once we were out the door. She would sneak on the booster switch – the expensive convector heater part of the installation, once the coast was clear.

She would also perk up when the home-help came in. Anna was parking her bike there on the way to school. The daughter said to me this day, 'Grannie's still got her moments.'

'Aye?'

'The home-help comes in to make the porridge. She says, *Thank goodness you've still got water, Mary. Been a burst up our way and not a drop coming out the tap.* Grannie says, *I can aye sell ye some.*'

The olaid had been dead cool about moving house to one where everything she needed was on the ground floor. As long as there was space upstairs for my sister when she came to visit. She had to have her living room fire, though. That was the condition.

'Dinna mind movin. Ken a need a that electric heatin but I like tae see a fire in the hoose.'

The last stroke left her tricky to understand and The Broch came back stronger into her voice for some reason. But she had a way of making herself understood.

So there was all that negotiating with the Disability and Improvement grants and conflicting regulations about ventilation and all. But the Morsø was installed, even if we couldn't light it.

The big, heated kitchen gave her a change of scene, with a set of glass double doors looking right out to the open. If you're not going to be out of the house much, you might as well see the clouds scud by. The shower had to be on Total Control, so there were safety cut-outs as part of the system.

When I made the tent of sticks and a wee hut of coal, her face just lit up. And then we were choking with the downdraft and there was nothing drawing. That's when I tackled the builder but no, he said, remember we'd gone from one set of linings into the top one to save taking the gable apart and…

His plasterer just gave me the slightest nod. He couldn't say anything.

That look was enough. That's how come I was up on the roof, with the brushes and wire and sash-weights on nylon line. You could only get the brush or anything else down a short way. You could say I was blazing. More than the flicking stove was.

You can think about it or do it. So I brought Anna along and issued her with a big magic marker to mark the spot on the inside wall. Just put an x where you can hear the brush scraping. And I got up on the roof again. Taking it canny, along the ridges, with a hard frost on. When I got down again, I found my daughter had placed her mark on the wall.

'It's not that far down,' Anna said.

'You're sure?'

'I'm sure.'

So she made her grannie a cup of tea and I went out to hunt down a cement-mixer.

It was borderline. I knew I could do that batch by hand. But time was getting to be a big factor in my life. And my mother's. It was a long day for her, stuck on one floor of one house. But I was trying to fix all this between Coastguard watches.

So I took a Stanley-knife to the new plasterboard in the upstairs room. That was a space she didn't need but then again she did. I'd to make sure the upstairs room was sister-ready. Whenever she wanted to come. Flights from Canada were getting cheaper all the time. Herself had been out there not long before the first noticeable stroke. Kirsty made the link with the Québécois cousins. The olaid came back with plenty of stories.

The taping and filling, throughout the renovated house, were the best parts of the whole job. A fine finish for show. The slates couldn't stay on the roof and the chimney couldn't take a fire.

So I went off round the corner with the trailer and called at Robert's. That was another visit, long overdue. Shit, I couldn't go in a hurry asking for a shot of his mixer. Robert had just got out of hospital. I knew he'd had tests and stuff so it might not be a good story. He lived on his own. Never mind the mixer, I knew I should just be going round there, checking out he was OK. But Robert was on another watch now and his new mate would be doing that.

So I didn't call by. I hired a mixer because my slater friend, who was now also the roughcaster and chimney-consultant, was due to come again that very afternoon. Everything had to be on site at the ready. That was the deal. And so I was going up the brae with the mixer in the trailer and counting off the materials. Additive to make the cement more workable, petrol for the mixer, and I was over the hill in the red estate car and everything was do-able. Then there was a noise I didn't understand.

There was a lot of glass in the car. I felt the breeze blow through it from the back. There was a neat orange shape, wedged in nicely on the back seat. The mixer had joined me in the car. So I got the flashers going and picked up as much of the glass as I could and tipped the mixer back up and out. This time I did tie it in, well chocked, in the trailer. It was a stable-door job because I was just round the corner from the olaid's. *More haste, less speed.* The olman's voice in my head this time.

Anna was watching crap on the telly, the stuff she didn't get to see at home. So it was the two girls in there together and I didn't even try to explain what was going on. That was a pity because my olaid would have quite liked the story of the mixer getting a comfy seat.

I'd just sanded the floorboards and sealed them. So there was no carpet to roll back.

The polythene sheeting went down fast. There was plenty of that left, the new traditional Lewis garden material. No new or renovated house on this Island is complete without some. Fraying offcuts of blue polythene weathering on the barbed wire. This traditional decoration might look a bit untidy to some people but it's a good wind-indicator. Quite decorative, too.

I knew that there was no chance of this renovated chimney drawing air in any wind direction, I just went tearing into that wall where Anna's X marked the spot. Soon there was dust and insulation everywhere. My oilies were abandoned outside the back door and I was down to the T-shirt, hearing the telly blaring below. The olaid probably wasn't even hearing the kango and Anna was just cool about the buzz because it was a bit quiet for her sometimes, round on Leverhulme Drive.

Sweat and dust were beginning to mingle and of course then I put on the mask I'd brought along with the Kango. After a cough or two. One day I'd sprayed bitumen on the exposed walls before the builder went in with the strapping and stuff. Not quite sure how that got to be one of my jobs. I could have been on Old Holburn and black Afghani every hour of my waking life instead of taking that dose of tar to my lungs in one afternoon.

Now I swung the five-pound club-hammer and I was soon into the upper section. Smoke bombs, aye sure. No wonder the sash-weights, and every other vernacular device, had failed to get through this blockage.

'Scalpel next, Da?' Anna asked.

And then she said, 'Good job I've just grown some more or you'd be sending *me* up there next.'

It was a crows' nest. All the years of hail and seepage and slow running tar had congealed it all into a material that was tougher than wire. No weights, no brush, no smoke, no nothing could have got past that. And the skeletons of three small birds with their recognisable beaks were still tight and close in a group right in there. They were preserved in all that residue. We put the nest carefully aside. I felt it belonged to someone.

We fired up the mixer then and trapezed through the living room with the buckets of thick-mix cement. That's what we say. 'Traipsed' sounds a bit flicking delicate, for the situation.

The troubleshooter was a man of his word but I knew that already. A more gradual curve of linings made the connection to the sweet, sweet airflow. The smoke could now find its sloping way up to exit over the concrete casting. Up over the other roofs of the Terraces and Avenues of all these generations of SY housing.

We packed expandable material around the liners. Then the blockwork did indeed fall into place. I did the clear-up and got the mixer and Kango back before five o'clock.

'That's a first for you,' said the girl behind the office hatch. She was maybe remembering the four Kangos and umpteen blunted chisels which was the net cost of the demolition of Charlie's four chimneys. Umpteen – that's one of the olaid's words – do other people say it too? Could be a title for a jig? – Umpteen Blunted Chisels. Or a Frank Zappa tune, if he hadn't also died young, from a cancer.

I couldn't bear to chase for the plasterwork specialist, the taper and filler. And that's a knacky job. Too tight a timescale to take that learning curve and I couldn't think of a favour or skill to swap with someone in the trade. When the haddocks and herring were still about, there was no such problem. You could give out a fry of line-caught fish. But the Minch was dead.

So I asked the olaid if she was up for paying for proper V-lining. Half-inch timber, so it could get nailed, direct over the strapping. We were into the reserve, on the budget as Gabriele reminded me, more than once.

'Is there anither air-fare in the kitty?' she asked. 'To git your sister hame again?'

I nodded.

She nodded.

'Fit else am I goin ti spend it on?' she asked.

Or stated.

She didn't have the fire on for Christmas but Hogmanay morning that Morsø Squirrel sent her sweet smoke-signal back across towards Denmark on a more mild airstream, from the west. Just a touch of north in it.

That night I had one last mission to do, before the New Year. I didn't have a drink till a bit after the bells. Instead I turned the key in the Type 3. Reversed her out of the garage. And navigated nice and easy towards the mansion of a builder.

I didn't ring the bell. Just left the gift-wrapped box, nice and prominent, in the back of the works' pick-up, in his drive. Under the stretched vinyl cover and beside the shovels. I left him something he'd missed. Something I'd found in a chimney he'd checked fully, top to bottom, bottom to top. A particular birds' nest. He could make a New Year soup of it if he wanted.

And sorry, but I can't leave you there. I found out a while later, Robert, my former watchmate, was lying exhausted in the house when I failed to open his door. He was back from treatment, with poor results, to find a burst pipe. Robert could usually fix everything – he'd done a spell in the building industry after the Forces and before the Coastguard Service. But he just didn't have the energy to fix anything then. His new watch leader did come round, took one look at the situation and moved him into his own house. A system working.

I'd get progress reports, at watch handovers, before slumping, already tired, into the driving seat or knocking off to chase builders or building control, engineers, surveyors, joiners or plumbers. Robert's ex-wife had come to stay, along with her new man, and unlikely though it sounded, the care and support was working as well as anything could. Aye, I'd be welcome, sure he'd like to see me, but remember he was at the morphine stage now so you couldn't be sure how much reaction you'd get.

Time passes at different speeds. The months were a blur of watchkeeping and arrangements and sheer physical graft. Good days and not so good days.

So I didn't manage to visit Robert's deathbed. I did go to his wake. I'd almost forgotten he'd grown up in Dublin. There was an old family tradition of well-heeled Protestant lads going into the British Army. Robert had been a Marine Commando before he became a Coastguard. He would never travel through Northern Ireland, to visit his mother, though he had never served there. I shook her hand as I left.

This was in a house just a stone's throw from my own mother's newly completed renovation. Robert was one of the kindest men I've ever met and I was privileged to work with him though I didn't even get my arse along to witness his pain.

Paper On Slate

It's possible that the generation before my own had a blind faith in education. Especially the members of that generation who only got the minimum of it, like my mother, my father, my uncles and aunts. I had the chance they never had and I probably didn't make the most of it. But I've a thesis brewing. What if you could combine their way of telling a story with the accurate details which come from research. Isn't that what good history books are made of?

I've noticed, when some people get ill they tackle it by gathering information in a very systematic and determined way. When I realised that part of the delay in moving my mother into a house specially adapted for her was caused by pallets of brittle slates, I began to find out more about the material. The research was never put to test in a court of law. In fact it led me up a ladder. But it seems to have found a story. Here is our starting point.

Papers, 1902–93, of or concerning Dr Lachlan Grant MD

See archive in National Library of Scotland

Dr Lachlan Grant MD (1871–1945) was a Fellow of the Royal Faculty of Physicians and Surgeons, Glasgow. He was Medical Officer for Ballachulish and Kinlochleven, for a time. He was the founder of the Highland Development League in the 1930s.

There's a wide gate across the wide mouth but it's padlocked shut. You can get in through a smaller side gate, so folk can walk their dogs. There are warning notices about sticking to the path. Quarries are dangerous places. Even disused quarries. It's pretty quiet in here now. There's still a lot of slate. Even though twenty-eight million of them were cut and packed and shifted out. There was serious money to be made from quality building materials. As long as you kept your overheads down. And of course if your workers kept *their* heads down.

Then there was the iron. Iron's a quality material as well. Corrugated iron is a bit of a rival material to slate. Victoria's Albert had a serious interest in the material, hence the tin ballroom at Balmoral.

The grading of slates is a skilled job. Remember how the blue-berry Penrhyn, one of the Welsh products, is graded by weight. So these are passed in piles, heavies, mediums, lights, as you go on up the pitch. To the apex of the roof.

The softer, saltier Easdale and the hard black fruits of Ballachulish – you work these Scottish varieties in a different way. So the long ones are down low and they get shorter as you climb towards the apex. And there are cheek nails here and there to keep them from pivoting on the single top nail. You get short heavies here and there near the top. It's what gives it character. All these fine Church of Scotland houses. The Mission House at Kinloch Resort and the one at Uidhe Bay, Taransay, that's Ballachulish. The Telford manses at Aignish and on the former Island of Berneray, which is now connected by a causeway to North Uist.

The slate lasts longer than the nails. The sarking – the wooden slats under the felt – will normally fail before stone. This structure makes a bed for Scottish slate. In England, they usually nail slate on battens. The ventilation is better but they rattle more.

The cutters worked in basic shelters. A sheet of corrugated iron was pinned to a few spars of timber to give them the most basic roof, while the blasting went on. (If that's not irony, what is?) That's how they broke into the mountain. The dynamite would bring down manageable slabs. Stuff they could work with. It would rain stones after a blast. They'd get used to it, swinging their own cutting knives, when all that was going on. Counting out their own slates.

Seated in the dust, in their moleskin trousers. They would swing the slating knife at the slab where they sensed the seam ran. Then they split and trimmed each individual slate. One man might cut two thousand of them in a day. Enough for half a cottage roof. He needed to keep that pace up, to get a wage. Rain was welcomed. It would dampen the dust.

Of course there were injuries. I wouldn't say they didn't blink an eye, when that happened, but injuries were common. Even if they escaped unscathed, the workers were prone to illnesses, caused by these conditions. It wasn't healthy, working in damp and dust, swinging heavy tools. That's what they did in Siberia and that's the sort of programme the refined architect, Herr Speer, organised for the Third Reich.

It was about the turn of a century. 1900. A good time for engineering. That's the year they completed the lighthouse out on the Flannans. They were doing things that just didn't seem possible. But there was a cost in illnesses and injuries. Working men were learning to get organised. But very few employers were willing to eat into their profit margin to help the march of social progress. So they just had to organise themselves. Dr Grant was not employed by the quarry owners. They were not far-sighted enough to see that the health of the workers was in their own interests.

The doctor would ask what was causing the coughs, the accidents. So he'd be worrying away at the company, negotiating improvements. They got fed up of him. So some bright spark decided they'd sack him. But how do you sack a man you don't employ?

We're speaking about a company that made its own rules. You couldn't just club together and buy a job-lot of tools. That wasn't allowed. You'd to supply your own but you'd to buy them from the company.

Dr Lachlan wasn't happy with any of that. He and the men became a strong team. When the company tried to exclude the doctor employed by their workers, the men all pulled together. It was a very early example of the lock-out. They took the bread out of their own mouths. But they couldn't hold out alone. And the doctor did his bit, writing for the campaign. The boys from the Clyde, they backed the quarry-workers. One day there was a visit from another man in a suit. His name was Keir Hardy.

They won but that's not the end of this story. This was not just about one quarry, gaining acceptance of one doctor's right to be there. Dr Grant broadened out the aims. The Highland Development League, the start of an idea for a Health Service – an entitlement not a favour – he was a leading light there.

I might have taken this research a bit further. As it stands, this is only an approach to a line of investigation. I was getting hungry for the details – the data that hints at the story. But I got wind of another cove doing a book on the same subject. Now I do realise that there is more than one work on the bureaucracy of the Third Reich, for example but the timing wasn't great either. There was a completion certificate to win and I'd need to organise my own working space. When I signed off watch I'd grab some rest then get up a ladder. I couldn't get the image of the slate-splitters out of mind.

The past lives of workers, nibbling at slate. The crimps putting the pressure on, gradually, so the slate snapped in the right place. An art to it. Like everything else.

I recently helped place some of their work on a roof in SY in the year 2000. It should last longer than the member of the generation sheltered by it. And it should also outlast those who graded the slates and nailed them in place, for her, even though we used galvanised clouts rather than copper.

Lax 1

I told the builder he could have the door from the yellow van. That was a bit of a score we'd acquired, for spares to try to keep the red one going. Our long-term project. We'd sell the Type 3 when the red van, last year of the Type 2, was roadworthy. That's the Hebridean idea of progress.

I didn't want anything for the door. But he wasn't to tow the van away. I needed the other bits.

He asked me again how much I wanted for it. I said that was OK, he'd have a bit I'd need sometime. Next time he saw me he put some notes into my hand. Worrying.

When I went out to the yellow van, for parts for the red one, the door wasn't there. Fine. But neither was the bumper I'd come for. And the factory-made towbar just wasn't there either. My watch-mate, Charlie, had got that for me quite a while back. Perfect for towing a dinghy. A long connecting bar distributed the load to another strong point.

It had been cut off at the connecting bar. Must have been done in the dark otherwise the guys would have realised it was only a U-bolt in the middle and two studs either side to take it out clean. I've done it with a socket-set in three or four minutes.

I had a look at the builder's blue, two-litre, Type 2 crewbus, when it came out of wraps. It had a newly sprayed bumper and a fitted towbar. This was no longer the standard, factory-built version that went all the way back to the rear axle to distribute the load. It had been adapted. I just asked him where he tracked all the bits. See that place you pass, near Ellon, on the Aberdeen road. You must have clocked a yard full of VWs. That guy was good for spares. If I needed anything, he'd have a look out next time he had the works wagon away, to pick up a kitchen and stuff.

'Aye, strangely enough, I need a bumper and a towbar.'

Weird things happen. One of his squad did us a couple of big favours. This was the guy who was ace on the grinder and spray paint. Another of these dudes, like Charlie, who can fix anything. But Charlie had got word of his promotion move so our dream team could not last much longer.

'You were looking for a nice stone slab for under the olaid's stove,' this cove remembered.

A piece of Penryn but not just any piece. It was part of the slate bed from the billiard tables in the castle. Guys were just throwing stuff like that from a height into skips. He'd another bit set aside for me, too.

That's how we acquired a section of the bed of Leverhulme's billiard table. It might even have been an original purchase for Matheson, the opium lord of the Long Island. Under new legislation it could probably be confiscated as the proceeds of that trade even though supported by the then PM of the realm. Of course we had to go to war in China to protect the interests of our merchants. It's difficult to say PM out loud without thinking of post-mortem but we're talking about Mr Disraeli, another prolific novelist.

He was the cove who coined the name McDrug for a character bearing a close resemblance to the fabulously wealthy Sir James Matheson Bart. You can't say the old PM's name without thinking of the Cream album. Disraeli Gears. Tales of brave Ulysses, how his naked ears were tortured, by the sirens...

Our heroes. But for the sake of historical accuracy it might be worth checking out Mr Clapton's reference to Enoch Powell's 'Rivers of Blood' speech. Total psychedelia was fine but it looks like at least one of those guys was against the idea of any more black in the make-up of the UK.

Talking of colours, think of the whin-yellow, the loganberry-orange and the raspberry-red of Type 2 VW vans. Pretty well the shades of the skoosh I used to find in cupboards in a pre-fab in West Road, Fraserburgh. I don't think any pineapples were damaged in the making of that pineapple-ade. We're looking at a coastal town situated not a million miles from the rural empire of a VW buff, on the outskirts of Ellon. But let's move on from that. It's circumstantial evidence.

Except that something even more strange happened. Now I wouldn't have said that any builder I've come across so far was in a great hurry to give you anything buckshee. The finishings were being put on the olaid's house just when I got the raspberry and cream van through the MOT.

With some help from Charlie.

'I never thought you would do it,' the builder said. 'And you found a bumper?'

'Aye,' I said. 'Just went for a Brazilian one from German and Swedish. I went over it with yacht enamel on the roller. Charlie Morrison's paint. Came up OK.'

'What did that ross you?' he asked.

'There's a word I haven't heard for a while. About a hundred notes,' I said.

It turned out, the original door I'd got stripped – to go back between the kitchen and the porch – was warped. No use. And the reclaimed flooring that Charlie and me stripped for facings so it had that proper old pine look – that didn't go as far as we thought it would. But the builder found a half-decent door and more wood and didn't charge for extras. Interesting.

I no longer have the appetite required for the maintenance of Type 2 vans. Our red one got legalised and went on for a few years but then we found severe rot in the chassis. Not impossible, just what you'd call beyond economical repair. And yet, if you had the time or money, you could have brought it back to near-new condition. The body might be like a machine but you can't really do that with humans. I'm in reasonable nick for my age, for example, but some parts have muscle damage which is beyond renewal. Like an area of my lower back. There was no drama. It didn't happen up on a roof. It happened when I was bending to stack the bramble fruits of Ballachulish, on a pallet.

Then again, there are generations of vehicles as there are of people. As far as I'm aware the Type 4 VW is a very common van, these days though there might be a Type 5 or 6 when you read this.

Willum's Mary

Her speech never really recovered from the big stroke. In The Broch they say a body has 'taen a shock'. Her eyes seemed to move that bit faster. So you had no doubts she was taking everything in. She got her home-helps trained. None of them would talk down to her. Otherwise the olaid would get aggressive. No wonder.

But you could tune into her new voice. She'd a memory for turns of phrase. I offered to get her to the kirk one week, if she wanted. We might need a shottie o a chair.

'A hope it's ane wi wheels you're speakin aboot and no ane wi electricity tae fry me,' she said.

The kirk means the Church of Scotland. Not the one on Kenneth Street. Definitely not the one on Scotland Street. Nor the Bayhead division, nor the new one, out Sandwick way. And of course the new Catholic Church, also on Scotland Street isn't in the equation. Hope you've got all that.

'No, dinna worry, Peter, loon. I'm nae bothered aboot goin tae the kirk.'

I knew she was worried about how long she could go without the toilet but she saved face.

'Last time I went there I got naethin but cheek. We'd just seen a coffin oot o the kirk and oer tae the men tae carry her. A neebor fae Westview cam up to claik. *You knew her well, Mary?* she asks. Aye, says me, weel enough, poor soul. She's at peace the noo. *Was she a good age, Mary?* the other ane asks. No really. I dinna think she was saxty-five. *How old are you yourself, Mary?* Saxty-four, I says. *My word*, she says, *do you think it's worth your while going home?'*

But the olaid seemed able to accept it when she lost this and that. As long as it was physical. Stuff got delivered to her modified house. It was the zimmer first. Later, we needed the Social Work wheelchair to get out of the house. We still called it a stroll when I took her round the block. She kept asking if I could understand her. She missed talking to Canada on the phone but she got flustered when Kirsty couldn't make out what she was saying. I told her not to worry, I'd let her know if she wasn't making sense.

I remember telling her about the time I went to borrow the tractor. We were towing a heavy boat to the harbour. A favour for a favour. Anyway, my mate was on the dayshift but he said to pick up the tractor – the grey Fergie painted red. But I'd to see his sister first. Aye, Portrona Drive, the urban croft.

Nobody came to the door when I rang so I went out to have a look at the beast. I was going to give her a warm-up anyway but nothing happened with the starter. Right then the *bodach* came running over. I'm not kidding, he was like a whippet. He'd been dozing in the chair, out the back door but he just woke up and came running.

'The battery,' he said. 'It's the battery. John's got terminals in a box.'

So we found them together. It wasn't long before I had one connected to replace the cracked one. But before I could step aboard, the *bodach* was in the seat and the Fergie was away and nearly took the gate off.

The daughter came running out then and waved her arms till he stopped and dismounted. She'd been on the phone. They had a few words and he went meekly back to his seat.

'John puts that cracked terminal on whenever he leaves the house,' she said. 'That's why he asked you to see me first. The *bodach*'s grounded. He's lost it for driving anything.'

You had to admire him grabbing the opportunity.

But when the olaid heard that one from me, she leaned over quietly.

'A wee word in yer shell-like. Am fair enjoyin the fitba an th athletics an th snooker on the telly,' she said.

'Aye?' I said.

'Aye, but promise me somethin. If you ever call by an catch me watchin the cricket on the telly, get somebody tae shoot me.'

She wasn't finished.

'I jist like tae ken there's enough tae cover the funeral. That's all we're needin in the kitty,' she said. 'But a dinna think there's muckle tae be anxious aboot. It's like my ain grannie. Grannie Bruce. When ane o the loons tellt her to behave herself or they widna bother aboot a funeral, she says till him, Weel if ye'll nae bury me for love ye'll bury me for stink.'

Noble Anvil

First, grow some dill and that flattish-bladed Italian parsley. If you've the use of some ground, use that, otherwise put a grow-bag in a fishbox. Plastic is fine. Wooden ones are collector's items now.

Go to a hidden loch. It has to be a long way from the road. It's best to go a few days after a decent rainfall.

Leave the fly rod behind because it will get in the way. Late season on Lewis, there's likely to be squalls too fierce to cast against. Worms are good bait if you can bear to put them on a hook. If not you could cast a spinner.

When you've caught enough for the number of people who'll be eating, leave. You're unlikely to get done for poaching with rod and line but they'll take your fish.

Have a dram and start cooking while you're still hungry from the bogslog.

Gut fish, leave heads intact and make several slashes across the thick backs so the seasoning and butter will enter the pink.

Stuff the cavities with as much parsley and dill, maybe chives, as you can fit.

Stuff more butter in the cavities as well as in the slits, or olive oil if you'd rather. A fair turn of pepper. A fair squeeze of lemon.

A grill at the top of an oven is best so they're kind of half baking as they're browning. Look for the skin crackling. Turn with care.

Best if there's some new potatoes, home-grown. If you don't have a plot of ground, you can grow them in a tub or inside a couple of tyres, holding soil.

You can dribble on the buttery juices from the pan, maybe with a drop of white wine stirred in but I wouldn't bother doing the cream sauce bit.

More greenery wouldn't go wrong.

Let's stay with this. Going to take a sea trout. Going out over the hill. This is research. You don't want to postulate a pattern too soon. You don't want to assume this is like that. This proves that. Or that causes this.

There are false friends in history as in language – words that you think you know because they sound the same but have a different meaning in a different context. Like 'cuddy', as I may have mentioned before – that mad way the mainlanders use the word for a fish to mean a horse. Just the one example.

The example in my own mind now is 'Allied Forces'. There was an occupation, of many countries, in lines out, in several directions, from something called Germany, at the time. These advances were halted, most notably on the eastern fronts. The lines of invaders were eventually beaten back, in Italy and in North Africa, as well as in the Soviet Union. These wars ranged over deserts and over vast, formerly fertile plains. Then a counter-invasion began in Normandy, France. This led to allied forces, advancing through western Europe, as the Russians advanced from the east. So it was also a bit like a race. But Allied Forces is also a computer game. Version 4.0 is best, Anna will tell you. It's also a term that's been applied to conjoined efforts to deal with the horrors that occurred in sections of the continent of Europe about fifty years after the recognised end of World War Two. The continent of Europe was still far from peaceful in the last year of a millennium.

A strong case was made for the urgent necessity of collective action of members of the Nato organisation, resulting in the bombing of the country formerly known as Yugoslavia, which took place between March 24th 1999 and June 11th 1999.

Atrocities which became known in allied countries as 'ethnic cleansing' but as 'Operation Horseshoe' in Kosovo, were documented beyond all reasonable doubt. Systematic human rights abuses directed at the Kosovan population were an obvious precursor of an escalation of violence against civilians. These actions were already well documented in the Balkan conflict.

This was officially confirmed in 2005 when the United States Congress passed a resolution declaring that 'the Serbian policies of aggression and ethnic cleansing meet the terms defining genocide'.

This is the obvious reply to those who point out that the decision to bomb, though taken jointly by Nato members and not solely by the USA, did not in fact have the backing of the United Nations at the time of its execution.

At the time, I'd alternate between the *Guardian* and the *Independent* for coverage of these conflicts. This also happened to be about the time I realised I couldn't juggle all the demands of being a decent coastguard, father, husband and son. So I quit the job. Thus I no longer had a meal break to spend in a rest room, catching up with a world outside the mapped environs of Stornoway Coastguard's area of responsibility. (Out to thirty degrees west and abeam the Outer Hebrides, as it happens.)

But my real understanding of the war only began when I ran away with the milkman. I was still living with Gabriele at the time but I'd like to summarise the points in my defence. Mitigation before litigation.

This guy hovered around on pay day. He was in no hurry to get the cash but would lean back and ease himself into Lewis yarning mode. He spoke of fishing. You could map the seasons by his stories. In April we'd be out into the Tolsta moor, way past the bridge-to-nowhere and he'd name the deep lochs which hid a stock of fit native trout. He'd describe the shades of their speckles and the depth of their taut bellies. The wide muscle in their dimpled dark backs. The pallid nature of the pink in their flesh, falling off the strong but delicate-seeming structure of light bones.

Later there would be word of the first salmon. Usually a grilse, a fish that's spent only about a year in the ocean, but a good eating size, about right for sending whole into the oven, in a tomb of silver foil, not much less bright than the flanks of the fish when it came into the side of the peaty water. Not long from the sea.

Finally, in October, there would be mention of sea trout. The late stock that sprints for the lochs at the tops of systems, the ones reached only by the strides of the fittest of guests.

'Where do you usually go?' I asked. And then, 'Would there be any chance of me tagging along?' and then, 'What do I bring?' And then, 'Only oilskins?' And then, 'No tent, no survival bag, sleeping bag, any of that?'

'You can bring a wee camping gas stove, for the tea,' the milkman said.

Of course Anna wanted to come when she saw me oiling the old reel. I was swithering because of course it would be as educational as anything she'd get at school. But it would also be illegal. Despite the efforts of that calm pipe-smoking MP of ours. At least he'd said his piece, 'Ladies and Gentlemen of the House, you must understand that in my constituency poaching is not regarded as a crime but a moral duty.' Donald Stewart, quoted in Hansard.

Let's try it out.

I'm sorry that we kept Anna from school on the 16th and 17th of October inclusive but it was for the following reasons. She was not available on the 16th because she was walking in to a certain location in the Uig District. This was a lesson in practical geography. She was not available on the 17th because she was sleeping all day to recover from being out in the hills overnight, followed by a three and one half hour walk over wetland carrying her share of a substantial harvest. This will be of benefit for her physical education. And here's a finnock for your own tea. — Peter MacAulay, parent.

This was composed but not submitted.

I went alone with my friend and so we had no need of notes. I had already drafted my notice to the Coastguard Service so that I could consider the possibility of becoming a full-time juggler. That was also composed but not submitted. The roles of son, husband and father all seemed to involve a lot of building work. Being a husband was also about listening to anxieties and pacing shores while doing so, glimpsing other people going out at sea.

So of course I wanted to bask in the milkman's beaming smile and enjoy his jovial nature as we slogged through mud. We had to take the wet route because the estate had been granted planning permission to blast a track out through the shorter, higher route. They always do get the permission. There would of course be a spare key for the gate, available for recognised representatives of the community.

The milkman is a fit cove, for one so heavily built. I was glad I didn't have the weight of camping gear on my back. But you hit a rhythm as you slog through bog and once the cold surface water has seeped over the tops of your boots, it's done and the layer warms a bit inside.

We were getting close to the top loch and it was late in the day. There would be about an hour and a half of daylight left. I asked why we were not going direct through the saddle but had to climb the nearest hilltop, right to the top.

'We'll get a good look from here,' the milkman said. 'Some of these toffs are keen. They might still be at it.'

We took a good sweep of the loch, through the glasses and walked on down the glen by the burn. It looked good. There was nothing moving.

The milkman was still cautious as we went quietly down and across to approach that loch, nestled under crumbling inland cliffs. He went straight to the usual bank – a long bed of gravel, broken by a few large protective rocks. We tackled up. I impaled a worm and put the rod back to cast. 'Impaled' is a funny word. In this case it means that I threaded the wriggling creature along the shank of a bent steel hook and made sure a barb broke its skin so that it couldn't fall off. Once upon a time, I made many cups of Darjeeling for a gentle Christian friend, whose studies of the sciences enabled him to explain to me how an organism such as a worm is incapable of feeling pain. I might not be able to argue with that but it can't be comfortable.

I was threading the fly line through the rings when the reel on the worming rod began to screech. You leave only a little tension on, so a fish can take some line if it pulls strongly. That way, a salmon or a hefty sea trout can't pull your rod and reel into the water. It's been known to happen.

I went for the rod and noticed the milkman was into a fish. The light was already fading but you could hear a decent splash. He reeled his fish in, before I saw mine and it sounded substantial. Mine would make runs and half leaps, when it seemed to be tiring, but soon a black and silver speckled trout was gasping, as its tail caused it to beat up the gravel. I pounced and took hold of a fish of about two pounds. I swung its head against a rock and it quivered. Then I reached out for the can of worms. The fly rod was abandoned at that point.

The milkman had three or four and I had two. Then it went dark. Then they stopped taking.

'I thought sea trout took in the dark,' I said.

'Well, they do,' the milkman said. 'At least, you get an odd one.'

That was the cue for the hail. You could just about still make out the anvil-shaped clouds, speeding to dispense their electrical discharge. A blast of sleet gained momentum as it followed the gradient of the glen and came right at us.

My fingers were shaking, not functioning properly as I reached for my oilies. More of the road-workers issue than the marine quality we'd need in this high loch, well up from salt. No wonder the sea trout were fit, negotiating that gradient. Hungry too. But it was maybe too cold for them to emerge from their sheltered lies to feed at night. Oh well, only about eleven hours dark to go.

When the shivers came, I had the thought, I'm here because I chose to be here and because I'm lusting after one of the finest fish of all. The look of it and the taste of it. But out in Bosnia and in the ruins of Sarajevo, people were huddling in weather that would make this seem like summer. And they had no home to go to, in the morning.

You get these moments of clarity and concentration.

'Do you want some tea?' I asked. But the milkman was dozing. He had a bit more insulation than me. A squat, well-built, unstoppable man. I got the flint in the lighter flicking and the gas flared. There was enough peace behind a boulder, to shelter it, till there was a boiling in the stainless pot. But I didn't pour it for a long time. I got my boots and socks off and held my feet to take in some of the heat from the steaming water.

In the morning we took another few fish. The milkman was twitchy.

'We'd better not be greedy,' he said. 'They'll take them off us if they're up here early.'

So we did the slog back. The fish got heavier as we walked. He'd judged that about right.

Twelve months later, I ran away with the milkman again. By this time, teams of forensic scientists were preparing to travel to the former Yugoslavia to investigate sites in areas coming under UN control.

'Same procedure as last year?' But I brought a lightweight sleeping bag and an orange plastic skin. My own body-bag. Once the bites tailed off, I dived in and said, 'Wake me up when they're jumping.'

I saw him not so long ago in Engie's. That's the petrol station where you also buy tackle. We made a deal for next year, if we're spared. But it wasn't only the milkman I met there.

I also bumped into the MP. Not the dead one with the pipe. This time it was the Labour MP who felt that the Kosovo air-strikes had achieved something worthwhile. We talked about the head-lines. The Middle East was looking unstable again. The Saddam issue was the crucial factor, he said.

'Well,' he added, 'the precedent is there. We've come a long way from being pacifists. We're up against aggressors with a degree of ruthlessness we thought we'd never see again. The systematic use of rape as a weapon. The herding of people into camps. That could ony be countered by collective action. And the precedent of a sanc-tioned air-strike is there now. The Nato bombing in Kosovo.'

On the other hand, I thought but did not say, a strong case could be made out for viewing the pragmatic Nato decision to drop deaths in Yugoslavia as an action which itself became a cause of escalating violence. Subsequent investigation by the International

Criminal Tribunal for the Former Yugoslavia confirmed that the Yugoslav security forces did indeed commit proven atrocities upon the civilian population of Kosovo. Many successful prosecutions at international courts proved that the evidence for these was beyond reasonable dispute.

However, the same body also found that the majority of these acts, which included mass murder as well as mass rape, took place *during* the bombing directed by Nato but not sanctioned by the UN, rather than before it.

I did speak then. I made the single point that any action had indeed to be collective, not only with the Nato seal but surely with the UN. How could you say it was OK for us but not for them? Them being Russia in Chechnya, China in Tibet, or any other occupying force.

The MP invited me to a Labour Party meeting even though I told him I was no longer a member and it wasn't an oversight. I said nothing but heard activist after activist warn him that he could no longer count on their support unless he distanced himself from his leader on the issue of the invasion of Iraq. He did not do that. The cove may have been unusual as a politician in that his public proclamations were identical to those he made in private conversation at the gas station. He saw his noble leader's determination to commit British forces to the second invasion of Iraq as a logical extension of the principle of collective action in Kosovo.

He lost his seat, next election, in 2005. Fast years. By that time I was looking more to our own wee shindig in Edinburgh for informed debate. It's just possible this might have something to do with an electoral system which kind of represents the votes cast in the make-up of the Parliament. Strangely enough, this is a policy once endorsed by the unseated member when he was engaged in dialogue with Liberal Democrats. I wasn't able to get excited about the little offered on the devolution menu of 1979 but I made sure I placed my vote in 1997.

The press put Labour's upset in the Western Isles down to local issues – like the closure of the fish-farm in Scalpay. I'd guess that the blushing Blair's marriage to George W Bush was a main factor.

We just sensed that our then-MP was a bit uncomfortable as a bridesmaid. Thus, a promising political career died.

Interesting though, that the policy of removing the successors of the Polaris class weapons from the Clyde was a clear part of the manifesto of the winning party. Also interesting that the same policy was formerly a key part of the Labour Party's manifesto, under Michael Foot's leadership. Somehow this had made said party 'unelectable', according to many commentators.

The percentage vote and the percentage swing are documented information. The interpretation of these figures is of course a matter of some debate.

Calbost

What a work is an island. What a greater work is a society of islands. A coherent group. The Monach or Heiskers, where Black John led the raiders to their own Point of Death and so became a hero. Flannans, twenty miles out from Loch Roag, where the lovers, who were not allowed to marry, made their landfall. They came ashore on bare Eilean Mhor and survived in that place, like the voyaging monks who had occupied the terrain long before them. Go down the searoad from there and out a bit and you'll find the St Kilda group. Hirta at first appears as if it's joined to the high stacks and Boreray. Then you come closer and each island becomes distinct.

Come home to the North Minch. You might have to run before a gale and find refuge in North Rona first, like the Steward of St Kilda and his wife. Gather driftwood to repair your vessel so you can voyage south to Stornoway in the spring and receive the greeting reserved for the few who've come back from the dead. And that was before the good lady gave birth to twins, conceived in that exposed place.

The Barkins in Loch Erisort. The Taransay Glorigs. The impossible Sound of Harris. When the Coastguard Tug contract was awarded, the Chief Coastguard visited and asked my colleague, a master-mariner, if he thought it was viable for a vessel of that draft to take a short cut through there.

'I wouldn't take a wheelbarrow through there,' my watch-mate said.

You can remember all the green-capped islands; the reefs, submerged, breaking, drying and covering but there are still sandbars to contend with. And these shift. The tides do what they want, when they want, washing back and fore through channels and interacting with the cumulative effect of ocean swells and Minch chop.

As an archipelago, the Shiants have it. That's what Mairi said, when she visited the new Ops Room. Management had found the cash to have a stand made for the huge Doppel binoculars, as a bit of a visitor attraction. These were a World War Two trophy that had come the Coastguard's way, back in history. But neither of us needed these fine lenses to visualise the coastal territory from Arnish to the Shiants.

Mairi is some talker anyway but I could sense compulsion in her voice once she started to tell me about the last time she had the boat out. I usually brought the tea into the Ops Room for a visitor but I caught something in her tone of voice. This was a story you couldn't start and stop between bursts on the radio. I got a few quizzical glances as I handed out mugs to my watchmates and brought ours to the restroom. I was entitled to my meal-breaks, on the twelve-hour watch system, though I didn't always take them.

Some coves don't understand about being mates with blones. And once you see through Mairi's tough talk you can see the fine line of her features. The Lochs girl with the Hispanic brown in her eye. Even if she cut back the black mane to give a post-New Wave edge to her look.

She was reliving things, once she got going. That's how come I can tell her story. I was content to listen. I'm not going to try to imitate her voice, just tell you what she told me.

This autumn, her father's marks had paid off again. She'd normally put the boat ashore, come October, but she knew she'd get twitchy later in the year when a decent frost would flatten the sea again. Of course she could get the diving-club inflatable down here, launching from the trailer. But some days she just fancied being on her own. Nuffink personal, mate.

That moment when you kill the engine and just let the boat drift in an offshore breeze. Her father's voice kept her calm. He was always surprised at her staying power. She'd been well wrapped up but most kids her age would find the autumn fishing a bit challenging. And she knew she couldn't come if he dug out the 303 and the ammunition.

He would have laughed at this technology she carried now. Her rods were near enough as fine as the one he had used for fresh-water fishing. He'd chase off with a bubble float and a Golden Virginia flat can of worms to see if he could pick up a late-season salmon or sea trout. These big walks to the distant top lochs of guarded systems – 'A bit much for my wee girl yet. We'll give you a year or two's growing,' he'd said. She still bristled at the disappointment.

Maybe she'd always been a bit of a gear-freak. The record player that could stack six singles high. The control on it to vary the speed. It still had a 78, as well as the 45 for singles, 33 for LPs. But this was a new model, bought from Oxendale's or J D Williams. The Sears and Roebuck of South Lochs. Her mother was always buying her trousers and blouses in crimplene or terylene. Any bloody ylene. Stay-Press, Drip-Dry.

The revolutions per minute reproduced your rubber soul. Norwegian wood. That's what she was floating in right now. Wasn't it good? Light pine. A biodegradable vessel imported, from Norway, a fore-runner of the flat-pack. Clenched together with copper nails and little caps. She'd had to back the heads of many nails with the ball from an old anchor-stock before himself had let her try the fiddly part. They'd swapped places. She was inside the growing boat and got the cap down over the projecting nail, using the hollow punch. Snug but not too hard. She hadn't been able to snip the first point off. He hadn't tried to take over but just showed her again, the twist you made with the snips. Not just squeezing. Then it was too easy and she was snipping too close to the cap. The rove, you called it. So there was nothing left to beat down to complete the rivet.

He'd given her the look she expected but didn't say a thing. Just punched out the first nail and then rummaged for a slightly thicker one so it would be tight in the drilled hole. And this time she judged it right. Then you had to listen to the rhythm of the hammers because the round ball of one tool, one side of the plank, was tapping against the other tool's light touch on the head of the nail. That one will do. Hundreds more followed. They'd swap jobs to keep the interest up. She did most of the riveting at the finish because she was light, standing in the fine boat.

After he was gone, the Rana boat needed some repairs. She knew what to do and could always find someone to back the nails. Cutting the new section of plank was scary but one of her father's mates had been a chippy in the Merch.

Her father's friend had showed her how to grind the rivet and punch it out. That way you got the bad bit of planking clear in one piece so it was your template for the new one. You didn't want to bother trying to scarf them in. It would be stronger and nearly as neat if she butted old and new together and joined them with a backing plate. Riveted through. See if she could get Kenny involved. He had a good hand for the tools. When it was steady.

Now she could identify every repair she'd made since. Some of them with help and some without. Most people who came out in this boat wouldn't spot any of the repairs. And she felt safe in the Rana because she knew every nail in it, the light, open Norwegian boat, built from a kit. She'd got the big, throaty Seagull firing and nosed out of shelter. Then she turned the small craft out, round the corner. She took it inside the Dubh Sgeir but the sea was still lumpy enough.

She might make Calbost of it but she wouldn't get as far as Loch Shell. She was remembering the day she took the Rana all the way to Molinginish, the shore that opens up, past the south side of Loch Shell.

From there, all the small islands in the Shiants group were distinct. When you were closer, details distracted you from taking in the overall shape. That was the day she'd found the carcass of a young sperm whale, up the shoreline.

Molinginish is a boulder beach, accessible from sea but a long walk-in. An old settlement had become a seasonal bothy. She'd beached the boat on that flat-calm day and found herself drawn right up to the beast. The whiteish leather had been scored with short marks. It must have been not long dead, otherwise she couldn't have come so close. Her strongest memory was the detail on that stretching skin. Years later she'd done Raku at the art class in the Nic and there it was, a ceramic impression, like that remembered skin but baked permanent.

Shape was also important. You had to judge when to stop working at that. They hadn't been able to fire the work down the shore, on a driftwood fire, as planned, but the teacher had linked with the techie department to set up an old oil drum as a kiln, fired by one blowtorch. Lewisian Raku. A metaphor for the fire which had produced all this exposed igneous rock. Volcanic activity, breaking from the tides, to form the Shiants.

As she grew, she was allowed to do more with the boat and more on the croft. She remembered the first time she'd been allowed to stay in the byre when a butchering was going on. 'It's not a proper deer, where are its horns?'

That brought out a laugh from himself and his usual accomplice. Then they'd bent back to the physical graft of skinning the hind. Later she'd seen this happen to a wedder but the colour of the deer's meat was different, darker and without the layers of yellowish fat. Sheep or deer or whale, the animal was something different, in death.

Her father's stroke, so sudden, so massive, they'd tried to keep the lid on the box. You don't want to see him like this. But she'd known she had to. She didn't care whether he was as pretty as he could be. Her mother too, she'd needed to see him. That maybe helped but she'd never really got over it. She lost her heart for living so far from town. The sheltered housing suited her fine. It was pretty social in there.

You couldn't look towards the Shiants without thinking of the bodies washed up on the shingle bank, the shore of rolling pebbles between these main islands. Her father would explain the song.

In *Ailein Duinn*, the sea captain from Stornoway must meet Anna, the black-haired daughter of the Scalpay merchant. They were promised to each other. His slim black ship of oak sets out from Stornoway but fails to reach East Loch Tarbert.

Anna cannot bear the loss. She composes the most painful expression of grief you'll ever hear. Then she succumbs. Her own coffin is taken for what they think will be its last journey, by sea, to be buried at St Clements', Rodel. But they're caught in a gale. Her brother, the skipper, decides that the living have to come before the dead. He lightens his vessel by casting Anna's casket adrift. So Anna's own sea voyage began out of East Loch Tarbert. Her body would be set nornoreast, which is the bearing of the Shiants.

But Ailean's vessel was overcome, close to the Shiants. His body would have been filtered through the outlying reefs of the group of islands, never straying far because the tidal effect, there, is cyclical. He was waiting for her. His brown hair and beard moving, like kelp, in the tides.

The force of the northern set is stronger than the ebb, south of the Shiants, so Anna's body had to move towards him. Both bodies were washed up together on that long thin neck of gravel.

Sure enough, they often sighted whales or dolphins in the Sound of Shiants. Big fish, small fin, her father had said to imprint the shape of the diving back of a minke whale. The orca was unmistakable, and usually there would be a tall male dorsal and a rounded female one. 'Do you think that's them?' he'd whispered. She could just about believe it. Anna had escaped the oak confines of her own casket.

She still heard the story in his own voice, no doubt about it. His catchphrases had soaked into the fabric of this vessel, like creosote. 'We'll try a jury rig.' Any kind of improvisation. She'd tried the phrase out at Cearsiadair school, last day of term. They'd all brought in records and the old Dansette player in the building failed to drive at 48. 'We'll just jury-rig it,' she'd said, experimenting with a single at 78rpm. A pile left by the older pupils who were now in the Nic. The Stones version of *Little Red Rooster*. Everyone reckoned the adjustment was an improvement. Soon everyone was asking for more singles at 78.

None of them were quite as good. Then she'd hit on putting on a Calum Kennedy Gaelic anthem – the teacher's choice, a 78 at

33. She always thought Kia-ora was a Gaelic name. The name of the ship in the song. Another success. The game was more popular than Monopoly. She could hear the speeded up riff in her ear now, above the swell. Sure enough, things just weren't the same in the farmyard.

Calum Kennedy had missed a trick. He was the local hero. He could have recorded a Gaelic version with the rooster transformed into the proverbial cow. As in, sad day we sold her.

'Time these bloody fish came on or I'll be singing it,' she thought. A passing boat would sight the drifting Rana with a demented singer giving it serious welly. They'd send the lifeboat to tow her in to protective custody.

'Talking of lifeboats, I'd better show my face back in the Ops Room,' I said.

'I was forgetting. You're running the watch now. I was wondering why you still had the tie on.'

'Aye,' I said, 'but you'll need to come back and give me the next instalment.'

She nodded. 'Part of my own job. Liaison visit. Your fishing vessel records are still way out of date.'

Nine Pounds

You don't go in to the bay at Calbost. Just stay out a couple of cables from the point to the north. Hold Eilean Mhuire at the Shiants just open on the Kebock. You're looking for about six or seven fathoms. You can feel the lead bouncing on the hard ground. That's the drift you want.

I might be a proper townie but Mairi and me went to the same academy of angling. She got her marks direct from her own father.

Now we were in nearly matching woolly pooleys of government issue or rather Agency issue. Mairi had her own laptop along. All the commercial boats registered SY or CY would now be on our own system. Phone numbers and addresses for skippers, owners or shore contacts, the lot.

'Yes, thank you. I will accept that mug of tea now, Mr MacAulay.'

She had a word with the others then followed me through to the rest room. Took a seat. I knew there was something else she had to say. She'd get back to that drift, up from Calbost. First she told me about diving at the Shiants.

Once you'd been down there, you could imagine it again, the territory under the surface. So that day, in the fast changing light, she could just make out the shape of Eilean Mhuire but she had this picture of the way the landmass continued under sea level. She'd dived there, in a calm, at slack water and found it as clear as anywhere except St Kilda. She'd been distracted from following the underwater topography by the sheer abundance of fish. Lythe and coalfish, up to ten pounds, swimming as grey-green individuals and yet so dense as to be one body.

Now, she had that imagery in her mind when she was fishing. 'I think like a fish,' she said. She would jig her chromed lure and vary the rhythm of it, to entice that big one to snap at it. She could see a yard of bronze, shimmering by the kelp.

She checked her bearings and knew she could drift a while before there was any risk of being drawn too close in. The wind was mainly westerly, off the land and the tide was slack. She'd got that about right.

Her own internal dials shifted from metres to fathoms, whenever she was afloat. She gave her line a good tug upwards and just let her lure fall, wriggling down again. The boat rolled in a wave and she thought it was the kelp gripping her big trailing hook. But then there was that nudging, shaking and the rod tip bent till it was right under the surface.

She felt the dive of a fish that had to reach the kelp to live. Don't let it fall off till I see what it is. Only now, she realised how keen she was to take a fish from the old marks. Just the one would do. She was desperate to know what species she'd hooked.

She knew from the job, the Spanish want hake. That's what drove them all west of the Hebrides, whatever the weather. English folk want cod. In Iceland they export the cod and eat the haddock. Norwegians don't turn their noses up at coalfish.

When this fish plunged again, shaking its head like a labrador, she was picturing it, tethered. The diver in her was meeting the angler. It was a ling or cod, she'd bet that now. A lythe, even a big one, would swim with you then dive again. This was a steadier resistance and an impatient jerking. She just held while it did its best to shake free. Then she recovered line between the strongest tugs.

There was something strange about the drift of the boat. It couldn't be big enough to be towing the Rana, surely. Maybe just acting like a sea-anchor. That was possible. Now she was watching for a first glimpse. The glint of her own lure would show first. They went for the flash first then smelled the oily bait and saw the whiteness of the strip of squid. Her father's trick. He had a collection of lead rippers. You had to shine them up with scrapes of a penknife.

She preferred chrome. The door-handle of a Ford Anglia used to be the business. These parts were thin on the ground now and in demand for restoration jobs. Her present stock of lures was made from the leftovers of a set of pram wheels.

She was kind of an acceptable aunty, making the fish-box cart with the brother's kids. That was only a few months back. The big bro was a few years older. They'd never been that close but he'd settled down, as they say when they mean mating. Twins as it happened. She'd noted the big looks from the mother but she'd never said it, why don't you find a man you can depend on and do likewise?

But she didn't mind taking the twins for a while. She'd let the toddlers bash in hundreds of nails to fix a board to a box. Property of Kinlochbervie Fishselling. Not now it wasn't. 'Don't you go getting hammer-rash.' That was another fine phrase he'd got her into. The wheels were still on their axles, the chassis of an old pram from the shed, with the rest rotted away. She'd realised then she could even get the brake working if she ran a pulley and jury-rigged a ratchet and lever.

She'd had to trim the original chrome lever so it wouldn't catch the ground. So there she was, asking the kids to stand back for one moment, please, *madame et monsieur*. The metal was hard on the hacksaw but she had the technology. The aunty with the angle-grinder did her stuff. The niece and nephew had been impressed while the sparks were flying. They'd be even more impressed if she could bring them the fish that was clinging to the lure she'd made from the offcut of that lever.

Whatever it was. It was still diving and keeping just out of her grasp.

Playing with kids was OK. They weren't babies but kids. Babies didn't do so much for her. Her own chance couldn't have come at a worse time. It was going to be difficult enough, chucking the public service security to set up her own IT consultancy. She knew she had to pay off the home improvement loans first. Kenny was cool about all that but then she'd realised she was late, that month. She'd been sure even before the test. If she was going to get something done, it would have to be fast. She'd known for a fact Kenny wouldn't have been able to handle the thought of losing it.

Now the fish was showing. Too compact for a ling. Even the white barbel, under the chin, was distinct. Not the kelp red of the *bodach ruadh*, the resident rock cod but its deep-sea cousin, come inshore for the winter. No gaff aboard.

She'd be fine. She was remembering how she'd taken the neglected tackle-box in hand. She'd shone up that lure, rubbing polish over the pitted bits. The falling verdigris. Renewed the trace with fifty-pound nylon. She'd replaced the rusty hook with a new forged job. None of your fine finicky ones, designed for anglers on wide craft, bristling with landing nets. She wasn't a real angler after all but a Lochy who wanted the glory of bringing home the dinner. This one fish would feed a few folk if she could get it in the boat. It had to be close to double figures.

Now. She got a hold of the trace and timed the pull with the roll of the boat. She just knew it was going to fall back but her new trace held and the cod was on the boards puking pinkish slime and venting it at the same time. Gorged on shrimp and prawn. As good a fish as you got, this side of the Island. About nine pounds. Salmon or cod. That was a good weight.

Her own stomach was tight. Knotted. And only then did she face the fact that she was on a lee-shore. Disorientated, she looked back to the Shiants but they were gone. The wind had veered to north and a bit east of it. Something strange was happening in the sky. It was too bright, under fast darkening clouds. The wind doesn't often shift as far as that in the time it takes to bring a decent fish from the bottom. She was observing cumulus nimbus. Cu-nim, the airman's nightmare. Big anvil-shaped clouds ready to spit hail and thunder.

If this was the movies, the music would be getting up. Gaelic gospel, your cue has come.

The only music she wanted to hear was the husky tone of that motor. She'd been drifting without it running because two-strokes weren't so keen on idling for too long. She'd stopped it her father's way, fuel cut off so everything in the bowl of the carburettor would be used up. So now she'd need to flood it, choke down. Mairi could hear his voice.

'If it's getting fuel and there's a spark, it's got to go.' Her father's lessons for the circa 1944 British Seagull applied equally to the circa '89 model she'd bought new, with her Civil Service paycheck.

She was close to hugging this motor, bought in the teeth of the best Far East competition. I'd helped her source the unit. The QB Seagull was no longer modestly stamped 'The Best Outboard Motor For The World' but you could recognise it was from the same stable. The design had been passed to Queen's University, Belfast. Nothing to do with politics or bolstering the Union, just that these guys were best when it came to two-strokes. The design remit was to keep it simple and rugged. Bronze and brass where it mattered. But it had to be a bit quieter and more fuel-efficient. So we were progressing to a 50 to 1 fuel mix when the opposition were on 100 to 1 or oil injection. But the fancier engines had more to go wrong with them. This was the business and it would take her clear, out of this mess.

The cod was still gasping on the boards. Normally she'd have hit it on the head at once. The gills were heaving, doing their best to find oxygen. At least the spray was keeping it all moist. It wasn't like a conger that could stay alive for hours out of water but only a minute or two had gone by. She had it in her arms. Strange thing, the weight of a fish and the weight of a baby. A good nine-pounder.

Anchors

I put the kettle on again and let Mairi get her breath back. I told her there was no hurry. We just sat in silence for a few minutes. It wasn't awkward. Then she carried on with her story.

She held the fish and could feel the muscles moving, see fins bristling. She knew she was risking the remaining stability of the boat by leaning over to release it but she couldn't just ditch it over the gunnel. It had come from shallow water so the swim-bladder would be intact. Sure enough it dived, with power, and was gone.

It was ale you needed for a decent sacrifice to the sea gods. They had access to plenty of cod. Or maybe not. Protected species, now, on the Grand Banks. Endangered species in the North Sea, if you believed the scientific officers' reports.

She sighed when the Seagull fired second pull though she'd known it would. But she'd left the throttle full on when she'd shut the fuel cock, earlier. So now it was roaring in neutral. Not too nice. She went to throttle down, the black thumb-lever still the same shape as the old chrome one. The engine shouted at her. Her onshore drift was increasing with the northeast squall.

Fuck.

But she was seeing how the throttle cable was a bit kinked. She'd sprayed it with liquid grease. This was just lack of use. There just wasn't enough time to get out, anymore. Maybe she was missing her man's contribution more than she'd thought. Her right hand went to tweak the throttle, get these revs off. But she was too slow to respond to the urgency of that screaming pitch. Slowed by memories.

At last she remembered that the QB had a stop-button and went to press it just as a thump and a squeal came from within the cast cylinder. A painful, crippled movement continued, sounds she'd never heard from any engine. It would be pretty damn messy in there now. Seemed like an hour but it had probably only taken under a minute to destroy her pride and joy. The motor was dead.

She was calm now, studying the green ones starting to roll in with white crests on them. A low roar was sounding above the slap of smaller waves on the clinker boards. This was the breaking and turning of building seas on the lee shore. She was one of the few swimmers in her class, at school. Her father had persevered, showing her all the breast-stroke movements at home, then taking her to warm rockpools he knew so she'd put them together. It wouldn't help her now. With that surge she'd be ingesting more water than air. OK, there was oxygen in water but even the old guys couldn't show her how to extract that.

Hell, she was close to the rocks. What was the village tale of the fellow up for his mate's ticket, getting questioned?

'What would you do if you found yourself on a lee shore with machinery failure?'

'Drop anchor, sir.'

'And what would you do if the wind rose to Gale Force?'

'Let out more cable and drop another anchor, sir.'

'And if it rose to a nine?'

'Put out another anchor, sir. With plenty of cable.'

'And a storm ten?'

'Have to put out the fourth anchor, sir.'

'Yes, and now can you tell me where you're getting all these anchors?'

'Same flicking place you're getting all that flicking wind from.'

As she was remembering, she was knocking in the pin at the stock of the fisherman anchor, always ready to go, at the bow. Three fathoms of chain and plenty of nylon warp but it wouldn't be enough, in this swell, unless she was lucky. As the warp was hissing out she looked for anything that would do for a second anchor. So she moved astern, with the spare rope and made an anchor bend

– a round turn but the first half hitch also goes through that turn
– fixed to jam below the cylinder of the nearly-new outboard. She
couldn't resist one more pull of the cord just in case some seizure
had been freed and splintered shards of alloy had healed themselves.
They had not. Her fingers were working on the clamps holding
the engine to the transom. No snags. So she put her strength into
lifting engine, bracket and all, and dropped it over.

A moment of slack when it hit the bottom. She grabbed some of
that line and led it round, crawling her way to the bow. She let out
still more line, running through the fairlead so there would be no
dangerous chafe. This would let the Rana plunge nearer the rocks
but there was more chance of holding the ground.

She breathed deep, now both lines were tied off. That fixing
point. What was its name?

'The bitter end. From the Dutch word *bitts* – that part where
the anchor is secured. You see it wasn't only silver we got for our
herring.'

All these things she hadn't even realised she'd picked up from
the olman.

Her voice was sounding out loud but not shouting. Singing. Best
Church of Scotland voice. Nearest you'd get to a good going Baptist
choir in a hundred mile radius of Garyvard.

'Will your anchor hold in the storms of life?' And the reply.

'We have an anchor that meets the strain, steadfast and sure
while the billows rain.'

Billows sounded a bit soft for these short, violent bastards. Was
it her imagination or were they easing? She was swinging bow-in
to the seas now. The gear was holding. The sacrifice might not be
in vain.

Someone might have seen her leave and reported her caught
-out. The SY lifeboat could be belting down here at eighteen knots
with the wind behind her. U.S. Cavalry job, bugles blasting. The
boys would find her, giving it laldy with seafarer's hymns. That
would be a performance, all right. Who was she kidding? The
report of the overdue boat would not be sent till nightfall.

Another wee precaution. She took up the fat buoyancy aid, from under the thwart. She carried it but couldn't work in it. Now she wrestled it over her bulky oilskin jacket. She was between a rock and hard place. Miracles were getting scarce.

But she might not need one. The savage edge of the front was through. There was still fierce power in the squalls but there was some breathing space between them now. Maybe she just had to bide her time. Hang on, the Silva compass was in the inside pocket. She couldn't see a mark to line up but if the bearing to the point was constant, her anchors were holding. Norwegian wood. Wasn't it good?

Call it zero one five. Wait a few minutes and check again. She was about to take away the eight degrees for variation then laughed at herself. No point in translating it to True. A constant bearing is a constant bearing. She wasn't going to plot it on a paper chart.

The seas were no longer breaking. You could still see them coming. Dirty lumps of grey water. There wasn't much white showing at the tops of them. The wind was right down again and returning to the west. The flood tide north would start any time now. She was going to get out of this. This boat was light enough to row well. That wind would take her out clear of the point and then the tide would help her along. She could sneak into Mariveg, the south entrance and moor the boat there

But she couldn't afford any pissing about, trying to recover the engine. It had done its work. She had to let that rope run then haul up that anchor if it wasn't snagged.

It wasn't easy to get momentum against the run of the swell. But the Rana boat is a light craft and the low freeboard helps when it comes to rowing. She got her craft into the safety of Loch Mariveg under her own steam. Own muscle, anyway.

The Black Pram

We're in the shed at Griomsiadair. It's a lean-to. It's a temporary structure that will last longer than the house. It's corrugated iron on a timber frame. Same as that dance hall Prince Albert had built at Balmoral. And that's still hanging together. Available for study by PhD students, assessing the longevity of materials. Older sheets, they say, last longer. New steel sheets are thin and come with sacrificial coatings of zinc or protective ones of plastic.

The shed was fixed against the stone gable of the home-built house. There were some fine wooden-handled tools still hanging from resilient nails. The wind came through the chinks but maybe that airflow helped to preserve it. And the tools. That's where Ruaraidh and Angus devised their projects. I was a bit preoccupied with blueprints for that elusive New World Order when they were unfolding the plans for the pram.

Plans are only a potential. But drawings can be beautiful in their own right and of course more perfect than the finished product could ever be. It's not so long since I've looked closely at a steel yacht, designed in the Netherlands. She had a very tidy Perkins diesel, recent electronics and decent sails. Self-steering gear. She was going for a song at a time when I'd been getting a fair bit of work. I had this daft idea: Anna and me could do a proper cruise. Ireland, Galicia, Azores, places like that.

I've seen the plans from Van De Stadt, and the lists of specifications. I've seen the paperwork for importation of cut steel plate, coated and delivered to an address in England. But I've also looked closely along the waterline and seen the buckling between the frames. That syndrome is known in the trade as the hungry-horse look. I'm informed it's usually only cosmetic and due to distortion from the heat of the welding.

And even if the ship has been professionally built under the supervision of a naval architect, repetitive pounding through seas will cause some buckling of plates. Think of it as the ship's memories of her experiences.

Anna was gentle with me but pretty clear when I sounded her out. It's not that she didn't fancy it. But what she really wanted now was a pair of river kayaks on the roof of a VW van. The faster the water, the greater the rush. She knew it was a sort of addiction.

Good job I phoned her before doing anything daft. End of the year, I was skint again. Unscheduled repairs to roofs and wheels. The ideal gets dented. When it comes to shaping the ways of the world I think, so far, history shows that the idealists are dangerous. It might be OK on a scale of villages or towns – New Lanark or Leverhulme's Port Sunlight. Maybe it's even possible for whole islands to tick over without too much bother. Once you start invading other places to spread the religious or political word it's ratshit dot flicking com, *a ghràidh*.

Take Napoleon. He was well into the whole picture – legal code and all. Couldn't megalomaniacs be more like boatbuilders – the ones who build by eye – smoke a lot of roll-ups and do a lot of standing back and looking at the lay of the planks? That would maybe reduce some of the damage they cause. But then they couldn't really be megalomaniacs.

I'm going to propose that there is a significant difference between those who seek to impose their order by weapons and those who are motivated to do it by eloquence and charisma.

Can we agree first on the similarity – both roughly-drawn types believe like crazy in what they're doing? And of course some leaders of men and women are capable of alternating between both strategies. Not my own cup of rhetorical tea but, never mind the words, look at the presentation. I'd go to Chaplin's *The Great Dictator* for the definitive analysis of Adolf Hitler's body language. Passionate and persuasive, if a little OTT for my personal taste.

But it's the tone of voice that gives you warning of the horrors to come. Think of the hate bursting through Adolf's tight-arse rhetoric. But that's the end of this digression. I was going to number them for the sake of order, the digressions I mean. But then they wouldn't really be digressions. Let's go back to the idea of blueprints, for vessels, rather than societies.

A proven design has to be achieved in suitable materials. These will be selected according to function, budget, taste and availability. There's also the crucial factor of time – you can't use a material that hasn't been invented yet. Some materials have been around longer than others. Wooden boats can still be competitive, in everything but cost. There are now also many ways that timber can be adapted for use in boatbuilding.

Some years ago, two friends were plotting construction in a material that was new to them both. Plywood has been around for a while. Layers of pressed timber are glued together to form a composite which has very good structural properties. Durability can be an issue but it depends on three main factors. The quality and species of the timber to start with; the number of laminations, with a large number of thin being stronger than a small number of thick; and the quality of the glue which joins them. Marine grade plywood uses particular glues and more durable species of timber are usually favoured over others.

A sheet of plywood comes in a standard length which is 2.4 metres (call it eight feet in old money) so there are some issues when it comes to joining sections. Angus was always researching and inquiring and came up with the plans for a simple vessel which had come out of tests very well. It was based on a proven shape – a Norwegian pram-dinghy. There will now follow a short description. Should you wish to proceed to the less technical parts of this story, please omit the following two paragraphs.

Thank you for continuing. A pram-dinghy is by no means unique to Norway but is very common in the sheltered waters of the fjords. The form is also prevalent in other parts of Scandinavia, particularly Sweden. Several Norwegian boats were imported into the Hebrides on the backs of fishing or whaling vessels. They were used as tenders. Rather than take them home, these would be sold off to local crofter-fishermen, as inshore rowing boats. Replacements could be obtained very cheaply or just built, on return home. Timber was cheap or free because in Norway, certain varieties of timber are easily available because the stuff does indeed grow on trees.

The design is based on efficiency and ease of construction. Planks, solid timber, or in this case, cut from sheets of plywood, run the whole length of the boat. They end in a blunt piece in the bow (front) and a blunt piece which becomes the stern (back). So there is very little twist in the shape. In Norway these are usually made from quite wide boards so there are only a few planks on each side. Because they overlap, this adds strength so only a small number of additional frames are required as stiffening and strengthening.

The plans which caught Angus's eye merely adapted that principle to plywood construction. Frames were set up first and the joints between plywood planks were designed to fall where there was supporting timber framing behind them. Fastenings would be dipped in protective gunge. So the boat was planned to outlive the creators.

I was away on travels while these gentlemen plotted and drew and assembled materials. So the summons only came when I was home from Uni, at Easter. 'Never mind the peats,' Ruaraidh said. 'There's painting to be done.'

So that was my share but I didn't get to choose the colours. The hull was black and the wooden trims at the gunwales and bow and stern were signal-red. The oars were black with red bands. She was a fine, simple shape.

All went well until the launch. She was light by the heavy standards of the time. Light enough, just, to be carried or dragged down the croft and put into the sheltered water of the inner loch, the Tob. The boys (translated as 'old guys') had a bit of difficulty carrying her down but there were plenty of cousins so they could stroll behind, carrying a rope and a bailer. They wouldn't need the bailer though, because she wouldn't leak. She didn't. When you launch a clinker boat for the first time, or if she's been out of the water for the winter, you expect water to gush between the boards until they expand. The pram was tight because the joints were bedded in suitable material.

The problem occurred when the boys sat in their new vessel. That's when they realised they were getting old. Each of them also knew then that he didn't want to die for a bit longer.

'Shit, she'd roll on wet grass,' Angus said.

Ruaraidh spoke in Gaelic.

'Oh well,' the watchers said.

I tried to intervene as gently as possible and say that some things you had to get used to. She'd never be like a beamy Lewis boat but this was a different style of rowing. She might seem tippy at first but maybe she'd stiffen when she leaned a bit.

The boys weren't ready for such advice.

'Pity she's too big to put on the mantelpiece,' someone said.

One of the boys used her that summer, to go out and back from the net. Someone else used her another year to get out to his swinging mooring about fifty metres out. That was about it. The boys had planned to take her over to Loch Orasay where you could still sometimes net a vermillion charfish. But they lost heart.

Not quite twenty years after the launch day, I bumped into old Angus in the Poy-oy. The postoffice. That's one word. That's how you say it. This would be about a year after Ruaraidh shed the mortal. I was a bit shocked at how frail Angus looked, leaning on the stick, but I hoped I didn't show it. Things moved fast.

'Make me a silly offer,' he said. 'I'll give the money to Kenny's young cousins for the painting they've done over the years. They've kept it up. But she's not been out.'

That's Lewis cousins he was talking about. Could be termed third or fourth cousins, on the mainland.

So we have to ask ourselves, how come I never had time to bring Anna over, to visit folk, out of town, while we were working away on our own extensions or on the olaid's house? But I did have time to take her to see this craft. The paint had protected the ply. There was some rot in the stem and stern. Some rusty screws because they'd built her before stainless steel fastenings were widely available. She belonged in a museum to document the shift of technologies. Construction of small vessels in the transition from Scandinavian lapstrake construction to epoxy-based glue systems.

We took our time on the repairs. I didn't have access to a big shed then so the jobs were weather-dependent. Angus wasn't interested in my reports of the oak replacing cedar at the top of the transom. He wanted to know what the colour scheme was now. 'Pale blue with a maroon trim,' I answered. He gave that the OK.

We gave him the photo. The pram moored calm among the rushes. We hit on this plan to row round Loch Orasay. That's the deep loch. Deep enough in places to hide a stock of surviving Arctic char. Well, I don't think the fish live for ever but the species continues here as it does in a very few other localised environments in Scotland. And in Lake Windermere. In Iceland they grow big. In Lewis they average half a pound and they're usually netted. I served one up to Gabriele the night she came off the ferry to stay. I'd been given it by Ruaraidh. I'd been a bit anxious about the local reaction to my German blone, even if she was going to go down well at the first footing – tall, dark and handsome.

The fish looked better than it tasted. It had been in the freeze a wee while. It wasn't at all bad but we didn't get far into the second course. Prawns, of course, since you ask.

The remains of the Lewis char and the prawns made good breakfast material.

Don't think we ever told Angus about our first adventure in the pram, after Anna and me had made a few repairs and painted her up. We went out to lay a running mooring in the loch. I'd heard it was deep so I brought along plenty of rope to go to the chain, shackled to a big single-point mooring – a dense piece of scrap steel that would bury itself in the silt and mud. What age was Anna then? She could swim better than me. But I delivered the lecture. One loop of rope and it's death. Once that weight is going down there's no stopping it. The line has to pay out smooth from the bucket. We're at the other end of the boat. No feet, no gear, no nothing near it.

'Just like dropping anchor, Da?'

'No, I can haul the anchor back.'

'Have you checked the depth?'

'Well, no, but we've plenty of length in the rope. Plenty to spare.

We'll tie it off to size after.'

It went over. No hurry. We balanced the pram and watched the line pay out smooth as you like and go on for ever till the float went over as well and disappeared into the still loch. Anna was curious. She looked over for herself before saying, 'What happens next, Da?'

I said not to worry but I was going for a wee swim. Just in case the float was a few feet under the surface. I can swim to about fifteen feet. Well, I could then. There was no sign of the luminous white plastic. Anna refrained from laughing till I was in the boat again and we hadn't tipped.

'It's a wee bit deeper than I thought,' I said.

'So we've achieved exactly nothing,' she stated when I got my breath back. She was reading a lot, these days.

'That's not quite true, young woman. We've done our bit to tidy up the more industrial streets of our metropolis.'

'And chucked it all in the country instead.'

'Can you see that hunk of scrap?'

'No, but I know where it is.'

'OK, but neither of us are seeing it again.'

'Probably not, Da.'

So we went for a row and trolled some flies round the loch. Never saw a fin, char or trout. Forgot to tell you what the char look like. More red than brown. Spots are more gold than black. In fact the red on the one I saw and cooked for Gabriele wasn't that different from the red that used to be the trim on the pram-dinghy.

When we were in a shallow bay, we put all our weight to one side, to test her out. The pram leaned right to the water and then became stiff. We could balance her like that, leaning right over. That's why Ruaraidh thought it was a good design for Lewis. It was. Once you got used to that quirky leaning thing that happened before the shape became a wedge on the water and stopped her rolling further. The old boys just lost their confidence too soon.

We got a bit of work done on the dinghy trailer – same one we used to move her from my uncle's croft. Not that light a boat, really. The keen builders, of course, hadn't been able to resist using some superb quality Oregon pine at two inches thick for the thwarts

– that's the seats which also brace the whole upper parts of the boat. It came from old doors from a posh house. A dead house on a tidal island.

We put a sail on her. A gunter rig – short mast but a fair amount of cloth – the rig came from Gabriele's old dinghy project that wasn't going to happen. That sail had never been used. We got given a wee jib. Perfect. That was my part in the joint enterprise. Anna would have to teach me the finer points of sailing. I'd fallen right into the trap of leaving the finesse to Gabriele. It was getting more and more difficult to get Gabriele out and about for longer than a short walk. There was a name for it, at last. They called it M.E.

We fixed the step – the housing – for the mast so it could be taken up and down, no bother. Anna and me jointly man-and-wom-an-ufactured a decorative wee rudder with fish shapes for cheeks. We tried her out on the Barvas loch. There's a few rocky bits but most of it is sandy bottom and the water's warm.

You're hearing the roar of the west side surf over the machair. I knew one hell of a story about that but now was not the time to share it with my daughter. All that wind, all that power, gets huge boulders rolling to smoothness along the outside beach. But that's not going to bother you as you're speeding about on the flat, brackish water. The pram took off.

I wondered how she could be so fast and then thought, yes, maybe because she's so bloody long, thinking of the bit hanging over the end of the trailer. But the pretty rudder wasn't that effec-tive. In fact, as she went like a dart for the shore, it was all getting a bit worrying.

We found out you could turn her by getting our combined weight where it mattered and using the sails. Keeping pressure in the main to take her towards the wind. Let that go and get some power in the foresail to take her off the wind again.

We managed to turn with only a few inches of water left. No harm done – and even the rudder escaped damage. Simple, really. Routine tack. Fuck.

'Da, I thought you promised Mum you'd be watching your language when I'm aboard.'

'It's all about appropriate words for the situation, esteemed daughter.'

Warm rain came on and the breeze got up and we found another problem. She was stable enough, hard over on one side, accelerating away but the water came in. There was the traditional, sawn-off Duckhams plastic oil container, with an angle in the cut so the handle remains. This is a design common to west and east Lewis and which had taken over from the Nestle's baby-milk tin, which was traditional in the days of my youth. These came to the Island about the same time as sliced bread. It would be worth studying the style of improvised bailer, island to island, Gigha to Unst. These are fine examples of applied physics. Amazing how you can think all that in the second it takes to grab the bloody thing and get it working for all you're worth.

They race boats this way in Shetland. As long as the bailer can keep up with the volume of water coming in, they reckon the boat can take a bit more yet. Anna was grinning from ear to ear. Then laughing out loud. She got me started. Good job there wasn't anyone out for a wee stroll in the force six.

We took her out in the loch a few times then put her on a running mooring, far side of the hoil. She proved a good rowing tender – but there's a tidal bar. Anna was getting into the fishing. So we cut it a bit fine for getting the pram back to her mooring. That bar of shingle was showing. No worries, we could just pull her across. But remember these heavy thwarts. It was a fair old push. Anna was taking the painter and leading from the bow. Then she said to me, 'Da, you know some people just take their dogs for a walk on the shore. They keep their boats in the water.'

We had another good day on the Barvas loch. It was a bit stony at the edges but fine when you got out. We got a bit casual about leaving the boat but not the gear up there.

Some kids from the village took her for a jaunt. Fine, but they left her untied, banging against the stones. Not so fine. Not a difficult repair job but it took a while to get round to it. Anna was into other things by then. There was a couple of changes in the air. The days of our carefree pottering were numbered.

Steel

Willum had done well for himself. He'd got out of the Academy and along to the Buchan College as soon as he could and got to grips with his navigation. He worked through his second mate's exams, sponsored by the company, then quit and went trawling. But he didn't just jump on a boat as a deckhand and go straight to the money. No, he did the one-year course in Aberdeen and picked up all the skills, the netmending and wire work and shut his mind off when the lectures in basic seamanship went on. He didn't appear aloof or anything and the younger guys kind of looked up to him. He was a skipper already, in waiting, and everyone knew it. The last days of the trawling in Aberdeen were rough. The fleet was run down or looked it anyway. I went along to the market once, took my flat-mate, Robbie, with me, to ogle at the catch and eat dripping rowies with the rest of them, the porters and salesmen. That was the starter, for breakfast, before bacon rolls, served with a bucket of instant coffee. We saw a taxi or two arrive. A skipper was rounding up his drunken deckhands while the engineer was coaxing the machinery back to life. They'd be in debt again. They'd need to make one more trip, Iceland way. The cod war was over but the UN deal was going to keep most British trawlers 200 miles out from the coasts of Iceland. Working conditions were just not that great.

Willum had done his stint on the rustbuckets. He earned his ticket and saved up his deposit. He was up on the game, the shift away from Aberdeen to working the west coast.

'See that catch, swinging in now, teuchter?' Willum said, 'Rockall warriors. We got them over your way. Dinna ken fit way your Stornoway trawlers willna gang oot fir their share o it. It willna be oot at Rockall for lang, fishin the likes o this.'

The warriors were the cod themselves. One to a full box.

That's how he made his money. He was canny with it too. Of course he had the nice motor. The girlfriend, Sheila, kept the seat warm while he was at sea. It was always parked away from the harbour, out of the salt.

I only spoke to him on the VHF once. Coastguard to fishing vessel. When we got to the working channel I could talk normal.

'Just heard you calling the other boat and thought I'd shout you. That's Willum, aye?'

'Aye and I think I'm talking to the teuchter cousin. Are you nae bored in there when there's a picking to be had oot here?'

'You're out Kilda way?'

'Well, I'm jist not free tae tell onybody exactly the whereaboots o this vessel at this moment but I can tell ye noo it's no that fine a mornin oot here.'

He was in the fish again.

I saw him only the once or twice in The Broch, in the new house. He wasn't that much for the drink but there was a dram out for us both as he spread out the plans. Folk were saying it was a done. Aye, the Aberdeen trawlers were done but plenty Broch and Banff boats making good livings working out of Kinlochbervie. The crewbus was parked outside. He knew I liked VWs and he fired up the turbo-diesel so I could hear her purr. A Type 4 Caravelle. Oilskins were left on the boat. The lads all had a shower when they landed. And a hurl back to The Broch for every second Sunday.

He told me KLB was second only to Peterhead for white fish. Aberdeen was done. Ullapool was booming with the Klondykers, the shotties o mackerel.

This was the new ship. Steel was the way to go. And the blue-prints were spread out. Willum took me down to the engine room first, of course. Twin Caterpillars. Then we took the tour right up to the bridge. You couldn't call that a wheelhouse.

And then he said, 'But I'm off down the road to pick up young

Andra. I've only the one loonie. Indoor fitba – that's his thing. I like tae pick him up. The Broch's no the quiet place you kent on your holidays. You just talk your Dostoyevskies wi Sheila. She's back til teaching English. At the Academy. I couldna wait tae git clear o it.'

And we did. And I met his lad, also Andra, named after his grampa. 'So,' I says, 'if I've got this right, you're Andra's Willum's Andra.'

'Aye.'

I hit it off with Sheila. We were soon on the historical novel. Sheila was saying how she could get right inside Raskolnikov's head. Everything just builds up. 'Yons like a symphony playing in somebody's mind and the thocht process canna be shifted nor stoppit. So it hid tae end in the swinging o an axe. But that's jist the beginnin o the mental journey.'

The next few years did definitely accelerate. Willum's new ship had her dents but she was still shiny red. Signal red, I think, with that hint of international orange. A safe colour. I was hoping maybe Anna's team would get to the semi-finals in The Broch and maybe she'd be playing against her cousin. Five-a-side is a big event these days. But it didn't work out quite like that.

Willum was tied up in business. Nearly as restricted as his ship. The bank was squeezing him and the Fisheries Officers were on top of the vessel. Every vessel. KLB was a quiet place and a lot of the stuff coming through Peterhead was imported from Iceland. They caught their own fish these days. Who could blame them?

'We should hae done the same. The Common Market was a richt for the farmers but the fisherman was payin the price,' Willum said.

The VW Caravelle, out the door, was the same turquoise green colour and, I was amazed to see, the same reg. And it wasn't a customised plate. The skippers would have the boat's name on the plate, which went from vehicle to vehicle, changed every year or two. There used to be money in the East.

Anna's team did get to the semis and they did play The Broch. She didn't meet her cousin. She asked about him but people just said no, Willum Sim's Andra hadnae been aroon the club for a while.

She didn't have to go to church on the Sunday though most of her mates did. She just said she had relations to visit. She had her dinner with them but there was still no sign of Andra. Sheila told her pretty well straight out. Anna was shocked by it all. Good that she heard it though. And she reported it back to me.

'Ah dinna ken fit like Stornoway is these days, but The Broch has its problems. Ane big problem. You must have heard we're bein cried the heroin capital o Scotland.

'Some of them are bairns still. They smoke it. They're thinkin that wilna dae much. Then they're gettin sick if they dinna get it. That's when they start injectin, tae get the maist oot o the bag. Your young cousin Andra has a these pals on the boaties. They dinna go tae the pub these days, they hiv pockets fu o cash and they go and git a bag for the weekend. And the ones that dinna hae the cash, they lie an steal. There's nane o them you could trust.

'That's ane o the reasons Willum is thinking o givin up the boat. It's that dangerous like. He disna ken if the loonies aboard on a Monday is still high. If they've sneaked something oot wi them. An there's wires runnin an swell runnin and there's been a hell o a number o accidents. Mair than ony time.'

As my lawyer and former classmate advised me, when I thought of tackling a certain builder, justice is for the next world. This one is all about probabilities. Sir James Matheson was only able to become a benefactor (mainly to himself) by distributing drug-fuelled havoc in Asia. There might have been some Old Testament justice if Stornoway had been hit by the epidemic which ravaged The Broch and Alness and other unlikely towns. Or maybe it *has* been bad enough here. Just that you're out of touch with it, another stage of your own life. A guy was done for taking a serious amount of cocaine across the Minch, not that long ago.

It was Sheila on the phone.

'It'll be a very quiet funeral. There's no need for you to come over but you've kept up wi your Broch relations and Willum thocht you'd want tae ken.'

I thought of old Andra, the one surviving brother of my mother.

I'd missed seeing him, last visit. He'd also had a stroke. He was recovering but he was in dry dock at Foresterhill Hospital. I didn't make it through to Aberdeen.

'No no it's nae your uncle. Aul Andra is nae baud. He's an army o hame helps and he's gettin by. I hiv to tell you, our ain young Andra has passed awa.'

A Funeral

I booked into the Alexandria Hotel. It wasn't very expensive. I was anxious, driving down on my own. The hail was lying. I had the estate car which looked like shit but was mechanically sound. It looked after me fine. I was knackered and didn't even go out. For a while, driving, I was thinking of the chip shop where you can ask for lemon sole rather than haddock but I was beyond that now. I'd picked up a sandwich when I stopped for diesel and I had that with the tea, in my room. Shit, UHT in plastic tubelets.

Das Boot was on the telly. I'd never seen the whole film. Men trapped in a steel cylinder. Now that must be close to Hell. A crew with a skipper who never gives up. But it's the engineer who saves the ship. The ironies build up at the big parade. They're about to get another batch of medals. But an air-raid comes and they all die, on the surface, in port. I never watched telly at home. I'd spend most evenings in the workshop itself or else leafing through files in the storage area up above it.

I'd thought I might have a view of the stretch of coast between the harbour and Broadsea, where Willum had once let me work the wee yole when he hauled a couple of pots. But now, I looked away from the sea to a row of houses that had been handsome once.

These must have been a big step up for folk like my roller-skating, singing and dancing grandparents. They'd stepped up to one of these, inside cludgy and all, from living with all the eight bairns piled into one room.

These same houses were boarded up now. Sheets of ply were nailed across where the windowpanes might still be. Talk about seeing through a bloody glass darkly. I think that was Paul rather than Peter. You could see a bit of coming and going but not much. One door at least could still open, in the block.

I remembered where I'd seen something like this before. We'd driven through the streets of Belfast on our way to a music festival in Dundalk, when I was a student. There were houses boarded like that. And I'd seen worse later in Derry, a visit for research. I'd decided that events were still all too close to be a suitable subject matter for a dissertation.

The *War of the Worlds* robot feet on the electronic watchtowers. They were surveying the estates. You could see a bright sprinkling of tricolours and Palestinian flags. Over in the rival estates, the Loyalist side, they flew Israeli flags in response. A few years later, I saw an exhibition where a Scot called Alec Finlay had asked to replace all the national and sectarian emblems with printed studies of wind-blown clouds. It was a reference to Basho, a Japanese poet. It gave a calm feel for a short time.

Back to this war-zone in the town that used to be our family's El Dorado.

Young Andra was a casualty. They say some people have greater tolerance to addiction of any sort. I thought I was like that with the tobacco and the dope but now I'm not so sure. Some people get hooked faster and get off it earlier. Folk like me maybe take a long time to succumb to their deep wants and then have to give in to them.

I only ever really knew one guy who'd had a full-time addiction to opiates. I'd never heard from Torcuil, my old angling mate, since he left the Island all these years ago after burying his girlfriend.

Once, I stopped the car on the quiet street in Coalsnaughton. Off the main road. I used to reach out to Torcuil's along the railway line. Sauchie was in the news too, for a few days of tabloid headings. A Scottish Republican living there was done for carrying arms. I might have gone to school with him.

But this time I was on my way back from a Coastguard training course. I'd brought a rod along, to cast a spinner in the sea at Highcliffe, in the hope of catching a sea bass, a fish I'd never seen in the flesh. Of course we went for pints when the official day was done and that was the real training, maybe even the therapy. Amongst the shop and the gossip, the stories of incidents. So I never wet a line.

I'd turned off before the Forth Bridge and crossed at Kincardine. I'd got the bus out there once, from Sauchie, to catch dark flounders we didn't risk eating. I found the road up to Gartmorn Dam. There was something different but I couldn't put my finger on it. I thought there might have been more pike fishers about. This was getting close to winter and I cast the spinner out near the island, the place where Torcuil took the big pike. Something wasn't right. I folded the telescopic rod and walked all the way round to where the burn ran in. The water was high but the ripples and deep browns were the backs and dorsals and adipose fins of trout that still had the spawning instinct.

Folk must have netted the pike and perch and restocked the dam – but not with the imposter rainbow trout, peely wally shadows of their North American originals. These were native browns, bred for the entertainment of fly-fishers. Probably Loch Leven stock, in genetic origin, like the trout shipped out to India to stock the clear Kashmiri streams.

I was lucky not to get arrested on two counts – spinning in fly-only water and out-of-season with it. So I watched and noted the change of circumstances. The condition of the place had not remained frozen in the same state it was in that year the teuchter went home. I drove away from the Dam and out the road to Coalsnaughton. Parked just along from the large detached house. I had no way of knowing if Torcuil's mother was alive or if her son was clean now or even still on the planet. It might or might not still be the family house. Courage failed me and I didn't leave the car. I drove on before I was reported as behaving suspiciously.

Old Andra's bairns helped get his wheelchair into the kirk. He wasn't going to make it to the graveside. The service was as good as it could be. The minister had known young Andrew personally and seen him develop into a potential leader, potentially a great sportsman, with a very winning personality. Sadly, Andrew's case was like many others in this town at this time. We would have to hold together as a community and look to see what we could do to help without having to assign blame. There were guilty people of course and they brought a plague as surely as if they had brought bacteria to the town rather than drugs. But once a new group had succumbed they also became dangerous to others. Because the habits of one fed on the habits of another.

In that same way, we had to be aware we were in possession of a more powerful source of change. In that same way, we would use our interdependence to counteract the threat to our community. We could only continue to offer support to our neighbours like Sheila and William and think of them and be with them at this time.

I went to the graveside. I threw my handful of sandy soil and I shook hands with my cousins. I didn't go back to the house. There would be plenty and they could speak whatever comfort they could, in their own language. There were others who had lost their children or as good as lost them. I said I was sure they understood I'd need to get moving towards the ferry. They thanked me for coming. I sent the wishes of my mother at home and my sister from Canada.

But I had one more night in the Alexandria. It was too tight to catch the ferry. Anyway, I wasn't in a hurry to get back, this time. This was a very rare patch of breathing space. This time I did queue for crisp lemon sole – the olaid's own favourite. It was firm and sweet, steaming when you split the batter. But then I bought a reporter's pad and a twinpack of Mitsubishi pens. A half-ounce pack. Some papers. A lighter.

I walked out for the paper, before breakfast. I'd written what I'd needed to write. I didn't need to show it to anyone. The shop had a metal grille over the window. I thought of knickerbocker glories and bright Broch Candy.

For some reason I took the *Fraserburgh Herald* as well as the *Independent*.

I had fresh grapefruit then real porridge and a smokie with a poached egg on top. A buttery roll along with it. They called them rowies in Aberdeen but my Broch granma called them butteries.

There's a lot of luck in how things turn out. Our gang sniffed solvents once shopkeepers started withdrawing the bottles of tincture containing opiate from the SY shelves. Soon they withdrew shoe-conditioner too and limited the supply of glue. That's when someone sussed out the active ingredient could be drained into a lemonade bottle, in the Mill.

Most of us got away with streaming eyes and short-lived bouts of paranoia. But we'd set the local precedent. Did that mean I had a share of the blame for the lonely death of a kid who went on to do what we'd done, out there in Sir James Matheson's overgrown gardens?

I read through the local paper, looking for signs of something I recognised – The Broch of Jimmie Sinclair's ice cream. There was a paragraph referring to the cause of death of the youngster whose body had been released to the family last week. The body had been recovered from Fraserburgh harbour by police divers, following a short search.

Persons were being questioned by the police in connection with the incident but no arrests had been made. It was thought that there had been a scuffle and there was some suggestion that the incident had some link to drugs. The deceased was a known user of heroin.

The cause of death, however, had been found to be by drowning.

The Barvas Shore

This is the story I heard from a distant cousin of mine. A *Siarach*. West-sider. This was my last year in the Coastguard Service. You're not going to hear about any incident we co-ordinated. But I'll tell you a story I heard on watch. Courtesy of the master-mariner who became a trainee. I've got one for you. I'm passing it on, he said. This is it.

There was a blind woman in the village of Barvas. She had sons. The eldest was on the village boat. The Barvas men never went to sea until they heard that the fish were running. The risks were too high because the surf comes in strong on a steep beach. There's nowhere to run for miles and miles, north or south.

They went for the biorach, the piked dogfish. Fish everyone else thought were a menace, tearing herring nets. But, on the west sides of North Lewis, and off North Uist too, they went out with longlines to take the biorach. They dried and salted them. Sometimes they'd be smoked. Sometimes they'd be buried deep into the frame of a coil of hay so when the wind blew through the haystack, the grey sharkskin wrinkled and dried too. So the fish was preserved.

The word came from Bragar and from Ballantrushall that the biorach were running. So the Barvas boat was out with the rest of them. But they were all caught in a sudden squall. They didn't manage home in daylight. So the whole village was out there on the beach. Lanterns held up to help the boys find their way in. Everyone was scanning the white line of the surf, hoping to catch a glimpse of red sail.

But the mother of the skipper was searching with her hearing. Remember she was blind. She was noting the fall of the stones, great round boulders being shifted and running back down the slope. She heard a sound that was different to the rest. She knew it was him.

So she was the first to perceive that her son had come back. The shock brought her sight to her. So she saw him. She saw her son for the first time when his body was returned to her on the Barvas shore.

The Sister

The sister and myself were always one thing or t'other. When we got on we were best of mates and when we fell out we did it in some style. I remember one time the minister calling by, for a routine visit. Up the road to Westview Terrace. He was the cove with the moustache and a big smile. He had no objections to me bringing a book along to the services to keep me quiet, instead of kicking my heels. He did suggest *The Water Babies* might be more suitable than some of the texts under my arm.

We were squared up shouting as he walked through the door. The olaid was only next door for a Nescafe and a fag. It's a wonder she hadn't heard us. The minister spoke softly, calmed us down. I found out, a lot of years later, he translated Burns into Gaelic.

The sister took her chance to build a new life in Canada. This is a traditional route for emigration, over the years, in The Broch as well as the Islands. It worked out for her. Nursing was a better career there than here at that time – with proper coffee on the go, non-stop, along with first-name terms. You couldn't return to the hierarchical systems of the NHS after that. Or the coffee.

When she said that, I thought of the paramilitary motifs of my own trade. I was a servant of Her Majesty. I might be there yet if it wasn't for the residue of post-Thatcher ideas in the public services. You spent so much time accounting for your time that you had very little time left for watch training. Or team building. Or yarning, which of course is both of the previous items combined.

How can you say how resentments build up? My mother's eyes would light up when her former cycling partner would arrive from the airport. Not on the first night but on the first day, the sister would rearrange the stuff in the cupboards in the kitchen. OK, she's a woman and I don't know much about them. I know more about trout really or I used to at least.

The home-help would be on leave when the sister was staying. Kirsty had her own systems. And they did seem to work.

The olaid made it pretty clear. She wanted to stay in her own house right up till she was taken to the hospital to get ready for satellite re-entry or whatever was going to happen next. If anything.

For me, the sister's visit was a time to catch up on this, that and the other. And I'd messed up in style not once but more than that. The appointment for the podiatry department was an outing for the olaid. Not a hassle but a wee excursion. I forgot at least one appointment.

The stroke club annual Christmas dinner was a laugh with other people of like mind and body. All of them had plenty of bloody marbles, nothing short there, and they all relaxed in each other's company, flirting and chatting because they didn't have to pretend. Knew they didn't have to prove they were compos mentis, even though they talked with a slur or had lost the use of some muscles. In that setting, they didn't have to prove a damned thing. A crew, a team. Similarities to the angling society or the boat-owners' association. The legion. You could rant about your obsession without worrying about being abnormal.

I had a grand time the first year I went. The olaid had the home-help pin the next year's invite up by the mantelpiece in good time. She knew it took time for things to register in my mind if I was doing research or on the tools. She reminded me more than once because she knew what I was like.

But I still got involved in a moorings operation, because it was the only day, for months, the tide would ebb far enough. After you've lost one boat from a mooring dragging, you lie awake imagining wear and chafe and unrelenting forces on the points of strain. The black pram was a modest craft but she was a link with my daughter and she was a link to my uncle and a connection with my surviving mentor. So I came dashing up the road far too late. I could still have got my arse down to the Caberfeidh Hotel to grab the pudding and say sorry and join in the banter and wheel her out again. But I was stinking of SY hoil mud which smells like nothing else. But not as bad as the shame. I hesitated at the door when I realised I was late and the olaid was down the road in the minibus.

So part of the tension between the sister and me was sheer simple guilt. I could see how the blone's professionalism was showing up and how my own was wanting. And now that I'd finally quit Her Majesty's Service, that made everything worse. Of course you'll have plenty of time now, folk kept saying. They just couldn't know that you'd never have less, first years of trying to establish a wee living for yourself. Of course the more Gabriele would say, 'We can get by even if you don't earn anything at all,' it made it kind of worse. She was teaching German, part-time. But she had good weeks and bad weeks. I was chief cook and bottlewasher.

So it was a crunch when the sister quietly said that she would only be going back to Canada for a fortnight to tidy up loose ends. She was needed here full-time for this stage. Because I knew somehow, somewhere beyond conscious thought, that she was right.

Don't know how it came to writing notes to each other. Talking via the home care system – home-helps to give respite to the sis so she could get shopping and get to the few vestiges of normal life. Gabriele and me just somehow stopped having her to meals on her night off. There was a very intense night when Kirsty was round and she just started reliving a case of hers, caring for a terminally ill child. Anna was very sensitive these days and Gabriele and myself were taking turns at trying to catch my sister's eye. But she had to continue.

Now I know she had no choice. Maybe the timing could have been better. But the need to tell it just surfaced right then and that's how it was. Better than leaving something that should be said, still unsaid. I think I knew there was something else between us we hadn't dealt with yet.

Once the note-writing starts, the game's a bogey. You've lost it. So I would time the visits down the road to when she wasn't there – 'Phone me when you're going shopping and I'll go down then.'

That was good in a way because it meant a continuity of company for herself.

Latterly there were some signs that even the invincible Kirsty was under some strain. She was just needing nights off, out at the movies which weren't available then in the city of SY. She wouldn't take a drink. And it wasn't going to get easier. The olaid had been diagnosed with a cancer in a kidney. But it could be very slow-growing in a person of that age and it was quite possible that a different illness would appear before it reached a critical stage.

After the last identified stroke the olaid got periods of amazing clarity. She was able to go back for miles in the long-term memory and of course she'd have to ask you more and more about the plans of the day every five minutes. But I'm a bit like that myself at my tender age.

She'd also wake up after two hours of sleep and need help to get to the toilet and then to her chair. And the sis was just cream-crack-ered. So I was forced to climb down from a standpoint of saying I just couldn't work along with my imperious sister. We figured out something like a rota.

Things had happened quite suddenly with Gabriele's mother. That was only a couple of years back. We hadn't been there to see the slide down the slope. But we were all together at the funeral. I suppose the olaid's journey was more gradual. But this was another stage.

The first night was tough. My olaid was near aggressive a couple of times. She'd got so used to a way of doing things. Just as well the sis was staying with a mate out of town or I might have had to go crawling for help. The second night, we'd got to understand each other a bit and I'd discovered the right channels on the all-night radio. We had it purring away with the Morsø glowing fine and it looked like we'd all sorted out a workable routine. But there wasn't a third night.

Kirsty phoned me. A swelling. She was frightened of a blood clot so the ambulance had taken our mother in. We agreed to stagger the visits so the olaid would have the maximum company. The sis sounded bloody tired.

The old girl was clear and funny. She couldn't cope with the dry heat and wrestled to get her cardigan off. Most of these nurses liked things tidy and full of decorum so they kept buttoning her up. She'd scowl.

When she got hit by an infection on top of every other bloody, shitty thing she was trying to deal with, they moved her to a side ward with one other patient. I could read the signs. I remembered side wards from a previous career that had spanned a full year.

So there wasn't a lot of need for decorum any more. She kept going way beyond what they thought was do-able by adopting a mission. After breakfast – well a spoonful of porridge flavoured liquid – she'd start on the first button of the cardy. The Count of Monte Cristo had nothing on her – that used to be a favourite book of hers. By my next visit she'd have the cardy off her shoulders and was feeling the cooler air around her chest. And grinning away at the victory. She'd tip a big wink to me. A rebel with a cause.

That struggle gave her a mission and so an extra week of life. It mattered. I cancelled an outboard servicing course because she wasn't going to come out of this one. But what a fight she gave. I've seen fresh run sea trout give up easier than that and they don't come much tougher or bonnier fighters.

So then you could just about believe she could last for ever. Like her brother. I left in the evening to get back to some weather-dependent jobs. I had the roof off a porch.

But I took the mobile. So I was up a ladder, catching the last hour I was going to get away with a fibreglass skin, when I got the call from Gabriele. The hospital phoned. It might be an idea to get down sooner rather than later. I phoned the sis right then too.

And soon we were together in that room with the olaid. She might have seen it, might have not, but the sis told me she'd got it across to her a day or two before, that we'd buried the hatchet.

Maybe that gave her another day or two boost so Gabriele was able to come in to say goodbye. And I was happy when Anna said it of her own accord. She wanted to see her grannie. Yes, she knew what the score was. She came in with me.

A couple of times Anna had sorted the whole show out before

me or the home-help arrived. Incontinence pad changed, the whole lot, no fuss. If that wasn't an intimacy, what the hell was?

The olaid made it as easy for Anna as it could be. She got her laughing – I forgot what the crack was but they could still be good. The nurses just loved that mother of mine, knowing there would be a smile and maybe a whispered crack as well.

Parents, parents. That's what they're supposed to do. God's sake, show the offspring how to do things right. The Broch woman who bore us showed us how to die.

The sis says, 'You know, I could do with a smoke.'

I hadn't seen her smoke for years. So I went and rapped with one of the auxiliary guys. He looked like a surfer and sure enough he had the makings. We might have got some blow from him too by the look of the cove but we didn't need that now.

So I kept my sister company when we went out the back door. The fresh air was good. Then I found myself skinning up – well a single-skin tobacco smoke. Lit up and passed it to her. I didn't want any more but it was just that connection. The sis didn't say anything but there was a lot in that nod.

It was my watch when the change in the breathing came. I just went over and gave the sister a squeeze of the hand, enough to take her out of the catnap. She nodded and came over to join me, our chairs up close.

'I think she's going,' I said. And then, 'I think that's it.'

We weren't in a hurry to go for the nurse. And when I did go over she just nodded to me to say, 'Yes, that's it. She went peacefully.'

My sister never said she was a nurse or anything.

Kirsty and me, we haven't had a bad word since.

Splitting up stuff, any of that – nothing was an issue. Our mother was a magician. Bloody funny with it.

Rebirth

I'd very much like to tell you now of the process whereby a vessel can be born again. This is a technical operation but the main requirement is neither nails nor timber but, my friends, it is faith. If you take a *cuirt* along the shores of Goat Island or Griomsiadair, or enter through the locked galvanised gates of Renfrew or Govan, you will see an abundance of projects. These will be directed at vessels of differing dimensions and type but most of them are unlikely to be completed.

Money is often a concern and we have to concede it is a factor that must be considered. But that is not the main requirement. The proof of this is the number of neglected vessels owned by those who have amassed large shares of the world's gear. But these owners of vessels and of gear may well be short of time and are almost certain to be also short of faith.

I cannot say that all vessels are capable of rebirth. First the carcass must be found. *Titanic* was found, though she has not, as yet, been raised. The streamlined *Isadora*, of the six-metre class, built to international rules, and last seen going bow-down when under tow at Kyle of Lochalsh – she was never found. There was thus not even the solace afforded by wreckage to grieve over. There was no opportunity to take mementos. Only memories remain.

We could consider example after example but friends, we must not lose the intention of this treatise, which is to prove that rebirth is a possibility. Not a waking dream but a thing you can touch. Better to believe without specific example but as we all have an aspect of the psychology of Thomas – the disciple who admitted doubt – we can study the case of one unique vessel. Should you wish to do so, you can rub a finger along the last part of the skeleton of the old and witness where it has grown up again from the very keel to be made almost entirely new. But faithful to the curvature and dimensions and displacement of the old. Like the *Titanic* herself, this example was first brought into this world in the year 1912.

She was a whole boat when she was completed but she was still called a 'half-*sgoth*'. A *sgoth* is just a skiff, as time goes by but there was a large class, a three-quarter class and a half class. At the time of her building, John Finlay MacLeod would have been helping his own father build these craft at Port of Ness. Maybe his olman's eye was on his work but I'm guessing he was already trusted to complete the smaller craft. There are records of the vessels they built and the length of their keels, the names they were given. But the meticulous notebooks don't tell a whole story.

Peace and Plenty survived because she was blessed with such a fine shape that everyone who had anything to do with her was affected by her beauty. Of course, such beauty is dangerous. There's a tradition in Scotland that you don't want to make a working boat beautiful beyond the appeal of a good line, well maintained. A decorative touch is allowed – the yellow arrow at the end of the cove line; the scroll around the name, repeated on the wheelhouse. But if you go beyond that, she might be claimed by the sea, for herself. The Scalpay herring boats must have come close to the limit, with their dozen coats of varnish and their perky canoe sterns.

It's a good thing that *Peace and Plenty* was used to set lines and creels and nets because the wear and tear leaves scars and scuffs. Some of these go deeper than any paint can cover. When you scraped to investigate possible rot you would find that the layers of paint would make their own map and their own historical documentation of her story. As you rubbed sandpaper, the way she would once have been rubbed with the skin of a dogfish, you would see the contour lines. There would be a deep flag-blue giving way to a shade of maroon, named 'Bounty'. There would be Admiralty grey and there would be Baltic blue.

You would discover evidence that her mast and her oars were carried in different positions, over the years. So you could imagine that sometimes she might have carried a sail, on spars that could fit inside her hull. And at other times, she may have lay snug at anchor, in the bays of Harris or the inlets of lochs so a taller mast could be stepped. Whatever their shapes, these sails would once have appeared white as cumulus cloud but later they would have been treated with the boiled bark that preserved herring nets of cotton. So a rich russet colour would develop. Suffice to say that our concern here is not with the rig or performance of the vessel. It is possible you will encounter such details elsewhere, for in her own country she is famous. We are concerned with the very fabric of her body.

We must demonstrate now, by this single example, how such a shape can be made again. I must remind you that we left the vessel apparently dead. Her keel was intact but her planking was torn apart and her ribs were shattered. The breasthooks, fore and aft, were torn asunder from her bows and from her quarters. Although I knew that her soul lay not in the lines which gave her shape, I also knew that the preservation of these lines was a homage to her history.

For many years I was custodian of the remains of *Peace and Plenty*. She was transferred in the registry of vessels to the name of MacAulay. A vessel is owned by alloted shares, there being sixty-four shares to a ship. As my own mother provided one half of the purchase price she was entitled to one half of the shares, being thirty-two. In return, she asked for a small share of the catch. She requested a lobster. I never did pay that debt with an indigo scavenger. And it might be very difficult to do so in the future, even should there be an abundance of them come, in traps, over her gunnels.

This is the story of her resurrection which took place many years after the extent of her decay was identified. With reference to our previous discussion of matters of faith I concede that it would be better if we could agree that her gospel is the memory of her own way through water. But some of you will be, like me, in the camp of the doubting Thomas. Therefore I must endeavour to lead you to a site where you can place your fingers on her renewed ribs.

They were making a film about the rocket-post experiment which took place on Scarp. But they were shooting it on Taransay. Just a little more scenic and the village could be recreated in canvas and paint. There was even a little graveyard and you had to touch the stones to know they were cloth. There was to be a boat scene. The company was attempting to assemble a flotilla of craft, contemporary to the time in the script, just before the outbreak of World War Two.

These were good days for joiners but, as I found, also good days for guys with a good grasp of Kelvins and Listers, Seagulls and Sabbs. Perhaps a recent refugee from the Coastguard Service who had a power-boat ticket and an appetite for shifting boats about.

It was all cash on the table. It would go to help a family find a substitute for *Tante Erika*. A few optimistic mates had looked at the wreckage of our British Folkboat over the years but I'd begun to give away the viable salvage, like the nearly new sail. Of course I'd got the Yanmar going. Once the corrosive salt water is flushed from the innards, you flood the motor with the stuff of life – diesel itself. Of course you take the starter motor and other bolted on electrical components to the alternator-doctor who lives in Newvalley. There's no need to visit Silicon Glen.

After the coughs and splutters, you nourish the turning motor with new oil and wipe with clean rags and coax her to sweet running. After all that, the last thing you want to do is to leave her idle so of course I'd given her to the guy who'd stored the wreck of the vessel which had contained the unit. Anna still hadn't given up hope but I knew I could never trust her life to a vessel with a keel that might have shifted, even if we replaced all the bolts. Better to build an entirely new vessel on a wooden keel we could examine throughout. An open boat is like an open book.

That movie helped us on our way. Anna made a bob or two herself, starting to save up, thinking ahead to leaving for Uni. We gave old, dry vessels first-aid with battery powered bilge-pumps. We rafted up the maimed with the mobile. We did everything we could to slow down impatient people who were rudely manhandling the pride and joy of Hebridean maritime heritage. We took care even if we couldn't always take charge.

This is the story. The island of Scarp is reached by a short boat journey across a Sound that can get out of hand pretty fast. A German engineer visited the Island in the late 1930s. He proposed that the mail be transferred across the Sound of Scarp by rocket. An experiment was set up. Special stamps were printed. There was publicity.

The mail was charred but the rockets flew. This created interest from the German government. Gerhard Zucker was required at home in the service of the Fatherland. He had scruples and wanted to insist on the peaceful application of his work. But he had family who could be put under pressure until he complied.

Maybe now it's difficult to separate the layers, like the histories of repairs on old boats. A true story becomes the fiction in a film. There is documented evidence that Zucker went into the Luftwaffe on return to Germany. In the film, he chooses to stand before a firing squad.

Of course there's also a love affair and a beached whale and a charming poacher and a landlord who really does have a heart. And great scenery in grand weather. The pressure to return to the fold of Nazi Germany is provided by guys landed from a U-boat in a vintage rubber dinghy. They wear excellent coats and doubtful accents. I happen to know from no less an authority than a master mariner from Dundonnell (now deceased) that this is the most plausible part of an unlikely dramatisation of a powerful story. Though maybe the souls of the separated lovers (Hebridean archetype embodied in the song *Ailean Duinn*) did meet in another element that is not terra firma. See also the motion picture *Rob Roy* for use of the same song but somehow transposed to a dry land situation.

We are dealing here, in the film, if not in the documented life of Zucker, with an aspect of death which was only hinted at in the legend of *Ailean Duinn*. Now the souls of the lovers can be observed as carried by soaring eagles in the slow final shots of *Rocket Post*. So, in this case, the transmutation of the human spirit into the animal world happens in mid air. A bit like in-flight refuelling. The pinions of a pair of well co-ordinated eagles ride the thermals over a Hebridean maritime landscape.

We had a breezy day for the rehearsal and probably the best traditional boat festival which will ever happen in the Outer Hebrides. Bright varnished craft were dulled down with black emulsion but they still looked good. We had to make sure the Yamahas and Suzis were carried on the side that wouldn't be seen.

But those of you with a healthy interest in sailing or historic vessels or both, don't hold your breath when you watch the movie. They couldn't get a camera on us that day. The next one, there were other priorities and the few minutes of film were edited to a fraction of a second of a convoy of various sails flapping in a calm while the boats nonetheless surge along with remarkable bow-waves.

The fees were, however, paid as agreed and we were very well fed. After all that fun, we had a conference which decided that the remains of *Tante Erika* were more viable as spare parts. So we only sold our aunty and not our grannie. I could phone my boat-builder mate to ask him to cut the planks to the lines he'd taken already. We still had the original keel in store, along with fittings and examples of her parts, such as knees and breasthooks.

He said he'd ring me back when it was time for the frames to go in. That was a two-man job and I could save the cost of hiring someone else. That way she would be affordable. We could save another cost if I trusted my daughter to get us across the Minch under sail alone. I could install an inboard after that, in my own time. The fitting out is where the costs could escalate. The boat-builder advised me to keep everything simple. He's no longer in business, by the way. I have a feeling that the remote situation of his workshop was not the issue.

A kind Fisheries Officer handed us what might have been the last dipping lugsail still stored, dry and sound in the Lochs area. We could have a new synthetic one built on its pattern when I'd made my fortune as an engineer. Till then, this would get us sailing. And there were spars to go with it. She'd get one of the boys to drop them off in Ullapool.

Anna bravely stepped aboard the ferry carrying the anchor from *Tante Erika* over her shoulder. The purser didn't let her away with that. 'So you don't trust us, young woman.' Next week, when we came aboard, carrying our own valise life-raft, also sheltered from our storm, he just shrugged his shoulders.

Thus *Peace and Plenty* was resurrected. She's a new boat on the old keel. Of course it was miraculous. The last few planks were a bit more freestyle. The final shape came out of the rebuilder's head but it was influenced by the grain of the larch. Whatever the mix of heredity and environment, the shape is sweet.

When it came to insuring the boat which was now a structure comprising new planks, from the old shapes, built on the old keel, with her ribs and almost everything else renewed, the insurers asked to know the date of the keel. 'It's documented as 1912 in the Fisheries Office records,' I said. 'Then it's still a 1912 boat and must be insured as such,' the voice on the phone said. So that was official.

Gabriele came across for the launch. No kidding, she was for renaming the boat *Tante Erika*, transferring the nameplate now propped up by her side of the bed. It was Anna who said we'd done enough tempting fate.

But she insisted on *Sekt* rather than whisky, which was fair enough because Anna liked that too. Our shakedown trip took us across to the jetty at Badluarach, along with all the leftover paint and tools and debris. Her planks had been kept damp in the warm weather and she took hardly any water in. We packed the materials and gear in the back of the van and Gabriele set off to catch the ferry. Our own crossing was gentle, with the builder proving his faith in the joint between old and new wood by coming along for the sail. When the wind fell low for a time, we trolled lines for mackerel.

They fried in their own oil in a pan which fitted neatly into a metal bucket with a simple camping gas burner underneath. We watched the shapes composed by the Shiant Islands alter as our angle on them shifted. When it blew up a bit more than we wanted, on the Shiants East Bank, we dropped some sail and rolled it smaller. So we glided into SY hoil, rested and fed. The boat didn't take a drop in, between her planks nor over her bows.

I did some research and found that the sweet little Scaffie, *Fidelity*, was awaiting her own resurrection, in Stonehaven, though she hadn't been buried yet. She was under cover. But her Ducati diesel had not done a lot of work and could well be available. Wilma thought James would have wanted me to have it.

'Aye, he passed away a couple of years ago now. But our own wee madam is fair excelling as a piper.'

Our sheds and greenhouses and new lean-to had somehow filled with stuff. I had planning permission for my garage with a difference. It would be clad with reclaimed natural slate on the gable. A velux window set in there, opening to a mezzanine. There would be an oily area, but also a shower. So I would no longer get in trouble for carrying the residue of projects into the house proper. Or the garden shed proper.

So the site-shed at the olaid's housing project became my operating theatre. We were letting out her house now. The house had served my mother's late life needs for about ten years. Where had they gone? The temporary shed beside it had survived my mother.

Broadband was coming to town and I was able to find all the bits to recondition the single-cylinder unit which was uplifted from Stonehaven. An air-cooled engine had its appeal. Apart from the Dietrich-like throaty tone, it meant there could be two holes less in the boat. No need for a raw water intake or exhaust outlet. There was just too much detail in the work to keep Anna motivated.

'Dr Frankenstein, I presume,' she said one day when I got back into the overalls, after helping her with the history essay. But see that moment when we ran the Ducati, on the bench – that should have been enough to cure Anna of that unhealthy fascination with unreliable forms of propulsion, like sails.

The neighbours thought it was criminal, the idea of putting an old engine in a new boat. You see, they didn't believe that she *had* been resurrected. If they could make that leap of faith, it was too much for most of them to see that the same miracle could happen to machinery. But the choice of motor was a matter of money as well as the thrawn tendencies of Lewis culture. There were changes brewing, in my own life.

Gabriele was not encouraging. 'You'll be moving in, round the corner, soon,' she said.

Two Bridges

Anna and me were always big pals. I mean, we had more than one adventure. Stuff that should have put her off any kind of boat for life. An overnighter in the Folkboat after the waterpump on the Yanmar packed in and I didn't have a spare aboard. It was long tacks against a strong headwind. She woke to see me straining to read the compass bearing.

'Would it help if I called out the numbers, Da?' She did and it did. She'd also tell me when we were getting too close to the wind and when we were falling off too far. She had a feel for it.

Her mother was anxious, meeting us in the morning, but Anna was beaming because she knew she'd responded to the challenge of it. She can always come out with that winning smile. Those who don't know her so well would think she was happy all the time.

But she's one of the driven people. A side order of desperation in the pleasure. Competitive sport only does it for a while. It's the challenges you choose for yourself. The Corrievreckan in a kayak. Pentland Firth in a dinghy. The unclimbed mountain in Turkey. The Ducati in the *Peace and Plenty* was just too easy.

On the day when everything changed, Anna and me were for keeping going. Her mother knew enough was enough. She was close to her own limit. The rain hadn't eased. The burn at the head of Loch Langabhat was so swollen you couldn't see the spawning salmon. We went most years to watch the fish swirl in the head-waters. Late November to early December. You usually see a fin or two first. The dorsal cutting the burn. Then you see the soldered flank turn in the blackish water. Light enters and the water's clear and the details of the fish come out. You see the hook in the jaw of the male, the maroon spawning dress. Then another and another and the pool is heavy with its fish. They don't have an option. If they live, they come back. Sniffing each current till they find their own river, in from the Atlantic.

Gabriele took one look at it and was for going back. She wasn't going to try crossing that burn. More like a river now. Anna and me were right up for a push. We could do the circle. Up our wee Himalayan path – snaking up Stulaval. It would get easier then, as the faint track followed the flat high ground. Then we'd cut across, to take the fork down by Loch Voshimid. After that, it was downhill along the Land Rover path to the Hushinish Road. She and her mother were always going to mountain-bike that one. But Gabriele had good days and bad days. You couldn't make plans. And the father and daughter could check it out, on foot.

Gabriele really was cool about walking back the same way – that would do her fine. She'd rescue the car and pick us up at that point on the Hushinish Road.

'You two won't be happy till you get soaked right through,' she said.

We'd storm it. The rain gets you walking faster.

We waved goodbye to the shape of Gabriele, taking it slow back up the rise to the path. We went to find the best route across. There was the foundations of a long-gone bridge. Very green grazed ground around that, standing out from brown, shining in the dreich late afternoon.

It's the first step in, when the cold hits your toes and the pain is sudden. Then it goes dull. The water warms in your boots and it's bearable. Then you don't notice. It's normal. I'm wading the ford and then my pole is going too far down. We should turn back. We'll have to find another way.

We both pace the bank. Not looking for salmon now but for a route through the shallows. I see one and go. Between rocks, the pole dips again but I push for it. Lose the footing, right close to the other bank. I dive for it.

'Hey, Da. Nearly a dry capsize. Nice one.'

'Kind of you to say so, girl, but I'm not as bloody dry as all that.'

Anna is across already, learning fast from the mistakes of her olman.

That was bridge number one.

Well, the bridge wasn't there any more but the ford was. We pause. I'm shivering but if we walk at a gallop I'll be fine. There's still a way back but it's borderline now, for catching up. We'd arrive in time to see Gabriele drive off to pick us up from somewhere we wouldn't be.

I think of the crossing before Loch Voshimid. Another trickle that could bring forth a yield of adrenalin today. I pause again.

'Do you think we should turn back?'

'Let's just go for it,' Anna said.

We do.

The responsible adult and his daughter get euphoric, warming up with the incline. Some pace. We strike out with the rhythm of folk who've been cooped up. Tasting the elements again.

We pause and look up, scan the skyline. You seldom walk this way without seeing a golden eagle. We'll hear stags soon. I see the lines of white descending from the ridges. Places where I don't remember any burns. Deep down, I'm turning over the options in my head.

We could still go all the way back. Wait for Gabriele to realise we're not going to appear on the Hushinish Road. Or else we could skirt round the next burn. Get up the east side of the ridge and follow it along the high ground. Along the watercourse. Dark wouldn't be long away but the ridge would keep us right. And Anna's an ace on the Silva compass.

Then we hear the roar of water. We look at each other but don't alter the stride.

We'll take a look at it, anyway.

This is bridge number two.

I'm trying to consider the option that's it's a no-go. I've struggled to find enough water here to fill my hand for a drink. Remember the Bible story. David or Joshua or some other heroic leader has more men than he needs for the mission. So he gets the squad to drink from a stream. Those who cup their hands to drink are taken. Those who lie down and lap are not. Since the Clock School education, of stories, singing and sums, all by a coal fire, I've cupped my hands to drink. You wouldn't want to miss out on a wee adventure.

'Can you see the path, Anna?'

Neither of us can. The noise is bad news. But the bulk and shape of the water is scaring us too. The colour is muddy or peaty but it's charging over the concrete bridge so hard that the foam is thick. It's a rapid, going over as well as under a bridge. I'm trying to remember what the bridge is like. There's nothing visible. It's only there by implication in the water-flow. I remembered it being a basic concrete casting over wide pipes but I'm not sure of the detail. Anna is already testing the edges. She finds solid cement-work under her boots. 'It's all right, Da, we're on it.'

'Aye, but how wide is it?' I feel with the walking pole. I'm tentative. Anna borrows it and prods. She hands the pole back. We reckon we've got it. Too much froth to see anything but there's no more than a foot of rapid water flowing over the bridge. Likely less. Anna links her arm in mine like when she was a kid. Now she's already higher and heavier than me.

'Come on, Da, we're going for it.'

But I'm the more cautious, elder one. I keep feeling with the pole, anxious to know the concrete is down there. But our slower progress does not give us enough momentum so the weight of water is driving us across to what must be the limit of the under-water walkway. Too late, we move faster and try to adjust our line upstream. Like vessels steering a course to allow for leeway. But it's not wind, it's water with the power to drive a turbine. And we over-compensate.

It's a big shock when I'm down. Seeing Anna in the water beside me. We're gasping. I feel the weight dragging me. See that Anna is lower than me already. My face is very close to hers. I've caught her eyes with mine.

Things are fast and they're also slow. I'm seeing something pretty close to panic.

'Take a deep breath.'

I hear my own voice giving the advice to my daughter.

It sounds calm.

And then I gasp air, too.

We're both down.

Then I'm up again or my head is. All the rest of me is being thrust against what must be the bridge. We're on the wrong side. Upstream of the concrete and the pipes.

I'm thinking that, very fast.

Then I see Anna going down again and I'm losing her.

I'm trying to dive, trying to chase her.

But now I'm in the full weight of water and there's no breathing.

No thinking.

I'm away.

Then I'm getting breath. It's in at the edge.

My boots are finding stones. I'm sick in my guts. In my heart. I don't want to get out of the river. Anna's in here.

This is where I stay. I'll get breath to dive again.

'Are you OK, Da?'

She helps me out. I suppose I must be exhausted because I can't help much. I used to help her eat, clean up her shit. Now she's coaxing me out of the water. It doesn't feel cold any more. The air feels cold. My stick is gone. Anna worms in under my shoulder and half hauls me up away from the wild wet.

'I thought I'd lost you,' I said.

'I thought I'd lost *you*.'

So we hug a bit and the warmth is good.

I know we have to get moving. The cold is going to set in and there's not a lot of light left. We're going to have to bomb it down the path.

'Any injuries?'

'I'm fine, Da, what about yourself?'

It's a bit difficult to get a full share of weight on one of my legs. The other is OK. I feel something that's a bit like pain under the numb stuff. Can't decide where it's from. I rub my legs and the juice is circulating.

'Fully operational, blone. Yourself?'

'Fit as a butcher's dog, cove.'

'Well, what are we waiting for?'

So there you are. Bridge number two. It's behind us now.

Bridge Number Three

At first everything is stiff and then you're through the pain. It gets euphoric again. The elation kicks in and drives us down the track past Loch Voshimid. The shapes of the hills either side of the glen getting bolder as the light is lost from the sky.

'You know this is where the last waterhorse was killed?'

'I thought that was in Uig. Other end of Loch Langabhat. I know you only ever tell me true stories, Da, but a girl could get confused.'

'Aye, depends where you're from. The versions.'

I tell her the short synopsis of the three-day struggle and it gets us down the hill a bit. The waterhorse preyed on cattle that strayed too close to the edge of the loch. It would lure a man or a woman on its back and dive down deep. I was trying to distract my own self though, keep the gnawing muscle-pain at bay. Anna was doing fine now.

The limp wasn't holding me back much. 'We're grand,' I said.

So we were, till I saw what was coming, next. This time Anna must have seen something in my eyes.

'We can go round this one,' I said.

'We're going over it. It's not that big. I can see the route this time.'

You know how it is in the stories. The pattern of three. There's always a twist when it comes to the third and last part of the pattern. A story like that has a form that's as strong as a good bridge.

That's why the shape of it stays so clear, in your mind.

While I was trying to think straight, Anna was studying the run of the water.

'I can see where the bridge is,' she said. 'There's only a few inches over it.'

'I don't have the stomach for it,' I said.

She put one boot out to make sure the structure was where she thought it was. Then she left me and took it at a run. There was nothing I could do to stop her. She was across. 'Come on, Da, you've got to go for it.'

I ran for it.

We were both on the other side of this burn and laughing like crazy. Then on again, walking at speed, coasting on the relief. There's a catch in every story. Like my olman's tweeds, no two were ever exactly the same. Like Coastguard search and rescue missions. When I was put in charge of my own watch, I'd tell my trainees, there is no such thing as the standard task.

At least one of us had entered the water at each of the first two bridges. We both got away with it on the third one.

Anna is no daft when it comes to the outdoors. She's been through mists and fogs and snow on Duke of Edinburgh Awards and stuff. She knew we had to get off this hill soon. It was half-light.

We didn't bring supplies because it was to be a fast slog. The chocolate was gone. I could feel the start of the wobblies. The blood-sugar thing. The combination of using different muscles – and needing more calories than you've supplied to your body.

And then I could see the tail-lights. They were moving so slowly. Like someone was looking back all the time for others appearing off the hill, waving their arms and shouting to stop.

We did all that but no-one saw us.

We were both a bit distressed at that stage. I couldn't stop shivering and the pain in my legs was kicking in. The adrenalin stage was over. Then we stumbled on the flask and the note. Left by Gabriele in a poke on a post. She'd be driving back to check the other end of the route now, thinking we must have turned back. It was sweet cocoa.

Nice one. Everything but the St Bernard. I didn't fancy brandy at that point. That's when you know it's getting serious. When you don't fancy a dram any more.

I knew then I couldn't walk any further. I was done. I gave in to it and sat on my sodden arse. The hot drink with its sugar and milk helped a lot. By the time Anna was ready to walk to find a house she could phone from, to tell the police we were fine, the car returned.

Gabriele had driven all the way back to the Loch Seaforth end but we weren't there either. She was getting seriously worried.

The heater was on full-blast. Anna and me were playing it down. 'Aye, we had to make a detour or two round a burn or two. Sure, we both got soaking wet. And the olman had a fair stab at pulling a muscle.'

Anna seemed completely unscathed.

I got a shock when I got into the bath. It wasn't the change of temperature. The bruising was already up. It was the extent of it. I'd only noticed the specific pain from one upper leg, transmitted down. It was the mass of purple and yellow that showed I'd been driven against an underwater bridge.

But when Anna went down, it was suction. She was less marked but more scarred. She told me later she did have nightmares about being sucked into a pipe. It's difficult to tell anyone about the forces involved. Past a certain point and there's no coming back. Nothing could come back against that weight.

She showed me the website. One of her number got given a boat, gratis, from a company. That means the group's exploits are being noticed. I see the tiny red dot emerging from waterfalls. I know it's Anna's helmet.

There's more than two versions of the waterhorse story. Like the last wolf in Scotland, there were a few last ones killed here and there. No shit, I don't think they're all dead. It's not so bad if you come out bruised. You've just been in a battle, what would you expect? It's the guys who come out of the turbulence without visible signs of a struggle. Even if you weren't a Da, you'd worry about that.

And I knew I'd done exactly the wrong thing by playing it all down so Gabriele didn't get more anxious. It would have been better if we'd told our full story at the time. My uncle Ruaraidh made the effort to teach me that, while he was preparing for his death.

I did hear later that Anna eventually did tell her story. It was a sea-kayaking trip, with an overnighter in a bothy. People were talking about close shaves. A mate of mine told me that everyone fell silent when they heard Anna tell it.

Good that she told it. Not just because it's a warning.

Andra 2

I was set to hand over the old Peugeot estate to Anna and her pals. They were adventurers and it wasn't as if a bit of brine dripping from dinghies or boards or kayaks was going to do a lot more damage. She ran fine. So it was my last road movie with the workhorse. I had some stuff to pick up on the mainland so it was a chance to see Andra. Sometimes you just need to get off the rock.

I don't care much about distance when I'm got some wheels under me. Dead easy. I tried to phone, before I left home, but got no answer. It was the evening. Maybe the home-help got him to his bed soon after his tea. I could have got the number from the cousins but I was going anyway.

The car wasn't booked on the ferry. The guy kept me in the standby area till the last minute even though the boat wasn't that busy. The bite of April.

And I wasn't booked in anywhere. I couldn't see a big push for weekend breaks by the North Sea this month. But the Alexandria was boarded up like its neighbours. Then I saw the posters. A gospel music convention. There might not be a bed in town. I could phone Willum and Sheila but it was a bit awkward – he might be at sea. She might be involved in the festival – she was quite strong on the church. They'd be bound to ask how Gabriele was doing. I wouldn't be able to say, 'Nae baud,' and move on.

No big deal, I could run out of town and get a bed in Pennan or out Inverallochy or even Peterhead. Pennan could be booked out too. This was a holiday weekend, for some, and *Local Hero* left its mark on that village. People still wanted a photo of themselves standing by the phone box. They'd get lashed with spray there tonight.

But I knew I'd better get my arse up West Road pretty soon. I went the long way, past the signs for the lighthouse museum, leaving Glenbuchty Place between the sea and the main road. Took a left before the seaward road that used to lead to the gut-factory. You never got that smell now, in either The Broch or SY. My grampa used to call the street with the big new houses, further up the road, Fishmeal Avenue.

I was just round the corner from West Road but the prefabs were gone and my bearings with them. There were new blocks of flats between the boarded up old houses and the more prosperous outskirts.

I looked at the dashboard and saw it was near seven. I shouldn't have stopped to walk along the beach, earlier on. I remembered the frapping red flag that warned the waves were too high for safe bathing. The surfers had a blazing gellie going in the dunes but they wouldn't call it that, these latitudes.

One house looked like it might be the one. I knocked. There was a chain on the door. It opened enough for a wifie to tell me, aye, Andra was on the go all right but he bided off that next wee close. Looked just like this one. I might be ower late though. No, no, he was keeping a richt for a man who'd had his quota o strokes but these home-helps just did the rounds richt early.

The house looked dead. The buzzer worked well enough but nobody came. Then someone went by.

'Aye,' the man said. 'Andra Sim's house. For sure. No, no, he'll no be in his bed but you'll no find him in, this time o nicht. Try the Elizabethan.'

'Not the Legion?' I asked.

'No, he disna drink there ony mair. Elizabethan.'

He pointed the way. I left the car on West Road and walked round the corner. There was a concrete building which looked like it could be of pre-fab construction but it had black painted mock timbers. This could be it. They had a board with special drinks offers on for the football. He'd be here.

It had all sorts of sightlines and corners and more than one screen. I had a fixed idea he was here but I couldn't see him. I was being careful because even big characters can shrink after a stroke. I still couldn't see him.

'You in fae the match?' someone asked.

'No, I'm looking for my uncle Andra. Andra Sim.'

'Andra disna drink here ony mair,' the barman said.

'Is he back at the Legion?'

'Ye'll find him in the Sultan. Just off the main street, ken at the front.'

'Before that drop down to the harbour?'

'Aye, that's it. He'll be in there.'

I thought I knew the way. Drove towards the sea-front. Parked the Peugeot.

I walked up and down the street and I couldn't see a pub called the Sultan.

Time was marching on. I asked someone else. There wasn't a lot of people out on the street.

'You've just walked by it. Can you no see it there?'

I looked back to the Saltoun Arms Hotel. That'd be it then.

I found the opening to the public bar and took a deep breath. There was a screen on with the warm-up to the match. Commentators were speculating. Alan Hansen was looking chill as ever. That's the guy the Latin teacher wagged his finger at. Alan was always a bit more cool than cool. He came sauntering in off the pitch at Lornshill. Another Academy though folk down there still called it The Grange. That was real Rangers and Celtic country. Of course, we had to shout for Rangers.

'Do you think, Mr Hansen, that football will ever put bread in your mouth?' the Latin teacher asked.

I wondered what he was earning for this appearance.

And then my eye went to a figure on a bar stool. He was wearing an Aberdeen strip and his arms were in the air. He was leading the pub in the warm-up singsong.

'Andra?'

He took a few seconds but he was clocking me all right.

'I might have had a bit more hair last time you saw me.'

'I ken ye jist the same. It's Mary's loon. You still have the bloody look o her too but you're no jist as bonny.'

'You're not looking too shabby yourself for a man I thought might be lying down.'

'Am no lying doon yet, loon.'

I bought him a whisky and I took one too.

'And your mates?'

'Dinna bother, loon, we're in a big school here. We're the breakfast club. But we werna in this morn and we might not be in the morra morn. But then again we micht. I dinna drink at hame ken but I like tae get the news here.'

I asked around and bought a rum here, a half pint there.

The barmaid came over. 'Your uncle's eyes fair lit up when he saw you,' she said. 'He'll be speakin aboot it for days. How did you find him?' 'Well, I had a couple of stops along the way,' I said.

'He's great for the singing,' she said, 'Leads them all at it. Then Willum's wife comes for him or he gets a taxi. He's nae bother.'

I floated between getting a yarn with Andra and getting the barmaid's news. There was a fair chance my last surviving uncle was going to live for ever.

'Start the bloody clock again,' he said. 'Am ready to go roond again. Ah please masel and a dinna harm naibody.'

Then he leaned over to tell me again, he didna drink at hame. A thing he jist didna dae. But they had a wee club goin in the morning. That was his usual. The taxi took him hame in time for his dinner. The hame-help had it ready for him. He wisna dain bad.

'Nae baud,' I said.

'You've a smatterin o the lingo,' the barmaid said.

Did she know my cousin Willum? Fishing skipper.

'Willum that lost his boy? He just lost hert. Finally gave up and took the boatie across to Denmark. Ten year aul, the boatie. Jist eligible for the decommissioning. Young Andra, he wis a fine enough loon fan he wis young. Jist went the same way as an affie number o oor loons. Quinies too. Some o them were worse if onything, when it got a haud o them. Quinies my ain age. Ah ken them. It's levelling oot at last. The toon is turning the corner.'

Too late for some. Like young Andra.

'Did ye see that programme on the telly? They were following the skippers, takin the boaties across for brakin up. There was a line of wheelhouses, all bristling wi aerials, a hale lang street o them, stretching oot. Men were in tears.'

'You're fair in the know when it comes to the boats.'

She told me she'd always followed them. Who was building fit. Who sold fit. This one awa to the West Coast. This skipper having a new boatie built. Then it was this ane oot, that ane decommissioned.

'Any lassies on the boats? There's a few lassie deckhands on the creel boats, down Mull way.'

'Ken this, ah wid hae done it. Nae jist for the money. I wis interested. Still am. I asked a few skippers would they tak me on. Ane o them says aye quinie, ye can start next week. *Deckhand?* I says. *No, sex-slave*, he says. They jist widna tak a quine seriously.'

Aberdeen scored. Andra's arms were in the air again. When the roar died down, I asked her if she knew any B&Bs.

'Are you needing sorted the nicht?' she asked.

'Aye.'

'Jist a single?'

'Aye.'

She made the call and I was fixed. No, I wouldn't have another dram. And Andra wouldn't need the taxi tonight. I could drive my uncle along the road when he was ready. Help him in his door.

Andra had one for the ditch after the game. I asked him how Willum was coping.

'Weel, he's a gem o a wife. That Sheila. But ye ken that yersel. The boatie wis jist steel an paint an wiring. Plain enough when you see them gettin rippid apairt. He's at the book-learnin agin. Back at the Buchan college. He's gey handy wi the electronics. He'll nae be stuck.'

His father wouldn't be stuck either.

'You're talkin wi a man fae wis at El Alamein. An so was Mary's man, yer ain faither. Nae a thing tae dwell on. Victory or no. Ships o the desert were nae bloody camels, loon. When a tank wis takin oot, it wis something mair than steel an wiring. There were men in there. Loons, mair like. We were a jist loons.

'Shermans an Spitfires an Stalingrad, that's fit made the difference. Rommel wis cryin oot for petrol an tanks an men afore an eftir he was awa hame sick. He wisna gettin them because they couldna brak through at Stalingrad. An oor aircraft were droppin torpedos tae tak oot their tankers. An oor Spitfires were no daen they gentlemen's dogfights, they were straffin the Stukas on their ain fields. That gave us hert.

'So I'd to bite my tongue monys a time loon wi a your talk on disarmament this an that. We were caught oot in '45. We turnt a coarnir at El Alamein and the Fifty First wis there and your faither an me wis there alang wi them.

'So I'll jist alang tae oor breakfast club in the mornin and sing the day in an nae bother naebody. An it's very fine tae see ye loon, Mary's Peter in The Broch agin.'

Analysis

It needs analysing. It needs an analyst. I should have gone out to dinner with that nice one in the bobbed curls and the leather trousers.

'You can tell me anything. Anything.' In a strong French accent but I don't think I imagined her. We met at a history conference in Edinburgh. This was her hobby. Mine too. To my own surprise, I got it together to submit a paper in time. To my amazement, it was accepted – *Health and Industry: the case of the doctor employed by the labourers at Ballachulish Quarry*.

But her English might not have been quite up to my complexities. My French certainly wasn't up to her own individual nature.

But maybe I was learning. When should a guy choose the impossible when other options are available? Because he doesn't admit to himself, for years and years that they are – or were. That's what history is. Things you can't change. Flashback time, again.

We're outside the Arts Lecture Theatre, Aberdeen Uni. The Film Society has shown *Les Dentellieres*. Sad and beautiful and maybe a touch on the lush side but recommended by a certain very distant German woman who spoke English I could understand very well. And she might have picked up Hebrew too, in that year on the kibbutz.

I was not long back from a train journey to Cologne. It had been a disaster worthy of a wry continental film. I came back, tied up in knots of tension and worried about eating and worried about everything. Maybe I was like that before I left Aberdeen. I just knew about it, when I stepped back on to that platform with a tight gut.

I was no longer a shift-porter with people putting money in my bank account. I spent most of these earnings on a souped up Mini, registered and insured in my mother's name. Then there was the fishing holiday, staying with the couple on that Finnish island. Before leaving the home island to finish the degree. The olaid liked the car because it was purple. She put up with its attempts at roaring and the banter from the bowling club folk because we could go for spins in it.

I was just too proud to get my arse out again to the phonebox at Bridge of Cowie. I only had to tell the olaid I was writing all these letters to thon German blone I visited on the kibbutz. And I was a bit short on readies except for the trains. I'd paid for them already.

'Can you help me out?' How difficult would that have been? But I didn't say any of that.

So I was uptight about money the whole trip and I didn't realise there was more train fares to find, along with her schedule of people to visit. Gabriele had arranged things so it was busy enough to be not too personal. We were both being cautious.

But even if cash and eating and everything else were OK, it's clear as the olaid's crystal sherry-glasses that this was not going to be an easy voyage. When I say it's clear, I mean it's clear now. Not then. Amazing bond you get from coping with stuff. The unexplained loss of a parent, in her case. And the sudden death of one, in mine. All these long letters. Both of us.

There was more to it than that. The powerful forces of fishing and dancing. Gabriele had come over to Aberdeen for the Folk Festival. She'd come along when I took a sea trout on the fly, from the Ythan estuary. She found some wild mushrooms she knew and trusted. It was a fine meal.

And the eightsome got us both out of ourselves, birling like dervishes. Holy shit, looks like the guys in the hats are right about that one too – dancing is dangerous, puts your very soul in jeopardy. I used to think Jeopardy was the name of a town. Maybe near Cairo.

It's now we need my friend from Marseilles. No kidding, she's a psychoanalyst with a passion for history. This is the question I failed to ask.

Is this well documented and normal, this way of not really coping with the death of a parent? Looking like you're doing pretty good – the family meals, the compensatory building of a stronger relationship with other family members. The semblance of balance. Until about a year later, the nosedive comes. Like a plastic Stuka fallen from its fine string of monofilament fishing nylon and heading for the carpet.

The dive manifesting itself in broken sleep, manic behaviour, eating disorders, falling in love. With people who live in other countries. While the near ones are reaching out for you.

Does everyone's mind work like this? Digression and flashback. Come back with me now again, outside said theatre, in a daze after said film, recommended by said woman, not quite a girlfriend. And you have to forget that there's nearly a quarter of a century between where we are now and the scene outside the film.

I've one hand on the drop handlebars and a present, live young woman says my name. She wants to talk about the film. She wants to go for coffee. This is not correspondence. It's not my imagination. She's breathing.

She walks like a dancer. Talking and strolling with her, I now know the phrase. I didn't know it then. '*Ca marche comme sur des roulettes.*'

It's going on rollers, man. The sister taught me that one. She said I needed at least one cool phrase, in French.

I don't look her in the eye because I'm somehow aware I'll fall in there. She's slim and has elegant fingers, elegant everything, cropped hair and fine features. My eyes are caught by the way the black on the backs of her hands shifts to pale along the fingers.

She didn't come to lectures very often but we got talking after a seminar. Then I saw her in the launderette. Not a very beautiful one. She told me she was jealous of me. Why? Because I knew where I was from. She remembered my piece about attitudes to the Chinese opium trade. My approach was a study of recorded statements referring to the proprietor who was seen as a benefactor because of the obvious economic benefits from spending some of the proceeds on my home island. I'd suggested that we could, by analogy, also look more closely at how the slave trade was perceived in Scotland. Maybe a study of letters to newspapers by prosperous residents of a relevant trading town.

People looked at her and saw a black girl with a trace of an American accent so assumed she had a strong cultural identity. But her parents had lived amongst the leafy courtyards and stonework and university culture of Oxford for a part of her upbringing. She spoke with a nice accent. She didn't know what African-American meant. She didn't know who she was.

And all I could find to say to this handsome woman, engaging with me again, was that this guy was coming round to the flat tonight. (I was back in Aberdeen city for the last year of Uni.) And I should be heading home in case I missed him.

He was one of the travelling people. He was a relative of my landlord. I wanted to meet him because he could direct me to all these recordings of stories and songs and history which had been retained by the travellers – the outsiders – when they'd been lost by most other sectors of Scottish society. He could just open his mouth and there you would have it, all that knowledge. All these stories.

This is another of these moments when you know just what you should have said. 'Jump on the carrier. There's my jacket for a cushion. We're going to hear some history, first-person narration. Three on a bike's a bit of a crowd but two's a piece of piss.'

But I just said I'd love to go for a coffee but someone was coming round and I needed to get back. I couldn't settle into all these stories I heard that night, because I kept thinking she would have been in her element.

But I was to dance with her twice. Once, she and her flatmates were having a party. I didn't usually get asked to parties because people knew I didn't drink and was serious. But I was pulled along by a group, doing the course.

She grabbed my arm. 'Drink?'

'No, ta, I'm fine.'

'Well, let's dance then.'

'OK.'

She tried to get me to stay when the others were leaving. I used to wake early, these days. Get up to make the most of the time when your thinking could be clear. 'You're not really going now?'

But we did meet again, maybe two years later, not long after I'd finally got together with Gabriele. I'd come back to Aberdeen to see different friends to the ones she'd come to visit. But we went together to hear this band. We'd both been planning to go there. It wasn't a date. But there was dancing. We were still very compatible dancers. I didn't walk her to the door of her pals' flat. Just to the corner of the shared road.

I hope I had the good grace to kiss her the French style. By which I mean a brush of each cheek. I don't think I did. Of course, I now know I loved her, after these half-conversations. I think I still do. I haven't heard of her again, since.

Who says men don't find out their own feelings? In my case, it only took some years. Funnily enough, that quarter of a century again. My analyst friend might tell me that's about average in male behaviour. And fear is pretty common too. The sort that kills a relationship that's going to go and throw you off a course you're pretty well bound to take. Even if you think you're a nonconformist.

So of course, as part of the slightly late mid-life crisis, I was lost for a time in the eyes and voice of another slim, black lady when she visited that same city to sing in The Lemon Tree. Don't get me wrong. I saw the singer's individuality. Her face did not look at all similar to that of my student friend. She was an artist, not a historian. I was not at all conscious of making comparisons or returning to an intense period in my own life. And I was not yet ready to admit to myself or to Gabriele, out loud, that you can only live in a state of sustained tension for a limited time.

The way you lie awake, night after night, composing songs which won't be sung. Certainly not by the petite diva from New York City.

Of course I could always have sent them to her, which might have improved the chances a little. Like buying a lottery ticket increases the odds marginally in your favour.

Then again, maybe I was almost aware that it was another cropped African head I was really seeing and another set of quite pale fingers, equally expressive ones, moving before me when the world was a bit younger.

Something inside your skull activates some gland or other so one desire damps down another. It's a force for defence in that it attacks love. It's lethal and in fact capable of killing passion before it has a chance to start.

So the death I'm discussing in this paper is without question a murder. I don't even have to consult my lawyer mate, to confirm this. It's quite clear that a real possibility of love was killed by wilful avoidance.

And now, so many years later, it seems that you're still quite capable of disregarding the lessons of your most personal history. A bit like the Griomsiadair boys (that's the old men, remember?), heading out into the Minch when the great, black drifters are running for harbour. But do you think we can be too hard on ourselves?

When I fell into deep conversation with Emily, the singer, I was not yet ready to admit, consciously, that I needed the kind of space that is not created by building physical structures but by clear thinking. Even if I'd already taken that step, I'd still not been able to sit down and talk it all out with the woman who bore a child we made, together.

I'm suggesting now, without the advantage of professional advice, that a less conscious part of you is really making the connections. But it also informs your conscious self, eventually, so it too has a chance of coping with them.

That's conflict.

There is one piece of documentation.

It's not objective but it is contemporary. I found a scrap of paper in the flyleaf of a notebook. An attempt to keep track of a project which was in danger of getting out of control. I knew at the time the building work, for my mother, could easily get out of hand. But I didn't have a clue what else was going on, in my head.

I don't think this is a love poem and so I can copy it here. I don't think it's really addressed to either of these two black women I met, all those years apart, in Aberdeen city.

At last, I do know what it is. It's a town boy's version of all these Gaelic songs of separation.

Song for Emily

Don't forget
to send me a wave or two
from the other side.

Just dip
the pulse
in your long fingers
to the churn
of Manhattan.

It won't be instant
but of course I'll sense them
arriving in
at our own west side.

Emily

Gabriele and me were at the settlement stage. That's another way of saying we were arguing.

She cut across the discussion of practical matters, 'You couldn't let go of your need to be part of a congregation until you'd found another relationship. And you couldn't admit you wanted to break from me until you knew there was the possibility of somewhere else to go.' A neat analysis. Worthy of a devotee of the mistress of irony, Jane Austen.

Guilty as charged. Maybe I didn't need advice from the blone in the leather breeks after all.

Gabriele and me should really have had the argument of the two Janes. Maybe it's already been fully explored but excuse me, I couldn't get into reading interpretations of interpretations. I got to the end of *Pride and Prejudice* but I found the certainties of the moral framework pretty offensive. All these manners. But that Jane Eyre, she's some character. Charlotte Brontë brings you into passion and banter and a fight for justice. I never read it at Uni. It was the daughter, educating me. I felt I was being drawn into a female mind.

But I can hear Gabriele's counter-argument. If I'd learned to know my own true self, I'd have found ways of expressing it earlier. Aye, as long as these were prudent ways. Jane Eyre's expression is not always that prudent. Thank the Lord or anybody else you deem appropriate. And I can also hear the daughter's warning about trusting unreliable narrators too far.

There is a radio 'pro-word' or convention, 'Prudonce'. In the context of radio traffic during a distress, a vessel can remind other vessels to keep other transmissions off the distress frequency.

But we had not really admitted, out loud, that our marriage was in distress. Maybe Gabriele and me always did have a different way of looking at things. That worked well enough for long enough.

You know in yourself when it's time to shoot the crow. Maybe my thinking is still coloured by Westerns. When it's time to go, these guys go. There might be an 'Adios amigo' and that's about it. But when you've been building up property it's not that simple. And when you've made a child together, it's impossible.

I had the vasectomy soon after the birth of our wonderful daughter because we were both sure this was plenty of responsibility. Knowing the dangers of spoiling the only child but also knowing that so long as we in the West think that people in other countries should restrict themselves to one, but we ourselves are exempt, then the planet won't hold us. And it's an easier op for a man than a woman. So they say. I'm only one guy and have only ever had the one op. So this is not a very scientific bit of data but I can tell you now it wasn't that painless even though the local policy was to give you a general anaesthetic rather than a local.

It's all going woozy and you recognise the orderlies from the sea-angling club. One of them is whispering quite loud to the other, 'Is that the bit we cut?'

The other says, 'Not sure. Maybe it's that bit.'

So you just get it together to say, 'Thanks, guys,' in appreciation of the double act.

It was bloody sore for a few days after. Make your own considered decision, gentlemen, but don't believe all the propaganda.

I can't plot for you the graph which would indicate how a couple had the security to build so much up together and then reach a point where separation was inevitable. The duration of the niggles which become arguments. The shockwaves of said arguments as measured on something you could call a Richter scale. The length of the sulks, the frequency and duration of love-making. The incredible difficulty in doing anything spontaneous.

It's easy to be analytical afterwards, even if the history is your own one. But something in my inner workings took charge, at the time.

I would wake and it wouldn't be due to my wife's snoring.

I was troubled and didn't know why, at first.

Then I began to tune in to the signals coming from New York. That's just down the road from Leverhulme Drive. You swing a right at the first roundabout then take the next left. Take the West Side road and stop before the sea. It's out there and I was hearing a whistle from Emily. One evening and the following afternoon, I'd fallen into the deepest of conversations with that Irish-African-American blone. But we didn't fall into either of our hired beds, please note.

I'd got a grant to attend a diesel engine maintenance course. My thinking was this – if the bottom falls out of the Scottish Fishing Industry, there could be a lot more berths for sailing yachts. These now come with pukka lightweight diesels. They get hardly any running so they need more maintenance and repairs. That's an opening.

Gabriele kept asking, 'Why do you need to do this?' She said she had enough for us both, between her scheduled hours and the inheritance. I must have had more doubts than I was admitting because I knew I needed to sort out an unspectacular little income.

It was over in Aberdeen and I was in The Lemon Tree. Emily was the support act. But we were looking into each other when she was playing. I had the idea that she'd clocked me hanging on the notes and the lyrics and she'd started playing for me in particular. I had one glass of wine with her but we just tumbled into each other's phrases. A petrol engine has to keep sparking and exploding. A diesel is different. Once that fuel comes under sufficient pressure to cause a very fine spray, delivered by the injectors, the cylinders will fire and the flywheel has to keep turning and turning. So steady. So little strain. There was a brush of lips on each side of her face, at the door, but I'm still feeling each one.

She turned up for a coffee along at the art gallery next day, to keep that conversation going. Emily replied fast to the first e-mail. But I knew to be wary of the Send button. If you write a letter you have to make a step or two to post it.

I woke up thinking about her. I heard the tune, in my head, every night for about a year. Gabriele was sleeping a lot these days, in the afternoon, when she could, after work or at the weekends, as well as the evenings.

I wasn't sleeping that much.

Something was happening to my memory. I realised it first, the week after the olaid's funeral. We'd had a good week with Kirsty. I'd seen her off on the plane that morning. The sorting out could wait. The jobs on the boat and our own house had been dropped while I got the olaid's stuff sorted, alongside the sis.

Then I returned to my tinkering. Fine-tuning the installation of the restored small diesel in the restored *Peace and Plenty*. We were soon back in commission. I was out in her, on a fine day, at the mooring. Bright sunshine with warmth on my neck, in the harbour I know well. I began to be aware that I was lonely as fuck and I couldn't remember where the third strand of the first tuck of the eye-splice went.

This is a job I've done thousands of times. And I tried to be methodical and slow it all down but it just wasn't working.

I remembered I'd still got the brick aboard. Think they'd just stopped calling them cellphones then. There was a good signal and I phoned a friend, another sea angler and said, 'This sounds daft, I'm doing a job at the mooring and I've forgotten how to do an eye-splice.'

'You're the guy that taught me it,' Michael said.

'Aye, but the mooring's half done. The rope is cut and the tide is rising. Are you busy right now?'

'I'll be over,' he said but he didn't hang up. I didn't, either. Then he said, 'Remember I used to be a fisher of men?'

My voice said, 'Aye, you were the Piscie minister in the New Wave tweed jacket. Deep purple.'

'Yes,' he said, 'I was an Episcopalian priest. I think you're suffering from post-bereavement stress and it's perfectly normal. Can you pick me up in the dinghy?'

The former priest did the splice before the tide covered the link. The mooring was saved even if the fate of its owner was in the balance.

During the day I'd be functioning fine. Or I'd be thinking I was. At night I'd be lying awake beside a sleeping wife. I began to compose letters to a woman in New York. They were more direct than any e-mails I sent. But I never posted them. Even the e-mails petered out.

There's a bit of luck enters everything, good or bad. You saw that often in the Coastguard Service. Some guys got away with it, others didn't. Both Gabriele and myself lost our fathers at much the same time. Later we lost our mothers within a year or two of each other. Maybe we could have supported each other better if there had been more of a gap. To the outside world, it probably looked like we were both coping.

We kept buying bikes for each other. They kept getting rusty, outside, unused. Maybe there was a good winter's day and she would cycle to work but the next day she might be exhausted, for no reason. I'd get my own out but salt would get into the chain and gears and I couldn't bear the thought of all that damage. I built a bike-shed but I didn't go cycling with her. Maybe all our sheds, in all our drives and crescents, are home to nearly new bikes, seized from lack of use.

My Piscie mate went off to try to start a new life in Edinburgh with a woman he met in the *Guardian*. His wife had already found a Lewisman with shining eyes and a Gaelic voice, from the next village. So, pretty soon, after the messy business of the filthy lucre, everyone was pretty much happy. Michael told me this was nothing really sudden. It had been on the cards for a while. There was a bit of history. And it was a good few years since he realised he had lost his faith. The usual issue – reconciling all the suffering of the innocent with the idea of a Being that still has influence over his creation. And if he doesn't – if he just set the whole thing up with man's freewill as a mixed blessing, then what's the point of praying?

He called me up from his new life.

'I'm amazed this number works. You're not still on the brick?'

'No, it got salted. Anna fixed me up with this new one and showed me how to do the brain transplant. The phone's I mean.'

'Sure. Look, Peter, I don't know if I should be telling you this but…'

'Aye well, you'd better, now.'

'There's a gig in the Jazz Café, Friday next. Chambers Street. Just round the corner. A sultry New York visiting artist. Wasn't that when you were thinking of trying to come down for a break?'

'Not a black Irish singer-songwriter with a leaning towards jazz but sounding nothing like Joni Mitchell. One who did a Scottish tour before, culminating in the Lemon Tree?'

'The same.'

We had of course shared our stories.

I went down the road.

You think you've come to look into the eyes of another but the reality is that a real breathing person would have to conform to an impression that's been developing inside your own head. The e-mails, back and fore, with Emily had kept up the urgency, the dangerous spark of language. This time, we didn't flow. Maybe it had something to do with the plan to give Anna a lift back up the road. She was just finishing her first year in Newcastle. Literature and film studies. This awareness just reminded me I was not a free man.

I came out of a year-long dayandnightdream on the sitting room futon in the Drummond Street flat. Michael was holding me by the shoulders to contain the sobbing.

'Sorry to wake you,' I said. It wasn't something I could control. This was a space I'd never been in. Not even in the hallucinogenic days.

I thought I was lovesick for the woman sleeping somewhere in this same city. Michael told me I'd been sobbing for hours. He didn't want to break into something I had to do but he couldn't leave it any longer. He'd seen me scribble in the jotter, bought to take notes for the conference. History, this time, not engines. Pity the psychoanalyst wasn't there. Or maybe just as well. He showed me what I'd done. The pad was chock-full of intricate doodles, working it all out.

Like the splice. I was nearly there, he was sure.

'You're not fucking unique, you know,' the Piscie mate said. 'It's just about one year after your mother's passing. I don't think your anxiety is about love. I think it's about death.'

He wasn't finished. 'Something I've been meaning to ask,' he said. 'The Coastguard job. You must have seen a few missions with a sad outcome.'

'Aye. A few.'

'Did you get counselling?' he asked.

'Don't think that was invented, back then. The Civil Service did welfare stuff but I never heard anyone offer counselling,' I said.

'Did you ever talk about them – the jobs that didn't go well?'

'I made reports. You got a paragraph – maybe two – to tell the story.'

'Did you talk about them with your watchmates?'

'One or two.'

'One or two jobs or one or two watchmates?'

'Both of these. Just the guys who were on watch at the time. The guys who'd been through it with you. Remember we were only the co-ordinators. We didn't go out into dangerous situations and get cold and wet.'

'It might have been easier if you had.'

'I did jot down a few notes once. One night in The Broch. I was hearing the voices.'

'Maybe you need to go back to that,' Michael suggested. 'Find a form for it. Just tell the story.'

Siller Morn

We've talked about the number three in stories. There's a pattern but something usually changes at the third repetition. When I became a Regular Coastguard, I had to learn Morse Code. It went off the syllabus about a year later but of course 'dit dit dit, Da Da Da, dit dit dit' is with you forever. That's another one you hear on mobile phones now. And for years I'd been formulating Mayday Relays and Pan broadcasts, for exercise or a few times, for real. Even in Routine radio communications the name of the vessel is often repeated three times, until contact is established.

We had an alarm bell in the restroom. Part of the twelve-hour watch system allowed you breaks where you could inspect the backs of your eyes after you swallowed your soup. Your mate gave you a buzz, when your time was up, in case you'd dozed off. But if it was a job, there would be three short blasts. At sea, that means, 'I am operating astern propulsion'. But, if I was on watch, I would lose no time getting back up the stairs.

Once or twice I entered the Ops Room with the radio pro-word derived from the French for 'Help Me' on the air. But this night, no Mayday was broadcast until we put out the Relay. And it was early into the watch. No-one had taken a break yet. We were all occupying ourselves, with the routines. Forecasts and working out the ephemera – like sunset and sunrise times, corrected for our location.

The red light went, on the desk. That was the ex-directory line. 999. Another pattern of three. My Senior Watch Officer tipped me the nod. I took it. He monitored the call.

It was the harbourmaster, Kinlochbervie. 'It's the *Siller Morn*,' he said, 'the FR registered *Siller Morn*. She's on Glas Leac. She'll need your team. They'll need to get a line to her.'

My form had the name SILVER MORN in my printing, with a ballpoint. My SWO had it down as CILLERMORN. Behind us, a multi-track tape recorder stored every phone conversation and every transmission on radio.

The harbourmaster was calling from his home. He had a VHF in the house and he'd heard the boat calling his mate on channel nine, just when he was thinking of turning in. Something in the voice made him listen. It was all low key but he was on the rocks, asking for a hand. Maybe a wee tow off.

I looked at the weather forecast written out on the board. Not too bad. But the tide was falling. 'What's it like with you?' I asked, on the line with the red button. We were sitting the other side of the North Minch.

'Not a terrible night but the boys are saying there's a big enough swell running. She's bumping. We'll need to get something to her.'

'Is there another boat close?'

'The *Siller Eve*. They work together. Brothers. Sister-ships. They're talking to each other. I'm hearing them now. They're up close.'

The panels of switches on our desks selected the different VHF aerials so you could receive or transmit through the same set of headphones. You could never get complete coverage of all the bays and sea-lochs but my SWO selected channel nine on the aerial closest to the scene. There was a very broken transmission. Nothing you could follow.

'Do you want me to ask them to chop to sixteen?' the harbourmaster asked.

My SWO shook his head as he dialled up the Hon Sec, Lochinver lifeboat. That's the launching authority. He requested Immediate Launch.

'No. Ask him to relay everything he can. Too chancy to chop channel now.'

So I got him to pose the standard questions one by one, the number of persons on board. The life-saving apparatus carried. The weather on scene. We asked him to instruct the skipper to make sure everyone was in their lifejackets.

I could hear the harbourmaster's voice speaking on his radio set and a crackle in response. The delay was sore. I was still holding on. Gripping that handset.

My SWO rung the team to call them out. He'd written down 'Glas Lek'. He was on the chart table. I was drafting a Relay. 'Pan or Mayday?' I asked.

Right then, the voice came back to me, down the line. There was a notch of difference in the tone.

'I'm understanding it's difficult to get at the life-raft and life-jackets. She's listing now. The tide's falling away.'

'Mayday Relay.'

I nodded and wrote it out for the Auxiliary to transmit on sixteen. We should send a telex to the Coast Radio Station so it would go out on the big-set. 2182 kilohertz. Long-range radio. But the red line was our only direct link now.

'Just keep that line open. I'll get a lat and long for the Relay. Might need a chopper. I'll need to call the boss.'

I didn't have the weight that watch. I was thinking ahead to the order of events, the procedures. My SWO was at the chart table.

'There's a Glas Leac, Lochinver,' he said. 'Sure it's KLB?'

I confirmed it with the harbourmaster.

'Got it,' he said. 'Approaches to the harbour.'

I remembered there was also another reef of the same name, out from Ullapool. A hazard of the same name out from each of the three main harbours in northwest Scotland. If you only had the name to go by, you'd be in trouble. The harbourmaster's voice came back on the open line. I relayed the gist of it.

'It's definitely the KLB one and they can't get right up to him. A hell of a swell. They need to get a line to him.'

I repeated what I heard, out loud. My SWO activated the line to RCC Edinburgh. That's a military control centre, in Pitreavie, near Dunfermline. He requested a helicopter. Passed the position. The aircraft would normally come from RAF Lossiemouth unless the rescue chopper was already out on a job. It was peak-season for mountain rescue. I heard one end of that conversation too. But I could guess the other. I'd heard it before.

The clear night. The air temperature. The time of year was against us. The Sea King would have to go north about. There was a significant risk in going over the mountains, the direct route. The danger of icing. We didn't need to do any speed, time and distance calculations for that one.

We all knew it was going to take three hours plus.

'Time to talk to the boss,' he said. 'We could do with a hand in the Ops Room anyway.'

It was going to be a busy night. The scramble was confirmed and the Duty Officer was coming in to give us a hand. Our Auxiliary was putting out the Mayday Relay on three different aerials. Her voice was calm and not too fast. They call them Ops Room Assistants, these days.

'Five persons on board. Requires Immediate Assistance.'

Other vessels would not be able to offer much help if the sister-ship with a brother aboard couldn't get close enough. But procedure has to be followed. And there's an element of luck in what's in the vicinity. A Fishery Protection Vessel would have a fast dinghy aboard. That could get close. My SWO was driving the telex. I was still hanging on to the handset linked to the red line. Our only link with the casualty.

The Auxiliary was handling the traffic on sixteen. The buzzer on the outside door sounded. The duty officer came through the door. 'Just carry on guys. I'll get the picture from the signals.' He looked at the position on the chart.

As the name *Siller Morn* was repeated again, on our broadcasts, along with its Fraserburgh fishing numbers, I got a whiff of nausea. Fathers and sons. Willum didn't want to make it difficult for his loon Andra. He'd a cousin who was pair-trawling and doing 'Nae baud like, alang wi the brither.' That's where I'd heard the name. That's why I'd recognised it over the crackle of the links in communication.

But the lifeboat was on its way and we could just about talk to him on sixteen, a bit broken. We'd copied his checks with Wick Radio on the big set, 2182. It was quite a steep sea. They were barely making their eight knots. It would be a couple of hours.

The *Siller Eve* tried firing a heaving-line, from a canister but it blew back in their faces.

The chopper came up on channel sixteen. 'Rescue 137 airborne from Lossiemouth, best ETA 2 hours 55. I say again ETA 2350 GMT.'

'Fuck. Will I pass that on through the 999?'

My Senior Watch Officer shook his head again. 'That's not going to help them, to know that. Just ask your man to relay that the chopper is airborne. On its way to them now.'

The Ops room settled into an urgent rhythm but under control. I was maintaining the log of actions and times while my SWO followed the procedures of information-flow. The 999 line had to stay open all the time. The radio set in the harbourmaster's house was still our best link on scene. The boss was informing higher authority. We heard from the coast team on channel zero. It was taking a long time to lug the gear over rocks. They couldn't get the Land Rover anywhere near. Even with the big rocket, there wasn't much chance of getting a line out to them.

If you don't have direct experience of a thing, history can help. The largest ever number of souls rescued by breeches-buoy took place on the Isle of Lewis, not that long after the Second World War. The *Clan MacQuarrie* tried to outrun a storm by going west of the Hebrides rather than face the short steep seas of the North Minch. She came ashore and all the crew were taken to safety on that tense hawser. There's a big and a small rocket, to fire a line out to a ship. I was trained to rig at least three varieties of shore-rescue tackle. We'd fired the big rocket on a couple of training courses. Once it had made a sweet arc in the air and another time it had left a strange trajectory.

'Shit, that would have taken the wheelhouse off,' someone said.

One member of our course was stationed in Belfast. 'I hope the boys in the balaclavas never get hold of these bastards,' he said.

But I was aware of another incident, come to me through oral history. I met up with a man I'd met as a child when the Coastguard depot was on Leverhulme Drive. We were on a search planning course, the days when you crunched the vectors of tides and wind history into an electronic calculator. Computer-assisted planning was to come a few years later. A well-run course left some space for yarns. The man who had pulled my father out from a collapsed bunk on a stranded ship was now an instructor.

As he put it himself, he was in 'the kiss-my-ass latitudes' on the run-down to retirement. But he could get his experience across. When he was stationed in Stornoway, a ship carrying salt grounded at Branahuie Bay. Aye, where the Nato jetty is now. He was Officer-In-Charge, on scene. The shore is shingle and the surf was breaking over everything. They could talk to the ship on VHF. He knew they'd never get the hawser tight enough in these conditions. He knew it would be dangerous to pull men through that surf if the breeches buoy was in the water. So this is what he did.

They did get a line out over the ship. Then they kept it simple, got the crew to pull out a heavier endless loop of rope. He asked the Captain, on VHF, to inflate a life-raft and secure it to that line. So it went back and fore, carrying everyone to safety. There was one casualty. It was the ship's cook, he remembered. A big, big fellow. He'd suffered a heart attack, from the shock. The rest of the guys were fine. They only got their feet wet.

Once all the initial action is taken there's usually some thinking time. I'd visited Kinlochbervie. I knew our team had a link to a fishing vessel working out of that harbour. If the team had gone out on that boat, with the rescue gear and the smaller rocket-gun, to fire out the light line, we might have had a chance. You could call that the benefit of hindsight.

The crew of the *Siller Morn* never did get to their own life-raft. The lads couldn't get hold of their lifejackets. That was before fishermen started wearing suits with insulation and flotation.

Our last message to be relayed asked the crew to get hold of any bit of buoyancy they could. Anything that might help keep them afloat. Anything that would show up in searchlights. I heard the crackling from the radio, over the phone. Still on channel nine.

Then it went very quiet.

I was freed from that phone and took my turn on radio, broadcasting the search area. All communications were now on channel sixteen VHF and 2182MF, as per the book. It was still some time before the chopper and lifeboat were on scene. We went from nine-knot boats to eighteen-knot ones in a very few years. Not soon enough. And this was before RNLI lifeboats could deploy a fast, inflatable boat to get up close when the larger vessel could not.

The chopper, Rescue 137, spotted some of the fluorescent debris in the water, soon after arrival in the search area, as per the ETA. They asked to minimise communications as they sent the winchman down. After about ten long minutes they reported that they had recovered one of the crew from the water.

'Rescue 137, Stornoway Coastguard. Do you want us to arrange an ambulance to rendezvous? Over.'

'Coastguard, 137. Channel zero. Over.'

'Roger. Zero.' (Channel for dedicated Search and Rescue Units only.)

'Coastguard, 137 on zero. Sorry but the condition of this man cannot get worse. We'll keep searching. Conditions are not very good on scene and we don't have that much fuel endurance. Over.'

'Roger, 137. Coastguard out.'

A sick feeling in the stomach. You can't let that into the voice you use on the phone or radio.

So the night went on. Between the lifeboat, the sister-ship and the chopper, all five bodies were recovered. What was left of the *Siller Morn* slid off the reef and the wreck was quickly broken up.

My SWO attended the Fatal Accident Inquiry. It was judged that all action which could have been taken, was taken.

But my first SWO and mentor, Seamus, had been returning casualty reports for years. They'd often drawn attention to the gap in helicopter coverage on Scotland's northwest, particularly when there was a danger of icing in the winter months. A survey was commissioned, based on drawing the radius of helicopter response times with reference to probable survival times of a person immersed in water. After that, a contract was awarded, for Coastguard helicopters stationed in Stornoway, Sumburgh and in Lee-on-Solent. They are all still in place. Too late for the crew of the *Siller Morn*.

The MP for the northwest mainland area, co-incidentally named MacQuarrie, led a successful move to make the carrying of electronic radio distress-beacons (EPIRBs) mandatory for fishing vessels over certain dimensions.

My cousin Willum's lad, young Andra, was not aboard the *Siller Morn* that night. He should have been. He'd failed to show up to catch the minibus when it left from The Broch after midnight on the Sunday. As you know, this was only a reprieve.

Smoking

Smoking is dangerous. So is sucking sweets. I liked to go to get my father's packet of Players from a pocket of his jacket, hung in the hall. One night he brought home a cigar in a tube. I liked that smell better. Another night he said he was stopping. He just did. Like that. But he started sucking goodies – boilings and mints. He never stopped that. I got hooked on toffees for a while but I've told you about that. I still like it when my nose catches the sweet stink of resin, lingering amongst the tobacco exhaust, in the narrows or round a corner in the streets of our island city. The purpose of smoking, when I was young, was to take dope.

I'd already been taught about smoking, at school. This is how. The science teacher with bobbed dark hair and a close fitting, medium length, tailored skirt and kinky boots spoke to us about particles. Kinky boots weren't that kinky. They were just black ordinary boots with flat soles. They started just below the knee. I don't think hers were anything special. And I don't think they had heels at all. It's partly Emma Peel's fault. Mind you, the original designs for her *Avengers* outfit are available for scrutiny. Her leather costume was adapted to be more suitable for view before the evening watershed. She was tall enough anyway, without the spike-heels. So was my science teacher.

You looked up to her for sure when you were called out to hold out your hands; the science teacher, I mean. I never got belted by Diana Rigg. I can't remember if I had to cross my hands or not. Some asked you to and some didn't. It was better if she didn't because she might just touch yours with the tips of her fingers so you stretched them out further to receive the strap. She'd put the tan leather Lochgelly right back over her shoulder but it wasn't that hard when she swung it down so the tails wrapped round your fingers. I think her strap had two tails. Most belts did but I've seen one with three. And most I saw were tan, not black.

Then usually you had to hold out the other hand. That was about it but sometimes you were instructed to change hands until you took a total of four of the belt. I never got six. It was usually the deputy who gave six and you didn't see it done in front of the class. Only once we were all assembled in the gym to watch the boss himself give six to an older guy. I don't know what it was for. He was a hero.

But we were gathered round the Bunsen burner, quite close, so we could see smoke particles in a tube. She probably didn't smoke normally because the cigarette didn't come from a packet. She probably just got one from another teacher for the experiment. She just struck a match and lit it and blew smoke into the tube and put it out again. There was something about the sight of the white from her mouth and the flick of flame and the brief, brief smell.

It was a different class but I remember the glossy photo of the lung. We were shown a smoker's lung. I still remember it. Heart transplants were becoming more successful after the first operations by Professor Christian Barnard, in South Africa, but I don't think they'd been able to install a new lung yet, without it being rejected.

So that lung had come from someone who was certainly dead.

It felt good being that close to that teacher. She was alive all right. I must have been about fourteen or so. These were really hard times. I didn't find the knack of masturbating but it came out one night, in sleep. I can't remember the detail of the dream.

It's still strong when it happens; sensing the smell of a woman, I mean, not a wet dream. You just realise you're close enough to sense the breathing. I'm going to tell you about being at a do. It's the civil equivalent of Combined Services. Nothing military, though guys from the TA and the ATC might have been there. Definitely a leader from the Boys Brigade and that's more military than any of them. I'd already been a year or two out of the Coastguard Service but one day I got a phone call, requesting my jacket.

Mairi Bhan was going to this shindig and she had nothing to wear, darling. 'What's wrong with your orange boiler suit?' I asked. 'And you'll be coming in town on the Fergie.'

'No,' she said, 'it's a posh do. So I'll need to take the Fordson Major.'

She never asked me if I'd seen Kenny lately. She just said, it should be a good night but it would be a gas to go in uniform and the Fisheries Office sweatshirt just wouldn't cook the mustard.

'Cut it,' I said, 'you don't cook it. You cut it, in the town. Out beyond the grids you probably boil it for six hours with a change of water.'

'Are you going to keep this shit going or are you going to talk to me properly?' she asked.

'I'm going to keep it going. It will be unrelenting.'

'In that case, you can come,' she said. 'You'll catch up with your old mates.'

She just wanted to borrow my number one jacket, the one with the brass buttons, if it wasn't on a scarecrow yet. 'We don't have scarecrows on Leverhulme Drive,' I said.

'Are you still living there?' she asked.

'Sort of.'

But the uniform jacket was available. It was still pressed, in wraps in a cupboard. A couple of the other local guys had gone back to sea. So it wasn't just me got pissed off with being told how the Hebs were like this or like that. But there was still a few guys I'd like to see. I'd paid for the jacket out of my wages so it belonged to me, though I was supposed to hand in the buttons when I left. I thought I might just run the risk of being prosecuted for failing to remove them.

'If you behave yourself, I might just shine up the buttons for you, before handing it back.'

So I dropped the parcel round at her office, just left it for her there. And aye, it was time to catch up with the old colleagues. Most of the job was a waiting game but we'd ran a few casualties.

You know that feeling? You see someone you know well but it's like the first time you're looking at them. I was half aware of Mairi's style. And I knew she was in good shape. But I looked twice when I met her along with a few folk in the County Lounge. It wasn't just my own eyes went to her. The jacket fitted her snug so the buttons were done up, looking formal, not just a mock-up. It was a bit longer on her than me, but not by much. She'd grown the hair a bit and had the ponytail tight so the smooth dark strands were slick against her face. She had the dark skirt and dark shoes with heels but not stilettoes. Nothing fancy. Just total class.

'You scrub up well, blone,' I said.

'Yes, but we could do with a bit more braid.' As she held up her cuff to show the one rosette.

'Aye, I never hung in there long enough for another ring.'

We all had one drink and then we were along the road to the Crow's Nest, top of the Legion. Then I was circulating, playing it cool on the vino collapso. Spacing it with water. I wasn't sober but I wasn't drunk.

'You don't mind a smell of smoke on your jacket?'

'You're very considerate, my dear.'

I don't know why I followed her out. Just maybe there was a memory of the snatch of a roll-up with something worth inhaling. But I'd only had a toke of a joint a few times in twenty years – just for the memory of it.

And she was in a wee gaggle of folk. Some I knew, some I didn't. Maybe I was curious to catch the yarn in the community of smokers, the lull from the music. And it was a stunning evening. Yes, you do get them in SY. This was one of these clear September nights. The year was changing. The temperature was dropping and the visibility was burning with clarity. Stars were jumping.

Everyone was saying stuff like, 'I'm seeing you in a new light, girl. It hangs better on you than on that lanky bastard.'

Affectionate things like that. And then I caught the image. She wasn't milking it too much. Just lingered for the right pause for effect. She brought the tube out of her inside pocket and twisted the red cap off. Time for a Havana. That was another coastguard connection. A very old-fashioned present. Sometimes we got a bottle of malt for the Christmas do. This time there was a box of Havanas but not many takers for them. So the guys had shared them out with the neighbours in the Fisheries Office.

It wasn't a huge one, and not one of these really fat ones either, but a proper cigar. I always liked the smell of them. The first smell, before it fades to bitter. She placed it in her mouth and I wished I had the Zippo lighter but someone else clicked a Bic and she was away. Just that surprising first burst of smoke and then it was natural.

'I thought I'd better bring something appropriate to the rig,' she said. 'And the Old Holborn tin didn't quite fit in the pocket.' She took a draw and let the smoke out over her lip, very slowly. She was enjoying that.

The others were settling to their own chats, they were a bit further on than me. Mairi was sober. Maybe she'd had one glass. She was driving back.

'You might as well have a taste,' she said. 'Be a bad lad.'

She held it out for me and I felt the curl of smoke roll round my mouth a bit. There was also a tinge of her. We were standing close enough for that. In the huddle.

She passed it on then, like a joint. The smokers were all up for trying the Havana. And I was back inside with her.

The room was full now so it was impossible not to be touching someone. I knew when I was touching Mairi Bhan. There was no need to move. I wasn't hard. There was just a gentle pressure, maybe hip to thigh. We stopped being social. We just talked to each other. The usual stuff. Boats and fish and fathers.

We were outside the door when my lips found hers. There was still a taste of the cigar. It was not unpleasant.

Gabriele and me were ten months into the 'see how it goes' period. We'd agreed on a year. We were getting on a bit better but sometimes I'd sleep the other end of town. Right at the edge. A cousin had a house there and I'd keep an eye on it when he was at sea. We'd agreed to keep letting the olaid's house till the books balanced. It's difficult to admit you need breathing space and even more difficult to admit that something you thought was forever might not be. I might not have been able to do it at all but my inner brain started talking to me. It kept me awake at nights but it was talking in riddles. It gets easier once it registers that you're not the first one to go through something like this.

Stop. Look around. Here it comes. But I think I only had two nervous breakdowns. One about a year after the death of my father and one a year after the death of my mother. Quite symmetrical.

The second one was a bit confused with the issue of achieving the aforementioned fifty years of ageing. Once you admit you're going to die, there's a few experiences you want to have first, if you can squeeze them in.

I signed up as crew on a tough delivery trip, along for the ride to nurse an old Perkins. Second night in, I realised that three out of the seven of us were up for it because it might be the last chance of a big seagoing adventure. Not counting me.

One heart condition, one cancer scare and one living very close to clinical depression. About the usual. I wasn't feeling that great myself but I came off that boat counting my blessings.

'Did I hear you're staying over at the Battery?' Mairi said.

'Time to time. I'm there this week. Bit of head space.'

She held my eye and said, 'Shit, I could have tried that Châteauneuf-du-Pape. I'm not driving, am I?'

It wasn't really a question.

'No, and we don't have to find a machine either. It's a snip really.'

Then we were walking, on the way home, just leaving her car across the road. It wasn't just a matter of miles. I knew why we weren't going to Garyvard.

It was exciting and calm at the same time. I was peaceful when I did fall into her hold. Yet it was her eyes holding mine all the time, never wavering. Her nails made direct contact too and this was signalling. You never knew when you would sense that sharpness. I was responding to her and I was aware of when she wanted me to drive and when to slow. I lay inside her just pulsing and waiting for her signal to move strong again.

I've never known such ease with someone along with the excitement and with such sadness at the same time. She didn't say anything. There was only different degrees of touch. I don't think either of us wanted it to stop but it wasn't over with our little deaths.

I think I knew that this was also the death of at least one friendship and possibly three. And that my marriage really had died in one form quite a while before. Now that calm and desire were happening at the same time again, I knew that part of me was coming back to life. And part of me was killing things.

205

I'm going to try to persuade you I only bought the car for the towbar. But you might suspect there were other reasons. The Peugeot diesel engine is a famous unit. It's known to be reliable as well as light and powerful. The family of small diesel-powered cars were the only European products that could seriously compete, in terms of reliability, with the Japanese opposition. The 205 had a compact, light body and was quite famous for its get up and go. Maybe the 306 is similar and maybe that model too is obsolete by the time you read this. But, like the Austin A-Series engine, maybe that famous diesel unit has not changed essentially from badge to badge.

I just thought you might want to have a bit of power in reserve if you had the weight of a dinghy on the back. The wee car had power all right. I have two endorsements on my licence to prove it. There was no drama. Both were over on the east coast between Inverness and Aberdeen. I was on my way to old Andra's funeral the first time and on my way to rendezvous with a Fisheries Officer who was on a course, the second. The first time I just failed to notice where the fifty zone ended and the forty began. And the second incident was similar, forty to thirty, which sadly appears to prove the general premise that the human animal takes longer to learn stuff than a rat in a cage.

The 205 had none of the vroom vroom you heard when you touched the throttle of the olaid's purple Mini. But I liked the shape of the body of the small Peugeot and I liked the shade of red. It was a bit noisy but Anna had helped me install a decent CD player. I was able to arrange things to pick her up in Edinburgh or

Inverness, a couple of times. We played disc for disc as we drove home together. You always call the Island home. That's not conditional on where you're living most of the year, or your state of mind.

Anna introduced me to Tom Waits. And a Tuvan throat singer who sounded very like him. And I happened to have *Willy the Pimp*, sung by Captain Beefheart on the Zappa album. She was amazed at the similarity. The lyrics are astonishing too. 'Da,' she said, 'I trust they *are* satire.'

The daughter also said how her tutor quoted a dude called Matthew Arnold: 'Criticism is comparison.'

I was able to make the bonfire when I got home. There was a short-term let of the olaid's house and I was able to cut it shorter. My former colleague, gone back to sea, was home from installing offshore wind farms in foreign parts and the house on the Battery didn't need minding. I had nowhere else to go but I still felt a bastard. Now the lyric that was in my head was *Dear Landlord*. It was me putting a price on the soul of another.

This was the time to perform certain actions. The letting agreement had been that one upstairs room was reserved for storage of the remainder of my mother's possessions. Kirsty had already sorted the most personal stuff. Now Gabriele helped me go through the rest of the drawers and boxes. We set aside some more family photographs and a few more keepsakes.

We had the seat of the old estate folded down, so she could get a good load to the skip at the dump. She was quite cheerful, once the pace got going. There's an element of relief in carrying out a duty like this. I'd done runs to the dump, myself, after the death of Ruaraidh.

While Gabriele was away, I looked once through the box of unsent letters I'd kept in the top room in this house and then I threw it on the crackling pile. She came back to find me standing by the wee gellie. Something caught her eye, maybe my handwriting.

She picked up the charring sheets of A4, in the same way as she'd gone through a few generations of a family that she was connected to but wasn't her own. She read from one sheet. She didn't have to. It was in my head. Still is.

The tin of Old Holborn
Shakes like a rattle.

I'm looking for the quietness
Before I exhale.

It comes before the bitter
And the fear of the dull.

You got to take
The time it takes

To roll the single-handed roll
Before you dream of raising stakes.

Six deep clean breaths
Were not enough.

I circled the box but
I posted the letter.

I'm not hell of a sure
It made anything better.

You stop for a smoke
You eye the horizon.

You watch the land fall,
The ridge, a bare backbone.

'That's yours,' Gabriele said. 'Your handwriting. You've never showed me any poems.'

'Songs,' I said.

'You don't sing,' she said.

We stood for a while. I poked the bonfire.

'Is there anything you want to tell me?'

I told her I'd started smoking again.

'You could have left that out of the midlife crises.'

By then I knew I wasn't really in love with Emily but I did know that something deep in my brain was telling me I couldn't stay where I was.

Gabriele asked me to tell her about the letter.

So I told her I'd tried to make explicit a longing that thought it was a desire. Maybe it's not unusual to write or do one thing when you think you're writing or doing another.

It's not only the daughter who can cite previous discussions. Now I'm not comparing my songwriting attempt to the novels of Tolstoy but there's an essay by one Isaiah Berlin, quoted to me by a fine man who urged me to read the unfashionable Sir Walter Scott and then *War and Peace*. A literary detour from the chronological progression of history. You had to take one course in another discipline so I signed up for 'Scott and the European Historical Novel'. I fell in love with Jeanie Deans and now my heart is in Midlothian.

Berlin says that there are two kinds of novelist – hedgehogs and foxes. A hedgehog has a purpose and plods methodically along a route. A fox is wily and twitchy and sniffs at the details. So you have novels in which histories are expounded and novels in which the complex motivations of individuals are examined. Tolstoy is a great novelist because he's a fox who thought he was a hedgehog.

I think I might have told you Gabriele and me decided to give it a year. At least. I also told you I jumped the gun by two months. I can't say now if waiting out a further eight weeks would have made any difference.

But I can chart the exact moment when our union became only an alliance of mutual convenience, applicable for certain situations at certain times. Some of the time we talked some sense but mostly we just talked for far too long. Of course, most guys would say that.

But it came to property and it was taken as read that there was no reason at all why we should start off with a premise of sharing things out. I was the one who wanted change so I had to pay the price. Now in principle that argument sounds fine but I'd been working twelve-hour days on property development for a bit too long and now I wanted to get what was left of my brain on to other things.

Pity I didn't reach that conclusion before stripping two more roofs for enough slate to make the hippy-dream, garage/workshop/sleepover-centre/sanctuary. And it's perhaps a pity I managed to service enough marine motors that year to pay the joiner.

It was not really about making an independent living, out of the shelter provided by Her Majesty's Service. Tinkering with engines is grand for a hobby but now that I'd done it for real a few times, servicing auxiliary engines, I knew it was never going to be enough to satisfy me, even if there was a sound business there for somebody else. While the oil was draining I'd be thinking back to something started in my own mental journey but nowhere near completion.

I'm not going to tell you now, the specific subject I had in mind for my mid-life thesis. In general terms, I wanted to look closely at one period of change in one part of Scotland. To examine contemporary accounts, in letters and records which might have escaped close scrutiny. Because there's still something to be learned by going into that level of detail.

It was a hope that nearly died in a Peugeot 205. Gabriele put the brakes on any open discussion of the principles of our settlement and I put the handbrake on. It didn't happen just like that. She was driving and I asked her to stop please because I had to get out. I had to get some air. I've heard since that these symptoms are often termed a panic attack. She said, no, I couldn't get out, I wasn't getting away with that. I said I had to get out, no really, I had to. She said, 'No.' I said, 'Gabriele, I'm going to put the handbrake on now because I honestly have no choice but to get out of this car right now.' That's when she accelerated.

It was a class wheelie. Well, it would have been after about two a.m. when there wasn't so much chance of something coming the other way. This was about twelve noon. Now I did tell you that Westerns have left their mark in SY culture. Along with James Cagney. Hell's teeth, it was more like the Blues Brothers only we missed what was coming to us.

A better way of putting it might be that the poor driver of the oncoming vehicle (on the correct side of the road) was spared injury to himself or his property. We were lucky he'd said his prayers that morning, the only possible explanation for missing us. But thank God he was still so shocked he never got our number or was too shaken to report us.

I decided that evening I wasn't going to buy my former classmate, the lawyer, a Laphroaig and pose a hypothetical question he might have heard a dozen times. I decided that continuing dialogue with Gabriele was essential because we'd somehow managed to make a baby together and raise her between us for a good few years. The baby was now a sharp and aware young woman and in the process of getting educated in a country where they charged tuition fees. If I didn't manage to pay half of these costs, I knew I was more and more tied to a woman I could not lie with any longer.

The death of our marriage was about to mean the birth of my new career. I didn't run away to sea or run back crawling (an interesting combination of movements) to the Coastguard Service. I was probably qualified to drive a cab in Cairo after my half-share of responsibility for that incident.

Instead, I did what comes naturally to a historian by training. I went back to pick up a strand of my previous life. The pace of a busy kitchen used to give me a buzz, even when I was only washing the pots. It was time to get back on the pans.

So I got my foot in a door that was open to visitors who wanted to taste local produce rather than ostrich steaks. I had to cook these too, a couple of times. But usually they trusted me to choose the fish of the day and have my wicked way with it. Megrim and tusk made regular appearances on the specials board.

I might have cooked for you already if you've dined out in SY. They say I'm good at what I do. I respect good fish.

Invitation

It was time I phoned Kirsty. I'd sent some books, a few small things around New Year. I was never going to make the Christmas Airmail deadline. I was burning the late lamp oil, doing a bit of research, so the time difference wasn't a problem – minus five hours.

Quite civilised. She was off shiftwork now.

It rang and soon there was a person on the end of it. Her twang seemed more pronounced. Not much Lewis in it.

'*Ici ton frere*,' I said but that was about my limit. Even without the accent and the lack of hand and lip movements. Her voice slipped back a bit.

'Now I'd know you're an Islander,' I said.

'Yes, a Montreal islander,' she said. 'West side though, so there's a lot of English spoken. Suppose I should have settled down the coast in Long Island. Hardly a change of address then.'

There was a bit of a pause, nothing awkward. Kirsty said, 'Is everything OK? I mean, it's good to hear from you but...'

'Aye, no worries, Anna's fine. I know, you're expecting something wrong. It's not like we talk every day. And yourself?'

'Back to routine.'

'Yes, Gabriele's OK – well, physically anyway – we know a bit about that now, the last parent passing. She's never really got back on track. But that's kind of why I'm calling.'

'You're no longer living with Gabriele?'

'That was quick off the mark.'

'Well done,' Kirsty said.

'What?'

'Well done. Nothing against Gabriele but...'

'Most people said they were surprised.'

'You made too good a job of putting on a show.'

'You saw that?'

'I saw you were under a lot of strain. You can only do that so long. Part of my job is to see that, remember. Doesn't give you immunity, though.'

'And how are *you* doing? Really.'

'Well, strange thing is, brother, I've been thinking of giving you a ring.'

'Everything OK?'

'A bit better than that.'

'So what's your news?'

'An invitation.'

'Not a head to wet?'

'Hell no – a bit late for that. A ceremony. A civil ceremony. A marriage in the law.'

I don't think I said anything.

'You're shocked?'

'No, just didn't see it.'

'Well I could have been more up-front earlier. Suppose it was that religious stage. First it was the Bahá'í list of beliefs. I remember the exact phrase, *does not condone homosexuality*. Then it was the hardcore Christianity.'

I went quiet.

I was back there, in the students' union building. They did a decent, cheap liver and onions. People were always giving out leaflets.

A gay activist challenged me head-on. Very reasonable arguments. He said, 'This may not be directly relevant but please take a look.' I said, 'I'll read anybody's viewpoint of anything.' He said, 'Thanks a lot.' I knew the tone in my voice had come out all wrong because really I couldn't claim to be open to his viewpoint. He'd clocked that. I ducked and dived.

My sister's voice came through again. 'So you weren't at one with the party line when you were still going to the Free Church? You told me you were there for the psalms and the stories. I remember tackling you on the letters in the *Gazette. The whore that is Rome. The plague of homosexuality*. But that was pretty much the official line. You dodged that, too. That's a lot of strain.'

'I always kept the L-plates on. Never even tried to go forward to take the test on dogma.'

'No wonder you were such a tight bastard. Do you remember when Free Kirk councillors were lobbying to cut the grant to the film society because they showed *My Beautiful Launderette*? The hardcore wanted to refuse them the lecture theatre in the school. I was home then and so were you. You were talking about histories of oppressive regimes but it was me who wrote the letter in reply. How the film was not *about* homosexuality. It was a political film about values in Thatcherite Britain. The correspondent had just proved the absolute need to show such films. And by the way, I thought the boys were quite funny and cute. But you must have wondered at my own lack of boyfriends?'

'Suppose I thought it was career. You knew what you wanted to do. Nursing, then the District, then the Community. Then Policy. Sharp cookie dot com – the Canadian sister. The two languages. But...'

'And you never guessed from my letter to the *Gazette*?'

'I think I was too bound up in the values of Thatcherite Britain. Who was it said her legacy was that greed was now legitimate? I was arguing against it all while I was developing the property. But I could see it, at work. You saw it in the detail.'

'Give me a for instance.'

'For instance, I got a mooring transferred to a colleague with a boat. Free, gratis. In the firm. He got a shift back to the mainland as soon as he'd done his three years and the boat had never been on it. I knew someone else looking for a spot so I said, will we just pass the mooring on? And he says, well he can have it for a bottle of grouse or two. He'd never even seen the bloody mooring.'

'That would be a cove from away, then. See, I can still remember the lingo.'

'I'll give you one more. Another guy lends out the garage he isn't using so we can fix up a boat. Very decent. We give him and his wife a bottle of champagne, real McCoy, rather than breaking glass on the bow. A new lobster creel falls off a lorry outside his house. He traps it and asks us what it's worth to us.'

'That's a for instance. Should be one word. Maybe it is in Stornoway.'

'Tell me about your lady.'

'About time you asked that.'

'Please.'

'OK. Denise was born in Paris. Algerian father. Toured Québec with a dance company. Stayed.'

'So how long…?'

'Have we known each other or been living together?'

'Been an item?'

'Fifteen years.'

'What?'

'Poor line, is it? No, but there's been ups and downs. Time out. That year, looking after the old girl. That was for me too. Working things out. Remember Canada's a federal set-up. Québec has had civil ceremonies since '92. I proposed right away. Denise wasn't ready. I thought I'd lost her.'

'So poor old Mary was more stable than her carers?'

'I think she might have been.'

'Hell.'

'So are you coming over?'

'It's a fucking long way in the *Peace and Plenty*. Need a tanker behind us.'

'Remember the Wright brothers?'

'Just bought a house, with the settlement. A daughter still at Uni. There's nothing in the kitty. I've a slate roof over me, roughcast walls round me and nothing else.'

'All you need.'

'Aye. Trying to build up the work. I'm on the pans these days. Sous chef. Relief chef. But getting a wee bit of a name in the town. Got to keep it going. I really fancy getting over though.'

'I'll book you the flights. My treat.'

'Look, really glad you asked me. Call you back on that one, OK?'

'OK. Don't leave it too long.'
'I won't.'
'And Peter?'
'Yeah?'
'I like you in skeptical mode. Don't let it go.'

I went for the pouch when the phone was back in the dock. Crossed to the window and let a bit of night air in.

Shit, I was supposed to be looking at past human experience because something might be gained. The idea was to compare what's happened in different places at different times. When I was studying interpretations of events, I was suppressing my own powers of interpretation. I wasn't the only believer who ignored the awkward bits. How many good Christians in the Third Reich reluctantly abided by the State restrictions rather than face the show-down? And there are the good Communists who noticed the shadows of their comrades as they disappeared. But kept quiet. They couldn't have swum against that tide. What good would one more death do?

The lessons of history? You're not the only one. And hindsight does indeed help. Now for our homework question. At what date did sodomy cease to be a crime in the United Kingdom? It's easy to forget that too.

Not soon enough for Alan Turing. He was a main player in the battle of the Atlantic. He was largely responsible for designing the computers which led to reading transmissions encoded by Enigma machines, when enough clues were provided. It takes time, even for mathematical geniuses. The breakthrough, from a captured codebook, happened late in 1942 but it was midway through 1943 before the numbers of lost ships fell again as the moves of the wolf-packs were anticipated.

On the 7th of June 1954 my sister was already out in the light and I was a twinkle in the olman's eye. Alan Turing died from cyanide poisoning. The verdict was suicide. He was facing prosecution for homosexuality. It took until Gordon Brown's leadership for Her Majesty's Government to apologise for that treatment of a man who had put his mind into the fight against fascism.

Fabric

I'm not really a sailor, not like Anna, but the relationship with *Tante Erika* did something to me. It must have done because I've woken with the sense of cloth on my hands. Terylene doesn't do it for me. It sounds a bit sexier when it's called Dacron. You think of these rows of zig-zag stitching. Sometimes they're picked out in a pale orange shade against the off-white. You can see why a company markets clothing and kitbags made from sails that would be dead. But Dacron is merely a trade name for common or garden polyester fabric, in the version first marketed by Du Pont fabrics.

When you're not fully awake, your mind works on good bearings. Glides. Like rope through Harken blocks. Small and light items of racing hardware, they're definitely sexy. For a while, there was no doubt about what to get Anna for birthdays and Christmases. Anything that might get a dinghy going faster. First, there is the material to consider, in lightweight metals or innovative synthetics. Then there is the design element where material is removed wherever possible. There are more holes than metal so it is as light as it can be without sacrificing strength. These are elegant structures and they function well. I understand the attraction but my own kink is the retro sense of soft tan sailcloth. As long as I don't have to depend on it for propulsion.

In fetishist terms this might be equivalent to silk stockings with seams at the back. The period detail would be about right. Then nylon arrived. When it was available. Not really a cargo priority aboard the liberty-ships which were escorted across the infested North Atlantic.

I accepted custodianship of what must be one of the last sails to be manufactured on this Island. Mairi Bhan was storing it in the house in Lochs. It had come from her father's shed. There are layers of repairs but most of the stitching has been done by hand. She thought my attic was the place for it – returning it to where it might well have been made or repaired. A loft in a house close to the hoil.

Maybe her thinking was that the best way to make sure an object is looked after is to keep it in use. It was briefly back in commission to drive *Peace and Plenty* home across the Minch. Now I was trusting the little air-cooled Italian job.

I did think of giving the sail to Gabriele and Anna but it's too valuable for everyday use. Whenever the Historical Society have a display relating to this Island's maritime history, they know where it is. There is a characteristic smell, maybe from the last time it was treated, and the cotton is quite soft to the touch among all the hardware.

Go far enough back and there's Captain MacDonald from Great Bernera. First, he'd ask the mate to go aloft to check the rig. Then he'd hoist himself up on a wire and study the details for himself. If he was satisfied, he'd really drive the ship, the Clipper *Sir Lancelot*, till the mate was shaking with nerves. But he'd inspect every detail himself first. Even MacDonald had to order the sails reefed, when the winds climbed the scale. That's the image. The men are spread out along the yard with only a boot on a rope to brace themselves. They pull away at sodden canvas and shake the hail off the cloth. So each seaman can tie his pennant that will help reduce the area of tensed wing, which will drive her through building waters.

It wasn't so much later that pioneers tensed the fabric to make a fixed shape that altered the flow of air and therefore the comparative velocity of it from one side of a wing to another. Soon after that, spluttering motors propelled these coated skeletons to stay in the air that bit longer. Until Bleriot crossed the Channel and Lindbergh covered 3,600 miles to land the *Spirit of St Louis* in France.

And it came to pass that seaplanes and aircraft with wheels that dropped on struts, were stationed at Stornoway airport during a large part of the Second World War. You know that one of the bombers failed to return from the South Lochs area of Lewis but, much later, a Shackleton, named after the great survivor, failed to clear a south Harris mountain during a social expedition in the 1990s.

And further out west, forty miles clear of the Sound of Harris, more than one aircraft failed to clear the hidden high ground of the St Kilda group of islands. But there is one more story of one more aircraft which did stay in the air until the west coast of south Lewis was under it. Then it collapsed, between the end of the road in Brenish and the end of the road in Hushinish. Very, very close to the territory selected to be of use for the development of rocket science. But this wasn't just a movie. Neither was the rocket-post adventure, in its original form.

I got this story from a tall young man who died young. An Auxiliary Coastguard. I missed his deathbed and I also missed his funeral. I was told off for it too because I was on the Island at the time. 'You should have been there.'

I said nothing because the former colleague who said it was right. I'm not expecting miracles at my own deathbed, if it happens that way. If I haven't set aside the time to say, 'What can I say?' then why should any bastard bother to remember me?

This dead man, who was gentle and enquiring and liked to take photographs with a long lens, was interested in aircraft as well as shipping. This led him to meet a former American airman who was returning to Lewis to visit the territory where he'd been stationed. This was his story. I'm filing it as a report, as I remember it, as he relayed it to me.

A given example of a given aircraft manufactured at the later stages of the Second World War crash-landed in a remote part of the island of Lewis. This was in the southwest, where there is no direct access by road. The tracks stop at the village of Islavig to the north and at Hushinish to the south. There are small settlements in the fiords charted as Tamnavay (pronounced Hamnaway) and Loch Resort. These are serviced only by small vessels. There are no pier or landing facilities.

The aircraft under discussion was the latest development of its type.

It could be considered a prototype. Therefore it was essential to ensure that none of its features could be seen or recorded by any non-authorised persons. In addition, the wreck contained the results of much development work, which was of sufficient value to recover.

The option of a controlled explosion was considered but the opportunity to examine the distressed components was judged to be of sufficient importance to warrant special treatment.

That phrase could well have been used in 1944 or '45 in official reports on the Allied side, by a writer oblivious to the specific meaning the phrase possessed, in its German version, in documents signed by very senior SS officers.

That treatment came in the form of a road. There was no necessity for a section of *Autobahn* on Lewis, to bring the wreck out. That was only to come much later, thanks to European money, granted in implicit exchange for a lot of dead fish.

As I understand it, from the memory of an airman as passed to a colleague now in a condition which makes the checking of detail something I think we can safely term impossible, the road built to enable removal of the remains of one aircraft was nothing ordinary. It was engineered so that light vehicles could access the crash site and transport the shell. It may have been removable tracking. It may have been part of the development of a system which could prove useful in moving instruments of transportation and death across what was left of the continent of occupied Europe. D-Day was coming soon.

There may be traces left between two road-ends for devotees of industrial archaeology to catalogue. It could even be that the Uig road ended in Brenish rather than Islavig before the pioneering track left a foundation to surface later. But I don't know and I do want to carry on with the story, rather than research this detail further.

Except that this is really the end of that story. It's a bit abrupt, I know, but *c'est la guerre*. Aircraft became more ands more efficient. Sir Frank Whittle's jet engine idea proved viable. Except we now know it's not sustainable but we still use it anyway.

You know all about the Allied advance through Europe, concurrent with the advance of the Red Army. Many Lewismen had been imprisoned in what is now Poland since their capture at St Valery while others escaped at Dunkirk. There's the story of the two guys from SY who escaped from one such camp and walked or brass-necked their way to the Baltic only to find the harbours frozen over. They could row and sail and start motors but they couldn't skate on thick ice. 'We'll try again in spring,' they said.

They gave themselves up before they starved and so joined the later Long March, a few steps ahead of the fast Russian advance. One autobiography, written in Gaelic, describes the mountain of sugar in the outskirts of a smoking city. It might have been Hamburg. Described by my own late olman as Churchill's Revenge for Coventry. Quite a long name. One German officer marched the thin men to the site of the bombed sugar refinery. They thought this was their end but no. They were allowed to gorge on the syrup-like residue till they had energy to continue.

There was no huge tragedy like the loss of the *Iolaire* as the survivors came home. Only a large incidence of dysentery and some isolated accidents. One vehicle skidded off a high bridge into a gorge. The uncle I never met was aboard. He is pasted into later history. Amongst all the boxes with photographs in frames and photographs in albums, there is one that haunts me. It's the golden wedding of my Broch grandparents. The last image of the lost brother is superimposed in a gap in the line of brothers and sisters.

When does a story stop? I've got one more for you now. It's a jump but I can make a good case for its relevance in respect of our discussion on structure and the framework that is essential to most vessels or modes of transport.

My olman did say more than once that the body is like a machine and I'm not going to argue with him just because he's dead. When a body is under strain, it's component parts can fail. It's not always the skeleton or the flesh on top of it. It can be the mind within it. If you've ever been awake for most of a night and been unable to jump free of a needle caught in the groove of a repeating record, you'll appreciate that.

And that's where we should leave it but I won't. I'm taking you back to a crash site we've visited already. I can't really take you to that one past the Uig road-end and I can't take you up the hill in Hirta because I haven't personally witnessed wreckage in any of these places. I have seen tangled propellers by the pier on Hirta. They're tidying up the Second World War relics though the cold war portacabins are still in use.

But I have personally sensed the remaining relics in the crash-site in the inaccessible hills of South Lochs. So come back with me to the shell of an aircraft which has shed its belts of ammunition, in knotted moorland. These came from machine-guns, now seized. And of course the ghosts, snug in their flying jackets, shrug off the mist that is often dense, round about five hundred feet up from sea-level, in a position round about five eight degrees north and six thirty west.

Some ghosts are more prominent than others – coves I failed to keep in touch with and failed to visit. I never managed to shake or touch their hands. I have at least to pass on their yarns.

But of course it's easier to tell you, about the tangled wrecks of aircraft on hills. Shipwrecks are more difficult for me. Less distant. My olman never talked directly about being trapped in either a tank or a bunk. I heard the details only when someone else drew them out.

Mapping

I was missing the driveway more than the village of outbuildings but it felt good to be back in the sway of the town. You could say I'd never been out of it, but it wasn't about where you were laying your head. It was about being hemmed in. Anna was off to Newcastle. I said the Geordie accent would blend well with SY. I made my own move, not long after. It was a shit time, some ways. Gabriele wasn't in a good state. I'd lost my own buoyancy. I was sluggish in the water. But some mornings I woke with a sense of relief.

When you're unsettled, you go out on walks without being definite about where you're heading. Or you find you're in the car that's stopped in front of a workshop. You have to re-map your own home town for yourself.

There's one Italian café left, out of the three or four, including the one where you received very sound advice along with the coffee. The shoeshop (and centre of moral philosophy) has been converted to flats. The blacksmith is still inventing things and contradicting the pattern of economic activity still somehow generally accepted in the developed world. When you ask him what the damage is, he says, 'Bring it back when you're finished with it and I'll make it into something else.' And the hoil is in the throws of shifting from a haven for commercial fishing vessels to catering for leisure activities.

I stroll down there most days. I like the colour of the big boats. They're ageing as fast as me and one by one you simply notice that there's a name you're not seeing. Al Crae never fixes a black-bordered notice in the butchers, for them. There was no funeral to mark the passing of *Braes of Garry* or *Sonas* or the *Golden Sheaf*. Their remains would take a bit of carrying, even if a big squad turned out to share the lift. Could be an argument for cremation, there.

The *Sonas* kept her varnish finish later than most. She might be pulling gear round the bottom of other UK coastal waters. Her larch planking is maybe what inspired me to keep to the natural grain of the timber in the rebuilt *Peace and Plenty*.

Once, I bought a painting that caught the changes in the colours you see round the hoil. It was in the Save The Children, when I was kitting out my hideaway with coffee cups. It was briefly installed up on the crisp new mezzanine library, over the workshop on Leverhulme Drive. That's before I realised there was no thinking space in that building either.

I look at a particular orange in Donald Smith's arrangement of components of heavy vessels and a mizzen sail across a weathered gable. His later paintings show the more bold colours that come from the cans in the Fisherman's Co-op. Teamac – made or mixed in Scotland.

The prawns from the trawlers don't go direct to Spain. That market's served by the neat and careful creel-boats. The selected crabs and lobsters, fit enough to travel far and maintain the standard of Hebridean shellfish. And some of these creel-boats were built not so long ago of Scottish larch. Before architects started specifying it for eco-friendly cladding so it's well nigh impossible to find boatskin-grade timber in the north of Scotland. Great broad planks of larch are imported from Siberia now.

But the *Peace and Plenty* has three sections of snug sawn frames. Cut by the cove, from wind-distorted oak and larch, found with the grain that meets the curvature of a given shape. Found amongst the storm-felled timbers out The Grounds. Larch and oak amongst the rare breeds – the russet-grained yew and the cypress that still smells like retsina.

The few trawlers still go out on days when the wind dictates that the new old boat has to stay tied up. You don't want to get rescued by your former colleagues, even though it's good to keep guys in jobs. The fisher-boys are generous. One of them will throw you up a few flatfish from the debris on deck. Obese seals cruise in the decklight-lit waters as the sifting and sorting continues. It's not herring guts that ferment in our mud now, it's the antennae of small nehrops and immature whitefish. You sift through the muddy shapes and touch the rough skin of a small turbot.

I might get a John Dory, though the larger ones are set aside now for the mixed box for another specialised supplier.

'We can't sell one of them, on its own. Is this any good to you?'

I took that one home.

My Episcopalian *amigo* was back up the road to sort out some of his affairs of this world. Rented property. I steamed the fish for us, cutting insertions so the flanks could be filled with slivers of ginger and lemongrass. Slices of lime go down its gob and into its belly. The spring onions go in after the Sauvignon Blanc and stock. I've seen us eating the tail section first, with a touch of the green-top soy sauce. Then it goes on for another minute so it heats up again and the thicker parts will be cooked, till the red at the bone goes pale. And the reduction is intense, to hit the grains of rice and give that background taste which does not dominate the delicate fish.

Colonoscopy

I'm more worried about saying the bloody name of the job than
I am about the job. You've to make an appearance at the surgical
ward. But you only get changed and recover in the ward. All the
action happens downstairs. But you go down in a lift, trolley and
all.

I'm changing into the gown – fastened at the back, like a wetsuit
but it's nothing like a wetsuit. Except for having to stretch for the
ties or getting some help.

I'm recognising the voice of the big guy talking to the nurse.
His symptoms have cleared up so he reckons there's no point in
going down. That's what they call it here. Believe me, the term has
got nothing to do with oral sex. He's turned up anyway and they're
trying to get a doc to see him. It's a conveyor belt of jobs so it's not
easy. Maybe he'd better just go down.

My symptoms aren't so bad either. I got scared when there
was blood round the bowl in the morning. I got the outside area
checked. My arse, not the toilet. No sign of piles or anything, so
they want to know where that blood's coming from and why. Then
there's blood in my mouth. And I'm crapping more and softer than
I should be. Maybe losing a wee bit of weight and I don't have a
lot to start with. So they want to have a look next compartment
up – the bowels.

I've mucked it up already, before the New Year. I got three dates.
Changed one. Forgot all about the second – till the morning I was
supposed to go in and that's no good because you've got to do
a treatment first. And of course I didn't read the instructions on

the laxative properly, the third time unlucky, so there wasn't much point in going in. To go into the ward, get changed and go down. So that was me off the list till I went to the doc about something else and she said I'd better get that posterior of mine back on the list and get it checked properly.

So there I was. No solids since midday Sunday. Just green tea and water and the sweetened solution that turns everything into liquid. You know how they told you at school how mostly everything is water. Well, I believe it now. Steak, sausages, anything that looks solid. It's not really.

Back to the waiting ward. First I recognised that tall guy's voice. From the harbour. The boat-watchers society of the city of SY. Then I caught the twang of the twin-port man. That's another popular club, the classic vehicle brigade. I'm just going to call him my neighbour because operations are a wee bit personal. Mine's a colonoscopy. I kept calling it other things but the auxiliaries and sisters and porter kept correcting me.

Cheery guy, the neighbour in the ward. I knew, first hand, he had a good bedside manner himself, if the parts were going to be expensive. Breaking it to you gently. Usually he just took bits from one he'd dismantled earlier. I could hear him now, keeping up the banter with the nursing-auxiliary. Weather outside, change in the seasons and how life was in general. I didn't want to interrupt his flow but I did want to know if he was still into VW engines.

Beetles, Type 2 vans, Karmann Ghias.

One trolley was ready, parked at my neighbour's. I couldn't see him, because of the all-round curtains. Then the chocks were away. I caught a glimpse of it, passing a gap in my own curtains. He was being wheeled to the lift. The style of driving the trolley is good for a minute or two's discussion along the way. It's hospital etiquette – a thing you've got to do, discuss the driving. Award the points. I used to swerve a trolley round the round myself. Just for a year. A lot of years ago.

'I think you've a deal going with the painter,' someone would say. 'Hell, the plasterer, too. Shit, the brickie as well? You're keeping them all in work with that driving.'

So time passes and the cove who was pushing the trolley is going to be lying on one very soon.

Never mind going on or off the trolley. When you're lying down, the mind can get into athletic mode. Before sedation. Or maybe it's the first stage of sedation, before you let go completely to it.

I'm going to speak to you of the beauties of the VW twin-port engine. Mounted at the back. Guys like that cove who was in the neighbouring bed – they can drop one of these beauties onto a trolley-jack to change a clutch. In about twenty minutes. It's a good idea to feed the throttle-cable through first before you re-connect it. Otherwise, you'll need to drop and jack-up the whole unit, over again. You'll be quite intimate with every nut and bolt but you won't be popular with the mate who's giving you a hand. If that happens to be your daughter, you'll be lucky to remain alive.

Listen to the word. Listen up now. Hear the dulcet putter. Right enough, they might not be all that fuel-efficient by today's stand-ards. But then there's the issue of life expectancy. And they can be rebuilt. Which was our man's forte. And maybe still is.

Lewis sheds. Sheds, all round the coast of the British Isles, host these fine machines which were manufactured pre-1979. And you will find them throughout the continent of Europe and in all other continents, with a very high density in North and South America. I was thinking of the time one chassis needed complete reinforcing to get an MOT – you don't get them in a lucky-bag any more, that piece of paper I mean. Well, the chassis neither. That's not exactly a spare part. So someone might put a tarp on a motor on a pallet and it's waiting for the day someone else has a good body and an engine that's done its work. Very frustrating thing. When the driving force is still sweet as a nut, steady as a Singer, and the joints, the spine, the very chassis of life is rotten.

OK, I was infatuated with a purple Leyland 1275 GT Mini for a wee while. But when you look at it now, what do you expect from a repressed twenty-year-old? Vroom vroom. A slightly older model with a bit of flash and a touch of fading class.

Never really went in for the RS 2000 ambition or the bright

yellow or red American Auto. Pal of mine had a big motor for a while. His pay was getting transferred into the bank, tax free. He had to spend it on something. But you'd need a tanker behind you to get the length of the Island. He gets as far as Glasgow once – maybe to get rid of it. Pulls up at a gas station. Attendant whistles.

'Nice motor, son,' he says. 'But must be costing you a fortune in… Durex.'

That was the same guy who sidestepped all that unapplied maths and physics and did navigation at the Castle. Him and Kenny F led that way but I didn't follow. I heard he jumped ship in Aussie not long after he gave me a practical lesson in berthing boats.

I heard there was a car chase and then a spell in jail. And a woman. I met him a year ago and asked him if it was all true. 'No,' he said, 'it was the USA.'

He came to, upside down, held by the seatbelt. Looking at the boots of a trooper. Noticing the sweet MaryJane dribbling out of the traditional top pocket. Gravity was a mixed blessing. There was about enough for one joint but there was some law about inter-state drugs. And his wheels were now across the border. This was New York State and he was caught by the short and curlies.

So he made a deal and got deported. He lost the car and the woman. But he got out of jail. A spell on dry land. No shipping company would take him on then. He was in Tehran when the revolution happened. Pictures of the cleancut Shah one day and the cove with the beard the next. Time to get out. His brother went travelling, too. Different directions. The bro was in Kabul when the Russian tanks rolled in. Crazy times. Lewismen should really stay at home a bit more. It's maybe not their fault but stuff like that just happens all around them.

But that was a diversion. We're back to remembering twin-port motors. It was slow, stately motoring for me, after that one throaty car. Anna loved the vans. She was very good at reading out the instructions from the Haynes manual. See that moment when the motor we'd rebuilt spluttered into life. We did a wee victory dance round the drive. The olaid was up to have her dinner and she was killing herself laughing. Nearly fell out of the wheelchair.

But the twin-port man who went down a few minutes ago – he was VW trained. Never seemed in a hurry but the diagnosis would be sound. The cure would work. Mechanics is simple, he'd say. I can understand engines.

The tall guy decided he might as well go down on the lift, get the check done.

Lying there, I was remembering conversations past. But I was also thinking of my own blood, seeing it in unexpected places. Tasting it in the mouth.

Maybe when I'd meet the twin-port man again we'd talk about our operations. Maybe not. I could ask him to look out for a decent Type 2 VW project. They cost serious money now, in good nick, but Anna was keen on finding one. That would be an incentive for her to pass the test.

But that engineer with the gentle touch was out the door by the time I recovered. I hope he got a good result, his operation I mean. Mine was OK. That test was OK. Just something to keep an eye on. So to speak. I wonder how the tall guy from the hoil got on. Just as well to go down, get it checked. An MOT doesn't last forever.

From: annarichmac@hotmail.co.uk

From: annarichmac@hotmail.co.uk
To: historymacA@btinternet.com

How's the Da? What's fresh, cove?

I did sit down with paper and pen but it reminds me too much of school and exams. So I hope you can accept this as the letter I promised.

And if you just mail back and say, You're seeing it all blone, I'll get in the kayak, up the road and swing a cheeky left at the top of Scotland and dive down to give you a scud on the lug. So there.

I know you're still in the huff I didn't pick anything historical for the dissertation. I know you had good ideas and I know you could have helped me. But you know too it's something I've got to do on my own. You're as bad as my olaid. She wants me to concentrate on Jane Austen of course. Maybe that's historical enough for you too but there's a slight problem. I don't care which of these boring daughters gets the guy in the end. In fact I don't fancy any of the guys. It's like the characters are all queuing up and jumping through hoops, set up by the author.

So yes Da, the course really is working out OK. Just like you said on the phone, I'm getting supported to study the literature of lies. Poetry, fiction and film. I still remember your own suggestions. Correct me if I'm wrong but –

1. Napoleonic wars from the perspective of the Highlands and Islands women left to run the crofts.

2. The '45 rebellion as seen by the effect of post-Culloden measures on the daily lives of surviving women in the Highlands.

3. The role of women in the Vietnamese war.

I know you did the historical novel for a module of the history degree and the *bodach* Tolstoy is the dude for you. Why do I know this? Cos you've only told me about twenty times. I don't think you did Charles Dickens.

I've scanned an essay and I'm enclosing it as a Word doc so you should be able to read it OK. I've a feeling you're going to like this one. It's the novelist Nabokov talking about Jane Austen. He says it's possible to achieve something near enough perfection if you do it on a small enough scale. He talks about a fan by Fragonard with delicate drawings. He says the mistress of irony is like that. But then he talks about the rough texture but the big scope of Dickens.

Now that leads me to the question. Are you still in the stone age of the movies? VHS bricks in the machine? Or have you got a DVD player now? Cos I'm going to ask you to get me David Lean's *Great Expectations* with Finlay Curry as Magwitch as the Christmas present. Everyone stood up and clapped in the lecture theatre and I'd like to see it again. But then I'll post it on to you.

Just to prove that I'm ignoring all attempts by respective parents to steer me into fulfilling their incomplete destinies – please know that my dissertation is likely to be on a completely different topic. So your conditioning programme, verging on brainwashing, has been a dismal failure. It's completely accidental, our similar opinions on the work of Ms Austen.

OK I'll let you into the secret. Fish. Don't tell anyone but there's a lot of fish in Scottish literature. Take herring – another scan winging up the broadband to you – Alasdair Reid's *The Colour of Herring*. Then there's the Greenock bohemian, W S Graham, in St Ives doing *The Nightfishing*. Norman MacCaig talking about the drifter *Daffodil* and basking sharks and trout and stuff. OK OK there's Ted Hughes' *Pike* as well which shows this obsession is not unique to Scotland. But doesn't he come salmon fishing on the Grimersta now he's a wealthy literary gentleman? I should include the poet who fishes the same water as us, even though he pays for the privilege.

Enough of work. Enough of life. Let's talk mechanics. You seemed to hit it off with Les, that dinner at Mum's. Or maybe it was just that no-one else was up to speed on the merits of VW engines.

Yes, we're still together, very much so, since you won't ask. In fact we're well into a shared project. Excellent distraction-therapy, coming up to finals. Beats watering the cactus. Naturally I've totally disregarded your sage advice on the subject of vehicles.

Yes, you've guessed, Les and me have found a Type 2. Not a split screen but the early one with the wee dinky lights − L reg. Tax exempt, if we ever get the show on the road. Les has the driving force purring away on the bench − the advantages of the air-cooled engine. But some body-parts are missing.

We won't find them in bonnie Scotland no more. No nor Deutschland or the Netherlands but wait for this one. Did you know that merchant ships are carrying front and sliding doors and sills and snub side wings over oceans?

Ageing parent, the people's car become the people's van is worth serious money these days as a restored but mainly original model. We couldn't look at buying one but I think we're going to make one up, out of bits.

Please don't be flattered into thinking any of this obsessional behaviour has anything to do with any interests or character traits of your own. But we might well have a camper-van to take the kayaks and ourselves where the waters run. Maybe not Babylon.

And Da, all the best − really − in the new house. But don't be offended if we don't stay the night − family house and all that. The old Leverhulme Drive. Don't worry, your masterpiece of a garage-library combo will be well used. Designer-sheds and glasshouses and all.

I've nearly forgiven you for throwing out that starter-motor and giving away the bumper. The heat-exchangers will take a bit longer, to forgive. Do you know what they cost these days? Could you not have cleared out some files and folders instead? But I suppose it's a part of Grumpy Old Man syndrome.

You're going to be a classic but will you still cook for us please? Your calamari is flicking awesome. If you have the same gentle touch with the ladies, you'll be OK. Have you figured out that new mobile yet? Don't leave voicemails. I can't afford to pick them up but txt me please. Don't even try with the abbreviations. Xxx

From: historymacA@btinternet.com

From: historymacA@btinternet.com
To: annarichmac@hotmail.co.uk

You know that song Dick Gaughan sings – No gods and precious few heroes. Think it's by Brian MacNeil. We've both just lost another hero. Dickens – the one with heart and social conscience. Aye, up to a point. I've been reading about John Rae – the Orcadian explorer. He brought relics and accounts from the Arctic to London. These revealed the sad end of the Franklin expedition so there was no point in risking more lives in continuing the search. But the Inuit described a scene in full. It included a description of wide pans and boiled and charred bones – they weren't all animal ones.

The more sensitive details were confined to his report to the Admiralty. They didn't want to spend any more money on impossible rescue missions because the Crimean war was going to be expensive. So they made everything public.

That's why Lady Franklin brought Dickens into the war-by-correspondence. This was a slur on her missing husband and Rae had to be discredited. He was only a rough-spoken Orcadian anyway. Even if he was a doctor and a good shot he was not far from a native himself. There are physical objects as evidence but most of the knowledge is from people's accounts. Rae had respect for his informants and his translator. Dickens had his own views:

'We believe every savage to be in his heart covetous, treacherous and cruel; and we have yet to learn what knowledge the white man – lost, houseless, shipless, apparently forgotten by his race; plainly famine-stricken, weak, frozen, helpless and dying – has of the gentle-ness of the Eskimaux nature.'

Bloody hell, he'd have been ripe for Mosley, if he'd lived on.

But I'll get hold of *Great Expectations* all the same and look forward to it coming back this way again.

Your dinner is booked.

Love, your olman.

After a Storm

It might have been a room in someone else's house but it was home for me, for a time. Home is where someone holds your eyes and doesn't need to look away. And when there is that security there can be exploration and you don't have to go out into the hail to have adventures. When one or other, turn-about, just takes as much pleasure in finding what's giving pleasure. No-one keeping a score.

When you know most of a given territory intimately, then there's a different pleasure in returning to the familiar.

Mairi, it was as if desire was its own fuel. No matter how much I let go to it, you would just need to look at me, or cup my balls and it would build again. But even less of a hurry. Just letting your words wash over, the Gaelic and the English and the ripe, ripe swearing. You're the out-of-town alter-ego, and you've enough of the male to be a mate and you're sex on wheels.

There wasn't a shadow of the other mutual mate from Westview, not in that first bed. It was when it was time to get out of town, the problem was clear.

It made sense. It was your family house and set back from a fork of Loch Erisort. Not quite, up a creek. Everything including V-lining, painted in a grey-blue eggshell and bordered with the oiled beading of dense Oregon pine, reclaimed from the stripped interior of your own house. Remember he showed me it, your former paramour and joiner. All these hours of sifting and shifting and stripping paint from sufficient sound timbers to return some of the old to the renovated crofthouse.

That reinstatement of old parts of a house – it's seldom done by locals. It's more usual to let the old walls fall in and build the new beside it. So the blockwork gets coated in peely-wally Skye marble dash as new structures erupt from the heather by older layers of habitation. The new-build is probably on the site of the former outdoor chemical cludgie. And the rubble from the blackhouse is thrown in the found or else it becomes the basis for one of the outhouses.

I know it was your father and mother's house. I know the market is currently depressed after a brief boom and you'll probably never get back what was put into it. I even know that you probably have to live there. But I can't let go to you there. Even though I just have to catch the steady blue in your eyes, so close that I'm aware that the colour also has traces of maroon and indigo. A really romantic Lewisman would say you had eyes with the hues of herring scales.

But I'm still not going down to Garyvard. Even if it does now have a nearly passable internet connection you can just about legally term broadband.

Every bastard I know would say it was a matter of time before it fell apart for you two. When Kenny F hits it, he hits it. But Kenny told me what broke him and what tore your relationship apart, long before you did. It's like any other history now. There's no way of knowing how it would have turned out.

Please know that our year together is replayed in my daft brain so often that it's like there's a tape inside my head between my ears. Do you remember, love, that line in the soulful ska rhythm of Mister Desmond Dekker. This weird memory of mine again. This is what sticks.

After a storm there must be a calm
You catch me in your arm, you sound your alarm
Poor me Israelites

Fucking impressive. That's a cove who knows where he's coming from. He knows his grammar. It's got its own structure and he's cool with it and if any other bastard ain't, it's their own tough shit. But I don't mind it being your home territory. Believe me, I'm clued up on the balancing act of looking after the domestic front and earning the money to finance it all.

But the cove who did the digging and the demolishing and the salvaging and the bringing together of something more than a shelter on your family croft, happens to be the cove I prayed with, over porridge with treacle, in Westview Terrace.

That's a guy who knows he's got to stay in London town. For now. There are warnings. He was home for the funeral. One of our gang. Don't think you knew him. Kenny and me talked about menfolk and about mothers. Sipping tea and scoffing salmon rolls in the County when we came back from Sandwick. You lost your own mother too, not so long ago. Maybe that was more difficult for you because you were so close to your father. You'd be bound to feel guilty about not knowing her so well. I got to know the olaid better after the olman just dropped.

I called by once, to see Kenny's mother. She kept asking what I was up to. I suppose next time I see the cove, we'll be burying her.

She knew I'd split up with Gabriele and all that. She's compos flicking mentis all right and a bit more. She still didn't see why her own son left that girl from Lochs, the one with the steady job. 'A bit wild all right but so are we all. Well maybe not me,' she said, 'but you boys still are anyway. Daft with it. You don't know when you're well off.'

She said Kenny was working at a Citizens Advice Centre in Brixton. You could say he was well placed. He must have experienced a lot of the issues.

I'm lusting after your way of speaking, Mairi, and I'm desiring the friendship of your body next to mine. You haven't put on an ounce. You probably never will. And I never really noticed you'd caught up a bit, in height, till you were wearing the jacket, tailored for me. But I like you too much to ask you to do things like making plans. Maybe you've got to stay with that house in that place. And I've this strong feeling in my bones that it will need to be a cove from away, that stays in it with you. May I say that I think you've made an excellent choice of vessel. I was very happy to inspect the machinery aboard it, with no guarantee and at your own risk, of course. But I'd be surprised if you had much serious bother with that installation. A clinker crabber by McCaughey of Wick is built for working the Pentland Firth so it should look after you in the North Minch. That red Mermaid aboard is a marinised Ford and the spares are easy to get hold of. There's an electric start and a heat exchanger so the sea-water cooling won't come in direct contact with the aluminium parts in the engine block. It all looks clean and well cared for. The oil's been changed recently.

She's a beauty and a total bargain. If the famous personal advertisements ask for a picture of your own boat, you should do very well for admirers. You've even got the old Rana boat for a tender.

Logic is pointless. I know that there are formulae for deciding the value of a partner's work and compensation for the opportunities lost while you're slaving away at house renovations. Things that are negotiated in proper Settlements when one person doesn't just admit quite suddenly that he's got to get out. I know the need to stride away from all that aforementioned V-lining. Because emotion has entered between the very tongues and grooves.

And it wouldn't do any good at all, presenting your ex-partner with a wad of digital cash as an acknowledgement of the labour he put into your project.

I've come up in the world again. Sold the olaid's house and bought one right back where I started. Between the County Hotel and the Free Kirk. And there's a low-roofed room at the top where a pile of papers and printouts is building up. But I've a feeling right in my weakening bones, that you won't be able to cross this worn threshold, unless I can accept that history really is the past and it doesn't matter who nailed planks on a wall.

But I don't think that way.

Bits of wood have their own history. Some of that's connected to a guy we're both linked to. Remember, his uncle taught me the marks. Old Angus with the sellotaped glasses. Far-seeing Angus. I've learned something.

There are all too many camps of detention on this planet right now but let's go back to 1945. This one was not designed as a death-factory. None of the camps within Germany's pre-war boundaries were, though executions took place. The most efficient death camps were all in the occupied lands. Work camps were pretty good at that too, the ration calculated to keep the captives going for a few months till they dropped. Plenty more to take their place. Death by starvation and disease was a by-product of the concentration camp, not the main purpose. Two men who knew each other, both private soldiers, stood at the entrance to Bergen-Belsen. I've heard it said, but not from either of them, that the stench put the fear into you even before you saw what you saw.

These men had come a long way from their communities of crofts, on either side of Loch Erisort. I don't know if they made their own pact together or if each came to the decision on his own. There were some things you wouldn't talk about. Angus was one of them. And my uncle Ruaraidh was the other. My father's own experience was different but he never talked about it either. At least, not to me. Your father kept his silence, too.

Ruaraidh never told me he'd helped to liberate Belsen. Angus never told Kenny, or me, what he did in the war. It took a bit of research to find this out. I know that fact now. But there's no way I'm able to imagine what went through their minds when the gate was opened.

Stoves 2 (verses 1 to 3)

In the beginning there was the Modern Mistress. In the rural areas these became dominant. The stove-pipe would be held by a score of cubits of cement and would project through roofs. And the construction of the roof would vary according to the materials available at the time of construction, or according to regulations relating to dimensions and spacings at the allotted time. And the materials of the roof skin would vary from the quarried slate of Ballachulish or Easdale to the Eternit branded tiles which no longer contained an element of asbestos, as was the practice in former times.

But, for those who ventured further out from the environs of the burgh, passing over many cattlegrids, there were to be found ranges and boilers designed to run on any solid fuel. And peat was sufficient unto the needs of the Rayburn. But not of the Aga which was installed only in the stately houses of those who could deliver silver to the merchants in return for fuel. Some of these appliances could be adapted to run on heating oil which, in the latter days, was supplied free of Value Added Tax. As was the solid fuel equivalent. The cost of peat was an annual permit, which was cheap and your own labour, which was not.

But the German process, carried out in the vicinity of the city of Essen, which burned off slag and left potent nuggets, provided in these times the potency and longevity necessary to maintain the temperature in cast iron whilst their owners and benefactors were at lawful occupations. Or at recognised institutions of education.

And this was named Anthracite and Extracite and Taybrite. And these fuels were supplied in sealed plastic bags in units of kilograms measured out on scales of approved make and type. And these would be inspected at regular intervals according to prescriptions laid down by local authorities. According to the guidelines also writ large by national authorities.

And merchants of the name of Ossian and MacIver thrived and prospered.

And the populations housed in Nicolson Road, in Morrison Avenue, in Stirling Square, these also thrived. Many went forth from there into the wider worlds of merchant navies, of hospitals, of hotel kitchens. And back out across the numberless cattlegrids, the rural populations also thrived. But the nature of the thriving, far from the city of Stornoway, varied according to a host of conditions. The furlongs of distance, out from the metropolis, being a major factor. As was war and rumour of war in the eastern extremities of the continent of Europe and in the maritime environs collectively known as the Middle East.

So every time the oil price went up you'd get a big rush for peat-permits.

Ranges and Agas, not so hot on peat, would be available for fifty quid a throw in the two-minute silence (*Stornoway Gazette*). And conversion kits for Rayburns would be available again, a grate and a riddle, for those who couldn't remember which box they'd hidden the bits in, when the oil wick was installed after the last crises was over.

Thus the history of the late twentieth century, with particular relevance to the price of a barrel of oil, from under the desert or under the sea, could be accurately plotted by careful scrutiny of adverts for stoves in the *SY Gazette*. Sorry, OK, perhaps with cross-reference to the *West Highland Free Press*.

I didn't move down to Garyvard. It was too big a step for a cove from town. Too big a one for me anyway and I think you know why. I couldn't live in the house we'd done up for my olaid either, though that would have made more sense. It was in our joint names but Gabriele signed over her half-share on condition that I signed over everything at Number One Coastguard Cottages to her. That included the garage-library combo.

There was a chance of a place on Kenneth Street so I did the quick-sale thing rather than hold out till I found someone with a similar set of requirements to the olaid. The buyers probably ripped out half the alterations.

But I'm now strolling distance from the hoil and the wee Co-op. The arts centre is two minutes along the road so the movies are back in town. I might not be the only one with a desire to move back to the street I was born on. Well, I wasn't born on the street but in a flat in a house on Kenneth Street. And I returned there.

Stornoway has the architectural integrity of the average Scottish cemetery. Dead centre of the town as they say. There are no planning requirements to install memorials which will chime with the proportions or visible finish of the neighbouring one. Therefore there is considerable interest in strolling to study the erections we've left behind. Down in Sandwick, you'll find tall marble pieces with draped urns. Compact black granite slabs with a pleasing half-moon curve at the top and a gold anchor or rose. Root further back and there are horizontal slabs of slate, fenced with resilient wrought ironwork.

There's also a few jumps in the skyline of Kenneth Street. The jail is quite classy now, with sympathetic larch or cedar cladding, left to weather. There's plenty of glass but of course you don't get to see the guys behind bars. It's the upper storeys which have transparency. Like when the cannabis plants, kept as evidence in the cop shop, were lovingly nurtured by some cleaner and you could see how much they flourished and sprouted day by day as you passed them by. But you don't get any hint of the guys in the cooler for a night.

The sergeant's house is no longer that but it's still there, a block along, after the intersection with the steep Church Street. It's pebble-dashed, like a lot of the council houses. Then there's the big car park and the big Free Church and the hall where you give blood. Next there's a run of houses, stone under rendering. There's a potted history of late twentieth century window design, with particular attention to long dormers in the roof.

But then there's one house with proportions which look fair and original. Two sweet storm-windows ascend from a simple but elegant roof of native Scottish slate. The nails are probably sick, of course, because few people think of fixing slates with copper clouts, which will last longer than the zinc-coated clouts which will rust before the slate has been worn down visibly by hail and frost and the gusts that sweep and probe all of our roofs.

The profusion of chimney pots is a clue to the histories of shared occupancies of this town house. It would have been a merchant's home, with its own community of offspring, aged relatives and servants. But when I viewed the interior of the house, there was a gas fire that looked cold, surrounded by a matt aluminium sheen installed at level two.

As the *cailleach* who sold sailors the string with the three knots of wind said, you men are never happy. You'll be wanting more breeze so you can untie the second one. You'll get as much breeze as you can take. But don't dare even look at the third. So you know right then they'll let the third knot go and they'll end up back where they started.

And I'm saying, I hanker after a real flame and the top floor could take it. You can't live with a fire that looks cold. And these days you can't just install gas or solid fuel stoves without reference to the rulebooks. I thought of developing a hidey hole, warm and illuminated by natural light through the sweetest windows, thinking of Anna, installed here for visits, with a developing library all to herself when she'd come here for an overnighter. Though she hasn't managed it yet.

But when I'd broken into the painted boarding that covered the fireplace and excavated the wide aperture in the stonework, I encountered a problem. After crawling my way upward, like the early Victorian chimney-sweep before the enlightened Mr Kingsley's fictional discourse, I found a mess of plastic bags and loose rockwool and any shite that would stop cement from falling further. When I approached the problem from the opposing angle, and got up on the roof to install the new ceramic can, I found the gas vent went through the only viable chimney. I'd been in a similar situation once before.

The small incident is of course a reminder of the main lesson of history. Are you ready for it? All I've learned. We take a bloody long time to learn from the past and then we have to re-learn it all again. Chimneys. Builders. Things are not always what they seem.

SY, my friends, is clearly not the environment for Smith and Wellstood stoves, of oatmeal hue, running on peat. But it is pretty damn good for kitchen-ceilidhs. We're only one street back from the seafront. After this morning I'm an honorary member of the International Fishwives Gossip Brigade. This distinguished unit didn't in fact fight in Spain prior to '39 but we certainly discussed it. And the present situation in the Congo did come up, along with a feasibility study into the installation of a woodburning solid-fuel appliance.

So the retirement plan, if I could ever afford it, could be strolling round the hoil to pick up stray driftwood. I could build little stashes so it would get a fresh-ish water rainfall to take the salt out until the arrival of an easterly wind to dry it. And a flame is better than a telly. When it's under control. The flame, I mean. The telly never is.

And probably won't be, ever again. Unless there's a return to the Westview (SY) and the West Road (FR) tradition of folk gathering in the same room, to watch the big game or the fight. Kitchens and living rooms all had flexible walls in those days. There was no limit to the number of folk you could squeeze in. I don't think many modern homes have these, now.

But I'll tell you what this town house does have. You don't clock it from the outside, unless you've a strong neck. Let's return to the fine detailing of the elegant storm windows. You don't want to present too wide a span of glass to the SY elements. But there's more to the design than a series of small panes. Above them there's a hook, embedded into the stonework, anchored so that at the time of fixing there could be no doubt as to its strength.

The double bank of interlocking windows was at one time capable of opening right out to leave a surprising span of space. So that would be for hoisting in sails or nets for repair, in joined attics, over the domestic areas. Possibly. But it would also provide for an exit as well as an entrance. And for a situation more likely than a fire.

You see, the stairway up to this level was so tight in the turns that it would be difficult to transport certain items up and down it. Things you could bend or squeeze would be all right. But not long after you're dead, you'll be stiff. So that hook is to hang your coffin on. So now there's a chance that it would be quite practical for me to die on Kenneth Street, at a (hopefully) decent interval from being born on it. Or, more accurately, to die inside a particular house on Kenneth St.

From: annarichmac@hotmail.co.uk
To: historymacA@btinternet.com

Dear Da

This is another letter. I'm typing this one too and I'm going to e-mail it. But it's a letter just the same.

I've seen it. *Culloden*. Peter Watkins – the guy who made *The War Games* for the BBC. Then they banned it. That's the one, isn't it? You told me you saw *Culloden* when it first came out. When the clansmen and the black and white redcoats talk straight to the mike and answer the questions. When did you last eat? What do you own?

I saw it in Film Studies, the week after *Ashes and Diamonds*. I can see why they programmed them that way, two war films, a documentary and a fiction. I thought *Culloden* is also like fiction. It's not just that the events seem impossible, so crazy. It's the way it's made. The film-maker comes in from above, the omnipotent author guy, just like the nineteeth century novelist. And I might have heard you argue some-thing like that yourself, with three glasses of vino down you. Tolstoy says more about the 1812 campaign when he's telling a story – lies, if you like.

But *Culloden* is a flicking amazing film. Glad I went, though I was wiping the eyes. Very girly. But some of the guys were sniffing too, on the way out.

Next week, it's Bill Douglas. You should be doing this course. Remember I watched one of the trilogy with you. Heavy going but the both of us glued to it. Did you ever see *Comrades*? It comes later, on the bill. His big movie. I know you're skint but why don't you get the bus down. It's about the Tolpuddle martyrs. But it's not a documentary. It came out at the wrong time and it's pretty long. My lecturer says it's really worth watching. I'm definitely going for it.

So it's been a thoughtful week, Da. And I think I know what I want to do. After Uni. And it's not a flicking PhD. Not an MLitt neither. And I'm not winding you up when I say I know you'd come up with a dozen great topics.

It's teaching, Da. But don't think it's English. Even at Uni there's a lot of getting fed with spoons. The students who do best – they spot the questions, read the lecturer's books and just come up with a small variation. I could teach people how to do that but I'm not going to do it myself so be warned, the degree will be mediocre. Not mikalor or however you write it – not miserable like a puddle of drizzle – just medium.

I know you think I'm spending too much time on the water but that's where I'm coming from. Oops, yes, I know we've all come from a womb. I can hear your interruptions before you say them.

I want to teach kayaking. I've been doing it at the club, after freshers' week. Taking the baby paddlers. It's amazing. You watch them achieve something they couldn't manage at the start of the lesson. It's just something I can do, help people to get a skill they might never get, on their own. That's it. After four years of studying criticism, I know I'm not that into theory.

It's another year at Uni – the postgrad, Outdoor ed. A fair bit of crap, of course. Big chunks of serious Scandinavian meditations saying obvious things about the great outdoors. Just about as boring as some of these old Bergman films you persuaded me to watch with you. Summer with Monika was OK. But I'll have a good qualification. Don't worry, I won't need any more cash from you – I know you're pretty stretched. A girl can see the signs. It's in Edinburgh, which helps. Mum's doing OK. Her job's come through the cuts. Plenty Eastern European folk in SY needing a hand with their English. Know you

don't see that much of her – cos you're cooking on gas for a crust –
but she's sailing again. Regular crew for a cove with a cruising yacht.
They're talking about Norway. She's cut her hair short and she's
looking pretty cool.

My own paddling is coming on. I don't do much at sea, these days.
We keep tabs on rainfall and river levels all week then go chasing
new runs.

Things are all good with me, Da. Only wee thing is Les is kind of slow
in coming round to the idea of another year in the UK. The van is
purring and he's hungry for the off. Even the Scottish rivers don't do
it for him. He's a man with a surfboard and he needs to use it. He's
talking about Ireland. I'm saying, what's one more year? And what
about Barvas beach and the Valtos break. We could be back and fore.
I can get work at home out of term-time. He's twitchy and getting
grumpy as hell. I think he might be for offski anyway. Maybe he'll be
back for me. The VW chariot carrying me home.

Have you joined the Sportscentre yet? I suspect you've not got round
to it and I'm going to nag you. Daughter's prerogative. Swimming's
the way. Stress in the kitchen and home to sitting on your behind
watching videos of old movies. It's a lifestyle but. The white thatch
suits you. Don't cut it short. The headband is groovy. Keep it on, out
of the kitchen.

Any chance of that monkfish with the red onion marmalade, when
I'm back on the rock?

Take care of yourself,

xxx

The Dream

Remember I gave you a bit of the history of the pram. Here's a bit of an update.

The pram is now outside the workshop on Leverhulme Drive. Why is it not inside the workshop designed for the purpose of protecting vehicles (of land or sea) from the assaults of weather? Other people had other priorities for covered storage. It was a bit of a mistake to build that structure on land you were going to leave. But I had not yet admitted that there was a need to leave, not even to myself.

All the seams are now epoxy-taped, to strengthen ageing joints. The plan is to put lighter, whitewood thwarts in place – well, bits of a staircase to be precise. We don't have an America's Cup budget. I don't really have any budget. The outside of the pram's been painted already, to protect the epoxy which, though a miraculous material, is subject to UV degradation, if not coated. The hull is no longer black but another shade of blue. Looking at the inside, I'm fair tempted to go back to black and signal red.

But the frost got into the transom, last winter. That's the board which forms the back of this boat, a vital part of the structure. So the pram built by the co-operative of two Lochies is in a critical condition. It's borderline. She's a life and death case but the operating theatre is still occupied with other people's projects. If I could step back a few yards I could tell you she's dying gracefully, fading into the grass. But a certain builder thought that, of a certain Type 2 VW, which lived to go 'put-put' again. For a time.

Shit, boats. What are they like? Stories are just as bad. Tangents are the main issue of West-Coast storytelling. This is like we're standing at the door. We're up from the table. The yarns ain't over yet and we're standing at the gate outside. It's a fair night. It's time for the purpose of the visit. You never hear it till folk are just about at the gate.

Now I need to describe a dream. Not last night but the night before. No, none of that, foot in the rope stuff. A weight falling through water and a line rasping out behind it, as far as its length can go. That's a waking dream. So it should be. This was different. I woke up sweating. I have to tell you why.

The dream is, I'm on Isle of Skye. The neighbouring island has got a few decent hills, it's got be said. And a couple of impressive sections of spate river. I'm casting a fly. Maybe that's why I'm there. The adrenalin surges when you see a fin in the water. Just like when you lean back and brace with your boots against the cliff, trusting the rope. There's tension involved. But now it's a rod and line, cutting through the water and a shape you can't see powers up below the surface. It's so strong it's got to be a salmon.

But it's the Norwegian pram that comes up from the vortex under the fall. With her trim in signal red again. How could she be under the water? But the transom – the back bit – is missing. Just gone. Nothing makes sense. How she got across the North or the Little Minch. How she got up a river. How she's back to the pale blue that's close to silver, under the black water.

A boat has a pattern, whether it's built from plans or not. It's got to be symmetrical at least, for fuck's sake. But I don't see any pattern to this story. Why she should come up in my dreams, with her stern ripped apart. It's more like a story my mother once wrote down. A Land Girl following a memory of the loom of a lighthouse.

I'm awake and shaking and just about to get into the van. I want to get up the road and make sure she's still settled into the grass, by the workshop. Not a smart idea. That would go down really well. Arriving in the middle of the night at the building I've signed over, with everything else. So my wife will agree to transfer her half-share of the olaid's house, to me. So I can buy another roof, a few more streets away. No-one is going to give me a mortgage on the strength of my business record or my cooking abilities. Slightly better chance on the second of these.

There's something else behind the dream of the pram in the limbo of turbulence. It's another story. I heard it from one of the cleaners at Uig School in north Skye, from the grannie of one of the pupils. Not yesterday. A Coastguard liaison visit. Some guy had the crazy idea that there could be a bit more dialogue between staff on different Scottish islands.

So here is the story, the way I remember it told to me. In the interest of historical accuracy, I did some research in Portree Library and found a contemporary account of the same incident. I photocopied that and you can find it somewhere amongst these papers, as a comparison. But this is the way I remember one woman telling it.

In the 1870s there was a big flood in Uig. It had been a dry year from the start. Then, late autumn, all down the north coast, the rain fell and fell and there was no stopping it. Portree Square was flooded. Everything was.

Up the hill from Uig, the two burns were rising – the Rha and the Conon. There was a graveyard there, near the Conon, above the bridge. It was flooded too, of course but not just under a shallow covering of water. The drive of the flood took the turfs off and boulders and soil were tumbled with it. Soon the coffins were disturbed. Some were driven against the stones and splintered. The recent ones floated and these were carried below, on the torrent.

Well, the two burns joined up, right behind the bridge, making a loch where there wasn't one before. The last man who got across safe and sound, well, he was a relative of ours and he went on to become a missionary, so maybe there was a reason he was spared. I think he went to the Andes. They called him 'the man of the mountains' when he came back to Skye.

Anyway, there was a proper stone house down where the wood is now. The factor lived there. He was the one who collected the rents. He'd been none too kind about it, either. But still they warned him to leave. His house was on an island, between the lines of the burns. But he wouldn't budge while he had the chance. He'd weathered worse, he said.

When the bridge broke, the weight of the two waters swept down, bursting through the factor's back door and out the front. That man who'd caused so much misery was swept out of his own house to meet his end. Some say that the coffins from up the hill went floating through his house with him. This was the home of the man who was partly to blame for putting folk to rest there, a while before their time.

Turbulence

These boats are toys. Reds, blues, purple and green. Mixes. Marbles. Spots. There are trailers with stacks of them but mostly they come in pairs or threes, a family, huddled on the roof rack. Don't think kayaks. Sea kayaks are long. The length and sleekness give you speed. Guys have crossed to Flannans, Kilda, Sula Sgeir, North Rona. They make them from all kinds of composites these days, resins and strands of lightweight matting. Same kind of principle as the skin stretched over a delicate lattice of bone or bleached wood. Strong as hell.

They say an Inuit paddler arrived in Aberdeen around 1720 but died shortly afterwards. There is indeed a fine example of an Inuit kayak in Marischal College and it can of course be accurately dated. But the story of its acquisition needs careful scrutiny. There are records of Dutch whalers landing Inuit people and vessels, captured alive along with the dead whales. I don't think you can say that the documentation proves that anyone paddled all the way from Greenland to Aberdeen.

I couldn't tell you the difference between surf boats and river boats. I know they're both short so they can spin in a tight space. They look squat, maybe for buoyancy so they should come back up when the turbulence just drives them down. Anna does both. Surf and rivers. Mostly rivers these days. She told me about this meet. A memorial. Surfers, climbers, paddlers all do that. Folk remember someone killed on the mountain, or in the water, by gathering in mass.

I think most people believe in remembering.

I hadn't clocked it was Invermoriston. Great Glen. Not consciously, anyway. I was just driving the same way. Working in Argyll. The obvious way to go. I pulled in right away. My car looked conspicuous without a roof rack. I was maybe intruding. But folk were still arriving. Stalls were set up. I had a look around for the old Peugeot estate I'd given over to Anna. No sign of it.

I walked down to where other cars and vans were parked. More were arriving, all the time. It was a big event. I sent a text. She would be driving. This was definitely the place. But she'd been down in the dumps, last time we'd talked on the phone. The boyfriend had told her he wanted some time apart to think things out. So maybe she didn't have the stomach. No, all the more reason she'd be here. The alternative family. The community of river boats.

I thought of getting coffee. Waiting. There wasn't a ferry to catch tonight. But I did have a rendezvous to make. The scenery should have been in black and white. Ealing era. A meeting in Ardnamurchan at the Strontian crossroads. Mairi was coming back from Mull. She was getting a fair bit of work now. Helping folk who worked from home in areas where the broadband was slow or iffy. I didn't have a job to do. The trouble with independent boat-builders is they're usually very creative so they install the engines, themselves.

But the weather had been decent and tourists were prolific. The pound was low in Europe. Ferry fares were down, with Road Equivalent Tariff for the islands – the ones with falling populations, anyway. Orkney and Shetland didn't qualify. Nothing to do with the way they voted.

I'd done a good few shifts on the pans and had the ferry fare for the 205. We could meet up and stay with mates of hers. It might be easier than when we were on the Island.

So I'd to get to the crossroads by a definite time. And right here now, I could be intruding. The text was enough. Just so Anna would know I was thinking of her. Doesn't matter what you say. I wanted her to know I'd thought of her. Simple as that.

It was sun after rain. Pretty ideal for these guys – or maybe they needed a week of torrents for some of the runs.

I got that chill again. The lazy wind, as my olman called it. Goes

right through you. Can't be bothered to go round you. The subma-
riner's gansey wouldn't help. It was in the car, picked up in a classy
thrift shop in Inverness. A fiver's worth of ex-Admiralty contract.
The big chill's worse when you're close to lively groups. Worst of all
when you're living next door to the action. You're a step aside. Cars
dropping folk off. Chinks of supermarket bags with bottles of beer
and wine and gin.

But I was off the Island and still feeling that chill in the marrow.
Movement helps. I got back in the car.

The flashing and siren registered just after I pulled out. I indi-
cated and pulled back in, to let the ambulance get ahead. The car
in front did the same. The way was clear now for the emergency
services, speeding down the road. That was the punch in the gut. I
was winded. As sure as if I'd just been driven against a submerged
bridge by a mountain torrent.

It was a fine day. Just into September. All these paddlers, a
UK-wide community, they were gathering here like Jacobites. Bit
more tasteful though. Thousands of tourists were still going up and
down the road. But that's what being a parent is. First you think of
your own. A red Peugeot estate with the front crumpled in. Then
you think, whoever it is, it's someone's family. But that's the second
thought.

You'd think, after the experience we'd shared, that water should
have been something for her to fill the kettle with. But she went
from sea kayaking to rivers. Then the specialised stuff. Studying
the rainfall, the snowmelt. Reading the gradients on the OS map.
Looking for trickles that you could paddle in a spate. She has a
talent for reading what's under a weight of water. She's good at
sensing the obstructions.

Sure she knows there's risks. But that's not a simple equation.
There's risks in everything you do and don't do. The minibus went
over on the way to a river. No-one was hurt.

It wasn't *her* car in the road accident, that day of the commem-
oration. The incident that got me started on all this. I don't know
the story behind the flashing lights, that day. But they would have
affected someone else's family.

Ceramics

It's explosive. There might not be a lot of mass. Velocity neither. But it's enough. So when a ceramic object falls four feet or so from a kitchen worktop and hits the stone floor, it will shatter. There might be large bits, might be small. Usually it's a mixture so you have to get the hoover out, whether the floor is ready for the annual dusting or no. But just for a minute you're looking at a bit of your life, distributed all around the floor.

This morning it was the teapot. This also left a small, damp heap of soaked lapsang-souchong leaves. No smoky smell because you've already imbibed that. As my housemate's mate said, Laphroaig tea. It's the residue. The damp dross. My spliced three-strand rope handle is, of course, intact. That was a repair made about twenty-odd years ago. The lid, a darker and less matt clay than the rest, because the original lid took a dive some time back – that's whole except for a chip. So it could be worth putting aside. But the terracotta unglazed clay pot has been in every address since the student days. It was in the cold Torrey flat and the room above the Brig o' Cowie.

It was in constant service because I didn't drink alcohol in them thar days, Jim lad. I was intoxicated by rhetoric. But there was the possibility of calm in the spaces between words.

The Edi Thompson bowl was very good for drinking tea. It was a comfortable shape in the hand. It had an unglazed ribbed line and then the smooth area went from something between Harris agate to Ross of Mull granite, maroons to pinks. It's possible I might have sipped a dram from it too because it seemed I no longer needed to look for the rest of any bottle that was open. It took a good few sips to acquire a taste for malt whisky. I'd been reared on black rum, the sea angler's preference, as the spirit of choice before I stopped drinking at the age of seventeen. In those days the choice of rums outnumbered the whiskies on the gantry in the Criterion Bar.

After the Parkinson's set in, Edi was not going to be making more pots. So it became precious. I stopped drinking out of it and that's when my bowl took the plunge as my sleeve caught it on its shelf. Edi was a librarian at a music college. He was deaf and a very good pianist. He was a keen climber and settled in Harris because of the hills that go straight up from sea-level. The ones that have no intrinsic landscape value, as quoted by the landscape consultant employed by the multinational company which wanted to develop the superquarry by wiping out a mountain. Would that have been a death? If the constituent rock had been shifted in ships to be laid as the foundation for new highways? Or simply a transfiguration.

Edi was gay and once wrote a brave letter to the *Stornoway Gazette*. As my own sister did but his was more of a direct statement, arguing against intolerance. He's under the ground on the west side of Harris now. You can't bury anyone on the east side. Not deep enough. Not without blasting equipment. They call the east side road the Golden Road because it cost so much to explode its snaking route from the gneiss. The 'golden grave' has a ring to it. Instead, they have the funeral path, east to west Harris. Each cairn is a dram-stop. There's quite a lot of them.

It might have been after that breakage, I housed Mairi Bhan's two raku pots in respective deep alcoves. They might be out of reach of glancing scuffs from elbows. Neither of them has a function. They both have a shape but you couldn't say what it is. I mean, not the way you could say a buoy is cylindrical or its top-mark is a can or a cone. I put some gnarled twigs in one for a while but I took them out again. The pots are what they are. They are their own stories. I love them. I don't mean I like them.

The daughter won a fine bit of stoneware made by the Island pottery with the longest standing. It used to be Stornoway Pottery though it was out in Benside, Laxdale, from 1974. Now it's Borve pottery and it is made in Borgh (same name). The West Side Borve, on the road to Ness, not the Harris one. It was a sailing prize and she won it with her pal in the plastic dinghy. I should be able to tell you the type. But I can't. Anyway, that piece of artisan's porcelain took a dive too. I wasn't responsible. I only visit the Leverhulme Drive abode by prior arrangement. But I saw it was in bits, set aside for a repair job that would never happen.

Now the amazing thing is that I won a very similar stoneware plate by Borve Pottery in a sea-angling competition. It was an accident and I'm a bit ashamed of it. I gave up competition fishing about the time the old king died. But there was not a scale to be seen on the east side so the cheapest way of getting out to feed a portion of Kenneth Street was to renew the membership for the Danglers. I didn't know it was a competition. I was thinking of dabs for the neighbours, a ling for the *cailleach* along the road, a haddock for the ex, a *cnòdan* for myself. I just knew it as the word for the fish. I didn't know it was Gaelic. I didn't know if it had any accents or not. I had to look it up. I already knew that *bodach ruadh* were red codling so I knew *cnòdan ruadh* was the red gurnard. Anyway, you get points for catching different species of fish, these days. I scored, big time.

Anna broke her collarbone. Outdoor pursuits. I went to visit her and took the plate in the packaging it came in. A replacement for her shattered trophy. I didn't have space for it anyway. Very bonny packaging. Aye but not plastic, not rainproof. Nothing's Lewis rainproof anyway. I didn't realise the bag was getting soaked. The bag with the plate and, of course, dark chocolates on top, grapes and all. It parted and that mass and velocity thing happened. I picked up the sodden base and wrapped it up with the rest of the debris. I couldn't just leave the sharp bits on the pavement. And I didn't find a bin and some sisters could be strict about visiting times, at least they were in the olden days and that probably hadn't changed, so I kept on going and found myself explaining to Anna why I was carrying in a sodden bag of shards.

I said sorry I'd forgotten the Araldite because it was a kit, a puzzle really, to keep her occupied for an hour or two. That seemed to hit Anna's fairly individual sense of humour. The daughter said it was exceflickinglenté but that maybe needs a note which is coming now:

(NB SY grammatical structure: the breaking of the conventional word with expletive insertion in its polite form, followed by a pan-European echo of French or Hispanic connotation – a nod to our neighbours down the searoad – as long as you work the tides – if you don't you're not going to get there, Bilbao or Vigo. Unless you've got a Kubota under your deck.)

So that's really it then, the deaths of pots. I never did own a Bernard Leach one. He was a Bahá'í. I know a lot of kind and wide-looking people who are or were. He learned about the Faith through an artist called Mark Tobey. An abstract expressionist, who made white-line paintings, a bit like calligraphy in Arabic but out of conscious control. Leach wrote a modest book called *Drawings, Verse and Belief.* I returned to it often. He worked with Shoji Hamada. The Japanese master did the raku with a proper fire. But the blowlamp and oildrum method is quite in keeping with Island historical traditions of using what's left lying around. I might have told you, that's how Mairi made them, in a workshop at the school.

I've got the house to myself again. There's a lot of space for one guy but not when it fills with files and books.

Plagues

We're all conversant with the device of a flashback by now. You've been to the movies even if you haven't been daft enough to trip out on LSD. So let's go back to Keitel's memoirs, written at speed when he knew his days were numbered. I found myself returning again and again to that period – the closing stages of World War Two. A lot of the killing happened near the end. I thought of two friends, Ruaraidh and Aonghas, Roddy and Angus. I did go to visit Angus once, in the sheltered housing. But he'd been moved to that place on the outskirts, just back from Broad Bay. A suburb that used to be one cattle-grid out. I was warned he wouldn't recognise anyone. He needed total care. Instead of going there to read to myself and to be able to say I'd done it, I kept going round to the library or downloading pdfs.

Hitler's Field Marshal mentions the plague. Not by name and not in detail but he refers to a conference when the *Führer* was looking closely at a research programme into biological warfare. Keitel seemed to have found this way of prefixing his orders with a protective introductory phrase, when he was troubled by the suspicion of a moral scruple. 'With extreme reluctance, the *Führer* has felt it necessary to…' sort of thing. As a former civil servant of Her Majesty I recognise a technique which was known as 'covering your arse' in the trade.

Flash-forward again and the evidence is overwhelming. Saddam Hussein was using chemical warfare against the troublesome Kurdish minority. That would be his administration's version of 'special treatment'. The dates tell us that this was weel kent many years before he became an official tyrant. When an alliance between the USA and UK administrations gelled to the point of mutual support (and indeed admiration), this history seemed to gain a sudden topical relevance. The question of the presentation of evidence that weapons of mass destruction, held in Iraq, amounted to a significant threat to the rest of the world, is outwith the remit of this personal diary. For now.

Strange thing though, that Robin Cook, then Foreign Secretary, could see clearly enough to tender his resignation. Unlike Field Marshal Keitel, who felt that such an act would be dishonourable, at a time of national crisis. Instead, he remained in command and made his weak protestations.

Of course Anthrax Island will be in your own ken. Britain's wartime experiments in germ warfare were filmed in that early technicolour that's got its retro atmosphere. A special flock of sheep was taken to Gruinard and observed, as the anthrax bombs were delivered. You can see the beasts fall and the carcasses being burned. So it was a successful experiment.

You can also see an attempt to tidy up. I think researchers were surprised that the spores in the soil were so persistent. Warning signs were kept in place until near the end of the twentieth century. There was a prohibition on landing on the island. It's remote enough anyway, of course. Yes, from London. It's under one mile from the nearest point on the west coast of Scotland.

Protesters placed containers with soil from Gruinard in prominent places, in the 1980s. Ministry of Defence personnel were sent to the island with protective clothing and enough formaldehyde to preserve shoals and shoals of sharks.

After further tests, the island was provisionally announced as safe. The Coastguard was informed that restrictions would be lifted. Next time a lobster-boat had machinery failure and it looked like the crew would drift on to Gruinard, I had no official reason, as a Coastguard Officer, to inform the MOD. But I thought I would anyway. This had been the procedure all my years in the Service. There was a bit of a flurry. 'I thought you guys said it was safe,' I said on the phone.

'Yes, safe for sheep,' a voice said.

But tests for safety to humans were incomplete. Unfortunately, these guys got their engine going again, otherwise the MOD might have got their test results, free of charge. Which is exactly what happened in a more recent British experiment in chemical warfare.

Now I'm taking it you're with me so far. No challenges on the story of Gruinard Island? But we're going to leave World War Two history behind and move straight into the Cold War – well I should say we'll move back in there because we've had an encounter or two already. From Melbost to Rügen.

It's 1952. The pertinent department wishes to conduct an experiment into the feasibility of spreading bubonic plague to an unspecified enemy. But this is clearly going to be a sensitive issue so a remote location is required. As Gruinard was still a prohibited area, due to continuing contamination, it was almost certainly considered. But from a scientific point of view, you clearly need to limit the factors under scrutiny to one at a time. The continuance of anthrax spores could complicate results. It could also pose some nuisance to personnel involved in the new experiment.

So caged monkeys and guinea pigs were set afloat on rafts in Broad Bay. (You may choose which is nearest to the human species, but please choose carefully and be willing to reconsider when you hear the full story.) Yes, that's the same Bay, to the north of the Eye Peninsula and touching on Stornoway Airport. It was a very productive haddock fishery at the time. Smoke floats were used as a means of letting loose the airborne plague so it would contaminate the rafts.

However, a Fleetwood-registered trawler ignored the warnings that special operations were being conducted in the area and steamed through the whole experiment. In one sense this was disappointing but in another way it was a blessing. Clandestine means were used to keep the vessel and its crew under surveillance. Her radio traffic was closely monitored. Luckily the crew went ashore, home in England, and mixed in general human society before they knew they were at risk of carrying the plague. This was the ideal situation to monitor the effectiveness of the airborne method of disseminating this form of organic warfare.

The crew fared very differently to the flock of sheep on Gruinard. There was no report of ill effects beyond the normal hangovers you might expect from the first night ashore, to wind-down, after a long voyage to the Hebrides. You'll have to make up your own mind about how far to trust your unreliable narrator, a figure common to the disciplines of both literature and history. Would I tell you any lies?

Anyway, it's not as simple as that. There's the matter of presentation. Let's move forward from the Cold War. Let's look at Iraq 2. Not the Kuwait reason for attacking a tyrant who was himself attacking that model of democracy. But the time when a logical case had to be made out for 'finishing the job' in response to terrible events in the city of New York. But the UK's involvement could not simply be seen as the inevitable result of a strategic alliance (cf causes of the First World War).

I don't know why HM Government could not have simply raised the issue of the treatment of the Kurdish minority. Maybe they were a bit too distant. Apart from the contrast in habitat, maybe they were in fact perceived to be a little too close to the Inuit savages dismissed by Charles Dickens as that bit less than equal.

Enormous pressure was brought to bear on certain individuals who had the duty to collate and present objective information on the likelihood of the Iraqi regime's possession of Weapons of Mass Destruction.

The information was not sufficient unto the needs of certain politicians. They required a proportion of bloody presentation with their pound of flesh. Leverage is applied by different methods. Different individuals have different capacities for resistance. Dr Kelly was the scientific adviser and therefore the key player. He was also a member of a religion which I happen to know holds human life sacred, in a similar way to Roman Catholics. But a member of the Bahá'í Faith appears to have taken his own life, under the enormous forces of conflicting duties, when instructed to put a bit more effort into the dramatic presentation of limited facts.

Lead-Line

I don't know what this collection of writings was meant to be. It's just happened. Made without any plan. So it might indeed be like boatbuilding by eye. But there's a big danger in that. The possible gain is fluency of line. The risk is that you come up with a shape that's not quite there yet. It only suggests what you should make next time. This is degenerating into a diary – a life story. That suggests there ain't gonna be no next time, to make it better. Building by eye – that takes a lot of tobacco. It's the standing back. You watch these guys at it. There's a lot of stepping aside and looking at the way the lines are developing. You're at a serious disadvantage if you don't smoke. The guys who don't, they're all big talkers. That's what gives them the space – but it's not as meditative as smoking tobacco.

This kind of diary's a good aid to thinking. Like taking time out to make a roll-up. Masking the tea. Do you use that phrase other places? I've heard an English colleague talk about letting the teabag mash. Up here, we let it brew, let it brew, speaking words of wisdom of course. A wee bit heat under the pot. Got to be a metal one. I don't like aluminium. I do like blue enamel. Well, it was blue, once upon a wenter. Hell, that's another word I've not heard for a while. Where did that one come from? Westview Terrace?

There's a difference between yarning and telling stories. The Old Testament is better on stories than rules to live by. Not everyone on Lewis would agree with me on that. But I think a parable is its own meaning. The word we use here is 'powerful'.

It doesn't have to be like anything else to work, the vineyards, the seeds, the stony ground. The stories carry you along. The images are not decorations. They're the meaning as well as the means of telling the story. There are layers. A good yarn also has layers. A story has its shims – moulds or templates. A yarn is a discovery. It's only after the words have come out, you know what you're getting at. The literary daughter's been keeping me posted, over the years. It was James Kelman for a while – the stories more than the novels. Did you know that his daughter is eligible to play for the Lochs football team? I liked a lot of these stories, a line getting unravelled.

Then there's that Carver guy. I got into some of them but I thought some others were a wee bit tight. Anna thought the sun shone out of his bachoochie. Last time I saw her, she brought me a page from the *Guardian*. Turns out it was this editor insisted on cutting and trimming Carver's stories. Getting them tighter. But the old Coastguard in me thinks in terms of losses as well as gains. I don't think tighter is always better. I liked that paperback with the black cover. Think the name was in red. Japanese writer. Anna brought me a thick novel too but I didn't get going on that. The Murakami cove. I've read the stories a few times. I go back to them. You're discovering something, along with the guy who wrote it.

Red and black. Funny thing is, that's what the kitchen was like just before she came. Like a trailer for the movie of the book of the stories.

I wanted to get the kitchen half-decent. And the downstairs bog. OK, the smell of parazone would make it obvious, this wasn't the normal thing. But even bohemian townies have got to maintain some social graces.

It took about a week to get sorted. You don't see how it builds up. I had the energy all right. Just needed a lot of sitting down. In between moves. The cooker and the pans were not too bad, to start with. I got most of the rest done but then I got sidetracked.

I wanted to hoover the floor. It's slate tiles. Maybe Spanish. I like this black floor. I just wipe the brush over it. But I opened the window and all that light showed up the crumbs and dust and fluff. So I opened the box. It's been in the hall cupboard for a while. Gabriele and the daughter had this wee conspiracy, the joint Christmas present. A couple of years ago. It was still in the cellophane.

I don't know how much the daughter chipped in but it was from the pair of them. A Dyson – no bags. I've been meaning to fire it up. The old wee hoover died, a while back. Only thing is there's no road wide enough for it left in the house. Where did all these books come from? You leave books and papers and discs behind you in a former address and you fill the new place up as the years whirr by. But you know the right answer to the question – amazon. co.uk. Will all our desired goods soon be shipped from three warehouses, each bigger than a football stadium? Better make that four – Northern Ireland will need its own and it all seems pretty much settled down for now. Who could have imagined that, in the 1980s?

A fellow called Colm Tóibín provided the reminder, lest we forget. There's accents in his name. He writes lies too – novels. Anna thinks a lot of them. I haven't read any of them but I did read his account of walking the border, posted to me by said daughter. *Bad Blood* shook me, even though I read it when it looked like the worst was over. One day, a van is stopped and the Ulster Defence guys pull out two Catholic guys and kill them. Might be a reprisal. Next day another van is stopped. The guys in the balaclavas ask if there's any Catholics in there. There's one amongst a dozen or so. The boys try to protect him. He's a good neighbour. But he's told to get out of the van and keep running while the rest are gunned down. It's the other side. Maybe it was Mandela's team showed the way, Truth and Reconciliation.

'You live twenty yards from the back of the library. Could you not just borrow the books? Or read then in there?' That's what the daughter said. 'No,' I said. 'It might be out of hours, when you need the link to the next piece of information.'

'The magic internet?'

'Aye, handy tool but I need the printed page to get right deep in there.' Photocopies and print-outs are good but they don't half mount up. As bad as books. So it's a bit like close-quarters pilotage, getting from one room to another, in here. A bit of a slalom course through the methodical piles of research material. Shove them all aside and I'd be in trouble. Lost, in fact. I admit it's a bit dusty and that's not so healthy.

So I had to get the kitchen-to-bog route sorted. A realistic objective in the available time. The dinner was easy.

Only thing was, I came across the old handline frame, loaded with thin red cordage and a sounding-lead. Mark 1 echo-sounder. Very low on battery usage. Anna was beginning to see the light. She's been giving the *Peace and Plenty* a run when there's no breeze for sailing. She came back with a lythe and a couple of *cnòdan*. She was talking about a sounder, to spot the reefs when the drizzle's obscuring the landmarks. 'Of course I remember the war memorial on the turret and the tit on the hill, Da.'

I'm not going to start drilling a two-inch hole in the bottom of the boat, for the recommended transducer, in bronze. You can get a hand-held thing these days but that's all a bit fussy, getting someone to hold a tube over the side and keep it steady. So I thought I'd just give her the lead-line. You'll be amazed to hear it's daughter-friendly, in metres, not fathoms. Two knots, two metres and all that. No codes.

But the frame was bust. I mean that whitewood was only about seventy years old – we should take it back to the shop but the receipt might be tricky to find. What a boorach that line got itself into – with tight circles in tighter ones. See once you get involved, with cordage and gear. I don't know if it was the dangler or the Coastguard in me kicking in but I started unravelling. Every chair in the kitchen was commandeered. The way my mother used the backs of them for hanks of wool to be made into balls for knitting. The trick is to tease all the tight bits out, so the loops are longer. Then you see what's fallen into what.

I stopped for breath. OK, you could call that a *ceò* – a wee thoughtful drag of a roll-up. Tobacco Kills. But it's been a friend to me, last few years. It's an action, an aid to thinking. I don't know if I could have thought things out without that space. Tea and coffee are good as well.

The thin braided line was in a very strong shade of red. Just like the red in that book cover. I remember looking for the traditional brown, the stuff you normally used for a handline, then I saw that the red polyester cordage would be thinner for the strength – better for a sounding-line. Less drag. Now the coils and loops made their own pattern over the black slate. I did nothing but look at it for minutes and minutes. Maybe longer.

I was still in the photocopies and print-outs. The memoirs of the Field Marshal.

Keitel knew the game was over in '41, once nobody had been able to dissuade the *Führer* from the invasion of Russia. After that, the only chance of victory was to take Moscow before winter. When that didn't happen, geography and numbers would make the result inevitable. But he'd no thought of resigning. He was still looking at the chessboard – if there had been a swift strategic withdrawal at Stalingrad... the formation of one short line of defence which could be supplied and reinforced.

But these things had not happened. So the Red Army broke through. When he says that Germany lost a whole army, he's looking at a map and the bulge of a line. There's no word of all these soldiers of skin and bone, in a slow march into fenced off areas. Just like all these Red Army troops photographed as prisoners in the Volkhov Corridor, a few years before.

There are these weak protestations to Adolf all through. But Keitel never considers standing down. Like when there's an outburst of rage from the Boss, at the mass escape from Stalag Luft 3. They must be taught a lesson. Special circumstances. Special treatment. Hence the orders which will allow for the execution of prisoners of war who are following their duty to attempt escape.

So that's what was behind Steve McQueen doing the jump over the wire. Or rather Bud Etkins. And it wasn't a BMW. It was an adapted Triumph T110 with strengthened forks and a few tweaks to make it lighter. McQueen took lessons from Etkins and became a competitive driver of racing bikes. But they didn't let him do the stunt in the movie. The machine which became an icon was resuscitated, years later for a museum-piece. And Triumph collaborated with McQueen's estate to launch the Bonneville T100.

Did you know that there was another production motorcycle based on a machine which became a historical object? The Harley Davidson MT350 is called the Corporal Lee Scott in remembrance of a soldier killed while serving with the Royal Tank Regiment in Afghanistan in 2009.

Please excuse the length of that loop of red cordage, teased out of the fankle. It will fall into its place in the sequence. We're back in the main strands. There's street-fighting in Berlin. The deaths of all these youths continued even though it was clearly impossible to stop the advance into the city. The certainty of the outcome did not prevent Keitel from driving round the city outskirts, berating the shirkers and calling back the retreating gunners as the whole show was closing. As his leader was preparing to put a pistol to his own head. As Frau Goebbels fed cyanide pills to her beautiful children.

I'm still seeing the red loops on the black floor. The blood of Russians and Germans and Ukrainians and Belarusians, Latvians, Italians and Romanians. (What did you make of it all, Queen Marie, first monarch to embrace the non-political Bahá'í Faith?) And men from Alsace-Lorraine, drafted in with a bit less freedom of choice than the Field Marshal. And the Polish and the Czech and Slovak and Yugoslavian and Hungarian and Austrian citizens. And all the other lost souls, of named states or the stateless ones.

I did listen to the daughter. I did go across the road and round the corner to enter the front door of the library. There were two display boards, just inside. One was new fiction. One was recent non-fiction. I picked up *Bloodlands* by Timothy Snyder. It's an account of the forces acting on the territories between Berlin and Moscow. Between the end of the First World War and the end of the Second. Stalin's realisation that the tool of famine was an efficient means of fighting his own ideological war. Hitler's dream of the same Ukrainian bread-baskets feeding his chosen people. Their means of eliminating those who didn't fit in to the plans.

I read the book in long bursts between coffee and sandwiches. I returned it and followed up some strands on the internet.

There's a charity which even now is excavating the ground in the Volkhov Corridor, and sieving the swamps, to trace the tags which still hang round the necks of some skeletons. These can then be properly buried and their descendants, whatever the nationality, informed of the location of their fate. That's what's between the black lines of Keitel's soul-searching on strategies.

My own vocation could well be in teasing out a few remaining tangled lines. There's more to be done yet on the Eastern Front but, for me, that's a bit like poaching. This research is the province of a former classmate of mine, a man elated by swimming in cold sea without the benefit of a wetsuit.

At my age, I'm allowed to leave all that restless exertion to the daughter. That's the swimming, I mean, not the research. Mind you, her mother ran the London marathon last year. Anna told me Gabriele was back on the bike, the drop-handlebars. I'm happy she looks like winning her own battle.

I can hardly walk to the bloody end of number one pier. There's a big gate halfway along anyway and it's not the same since the Art Deco transit shed got removed. It went out in style, with half the island turning out to dive into Norman MacDonald's community play, *Portrona*. A Hymn to the Herring.

I'm going to go for my own marathon. I've got as far as writing to Aberdeen Uni. They were interested enough to offer a meeting. We talked over a few ideas for sustained research. The focus has to be tight. There won't be another lifetime to search the nooks and crannies.

I thought of a close analysis of certain types of machinery in warfare. The motors which propelled invading and retreating forces in the Second World War. But a lot of that is covered, now. Then there was the aftermath. Did you know that Rolls Royce sold a large number of small jet engines to the Russians? A very competitive version of the Mig fighter used them. The word is that our American friends were a bit offended by this trade.

There's still a lot to be learned from Korea and Cyprus. It's amazing what we find when long-held documents are released. Suez is an interesting one but how can you compete with that great movie, *The Ploughman's Lunch*. Fiction, though it is.

But I knew what to go for, in my own kitchen, as I realised the filter in the end of the rolly-up was dead in my hand. It was the inner journey of Keitel that fascinated me, as much as his own presentation of the events which can be verified. How people justify themselves. But maybe it's time to look a bit closer to home. Bonny Scotland, we'll support you evermore. Aye but good to face up to the fact that folk's attitudes are also a matter of fact. Maybe attitudes shape future facts.

You ever get the feeling that you were on good lines a long time ago? You were in the groove. You just didn't realise it.

Scots were never blameless. Nobody was or is. It's a sliding scale. Maybe we can agree to place Hitler pretty close to the extreme end of it. The victors agreed to hang Keitel and put Hess in jail for life, meaning life, despite his descent by parachute to Eaglesham on the 10th May in 1941. Churchill considered him of unsound mind, rather than guilty. They didn't shoot the deputy but his signature was on an abundance of orders before his wilful attempt at a peacekeeping mission with the fourteenth Duke of Hamilton. Hess might have been spending a quiet evening with the family the night they burned the synagogues but he'd already signed the Nuremburg laws and the banning of Jewish doctors and lawyers. I've not managed to shift from the World War Two period yet, but bear with me a little longer. A last fankle. A persistent, twisting loop.

You might also come to a stage in life when you want to fit things in. Just in case you don't get another chance. There's no suggestion that the Duke knew he was the key to a negotiated peace which would have mitigated the extremely worrying plan to invade Russia. The Duke was in charge of air defence in Scotland. Now there's a subject for connoisseurs of conspiracy theories. Could this explain how Rudolf Hess's Messerschmitt BF 110 eluded British guns and fighters?

The answer is no. Excuse me mentioning my particular sphere of interest again but engines are relevant. Hess had learned to fly after recovering from his wounds in the First World War. Test pilots at the Messerschmitt factory allowed the deputy free access to their latest developments. So he might have started off on a moonlit night with heavy long-range tanks but by the time he swung a left off the North Sea airspace, he was flying a very interesting aircraft. He was fast and high, driven by a pair of Daimler Benz, twelve-cylinder, fuel-injected petrol units. That's a lot of energy under your wings. One of these engines survives and is on loan to a museum in Scotland.

It looked like Hess was going to live forever too but he didn't. The original plan was to scatter his ashes to the mercy of the four winds but the body was handed over discreetly to his surviving family. His remains were buried in Bavaria but later uplifted again after the site became a place of pilgrimage for neo-Nazis. If I said that there was a memorial stone in polished black marble at the site of the aircraft crash, on Scottish soil, would you believe me? And if I quoted the engraved words as 'Brave heroic Rudolf Hess', would that be completely implausible?

How far along the sliding scale do we place the man who was to hang himself with an electrical cord at the age of ninety-three? He regretted nothing a long time before Edith Piaf. He was the ultimate believer and his faith was blind until he knew his hero really did intend to take the holy mission eastward in '41. Then again, the purpose of the invasion was not that clear. First there was the mythology of Madagascar as the place to contain the driven Jews. Then there was the far lands, the eastern edges of the former Soviet Union. The Bolsheviks would be destroyed. The bones of the commissars would fertilise the grain-lands of the Ukraine. Comrade Stalin had already done his bit in arranging for the starvation of millions who would be in the way of the true citizens of the Reich.

Since the lightning-war ground down to a more gradual way of terror and death, the mythology had to change. The killing of Jews had to become the prime reason for this war, since it was impossible to take Moscow or break through at Stalingrad. Hitler was a hoor of an orator but a shit storyteller. I've nothing against making it up as you go along but his narrative of a purpose is tied up in knots. Once the policy was formulated, the use of all these resources at killing pits, ghettoes and transports and death-factories was justified. Even a generation later, my most liberal heart couldn't bleed too much for those sentenced to death at the Nuremberg trials or after. And a less smooth history teacher in the Nicolson Institute, Stornoway, was to ask more difficult questions than any which might come up in the Higher exam. Sixth Year Studies, even.

The subject of capital punishment led to a comparison of the ideas behind the words 'justice' and 'revenge'. 'So what about Brady and Hindley?' he asked. The image of the second of these is also a historical icon with a length of hair sweeping across a partly obscured face.

Courts are now deciding on levels of compensation paid to workers deported to keep German industry turning, between the bombing. Some chemical companies had to produce the gas that would make industrialised killing more efficient. BMW made aircraft engines as well as army motorcycles. Sadly, we have to admit that Volkswagen Beetles were part of Nazi propaganda as well as the later war-effort. But if we notch up that score we have to look at the man behind the rally Escorts and all these Cortinas. Mondeo sounds neatly universal but Henry Ford published a collection of his strongly held views on the subject of the 'International Jew'. Maybe it wasn't so original, his theory that the Jews were the real cause of World War One, but it still won him the Grand Cross of the German Eagle, in 1938.

It's not all about nice motors. Clothing plaid a part too. So to speak. Hitler wasn't too pleased with Leni wasting all these rolls of Agfa and Kodak on Jessie Owens. But when it came to *Triumph des Willens* (*Triumph of the Will*), how could she have infused all that drama into the depiction of the court of the war-gods, if her subjects had not been so very well dressed. You won't find it difficult to believe that the Hugo Boss firm manufactured clothes for the Nazis, from the plain brown shirts to the black uniforms of the Waffen SS officers. Who says that 'Dead men don't wear plaid'?

I have to point out that the uniforms were not designed by the Boss firm. They only made them. Working to specifications. With forced labour.

When you're trying to sort out line that's fallen off a frame or a spool, you have to be willing to tease out every element to the full stretch. But you're looking for the cheating heart of the issue. That could be an accidental knot, in danger of being unique. You might never come across one quite like it again. But it's going to be difficult to find. Each section of the problem will draw you into it. I'm thinking now of the film-stock of these documentaries, the amateur and professional movies which have caught more than they aimed for.

Kodachrome is about to go out of production. Super 8 is now an expensive atmospheric alternative to digital. The study of the fate of one company could be a tool to use to examine the shifting attitudes which lie behind votes and party memberships. How guilty was Leni Riefenstahl along the slippery scale? Should Speer have been released? He was known to be a cultured man so his dedication to the cause gave the more obvious thugs some credibility. He managed the slave-labour programme even if he didn't work out the starvation ration. He didn't live to be over ninety like Hess or over a hundred like Riefenstahl. But he wrote his version of events.

We seem to be back with the issues of crime and punishment and the elusive notion of justice. Let's not forget that a terrible murder was committed by an individual or individuals in the midst of God-fearing Lewis people. The culprit might not have been from outside our circles. And the culprit may have been protected by others.

Over on the mainland, a minister of the kirk, in civilised Cromarty, was an outspoken defender of the trade in slaves. He wasn't an outsider. That's the thought which stayed with me, after I'd considered the incredible but true journey of Herr Hess. I needed to get back to the internet, once I'd cleared a tangle, cleaned a route to a toilet, cooked a dinner and had a conference with the literary daughter.

I can't leave you in suspense. I got to the root of the fankle. You get through a slough of despond where the temptation grows. You've got to resist making a cut in the line. You then have two angles of attack but that's a divided front. And we all know the dangers of that now, don't we? A fisherman's bend will make a strong join when the problem's been solved but that's a confusing thing in a line where knots mean depths. After one long, long loop was pulled through another, the problem fell apart. I was able to wind an unbroken red cord on a solid piece of timber and present it to my daughter, with said sounding-lead attached. An aid to navigation and angling. Intermediate technology.

I also removed the machine from the box and dysoned in the disaster area. I'd been a bit scared Anna would roam outwith allotted territories and find that box unopened. So I was able to remove much of the dust from the lower regions of the kitchen terrain.

Since you ask, I did monkfish seared in light oil with a sprinkle of fresh red chilli. A few drops of the light Japanese soy sauce, the one with the green lid. Served with a *jus* made from the backbone of the fish, with other trimmings from other species and lemongrass and coriander. But not thickened, so it's a soupy bath for the rice-noodles. I think she enjoyed it. Once she'd opened every window she could get near. Must have been the chilli oil. A lot of folk can't handle that. Suppose I'm just used to it. And the tube on the Dyson wasn't really long enough. There's an extension do-for you're supposed to use for getting into inaccessible pinnacles. I couldn't cope with that. I think I made a decent effort.

Language and Literature did lead into Outdoor Education. Anna could be doing expeditions in Canada and in Alaska. Sounds like there's two women across the pond she has to meet. She never really had time to develop her relationship with her aunt. I told Anna I sent my sister and her good lady *Bothy Culture*, *Hardland* and *Grit* – a hell of a trilogy of albums, mixing heavy dance beats and samples from the voices of Scotland, sung and spoken. A lifetime's work in a short allotted span of years. Martyn Bennett. I also put in a book by the mother who outlived him. Margaret Bennett has been noting and recording the songs and tunes and stories from a Gaelic culture, surviving in Cape Breton and Québec. A couple of generations' work in one jiffy bag.

In The Fish Shop

Now and again I give my custom to the fish shop. There's Ronnie Scott's which is not a branch of the jazz club but is a fine source of rhythmic conversation. I used to enjoy the stroll out to the industrial end of town and a yarn as I selected something for the restaurant and something for my own lunch. I've taken to having my dinner in the middle of the day, the way I did growing up.

My Da, like most Da's who worked in town, would come round the corner on his bike and the stew would be ready.

But I've taken to the route round Lazy Corner. I used to think the turn in the hoil was called that because of the railings. Whenever there's a railing in Stornoway there's some old guy's foot leaning on it and the other straight beside it. You take a look for yourself. It was a Skyeman pointed this out to me. It's what we do. Though I'm not an old guy yet. On a good day there's a couple of coves yarning though storytelling is of course a thing of the past, they tell me.

It's called Lazy Corner because that's where any debris will collect. The tide is slack there and the rainbow of diesel will lie on the surface for longer. I went into the other fish shop, by the fisherman's co-op. There's a fellow in front of me but he waves me on. He's in for a yarn with the guy behind the counter, before he buys his fish.

'It's all from the east coast the day, Peter, the boat's haven't got out.'

'No, it's been shit weather,' the other fellow says.

I knew his voice. 'Well, hell, it's yourself. Remember all the Broad Bay haddies you flogged from the Bedford van,' I says.

'Yes and I used to give you and your pal a spin round Westview and drop you off on the corner of Leverhulme Drive. That's where you are now, isn't it? Still with the Coastguard?'

I told him no, I was working for myself now and living round the corner from here. 'Think of all the lorry-loads of whitefish we sent from here to Aberdeen market. The by-catch from the prawn trawl.'

'Where did it all go? What happened?'

The former fish merchant looked younger than me. He took a look at me and he said, 'You don't half look like your olman. Sound a bit like him too.'

'So is that you getting younger or me getting older?' I asked.

The guy who was serving was also from these streets. This was his retirement job, three days a week and this was why he was doing it.

'You used to work with old Seamus, didn't you?' he said. 'He didn't last long after he retired. There was some characters in the Coastguard, then.'

'Aye, first watch with him, he taught me how to skin a rabbit. Tying a bowline behind my back came later.'

I was there again. That first cut with his neat small knife of German steel. Seamus showed me that. Then he told me to get my thumb in between the skin and the meat and left me to get on with it. I looked down at the skate wings, through glass. They would be local and skate doesn't have to be as fresh as other fish. My old neighbour behind the counter was the man who showed me how to skin skate. A small cut. Just enough to prise your thumb in. It's a bit tougher on the hands than a rabbit. But I didn't buy a skate wing. I knew I shouldn't be eating a big slab of butter and probably not the capers and balsamic either. It wouldn't be the same without the old *beurre noir*.

Then I saw the razors.

'Somebody diving for them?'

A guy brought up in the town, a guy who should know better, got done for wiping out a whole bay with some electric gadget. It was worth checking.

'Aye, there's a cove getting a few from Broad Bay'

'I'll take six and a few of these mussels.'

'What'll you do with them, Peter? He's good on the pans, this one, so they all tell me.'

'I won't know till I start. But maybe I won't steam them, this time. Had some in a Chinese in Edinburgh. Sort of place all the specials are in Chinese script. I asked for the fish dish one day and got razors. They just roasted them in garlic and chilli and a touch of soy sauce, on the half-shell. Slit them and gut them and throw them in the oven in some warm oil.'

'I thought you'd go out for the shellfish yourself,' said the cove who used to have the Bedford.

'I used to. Over in Lochs for the mussels and down Holm for the razors. I suppose I could time it to get the airport bus down but I'd rather come in here than dodge the hail showers.'

'Hell, I'm still seeing your father in you.'

'And you still look like you're ready to charm the *cailleachan* of Kennedy Terrace, from the running board of that van.'

'Where did the years go, Peter?'

The conversation got something going, in my head. I had to sit down, after I got through the door, once I'd put the bag of razorfish in the sink. Catch the breath. I never even put the kettle on. You know when you can hear yourself thinking.

At last, I knew what I was doing. The strands were all there, the same way the olman's warps and all those bobbins of wool were delivered to his shed. 'Christ, I'm weaving,' I said to myself.

A Liberal Consensus?

A re-examination of attitudes to the Slave Trade in Scotland with particular reference to records pertaining to The Royal Burgh of Cromarty and its surrounding districts

THE PHD THESIS OF PETER MACAULAY

INTRODUCTION

Estate owners in the colony of Guyana were in the habit of transferring the names of their home settlements to the Guyanese areas they held jurisdiction over. Scottish names were also given to many people who were brought to these estates to work without payment. Strong connections with the estate owners' home regions in the United Kingdom were thus maintained. This might help to explain why the burgh council of the trading port of Cromarty opposed the abolition of slavery. It is interesting to set this clearly recorded standpoint against the background of wealth and culture still visible in that burgh, a significant seaport at the time. It is also very tempting to make comparisons with other administrations in which the most repressive of edicts were issued from the most refined examples of balanced, neo-classical architecture.

The mercantile architecture of Cromarty has still a high degree of integrity. In this thesis we will be examining the declared written opinions of senior members of that community with reference to the Parliamentary Bills which eventually made participation in the slave trade illegal within Great Britain.

Those who voted for such declarations, at the level of the burgh council, were by definition (according to the franchise at the time) those with wealth and so with vested interest. There is of course no record of how farm workers or dock workers or serving girls thought. This thesis begins with full acknowledgement of that limitation. However we will look at one particular life-story, not because it is typical but because detailed records of its circumstances still exist.

One Hugh Junor brought a daughter and a son back from that coast of Guyana. He did not bring their mother. The children were called William and Eliza. They were half-casts, in the terminology of the time. Both attended school on the Black Isle. Eliza is still there. She was buried in Rosemarkie. Her brother left that area. He did not go home. Who could say where home was for William Junor? But it seems very likely, from surviving records, that he might have found somewhere more welcoming in Buenos Aries.

The case-study of his sister will be studied more closely. Her father married. Her father died. Her stepmother married again. Her new husband was the Reverend Archibald Brown. We might well expect that support and protection would have been offered Eliza, from that man of the church, now her legal guardian.

The Reverend was a pamphleteer and activist but one who supported the slave trade. He is described as clutching a drawing – elegantly done but for a practical purpose. It showed how best to pack the hold of a ship with live cargo, for the maximum profit.

Eliza was forced to leave the area of the Black Isle, for a time. Later, she and her own daughter returned to Fortrose, where they were to make their living as seamstresses. They marked out their own will to be there, on that peninsula. This was a woman who had once being taken over oceans by her own father, leaving her natural mother behind.

This is a story but it has been gleaned from a range of extant documents and records. These have suggested a line for further research. The following thesis will attempt to gather and present a wide range of recorded statements and comments, not previously collated and all relating to the trade in slaves, with links to Scotland, prior to the legislation to free all 'owned' slaves in 1833.

The various Acts of Parliament, to abolish the trade, driven initially by William Wilberforce, were of course passed in a series of gradual measures. The conclusive Act only completed its passage three days before the death of the principal instigator of the process.

In a Scotland now entering the second decade of a new millennium, it is all too easy to take a fabled liberal consensus for granted. This thesis will give documented evidence of attitudes to one single issue, close scrutiny. The study will be limited to one small part of Scotland during the period 1800 to 1833. We will examine recorded statements, minutes, letters and published texts with a view to summarising an accurate record of local opinion, for and against abolition of the trade and freeing of slaves in the regions under the British Empire, at the time.

Will and Testament (revised)

Western Isles Hospital

Hell's teeth, that last will and testament set something going like a train. When I say the last, I mean the first one. It got a bit much. I had to lay it all aside. Picked it up at different times and then other stuff happened. Years and years of other stuff. You know how a dictionary is out of date as soon as it's printed.

I'm reminded now of the notes on the form which set the whole thing in motion. Off and on. Lengthy though they are, these musings can't claim to be the product of any perpetual motion. Efficient we can sometimes do but perpetual is tricky. Not even the blacksmith down the road has managed that yet, though he's come close. It's maybe no accident that the typeface used in Admiralty charts, for general information, is Perpetua. Come to think of it, the one used to highlight warnings is Univers. Modest people, the Admiralty, as represented by the Hydrographic Office. It took them a hell of a time before they acknowledged the significant survey work done by one Dr John Rae, of Orkney. Not a naval officer.

The practical stuff in my first attempt at a Will is a bit out of date now so I'm going to have another go at that now.

TO WHOM IT MAY CONCERN, please accept this as the last and final document to the date fixed thereon and signed by myself and witnessed by my friend the Reverend Armitage, who you may be interested to know is now back in the fold. Or operating the gate to the fold. Anyway, he's got his old job back. I don't think you have to believe in God to be an Episcopalian minister. Or priest.

The most important thing to say is that the cod appear to be coming back. Well, not the same guys exactly, but their progeny. I left a few behind in the fridge in the townhouse kitchen. I hope the message got out. The key's under the usual stone. People still drop off fresh fish when they know you're not well enough to catch your own. They came from the west side, of course. The Minch has still not recovered. You might not rate cod but these were line-caught. Their delicate frameworks were not crunched. So the mottles and marbling changed in tone from a kelp-tinged russet to best butter. The very tint of the pats you'll find simply wrapped in greaseproof paper.

You hear more of the news when you live close to the hoil. I can tell you the thumping big cod are being taken on the searoad to Muckle Flugga. Balta Sound is still sad. The sailor reported that there are only a few saturated timber piles to hint of the bustling piers, the commerce and banter. We have to imagine my Lewis grandmother, and maybe my Broch one as well, taking their picnic on the Sunday when the boats' ropes remained secure on the rafts of black fishing ships.

Outskerries is a rich looking place, though, he said, and the port of Lerwick has all the signs of a Scandinavian city, with oil revenue stacked in the warehouses. The trawlers and purse-seiners rise high but they have to remain tied up on designated days (not necessarily Sundays). So the mate returns to Whalsay or Outskerries to whitewash his house again and set a few creels with the lad. The surviving trawlers, sheltering in the home haven, show more and more signs of terminal decline. Their registrations are seldom SY. Most were bought after doing their short commercial life's work on the east coast. The BF or FR ship is patched and paint is thrown in its direction now and again. There are exceptions. There's a fine AB whalebacked boat in signal red and a timber ship with an all-over deck casing of steel that's well painted in a very fetching lilac. The skipper's a cove, not a blone, but pride is taken. Most of the voices you'll hear when they're mending nets are Romanian or Bulgarian but there are also deckhands from the Philippines.

So what's so different from the hotchpotch of voices you might have heard in the days of the great herring trade – Ukrainian or Russian or German or Polish or Swedish or Danish or Cockney, or Geordie or Buchan or man of Hoy or any other tone of any other trader who has passed through our hoil?

But I'm not going to prolong the rant. You already know the predisposition of the Long Island male towards preaching. Even if the faith is skepticism.

FIRST, the menu. The most important thing about this Will is the gathering to read it so we'll try to make the most of that. I hope my surviving friends will have made the arrangements for the scoff to take place in my house on Kenneth Street. Gurnard and mackerel. Serve them up as Hebridean tapas and this is how, if you will. There will be enough in the kitty for a *deoch* of choice to wash it down.

I'd like you please to fillet the gurnard – red ones or grey, doesn't matter. But conserve the carcasses to produce a stock. If it's not too fancy a term – can we call it a *jus*? Anyway, a reduction of that stock with a bay leaf in it and some fino sherry. Take parsley from the boxes out the back door.

Then please tap them dry on a clean cloth. (Is that why they're called tapas?) Moisten them again but with lemon or lime juice or both. This is an anti-scurvy device but it also brings out the taste. Maybe some finely chopped fresh chilli but not too much. Take some fine polenta flour in a separate plate and season it. If there's any of the black designer-salt left in the jar, sprinkle some of that in it. It won't taste much different but it will look very fine. Failing that, substitute a good twist of black pepper but if you do, you probably want to leave out the chilli.

A fair bit of clear oil, nothing too strong-tasting in itself and not too hot but enough to crisp the polenta coating. Drain and serve with a few spoons of the intense *jus*, in a separate small bowl, as a dip.

Grab your own bit for quality control and get on with the mogs (AKA in SY as mackerel, runag, mogerero). If they're small fish, the sort we seldom used to see, but which taste even sweeter, cut slits in the flanks so the flavourings enter. If they're large, cut a fillet from each side. The head, backbone, guts and tail will come off in a one-er but don't keep them for stock. Ideally you want to get them in a pot as soon as possible but the other kind of pot. Just take it aboard a small craft and row far enough to take shrimp or prawn or crab from the mouth of the Creed. (The river.) As my olaid once said, a visitor to SY heard the phrase The Mouth of the Creed and wondered what cultish religious practices took place in this town.

Have the oven quite hot. Sauté onions and garlic and ginger with fresh ground masala, composed to your taste. But please consider splitting some cardamoms and getting the seeds in there. Smoky paprika is good for the look as well as the taste. Tumeric is a bit powerful but the smallest hint is not terrible. You can stuff the cavities of the fish with a bit of greenery – coriander is good but please, not the individual packets air-freighted in from Israel.

With luck the conversation will be going full pelt over the first course, so the mogs will have a chance to bake till they're about as crisp as they get on the barbecue. Remember, that's not cats. I'll never get that way folk on the mainland use our words for fish, for animals.

Someone nearly as fussy as me should attend to the basmati so it should be steaming ready with something close to a crust happening at the base of the pan. And the dhal should be Beluga black lentils or, failing that, I'd go for Puy. I realise that these staples were probably not grown on the Peninsula or anywhere else on our own long Island but it seems a bit more sensible to import sacks of these, slow-time, than flying delicate sproutings around the globe. Plus, it's good to keep some mariners in trade.

If you can't get hold of mogs, I'd go for megrim. A firm and tasty fish and more common in the trawl than lemons or Dover sole.

As to music, we may have done that already. A small but select gathering. Sorry if you missed the tunes. We were blessed with fiddle and guitar and chopstick percussion, not long before I made my exit from Kenneth St. I had a feeling I wouldn't need to make a return booking for the cab.

I could have given the cancer of the bowel a good run for its money but they sussed out I've had poor lungs for some time. The heart wasn't that great either. I thought I was eating a healthy diet of fresh fish. I thought that using butter again, for a fair number of years, rather than the low cholesterol oils and spreads, was quite balanced.

When I failed the MOT they advised me that prawns and scallops are very high in the bad sort of cholesterol. 'How many years have you been living like this?'

'A couple.'

'And exercise?'

'I have been walking well-defined routes,' I said. There wasn't a lot of point in adding that these were between the kettle and the computer, avoiding the growing heights of papers.

I did take one proper day off, helping out on *The Real McCaughey*, in Loch Erisort. The usual deckhand was taking part in either the peat-revival or the religious one. The skipper was very happy to let me take the wheel for the day. I was just not fit enough to do any hauling or even sorting. But I could still steer the boat while he did all that physical stuff.

Davie is fishing a lot of territory I know. He finds the edges and borders where the big langoustines dig in. He has detail on his colour sounder and he targets these tight ribbons that have escaped the trawl and the dredge. He tubes the catch, to protect it, on its travels. I think he might know each prawn by name, the way he talks about them. Good job I help him out, when the Garyvard lad has skidaddled, or he'd probably be talking to them too. And come on, it wouldn't be a day off if I came to sea with coriander and lime and lemongrass. So Davie throws butter on the pan and sautés the smaller prawns in the shell. He hails his mate, back from his dives, and a bag of scallop shells comes over on the boathook in exchange for a bucket of our own catch. If Anna is back home, I make sure a fry of each goes round the corner for her and her mother.

We served up a wee starter of each, that last kitchen party on Kenneth Street. Anna was on an expedition, out of contact. Cambodian rivers. Gabriele sent a card but it included a note saying she was sure I didn't want her attending but bawling. She was right. Mairi and Davie came along. So did their lads. Mairi must have decided she'd left it too late to have her own offspring but the two lads came to the Island along with Davie. Their mother fell for an Indian traveller and she'd gone back there with him to discover herself.

The Piscie minister presided when I got a bit short of breath. Michael has kept up his wee property on the Peninsula. He claims to have an eye to the future but I think he's looking to a rise in Island property prices rather than any possible progress of his own soul.

In case you're anxious about an ending to my rant, to rival *Rocket Post*, can I confirm for you that Davie, the cove from away, has made Mairi a happy woman. I've a feeling that her computer consultancy fuels the *Ford Mermaid* but the boat's in safe hands when that cove drives her. His boys think she's cool and she seems really easy with them. Davie says they came back to life when they got going on the fishing and boats. I've shown them a couple of marks, myself. They take it all in.

Mairi has never got back in touch with Kenny. I've phoned him a couple of times. When the house was quiet around the New Year. My old mate from Westview is still on the tack except for the occasional break-out. He did up an ex-council flat in Brixton, now Grade C listed. He's been with the same blone for years but they don't live together. She's never been up this way. He says she keeps her own flat in another block, a couple of bus stops away. She just carries on with her normal life whenever Kenny goes AWOL. It's usually over in a week, these days. He must have something to come back to. I only got all this gen the week we buried his mother.

As far as I know Angus is still alive but not responding to anyone. Kenny did go along but he said he didn't think there was much point. He didn't stay long. Not a flicker. Our skipper is likely to outlive me but I think I've had the best deal.

Enough of the merry banter. It's time to talk property.

Dear Anna, love for you has been the sustaining and constant factor. But I'm not leaving you the house. You're doing not too bad, young woman. I've no idea how your mother will dispose of the empire on Leverhulme Drive. If all that stuff I built is still intact then there's a fair chance one or other building will provide some income. They don't belong to me, so I can't give you what I don't now have.

It was great to know you were making good use of the garage-cum-library. Not everyone would see why you'd need the both of them in one building. I've no idea what the arrangement is with your mother but you tell her something from me: if she's charging you rent for it, I'm coming back to haunt her. If she thought my obsessions were boring in life wait till she hears me intone the specifications of all these engines, as a ghost. It will be constant, the dimensions, tolerances, servicing instructions, repeating in her ears for the rest of her own life.

It seems to me that the legacy of that troubled architect who was the grandfather you never met, included a fine house and a fine boat which are now outwith the family. But he also left a pretty sensible portfolio of property and your mother's share should be enough to give you a good start. That's nothing to do with me but I'll tell you now what is. Because I made a shit job of explaining it at the time.

I was happy to put my own research on the back-burner when I knew you were on the way. It's nothing to do with being led to believe you were a son and heir, at the time. It didn't come naturally, biting the lip and taking the queen's shilling but it was a worthwhile job and it fed the family. It was right for the time but then I had to get out.

Living with your mother was like that too. Leaving her, wasn't leaving you. It wasn't really about meeting or re-meeting any other woman. My aspirations had become different to your mother's. Pity I didn't think all this out before putting up all these extensions. None of them provided space. Never mind, the shared equity from the Kenneth Street abode helped the both of us complete our studies. So I'm turning full circle, back to the faith of my labouring grandfathers, in education as the way ahead. The house did its job for me as it did in the past, for a good few folk now already in the land of the dead. But I no longer really own it.

Anna, *a ghráidh*, I think the ones that judge us might be our offspring or the ones nearest to that. I managed to organise getting a boat put back together but I broke up one family. I don't think it would have been any easier for you or your mother if I'd been able to hold on a bit longer. But you might say, what was so important that it was worth all that damage?

If I don't really think that spelling out details of past actions is going to make that much difference to the future, why did I have to get back to my subject? I'm sorry but I don't know. It just seemed to matter. We might have free will but I don't think I had a choice.

I regret that we missed a bit of theatre, in my box coming out the storm windows, up top but I hope that the idea raised a smile. What I very much hope is that I've passed on some stories to you.

A bit more practical stuff now. I suspect that a sensitive hospital staff might have legally helped me on my way, by omission or otherwise, and if so I thank them for it.

Young Al the undertaker, who's not that young now, nudged me one time down Sandwick and told me not to worry. The olaid bought a plot for me and one for the sister too. Bad manners to refuse a present so don't burn me after all. Go for the standard local option. Anna, you could probably have the sister's but it won't be much good to you either if you go diving down Victoria Falls or somewhere like that.

Mr Executor, there's a bottle of Jura to say thanks for attending to details though I know you'd help, anyway. Please toast the brave and perceptive Mr Orwell when you take the cork off that one. My good friend Michael Armitage, who is very worldly for a minister of any breed, advises me that it is possible that a suitable charitable trust would be able to retain the Kenneth Street house by sub-letting a portion of it.

There's been discussions on international exchanges. Residencies. It would be great if you were involved in some way, but it's also great you know what matters to yourself. If Michael's scheme proves feasible, I'd like to see a room left for the use of exchange students. Even though I won't be seeing it. But what about encouraging:

• original enquiry in the sustainable energy, wave and tidal action preferred – the wind goes up and down but the sea does that all the time

• historians who believe that harping on about the atrocities of the past may mitigate those of the future

• conservation of fish stocks by a return to working with lines rather than trawls

---

I did seriously consider seeing if we could do some deal with the Arts Centre, along the road. It's been grand to wander over for a yarn but their cinema programme has been depressing. I'd reconsider this bequest if there was an undertaking to show *The Last Picture Show* once a year. After all, it is about our home town though I don't know why Bogdanovich felt it necessary to transpose the thing to Texas.

Anna, help yourself to any of the vinyl or the books that are still about. And that's a nice record deck and amp by the way, if your mother's one is kaput. There's likely to be enough in the bank to finance an expedition you wouldn't normally do. I'd like to think you might have a bit more thinking and writing time between the treks and the paddles. You see I'm a normal Da with a bourgeois tendency, after all.

I hope you're not shocked by any of these revelations. I've at least two, possibly even three, lost loves in me but I'm pretty sure that most people do. Maybe the lessons of history are only worth serious discussion if we accept the premise that individual human animals aren't as individual as they think they are.

I still hear the voice of a young lady who had cropped hair and slim fingers. The memory led me back to an area of research which I should have pursued a little earlier. At the age of fifty-seven, I submitted my PhD thesis, which did indeed explore attitudes to the slave trade in one area of Scotland, up to and after abolition.

My own parents made sacrifices so that I had the chance of a University Education. Now I've used part of what might have been my daughter's inheritance to complete it. I can only hope that the published thesis is worth that. Let's face it, the economy is falling in about our ears. Development at this pace never was sustainable. In the present climate, we can never take liberal values for granted.

You can only analyse events so far. My olman found the hot metal catch to a lid that let him out of a glorified sardine can of a tank. Then he was remembered and found and led up from a collapsed steel bunk in a doomed ship. One of these incidents was on the North African continent and one in North African territorial waters. I suggest that this is not evidence of any divine plan but the accidental circumstances which are part of his own story.

Here's another one, since I've got an audience. I'm very grateful I lived long enough to read the *Guardian* of 22nd June 2012. By the skin of my teeth. And that Michael bought me a subscription. I was well enough for a couple of hours each day to read the paper and well enough to spout this response to the kind Macmillan nurse who plumbed it into the laptop for me.

We are of course all under sentence of death but the timing can sometimes be altered. Liam Holden was the last person in the UK to be sentenced to a legal death, by hanging. The measure was still available to judges in Northern Ireland after it was dropped (sorry) in England, Scotland and Wales. His conviction for the murder of a soldier in Ballymurphy, West Belfast, in 1972 was based only on his confession.

At his trial, Mr Holden described his interrogation by Army officers, before being handed over to the civil authorities. He told how wet towels were applied until he was sure he was going to drown. One of the officers in question had recently attended a training course in interrogation techniques. The jury was not present in the courtroom when this was disclosed. Mr Holden was not hung. He was imprisoned in The Maze until 1989. He has just been pardoned. Out of thirty-three similar appeals, twenty-six have, so far, been successful. Only four convictions have been upheld.

My own father was reprieved at least twice in his life, from drowning or choking. By luck rather than by law. If he had not survived, I would not have been born. I very much hope that none of you wish, in fact, that I hadn't been brought to life. If you do think that, please keep your opinion to yourself for an hour and enjoy the scoff. I hope the quality of the rice and dhal is sufficient unto the needs of the vegetarians who must surely inherit what is left of the earth.

How can we judge if we used our time well? But I've no doubts at all about so much of a second of the time we put in to raising our daughter. In case any listeners have been switched off for a while and are just waking up for the business. Here we go.

The Business

THE WILL OF DR PETER WILLIAM MACAULAY. I revoke previous wills and codicils and I appoint to be my executor the Rev Michael Armitage of 21 Drummond St, Edinburgh.

In the event of my death I wish my property to be distributed as follows.

1. Split cane three-piece fly rod by Allcocks with Hardy Viscount reel and all ancillary equipment to Ms Anna Richter MacAulay.

2. Beachcasting rod by Abu Svangsta with Penn reel and ancillary equipment to Anna Richter MacAulay.

3. Telescopic spinning rod by Daiwa (with Made in Scotland thistle badge) and Daiwa reel (unbadged but shit, you've got to give a bit of business to your economic allies) also to Anna Richter MacAulay with the recommendation that it be used at least once to pursue migratory fish without written consent.

4. Painting titled 'Bhalaich an Uisge' dated 1973, by the Lewis artist Donald Smith to remain in the house known as 35 Kenneth Street, if the reverend can clinch the deal to hang on to said house. If not, Anna it's yours and if you don't want it, don't give it to an Lanntair, who have failed so far to show much interest in this local artist's work but offer it for the public bar in the Lewis Hotel. Smith is a third or fourth cousin of yours, by marriage, via the Griomsiadair connection.

5. Any vessel that may remain in my possession at the time of my

death, to be offered to the North Lewis Maritime Society, without condition. They can sell her if there is not sufficient interest in maintaining her. Anna should feel no sense of duty to take responsibility. I love her dearly and am thus aware that she is addicted to windpower and kayaking. I have however made provision with my executor for life membership of Anna to the Stornoway Sea-Angling Club. And also to the Maritime Society, *Falmadair*. This trust operates several traditional vessels. These two memberships should enable my daughter to sail and fish to her heart's content without serious personal financial risk.

6.   To Kenneth Finlay Macrae of 42 Dumbarton Court, Brixton, London, I leave the set of cooper's tools which are on display in the kitchen in the Kenneth Street house. These were given to me by a trained cooper who was made redundant. With these go a copy of Morrison's transcriptions of oral tales, collected by him, in Lewis. He was a schoolmaster turned cooper.

7.   To Mairi Sine Nic a Ghobhainn, of Croft no 6, Garyvard, I leave the cloth-bound notebook which contains my recollections of the transits for fishing marks, located between the Shiant Islands and Tob Lierway, south of Arnish point. There are also drawings of the skylines which should aid identification of the marks. Mairi will know many of these already but I hope this helps pass them on to the children now in her joint care.

8.   To Frau Gabriele Richter, I leave nothing because she has already had more than enough stress from disposing of the possessions I accumulated either as an individual or jointly, during a significant part of my lifetime. If it had been in my powers to do so, I would have given her the body of her father to bury or at least a conclusion to that sad story. I think I fully understood the depth of this human need when Seamus MacLean, my mentor in the Coastguard Service, got hold of me to pass on a word of advice during his retirement party. He had a good dram in him but he made this very clear:

'Keep the search going, Peter, keep it going even after you've no hope. I used to dread the night shifts, down at Oban. A woman kept phoning, asking if we'd found her boy yet. Had we tried all the islands? That's where he must have got ashore.'

9.   To all those gathered for this reading I leave the case of white wine and the case of red, selected by Michael. I'm pretty sure I'll be resting in peace, fully confident that the corks will have been removed or the screwtops turned. The red will be breathing. Which is more than I'll be doing but please do pause to reflect that at a future date, you will not be breathing either. There will have been no religious observances made during this ceremony. It is, however, my duty to point this out to you at this time. Even though I'm only half a Lewisman, not a Hebridean but a Hybridean.

Cause of Death

Additional note – Michael Armitage
Friends, as appointed executor of my good friend Peter MacAulay's estate, I feel it my duty to add a few notes to Peter's very individual testament, as part of his legal last will.

Some of you may not yet know that, following examination of tissue samples, the cause of death of Doctor Peter MacAulay was listed as COPD. I was myself unfamiliar with the term. The abbreviations stand for Chronic Obstructive Pulmonary Disease. I understand that this is a term which covers various forms of blockage such as chronic bronchitis, emphysema, or both. It seems that heavy smoking and a dust-laden environment are both key factors which can lead to the development of this problem until it reaches an acute state.

We could consider it a mercy that Peter was spared further pain. However, it is also a great loss that a man who was hitting the stride of his intellectual development was taken from us. We have no alternative but to trust to a greater wisdom than we can presently perceive.

He would not have wished for too morbid a footnote to his life. However, I cannot avoid sharing the thought that the ironies involved in his death are very much in keeping with those of his life. He was a man who loved the sea and who indeed made his living for many years by helping to protect those in danger on or by the sea. He loved to cook and eat the produce of the sea. Perhaps, in this way, Peter revealed his truly spiritual side. Peter made it clear that he wished for no religious observances at this gathering or at his graveside. But he made no secret of his appreciation of the telling of stories in the gospels or of the pleasure he took in comparing the accounts of events given in them. Allow me to read a few words from the gospel of Mark.

> *And when the day was now far spent, his disciples came unto him and said, This is a desert place, and now the time is far passed:*
>
> *Send them away, that they may go into the country round about, and into the villages, and buy themselves bread: for they have nothing to eat.*
>
> *He answered and said unto them, give ye them to eat. And they said unto him, Shall we go and buy two hundred pennyworth of bread, and give them to eat?*
>
> *He saith unto them, How many loaves have ye? Go and see. And when they knew, they say Five, and two fishes.*
>
> *And he commanded them to make all sit down by companies in the green grass.*
>
> *And they sat down in ranks, by hundreds and by fifties.*
>
> *And when he had taken the five loaves and the two fishes, he looked up to heaven, and blessed, and brake the loaves, and gave them to his disciples to set before them: and the two fishes divided he among them all.*
>
> *And they did all eat, and were filled.*

I think Peter truly dedicated himself to an area of study he felt important, in his latter phase. This was a part of a major shift in his way of life. Latterly he spent very little time on or near the sea, apart from an occasional short walk to the harbour. His boat was very little used. There are no further extended pieces of writing in his diaries, either handwritten or on print-outs. I could find no further chapters stored in his computer. He seems to have found a focus at last and completed his research and the writing of his thesis in the comparatively short period of two years.

And yet, in a way, he drowned in his own house, in the dust which had encrusted all those folders and files. I was acutely aware of the smell of it, clinging to all his papers and books. As executor, I took all possible steps to contact the relevant parties. It proved impossible to reach Anna in the available time. I feel sure that Peter would have been glad she was able to complete her expedition. His friend Mairi attended with her family. His former wife was present, with her partner. A small number of former colleagues and members of Stornoway Sea-Angling Club, joined our gathering. His sister arranged for a large bunch of roses signed by both herself and her partner.

Some of Peter's stated provisions, particularly those relating to the menu, were somewhat challenging. But all involved carried out their duties to the best of their ability according to the availability of fish. I did my humble best 'on the pans', with Davie's assistance. You may have been confused by Peter's use of the word *runag* for mackerel. My research informs me that this is a Gaelic term for 'sweetheart'. This seems to be a transliteration of the Gaelic word *rionnach* (mackerel) but perhaps, for Peter, the two meanings are fairly close.

Peter was buried in Sandwick, by Stornoway, with no religious or civil ceremonials. A piper was however commissioned to play a selection of jigs and reels before the slow air of his choice. That is the piper's choice. My recollection of my friend's last verbal instructions, given to me before he underwent the operation for removal of the cancer, which had spread to a lung, was, 'Don't pin the piper down. He's very welcome to call his own tune, even if we can pay him.'

Executor's Notes

There follows a bound typescript, the PhD thesis of Dr Peter William MacAulay as submitted and accepted by Aberdeen University.

A copy of the full thesis has also been lodged with Western Isles Libraries but I have duplicated the introduction to the work in its place with the other documents – the writings and correspondence concluding with Peter's Will and Testament. These seem to have been written over a considerable period of time.

Two notes, written by Peter, are set out below.

'NOTE 2' FROM A COMPUTER PRINT-OUT
The memorial stone to Hess which was placed in Eaglesham was destroyed in 1993. To quote the words of a 'veteran' National Socialist and founder of the National Socialist Movement of Britain in 1962, C Colin Jordan: 'Their Asian leader, Aamer Anwar, West of Scotland organiser of the Anti-Nazi League (ANL), a communist front organisation devoted to violence, took up a sledgehammer and proceeded to smash to pieces the memorial to the visitor of 1941.'

'NOTE 3'
One further typewritten sheet was also found, apparently an appendix to the papers. This appears to be a transcription from the source, as credited, but to date I have not been able to refer to a copy to check this. I do know that Peter was fascinated by alternative versions of the same story.

From *The Great Flood of Uig, Isle of Skye, 1877*, D. Nairne, 1895
'Though the weather that prevailed in the Highlands during October was boisterous and destructive, the damage done in other parts of the country was so trifling in comparison that the deluge which occurred in October 1877 will always be known as The Skye Flood. It occurred on Sunday the 13th October, and wrought by far the greatest havoc in the north part of the island, where the rivers drain into the western seaboard. For destructiveness, the flood was unprecedented in Skye, the descent of waters from the hills, where the rain cloud seems to have burst, being sudden and overwhelming. The Conon and the Hinnisdale thundered down in terrible volume, carrying away bridges like matchwood, oblite-rating crops, sweeping flocks of sheep into the sea, and entirely changing, in several places, the face of the country. At Uig, the ancient graveyard was carried away, all but a small remnant, and hundreds of corpses, in all stages of decay, were scattered up and down the shore, or reburied under the debris, the result of landslips, which was carried down in hundreds of tons. Kilmuir Lodge, belonging to Captain Fraser, which stood on the shore of Uig Bay, was wrecked and the manager, Mr Ferguson, perished in discharging what he considered to be his duty, having refused to leave the lodge to take care of itself in the peril which began to threaten it as the flood rapidly gained in dimensions.'

Acknowledgements

This is a novel and so most of it is made up. It is set in geography which really exists and it refers to some historical events which are well substantiated. None of the main characters in this book are intended to represent any person, living or dead, though there are references to actual writers and artists, some still living.

The character of Anna is completely invented but I am indebted to my two sons, Sean and Ben, for some of her phrases, as children.

Gabriele is another invented character but I am indebted to several different persons' accounts of their fathers' survival stories, including that of Barbara Ziehm. I am also indebted to Barbara for some other phrases and incidents as I am to many colleagues and friends, over the years.

References to the tragedy of the *Iolaire* are indebted to research gone before. I was most influenced by the work done by Don Laing, Norman Malcolm MacDonald and Roddy Murray.

Some of the passages reflecting spoken Doric were tuned with the help of Alexander Hutchison. Alex Patience, from Fraserburgh, also helped bring me a sense of that town. Peter Mackay provided advice on the Gaelic. John McNaught, artist and printmaker, generously shared his ideas and research on the subject of Highland heroes and anti-heroes. John's own research as well as his story-telling skills, informed me of the astonishing history of the family of Hugh Junor and the documented records of the opinions of some residents of Cromarty at the time of the struggle to end the slave trade in Britain. The initial drafts of some elements used in this book were the result of a commission by Highland Print Studio, in response to an invitation from the director, Alison McMenemy.

The idea of the blowlamp and oil-drum method of Raku firing is lifted from observing the workshop practice of the ceramic artist Alison Weightman. I heard the 'Hybridean' gag from Sophia Dale.

Thanks to the following people who have read and responded to drafts of the book:

Elek Horvath, Robert Macfarlane, Lily Greenall, Sue Stone, Peter Urpeth and the author of the report he commissioned as then Writing Development Officer for Hi-Arts.

I am very grateful to the publisher Sara Hunt for the courageous decision to take on this work at a time when most publishers would not consider novels at all, let alone one of this length. My wife, Christine Morrison, has put an incalculable number of hours into listening to the whole novel, then reading many drafts, helping with continuity, formatting and proofreading.

The work could not have been completed without the support of the Scottish Arts Council become Creative Scotland and the Hi-Arts service become Emergents. I wish to mention the late Dr Gavin Wallace individually for the trust shown in backing my proposal to devote two years to developing work from draft versions of many years of prose writing. This novel was brought to an advanced stage during that period. A Creative Futures Residency, developed and administered by Shetland Arts, in partnership with Western Isles Libraries, 2011–2012 also contributed.

Further editing was done as writer-in-residence in the garden of Dora Morrison, Kittle, Wales, and aboard Ken Linklater's yacht *Rebecca*, on the road to Rathlin Island.

Back to the beginnings of this, my first novel, I am indebted to the great adventure of Thomas Crawford's course on 'Scott and the European novel' (University of Aberdeen). Some writing which has found its way into this book also found a first readership through the creative writing groups, 1979–1980, initiated by Graeme Roberts, also a lecturer in the English department at Aberdeen.

Some previously published short stories have been reworked into this book. I am grateful to my very first publisher, James Campbell, and subsequent editors of *The New Edinburgh Review* and *The Edinburgh Review; Stand; Waves* (Ontario); *Northwords Now;* ASLS as the publishers of *New Writing Scotland;* Polygon/pocketbooks as publishers of *Mackerel and Creamola* and *Green Waters*. Extracts were published or performed, as prizewinners, in the Baker Prize, run by The Reader's Room, Isle of Skye, and The Scottish Writers Centre (linked to Aye Write festival, Glasgow). Particular thanks to Alec Finlay of Morning Star Publications and Hugh Andrew of Birlinn/Polygon. Thanks also to Birlinn for permission to quote from Norman M MacDonald's *Portrona*.

Thanks to Christian Salvesen PLC and the National Library of Scotland, partners with the Scottish Arts Council in instigating the first Robert Louis Stevenson Award at the suggestion of Frankie Fewkes and to Catherine Lockerbie, then literary editor of *The Scotsman*, who provided important support in the year following the inaugural Stevenson residency.

The support of Donald Smith and the board and staff of the George Mackay Brown Scottish Storytelling Centre over many years has been a major factor in developing chains of stories. I was introduced to the work of Brown at Aberdeen College of Education and met him first, thanks to an invitation to read my own stories at The Pier Arts Centre, Orkney. His positive reaction helped give me the confidence to continue seeking to find a form for my extended work in prose. Norman M MacDonald, Iain Crichton Smith and others who were generous in their comments on my first gathering of short stories (*Living At the Edge*, Machair Books, 1981) also encouraged me.

Three commissions to write for theatre provided an insight into the development of character. I don't think this novel could have been achieved without that. The three Scottish directors, Gerry Mulgrew (*Seven Hunters*), Morven Gregor (*Brazil 12, Scotland Nil*) and Alison Peebles (*The Sked Crew*) all brought me into a rich collaborative game.

The views of Peter MacAulay and other characters in this book are not those of the author. Most importantly, I'd like to put it on record that I prefer brill to megrim.

Ian Stephen is a writer, storyteller, artist and sailor from the Isle of Lewis. His prose, poetry and drama have been published around the world and garnered several awards. He was both the first winner of a Robert Louis Stevenson Award and the first artist-in-residence at StAnza, Scotland's annual poetry festival. This is his first novel.